GUARDIANS OF THE MUSE

EDWIN RITTS

ISBN: 979-8-9864413-0-6

Produced by Publish Pros
www.publishpros.com

DEDICATION

*For my dear wife, Susie, who gave me the time and space
to get this all together.*

PART I

*"Suit the action to the word,
the word to the action."*

WILLIAM SHAKESPEARE

CHAPTER ONE

"Hardly anyone noticed when Chapman Billings opened his garage studio to a few friends on Sunday afternoons. There were few other distractions from the heat and isolation of Meriden, Alabama in the summer of 1936 that gave these weekend artists such serious pleasure. Billings, in a white smock and striped cravat would work in oil, perfecting his seascape imagery known to many through his respectable placing in annual county fairs. Harry Lloyd, dressed in his Sunday white shirt and bow tie, would be working in watercolor. Harry had spent one year at the Art Institute of Chicago before returning to Meriden to assume his place in the family's cotton business. His sojourn into the cultural life of Chicago had been at the behest of his mother who, when visiting, would accompany him on Sundays to gatherings of the city's newly formed Poetry Society to read poetry she had written in her younger years.

"The 'Billing's Bunch' was a distinguished group of the city's culturally advanced. Twice a year, the group sponsored public displays of their work—held for the first few years at the garage studio. To the delight and surprise of the artists, these events would attract a large audience, resulting in flurries of related artistic activity community-wide. Interest became so great that even the regular Sunday sessions began to attract spectators who would come to watch, listen, and partake in the aesthetic fervor. Attendance at these gatherings grew to such an extent that the artists could not concentrate on creating. Billings, their unappointed leader, formed a committee of several other artists and suggested to the city's governmental leaders that perhaps a gallery space for temporary exhibitions, lectures, and readings should be open to the public on a regular basis.

"Unable to find free or reasonably priced space in a downtown building, the group applied to the federal government's WPA program. To no one's surprise, the state's WPA coordinator responded by persuading the city to allow artists to use the lobby of City Hall for these purposes. The program would pay a modest fee for use of the space, the city would provide custodial services, and a WPA emblem would be displayed prominently on the front door. Within two months, the artist group, who now were calling themselves the Meriden Fine Arts Society, was operating a public gallery open three days a week, including Sunday afternoons, for events of artistic importance."

Finishing her opening remarks, the docent looked at the faces of those in her charge. This too was a group of Sunday afternoon gallery visitors who had come to the institution developed from that 1930s WPA project. "Our tour will begin in the gallery to your right, so if you will follow me…"

Mitchell Jenkins, who had been listening to the docent, knew that the evolution had been much more involved than the thumbnail sketch he had just heard. He thought of the progression of events and those who had shaped them as he watched the last of those on tour file into the first of a catacomb of spaces that held the museum's collection. Continuing from where the young woman's brief history had ended, he again began putting the puzzle together.

CHAPTER TWO

The initial gallery space was to move three times between 1940 and 1958. Its success became so public that the local artists who had been its instigators seceded from their own organization and formed a separate body open only to practicing artists, poets, and authors. In 1958, the gallery was moved to its first permanent location, a large home in Meriden on five acres lost by its owners through foreclosure. The Art Association, as they called themselves, had gone out on quite a limb to purchase the structure and was soon raising funds for emergency renovations. Through pressure from the association's recently formed board, the city appropriated modest funding for the structure's ongoing upkeep. The board invited museum personnel from Birmingham to speak at public gatherings on the importance of the visual arts as well as the significance to the city of this new cultural entity.

Three directors of the new facility would come and go in its first years. Each was better qualified than the one before, though none was able to determine appropriate goals or establish themselves as viable leaders. Chapman Billings, who with his compatriots had started this artistic ball rolling, died in 1959, leaving several of his paintings to the association. The gift was seen by what remained of the original Sunday group as an attempt to form the basis of a collection of artworks perpetually available to the public. To that end, Henry Lloyd, who was now running the family business, donated four of his watercolors and stepped up to serve as president the year their third director left to teach at a northern university. Selection of a new director became the principal piece of business for Lloyd as 1962 began.

Mitchell Jenkins was hired that spring. Though he had only recently graduated from the University of Birmingham, he had been highly recommended by the Birmingham Museum's esteemed director, August Cortland Bishop. Jenkins, with his young and attractive wife, Maureen, settled into the city that summer. He was to find that Lloyd and the board, who had done so much for the arts there over the last twenty-five years, were unable to take the association to the next level—museum institution. There were neither sufficient funds nor staff to make such a transition, and Jenkins, young and energetic, strained at the frustration.

He remembered the afternoon Bishop had proposed the position to him. Their discussion centered around the differences between Birmingham and Meriden, and the future for someone removed from the center of the state's artistic community.

"Culture in the South," Bishop had said, "is always taken with two lumps of sugar. There is always a certain gentility that surrounds even casual discussions of art here, unknown in other portions of the country. It has survived 'The War,' sustained a broken economy, and fostered a remarkable style of living. Your public is susceptible to charming advances and elaboration that if done well, will enable an arts institution to be elevated above other forms of industry."

Jenkins' first two years were filled with exploration. The mansion had weathered badly since it left the hands of its original owners. Plaster ceilings had peeled from the leaking roof, rooms had been cut into funny shapes to accommodate apartments in an attempt to make money. Solid walnut panels had been removed from the walls of what had been a vaulted music recital space and stored in a basement with mud floors. Leaded glass windows were broken and boarded over, and the grounds had been left to the torments of nature.

In all, the mansion had twenty-eight rooms, only five of which were deemed acceptable to be used by the public. Much work and time was spent those first years working on the physical remedies required to re-open the second and third floors. The mansion's history piqued the interest of the Meriden public, and Jenkins reasoned even if all interest in art were to stop, people would still come to see the restored house and grounds. He worked with a single purpose to finish as much of the restoration as funds would allow.

The local artist community still met together in an organized if somewhat loosely knit fashion. They generally welcomed Jenkins' arrival, even though the association was now in full charge of art activities in the city. He had fresh, new ideas about the current state of artistic expression, while many of their number had negative feelings toward the art developing in places like New York. Abstract Expressionism was bad enough, and Pop was thought to be outrageous. Those in Meriden who did dabble in the avant-garde did so with hesitancy. It was prudent of Jenkins to be tolerant of the doubters, for his early survival depended to a fair degree on their support.

While he had chosen administration, Jenkins had studied painting at the university, producing banal images of country landscapes in his studio courses. He preferred the work being touted by galleries in the Northeast—particularly the work of a friend and native Alabamian, Beau Britian. Born to share-cropping parents, Britian managed to make it through the state's limited public education program. Afterward, he briefly lived with an aunt in Birmingham before joining the Navy, seeing a bit of the world during his service. Using the GI Bill on his return, he entered the University of Alabama in Birmingham, taking courses randomly before finding himself drawn to studio art classes more than anything else. After two years of study, he left Birmingham to live and work in New York, finding a third-floor, cold-water studio with living space in SoHo.

In 1963, a painting he had consigned to a small gallery near his flat was seen by Herschel Marelli of Marelli Gallery, Inc. Marelli had inherited a sizable collection of European Impressionist paintings from his parents when they died in the early 1940s. He opened a gallery on Madison Avenue with the intent of selling off some of the works and eventually moving to Europe. However, he discovered he enjoyed the life of a successful New York art dealer, making trips abroad only as a tourist. Developing an interest in contemporary art and spending increasing amounts of time meeting living artists, he began to show the best of what he saw, building an impressive stable of artists and attracting a clientele of the wealthy and important.

The Britian painting Marelli took note of was entitled "Wall," a relatively small work that purported to be a series of bricks placed together as if to form a wall. The artist explained he was concentrating on the application of paint rather than an image. Marelli found the painting alive with possibilities, quickly purchased it, and asked the address of its maker. What followed was the stuff of which legends are made. Marelli visited Britian in his studio, purchasing everything he had hanging on or stacked up against the walls and eventually providing him a comfortable stipend to produce additional work to be shown in his gallery. Britian's first exhibition at Marelli was titled *New Wave* and sold out within two days.

The young artist and his dealer had a wonderful and mutually beneficial relationship largely unknown to most of Alabama. Jenkins kept up as best he could, but distance and his own ambitions kept their friendship somewhat fragmented. Fundraising for the building's renovations had been successful, brick-and-mortar projects generally were, but keeping the place open, funding his salary, and covering the cost of day-to-day operations were a constant grind on the organization's board and on Jenkins. By the end of his second year, he was faced with the decision of working to make the association part of a government agency's budget (as Birmingham's museum was) or leaving Meriden for somewhere else.

As a start, Jenkins began to initiate contacts within the city's modest corporate community. A number of these executives, he found, traveled extensively for both business and entertainment, sampling the world's pleasures. These individuals would be easy marks for Jenkins when talking about the New York art world and museums they may have visited. He did his homework on these people and their businesses, intent on building useful personal resumes. In the beginning there were three such potential benefactors. All were either in business for themselves or heads of growing corporations. From information at the local Chamber of Commerce and other sources, Jenkins determined their approximate gross incomes, their companies' gross sales, and the cost of their homes and cars.

The first was a physician. Dr. Abram Rubin had practiced medicine in the city for only five years when Jenkins made his acquaintance. Rubin had grown up in Meriden after moving from New Jersey with his parents and was initially interested in artwork for its investment potential. His early acquisitions were conservative, leaning toward figurative work more than landscapes or still-life paintings. Married with two small sons, Rubin found being a physician was more than lucrative for a man with only two weaknesses. Jenkins would soon help him develop a third, and cars and women would prove to be the least expensive in the long run. His first purchase had been a small chalk and pencil drawing by Arshile Gorky, and after reading in the press about the possibility of an art museum in Meriden, Rubin was quick to show the drawing to Jenkins.

To encourage this potential benefactor to invest in more pieces, Jenkins contacted several gallery owners in New York who handled Gorky's work and confirmed they would be quite pleased to meet with him and an interested collector when in the city. He then talked up a trip with Rubin for the two of them combining business with pleasure. They returned to Meriden the kind of friends that dark secrets make, two new paintings for Rubin, and with the association acquiring a Gorky drawing.

Jenkins worked next on expanding his new friend's artistic tastes, lending him books on more contemporary artists—particularly those in the stable of the Marelli Gallery—as well as getting him good seats at lectures in Birmingham by noted art historians, critics, and artists of the second half of the twentieth century. Rubin enthusiastically took the bait. Jenkins was careful to show his new collector only works he could afford, never anything out of his easy financial reach. To his credit, the good doctor began to develop his own attitudes about the artwork and began frequenting galleries on his own in New York and Atlanta, becoming more conversant about trends and new artists than even Mitchell Jenkins. Buying pieces became easier and easier, and returning to Meriden from his shopping trips more and more unpleasant. Not wanting to stay in the South or return to the Northeast, Rubin began investigating moving his family and practice to the West Coast.

Mitchell Jenkins' reaction to this news was utter frustration in losing someone he had worked hard to cultivate. For weeks he thought of every possible reason why Rubin should stay in Alabama. It became an obsession. Flattered by the attention, Rubin still spent an equal amount of time thinking of reasons for leaving. Finally, the offer Rubin had been waiting for came. He would join the surgical practice of a friend in Los Angles. It seemed a perfect blend of position and proximity to one of the fastest developing centers for modern art in the country.

Jenkins was crushed by the news. "Los Angeles of all places," he fumed. "Some museum SOB will pick right up on Rubin. I'll never see or hear from him again!" It was an unthinkable blow, but he immediately began plotting how he could endear Abram Rubin to him and Meriden after he was in California.

Calling a special meeting of the association's board ten days later, Jenkins began to outline the tack to keep Rubin involved. "With the board's approval we will undertake an ambitious acquisitions drive. A campaign will be run to raise funds for the purchase of American painting and sculpture, combining privately raised monies with federal dollars coming through the National Endowment for the Arts. Meriden is the right size and in an area of the country traditionally lacking in artistic incentive, making it a prime location for the NEA's funding."

He had contacted Britian as well as the federal program's administrator prior to his announcement, and the three had discussed the project in some detail. Britian promised to be an advisor to the project, and the administrator's delight in meeting and working with him clinched the deal, assuming Jenkins could get the association's board and Meriden's few benefactors to go along.

"This project," he continued, "will put this association—no, let's finally call it a "museum"—and this city in the forefront of the southern arts scene!"

There was, of course, much applause, for Jenkins was always supremely articulate when before an audience. After limited discussion, the board moved to approve the initiative, and a prepared release for the press was distributed. Anticipating a positive reception, Jenkins removed from his notepad the application he, Britian, and the NEA administrator had discussed several days before. The application called for a total grant of $30,000.00, an equal split between both entities and the maximum the NEA would provide. Then without pausing for breath, Jenkins moved that Abram Rubin be appointed chair of the project, which was immediately approved. The achievements of the day now behind him, Jenkins returned to his office to phone Rubin, who had already accepted the post if agreed to by the board. Rubin was now in pocket, and Jenkins was confident that after he moved to LA, Meriden would be on his mind. Still, with Rubin gone, he knew he needed to find others whose artistic interests he could encourage. Additionally, there was the need to find $15,000 to satisfy the museum's share of the funding per the NEA application, which went out with the evening's mail.

✵ ✵ ✵

The next two individuals on his potential patron list were not of his own age or temperament, but people of significant wealth and established artistic tastes. The first was Rudolph Bates, the successful president of Hall-Crowell, an automotive parts manufacturer that had recently moved a substantial branch of their operation to Meriden. Bates, formerly the assistant to the company's chairman, Russell Hall, had been sent to oversee construction of the new facility and its operation afterwards. It was quite the promotion for Bates, who had begun with the company as an engineer. The Meriden facility was to be the largest of the company's holdings, responsible for over half of its annual sales.

A tall, educated, and charming man, Bates had taken to the South readily, and to the surprise of the older Meriden residents, was enjoying the respect and friendship of the city's most prominent citizens. A skillful people manager, Bates enjoyed creating healthy environments for his employees. He took a personal interest in the construction of the new facility, both office and plant areas, with a particular eye toward areas where artwork could be displayed. The company's headquarters in midtown Manhattan allowed Bates access to many of the established galleries doing business there.

Russell Hall had spent much of his life collecting contemporary art, filling both his home and offices with works that were respectable and expensive, if not always exciting. Hall was also a benefactor to many museums, per the company's annual reports Jenkins acquired when news of the firm's new facility was first announced.

Bates and Jenkins first met over lunch at the Longleaf, Meriden's all-male private club, sitting opposite each other at the "Bull Table," reserved for businessmen. Bates was attractive as a potential museum board member, and Jenkins knew most of the city's non-profits were interested in him as well. However, he didn't press the notion, listening instead to the conversations going on, particularly Bate's comments. He was up to speed on the museum's activities, including the recently announced acquisition project, news of potential federal dollars coming through, and the financial goal for local fundraising.

As his facilities construction progressed, Bates would occasionally call Jenkins about the artwork he was thinking of including in the building's public spaces, and when it came time for their installation, asked Jenkins to come for a preview and critique. Habitually early for meetings, Jenkins amused himself wandering the building's huge lobby and was immediately taken by everything he saw. There were contemporary works from the collection of Russell Hall—a large abstract by the painter Al Held, a modest but strong Kline, a darkly forbidding Rouault, and on the lobby floor, a large, twisting John Chamberland sculpture made of car parts. Was he in New York suddenly? He was not, but surely wanted all he saw and likely more for the museum.

"What's your verdict Mitchell?" Bates's voice awakened him from his euphoria.

"Just wondering where I am Rudolf. These objects are amazing! Can the museum give tours?"

"Sure," Bates said, laughing. "Just let us know when you're coming and how many are on the bus!" He didn't know that Jenkins was only half kidding.

"Objects of this stature are going to make us look bad even with the new pieces we're going to collect. Maybe I can get Beau to negotiate some rock-bottom prices from his friends, but still, this collection is hard to beat."

"No need. Mr. Hall tells me he's willing to loan objects to your museum, as long as you carry the insurance!"

CHAPTER THREE

Mitchell Jenkins found himself facing his office door on the museum's second floor. It had been only twenty-three minutes since the docent had begun her tour, yet he had remembered years of his and the institution's history. Had it really been eight years since he had come to Meriden? Perhaps he had been there too long, though he still found every day to be exciting—except for the events of the last two weeks. He turned his mind from these thoughts and walked to the large windows overlooking a corner of a sculpture garden where a John Chamberland sculpture was installed. It was the one he had first seen in Hall-Crowell's lobby – now part of the museum's collection. He turned, pulled the curtain, and sat behind his desk in the semi-darkness. Again, he escaped into memories of years before, back to the lobby of the manufacturing plant, the artwork it held, and how he could parlay works from the collection to further the museum and his own goals.

✻ ✻ ✻

Three months after Hall-Crowell's Meriden facility opened, Jenkins' plans for a major exhibition from the Hall collection were complete. Russell Hall agreed to lend the Meriden Art Museum seventy works from the company's collection and his own. Jenkins and Bates made several trips to New York to select the pieces that would make the trip south. During one of these, Jenkins took Bates and Hall to meet Beau Britian and tour his studio. Hall took an immediate liking to a large painting the artist had recently finished and purchased it. He then insisted it become the centerpiece of the Meriden exhibition. Russell Hall was a quick decision maker, seeming always on the move to get to the next issue.

"Shouldn't Marelli be informed about this sale?" Jenkins said aloud, but as if to himself.

Russell Hall turned to him with a smile, "Herschel looks the other way when I make a purchase from one his artists...I'm kind of a silent partner."

Jenkins nodded his head as if he understood what Hall was talking about.

Hall continued, "We were friends before he went into the gallery business, and when he seriously began thinking of making the leap—well, I loaned him some money to get started. On very favorable terms for him, of course." Hall flashed another of his smiles. "If he has a good year, he pays some on the loan. If I see a piece of art from his stable that I like, I buy direct. Mitchell, this has been a wonderful morning and I am so grateful to you for setting the meeting with Beau. Rudy and I have some business to take care of now, but I'm wondering if you could come by my office later this afternoon, about four?"

"Absolutely. I'll see you then."

Hall and Bates left, leaving Mitchell and Beau suddenly alone.

"Whew!" Jenkins said.

✲ ✲ ✲

Russell Hall's office suite comprised a large portion of the twenty-third floor of a mid-Manhattan office building. Two corner walls were floor to ceiling glass through which anyone facing Hall could see city traffic moving north to south, east to west, the automobiles just moving blurs of color. Jenkins was waved in while Hall finished a call. He used the time to admire the art installed on the walls. To his immediate right hung a DeKooning woman in pinks and yellows; opposite was an abstract by Robert Motherwell; above a credenza hung a nice sized Pollack; and on the corner of Hall's large desk was a bronze maquette for a proposed sculpture by Milton Avery.

After the two talked about Meriden, the museum, and the proposed exhibition, Hall produced a few papers for Jenkins to look over and sign. They were simple loan agreements produced by the company's corporate curator and reviewed by the firm's legal department.

"No need to sign them all here, you can mail back the originals. Rudy has told me all about the exhibition and the related activities you two are planning. Mrs. Hall and I are uncertain if we'll be able to attend the opening, although we would very much like to see our new facility. Perhaps we'll be seeing you after all. In any case, it has been a pleasure to meet you, Mitchell. I appreciate you coming up here to meet with me, and especially your introduction of me to Beau Britian."

Hall said he would coordinate the objects getting to the museum, and with that, their business was concluded.

☆ ☆ ☆

In his hotel room later, Jenkins ordered a double scotch from the bar and brooded over the way he had been treated by Russell Hall that afternoon. Had he been the director of a museum in Chicago or Boston, he would have been given more time to impress Hall, though the Britian introduction and studio visit had been a hit. This was not the way he had wanted to end his meeting with Hall, and he felt he'd not accomplished enough. Bates had taken the afternoon flight back to Birmingham and the evening shuttle to Meriden, leaving Jenkins alone. He called Britian, but there was no answer. He tried several other numbers with no luck and settled for a night on the town. After dinner, he toured Forty-Second Street for several hours, finally bringing someone back to his expensive hotel room. After all, he had had the good doctor Rubin give him a preemptive shot of penicillin before leaving.

Mitchell Jenkins flew back to Meriden the next afternoon, and it was Saturday morning before he returned to his office. Awaiting him there were letters from both Rudolph Bates and Russell Hall. He opened the Bates letter first, which confirmed and summarized activities discussed on their recent trip—the loan of artwork to the museum, and a listing of the pieces with their sizes, media, values—information included on the agreements Jenkins had already signed. *Bates is covering his bases*, Jenkins thought to himself. Then he opened the letter from Hall, which he found was actually from his executive assistant. It said Jenkins would be receiving, by the end of next week, several wooden crates of artwork being gifted to the museum by Mr. Hall. The artists were not immediately familiar to Jenkins, but the enclosed slides showed pieces he thought looked competent and was very pleased by the gesture. Perhaps he had made more of an impression on Hall than he thought!

That November the Hall exhibition opened. Jenkins installed the seventy works throughout the building's galleries, and the exhibition's receptions were the talk of the town. He had in fact arranged for two – one for VIPs of the city and the museum's board, and one for the museum's membership, followed by the public the next day. To his delight, Mr. and Mrs. Hall did attend the first night's festivities, flanked by Mr. and Mrs. Bates, the city's mayor and council members, state legislators representing Meriden, and the state's lieutenant governor. The only major player missing was Herschel Marelli.

Both the Thursday evening reception and the Friday evening lecture Russell Hall had requested he give, concerning his love of visual art and collecting, had gone off without a hitch. Jenkins used both occasions to put Hall in contact with anyone who might be influenced by a passionate collector. He knew Rudolf Bates had caught the bug, and he was hoping Hall's comments might also sway his third potential patron, DeBain Howard. Howard was president and founder of SouthLife, the largest insurance company in the region, now also doing business throughout the South and West. He was a frequent visitor to galleries along Madison Avenue. Jenkins could tell both Bates and Howard began seeing themselves as the Russell Hall of Meriden as the festivities progressed.

As an addition to the exhibition's opening weekend, Jenkins had arranged, through Britian, for a lecture to be given by a contemporary art historian to bring the Meriden audience and the exhibition past the Abstract Expressionists and up to date. Britian's painting was the centerpiece of the exhibition and perhaps was destined to come to the museum's collection in time. The lecturer, Babs Horowitz, taught at Columbia, wrote essays and exhibition reviews for many of the popular art magazines, and was exceedingly liberal in her manner and politics. She arrived early in the week "to get a sense of Meriden, Alabama, the South, and its people in general." Jenkins met her at the airport, where she rented an automobile and accepted his luncheon invitation. She followed him to the restaurant, freshened up a bit, and met him at a table in the dining room.

"Well now," she said, sitting down, "whatever that is you're drinking looks pretty good. I think I'll have one too."

Jenkins signaled the waitress for two more cocktails. "I'll be pretty busy at the museum this week getting ready for our opening, but are there any introductions you'd like me to make for you?"

The drinks came and she took a large swallow. "That's very good of you, but I've made some connections already, and I like poking about on my own. Beau gave me the names of some folks in Birmingham he's still in contact with. I can't wait to meet August Bishop!"

"Okay then. You have my phone number should you need anything during your stay. Feel free to come by as we finish the installation or if you want to talk further. November is very nice in the South!"

✧ ✧ ✧

On Sunday morning, Mitchell Jenkins was at the museum early, supervising the placement of folding chairs in its large, high-ceilinged ballroom. He had not heard from Ms. Horowitz since their meeting earlier in the week, but he figured since she was a New Yorker, being loose in Alabama shouldn't be a problem for her. He expected her by noon for her talk at two o'clock.

Rudolph Bates had called him earlier, thanked him once again for taking such good care of all of the pre- and post-opening arrangements. "Mr. Hall is very impressed with Meriden, the exhibition, the handsome catalog you put together, and of course, the museum."

Smiling to himself, Jenkins remembered the twenty minutes he had first had with Hall in his New York office. "Sure glad to hear that, Rudolph. It wouldn't have happened without you coming to town. Hope you'll be with us this afternoon!"

By twelve thirty, Babs Horowitz had not come by to sort her slides, check the microphone volume, or arrange her notes at the podium she was to use. Jenkins started feeling that certain cringing in the back of his neck when his life was going out of control. By two fifteen, Jenkins was in a panic. Horowitz was still MIA, and the ballroom was full of people. As he rose to make some sort of explanation, he heard a sharp "Hello" from the room's entrance. Babs Horowitz staggered through the doorway asking politely, but loudly, for the "whites only women's restroom."

Jenkins' heart stopped. She had been taking in the Alabama culture and was not pleased by what she had found.

He rushed to the ballroom's entrance, intercepting her near the restroom door. "Where have you been?" he asked, pushing her gently toward a wall and quickly learning she'd been drinking when she opened her mouth to answer.

"Is it time for my lecture? I'm quite ready to deliver it. If you'll just let me powder my nose for a moment, I'll be all set."

He let her pass and enter the restroom while he went back into the ballroom to face the audience. He apologized for the delay, saying Ms. Horowitz had just arrived and would be with them in a moment or two. He again headed back to the ladies room door.

After a moment Babs emerged, her hair combed, her clothing straightened, but her eyes still a blur. "You didn't tell me Alabama was so exciting," she began sarcastically. "Now I know why Britian left for New York."

Jenkins was now openly sweating. The last thing he or the museum needed was for Babs Horowitz to walk into that room and preach about civil rights. Though still drunk, he knew she was very capable of delivering one hell of a damning speech about inequality, injustice, and the killing of the creative spirit.

"Beau Britian left here because he was creatively dying. Mr. Jenkins, did you know that? He was..."

Jenkins quickly guided her into a small room off the museum's largest gallery he had converted into a private study for his use after hours. There was only one door, which he locked, depositing Ms. Horowitz on the leather couch. He covered her with a cotton throw, shutting the door behind him. There was considerable audience commotion by the time he re-entered the ballroom, though perhaps only five minutes had passed from when he had first intercepted Horowitz and his return. His presence at the lectern quickly silenced the audience and he took command of the room.

"Unfortunately, our speaker this afternoon has suddenly taken ill and is resting." He took a breath, gave the audience his best smile, and delivered an impromptu but remarkable talk about Beau Britian and some of his contemporaries, as well as the educational importance of the museum and its growing art collection.

His remarks were well received, and after making small talk with perhaps a dozen people wishing to congratulate him on all he was doing for Meriden, he managed to get back to Babs, who was still sleeping. She remained in her drowsy state as he drove her later to the airport for her return to New York and was only semi-alert when she boarded the airplane. He didn't hear from her, but was not surprised when he found an article she published in *Art News* about civil liberties and the lack thereof in the South, which she then related to the lack of artistic recognition among minorities. Meriden, thankfully, was not mentioned, and only Abram Rubin guessed what likely had happened that Sunday at the museum and in her four days of touring Alabama beforehand.

CHAPTER FOUR

DeBain Howard represented far more immediate purchasing power than Russell Bates ever could. One of four siblings to inherit controlling shares of SouthLife Insurance, he had risen quickly to become its president. Along with two of his brothers who worked in other areas of the conglomerate, Howard radically increased the scope of operations to include offices in all southern states, as well as diversification into radio and television. Gross earnings at the end of 1967 were nearly one hundred million dollars.

With his stunningly beautiful wife Emily, he built a twenty-four-room mansion on the city's north end, which she furnished using only the most expensive Atlanta and New York designers. From a modest background, Emily found herself thrust into mainstream Meriden power and high society. It was a role she often found difficult to manage, though the financial means her position provided were much to her liking. Early on in their marriage, Emily had tried to be a Howard wife, hosting both family and corporate functions, giving birth to Howard sons and generally seeking to find a social equilibrium. Howard's company travel, vision, drive, and boundless need for expansion kept them apart much of their early married years. At first, she found this somewhat liberating.

Their sons were shipped off to prep schools as soon as they were of age, allowing an overnight in Atlanta or Birmingham for shopping, exploring art museums, or attending a play. When she began to feel constrained, she would enlarge her radius to New York, where there was a corporate apartment at her disposal.

Occasionally, she and DeBain would find themselves in Meriden at the same time. These were interesting encounters, for she still found him handsome, viral, and entertaining, and used these times to her best advantage. She knew he was seeing other women when away from Alabama, but it was allowed because she was seeing other men. As long as it was done discreetly and brought no shame to the Howard name, anything was allowed. On the occasion of the Hall collection's museum opening, both the Howards were home and decided to attend the evening's event out of curiosity, and because Russell Hall was somebody. Driving to the museum, DeBain asked about a painting she had purchased in New York, now hanging in their home.

"I had it hung where we live," she said.

"That's not what I meant. I like it. It's very well done, though I find it haunting. Who's the artist again?"

"Axel Logan," she replied, "and it wasn't very expensive."

"That's a very good bit of news," he said, smiling. "I like it more already!"

The museum was crowded when they arrived, and as usual, they walked off in separate directions. To her surprise, Emily found she was enjoying the exhibition quite a bit, though it was more contemporary than she knew DeBain would care for. She also found the collection of men in attendance quite pleasing and had no trouble surrounding herself with three or four in a corner of a quiet gallery. As for her husband, he lost little time finding the power people of Meriden. He knew they would be introduced to Russell Hall when he arrived and wanted to be part of that group.

Mitchell Jenkins spent much of the early evening greeting guests and making mental notes on who was with whom and what they seemed most interested in. It was part of his approach to people, to watch, remember, and, when or if the time came, act on what he knew. The Halls and the Bates arrived a tasteful forty-five minutes after the reception began. He found himself fascinated by wealthy people. They surely had problems like those faced by anyone, but their money gave them the opportunity to rise above and easily find solutions. Jenkins spoke to the Howards on their arrival, expressing his delight that they were both in attendance, then watched them part ways—she to the artwork and he to his peers. As always, Emily looked exceptionally well cared for, and he concluded money could take care of that just like everything else. She was watching him too. He was rough, she thought, but something indescribable in his manner she found attractive. She was sure other women thought that as well. She worked her way slowly toward where he was talking to a white-gloved widow of ten years.

"Mr. Jenkins," she interrupted, "this is such a wonderful event for our city, and what a great party you've thrown."

The woman he had been talking with was caught mid-sentence by Emily's interruption, and Jenkins, wanting an opportunity to talk to Emily Howard, didn't know how to handle the potential ruffled feathers of his original conversation partner.

"Why thank you, Emily," he said. "It's so nice of you and DeBain to attend this evening."

The widow smiled at them both and turned to begin a conversation with someone else.

"Actually," he continued, "its everyone's party. The kind of celebration I hope the museum will become more accustomed to having for our important exhibitions." He had recovered from his momentary awkwardness and was concentrating now on the wonderfully fitted dress Emily was wearing. "Have you had an opportunity to meet the Halls, Emily? I'm sure you will find them to be quite interesting."

"I'm sure I will," she responded, deliberately not speaking his first name, hoping to make him feel subordinate. "I purchased a painting several weeks ago in New York. It's a small watercolor by Logan. Do you know his work?"

Jenkins thought for a moment. The great realist, still painting his way through the Abstract Expressionists, the Pop crowd, and the New York critics; his paintings had recently begun to do very well.

"Certainly, Axel Logan has always been a fine painter." Jenkins remembered seeing one of his paintings on his last visit to the Metropolitan that the museum had purchased recently, setting off a bit of a rush on his work. It was a very simple painting really, its content full of ambiguous questions.

"It's nice to know one of his paintings is in our city. I'd love to see it sometime when convenient."

"How about Monday evening? You could come over around six for a cocktail. DeBain and I would love to hear how you put this exhibition together."

The invitation accepted, Emily Howard smiled, then was on her way across the gallery, picking up an offered glass of champagne. Mitchell Jenkins felt a surge of relief as she left. She was a bit of a puzzle. *Rich women are a different breed*, he thought.

The weekend's events had been more of a strain on Jenkins than he'd thought. Babs Horowitz had been a mistake, and he now realized Beau had recommended her knowing she'd be trouble. One of his little jokes. Yet he knew there was much truth in what she had said and written about. He was a Southerner though, and while he knew there was much wrong between the races still in the 1960s, his upbringing would not let his conscience prevail. He had a similar attitude about women. While his brain told him there were no differences in ability between the sexes, his upbringing had ingrained in him that women were made for only two tasks in life, and it was a barrier he just could not or would not get past.

He thought about Emily Howard on his way to their home the following Monday evening. He found her very attractive. Knowing she was at least seven years his senior did not seem to bother him, and he found that odd. Young women were more his style usually. Perhaps it was her sophistication that was attractive. He remembered how she had looked at the reception. Though it was fall and the evening's temperature cool, she was without a wrap. Her strapless white dress exposing tan shoulders had made him wonder where the tan stopped, if at all! He wondered too about the Logan painting he would soon be seeing. Perhaps it was a random, chance purchase. She had seen the painting in the gallery window, walked in, and bought it. The thought of that kind of free spending tantalized him. He had spent a few hours that afternoon reading anything he could find on Axel Logan and hoped he could remember enough about the artist's life to impress.

When Jenkins arrived, lights sparkled through the windows on the first floor of the large, stone home. It seemed to him it was much too large for two people, though he knew it saw much entertaining. He parked his car just past a wooded patio area. Two large German shepherds rose from their sleeping positions on the patio and trotted toward him. Normally Mitchell Jenkins wasn't frightened by dogs, but he was tired and these two did not look particularly friendly. *Well,* he thought looking out the car window at the two beasts awaiting him and slowly opening the car door, *at least they look well fed!*

DeBain and Emily Howard were awaiting him in a large sitting room in the center of the house. He had been greeted at the door by a maid, who took his coat and escorted him into the room. DeBain was behind the bar making martinis, while Emily stood by the mantle over which the Axel Logan painting was hung. *She's posing,* Jenkins thought. Perhaps the tableau could be called, *Woman in Blue Velvet Pants and White Translucent Top.* He smiled at them both as DeBain handed out glasses, then sat in a leather wing-backed chair.

"Well Mitch, what do you think of my prize?"

Jenkins coughed slightly at the question, wondering if Howard was talking about his provocative wife or the painting. "Definitely a Logan," he replied, mad at himself for sounding so stupid. "Looks very nice where you've hung it. Is it a recent work? Did you buy it at Serelle in New York?"

The painting was of a kitchen interior, dark with much use of the artist's typical green wash, and on the table was a blue pitcher. The pitcher gave the work its center, clear and distinctive against the ethereal abstractness of the background.

"The painting was completed just last year," Emily chimed in, "and I did purchase it at Serelle."

Jenkins was pleased with himself as there were several galleries it might have come from. "As a young man, Axel began showing at the Davis Gallery, I believe, in the early fifties. Not long after, the gallery closed due to Davis' death, and Logan kind of floated along for a couple years until he was picked up by Serelle. He also occasionally shows work at the Hamilton Gallery as well." Jenkins saw Emily was listening to his every word, while DeBain was fingering his martini olive.

"Do you think I made a good choice Mitchell?" she asked. "The painting was one of six the gallery had on view. I thought it the strongest of the group."

Jenkins smiled at her and nodded. "It's a very complete work of an artist who is finally getting his due. The curving line of the pitcher's side is what holds one's attention. It is so crisp and certain against the uncertain background of the room. It's of a good size, has weight and presence." He didn't know how much more he could say about the painting without revealing his personal views on Logan, an artist of whom he was not particularly fond.

"Do you think it will hold or increase its value?" DeBain asked.

Jenkins turned to view the work again before answering, sensing the painting may be a sore spot between husband and wife. "In this world, values are hard to predict long-term. There are too many people making decisions about artwork—critics, art historians, museum curators. The test of time is really the only arbiter worth consulting. Logan's been working constantly for some years, showing his work in New York, and he's soon to have a bit of a retrospective in a museum there next spring. With the Met's recent purchase of one of his earlier pieces, I certainly think it's not going to lose its value." He turned to DeBain, "You're not thinking of selling it so soon after it's arrival in Meriden, I hope. I haven't had a chance to borrow it for the museum!"

They all laughed at his joke.

"It certainly would be available to the museum sometime," Howard assured him, "especially in light of the Hall collection and the interest it is generating. I suppose you will be offered many things for exhibition that might become part of the Museum's collection eventually."

Smiles all around. Jenkins was pleased to move away from Axel Logan toward an area in which he was eager to engage—DeBain Howard.

"It's very difficult trying to build a collection distinct for Meriden, Alabama while staying within the limited financial means of the museum and the community." Jenkins had rehearsed this speech often and thought the time may just be right to try it out. "Certainly, the task would be easier if the museum already had a collection of objects it had been given over the years. The Met, for instance, has a worldly collection of things that have come to it without solicitation. In recent years they have had to turn down gifts, as holding collections is expensive due to storage, insurance, maintenance, and the people charged with caring for such a wide variety of collections. Did you know the Met has storage vaults running underneath Fifth Avenue filled with things that will never see the light of day? We simply cannot afford that kind of operation plus it's not in our best interest."

His audience was in wholehearted agreement, and he continued. "There have been things given and accepted from the time of Chapman Billings that are highly eclectic and largely worthless. Quality is the key to our collecting going forward. We must build a collection of objects that are unique and not found within our region. Just last spring the museum's board began thinking this way when they decided to apply for a purchase grant from the National Endowment for the Arts for work by living American artists. If we're successful, it will be a great beginning. Our recent Hall exhibition was created and guided by an astute collector with the funds at his disposal to acquire significant works from both new and established artists. We're not yet in his league, but we've got to think like we could be in time!"

Jenkins could tell the Howards were listening intently to his re-marks. DeBain was interested in the dollar amount of the federal grant request as well as how the matching funds were to be raised. He was thinking of how the family name could be linked to the effort and asked a few additional questions about gift tax deductions.

Sensing he might be close to hooking this fish, Jenkins continued. "The grant is a dollar-for-dollar match for a total of thirty thousand dollars if our request is approved." He noted the audible response from his audience, took it as somewhat of a good sign, and continued. "As we've defined our collection scope in broad terms, it was much easier to provide an overview of the works and artists we might go after. Had I known of your Logan purchase earlier, I might have included a sentence or two about Meriden having collectors interested in our area of specialization. For the purpose of this project though, I'm thinking it would be most advantageous to purchase multiple works by rising artists rather than purchasing one or two works by those already established. So, we'll need to be judicious in our selections. As you may know, Dr. Abram Rubin has been collecting in this area for some time and is a wealth of information for me. He relocated to California recently, but has graciously consented to work on the project as an advisor focused on West Coast artists. And of course, our fellow Alabamian, Beau Britian can guide us from New York."

DeBain said he was not familiar with Britian, to which Jenkins was only too happy to respond.

"Beau has become something of a shooting star in the contemporary art market and has already been very helpful in adding to the Meriden museum's collections through his network of friends in New York."

Jenkins and Howard continued talking, but Emily had zoned out. Financial talk bored her because it always led in the same direction. Wealth was a wonderful thing, she thought, but the scheming and fret-ting about it was not. She wondered how much money it took before wealth became joyful. Turning her attention back to the two men in the room, she began watching Jenkins more closely—his gestures and body language, expressing his passionate interest in art and his museum. Didn't he know this was rural Alabama? Half the people over forty have never been to school. The working class fought almost every effort to raise taxes for classroom education and school lunches—certainly they would never support art. Mitchel Jenkins didn't look crazy, she mused, and neither did he sound that way. She looked over to where her husband sat and knew he would contribute to this cause in the family's name, amused at how he made Jenkins finish his pitch before saying anything. *How many other wealthy Meriden families had he been talking with before ours?* Then her thoughts turned to Jenkins personally. *What is his financial position? Surely the museum can't afford to pay him all that much. How much of what he's been saying this evening is true? How is he in bed?*

Jenkins finished his remarks and was still uncertain as to where he stood with DeBain Howard. It was difficult for him to second-guess the wealthy. They didn't have to commit to anything quickly and certainly were sophisticated enough not to show their true feelings in a conversation like this one. Still, he always tried to predict their responses and now was finding their silence maddening. As the large grandfather clock in the hallway struck eight, Emily Howard returned to her place on a small loveseat by the window with a fresh scotch in hand, and DeBain cleared his throat to speak.

"Well, Mitch," he began, "I can see you have given the culture of Meriden, or the lack thereof, a great deal of consideration. I had no idea you and the museum's board were so active and eager to give our little town an artistic identity. You must know I believe governments can do more harm than good meddling in the private sector's business. Too many guidelines and red tape; they are going to ruin the commodities business before they are through. However, if they have funds to give away, I suppose Meriden ought to get in line—we're certainly more deserving than New York for instance, or LA. Don't you think Emily?"

She looked up and smiled at her husband and Jenkins. She was feeling more than slightly drunk, and since DeBain didn't like her this way in front of guests or in public, she didn't answer his question.

Howard cleared his throat again and continued. "We will certainly participate in the fundraising drive for your new collection. If it's possible, I'd like to make the gift through our company. I'm assuming there is some tax advantage to this. The Howard family has always been interested in art. My father had a small collection of paintings, not what I liked personally, but they seemed to make him quite happy." He stood and walked to the mantle and looked at the Logan. "This isn't the first piece of art we've purchased, but certainly the most expensive! I'll have our accountants call you early next week. They are likely figuring our corporate tax position right now and will have a good fix on the amount of the contribution we're in a position to make."

Mitchell Jenkins rose after a few minutes of thanks and appreciation and was escorted to the door by DeBain, who was talking about travel, the Hall collection and its insurance valuation. Jenkins was pleased to be leaving, for he was feeling a bit on edge, needing to get into the night air, maybe blow off a little steam. DeBain asked if he would be interested in making a trip to New York sometime in the next few weeks to look at artwork Jenkins might recommend for a Howard Collection.

"Look at your calendar and clear out maybe most of a week," he said. "Don't worry about the costs, we'll fly up on the company plane and we have an apartment there with three bedrooms. Think it over."

It didn't take much "thinking over." Giving it a week, Jenkins called DeBain to see if the invitation was still good. Two weeks later the Howards and Jenkins were aboard the SouthLife DC3 headed to New York – it was the most pleasant flight Jenkins ever made.

CHAPTER FIVE

Maureen Moses Jenkins was a flower of the deep South. The only daughter in a family of boys, she easily claimed the natural affection of her father and enjoyed every minute of it. She and Mitchell came of age in the same small Louisiana town during the 1950s. Segregation was a word that meant more than an isolation of the races in Opelousas. Not only were Blacks separated from whites, but sexes were also separated in the school system. Accordingly, Maureen attended the all-white Sandra Scott School for Women. It was where young ladies of good families were expected to go. Fortunately for its students, it was more of a finishing school, where Maureen developed interests that would last the rest of her life. Likewise, following the traditions of the city, Mitchell was schooled at the Rogers Military Academy in nearby Ville Platte. It was the school young men attended to prepare themselves for the mastery of their lives.

While Maureen was a perfect student, Jenkins was a problem, spending much of his adolescence on guard duty. He had been in and out of trouble as a youth, always in fights and the subject of gossip among the young ladies of Opelousas. He had few friends, and it was during this time, Maureen remembered, that the terrible accident occurred. It was something she still shut from her mind and refused to think Mitchell had any part of. She knew her initial attraction to him had been his reckless behavior, and that worried her. Both were vulnerable to seduction; the innocence of another time had blossomed into a natural curiosity Maureen expected he had already satisfied. They explored her curiosity the first time in the back seat of a car Mitchell borrowed from a friend after graduation. That fall, Jenkins would begin classes at UAB while Maureen stayed in Opelousas, waiting to be married so her life could begin.

It didn't take "Papa" Moses many evening encounters with Mitchell to conclude this young man was not the type to be content with lingering walks in the park with his daughter. It also didn't take him long to find the dirt road on the town's outskirts where Mitchell would take Maureen to spend evening hours on long summer nights. The car he had borrowed was a dark blue Hudson Deluxe four-door with an enormous back seat. Maureen Moses was someone he wanted now and was about to have again. In the moonlight, her face was flushed with excitement. Despite his growing need, he felt no real emotion for her, only that he was doing what was expected of any healthy young man. Maureen, while shy in the beginning, was now intent on repeating what she'd experienced weeks earlier.

At that instant, the car door jerked open. Mitchell felt the skin around his right shoulder pinched by the strength of a huge hand. With his belt unbuckled and his pants down to his knees, he was in no position to fight back or even free himself from the terrible grip. He was being pulled bodily from the car and as his head cleared the door, he turned slightly to see the hulking body of Maureen's father—one hand on him, the other holding a shotgun. Moses threw his captive to the ground as Maureen screamed.

"I don't know what's keepin' me from blowin' your head off boy." C.W. Moses held the shotgun inches from the side of Mitchell's face.

Maureen was sobbing and pleading with her father. "I love him Daddy! Don't kill him! Mitchell and I have been friends for a long time. We're going to be married next fall and we'll live in Birmingham by the college. It's what I want."

Jenkins tried to rise from the ground only to be kicked down again by the powerful Moses.

"You little bastard!" Moses shouted. "You've soiled my daughter. You're going to suffer for this like you never suffered before. No military school ever did to you what I'm about to."

Mitchell got to his feet and ran, jumping over the low brush that grew in clumps by the roadside. The suddenness of his movement startled Moses and gave him the advantage he desperately needed. He heard the shot gun discharge, the first barrel somehow louder than the second. Maureen screamed again as a third blast sent a flurry of small pellets into his left shoulder and he tumbled to the ground.

Mitchell heard the heavy breathing of his pursuer and tried to pick himself up from the soft earth to no avail. Moses was close and Maureen was with him. He was laying as quietly as he could, hoping the darkness would give him protection, when he suddenly remembered what Maureen had said to her father back at the car—*marriage?* The pain in his shoulder was now more than stinging as he got up and moved as quietly as he could toward the lake, where he could take cover and wash off the blood. He was a mere 100 feet from the water when Moses spoke.

"Hold, you bastard." The voice was low, as if Moses was standing next to him. Jenkins did as he was told. "Don't make me shoot again 'cause I'll drop you dead this close." Maureen was standing behind her father, her dress torn from running in the woods. "Real slow now, get up and walk back this way. We're gonna be real busy this evenin'. The three of us going callin' on Johnathan Mack, then maybe a doctor."

The three of them walked back to where the Hudson was parked, the back door still open. Maureen wrapped a blanket from the car around Mitchell's shoulder and he laid in the bed of Moses's truck. The ride to the Justice of the Peace's home seemed to take forever as Jenkins tried to shield his shoulder from the bumps in the road.

✲ ✲ ✲

Mitchell arrived in Birmingham a married man that fall. The couple found a small apartment off campus and set up housekeeping. Mitchell got through his classes and worked. Maureen took part-time jobs, much to her husband's displeasure. Wives were not supposed to work, but the money was needed badly. She did what she could to help, then she became pregnant. While he wondered how his life could get worse, he knew he was getting by somehow and resolved to do better as quickly as he could. Maureen would manage their home, and now their family, while Jenkins would manage his schoolwork and later a career—whatever that was to be—and he would succeed.

His interest in art had occurred quite by accident. Having to take a course in some artistic area, Jenkins enrolled in an introductory visual art class as a sophomore. He enjoyed the lectures and found the slide presentations calming. His interest blossomed into taking a studio course in painting, which was where he met Britian, enrolled as a "special student" and not seeking a degree. Britian was working odd jobs, painting at night in a run-down studio space he rented. Mitchell was particularly fascinated by both the intensity of Britian's time at his easel as well as the carefree lifestyle he and his artistic friends enjoyed. The atmosphere was compelling, and he wished his own situation in life would allow him total access to it. His junior year brought him a part-time job that would shape his future. He was hired as an assistant at the Birmingham Museum, helping with whatever needed doing, and in time coming to the attention of the museum's director, the venerable August Cortland Bishop.

A classical scholar, Bishop turned a cold shoulder toward contemporary art in general and the young "rabble rousers" who called themselves artists. His energies were channeled toward building a collection of French Impressionist paintings and was capped by the gift of a significant number of these works being made to the museum during Jenkins' employment. The collection required the construction of a new wing, funded in large part through government sources and practically insuring Bishop's tenure for as long as he chose to stay in Birmingham.

Throwing himself into the new project, Bishop charged his young assistant with overseeing all other parts of the museum's programming, keeping the daily activities moving forward. Running around and sometimes through other staff appealed to Mitchell's nature, knowing if he was doing at least a satisfactory job in the eyes of his new mentor, any flack he encountered would be overlooked. Bishop reasoned that in time Jenkins would grow tired of working in his shadow, but for now the younger man would greatly benefit from his experience. Though reluctant to consider it, Bishop knew his own time in Birmingham would someday end, and he wanted to make sure his successor would carry on in a manner consistent with what he had set forth. Secretly, he began making plans for an eventual Jenkins takeover. He never expected his protege to disappoint him by actually taking a job in Meriden three years later. The change in plans didn't worry Bishop too much as he knew Meriden had far to go to rival Birmingham in the eyes of the art community. Besides, he had not given up on the idea that under pressure, Jenkins would eventually return to take over.

✵ ✵ ✵

These thoughts of his early days and the extent of his growth in Meriden came to Jenkins as he sat in the Howard's Fifth Avenue apartment. Upon their arrival in New York, the party of three had taken in two of the major museums (admittedly quicker than he liked), had a fashionable dinner at 21, and attended a party at the apartment of television talk show host Jimmy Corning. Corning gave parties rather frequently to identify new talent. SouthLife was one of the show's major sponsors, thus the Howards' invitations to attend when in the city. His program being filmed in the afternoon allowed him and his guests to watch the late-night telecast on two large monitors.

The evening was quite memorable for Jenkins, who played the part of a quiet, polite Southerner to the hilt. There were US senators in attendance, as well as the mayor, a couple New York Jets linemen, actors and actresses, the rich and super rich. After circulating for a while, Jenkins settled himself into a corner next to a small group who were talking about art. The distinguished-looking gentleman turned out to be the director of the Museum of Modern Art. The frail, elderly woman was the artist, Grace Donahue. Jenkins had not known the identities of either of these two when he seated himself and was awestruck after listening to their conservation. He felt compelled to say something, not to just sit there nursing his scotch, but was at a loss, not knowing much about the current art scene in the Big Apple. Finally, he introduced himself and made a few comments about the exhibitions he had seen earlier that afternoon. He was pleased not to have said too much to signify his visitor status and was relieved to see Emily Howard stagger toward him saying something about leaving.

It was mid-afternoon of the third day of their visit and Jenkins was taking a breather in the apartment. DeBain had spent the morning at his New York office and Emily was out shopping. Jenkins had spent much of the morning at the Metropolitan, had a wonderful chili dog for lunch from a vendor outside the museum, and now was awaiting DeBain's return. They had set the afternoon aside to tour three galleries Jenkins thought might have works that could be purchased for the Meriden museum should the federal funding be approved.

DeBain had no real art bias, a fact Jenkins appreciated. One object seemed as good as another to him, abstract or representational, so long as it held its value with the promise of potentially increasing. Emily, on the other hand, had very definite tastes about everything, which sometimes ran to the extreme. She would prove to be a real test for Jenkins' sense of what a woman should be and how she should act. She'd tease him when sober, converting to slapstick when drunk. This constant assault added to his tantalizing thoughts of her; the harder it was for him to understand her, the greater his fascination.

At three thirty DeBain returned, and after a quick change the two men were off. He had lined up an audience with Herschel Marelli and two other lesser galleries Jenkins thought were still worth Howard seeing. He was encouraged by Howard's increasing interest in art and hoped to be able to attract him to works as a diversion to the Logan. On their walk to the Marelli gallery, Jenkins briefed Howard on the owner's importance in contemporary art circles and his discovery of Beau Britian's work several years earlier. Jenkins had never met Marelli personally, but Britian had greased the wheel a bit and made the appointment for his fellow Alabamians before leaving on a trip to Paris that he had told Jenkins "was so good for the soul."

Herschel Marelli was immaculately dressed in a grey linen suit. Though a small man, he was very trim. Jenkins admired the serenity of his attitude while being faced with two men he didn't know. He rose from his polished desk and greeted them as if they were old friends, and good clients. *Beau must have really done a job on Marelli*, Jenkins thought. *He must think I'm Orphan Annie arriving with Daddy Warbucks.* Smiling to himself at that thought, he hoped Marelli wouldn't push anything on DeBain.

They were offered coffee and seated in comfortable chairs of Italian design before Marelli asked about their visit to New York. DeBain smiled, admitting New York was like a second home as he was often here doing business. Then he launched into a conversation about the insurance business and the nation's economy amid an unpopular war. Jenkins noticed Marelli listening to every word and responded in kind. They seemed to be enjoying each other. *This SOB is really a cool customer,* Jenkins' thought, beginning to feel out of his element, whatever that was. He wanted to understand the world Marelli lived in where he not only could talk art, but also could hold his own talking about anything with someone like Howard. Jenkins knew he was outclassed, playing in a league he had only dreamed about, and he couldn't let his guard down. The stakes, yet undefined, were getting too high already. He felt woefully unprepared and began to panic. To retain an aspect of his composure, he rose from his chair to examine the Lichtenstein painting hanging next to him.

Sensing Jenkins' discomfort, Marelli turned the conversation to Meriden, the museum, and the Hall Collection currently on display. Again, Jenkins appreciated his old friend's briefing of Marelli and settled back into his chair. He began talking about his background, coming to Meriden, and the museum's progress during his tenure, joking about not having a Britian in the collection yet. He was unsure about talking with Marelli about the grant application. While his admiration for the man had grown since they entered his gallery, he wasn't sure how the government might feel about it. However, DeBain Howard did want to talk about the pending grant opportunity.

Marelli was interested but not overly anxious since every painting in the room was worth well over the grant's ceiling. "The Marelli gallery will be as helpful as possible in suggesting artists we think you and your board might wish to consider," he assured.

They talked for another thirty minutes and by the time they left, Marelli and Howard were fast friends with invitations for future visits and exhibition openings being scheduled. The two walked toward the gallery's entrance with Jenkins bringing up the rear.

As they walked back down Madison, Howard began talking about the audience they had just finished. "I was very much taken with him and enjoyed being there quite a bit. You seemed unusually quiet Mitchell, did I say anything wrong?"

"Not at all. I guess I'm still too much of a country boy to be completely at ease here. Herschel is a good man, as good as they come in this business. No one should be worried about the value of any work sold through his gallery. I just get nervous when anyone begins talking about money in sums larger than five thousand dollars."

DeBain laughed, saying he admired Jenkins' conservatism. "You'd make a good banker, Mitchell," he joked.

Between the time of his visit to the Howard home and their departure for New York, SouthLife had issued a check to the museum for five thousand dollars. Howard assumed Jenkins understood there could potentially be more funds coming the museum's way if he played his cards correctly.

The second gallery was even more to DeBain's liking. Its director had more energy than Marelli, and the artwork was not as contemporary. He and the director quickly became deeply engaged in a discussion of a bronze sculpture by Seymore Lipton. It was clear DeBain was taken by the piece as he talked about it the remainder of the afternoon and that evening over dinner. Jenkins was something of a captive audience as the two ate in the apartment, where DeBain proved himself an accomplished chef. Afterward, he went to a meeting with his New York executives, and Jenkins resolved to retire early. Emily spent the evening with friends.

Jenkins woke at one thirty in the morning to the sound of someone walking around in the apartment and listened intently to voices as they came closer to his bedroom. He clearly heard Emily's voice and felt relieved. However, there were at least two other voices, male voices, low and murmured. Then there was giggling and laughing. Jenkins rose and opened his bedroom door slightly, trying not to make any noise. He could barely see into the living room, but could tell the patio door was open as he could hear traffic from the street below. Only the bar lights were on, where Emily and the two men were taking advantage of the late night and each other's pleasant inebriation. Jenkins opened the door a bit wider for he could hardly believe what he saw taking place not twenty feet away. Crossing the hallway, Jenkins slowly peered into the dimly lit room. There, amid sofa cushions and bed pillows he saw Emily Howard and two young naked men enjoying stimuli of various kinds. He was at once pleased and shocked by what was going on, and after watching for a few moments quietly went back to his room.

Emily certainly did not look her age, and he was amazed at her apparent appetite. He wondered how she could be so uninhibited when DeBain might return at any moment. Then he wondered if she entertained in this fashion when back in Meriden. His thoughts were interrupted by a gentle knock at his door. Waiting a moment, he opened the door and found Emily leaning against the hallway wall. She wore only a silk bathrobe, unfastened. She smiled up at Jenkins who was visibly interested in her tanned body standing only four feet away.

"Did you enjoy the show? I thought about inviting you to join us but decided I might be pushing my luck with three. I thought you'd be out with DeBain tonight," she continued, her hand slowly rubbing the upper part of her right thigh. "I was a bit surprised to see you standing there. Really, you should show a lady more respect than to peep while she is entertaining."

Jenkins was at a loss for words, finally asking where the men were that he had seen in the living room.

"They're gone. Those boys need to get their sleep or they'll be cranky tomorrow." She laughed and pushed herself into his room, watching Jenkins become increasingly more self-conscious. *How long,* she wondered, *will it take him to discover he's standing in his underwear with an erection?* It made a wonderful scene, and she was enjoying every minute of it.

Jenkins was also wondering many things as he watched Emily Howard circle around him in her robe and heeled slippers. One thing he did not have to wonder about was her body. Even now, she didn't seem tired after all the "exercise" she just had, and in fact, was obviously looking for more. He thought of the large hands of C. W. Moses and how they once threatened his very existence. DeBain was certainly not Moses in stature but equally capable of hurting him in ways that could be far more harmful. Had Emily been anyone else's wife…DeBain represented too much potential to be lost over a woman, even though she was wonderfully seductive, now laying before him on the bed still warm from his body.

For the first time since she had entered the room, Jenkins looked her in the eyes. "They say three's company and I wouldn't have wanted to feel out of place." He smiled confidently for a moment, then discovered his lack of clothing.

Emily laughed as he pulled the bedspread around himself. "Are you really so modest, Mitchell? Certainly, at this time of morning we can afford to be a bit less formal. You really don't need to cover up on my account."

He smiled at her again, nervous and conflicted. Quickly, Emily was on her feet. She'd grown tired of his predictability. *Country boys are all alike,* she thought. She stood in front of him and lightly touched his bare chest with her fingertip. She liked his authentic build and wanted him to make a move toward her, but knew he would not. After a moment she turned and left the room as quickly as she at entered. He could hear her light laughter as she walked down the hall.

He dropped the bedspread from his waist and laid back down. He was sweating and angry. Getting up again he took three aspirin from the bathroom and got into bed. He fell asleep but it was not restful. The smell of breakfast cooking awoke him, and dressing quickly, he found the maid preparing a meal for one. After a bit of small talk, Jenkins asked where DeBain was.

"Mr. Howard's generally never here for breakfast. He spends his nights at his club."

"And Mrs. Howard?"

"She was up and out early this morning on her way to Italy. Said to say goodbye to you when you woke up and that you should tell Mr. Howard she'll be back in Meriden in three weeks."

Suddenly the morning was full of questions, none of which Jenkins could answer. His last day in the city was spent alone. DeBain had telephoned to say he would be busy and that Jenkins should meet him at the airport for the return flight. He knew his wife had gone to Europe and said little about it; she apparently did this from time to time. Jenkins spent the day visiting smaller galleries in the newly established arts district of SoHo, had lunch there, then returned to the apartment to pack. He arrived at the Newark airfield in plenty of time, and the co-pilot fixed drinks. DeBain arrived precisely at seven thirty for "wheels up." He looked tired, Jenkins thought, but was in good spirits as he greeted him.

A moderately sized wooden crate was being loaded into the plane. "If Emily can purchase art for the house, so can I," Howard explained. "You remember that bronze, the Lipton? Well now you know where you can see it again."

Jenkins was both shocked and pleased as the piece was handsome and abstract. "I hope you enjoy it. Perhaps an exhibition of his work could be organized sometime. We could even travel it to Birmingham."

Howard was listening but didn't seem particularly interested, and Jenkins decided not to push the subject—at least not right away. It was enough that Howard was interested in purchasing now, all else would come in time. He sat back in his seat enjoying his scotch, listening to the plane's engines come to life. It had been a good trip—just full of surprises.

The two men spent the next few years in an on-again-off-again arrangement, with DeBain calling on Jenkins to look at a particular art object that interested him. While they were sometimes not Jenkins' favorite works, he was wise enough not to discourage him. Sooner or later, the businessman would be needed to assist the museum in some way.

CHAPTER SIX

The years between 1969 and 1971 were ones of planning and austerity for the museum and expansion for the facility's burgeoning school, which was, after all, the reason for the museum's beginning in the first place. Jenkins had successfully convinced the city's governing commissioners the museum was a sustainable asset to Meriden and should be funded at least in part through taxation, as was done with the school system. It was a time of researching how local governments worked, in theory, and getting to know the personalities who in fact made it work. He began to compile extensive files on all city officials (elected or otherwise) to determine any personal interests or flaws that might assist in his pursuit of them. He became fascinated by the projections supplied by the local chamber of commerce and planning commission that showed substantial growth potential in the years ahead. A strong cultural component, they believed, could be a selling point for northern company executives eager to expand to an area where living expenses were low and labor relatively cheap.

Jenkins thought there was a better than even chance of receiving government funding, but at this stage in the museum's development, artistic education, not exhibitions or collections, would get his foot in the door.

Consequently, he developed a five-year growth plan for a full integration of the museum's educational capacity with the city's school system. The museum would provide a place for educational activities, as well as staff to coordinate with classroom teachers, while the schools would provide students on a daily basis. For his plan to succeed, current levels of private fundraising would never be enough; thus the need for government funding. The museum's leadership understood this but were reluctant to give up their operational autonomy to a bureaucratic entity. Jenkins knew it was his job to answer financial questions that might arise from the city and manage programming issues that were bound to come into play from his Board. With the museum's financial matters keeping him busy, Jenkins was posed with a second matter that would require his attention and capital.

The NEA purchase grant had come through for the full $15,000, requiring the remainder of the local match to be raised as soon as possible. Acquiring artwork for its collection was every museum director's dream—and Jenkins was no exception—yet it took him even deeper into fundraising. Asking for money from any potential source was a lot like prostitution, he thought, and as far as he could remember there had not been any courses teaching this skill when he was at the university. Perhaps the lessons could come from his mentor in Birmingham; surely August Bishop had experience in this area. So once again, Jenkins opened the lines of communication between the two institutions, which had grown a bit cold over the past months. Bishop was always cordial and interested in what his old student was doing, particularly when it related to expansion in Meriden. While convinced his own institution's place was secure as the museum of the state, he wanted to know if a rival was in the running. With his courtly manner and prestige, Bishop had mastered the fine art of keeping politicians in pocket to use whenever necessary. His was the luxury of using the telephone for requests to officialdom rather than having to meet with them in person.

✳ ✳ ✳

The intercom button of his desk phone was blinking furiously when Jenkins noticed it and stopped thinking of the past. His office, cluttered with the reminders of the present, had become his only refuge. He looked at the phone again. That will be Martha, he thought to himself. I wonder how much time I have? He picked up the receiver, and it was indeed Martha Dyer, his administrative assistant.

"Mitchell, the press has been phoning all morning, they want a statement about Ted's leaving. What should I tell them? They know you're in the building."

"Try to get me as much time as you can, kid. I've already issued a release. Make them wait awhile, and don't let them get to Taylor. I'll try to call him again."

Jenkins looked at his watch. It was evening in Europe, a hard time to reach anyone by phone. He sat back in his chair, removed his glasses, and rubbed his eyes, tired from the strain of the last few weeks. He thought again of August Bishop and the times he spent with him in Birmingham. He had learned so much from him. His mind drifted and his office faded away once again.

✻ ✻ ✻

The one golden rule Jenkins didn't have to learn from Bishop was to never let anything or anyone get too far away. People could always be used to some advantage, and he made it a point not to make enemies unless it was completely unavoidable. "Never burn bridges," was the advice he would give from time to time. In Jenkins' dealings with city government, this advice was particularly useful as the institution's history was remembered by older members of city council—memories that helped him strengthen his case for funding. Bishop had supplied information and statistics about the impact of local governmental support on the Birmingham museum that Jenkins could use in Meriden. Every opportunity was added into his plan, including construction of a free-standing art school, an outdoor theater, and expansion of the current museum facility on the available acreage surrounding the existing building. It was a strong effort, presented with an artist's colored renderings supplied by an eager local architectural firm. He also increased his rapport with the men in the community who consistently were involved with making new projects happen—members of established families in the city as well as the state. They were professional men of business, medicine, and law. Lawyers were his highest interest, as they could counsel him on how best to approach those who made the decisions on funding. By the time he was ready to present his case in hearings that would include six months of discussion and deliberation, Jenkins was fully prepared.

However, he was to achieve only part of his goal by early 1970 and came away bitter, since the city council had not been entirely convinced of his vision and had not given the museum the full amount requested. For their part, the council felt they were following sound, conservative government judgment. They were dubious of the growth Jenkins was predicting, but realized the young director had a concept worth funding at some level. It was a signal to Jenkins that his board and annual contributors would need to shoulder a greater share of the financial burden. Although disappointed, Jenkins would not retreat from his role in the museum's life or leave the city. With patience and the correct pressure applied, he still stood to become the August Bishop of the future.

The two men spent several days together as teacher and student, much as it had been when Jenkins was an undergraduate. He learned when dealing with elected officials and public money, alternate avenues to assure forward movement were essential. The strategies pertaining to something as seemingly mundane as the funding of an art museum needed to be well conceived and articulated to allow the person making the ask to act on many fronts, and to provide correct and ready answers.

Bishop understood the need for significant funding in Meriden. As a younger man, he too wanted to assure his own position in Birmingham by growing the institution he took over. "Make yourself seem irreplaceable," he told Jenkins, "essential to the museum's operation. When an institution is small, this isn't as important, but you have grown your shop noticeably and need to ensure your own position there by simply being visible. The larger you grow, the more secure you become. I'm sure you remember when I dealt with my own need for government funding, all that time I spent lunching with politicians, talking about the Impressionist paintings I was working to bring to the museum and how important it would be to the State. I think I just wore them down and they finally saw the light. You need to make your politicians believe the museum is just as important to their community as a library or a school or a new sewage plant. You need to be part of the annual tax budget."

The old man had always been pleased with the promise of his pupil. Through all the years he had been in Birmingham, Jenkins was the only one who reminded him of himself when he started out in the museum business. Museum business—an oxymoron if there ever was one! It used to be museums were run by the third or fourth sons of wealthy families. He would be connected with other wealthy families, and financial needs were generally handled over martinis in the confines of a private club. Directors studied art history and devoted their lives to research and travel, hoping to uncover the artistic find of a decade. But those times were over. Jenkins, Bishop thought, was perhaps the perfect combination of talent for the new order of museum directors. He did not have a vast knowledge of art history, but he had a sharp mind, understood how to accomplish goals, and he could talk to anyone. Bishop listened as Jenkins talked about his refined multi-year plan. It was an impressive undertaking for a town the size of Meriden. He smiled to himself as he thought of Jenkins succeeding him sometime in the future and how his experience in Meriden would be important. Bishop had long contemplated his own retirement from a career spanning over forty years. So many of his peers had faced their endings already, some expiring while sitting behind their desks. He was tired, he admitted to himself, but he wanted a few more years. Besides, his successor was not quite ready.

Jenkins had finished explaining his plan and was waiting for Bishop's remarks. The old man's eyes were slightly glazed over by his own thoughts, and his silence made Jenkins uncomfortable. In a few moments Bishop's mind cleared and he came back to Jenkins' funding issue.

"I have spoken to a few of my friends in the state legislature and had a brief conversation with the governor, who I think you know is a close personal friend. We all agree there is a way your museum could have a modicum of state funding that would be much more reliable than local money."

Once again, Bishop had dealt Jenkins a surprise card. He had no idea his mentor had taken his financial problems so seriously. He knew the governor and Bishop were close friends, childhood friends in fact. But the thought that Bishop had spoken to him on Jenkins's behalf without mentioning it beforehand was at once gratifying and frightening. He wondered who else Bishop knew in high places. How many times had his name come up in conversation with people unbeknownst to him? The thought made Jenkins very uneasy.

"It is our opinion," Bishop continued, "that you should pursue the establishment of your own governing commission selected by you, of course, appointed by the governor, and funded through the state. These people would be leading citizens in Meriden and sympathetic to your cause."

It was a loophole Bishop had found for him. He marveled at the political moxie of a man so revered in academic circles. This was the type of man Jenkins would have to become if he were to survive the years ahead. He thought briefly about the favors Bishop would request for helping implement this proposed legislative procedure. He wondered too who would be powerful enough to introduce such an amendment on the legislative floor, but Bishop had already arranged that.

"I've taken the liberty of speaking to the senator from Marion County, just east of here. You may remember him from those summer get-togethers we used to have at the lake house. Harry Noel is his name, used to hang around with my niece."

Jenkins well remembered the niece but could not place Harry Noel. He also remembered the summer staff parties at the lake. They would all behave tastefully until the old man left for his bed, then the beach would be littered with nude bodies in and out of the water. Maureen had hidden herself away during those gatherings and was glad when Jenkins decided to leave Birmingham for a quieter life in Meriden.

"Well," Bishop continued, "Harry finally got into the pants of that young girl and married her to make it legal. So now he's my nephew, making him easy to get to on most matters. He's agreed to talk with your people in Montgomery about drafting the necessary legislation. I believe your chap there is named Peters."

So old Bishop saw to it that his niece married a politician. I wonder what she has been able to tell him of the comings and goings in Montgomery. Jenkins confirmed Philip Peters was indeed his state senator and further a member of the art association and frequent visitor. He was the perfect person for the job, Jenkins agreed.

"There should be no opposition to the enactment," Bishop said. "You will need to work closely with these two until you are completely satisfied with the language and tone of the document. Once enacted it will be very difficult to change."

His head still reeling, Jenkins drove back to Meriden in the early evening after raising a glass of scotch with Bishop. His mind wandered back to those summer parties at the lake house. Bishop had always been careful to invite the same number of men and women to ensure a proper mixing of sexes after he went to bed. Jenkins wondered if the rumors were true about his watching the beach from his bedroom through a telescope. Bishop's niece, Jess Courtland, was the kind of girl one dreamed about, though a compulsive flirt. She'd flit from man to man, arousing each, then leaving just when they wanted her the most. He remembered the first time he saw her floating on a raft in the middle of the lake. Suddenly she stood up, waved to her admirers on the shore, slipped off the top of her two-piece, and tossed it into the water. She was careful to be far enough from shore so exact details could not be readily seen, and the guys dove in to get a better look. By the time they got there though, she had retrieved her top and was paddling away from them toward the opposite shore.

He also remembered the time he had been summoned to the lake house for an evening's conference while Bishop was dealing with the museum's expansion. He had arrived only to find Bishop had been detained, and there to greet him was Jess. She fixed him a few drinks, then seduced him. Leading him to a bedroom, she stripped off the few clothes she wore and proceeded to do things to him he'd only imagined. He fell into a deep, restful sleep until Jess awakened him.

"Uncle's home and would like to see you."

"He's here?" Jenkins managed. "What time is it? Does he know what we've . . ."

Jess tried to soothe his fear. "Calm down, Mitchell. I told him you were tired because he was working you too hard. Everything's fine. Besides, I'm on the pill."

Had Bishop been here the whole time? he wondered, *watching his niece put me through some sort of manhood trial?* He tried to put these thoughts out of his head but could not. He remembered other times when Bishop wasn't where he was supposed to be and seemed to know more about Jenkins than he should. His mind shifted to Maureen. He knew she suspected his infidelities since their marriage at the hands of her father, but also was confident she would say nothing about them. She knew how he was long before they married.

✲ ✲ ✲

It was the intercom again. "Mitchell."

Martha's voice was tired. He could see her in the office across the hall, dressed in a well-tailored business suit.

"I think you better take the call on your private line. It's Louis Sterling, and he won't take no for an answer."

Jenkins hesitated before he spoke. The tension would not go away. Sterling had been a friend for so long, he thought.

"Thanks, I'll speak to him. Pick up on the call though. I'll want you take notes. Lou! Sorry to keep you like that, but you caught me in the john. How are things with you?"

"Things are getting tight around here, Mitchell. That statement you issued should have been discussed with the commission beforehand. My people here are beating down my door to ask questions. As if that weren't enough, I'm getting calls from Taylor and Laura wondering what the hell Rudy and I have been keeping from them. All hell is about to break loose, and you are smack dab in the middle of it."

Jenkins held the phone and Sterling's piercing voice a few inches from his ear. "Lou, these are all circumstantial problems that only seem related. I've told the commission the facts, believe me, and under the circumstances there is really no problem. There may be a few people who want to make trouble for me, but we can weather those storms. As long as I have the backing of the commission, nothing can hurt us."

"But all those resignations," Sterling countered. "The press won't leave something like that alone."

"Malcontents, that's all. After they make their charges the press will come to me. I have files with enough stuff to discredit each one of them. They're going to wish they'd never started any of this."

"But that's only half the problem Mitch, and we both know it."

Jenkins could hear something in the background at Sterling's office. He strained to distinguish the sounds. "Lou, are you alone?"

Sterling paused before answering. "Rudy's here, that's all."

They're plotting, Jenkins' thought. I should have suspected that! "Listen Lou, just tell your people to come to see me in a day or so. I want to give the others enough time to hang themselves."

"What if they don't Mitchell?"

Jenkins hung up and called for Martha to come into his office. "Martha, I want memos to the file of Rudolph Bates and Louis Sterling. On this date in a telephone conversation from Sterling to me, I learned of their fears and suspicions of my administrative abilities and judgement." He went on dictating, then instructed his assistant to put a copy in each man's file. "When we get out of this thing, kid, I want those two bastards out."

The two looked at each other. She was the only one on staff who had stayed close to him and was the only one he trusted. She knew too much, but there was a reason for that. She left his office to let Jenkins make notes for the press conference he decided to call the following afternoon. However, he was in no condition to think about anything and put his pen down.

CHAPTER SEVEN

Creation of the Meriden Museum Commission took exactly four months to complete. Jenkins lost no time in contacting Senator Philip Peters at his Montgomery office to learn how this type of legislation worked, its manner and timing. He learned the new year would be a critical time for relations between state and municipal governments, with the latter wanting more control of local matters. Explaining the intent of the proposed legislation, Jenkins found a sympathetic audience in Peters, and the two of them, with input from Harry Noel and Bishop, worked up a document designed to give Jenkins the freedom he would need to operate a quasi-governmental agency doing business as a privately run one.

The commission would be made up of eight residents of Meriden County serving for staggered terms. It would have an elected chairman, and Jenkins would report to the commission on a regular basis concerning museum programming and finances partially provided by the state. It would be the sole governing body of the museum. Nominations for membership would be reviewed and appointed by the governor of Alabama, who would serve as an ex-officio member. The bill was an imposing and unique document, reviewed and refined by lawyers in both

Montgomery and Meriden before being introduced by Peters for debate by the state's bureaucrats.

Selection of the eight members proved to be the greatest problem for Jenkins. His first thought was to appoint eight men he knew would get along with him and each other. Rudolph Bates was a promising candidate, representing industry and regional growth. He also wanted men of community stature who had attended the museum's events or at least expressed an interest.

"Someone in the media, I think," he said to Bishop on a phone call. "Someone in construction, and someone who's good at managing money."

"You need to find several someones *with* money, Mitchell," Bishop responded. "Managing money is good, but having it is better. Sounds to me like you're on the right track, but they sound like a stuffy lot, all high up in the social and economic strata of your fair city. Perhaps you should consider lightening it up a bit; including a farmer or two might round things out."

Jenkins knew Bishop was being an asshole now but could not be defensive. "I'm not in Birmingham anymore," he admitted to his mentor, ending the call.

He was steaming! Bishop's remark about farmers was just the kind of putdown that caused Jenkins to question the sincerity of his old teacher and was more than necessary to make him see red. Settling himself, he began calling some of the people he had outlined in their conversation. The first on his list was Louis Sterling, editor of the *Meriden Challenger*. The paper had always maintained a responsible position in Alabama and had been purchased by the Knight chain in 1960. Sterling had come from Knight three years later. A social person, he traveled extensively, as did Bates, a factor Jenkins reasoned would be a plus. At least these two would be cognizant of what was happening in art museums across the country and perhaps even around the world. They would likely give credibility to many of his ideas. Sterling had quickly become part of the community and was a man of the South, with a deep Texan accent and a natural charm. He also had an interest in art and made respectable watercolor paintings when the mood struck him. However, it was his position that made him most appealing. The museum needed wider publicity for its collections and exhibitions, as well as articles featuring its students making and taking art seriously. Along with Bates and Sterling, Jenkins selected six other candidates for the governor's review—Laura James, Dutton Little, Irving Pine, Martha Neil, Patrick Hook, and Jack Wertzberger. James and Neil were two of the most promising women Jenkins could think of to name; James for her capital assets and Neil because she could be easily swayed by logical debate.

Jenkins needed to establish himself as the force behind the commission. He would come to find that most of the commissioners, as was true with members of the Art Association Board, had other lives to lead and precious little time for museum business. His was the sole voice at meetings and the sole architect of the museum's future. Of the group, Rudolph Bates and Laura James were the most important to Jenkins' overall strategy of self-perpetuation. The Bates connection to Russell Hall was obvious. He sought to use Bates as a conduit to assure continued contributions from this important northern collector whose name could be easily dropped with art dealers, especially in New York. Bates, on his own, had family connections to power in Washington and was on other larger museum boards. However, the financial resources of the James family proved to be Jenkins' biggest interest during the early months of 1970.

Taylor James had moved his family and his manufacturing business to Meriden in the late 1940s. The business was one of the first to manufacture specialty items from plastic. He had started as a chemist working for DuPont before the second World War. His development of petrolchemical additives led to a military interest in finding weapons applications. He left DuPont to explore these applications on his own, gaining backers through family friends of Laura's. Taylor grew his company in all directions, opening new markets in the South, Midwest, and West. Within twelve years, he turned the family fortune into a mega-fortune with gross sales estimated to be over ten million dollars. Laura was a gentle, careful woman who helped guide the company through its day-to-day operation, but still had ample time to serve as a volunteer for a variety of causes and oversee the upbringing of their only child, Morgan.

In the summer of 1969, Jenkins met Morgan James, who called to see if she might interview for any available summer positions.

"We have no positions at present, Miss James," he had said, "but you are more than welcome to come by and fill out an employment application. You never can tell what might develop."

With her mother on the commission, he couldn't afford to be rude; besides, he thought he should get to know the families of its members. That afternoon, Morgan arrived and was passed through to Jenkins' office by his secretary. Unlike her mother, Morgan possessed a naturally effervescent charm that disarmed everyone she met. The secret of her parents' vast wealth was well-kept with her, yet she projected the self-confidence of the wealthy. Jenkins found her pleasant and ended the interview after forty-five minutes. She had been very interested in the museum, its history and current programming. After a brief tour they parted, but she stayed to walk through the galleries. Later in the afternoon, Jenkins remembered to ask if she had filled out an application. "I should know if she's at least qualified to do anything here," he murmured, walking back to his office.

Jenkins forgot about Morgan James until he received a second telephone call from her ten days later.

"I was wondering if any positions had become available since we last talked," she said, then asked about any volunteer opportunities. "I need to do something over the summer, and money isn't really an issue. Getting out of the house is my main concern."

He said he'd ask his staff and get back to her, which he did the next afternoon, saying if she was truly interested in volunteering, she could assist him with budget preparations. Her performance the first weeks was fair, and small tasks he left with her were completed in a reasonable amount of time. Morgan was friendly and extremely interested in the job Jenkins was doing. She didn't talk much about her personal life or her parents, and while curious, he never asked questions.

It wasn't until several weeks later that a telephone call opened his eyes about Morgan. The call was from Taylor James, her father and scientific recluse. He was gruff, rude, and patronizing, making it hard for Jenkins to keep from taking an instant dislike to the faceless voice on the other end of the line.

"Jenkins," he began, "This is Taylor James. I don't believe we've ever met, but my wife is a member of your governing commission, and my daughter is working at that museum of yours. At least that's where she says she goes every morning."

Morgan had never mentioned her father in conversation, nor had Laura as he remembered. "Yes sir. Morgan volunteers here and is doing very well. What can I do for you?"

"You've got it wrong Jenkins, it's what I can do for you. What will it take to get her off my back? Just name the amount."

Jenkins looked at the telephone receiver. "I'm sorry Mr. James, but I'm a bit confused. Did you ask me to name an amount?"

"Come on now, let's not play games. My daughter comes home every night and complains that no attention is being paid to the museum and how hard you work at moving it forward. Whether you put her up to it is between you and your conscience, but if she doesn't stop complaining she's going to drive me crazy. So how much do you want?"

Jenkins still did not know what to say. He looked around his office trying to think of a reasonable donation from someone he'd never even met.

"Okay Jenkins, we'll play it your way. I'll send a check for ten thousand. Is that enough?"

"Oh yes, that would be a big boost to our..."

"Fine. Just be sure she doesn't complain anymore. She's really a handful sometimes."

The phone went dead. Jenkins, still stunned by the call, listened now to the dial tone.

✳ ✳ ✳

The following morning, Jenkins received a hand-delivered letter with a check for $10,000 made out to the Meriden Art Museum and signed by Taylor James. It was drawn from a local bank and dated with the current day, month and year. Jenkins had decided not to investigate James until a check arrived. If it had been a joke, he would be needlessly asking questions; if it were not, there would be ample time. Morgan James arrived for work by mid-afternoon that day. She did not seem overly interested in Jenkins, nor did she seem to know of the telephone conversation the day before. The two made polite conversation before Jenkins casually began inquiring about her family. He knew her mother of course, so he steered it more toward her father as his check represented the largest single sum ever given to the museum.

She was reluctant to talk about her father. "He has a manufacturing business here making things out of plastic."

Jenkins nodded. "I've not had the pleasure of meeting him. He must stay very busy."

She reddened slightly. "People say the ugliest things about Daddy, and it makes me so angry! He's not really a recluse like they say. He just enjoys his labs at the plant and concocting new products. He does get out and he travels quite a bit. He even enjoys visiting museums," she said, perhaps to create a common bond with her boss. "He doesn't like what he considers meaningless or sloppy; he's very much a traditionalist in that respect."

Jenkins smiled, listening to every word. He had to find out if Morgan knew about the donation and somehow encourage her to lay off her father. The situation could become a problem otherwise, and Mitchell Jenkins didn't like problems. Suppose the girl and her father didn't get along? Would she be upset about the gift and the real reason behind his giving it? If James didn't contribute in a like manner to other charities, she would certainly wonder why he had decided the museum should be so fortunate.

"Morgan, does your father contribute to local organizations like the chamber music group or the library? Do you think he'd be interested in a personal tour of our galleries?" *Shit,* Jenkins thought, *for ten grand he could own the place.*

"Did Daddy send you some money for the museum?"

Jenkins looked at her with relief. "Yes, he did, this morning."

"Was it quite a bit or a little?"

Jenkins didn't know how to answer. "I guess it depends on one's point of view." He laughed at his answer, wanting to be delicate. "It's a good amount actually, but I'm not sure your father would want me talking about it."

Morgan smiled. "Well, spend it. I can assure you it's good. My parents are quite wealthy."

Jenkins didn't like the tone her voice had taken and wished he had kept their conversation light. She was upset, but her mood seemed to clear.

"Perhaps you could use the contribution as a nest egg for the art school project you're planning. Daddy would find that a good, constructive use that would benefit the city." Morgan smiled and left to continue her work.

As soon as she was gone, Jenkins called a neighbor who worked at the bank, wanting to confirm it was good and to get his friend's impressions of James.

"Oh, the check is very definitely good. We don't see Mr. James in the bank very often. He's what I would call a sleeper on the donation circuit—very quiet about his assets, but his company did very well last year. Can't say I'd have figured the museum as an area of his interest, but you can definitely cash it. Would you like me to open an account here?" his friend asked laughingly.

"Actually, Herb, that's not a bad idea. Set it up as an account for our art school building project."

The two discussed interest rates and other matters, but Jenkins' mind was not on the bank—it was on Taylor James.

✳ ✳ ✳

The Art School project served many purposes. Primarily it was a tool Jenkins used to convince different constituencies within the city he had not forgotten his promises of what now seemed millions of years ago. The art community had been alienated, with many there feeling the museum was growing too quickly, and that Jenkins had forgotten the reason for its coming to be in the first place. The space currently serving as an art school was pitifully small, limiting the number of courses offered. Though fees were charged, they barely paid for the instructor's time. Jenkins promise to the school district that the museum would offer advanced training was still unfulfilled. He felt pressed to get the project moving to reduce his ever-present anxiety regarding his continued employment. There had never been any opposition to him or his tenure, no potential enemies he knew of, but he never felt really secure like August Bishop. A building project would be the kind of solid achievement he could point to as real progress. He had already discussed the project with a local architectural firm, and with the Jameses' money in hand, as well as what he had already raised, the school was nearly paid for.

Events started moving quickly. Construction began on the school, a project Jenkins threw himself into, wanting to learn as much about the process as he could from the architects, contractor, and even the project manager on site. Additionally, he was working in earnest now with Abram Rubin on the NEA purchase of artwork for the museum's collection because the time allotted for this project's completion was rapidly coming to an end. Jenkins thrived under this kind of pressure, however, and enjoyed being constantly on the phone with artists, their dealers, and Beau Britian. Through what seemed to be his endless media attention, he bolstered the museum's position and the importance of art to the city and state, quickly becoming the irreplaceable director of all under his domain.

He also lost no time in affecting a relationship and rapport with Taylor James. Morgan was still working at the museum when the first meeting between the two men took place. James was invited to inspect the plans for the new school and the early construction. Jenkins was still unsure about the relationship between father and daughter. In reviewing Morgan's employment application, he found she had attended one of the finest preparatory schools in the country. Certainly she had no problem with being wealthy. Still, she had been very reluctant to talk about her father. Perhaps she had a problem living in his shadow? He could only speculate, but ultimately decided not to invite her to the meeting. On that particular day, in fact, he sent Morgan to Birmingham, a trip she took willingly, thinking it of some importance.

The only importance, of course, was to Jenkins, who wanted no distractions in preparing for and conducting his meeting. He had never dealt with anyone quite like Taylor James before. DeBain Howard had been generous with money for the purchase of artwork, but Howard would be getting something in return, in addition to a tax donation. His name and that of his corporation would be visible to anyone entering a gallery and reading an object's label. James had given money to quiet his home life. He spent a large sum for something he could have brought about himself had he had the gumption. It seemed to Jenkins quite a different circumstance. There was much to be gained from a positive first meeting, and much to lose should it go badly. Jenkins took great care in alerting his small janitorial staff to have the building spotless, for it currently was his greatest asset. He decided not to talk too much about James' laboratory work since outside of chemistry classes at Rogers, he knew very little about science. He had not been able to discover much about the plant on his own, as security was strictly maintained. His telephone inquiries had been met with curt answers and finally a referral to the president's office, which he politely declined. He and James were to meet in the afternoon, tour the museum, examine blueprints for the school, and inspect the beginnings of construction. Jenkins hoped at that point he would know how to proceed. He would have no other guide to follow except his instincts.

James arrived precisely on time and found Jenkins talking long distance with Abram Rubin, who had unexpectedly called in a frenzy over the purchase of a painting he had just made. Jenkins was finally able to end the call by promising a return call later in the afternoon, but had already kept James waiting in his outer office longer than he wanted. Thinking about how he would apologize to James, Jenkins was momentarily struck by the sight of a man, much younger-looking than his sixty-three years, walking about the room with his hands sunk firmly in his blazer's pockets, examining in some detail the paintings hung on the walls. He did not look like a man of wealth. In fact, had Jenkins seen him in one of the museum's galleries he would have walked right past.

"Mr. James." He greeted his guest with an outstretched right arm. "I'm so sorry to have kept you waiting. I'm Mitchell Jenkins."

For a moment nothing happened. James was still looking at the painting opposite Jenkins' office doorway. He stood for more moments than Jenkins cared to count with his back to him, ignoring his greeting entirely. Achieving his desired effect, James finally turned, looked at Jenkins, and shook his hand. He had forgiven the delay, but made it perfectly clear that while games could be played with other men, Taylor James was treated differently.

"Jenkins," he began, "a busy man never works in a coat." He looked Jenkins in the eye. "Either you are not a busy man or you're wearing that coat to impress me. Which is it?"

His expression didn't change as he said those words. He didn't smile or offer any kind of consolatory gesture. He was serious and wanted this new acquaintance to know it. Jenkins felt the strong hand of C. W. Moses again on his shoulder. As he often did when faced with an unpleasant situation, he tried to laugh. Making a joke of bad circumstances often made him look the fool, but better that and have the awkwardness pass than have it linger.

"Just trying to look like a museum director," he said. "It encourages people to overlook my other deficiencies."

He ushered James into his office, away from the ears of his secretary. James took a seat on the office couch facing Jenkins' desk and chair. Jenkins removed his jacket and sat down in shirt sleeves.

"I have certainly enjoyed having Morgan here this summer," he began after an uneasy moment. "She has been invaluable, researching information for our upcoming budgetary hearings with the state. As you may have read in the paper, we're set to receive funding from Montgomery to help with the operation of the building here and the art school we hope to have online next year. With the assistance of the Art Association's board, I have proposed an outline for the next five years projecting an annual budget of $250,000 by fiscal year 1975-76. It's much more money than the association could possibly raise from within its ranks." Jenkins watched his visitor's facial expression as he talked and thought he detected James only half listening.

"It's not the only answer," James said to Jenkins' surprise, "but one that should provide a steady income as long as the state's tax base remains strong." *Perhaps he's been listening after all,* Jenkins thought.

"Actually," James continued, "you would do well to consider ways in which the museum could make money for itself in addition to what you receive from the state and projects of the association. I assume they fundraise in one form or another."

Jenkins gave his guest a brief history of that organization, indicating the private sector had only done so much financially. "For special events or projects, we can generate quite a bit of interest. The problem is coming up with enough events, and volunteer workers can only be asked to do so much. My small staff and I are stretched thin."

"You'll soon have some money from the state and should be thinking about additional staff to hire then. How many people do you have working now?"

"Four." He had hired a string of secretaries who he couldn't manage to keep for any length of time, a bookkeeper, a janitor and a part-time educator. He admitted to being overextended but still felt he needed to keep a personal hold on the organization's business. James' expression had not changed, and Jenkins was beginning to feel ill at ease with the man's seeming lack of emotion.

"I think you're making a mistake doing everything yourself. The times now require specialization, and unless you are vastly more qualified than your background indicates, you must learn to delegate authority to qualified staff to whom you give direction."

Jenkins' stomach was heaving. He did not like criticism, particularly when his own estimation of his work was very high. *What did James mean by commenting on my background? How did he know what my background was?* He wasn't going to give up any of his power and influence after working so hard to earn them. He smiled and gave a curt "yes sir" to James' remarks about delegation of responsibilities. It was his way of showing defiance in a respectful way. The two men got through the remainder of the afternoon in much the same fashion—James giving advice based on his manufacturing experience and Jenkins smiling and saying, "yes sir." They toured the building, which James disliked for its intended purpose; they studied the school building plans and inspected the construction site. James' general remarks were critical based on his own overall philosophy rather than on specific design concepts, making it difficult for Jenkins to contain his anger, but he managed a handshake as the two men parted. James, in his own way, had been perfectly honest and courteous to the young museum director. He thanked Jenkins for his time and suggested they get together again. Jenkins went back to his office, closing the door to hide his rage. He poured himself a double scotch and sat behind his desk. August Bishop had absolute power, but also had the scholarly background and presence to retain that level of respect. Jenkins felt the pangs of his own inadequacy, the same feelings he felt with his father. He left the museum late that night, after the scotch had washed those feelings from his mind.

✳ ✳ ✳

When Morgan James returned to the museum the following day, Jenkins was surprised to find she was very knowledgeable about the meeting between her father and himself the afternoon before. She was not at all angry he had sent her to Birmingham and acted as if she had not made the connection between the two events.

"I think my father was impressed with the basic concepts of what's going on here, as well as what you outlined to him regarding your goals and objectives."

He could tell she was pleased her father had not immediately disliked the museum, or Jenkins for that matter. He let her continue, for he wanted to know as much as possible about James' view of their meeting.

"Daddy is an urban creature. He hated moving from New York, but he knew he had to for the sake of the company and his future. The countryside just isn't as exciting as the bustle of a large city. You should see him in his lab at the plant though. I think he's able to forget where he is when he's there."

"That's how I picture him, but he must take time to supervise his manufacturing operation too. He has quite a few opinions on corporate structure. He must have a large staff, people who make a lot of the hard decisions."

Morgan paused before answering. "Actually, there aren't too many people involved at that level, just my mother and an aunt. They keep things moving along for him. Those two women have been with him from the beginning."

"Distribute authority," he had told Jenkins, yet only two women really helped him run his company, and one was his wife. He could picture James in his high-tech office, dreaming he was high atop a Manhattan tower, taking orders from customers around the world. Kind of like the Wizard of Oz.

"Your father seemed to know a lot about the museum, and about me," he said as casually as he could. "He must be kept very well informed."

Morgan looked embarrassed. "Please Mitchell," she said a bit defensively, "don't think that I've been doing a lot of talking at home. I'll admit to arguing your case for money and, I might add, the result has been rewarding. However, my father researches everything and everyone of interest to him."

The rush of emotion that had been building inside Jenkins was now in full form. He could feel the blood pounding in his head and quickly buzzed his secretary for a glass of water and two Alka-Seltzer. He told Morgan the antacids were for a bit of a sour stomach from the night before.

"I didn't get the impression your father cared much for the building or for our future plans. I had hoped he would be more excited about the art school project since he is helping fund it."

Morgan sighed. "I'm afraid he doesn't have much use for historic preservation. He thinks it's money thrown away. That's why he decided to build a new plant here instead of renovating existing spaces. He's very stubborn about that, and many other issues."

"I'm sure he is."

So, Jenkins thought after Morgan left, *Taylor James would rather see us build a new structure rather than work with the one we have. Well, who asked him anyway?* He had considered the museum's future many times and a move in location had never been part of any scenario. The former mansion was a one-of-a-kind attraction visitors came to admire. James would just have to be convinced to accept the plan as is. Jenkins knew he would have to deal with more men like this and would need to overcome their strong wills. He would rehearse potential conversations and create the right answers to every question that might be put to him. He knew he would need to enlarge his staff, especially as the school grew. Perhaps his part-time educator would consider managing the school full-time. She had taught school after all, and was easily led. He bristled a bit at the thought of full-time staff or, better said, trying to control them the way he wanted. He felt as if he was facing the second major abyss in his lifetime and wondered how to get across. The first had been decided for him that night in Opelousas. C. W. Moses had not been a man to reason with, and Taylor James likely would not be either. He would share his fears and hopes with no one and continue to impart only the information he wanted others to have. It was survival mode time!

In dealing with James, Jenkins had forgotten about the return call to Abram Rubin. He had been living on the West Coast for just over a year and, as promised, had written Jenkins often. The letters sometimes made little sense but did express his increasing interest in the art world. He found living in LA quite to his liking and fell quite readily into the fast-living set, making weekend trips to Vegas and commuting to beach homes whenever possible. He had also managed to work his way into several interesting galleries, becoming one of the elites in their growing coterie of art patrons. Jenkins marveled at the change in Rubin's responses to the art world. The Gorky was eons away from the paintings he was now acquiring and sending pictures of for Mitchell's critiques. He was spending every extra dollar he made to satisfy his inexhaustive artistic appetite. Jenkins knew if he didn't call soon, Rubin would be hurt and irritable.; he was not in a position to allow that to happen. He placed the call, catching Rubin in his office just before lunch, and found him not too terribly hurt by the delay.

"Mitchell, I've decided it's time I purchased something that would really give my collection some definition. I've decided, if I can afford it, I would like to own a painting by Beau Britian."

"Well Abram, that's a wonderful choice. Beau is a longtime friend of mine and an artist whom I greatly admire. But his work is getting very expensive. Marelli has done a great deal for Beau, including placing his work out of reach of a museum my size. Any painting would be much more than the entire grant we received from the NEA."

"I know they're high, Mitchell." Rubin's voice was now hitting a pitch that usually signaled impatience. "Especially here on the coast. That's why I hoped you could get me one direct from the source. You know, something he might sell to a friend of his old friend without Marelli knowing. I don't want to put you on the spot, but sometimes you have to ask favors. Besides, if a painting were available, it would likely come to you eventually. What do you say, will you think about it?"

"I really don't know, Abe," Jenkins answered truthfully. "I can certainly give Beau a call. He's been very sympathetic to us, so if he had something and thought it would eventually come this way, maybe he would sell one without going through Marelli. He's under contract though, and most artists loathe breaking the rules. I'll see what I can do. Anything of particular interest to you?"

Rubin laughed. "Actually, I'd like something like what was sold to the Modern last year—only in blues and greys and priced for a quick sale." He laughed again.

He has picked up some odd quirks living out there, Mitchell thought.

"Seriously, Mitch, I'd be tickled to get any painting from Britian. When are you coming out here to see me? The women are incredible, you just won't believe your eyes. Alabama it ain't! Just leave Maureen there for a couple of weeks and we'll do the city up right." Jenkins heard laughter again. "Oh Mitchell, one other thing. I'm sending you slides of several West Coast painters I've met whose work you might consider for your purchase grant. They're going to be big in a couple years and you can get their work now while prices are good. The stuff is very contemporary, very stimulating—just like living out here. I tell you Mitchell, the country is dead east of the Mississippi. It's all out here. Listen, I've got to go, something's come up. Actually," Jenkins heard a door close in the background, "someone has come in, and if you could see her, you'd already be off the phone. Hope to hear from you soon, sorry to go like this…well, not really."

The line went dead. Jenkins shifted in his chair and deposited the receiver in its cradle, reflecting on the woman who entered Rubin's office. He wondered if the doctor's preferences were still running true to what they had been on their last New York trip. If so, she would be tall with dark, long hair. She would have spent a great deal of time on her exotic-looking face and would be well-built, tanned, and wearing white. He liked his women in white clothing—perhaps it was a result of his medical training.

CHAPTER EIGHT

Maureen Jenkins was tiring of life in Meriden. She was ready for Mitchell to climb the professional ladder and leave Alabama. Mitchell kept her stranded; caring for the home was her occupation, and to ensure she was well-entrenched there he sired two children. His hours were irregular, sometimes working late into the night, yet he always expected to find dinner warm and plentiful upon his arrival. She recognized these had been busy years for him and understood his drive and ambition. He had taken a lifeless organization and given it the vitality of a young lion. It was his strength, and it was working. His accomplishments were real, as was her pride in them, but he gave her no opportunity to participate in the excitement. Her time with Mitchell was on Sundays or late in the evening after he finished his last phone call. It was hard for her to complain, considering the reason for their marriage and the struggles to get Mitchell through university. He had taken the job in Meriden at a fair wage for the time and size of the city, and she had watched him seize every opportunity. He was making more money than she thought she'd ever see, and Mitchell said the potential was still greater. Would they have married had they not been forced into it by her father? It was a question that nagged her.

Would Mitchell have married someone else from college, someone more interesting in a professional sense? She interested him physically, but knew he admired "smart" women. She also guessed he slept around. She knew of his prowess with the other girls in the school she attended, and she knew about the beach parties held by August Bishop after they were married. In Meriden, his conquests had been less casual and more purposeful, as if he could receive some benefit for the museum through intercourse. He was much too good a liar to accidentally say something incriminating and much too clever to allow himself to be caught, but she knew just the same.

He would be late coming home again this evening, having called as she was preparing dinner. She managed to salvage some of the meal for him and found the book she was reading the evening before. At ten o'clock, she heard his car in the driveway and walked to the bar to pour his scotch, then awaited his entrance. With a notebook and papers under his arm, Mitchell came into the house. His dogs had barked as he pulled in but were now quiet, and the children had not been awakened. He offered a "Hi, Babe" to her as he took the full glass and kissed her neck.

"Bad day?" she asked, trying to start a conversation. "You look tired. Why don't you shower while I get dinner ready? You have about twenty minutes."

Mitchell carried his drink into the bedroom and got into the shower. He felt a sense of relief at being home—it was a place that didn't matter as much as the museum did. It bothered him that Maureen wanted to work. A small, part-time job to keep her occupied, she had said when the topic arose before, but surely she had enough to keep her occupied, especially with the children. Besides, no wife of his would work! It was a decision he had made while at UAB, when she was employed to help pay the bills. She had worked in an office for two young attorneys, both of whom Mitchell suspected were after her. Then there was the other reason—his relations with other women in the community. He worried if Maureen became friendly with anyone he had, he could easily be caught. Maureen would have to be content managing the household and raising the kids.

He dried himself with the thick towels he had selected from a department store in New York and remembered the scratchy ones his mother always hung on a line to dry in the Louisiana sun. He loved having things better than his parents and better than most people living in Opelousas. He dressed quickly in a cotton shirt and the suit pants he had worn that day, then made his way to the bar for a refresher before entering the dining room. He was hungry and dinner smelled wonderful. He reflected on Maureen's overall performance as a wife. The house was kept clean, the furniture arranged consistent with the latest house magazines; his children were growing and healthy he assumed, though he had not seen them in three days; her meals were good—not exotic like the ones he had in New York, but that was to be expected

"Dinner smells great, Babe. How are the kids doing? I'm sorry I don't get to spend more time with them."

Maureen had gotten over being mad at him for the late dinner call. She didn't want to argue or be angry, only to have him to herself awhile and be the only thing on his mind. She gazed at him in his polo shirt and thought he had not lost any of his build, which was still attractive to her.

"I'd like to come by sometime and see the school building before it's finished," she said. "Would that be okay?"

Jenkins put his fork down and smiled at her. "Sure Babe, anytime you'd like. It's under roof with interior walls up."

It was the kind of answer she expected, with no time or specific date mentioned. He started eating again.

"The mayor said some nice things about the museum tonight on the news. Did you see him?"

"I was behind the scenes when he was being interviewed. There was a meeting of some Meriden legislators in his office and he asked me to join them. Seems August and the governor have been cooking up some museum complex and they want it started before the governor leaves office. Don't know all the details, but I'm headed to Birmingham in the morning to see Bishop and find out all there is to know." He looked over at her and lowered the tone of his voice. "Now before you ask to come along, I'll be up there all day and would have little time to spend with you. It would be quite boring. You'll be much happier here." He smiled at her and patted her hand.

She had not planned to ask to go but didn't say so. She knew he wouldn't want her along since he never had before. Maureen listened to her husband talk briefly about his day, then about a telephone conversation with the mysterious Taylor James. He had lunch at his club, a privilege only recently awarded him by the Art Association, and had worked through the afternoon and evening on the purchasing program he had to have finished by year's end. She was glad he enjoyed the pace of his days, being constantly in demand it seemed.

Finishing dinner, Mitchell wanted to work for a while on the final figures for the purchasing program. He talked to Maureen as she cleared the table, then patted her roughly on her backside, sending her into the kitchen. He spread papers out on the table and became lost in them. She watched him as she rinsed the last pan; she was in her world and he was in his.

"Mitchell, would you mind if I took the children to Florida for a week in December to visit my sister?" When he didn't answer, she put down the towel and walked toward the dining room. He was still bent over his artist list and color transparencies of paintings, and she wondered if he had heard her at all.

"Mitchell, I asked…"

"Yeah Babe, I heard you." He looked up at her in the doorway. "It's okay with me. I can get along, and it'll be good for you. Would you drive?"

She hadn't thought about how she would get there, only that she had to go. "I don't know, maybe Mandy would like to go too. She could help with the driving, or we could fly."

"Well you better figure out how you're going get down there. It's a long way to drive by yourself, especially with the kids. Even if your cousin can go, you know how she talks. I'm not sure she could keep her mind on driving for any length of time. Flying's expensive and your sister would have to drive all the way to Orlando to pick you up."

As always, he was full of questions and concerns. It was his way of making her look foolish and sucking the fun out of it, but at least he had said she could go. He watched her go back into the kitchen to think about how she would get to Florida. *Why did she pick that time to be gone?* He would need her in Meriden in December, when social events flourished. Attending alone would lead people to talk. *She'll get down there with that liberated sister of hers and get all churned up.* He put her out of his mind and again concentrated on the final NEA accounting documents he'd be sending to Washington.

With the assistance of Beau Britian, and despite the assistance of Abram Rubin, Jenkins had purchased twenty-three objects. To his amazement, finding the matching money had been the simplest part of the project, with DeBain Howard covering most of it with his gift. The remainder had been donated by five local families who wanted to participate once they understood the prestige receiving the grant meant to the museum and Meriden. Jenkins relished in the fact that August Bishop had never received this kind of federal support. It was something he had over the old fox, and it was the first time the Meriden Museum would own objects of some stature. Jenkins enjoyed pondering the publicity value of that fact. He would have the objects shipped before the new year and installed for a gala and exhibition shortly thereafter. Hopefully it would remind those in attendance of the Hall collection. Perhaps he would invite Bishop. It was getting late. Maureen had gone to bed an hour or so before and he felt himself tiring, but his mind wandered back to the morning's meeting with the mayor that prompted his upcoming trip to Birmingham. *What had that been about? A state-run museum facility? Why hadn't Bishop telephoned about this before?* Jenkins had called as soon as he returned to his office.

"I just had an interesting meeting, August," he had begun, "about something I think you know about. Something proposed for Birmingham."

The old man couldn't be bothered to get excited over Jenkins' questioning. He simply asked if Jenkins could meet with him in a day or two and that he would explain everything.

"Now don't ruin your lunch over it, Mitchell. You know I wouldn't do anything to harm you down there. Just come up and I'll explain everything."

✵ ✵ ✵

It had begun raining early in the morning and continued in a steady grey downpour all day. Mitchell Jenkins disliked the drive between Meriden and Birmingham. It was flat, long, and a complete waste of his time. He did enjoy getting away from his desk though, and this morning he particularly enjoyed getting away from Maureen. She was fast asleep by the time he had entered their bedroom the night before. Normally he would have woken her because he'd had a long day and needed the release sex always brought him. But he knew she was mad, and he refused to beg her for sex knowing it was easy enough to get from other sources. She had been quiet when he saw her that morning, still thinking about Florida, working the trip out in her mind. He left early, not stopping for breakfast.

Jenkins stopped by the museum before heading north. He enjoyed arriving there early in the morning. Everything was still, and the rain was clearing a bit, allowing a glimpse of the new construction and the wooded acreage beyond. He left last night's work with his new secretary to be typed into the government forms while he was away. He had gone through five secretaries in six years. This one was a good typist and spoke well on the phone, but he had hired her because of her looks and sex appeal. There was a little polish about her, but her true assets were all… up front. She was the kind of woman he'd always wanted to hire but was afraid to. That he had actually done it this time satisfied his feelings of security. All was still quiet as he left, thinking about his new employee.

She was twenty-six, divorced, and he was sure she had the ability to make a man do whatever she wanted. He cleared his throat and drove down the museum's winding driveway. *I should have asked her to go to Birmingham with me. It would have made the trip so much more interesting.*

When he arrived, the parking area of the Birmingham Museum was filled with cars and school buses. Children with their teachers were filing between the lot and the museum's entrance with military-like precision. They would be greeted by smock-clad docents, ushered through the building to see the wonders of its collections, perhaps see a film, and would later have lunch on the grounds. The fountain outside the main entry had been turned off for the winter. It was a useless contrivance, the whim of a past trustee. The building itself had been the spacious home of a wealthy cotton baron built at the turn of the last century. Like the Meriden structure, the building had been purchased by an active art association and converted into gallery space. Unlike Meriden, the idea had caught on in a big way, creating an atmosphere perfect for someone like August Bishop. Three subsequent additions had been made to the original structure, stretching over a full city block. Two of the three were accomplished during Bishop's tenure—the second one being the gallery areas Jenkins had assisted with. He found a parking space at the building's rear where the staff parked. He saw Bishop's car in a space bearing his name. *Still driving Cadillacs, I see.*

The service entrance was closed, so Jenkins walked to the museum's main entrance. He counted the galleries between the lobby and Bishop's office. The first housed a fair collection of classical ceramics donated by two Birmingham families who had spent time in Greece after the second World War and returned to invest in what was being called the "New South." Its black and white marble floor would be highly polished by the staff, the collection displayed in tall cases each containing one or two objects. It made for a very dramatic entry, setting the tone for the museum. Bishop always made much of this theatrical approach: "People must know where they are when they enter. They must be dazzled immediately, or they won't consider anything one has to show them."

The next gallery was exceptionally large, housing the collection of French Impressionist paintings Bishop had snagged from an East Coast collector. It was the event that sealed his tenure and created his scholarly bona fides. Jenkins always found something new to admire here. As much as he liked contemporary art, these paintings represented a time in art history he would have like to have lived through. Women were full-bodied and elegantly dressed, while the men appeared strong and powerful; the landscapes were mysterious and fanciful. Finally, he would pass into a corridor of prints that led to an unmarked brown door—the exit Bishop used so often to elude an unhappy trustee or newspaper reporter. It was the entrance Jenkins used to immediately access his boss once upon a time. Out of respect, he knocked twice and waited for the electric buzz, which only took ten seconds.

The book-lined office smelled of coffee and expensive cigars. It was part of a large suite of rooms that permitted Bishop an inner sanctum, meeting space, and board room. As Jenkins entered, he found Bishop on the phone. He was waved to a seat on a pillowed couch in the room's center. From there Jenkins could look through large side windows onto formal gardens. Even in winter the garden was beautiful, possessed of a melancholy stillness perfectly suited for the time of year.

His phone call over, Bishop addressed his guest. "How was your drive up? With the rain and likely some fog, I'll bet it was dreary." He rose from his desk and took a soft leather chair near the couch. As always, he was in a good mood, genuinely pleased to see his former student. "Would you care for coffee or tea? I can have either brought right in." Bishop used the telephone on an end table by his chair to inform his secretary he was not to be disturbed. "Yes, he's here now. Came the back way as usual... I'll tell him that for you." He put the receiver down. "My secretary has asked me to tell you that you are supposed to use the public entrance to my office so she may announce you. She says only my female friends are allowed to enter from the rear."

"Is it still Jeanie?" Jenkins asked with a smile. "If so, she's just mad because I didn't leave your last lake party with her. She was hot for me all evening. Must've been the punch!"

Both men laughed, Jenkins over the woman's advances, Bishop remembering how much vodka he had used in the mixture.

"I'm sorry you had to learn about the state museum complex from some damn city official in Meriden," Bishop said. "Nobody down there can even hope to know the real story and what it'll mean to Alabama when complete. I wanted to talk to you about it myself so you were ready for questions from the press, but my time ran out. The governor wants it started now. In fact, it was someone from his office who leaked the story."

"What state mus…" Jenkins started but wasn't allowed to finish.

"Now Mitchell, don't interrupt, just let me explain." Bishop settled deeper into his chair. "As you know, there haven't been many institutions of this nature. I'm fortunate to have been here so long that the museum sort of runs itself. Your operation in Meriden is probably the best of the smaller museums in the area, but the state's full resources are found here. The governor thinks the time for cultural denial is over and wants something significant built, a showplace where our citizens can come for art, history, and science in one place. The plan we're working on—and it's really still on the drawing board—is for a complex to be built around this building. The city will give the state the land north and west of this block. When completed, it will be the largest center of its kind and will employ hundreds of people with an annual budget of $10,000,000, supplied by the state. The governor believes he can get that money appropriated over the next two years, or by the end of his term. The complex will be a first for the South and rank among the leading institutions of its kind in the country."

Bishop was excited, and a bit puzzled by the look on his former pupil's face. "What do you think, Mitchell?"

"How's this going to go over with other agencies in the state? Can you avoid the jealously that is sure to arise?" Jenkins was still trying to process all he'd just heard and felt his temper flaring. Birmingham already got too much attention. The wealth the Governor was preparing to spend in the largest city would be better spent all over the state for the benefit of those organizations soon to be lost after the completion of this monstrosity.

"This is all a bit hard to fathom, August." He was stalling while he decided whether or not he could be frank in his response. "It's certainly very ambitious, but is it what you really want for the museum? You'll be swallowed up by the state. I'm afraid my reaction if I were you would be different from what I sense you're feeling about this plan. You've worked for thirty years to make this the finest museum of art in the state, and arguably in the South. I can't imagine you want it to be overshadowed by this proposed complex."

Bishop nodded slowly as Jenkins spoke, listening to words he would have spoken himself fifteen years earlier. "I understand where you're coming from, especially knowing how hard you've worked in Meriden. If I were your age again, I would likely respond the same. However, some good points can be made for consolidation, and I'm sure if you thought for a minute, you'd be able to come up with some of them. Egos don't diminish with age. I do care about what happens to this building and its collections, but I guess I see it from the inside. I would certainly want to continue in the administration of the museum after the complex's completion were I not already past retirement age. And I certainly want my staff carried over. But I'm tired and will be ready when the construction is done to turn my chair over to someone else. The monument to my success will still be intact, just amplified by its new surroundings. The excitement of the project will do more for the humanities and sciences in this state than has been done in all of our history. I won' preach to you about the benefits of unity as I'm sure right now you can't believe in it. You and your peers aren't going to like any of this, but the common good is something I think you should consider. Besides, the governor is set on seeing this through. He and I are old men, Mitchell, prone to dreams of greatness and legacy. You may not be able to see that now, but trust me."

Jenkins said nothing. The mayor of Meriden and both legislators hadn't been particularly happy about the project; not because of any special feelings regarding culture in Alabama, but because it reeked of higher taxes and the further establishment of Birmingham as the city of importance in the state. It was hard to work with pennies when big money was being spent with so little concern and even less discussion. Here was August Cortland Bishop, who for years had been the artistic sage of Alabama, telling him he was willing to give it up for the citizenry of the state, so they can come see the wonders of the civilized world all in one place. Bishop had never cared for the citizens of Alabama at large, only a small group of wealthy ones who could purchase objects that secured his place in the history of art museums in America. In his heart Jenkins knew he was no different, yet he was hearing these thoughts espoused by the one man who he had least expected to hear saying them.

"August, I just don't know what to say. It sounds like the governor has me and the other agency heads over a barrel. I really can't believe you're willing to turn this over to the state and someone else to run. There will probably be a director for each of the agencies involved and an overall director above them. Are you thinking of retiring from here and becoming the senior director? I hope you'll excuse my impertinence August, but that's the only possible reason I can see for you to be so eager for this to take place."

Bishop returned to his chair from getting another cup of coffee, listening all the while to his pupil. The true subject of the morning had not yet been discussed. He knew Jenkins would be unhappy about the project, but hoped he would react positively to the desires of an old man and friend.

"The change you describe did occur to me," he said, "particularly when I could see the governor was serious. The governor and I go way back to a time when life in this state was easy only if you had money. Fortunately, both of us came from families with money, his from politics and mine from farming and commerce. He wanted me to take the overarching position you just described, thinking I would be a natural and fair arbitrator when egos collided. It was only when I reminded him we were about the same age that he began listening to me about finding someone else to oversee what will ultimately become a monument to us both. I've grown increasingly tired of being here, and I want the last years of my life to be devoted to the things I like best. I want to travel again to Europe, to see the places I've loved all my life, and I want to write the definitive history of Impressionism.

"So no, my succession to a higher post is not the reason for my consent. I want out. But I do want the museum to be managed by someone whose judgement I trust, someone whose instincts are as good as mine. The job is going to require someone who is able to react to situations and bend them to his advantage."

He turned, looking Jenkins hard in his eyes. "Mitchell, I want you to run the complex. I want you to carry on my work and to rule over this new venture as I would—with an iron fist."

For emphasis, Bishop slammed his fist onto the arm of his chair. He startled Jenkins, who jumped at this punctuation. *Here,* Jenkins then thought, *was the Bishop I expected. The spark is still there.* However, the reality of what had been said had still not completely registered. Staring intently at his mentor, waiting for him to continue speaking, Jenkins realized Bishop was finished.

"Me?"

Bishop sat impassively, his lit cigar glowing in the soft light of his office.

"You want me to run the whole complex?" Jenkins asked, incredulous.

"Yes, the governor and I want you to run the complex," Bishop confirmed calmly. "We know you can do it. You are young, strong, and have good training and experience. You can't stay in Meriden forever. Your school is almost built. Believe me, my boy, boards have a nasty habit of looking for someone new after construction is complete. You must be tough to withstand the pressure to leave, and it'll be a while before they consider more building. You've completed a successful chapter in their history. It's time for you to move on, and this is where you should come—back to where you started!"

The old man leaned forward in his chair. He knew Jenkins would keep his traditions alive. Under Jenkins' watch, the Bishop name and his accomplishments would be remembered.

"I don't know what to think or say, August. This has taken me completely by surprise."

"No need for any snap decisions. I'm not quite ready to give over the reins, and the governor still has his work cut out for him on all this. But do think about the proposition, as well as the possibilities. Give it some time to sink in." Bishop stood and walked back to his desk. "I've prepared some reading materials on the project and the current financials for you to review. They'll give you a better idea of the scope of what we're thinking about. The position would be quite a big step in your career. Plus, it would mean a great deal to me to know you're caring for the work I've done here. But you must think of yourself first, Mitchell."

If the drive to Birmingham had been dismal because of the weather, the drive back to Meriden was little better. The air was charged with the electricity of excitement, indecision, and a little anger. Mitchell had declined Bishop's lunch offer, leaving his mentor's office with a box of papers, budgets, and architectural sketches. He wanted to read them before driving back, knowing he wouldn't be able to concentrate on the road without giving them at least a cursory review.

He drove across town to a park near the university. He'd been there many times before, but never alone, never in daylight, and never to read anything! The rain had stopped, but it was still damp. He opened his window slightly and turned off the engine. Bishop had done a very thorough job assembling the information. Jenkins found four bound documents, each explaining a specific phase of the complex. The first was marked "SCOPE" and provided more detail to the generalities Bishop had discussed. The complex was to be built on the acreage around the current art museum's building, embracing the disciplines of history, science, and the fine arts. These would be specific to the state of Alabama, but broad enough in scope to offer exciting examples of objects making national and world headlines. Over two hundred people would likely be employed, half of which would be professional historians, scientists, art historians, and educators. Each unit would have a director responsible for the operation of his discipline who would report to an executive director in charge of the entire complex. The folder also contained maps of the proposed sites, as well as renderings of proposed designs by local and regional architectural firms.

The second document was titled "FUNDING." It detailed the current possible revenue sources throughout the state. The proposed budget for construction and staffing was set at $7,500,000. As this was to be a facility for the people of the entire state, tax monies would be allocated, and funds from the state's tourism agency and federal sources would be earmarked for creating cultural centers for the study of the state's native resources. Information regarding salary scales for all employees was also included. Jenkins looked all this over slowly, saving the figures for the discipline directors and executive director until last. He was surprised to find the proposed pay scale was much higher than he expected. Finally, he looked at the projected salaries for the lesser directors and the executive director. His throat went dry. The figure was almost six times his current salary, more than he ever dreamed of earning in a single year.

He closed the second folder and went to the third, which was marked "TIMELINE." Here the governor's staff indicated the proposed project dates, from his first address and the legislature on the proposal, which had already occurred, to the time necessary to find a proper architect and general contractor, acquire land rights, and the actual construction; everything had been planned for, down to proposed opening day's festivities. Having been recently exposed to a modest construction project, he knew these dates would likely slide, but still he was impressed with the thoroughness of planning. Every second of construction, organization of staff, moving of existing exhibitions and construction of new ones, and art installations had been plotted out.

The final folder was simply marked with his name and contained two pages of formal stationery marked "Office of the Governor." The letter was a personal request to accept the position and assist him in seeing the project through. He stressed Mitchell could do more good for his state in Birmingham than anywhere else. He read the letter twice. It contained information about Jenkins and the Meriden Museum only a board member would know, presenting a glowing record of the Jenkins tenure. *How could this information have been gathered?* Even Bishop wasn't this close to the inner workings of his operation.

Fifty miles from Meriden, Mitchell Jenkins pondered the words the governor had written to him: "…the importance of this complex to Alabama is immeasurable in terms of the educational opportunities we know of today. I am tired of this state ranking low in studies concerned with our population's quality of life. It is time the state did something constructive for its citizenry, it is time this state examined its past while putting it in perspective. When complete, this project will do these things for the good of all…" Jenkins remembered the salary figure too. He thought of his desire to make something of his life, something that would make others impressed with a poor boy from Louisiana. "Think of yourself," Bishop had said. Jenkins thought of the opportunities in taking the position and the liabilities.

He didn't want to follow in the footsteps of anyone, especially someone like Bishop, whose footsteps would be large. Bishop had many friends in Birmingham who would remember how he did things and might object to the ways of someone younger and without the polish and historical art background of the older man. Jenkins wanted to make his own way. There was also the government to consider. The current governor felt this project was exciting and necessary and was willing to spend money on it, but he would be out of office before the project was very far along. What would happen if the next person didn't follow his lead and put a stop to it, or put it in the hands of an unsympathetic legislature? Bishop would be gone too, leaving no one to lobby for its continuance except Jenkins. Was Alabama ready for this kind of project, or was it the dream of two old men wishing to be remembered for their good works and not the other things that may not sit too well with history? These questions worried Jenkins, who was only now feeling secure in Meriden and content with the little empire he was creating. Still, the challenge of this offer and the money it would provide made it hard for Jenkins to turn down. Was this the favor Bishop had held back since he helped create the commission for the Meriden Museum? Had this been the old man's plan all along—make Meriden nearly self-supporting so Jenkins felt free to take the new position without regrets?

Jenkins cursed Bishop as he drove onto the museum's grounds. Though it was only six in the evening it was already dark outside, the winter air causing his car's exhaust to be visible through the rear window. He noticed his office lights were on, as were the lights in the adjoining office. Looking over to the parking lot to see whose car might still be there, he saw none. He parked near the building's shipping entrance and saw his new secretary's car. He wondered why she was still working as he unlocked the door and let himself in. Walking toward the light from the second floor, he mounted the staircase and found no one at her desk. The copy machine was humming though, bearing witness to her presence somewhere in the building. He entered his office and found her leaning over his desk, sorting the stack of pink message slips and finished correspondence. The skirt she wore was just tight and short enough to afford Jenkins an incredible view of her thighs, which were long and very firm. He tried to make enough noise for her to straighten and turn around.

"You're working late. Did I give you too much to do, or is it because you didn't do enough while I was gone?"

The young woman turned, straightened up, and smiled at him. "I was just making sure you would see all these messages, Mr. Jenkins. The typing has been finished for some time."

Jenkins didn't think much of overt formality in the office. All of his employees called him by his first name. "Who called, and how important did they sound? I'm really not in the mood to call anyone back this evening, but if you think there's something that needs to be attended to, I guess I'll do it."

He sat at his desk and glanced over the pink slips arranged before him. Looking up, he saw she was again leaning over his desk, her eyes also on the papers. He was waiting for her to venture an opinion when his eyes caught the expanding pucker of her open blouse. He traced the line of her neck down to her breasts held in place by her bra. They were much larger than he had thought, the nipples clearly visible as she moved her arm to push a message toward him. He touched the paper with his finger, bringing it closer to him, his eyes breaking from her body.

Again, she smiled and straightened up. "You look tired. Shall I make you a drink while you call? I found your liquor cabinet quite accidentally this afternoon, and I can get some ice from the kitchen. Is scotch what you drink?"

He nodded and thanked her for the offer. "Make something for yourself why don't you? I hate to drink alone." He looked at the message she had proffered. It was from Maureen. Jenkins smiled as he crumpled the paper in his hand and dialed the number. She was angry, having not heard from him since he left that morning.

"Have they turned off all the telephones in Birmingham? Did you forget we're supposed to be at a fundraiser for the symphony tonight? It was something you arranged and insisted that I go too. Are we dining there, or should I fix something? Honestly Mitchell, you don't think about me much, yet expect me to be ready for you at a moment's notice."

He knew she wasn't really mad about his not calling, it was about the Florida trip she had been brooding about all day. He didn't know what to say, but knew he had to find the quickest way to make her stop talking before the drinks arrived. The party was at eight; he had written it on his desk calendar then completely forgotten about it.

"Babe, listen, you're right. I should've called. It's been a long day and I have a lot to tell you, but I have to return some calls now and dictate some letters. We'll have dinner after the party at the club. Have something to eat to tie you over till then. I'm really sorry. I'll pick you up at eight." He could hear footsteps coming down the hallway. "I'd better go now—see you in a bit."

He cradled the phone as LeAnne re-entered the room. She had removed the clasp from her hair so it hung free around her face in loose curls. She sat on the couch across from his desk and placed his scotch on the end table to her right.

"I'll just put your drink here until you're finished," she said as she eased out of her heels.

Jenkins knew she was teasing him and wondered how far she would go with her act. Deciding to let her play it out, he looked again at the line of pink slips. It had been a busy day at the office. He found a call from Rudolf Bates, one from the school's architect, two from Rubin in California, one from Morgan James, and a late afternoon call from August Cortland Bishop. He drew all the slips together, arranging them in order of importance. He would call them in the morning. He looked over at LeAnne again, who had taken several sips of her scotch and had gotten comfortable. She was no longer holding her glass with both hands, but rested her left hand flat on the upper part of her thigh, slowly rubbing it back and forth. He watched her for several seconds before asking if there were any other things he should know from the day's events.

"Except for all the telephone calls it was a very normal day The reports on the NEA grant are on your right there in the grey envelope. I think I did them the way you wanted, but I can work on them tonight if you see an error."

Jenkins looked at the envelope, then back at her. She had raised her left leg keeping the right one straight. The effect was immediate on Jenkins as he rose from his desk and moved to where she had placed his drink. He looked down at her and noticed she wasn't wearing nylons. He could have sworn she was wearing some when he'd entered his office. He walked around and sat on the couch next to her.

"This is a very pleasant way to end a long day," he said, deciding to give her every opportunity to show her true motive for this cozy welcome. If she was just teasing, he would know in a few moments, and if she wasn't, he planned to take advantage of all her skills. "I hope you're happy here LeAnne. You've been keeping my work life in good order.

There's a solid future here for all of us now that there's a steady stream of funding coming in."

He had placed his left arm on the top of the couch's back cushion, holding his scotch in his right hand. He could smell the perfume on her neck and watched her tongue the ice in her glass. He took another long swallow then reached out to put his glass on the table. He brushed the side of her leg as he returned to his position, and she smiled at his touch. Her leg was warm and smooth. She was not just teasing, he concluded, and reached his right hand to her head, gently drawing it to his. It was a long kiss. He moved his hand down to caress her breasts and found them unencumbered by anything but the softness of her shirt. He moved his hand over them, feeling her nipples push against his palms as if ready to explode. She managed to wedge her glass between the cushions to her left and began to explore the bulge she found between his legs. He felt the room spin and pulled LeAnne closer.

CHAPTER NINE

The days between Christmas and New Year's came and went in a blur for Jenkins. The museum was closed both holidays. Maureen, Mandy, and the children arrived back in Meriden at almost the appointed time. They were full of talk of family and the beauty of the Florida coast. Maureen had managed a good tan, and the children had been amply cared for by her sister. He had never told her she couldn't go, and she had taken on the long drive, determined to make the trip. Once she was gone, he had delighted in accruing twelve-hour days at work. Most of the staff had been given time off and he was often alone in the building. The weather had finally turned cold, but the days were bright and the lightness in the office cheered him. He had not yet told Maureen about the proposed Birmingham position. She would welcome the change; for him, the money was interesting. He had done some good in Meriden, building a fledgling operation from nothing. He was not anxious to be involved in Birmingham politics and society, yet he knew Meriden would never grow much further unless something drastic happened. There was nothing on the horizon and that, more than anything else, made the move appealing.

Jenkins tried to think of something more festive to cheer him up. He thought of the impromptu holiday party held at a neighbor's the evening before. Jake Adams, the friendly physician next door, had come by with two bottles of homemade Christmas wine. He had apparently already consumed a bottle and was entirely too cheerful. He had long had eyes for Maureen and his current state gave him the perfect opportunity to express his amorous intentions. Jenkins found his neighbor's interest quite amusing, having often hoped she would fall for someone to counter to his own indiscretions. After drinking one of the two bottles, he and Adams decided to take the second one further down the street; and so the evening went. Maureen didn't accompany the two on their holiday debauchery, a blessing Jenkins would forever be grateful for.

After visiting two other houses and consuming more wine, the roving party, by now quite sizable, arrived at the home of the Honorable Thomas Chase. A Harvard Law School graduate, he had moved to the South during the early civil rights years of the late 1950s to offer legal services for Blacks in a downtown storefront. He escaped death threats and an office fire, becoming a well-respected trial lawyer and member of the Meriden community. His federal appointment came as no real surprise during the Kennedy years, though the publicity rekindled hard feelings among some. He was an excellent judge and, most importantly for Jenkins and the increasing number of neighborhood celebrants, he was the perfect host for a batch of drunken Christmas revelers. Before the night was over, Jenkins found himself in deep conversation with Chase about the growth of the South in the years ahead.

"Just ask anyone here, Tom." Jenkins waved his arm indicating the other neighbors assembled. "They will tell you the South is going to rise again. Very few of them were born here, they're Yankees just like you." He grinned. "But they're happy here. Everyone's making money, living well, doing what they please when they can, enjoying our climate and easy nature. But you know what they want? They want all the perks of the North down here. They want the stores and the schools and cultural attractions, everything that's good and exciting about the North, they want here. Hell! I want that too Tom, and I was born here. That's why I work so hard at the museum. As it is now, we can't compete. They'd laugh at me in New York if I asked to share an exhibition. That's the problem, Tom." Jenkins looked around the room again at his neighbors. "Nobody wants to pay for the things they want. And they don't want the state or county to provide these things because of the potential for increased taxes."

Jenkins didn't normally preach like this and felt awkward now as he and Chase walked into another room to escape the noise. Chase had purchased the largest house in the subdivision, a fact he suffered a great deal of teasing about. However, it was furnished poorly, Jenkins thought, as the two continued into a front parlor Chase kept as a study. Jenkins looked for personal articles that would identify the room's occupant and found nothing.

"Mitchell," Case said, seating himself, "I certainly agree with everything you've been saying. Meriden, like most of the South has come a long way in the last twenty years. It's remarkable, and the period we're in now seems to me like how it must have been at the end of the Civil War—the North is invading with goods, ideas, everything that catches the eye. The carpetbaggers are returning, and I guess I'm one of them!" Both men laughed. Jenkins had thought of saying similar words but hadn't. "The more people move down here from up there, the more change is going to occur. School systems will be modernized regardless of the cost, and who knows? People might be elected to government positions who will appropriate money for your museum. These are boom times, and we shouldn't stand in the way. People will pay for what they want, we just have to be sure what they want is best for them and for the South."

Jenkins was pleased with this last remark as it seemed to give Chase the humanity missing in his rather austere home.

"People in positions of power like ours," he continued, "have an obligation to our other citizens. We need to be careful in our actions, lead through example, and watch that the beauty of this land is not marred. Twenty years ago I wouldn't have said or thought these things. Back then I believed in individual destiny, in the fulfillment of everyone's own dream. I've grown wiser with time and pass these thoughts to you as a friend." Chase filled a pipe with a tobacco mixture he kept in a wooden box. Jenkins watched as he lit the tobacco, taking great care.

"I know what you're saying Tom, believe me. Most people I deal with daily haven't the slightest idea what they want from life and even less of an idea how to get it. I decided for them a long time ago about the museum and I try my darndest to achieve my goals regardless of the opposition. Once they see how good it can be, they'll support it, but it's up to me to ensure they're happy and to eliminate any problems that would stand between me, or the museum, and the final product. I can't talk to anyone down there, no one understands the full impact of the vision I have for that place." Jenkins looked at his watch. It was getting late, and he was suddenly tired. "Maybe we can talk another time Tom. You know, when you're not in court and I'm not drunk."

The two men agreed to do so and went back into the main room where things had progressed to a game of strip poker. The women had challenged the men, but the results so far looked as if both sides were losing with equal regularity and vigor. As Jenkins and Adams walked back to their homes, Jake began asking about the museum and its future. "I have a lot of patients tell me they visit the museum, particularly the new school building. I think it's going to grow!" He trudged further down the street, waving to Jenkins with a "Ho! Ho! Ho!"

✲ ✲ ✲

Finally, back at his office early on January 2, Jenkins relived his visit with Bishop. He still had not decided but knew that time was swiftly approaching. His intercom buzzed, breaking his train of thought.

"Line three for you Mitchell," LeAnne said.

"Mitchell Jenkins speaking."

"Jenkins, this is Taylor James. Do you have a minute?"

Jenkins sat up in his chair. "Certainly sir, what may I do for you?"

"I was wondering if I could come by this afternoon. I don't want to interfere with your schedule but would like to visit if you have a bit of time. Could we make it around three?"

"Certainly," Jenkins' mind raced to remember if he had anything going on at that time. "Come on by. Three will be good, I can . . ."

"Fine. See you then."

The phone went dead. *Abrupt bastard,* Jenkins thought. *I wonder what he wants?* It was nearing noon and he was hungry. He got up from his desk, put on his coat, and left the room, locking the door behind him. In an outer office a janitor was buffing the wooden floor and Jenkins asked how he was doing. He never really stopped to listen, figuring that asking was enough. He descended the staircase and spoke to the receptionist as he passed. "Going to lunch. I'll be at the club if I'm needed." Then he walked down the long hallway toward the outer door still decorated with a large red and green wreath. He hated the Christmas season, everything about it.

✵ ✵ ✵

Mitchell Jenkins was pleased at Britian's staggering artistic success. Journalists from New York were phoning the art brokers of Birmingham to gather background information on the southern phenom and would occasionally call Jenkins, who they were told knew him from college. He enjoyed this second-tier limelight and was quick to realize the importance of establishing a strong association with Britian. He also felt this might help in finding and purchasing works Britian had done while still in Alabama. With two hundred dollars borrowed from an association printing budget, he flew to New York to spend time with his friend and to see for himself if all the publicity was warranted.

He found Britian living a life few artists ever know. Instantly, it seemed, he was both a financial and artistic success. The community of artists among whom Britian had worked since arriving in New York were also finding a widening degree of respectability.

"The world may never understand my work," Beau had said to Jenkins, "because the critics don't really understand the final image is only a result. The process is what it's all about for me."

At his friend's urging, Jenkins spent an extra week there, enjoying the casual manner of Britian's life and sharing a bit of his celebrity status. Alone in Britian's studio he would allow himself free rein, perusing paintings stacked in hallways and paper scraps heaped in trash cans. He would often unfold drawings of proposed works and wonder if the city's garbage collectors were amassing artistic collections of their own.

"Mitchell," Britian began one morning after breakfast together, "the comely Ms. Horowitz is telling people you raped her while she was in Meriden. Says it happened in some little room off one of the museum's galleries while she was resting after having a bit too much to drink. She's not my type, but did you indulge?"

"I certainly did no such thing, though I do admit I thought about it. She arrived at the museum to give her lecture drunk as a skunk, could hardly walk, and I carried her to a little study I made for myself on the first floor. I laid her on a couch where she fell fast asleep and had to give the talk in her place. You'll be pleased to know I gave you good reviews!"

"I see. Well, I hope she isn't serious about a paternity suit." Britian laughed and carried their dishes to the kitchen.

It didn't take long for Britian's help to pay off. Wooden crates from New York began arriving monthly it seemed, and Jenkins, in the presence of the local paper's art editor, had his picture taken uncrating and examining the newly acquired treasures. "MERIDEN MUSEUM EXHIBITS THE 20TH CENTURY," the headline read. Like Britian, some of his artist friends were becoming wealthier and were finding the tax laws, to which they had never paid much attention before, were fraught with major obstacles for making donations of their own work to not-for-profit agencies, requiring attorneys and tax consultants. Under their guidance, it was determined that while artists could not gift their own works to receive tax deductions based on the fair market values of the work, they could gift works they owned by other artists. Happily, Meriden became a beneficiary, and the gifts kept interest in the city's artistic life active. Jenkins began feeling a lot like Chapman Billings.

✿ ✿ ✿

Taylor James sat in a soft leather chair that had been his father's. His office was cluttered with a lifetime of scientific patent certificates on the walls. It was his bastion, his safe place. He firmly believed money was made by those who had money. On the wall behind his chair was a map of the world, compliments of National Geographic. Marked with black pins were the cities where his company did business. Black was heavy up and down the East Coast, with additional pins scattered throughout the Midwest, particularly around Chicago, and in California. Pins were even scattered throughout Europe. His corporation, which had begun as a small business, was now among the top five producers of petroleum distillates in the country, and he ran it all from the facility in Alabama. It was his mission to see his ideas used by firms he owned or ones that would pay for his knowledge.

His only problem now was his own success. James and his immediate family owned and controlled ninety-nine percent of the operations, and tax laws were hurting them badly. At his last meeting in New York with the principals of the accounting firm he used, it was recommended that the company go public. It was an agonizing decision for someone who enjoyed total control of most everything in his life. Finally though, he consented. The changes were worked out within two months at the year's end. The game now was for James to give enough money away to create a tax loss, and it had to be done in a hurry. He was able to keep fifty-one percent of the newly created shares, but knew he had to create a board that would inevitably want to disperse their wisdom upon someone who clearly did not need or want it.

Jenkins returned to his office after lunch at the club. He had sat at a table with ten of the city's leading citizens—doctors, politicians, and business leaders—whose attention was suddenly focused on the museum and its future. He had not intended to lead the conversation, but didn't hesitate to do so with such a captive audience. Perhaps their curiosity stemmed from his not being like the others seated around him, providing a diversion from the usual talk of the economy. Regardless of the reason, Jenkins was always ready to share the museum's story. He suddenly remembered what Tom Chase had said about leading into the light. Walking out to his car afterward, Jenkins thought he might have taken the afternoon off had it not been for his impromptu meeting with James at 3:00. He would not keep him waiting this time and would greet him in shirtsleeves!

The two men sat in Jenkins office as before, one on the couch, the other on a chair. James was in a coat and tie, having been at his office all morning. He told Jenkins he was grateful to him for meeting on such short notice. They discussed the school's completion and the upcoming spring semester.

The conversation was light and a bit puzzling to Jenkins, the urgency of the morning's phone call not evident.

"Mitchell, I've come by this afternoon to talk to you about several things that have been on my mind for some time, since moving to Meriden in fact. I've become increasingly concerned about what people are calling the 'quality of life.' I mean, where are the opportunities for people here to be exposed to new ideas? There's a whole world out there to be experienced." James was sitting forward on the couch now, excited and into the subject of his visit. "When I was younger and living in New York, the world was at my feet. Anything I wanted to see could be found—the greatest cultural events of our time were presented in museums around the corner from where we lived. Now, I know New York can't be duplicated, but I think we could do more. We could be as good as Birmingham, perhaps better. Those folks up there haven't changed anything in years. My wife tells me you know what you're doing, but that the museum struggles to get ahead and has a long way to go before making the major league, so to speak. My daughter drove me crazy last summer describing how hard you work at making positive contributions to culture and education, the new school facility being just one example. Look, I'll come straight to the point, but this needs to be kept in confidence. Strict confidence.

"For forty-eight years my company has been solely owned by my immediate family. When I began working with the substance now known as plastic, nobody gave a damn about it. I did though, because I saw its future. I knew, or at least felt how it could transform our world. So I started my own small lab, and as things grew and we needed more space and a cleaner environment, I moved the lab and the headquarters for our operation here. Three months ago, my wife and I met with our lawyers, tax advisors, and accountants, and the decision was made to let the company go public, sell shares, and take on shareholders. I knew it was coming, but wanted to put it off as long as possible." James stopped for a moment and looked down at his shoes. "Anyway, the decision was made. Even after these legal changes, we still have controlling interest in the new organization, but we're going to earn much more money this year than I expected. Because of this large increase in our income, we're needing to give a lot of money away to avoid the long reach of Uncle Sam. I'm prepared to give the museum $2,500,000 over the next two years if you and your board will accept the gift. I would like the money to be used for a new building, not renovation of this structure. A building to house important collections of art, a building with a dynamic design—and it doesn't have to be constructed of plastic." He smiled at that and visibly relaxed.

"Did you say $2,500,000," Jenkins repeated slowly, "for a new building, here on this site?"

"That's up to you and the commission. I'd prefer someplace else myself. This site, the whole area has had its day. I should think after you consider the city's growth and the direction it's taking, you might prefer a new site. However, as I said, that's up to you should you decide to accept our offer. I don't mean to put you under any pressure, but I need to know something soon, in the next few days. All that really needs deciding is whether or not to take the gift, the property issue can be worked out later. I've prepared a formal letter of our intent and will leave it with you. Please contact whoever you need to as quickly as possible." James rose from the couch and placed a gray business-sized envelope on the table between them.

"I, uh, we certainly appreciate this extremely generous offer, Mr. James. I can't speak for the commission, but this is something we never expected. I'm completely stunned and don't know what to say. I had no idea…"

"I'll bet," James said. The two men walked to Jenkins' outer office and James paused. "Remember, not a word to anyone outside your commission about the gift or the reason for it. This must remain a secret until all the details are finalized."

Jenkins assured him he understood. The two men parted and Jenkins returned to his office and closed the door. He wanted a few moments alone to savor what had just happened and to think about his options. He took a sheet of loose paper and with a pen wrote the figure: $2,500,000. He analyzed the zeros, drawing little pictures within them. Then he began working out a construction budget based on what it had just cost to build the art school, which had hardly been used. *James really wants his money spent on a building elsewhere. Where would the funding come from to purchase the land? This is the best site, and expansion drawings already exist. Why move? James could be talked into reconsidering this site issue after the gift is agreed to. He seems reasonable.* He also thought of the possible problems that might arise over the state's funding. Perhaps they would understand this was a capital gift for construction, not operations. There was much to do, and time was slipping by.

His stomach churned as he reached for his phone's intercom. "LeAnne, I need to speak with every commissioner this afternoon. Start with Mr. Bates and leave Laura James to last. If they're not home, try to find out where they are and if I can reach them by telephone. I'll take the calls as you can make them, okay?"

He rang off. He hadn't meant to be curt but knew the less said, the better. The first call came in at four fifteen and the last at ten thirty. Jenkins was very cautious with all the calls. He led each of them to the only realistic conclusion, and with a unanimous vote clinched, so was his future.

It had been a long day. Half of the commissioners were still out of town for the holidays. He had expected their positive reaction to his news and tried to play a bit of the devil's advocate with them, though not hard enough to diminish their enthusiasm for James' generosity. He had been instructed by the commission's chair, Rudolf Bates, to telephone James in the morning and accept the offer. Bates would fly in from Chicago if necessary. Jenkins wanted a drink and crossed the room to his bar. He hadn't eaten since lunch and the scotch burned all the way down. He also realized he was very alone in the building, a building that might soon be replaced. For a moment Jenkins pictured himself in a new structure especially designed for contemporary art and suddenly realized this older building no longer pleased him

His phone rang. "Mitchell are you still in there?" It was LeAnne.

"Still at it," he said, "but I'm into the scotch, so I guess work is officially over for today. What are you doing? It's eleven fifteen!"

There was a pause. "I'm in a phone booth not far from you. Just got out of a movie and thought I'd call to see if you were still there, in case you needed anything. Anything at all."

Jenkins laughed, as did LeAnne on the other end of the line. "I could use a little help. I'll go down to the kitchen for more ice and meet you at the door."

So, the night would be longer still.

✲ ✲ ✲

Maureen was asleep when he finally arrived home. The house was dark, and the kitchen smelled of the dinner he had missed. He peered into the refrigerator to find ham, green beans, and cornbread. It was after two in the morning. His clothing was rumpled and reeked of the cigarette he had smoked in the car to hide the smell of perfume. He ate quickly, then decided he'd head for a shower in the guest bedroom and bed. The household mail laid on the kitchen counter, but nothing was of any interest to him. It was Maureen's responsibility to pay bills from the money he gave her. Jenkins enjoyed the house when it was quiet like this. It could be his then, though it was not what he would have chosen if circumstances were different. It was one of his recurring fantasies—a life without marital or parental responsibilities. The world could offer so much to someone in his financial position who was without obligations.

He had developed a passion for beautiful objects that truly surprised him. Certainly nothing in his background allowed for this. The young man his memory conjured was nothing like the man he had become. The past was an embarrassment he tried to forget. It seemed to him now he had managed to live through one trial after another, stumbling blocks in a life with little substance until he had moved to Birmingham. Then everything changed, though the life he tried to leave behind still clung to him. Maureen never expected to marry a museum director. The boy that night in his car with her had never expected to become one either, but he had, and their worlds had become more and more different. She should have had a simpler life with a simpler man, one who returned from work at five, who enjoyed hearing about their children, and who would aspire to nothing more than the maintenance of their household.

The hallway clock struck two thirty and Jenkins allowed his thoughts to vanish. He walked into the guest bedroom, stripping himself of the suspect clothing that would find a resting place in a large hallway hamper. He wished he could rid himself of other parts of his life as easily. The shower water was hot and felt good against his chest.

Maureen had awoken when Jenkins entered the house. She laid still, listening to the movements of her husband in rooms removed from the one they shared. They were comforting sounds, even though she hadn't seen him since eight the morning before. The love she had once felt for him had long passed. What remained were only a series of motions, one leading to the next. At this moment, her need was for his body. He was a very attractive man who worked at keeping his body fit. She rose from the bed and walked noiselessly across the thick carpet. Entering the hallway leading to the guest bedroom, she unfastened the silken pajama top from behind her neck, its softness making her nipples hard as it fell to the floor.

The bathroom was filled with steam, and the cloud-like atmosphere excited her further. Quietly she pulled the curtain to one side, peering in at her husband covered in soap, his skin pink from the heat. She reached inside and moved her hand across his thigh. Jenkins jumped, then turned to see her naked body.

"You scared me," he said, his eyes not able to look beyond her swollen breasts. "But it's worth it."

She soaped a washcloth slowly in her hands and reached inside to the man she had lived with for so many years. Earlier in the evening she had wondered what he could have been doing at the museum so late into the night. There were many possible answers, some of which hurt her deeply. Those thoughts were banished now as her need became stronger and stronger. Jenkins allowed the water to run again over his chest, rinsing away the soap, revealing the measure of his own excitement. Feeling his desire to caress her softness, he stepped from the shower, letting the water run into the drain. He lifted her into the air effortlessly and walked back down the hall into their bedroom.

CHAPTER TEN

As usual, Ellen Maxwell was at her office early. She had been hired by Mitchell Jenkins as a collection lecturer in 1969 and by 1971 was promoted to curator of education. Ellen grew up in and around Meriden. She married young and traveled with her husband throughout the South as he followed a career as a land developer. She returned to Meriden with a child and a divorce, went to college, graduated, then taught school. She was a strong woman Jenkins admired. He knew she was much more capable than the school system gave her latitude to be. Once hired, she quickly began developing lecture programs based on works in the museum's meager collection.

Jenkins also recognized her appetite for innovation. It was for this reason he would come to confide in her about certain points of museum business he considered important but not sensitive. He wasn't completely at ease with her sense of female liberation; she had not remarried and never dated. He maintained any woman not interested in the opposite sex could not be completely normal, but she was important to Jenkins for other reasons too. As a Meriden native, she knew many people who could benefit the museum; she also knew people who could cause the museum harm. He asked her to talk about both when issues developed, and the James gift might be one of those issues. He had become increasingly concerned with the social politics of Meriden since the new decade began. People seemed to be more vocal than in prior years, and increasingly more conservative. Would the gift be controversial? Would it be seen as elitist and thus a threat to the largely rural population of Meriden? He wanted some insight into probable public reaction and thought Ellen could help gather intelligence.

Discussing concepts in the abstract generated a positive reaction from Ellen. This ability was becoming a major strength that enabled him to hold a conversation without ever taking a concrete stand on anything. He practiced this technique whenever possible, often finding it amusing. Another important conversational secret he had learned was people who don't have strong beliefs are easily swayed by anyone who does. With Ellen this last strategy was sometimes difficult because she did hold strong opinions generally based on sound reason.

He found her working on a script for a new program for elementary school students. "Ellen, may I interrupt you for a few minutes?"

She looked up from her work and sat back. "Sure Mitchell, pull up a chair. What's on your mind?" She never offered him the female smile and laugh he was accustomed to with most women. It was part of the reason he didn't trust her fully, but overlooked it when necessary.

"You remember Morgan James? She worked here last summer, mostly in my office, helping with the budgeting materials for the state. Her father gave money to help with the school."

"Of course I remember her." She looked at him as a teacher does a pupil who is withholding something. "You certainly didn't drop by to test my memory. What's up? Did the old man give you more cash to spend on educating the masses in backward Alabama?"

Ellen saw Jenkins' expression change from his usual chauvinistic leer to blank hurt, to a belittling 'gee whiz' attitude typical of southern men who generally are not nearly as backward as they let on.

"He, Mr. James, is indeed giving us some money," he began with a smile that became a nervous laugh. "But not just for education. He's giving us money for the construction of a new museum building, and the commission has gratefully accepted the gift, which will be announced on the evening news."

Ellen, prone to her own dramatics, opened her mouth in excitement and let out a soft "wow." She prolonged the word for the proper effect, then asked how much he was giving.

"Two-and-a-half million. There are still a few minor problems to be worked through, but I wanted to get your reaction and see how you think the rest of Meriden is going to react."

"Well," she said, still staggered by the amount, "I don't rightly know. That's a very large sum of money. It's wonderful the museum was selected to receive their generosity. I really don't think there will be much trouble about our accepting it. I mean, the old families here will think James is showing off a bit, but they think that of all Yankees, rich or poor."

"It's the state's annual appropriation that's worrying me. James wants the construction to be on another site, somewhere more central in the city. I worked hard convincing the legislators in Montgomery of this building's historic value. Perhaps after moving from this building we could find funds to renovate it properly and operate it as a historic site separate from the art museum. That would benefit the community, and as the commission would own both entities, where the art museum is located shouldn't be a concern." He paused, thinking over what he had just said.

"Sounds to me as if you have everything under control, as usual. The news is really too astonishing to elicit much negative reaction. It's wonderful and will prove to be quite a plus for you I should think." She was getting to him with compliments, making him feel important. It was a tactic she used when she needed to get her way or to ease tensions. "Meriden just might amount to some cultural significance after all. A new museum building really is needed for many reasons. You better than anyone know the limitations of this structure. Even for educational programming it's difficult, to say nothing of its limitations for that so-called artwork you're buying." She loved teasing him about the works he purchased that she then had to explain to diverse audiences. "How about getting James to give something for education? I'd be willing to help with that."

"You'd likely have to do a bit more than talk. I expect Taylor James gives nothing away he doesn't have to."

As he got up to leave, Ellen Maxwell promised to do all she could to help mollify any negative reactions that might come from the day's announcement.

✳ ✳ ✳

It had rained much of the morning, and even now the sky was darkly overcast with the threat of more rain to come. The lights from inside the club twinkled. Jenkins looked at the high-columned, brick building that was the exclusive men's bastion. Taylor James had agreed to meet him at the club for lunch with whatever number of commissioners were in town. On their behalf, Jenkins would accept the gift, allowing the social atmosphere to cover any awkwardness he might feel. He had told Laura James earlier of the commission's overwhelming positive vote. Her membership was a concern in accepting a gift from her husband, even though he and it represented the private sector within the community. It was their money to give away to anyone they wished.

Jenkins was feeling somewhat trapped by events rather than being able to shape them. He considered his morning's conversation with August Bishop, whom he had called for a bit of feedback and advice. The older man had been surprised so much money could be found in Meriden and quickly surmised the acceptance of the gift would put an end to his attempt to get Jenkins back to Birmingham. He decided to try to use the situation to his advantage.

"Incumbent directors generally don't survive a major building program, Mitchell, because their boards typically want new talent at the helm. It might be better for you to come here as the new director of our project. Meriden can put its plans on the shelf for a few years while they decide what it is they want." He then asked when construction might begin.

"That's difficult to say," Jenkins said. "We're only accepting the gift today. There is some question over the building's preferred location."

"Then nothing is definite yet." Jenkins could sense Bishop thinking, wondering what he could say that might make Jenkins think seriously about leaving Meriden in the face of this building project.

"Well, this is an interesting time for you. I thank you for calling your old friend to alert me to the excitement down there. I want you to remember the offer here even considering this good news. We're not in the Northeast, you know. It will always be more difficult to make a name for yourself living in the South, so one must take advantage of all the opportunities that come along."

Bishop fell into one of his disconcerting long pauses. It was the type of dramatic effect that generally allowed him to have the last word. Jenkins counted the seconds and decided to abbreviate the drama.

"Being in the South didn't hurt you, August."

"Exactly so, my boy. But I didn't spend my career all in one place. I'll talk to you later. Enjoy your afternoon!" Bishop was off the line and Jenkins was sure he had walked into a trap.

Jenkins decided to go in and make sure the dining room was ready for the meeting. He had called the media, alerting them to be outside the Club for a major announcement at two thirty. The remainder of the day was filled with excitement as James formally offered the gift and the commission accepted. Jenkins spoke briefly on the importance of the gift to the museum as well as to the community, then assured everyone present he intended to work tirelessly on the project. After lunch, the press assembled. Again, there was a round of speeches. Jenkins returned to his office by five, tired yet exhilarated by the day's proceedings. The radio station was the first to broadcast the news, scooping both press and television. Taylor James, much to his pleasure, was being called a very generous benefactor and a patron of the arts. It was a role he would come to enjoy. For Mitchell Jenkins, it would become a time of endless meetings with many contractors hoping for a piece of the action.

The following morning he sat in his office alone. LeAnne had just come in to deliver the day's mail and pique his interest in the low-cut sweater she was wearing. He had enjoyed her the two nights before, even more than he had the first time. He wondered if he should fall in love with this woman or keep their relationship strictly based on sex. He was deep into these thoughts when his intercom button lit. LeAnne's voice was almost as breathless as it was when he had pushed himself into her.

"You have a call on line two."

"Hello, this is Mitchell Jenkins."

"Hey Mitch." The voice on the other end was clear and friendly, it was Charlie Scott. "How the hell did you pull that off? I just heard the news on the radio and can't even conceive that much money! Do you think he'd like to throw in on an advertising agency?"

Jenkins appreciated the call from his friend and knew it was sincere. "Charlie, I really didn't do anything! The truth is he needed to get rid of some cash and I was the most deserving son-of-a-bitch around."

Both men laughed.

"Well Mitch, I just called to let you know I think it's great!"

"Thanks Charlie, I appreciate your kind call. So how are things with you? Any change since that day we talked before the party?"

"Too early to tell, my friend. I think we'll know more by the end of January. Oh, by the way, Marie asked me to tell you any time you're in Atlanta…"

"Gotta go Charlie. I'll call next week, maybe we'll have lunch."

"Okay. Happy New Year!"

As he hung up the phone, Jenkins pictured Charlie sitting in his cluttered office. The morning's coffee pot would be half-consumed, its remainder sitting cold by the ashtray near his right hand. Torn magazines and newspaper clippings would be folded for his attention in one corner of the desktop while new copy would be taped together at its center. He would have smoked a full two packs of Camels by now and be wondering why he had no taste in his mouth. He was an intense man, one that needed to express himself constantly to avoid a complete breakdown.

Jenkins remembered the party they had thrown two Christmases before for clients, the talk he and Charlie had had about the firm's future and the unsettling news they were in financial trouble. As that afternoon wore on, he had watched the fire give out and listened to a blustery wind work against the rafters. He finally rose and began looking around for more wood. The afternoon's coolness felt good to him, and he gladly went outside to carry logs in for the night. He was enjoying being away from the museum, but his mind kept returning to the financial problems the advertising firm was encountering. They were still paying off the loan he had made to get things going and was due to continue for the next two years.

After several trips bringing in wood for the night, he lit another fire and stacked the remaining logs on the hearth. He then crossed the room to where the bar had been set and poured another scotch. It was then he heard muffled sounds coming from one of the small bedrooms. *Must be Charlie getting a bit of fun in before dinner*. After listening to the noises a little longer, he decided they were not coming from the room Charlie had entered. Carrying his scotch, he quietly attempted to determine the exact source of the noise. The sounds were seductive and came from the room in which he had placed his overnight bag earlier that day. He eased the door handle open ever so slightly to peek inside and noticed two figures on the bed, deep in the throes of love making. To his surprise, both figures were female. It had been quite a day—first the conversation with Charlie, then the scotch he'd consumed, and now he watched two pretty women making love! He felt a bit dizzy and needed to shut the door as quietly as he had opened it. His hand hit the doorknob, and the noise startled the two women who scrambled to cover themselves.

"I'm sorry," Jenkins offered. "I thought this was my room. I came in by mistake." He was grabbing the doorknob again to shut the door when the taller of the two women answered him.

"This is your room, Mr. Jenkins. Marie and I were waiting for you to come take a nap with us. We…couldn't wait on you forever, so we started early. Come in and let us help you relax."

Jenkins smiled and entered the room, shutting the door behind him. Both women were quickly out of bed, completely naked and beautiful. The taller woman, Jane, had what appeared to be a complete tan over her body. She had long, graceful thighs and large full breasts that hung on her thin frame like melons. Marie was only a few inches shorter and had a body equal to that of the other woman. Somehow, he had failed to notice earlier she was a very light-skinned Black woman. *Scott must be crazy*, he thought to himself as the two women approached him, *inviting a Black woman here for the party tomorrow. This is still Alabama!* Marie began undoing the buttons on Jenkins' shirt, pressing her naked breasts against his chest, the nipples warm and wonderfully soft. He had never been with a Black woman, though growing up in Louisiana he'd been offered several chances during his adolescence. Jane quickly removed the rest of his clothing and was busy licking the inside of his right leg. No amount of liquor could dull the sensations coursing through him as she worked her way up. Marie was behind her, running her long fingers over his torso in time with the movements of her friend who was on her knees. The two women eased Jenkins to the bed. For the next three hours Jenkins lived every sexual fantasy he'd ever had, finally falling into a deep sleep with both women. He awoke alone in the bed at ten thirty, smelling food being cooked and hearing the muffled laughter of one of the girls and Charlie. *That guy is going to get me into a lot of trouble someday.* Jenkins stretched out on the bed. *God knows what he has planned for tomorrow.* He rolled on his side to raise himself from the bed as the bathroom door slowly opened. Standing in the doorway was Marie, wearing a lace bra and light gray g-string. Her hair was brushed into a loose afro.

"Hope I didn't wake you while I was showering." She moved toward him. Jenkins couldn't help but want her again. "Would you like to shower before dinner?" she asked. "Jane and one or two other girls are in the kitchen. I got out of the kitchen detail because Charlie wanted me to stay here in case you wanted anything else before we ate." She was standing over him beside the bed. Jenkins looked up at the neat black hairs showing through the lace front of her panty.

He cleared his throat. "Well, there are a couple things you could do for me," he answered, noticing her eyes move down his trunk toward the movement under the sheets.

Marie slowly reached around her back to unfasten the bra with a single movement. With her other hand she pulled the sheet down, and an hour later Jenkins emerged for dinner.

✳ ✳ ✳

The city limits of Meriden were almost a perfect circle twenty-five miles in diameter. Within this circle, fifty-five thousand people lived. Of this number, half worked in the city itself, with the business district encompassing six square blocks bound by City Hall at the south and the only multi-story office building in the city to the north. This new structure, completed in 1967, represented the new Meriden—strong, growing, and filled with the desire to succeed. It was built by a western banking conglomerate, Endicott Enterprises, whose executives were convinced the South held great business opportunities. The Endicott Building rose like a beacon from the flat Alabama landscape. Its visage could be seen for miles in all directions. The city's mayor, Harold Stubbins, was anxious for growth and to accumulate the advantages of a healthy economy. A businessman himself, the mayor was able to see and understand trends within his community, including the city's business district. Entrepreneurs were clamoring for shop or office space near to or in the Endicott Building, while the south end was rapidly falling into decay. City Hall was part of the south end's decay. The building, constructed after the "War of Northern Aggression" but before the end of that century, had few amenities of the twentieth century. It had seen much change come through the city but simply was not the image of the "New South." In fact, many of the city's leaders deemed it a major hindrance to progress. The mayor and his staff worked to identify federal grants that might fund the construction of a new structure, as well as pieces of real estate on which to build it.

It took the mayor little time to find the property he wanted—a three-quarter acre tract located on the northern end, owned by the First Baptist Church. The property had come to the Church through the family of a long-deceased member whose great-grandfather had originally staked the land as a homesteader. The south end had traditionally been working-class and was in fact the city's birthplace. Plots of usable land were carved out of the countryside by English settlers moving west. Even then, the city of Birmingham was much grander than Meriden, its people and farms different as vast plantations grew, mirroring those of other southern states. Few settlers in Meriden could afford slaves, but at the war's conclusion, newly freed families migrated to Meriden, the town proving to be a safer respite than the larger cities in Alabama. Many built dwellings in the south end, and those who had learned trades opened their own businesses. However, their arrival caused an exodus of white families to the city's north end, eventually establishing residential neighborhoods with schools, shops, and churches that prospered well into the twentieth century.

These were the conditions in Meriden when Mitchell Jenkins and his commission announced the James gift. The new suburbs, like most such developments in the southern states in the early 1970s, were populated by mostly white people congregating in areas consistent with their financial positions. Mayor Stubbins, pushed further by his dream of relocating City Hall, found the cash to offer the church and hold the land until the city council could vote on his plans in the new year.

Taylor James read the reports of the mayor's doings with interest. He was astounded at his ability to channel funds for the purchase of land without the action of council. He agreed the old city building needed to be replaced, but wondered why the new structure could not be built on the footprint of its current structure. The church land seemed to him better suited for something else, something like an art museum. He knew of Jenkins' reluctance to leave the existing museum site but figured he and his friend Stubbins could be persuaded when confronted with a reasonable argument.

✳ ✳ ✳

Mitchell Jenkins spent the first months of the new year in early planning for the new Meriden Art Museum. James' generosity was much discussed in local press, editorials, and columns. He had given Jenkins and the commission free rein in the choice of architect. While several nationally established northern firms expressed interest in the project, the final selection went to a Montgomery firm that had done work in Atlanta. The daily business of the museum, its exhibitions, school, and educational programming were left to those staff who could best handle them. In conversations with members of the commission, Jenkins was often asked if he should not at least consider the possibility of finding an assistant, someone to help him juggle all the balls he had in the air. He viewed the suggestion with apprehension, fearing it was the first stage of the changes August Bishop warned would take place as the museum grew. There was no denying he could no longer participate as fully as he had been in all the work at hand, but still preferred to put this step off for as long as possible.

"Mitchell," Louis Sterling would say over lunch at the club, "physical growth is going to demand you hire more staff. The commission doesn't expect you to do it all. A group of folks who can take problems away from you will soon become a necessity."

Again, Jenkins would hear Bishop's voice telling him things would change, "regardless of your decision to come or go."

In the two years of its existence, the museum commission had formally met a total of eight times. Jenkins prepared extensively for those meetings, sending members an agenda and background materials on topics for discussion ahead of each session. The James gift though, was the single most important issue for discussion during their brief history. Jenkins never let any doubt of the importance of the new structure enter these discussions. His strategy with the commission was not to ask their opinion of a location or even give them an opportunity to discuss options. He would tell them his plan, going into specific detail and with as much information as he could generate to give it credibility. Then it would be up to them to come up with alternatives. Rarely did they find his thoughts or plans unsatisfactory. They were fine leaving it up to their director to hash out the location and the minutiae of the next steps forward with James, architects, and contractors. He was the professional after all, and they had confidence in his abilities. In a lucky turn of fate, Laura James drew a six-year term on the commission. Jenkins found it satisfyingly easy to let her presence at meetings influence the outcome of issues.

Taylor and Laura James sat in Taylor's home office waiting for Jenkins to arrive for dinner. He had become a frequent guest in the months following the gift's disclosure and was enjoying the growing confidence of his newly found patrons. To his credit, James wanted little said of his generosity, and he was not interested in becoming a figure of importance to the commission. His laboratory was taking as much of his time as it ever had, and he was looking at additional European investors. It was because of his wife that James decided to give the money once he found out he had to. Laura's interest in aesthetic affairs had long been supported by her husband. He enjoyed the objects she purchased over the years for their home and his office even if he did not always understand the artist's intent. The two had married in 1954, the second time for him. His first marriage was never discussed, and the daughter born of that union was never seen. Laura had been a good match for Taylor and his need for isolation.

Over dinner, Taylor was going to show Jenkins the result of an urban traffic study he had personally commissioned from the Stokes and Jamison Planning Engineers in New York City. He had only recently received their findings and had sent a copy to Mayor Stubbins that evening. He was also sure it would be reported in the press later in the week. James found the information very interesting for several reasons, one of which would prove beneficial to the art museum and its supporters.

Jenkins arrived promptly at seven fifteen. He had not asked Maureen to join him as he had on two other occasions. He found she didn't enjoy nor was particularly interested in business discussions, which distracted him from being on top of his game. The James home was a contemporary structure built for them shortly after their arrival in Meriden. Located in a wealthy section of the city, near downtown but in a park-like setting, it made the growing urban environment seem far away. The grounds were beautifully landscaped and cared for. It was the kind of house one could have with money, and Jenkins would sometimes find himself lingering in its gardens, surveying the beauty as if it were his. Winters were mild in Meriden and even now the air smelled clean with the hint of the coming spring. Jenkins strolled slowly up the walk to the front door, the lanterns along the path giving the surroundings an additional beauty he wanted to savor.

Anne, the Jameses' housekeeper and cook, met him at the door. She was a gracious, large, Black woman who had served them in New York. She had been surprised to learn of their move to Alabama and was not terribly anxious to return with them to her home state. "Good evening Mr. Jenkins," she said as she took his raincoat. "I hope you've had a good day."

Jenkins smiled at her as she crossed the vestibule to put his coat in a closet. He was a product of the South and had, as did many other of his ilk, very mixed feelings about people of color. While he spoke against segregation and for equal rights for all people, there was a part of him that believed the race to generally be inferior. He had grown to like Anne though. She had found her place in life and worked to improve it. As he and Tom Chase had discussed, place was not a simple matter of race or even sex, but a matter of mental capacity. It was a classification process used by school systems for years.

"Mr. and Mrs. James are waitin' for you in the livin' room. I'll show you the way…"

"That's not necessary, Anne. I can find them. Besides I'll bet you have more important things to attend to in the kitchen." With that, he walked down the darkened hallway to the large room at its end, where he would find his hosts.

CHAPTER ELEVEN

Ted Martin sat alone on a brown plaid couch facing two large windows that looked out onto maple trees. It was still early morning, and though he was dressed for work, the gallery had not yet opened. In fact, all the building's alarms were still active. He listened to the silence of the empty rooms transmitted through microphones to a speaker mounted in a wall of his apartment. There was no traffic on the street below, and he enjoyed the serenity surrounding him. He rose and walked to a bookshelf located at the bottom of an open staircase. In a small wooden box, he kept his cigarettes. He took one from the pack and looked through the glass door to his right that opened to a metal walkway on the building's second floor. It was to be a cloudy day, the kind that would later linger in a cool dampness before turning evening to night. It was typical weather in northern Ohio, the kind he had known all his life.

Hudson, Ohio was a quiet, small town tucked away in the Western Reserve, with houses that were mostly frame, painted white in the manner of New England. Also like New England, Hudson had a town square bordered on both the north and south ends with formal flower gardens maintained through the diligent persistence of three local garden clubs. Martin enjoyed walking through the town on mornings such as this.

On a straw placemat was the set of security keys to deactivate all alarms in the building. Before leaving on his morning walk, he would tour the galleries out of a strange loyalty to the shadows that inhabited the spaces when the lights were turned off. He unlocked the wooden door to the entrance of the largest gallery and gently pushed it open. The room was exactly one-hundred-twenty feet long and fifty feet wide. Its ceilings were open, exposing the heavy wooden beam work of its construction of over a century earlier. He walked through the gallery in the light coming from the clerestory windows above, listening to his steps on the gray linoleum floor. The gallery walls had been painted a deep maroon, the color the gallery's founder had used in an attempt to reproduce the look of red velvet. The collection, European genre paintings of the nineteenth century, hung frame-to-frame the length of both long walls. Martin stopped to look at a large painting installed at the gallery's center. It depicted the recovery of a child's corpse drowned in an ocean. Two large fishermen stood on either side of his colorless body where it washed up on shore. The child's body glowed in the shadow of the room, and he recalled listening to the first docent-led tour he had encountered after becoming museum's director.

The small, Sunday afternoon crowd had stopped in front of the painting as the docent began to relate the story of the drowning and the sadness the artist was able to portray. "The painting was made to commemorate this sad event that evoked much sympathy for the people living in this seaside English town. The boy was lost at sea when a storm blew up and threw him out of his father's fishing boat. The artist has chosen to use a very deathly hue of white to portray the child, though his cheeks are pink and his face in gentle repose. Perhaps the painting was a warning to other fishermen not to go to sea when weather threatens. Next, we see…"

Martin had asked the volunteer after the group had left how she knew so much detailed information about the painting. Her answer was that the information was contained within the painting itself, all one needed to do was look.

"The artist was moved by the sad event, Mr. Martin. He was a witness to the tragedy and recorded it for us on the canvas."

She was convinced of the accuracy of her account and the painting's history. Martin decided it would be foolish for him to dissuade her as accounts of this nature were common, he was sure, among all the volunteer guides.

Walking through the remaining gallery's contiguous spaces, Martin concluded the collections had spent another uneventful night, just as they had since Merton Osborne, its founder, died in 1911. He checked the exit doors, then left as he had entered. It was his custom to leave a small electric illumination on over Mr. Osborne's portrait, which hung alone on the large gallery's back wall. "Good morning, Merton," he said, closing the door. He crossed the building's side yard, walking past a garden of late rose bushes and into an alley from which he began his morning stroll. The alley was paved in brick and led past now-vacant outbuildings that once served as storage for the stone manse of Hudson's Methodist Church, constructed in 1800. *How had the countryside changed through the years? How vast it must have seemed.*

The Osbornes were settlers in the 1840s. They had arrived with other families who left New England seeking western land. Merton's father was a boy when his family arrived, establishing a general store and later building a hotel called the Olympian on the shore of the Cuyahoga River that ran through town. The hotel served as a summer vacation spot for wealthy residents of the growing city of Cleveland. Merton and his three brothers spent their free time playing by the river, pretending to be well-to-do vacationers staying at the hotel. He had a vivid imagination and was fascinated by the world outside the boundaries of his rural home. Guests at the hotel provided him endless information, sparking his early desire to travel.

During the Civil War, Merton served the Union as a telegraph operator stationed in Hudson. It was his mother's wish that he not participate in the fighting, a disappointment he felt deeply throughout his life. His oldest brother, a doctor, worked at field hospitals in nearby Pennsylvania. The horrors of war were related to Merton through his eyes. They were scenes he often dreamed of after hearing the accounts. His father died during the summer of 1866. His mother took over the hotel with Merton and his younger brother. At her death in 1873, the boys sold the hotel and its contents, dissolving their partnership to strike out on their own. Merton decided to leave Hudson for the cities he had longed to visit as a boy. By the age of forty-five he had become a man of the world, traveling through the industrial north as well as the many capitals of Europe. Little is known about this time in his life, except that when he finally returned to Hudson, he did so as a very wealthy man. He built the gallery to house himself and the paintings and curiosities he had collected during his years away. In 1898 he opened his gallery to the public.

Ted Martin had shared this information often during the years he worked at the gallery still owned and operated by members of the family. The gallery's history after Merton's death was sordid and not the subject of public information. There had been a series of trustees who neglected the structure and its contents, and the current trustee was the first to take a real interest in its history and collections, spending a portion of the endowment Merton had left on painting conservation by staff at the Cleveland Museum of Art. When Ted had been hired, much of the endowment went to cover his modest salary supplemented by a free apartment, and painting conservation was limited to one painting every other year. The current trustee liked this slow pace, the fact that little physical change took place at the gallery, that visitation was modest, and that Ted, like his predecessors, would likely move on after a few years of being choked by his no-growth philosophy.

CHAPTER TWELVE

Mitchell Jenkins found Laura and Taylor having drinks in their splendidly decorated living room. Laura had decorated the home herself and it displayed the gracious good taste of a woman of quiet sophistication. At his entrance, Taylor rose from the loose-cushioned lounge, greeting Jenkins with a handshake.

"Glad to see you Mitchell, and pleased you can stay for supper. I've a great deal to tell you about developments that will become known publicly tomorrow—things I'm sure will please you. May I build you a scotch?"

Jenkins thanked his host for the offer and allowed him to make one up from the large bar located just outside the living room. Laura was seated in a small wooden chair by a reading lamp, having just finished reading an article in a national museum publication Jenkins had sent her. It was about boards and directors and the increasing amount of support the first needs to give the latter as museums face the midpoint of the new decade.

"I'm sorry Maureen couldn't make it this evening, Mitchell." Laura put the magazine down to her side. "I enjoy seeing her. She is so beautiful."

Jenkins put his right hand in his trouser pocket. "Yes, she was sorry she couldn't come too, but had made a commitment to our daughter—a music recital at her school. Maureen does love to see your beautiful home." He stepped toward a small silver bowl holding salted almonds and took a handful.

Taylor held a glass out to Jenkins and changed the subject, for which his guest was grateful. "How is the architect coming along? Any new notions about his design?"

"We're still listing the areas to be included in the building and how they should relate to one another," Jenkins replied. "Browning and I are going to visit several museums together in the coming weeks to see how they are designed and what changes their directors would make if they could do it over again. But there is no specific design as yet. I had made crude drawings some time ago for a building on our existing site…"

"Come now Mitchell," James interrupted, "we both know the existing site isn't adequate for the kind of growth Meriden is expecting." He had changed little on this point. "We're in the new South now. In five years there will be so much prosperity here we won't recognize the Meriden of today. It's already happening in Atlanta, growing like a bad weed in all directions, and if they aren't careful, they'll eventually have all the problems associated with big cities in the North. Nobody thinks of little things anymore; Atlanta is going to have a sewage problem—mark my words—and nobody there is thinking about it."

Laura sat quietly in her chair. She had heard her husband's lectures before and knew it was best not to interrupt when he had a new audience. She watched Jenkins as he listened to her husband's ravings, probably thinking of something bright to say when he finished. She admired his ability to appear interested in what was being said—the same talent she had acquired over the years. She reviewed her life with the man lecturing on the sins of rapid over-development. As a younger man he spent all his waking hours in the lab. The opening of the company left even less attention for her. Oh, she saw him at work, but his mind was generally miles away. Her place in his life was set by years of struggle and the bonds of age.

She finished her sherry and motioned for Taylor to pour her another. He had finished his lecture, and both men were silently looking down, as if studying their shoes.

"Mitchell," Laura began, "do you think the Art Association Board will resist moving from the location they helped provide? I worry people will think the we're running roughshod over the art community in Meriden. I think it'll prove to be an issue on which you'll have to take a stand, especially since I'm on the commission."

He took a seat opposite her and leaned forward. "I believe the association and its membership are very much aware of the limitations of our present buildings. The current building has no temperature or humidity control, no lighting that meets museum standards, eleven openings of some kind or other on the first floor alone, no security system, and precious little available wall space for artwork. It's extremely difficult to attract quality exhibitions from important institutions with a facility that is so inadequate. It's also difficult to attract gifts from collectors here in Meriden or from other places. What was accomplished in 1959 was a good start, as good as the association could make under the circumstances. They had little money and no real direction. Their great accomplishment was to attract interested people into their sphere and hope someday, someone could do something better. Now that has happened, and I believe they'll back your and Taylor's initiative one-hundred-fifty percent. Together the association and the commission now have an opportunity to build something important for art in Alabama and the Southeast. The new building could be the focal point for so much activity, and not just Meriden activity either. The potential is limitless. I just hope the commission will see its way clear to allow me to remain here until the building is completed." He looked down at his scotch. "The rate of directors being relieved from their duties greatly increases after the completion of major building projects. If I survive, I'll be lucky."

"I don't know anything about that," Laura replied. "Everyone on the commission thinks you do an outstanding job. I certainly wouldn't be in favor of a change in leadership unless you requested to go somewhere else."

"You're very kind, Laura. I hope to do the job that will do credit to all of us."

Taylor James returned with his wife's sherry. He had been on the telephone, "Well, that was the mayor. He's finished the planning commission's report and is fit to be tied! That's why I needed to talk with you tonight, Mitchell. Shall we go in to dinner?"

Anne had set a set a wonderful table in a room Jenkins thought was the best in the house. Taylor took his place at the head of the long mahogany table with Laura at his right and Jenkins on his left.

"I had hoped Morgan would join us," Jenkins said. "Has she gone back to school already?"

"Left this morning in the new car her father bought her," Laura answered. "It was a late Christmas present that didn't arrive until just this week. I don't like sports cars, but it was what she wanted, and she has a way with her father."

Laura smiled and looked up at Taylor, who was pretending not to have heard the discussion. Sensing his wife had finished her jibe, he told Jenkins Morgan had hoped to be remembered by her summer employer. "She is really pleased that the commission accepted our gift for the building, even though she hasn't spent much time in Meriden since we moved here. Maybe she'll decide to live here after she graduates."

"I hope so," Jenkins answered, "we certainly need what she could add to the community."

He was smiling, but was nervous making small talk. He constantly felt on thin ice around James and kept his guard up. James had done a great thing for the museum and could do even more, but could just as easily do it harm. Jenkins was fortunate Laura had agreed to serve on the commission; she might be able to buffer her husband if he went on a tear. Anna began plating dinner and filled elegant crystal goblets with a vintage French wine. *This is a far cry from Louisiana. James could carry me far if I play him properly. It's way too early in the game to make a stupid mistake.*

"Mitchell," James said, passing him the wine cork for his examination, "did you know the mayor wants to move city hall from its present location to one at the north end of the business district?"

"Yes, I'd heard that from friends. He's even put city money down on some land, I believe."

"He put a deposit down on a parcel of land owned by the Baptist Church. What isn't generally known is his council secretly voted on the money for the entire purchase price and a check was issued. That land is now the property of Meriden."

Jenkins was only mildly interested in the developments of city government. While his relationship with the mayor's office was fine, no city money came to the museum. "It's hard to believe the press didn't pick up on that transaction since land deeds are public record. Sounds like Harold pulled one over on the boys at the *Journal*. How soon would construction begin? They have money from the Fed?"

"They do indeed have the money. The mayor also has, as of this evening, the findings of the city's planning board and an independent planning consultant indicating a move to the north end of Meriden would create a severe population imbalance that would surely mean death for the south end of the city. The study couldn't have come at a worse time for Harold, considering the city's purchase of the church land. But, better now than once construction began."

Jenkins couldn't quite figure the connection between the city's problems and the museum project. Taylor was leading up to something though, and Jenkins hoped the connection would be made soon. "It's just a study. The city doesn't have to go along with it, does it? What's the mayor going to lose if he goes ahead with his plan?"

Taylor straightened in his chair. "The federal money!" His face lit up like a man who knows a great secret and has just let it out. "He'll lose the federal money if he builds in an area that is detrimental to the growth of the community. The guidelines are very specific about this. Tomorrow morning the press will realize the basic findings of the planning commission's report. It will not be good for Harold or city council. They've spent a good deal of tax money they may or may not be able to recoup."

He looked at the other two at the table as he rendered the final verdict on the mistakes of Harold Stubbins. Laura sat quietly, listening. She wondered if Jenkins had figured out where her husband was leading the conversation. She didn't ask if Taylor had played a part in the developments he just outlined.

"The private traffic study funded by concerned citizens," Taylor continued, "showed that with the Endicott Building on the north end of town and the new city hall on the south end, a balanced traffic pattern could be achieved, giving new life to the southern end of the community. Downtown growth is inevitable, but its proper planning is essential. It's what the Feds told Harold from the beginning. What we must do, Mitchell, is figure out a way for the church land to be acquired for the new museum."

So, Jenkins' thought, *he has finally gotten to the heart of this conversation. James had given the matter more thought than I gave him credit for.*

"I could buy the land, of course, but I think that puts too much James money in the project. I would like to see the city take the initiative, though Harold is too confused now to know what to do. What I'm going to suggest to him is that the city deed the land to the museum as a gift. I'm sure there are plenty of legal ways to handle the transaction. The point is, the Commission could accept the land and construction on the new structure could begin as soon as you and the architect develop plans." Taylor James was pleased with himself. It was, in his mind, the perfect location for the new museum. "Meet me there in the morning Mitchell. It's the perfect site. I think you'll like it!"

Jenkins smiled and acted excited about the proposal, though he hadn't made up his mind to completely agree with it. If James had gone this far, he had probably already spoken with Stubbins about gifting the land. "It seems everything might fall together very quickly. I really don't know what to say, but like everything else in this new year, it's very exciting."

"I don't think Taylor expects you to say anything, Mitchell," Laura said, finally breaking her silence. "There's still a lot of ground to cover before the land can be given to anyone. Taylor sometimes makes very complicated things seem very simple. The downtown site might not be appropriate for its intended use, but even so, the city has to agree to give it up. As you alluded, they don't have to follow the course of this study. Surely Harold could get the money for a new building through commercial banking channels."

James didn't like having his plans questioned and gave Laura a harsh look. "In the first place, the city has already accepted the federal funding. To give the money back would make Meriden look pretty damn stupid. And if they're caught ignoring the guidelines and are forced to repay the government, Stubbins can wave goodbye to any future political ambitions he might harbor. In the second place, money on that scale is tight. Even if you can get it, and I suppose the city could, the interest rate is three times what the federal rate is. Stubbins would be crazy to go out on the limb for that kind of debt. The taxpayers would eat him alive next election. In the third place, the study is correct. The south end would dry up if city hall moved from there. Property values would drop and existing merchants would go out of business. Harold made his money in real estate, investments that are very substantial in that part of the city. He can't afford to move city hall from there, and I can't imagine how he ever thought he could! No, they will be forced to sell that land, or do something with it in order save the federal funding. Harold's going to be very busy with the press tomorrow, but by the weekend I should be able to get an audience with him and pitch our plan. Mitchell, I don't mean to rush you in this matter, but I believe the land can be in the hands of the museum by spring, and as you can tell, I'm fired up about our project. I'm not going to interfere, but I'd like to see something happening by next fall. Our attorneys tell me our donation needs to be in your hands before income tax documents are filed, so the land and our money could both come at the same time!"

Jenkins was beginning to enjoy the power of Taylor James, yet was wary of it at the same time.

CHAPTER THIRTEEN

It had been an uneventful day for Ted Martin, the kind he treasured. Eva Osborne arrived later than usual, giddy at the prospect of having lunch with friends at the new Reserve Country Club. She was also beaming with the news her eldest son would soon be discharged from the army and returning to Hudson to take his place in the family business.

"You know Ted," Mrs. Osborne said, "when James took his bride and left for the army, Mr. Osborne and I were sure they would settle in New York where her family resides. Mr. Osborne was so pleased when James wrote and asked if there was a position for him here. He will be the trustee when Mr. Osborne retires. We so want James and Lucy to take an interest in the gallery. I'm sure you will enjoy meeting them both. They're about your age and are such fun! When James becomes trustee, you and he can work together managing the gallery in the tradition my Mr. Osborne has started. Until he got the gallery, nobody took any interest in it at all, and now it's open to the public almost every day—just the way Merton would have wanted it." With that she looked over her shoulder at the portrait on the wall and gave the restrained smile she used when in the gallery, as if she were in a holy place.

Ted Martin never intended to stay there for his entire career, but Mrs. Osborne would never understand that. It saddened him to think of growing old waxing the gilt frames of the same paintings over and over again.

"Just by being here," Mrs. Osborne continued, "James and Lucy will breathe new life into the gallery. I'm sure they'll be full of new ideas for activities and will want to have parties here and special openings for exhibitions." She looked at Martin and her expression changed to a reprimand. "The exhibitions we've had recently have been a bit too contemporary for my taste. Particularly the last one. Those so-called artists from Cleveland. Mr. Osborne agrees with me on this. They were very nice young men, but their work does not express the historic intention of the gallery."

Ordinarily Ted wouldn't argue with the Trustee's wife, but since she was in a light mood about the return of her oldest son, he decided to chance it. "I'd have thought that exhibition would have been the kind of thing Merton would have sought to present in his time. He encouraged young artists, purchasing their work from time to time, and the opening brought many new people into the gallery who might have an interest in becoming involved. I don't think we can afford to turn a cold shoulder on the artists of our time and area. I'm sure your son would agree."

He did not go on further. Mrs. Osborne was looking at the floor, her light expression now completely gone. She was rubbing her hands together indicating she was unhappy, and Martin knew he had overstepped. He tried to say something that might nullify his opinions in her mind but could find nothing to say. She left for her luncheon with her face drawn, a cloud of angst above her head.

The remainder of his day was quiet. He followed the established routines of work that would get him through the days between installations of exhibitions and packing them for shipment elsewhere. The Osbornes had always offered to host opening receptions for new exhibitions, and Martin felt they enjoyed the activity these occasions generated. Mrs. Osborne's comments of the morning had not troubled him as much as her look when she left. He worked hard for the family and felt they should allow him more opportunity to express his thoughts and plans about how to expand the gallery. They always talked about growth but were never anxious to enlist help to achieve it. Mr. Osborne called mid-afternoon, as was his custom. He was in a good mood and joked with Martin, making him feel at ease after the morning's discord. At five o'clock, he closed the exterior door and walked through the galleries for a final security inspection. He entered his small apartment and opened a bottle of wine as the first drops of rain fell on the tin roof above his head. The rain was falling heavily when he heard the sharp ring of the gallery's front doorbell. Switching the audio speaker on, he could hear a car's engine, the falling rain distorting the sounds as other cars passed by.

"Hello! Is someone there?"

"Mr. Martin, this is Mr. Osborne, I would like to speak to you a moment please."

"Yes sir, I'll be right down."

He hurried down the staircase to the gallery's front door. It was almost six o'clock, and Martin wondered what had brought him out into this cold, wet night. Robert Osborne stood on the entry steps with the collar of his black overcoat pulled tight around his neck, his head bare. He glared at Martin as the rain fell in his face.

"Please come in out of the rain, Mr. Osborne." The words went unheard because Osborne had already begun talking as he stepped inside.

"I want you to know," he began, his voice a full octave higher than usual, "that no one speaks to Mrs. Osborne the way you did this morning. She is the most wonderful woman on Earth and doesn't have to be bothered by you or anyone else who cannot be civil to her and treat her like the fine woman she is. You and all those people who think they can take this gallery away from her are sadly mistaken. No one can ever take it away from Mrs. Osborne and me. I know you make Mrs. Osborne's life miserable. If I hear of one more incident of this type of behavior, one more time when Mrs. Osborne feels obliged to tell me anything you have said or done, you will be out on the street. There will be no two weeks' notice, I will have you thrown out. Do I make myself clear?"

Ted couldn't speak. Mr. Osborne turned and walk back out to his car, which was still running. In less than five minutes, he had managed to undermine his young director and give him chills. Ted had never been subjected to such a dressing down. Osborne drove away, leaving him standing in the gallery doorway. The wet street glistened in the night. He released the door and it slammed shut in the wind, rattling the lobby windows.

CHAPTER FOURTEEN

By the end of February, Mitchell Jenkins and John Browning had made five trips to museum buildings across the country and were finally ready to begin planning for the kind of facility Meriden should have. Jenkins enjoyed getting away on those occasions from the pressures of Taylor James, the commission, and the museum's daily operations, which had steadily increased. He had taken over a room adjacent to his office to use for the building project. Three times a week he and Browning would spend long afternoons there. Taylor James had accurately predicted the outcome of the city's land problem, with the commission gaining control of the parcel the city had purchased from the Baptist Church. Everyone knew an incredible amount of work would have to be finished in the months between the coming spring and late fall, and Jenkins set about accomplishing as much as possible with a blind indifference to anything else. He set new work hours for himself, arriving at the museum by one in the afternoon and working past midnight. He also renewed his relationship with LeAnne during this time, taking pleasure in her company two nights a week. His new schedule suited his needs and worked well, except when it was interrupted by morning meetings with James, or as was the case this morning, when he had to meet with Charlie Scott.

He had not seen Charlie since the night at the lodge two years ago. He heard from his friend that business picked up a bit in the new year but never got a full briefing on the agency's future. Charlie had called the afternoon before in the hopes of getting a few hours of Jenkins' time, but was put off until the following morning.

"Have some coffee ready and I'll be there by 9:15!" Jenkins had said.

"Twelve more hours won't make any difference!" Scott replied.

Jenkins had a sinking feeling in his stomach as he returned to the work room and John Browning after the call. Arriving at Charlie's office the following morning, Jenkins was surprised to find it empty. The desks and tables where people had worked were gone. Old campaign proposals were tacked to the central corkboard on the largest wall, but no new work was to be found anywhere. He let himself into Charlie's office and found his friend in a deep discussion with a young man he didn't recognize.

Seeing Jenkins, Charlie stopped talking and stood up. "Mitchell, thanks for coming, I know it has cost you some sleep! This is Carson Smith."

The two shook hands and Charlie poured a third cup of coffee.

"Still take no cream, Mitchell? I'm sure you noticed the empty rooms out front. I've had to let most everyone go. The firm is finished. Carson specializes in tax law and bankruptcy procedures. I thought his advice would be beneficial, and he's giving it gratis."

The meeting continued to be full of bad news. Charlie had managed to pay off some of the larger debts, but the firm owed many creditors, to say nothing of the bank. They had employed creative people and worked hard, but the money had simply run out.

"We can raise some money by selling equipment and office furniture—I bought the best. But that won't make enough to cover your loan. Carson has some ideas about how we can help you with that."

Jenkins hadn't expected any of this. It was a sad parting. To some degree each blamed the other for the failure but would not admit it out loud. After most of the debts were eventually paid or settled in some fashion, Charlie moved to Atlanta and was able to get a job with a large advertising firm. The two rarely saw each other after that day. Jenkins was present at the auction of the office furnishings. He watched as things were sold, feeling a chill down his spine—the same chill he had had when Biggs died.

✳ ✳ ✳

By May, John Browning completed the architectural plans, which were approved by the commission and ready to be put out for contractor bids. To Browning's surprise, six bids for the project were received from contractors in Alabama and Georgia. Because the funding came from a private source, pressure to take the lowest bid was not really an issue. In the end, a firm from Meriden was awarded the contract.

"We are lucky the bid was within budget," Browning told Jenkins in the privacy of his office. "I've worked with this outfit before and they're not as backward as you might think, though I hope they've considered the magnitude of the project and the exactness it will require. I'm meeting with the owner of the firm tomorrow, and you probably should be there too."

Jenkins agreed, returning to his office in time to take a call from Louis Sterling, who inquired if Jenkins could stop by his office for a drink after work. He enjoyed Sterling's company and promptly arrived before five thirty. Sterling's office was a fascination. He had worked in the newspaper business all his life, and the room was filled with mementos and awards. He was a very neat person, an oddity in a business traditionally operated in clutter. Since the *Journal's* take over by the Knight chain, the prospect of instant news had enabled Sterling to bolster the effectiveness of the paper in the Southeast and the state. Nothing had come easily though. He was currently struggling with a suit filed by the NAACP claiming rampant racial profiling in the paper's hiring procedures. Sterling and his assistants were at the center of the confrontation for weeks before consenting to make significant changes.

Both men stared quietly into their glasses for some time, each thinking about their problems and futures. Finally, Jenkins looked up. "I'm thinking seriously of hiring an assistant. Someone to take the pressure off me a bit." He knew this would bring a smile to Sterling's face. "It looks like we're going to be doing a great deal of growing in a very short time. My role is going to change significantly from what it's been, and someone will need to take charge of in-house matters, like our schedule of changing exhibitions. The collection will be growing too, and just the recordkeeping alone is going to be more than LeAnne can handle. I'm going to begin looking for someone, but in the meantime, I'll carry on as best I can and hope Maureen will understand."

Sterling found Maureen beautiful, as most men did, but had no idea what she was like beneath the surface. Thus he easily believed what her husband said of her. Jenkins was tired of dealing with her and made it known when she was not around. He professed not believing in the institution of marriage and would gladly be free again to live "a life without strings." He hoped she would take a lover so he could be free of her in an appropriately outraged manner. But as of yet, she had not obliged him.

☆ ☆ ☆

Jenkins parked his car under the covered rear entrance of the museum building, looking out across its grounds as darkness began to hide the trees in the distance. He felt hungry but didn't want to go home. Deciding to take a walk before going back to his office, Jenkins set out to the north of the building, past the new school now in full use for the summer semester.

He peered through a window on the ground floor where students were working on potter's wheels. Three young women were within view. They were turning small pots with their fingers, making the forms rise and not knowing how to stop them. *The best thing about pottery is watching those breasts hang over the clay. We should only enroll women for this class, it develops more than the mind!* He walked around the building, looking up toward the windows on the second floor. A large piece of canvas was strung over the window so the interior couldn't be seen. *They must have found a model.* He craned his neck, hoping to see the silhouette of a naked woman against the canvas. Waiting a few seconds more, he saw what he hoped for. The strong spotlight shifted from one position to another, and the model's shadow became visible. There was a strange familiarity about the woman's form. Transfixed, he lingered a few moments more and the model changed her pose. It was the movement that gave her away. "That's LeAnne!" he said aloud and looked again as the woman moved sideways. "I'll be damned," he muttered with a grin.

The night's air was more than warm. Lightning flashed, outlining clouds with a wonderful iridescence. Jenkins was thinking of LeAnne, remembering the last of their late-night encounters. He was close to the museum's staff entrance when he noticed a figure seated in the grass, a student from the school taking a break from the intensity of forced creativity. It was a young woman, her long, blond hair combed over one shoulder, striking a very dramatic pose.

"HI! I'm Mitchell Jenkins. Are you okay?"

She looked up and offered a guarded smile. She was pretty, perhaps 18, wearing jeans and a t-shirt. "I'm Lisa Waterman. I'm a student here. Just came out to enjoy the darkness and the light show."

Jenkins stepped a bit closer as the woman carefully crushed the stub of a cigarette. He couldn't tell by the bit of remaining fumes exactly what she had been smoking. She was smiling now, teasing Jenkins with her eyes.

"Have you been one of our students long?"

"Actually no. My family just moved here from Atlanta. I've taken a lot of art classes though and miss the museum there with its contemporary collections and exhibitions."

"You like modern art then?"

"Oh yes," she replied, "especially the work of Beau Britian."

They were magic words, and Jenkins was quick to respond. "Beau is a friend of mine. He'd be pleased to know you admire his work." He could see the instant impression he'd made in her face. "He's going to be an important artist and is well on his way to becoming one of this country's giants. There are a few of his pieces in our museum. Would you like to see them?"

"The museum's closed now. How would we get in?" She was laughing at the prospect of breaking into the structure behind her.

He sensed her intense interest in getting inside. "We don't have to break any windows. I have a key." He helped her stand, then guided her to the side door near his car. He unlocked the door and opened it slowly. The dim light at the receptionist's desk lit the way down the corridor. "See, it worked."

Lisa laughed and squeezed his offered hand. They entered the building like two conspirators, closing and locking the doors behind them. The cigarettes she had were not tobacco after all, and as three more were shared between them, the interests of the evening moved away from art.

It was a quarter past three in the morning when Jenkins awoke with a start, and he was alone in his office. He hadn't heard Lisa leave. He pulled himself up, noticing the Britian lithograph of the letter "W" had been hung upside down during Lisa's stay. "MMMM," he said, looking at it. He rose, walking naked out his office toward the bathroom that accommodated both sexes. It occurred to him that after all his time in Meriden, he had never walked through the building in this most appropriate state. He decided to send a memo to Ellen Maxwell suggesting a special program for nudists, and he would offer to lead the discussion personally. He spent fifteen minutes splashing his face with warm water from the pedestal sink. He decided he would sleep on the couch in the den when he got home and tell Maureen he didn't want to disturb her. Leaving the museum whistling in the stillness of early morning, he found a note on his windshield held in place by a wiper: "Enjoyed it." Jenkins smiled as he slid behind the steering wheel and fired up the ignition. A slight wind stirred and a few drops of rain began to fall. A set of taillights were barely visible at the end of the drive; the car turned left and was gone.

CHAPTER FIFTEEN

Jenkins worked through the remainder of the summer, feeling a growing excitement for the groundbreaking ceremonies. With Sterling's assistance, he successfully identified regional press who would be interested. Publicity was gradual but very real, and for Ellen Maxwell, who Jenkins had asked to define a proper protocol for the event itself, the pace was far too fast. Early on he had called a series of strategy meetings to determine how the ceremonies should be handled. Involving others in the decision-making process was not typical of him, and he was clearly not comfortable in the role. However, he did not want to offend anyone or be accused of leaving any stakeholder out of the process. He also reasoned if more people were involved, there would be more culpability if something went wrong.

It was during the second of these sessions that Jenkins introduced Taylor James to Ellen Maxwell. Though she and Morgan had become friends during Morgan's summer internship, Ellen had not met the patriarch of the "ruling class," as they came to be called by some staff members. James was invited partly out of courtesy and partly because of his growing stature in the community. Jenkins had learned very quickly that Taylor was not above twisting arms for things he wanted. Ellen Maxwell was asked to outline any areas of concern relative to the groundbreaking ceremony. Always efficient and composed, she delivered a basic summary of the kinds of activities to include, who should give speeches, who should be seated on the platform, and other details, proving her effectiveness in this type of role. Taylor indicated he would be honored to give some remarks or perhaps present a check to the commission chairman, symbolizing events that already had taken place. With much purpose the meeting continued, dragging on for a total of three hours, after which Jenkins thanked everyone for their interest and contributions.

Taylor purposely stayed behind, and as Jenkins waved at his last guest, he saw him take a seat on his office couch.

"Mitchell, that Ellen Maxwell has a lot going for her, very bright! Glad to have her working on this aspect of the project. What else does she do here? I mean she's on your staff, yes?"

Jenkins was surprised by the question about Ellen as there had been many points covered during the meeting that seemed more likely to be on the benefactor's mind. "She develops educational programming for children primarily, designed to help them relate to art. She's a very bright woman and has lived in Meriden all her life."

"Really? There seem to be very few of that ilk left in this town." He was not looking at Jenkins as he talked. He rubbed the skin under his neck as if needing a shave.

"Except for the time she was married. Then she moved away for a while."

"Married?"

"She's divorced now. Has a couple kids and lives just outside the city limits. A very independent girl, what they call liberated!"

"Very capable though, Mitchell. The kind I'd have in an executive position in my business. I've always found women are better at running things than men. You should let her do as much for you as she's willing to. She's attractive too, very nice indeed."

The two talked for thirty more minutes before Taylor took his leave. *Ellen Maxwell is capable,* Jenkins thought, *maybe a little too capable for my liking.*

He thought little of the conversation until Ellen called his office several days later to ask if he could stop by.

"I'm having a problem you might be able to help with," she'd said cryptically.

As he entered her office, he noted the odd smile on her face that broke into nervous laughter as she moved her hand in a sweeping fashion toward a dozen roses in a crystal vase.

"Well, is there something you need to tell me?"

"They're from Taylor James. Came this afternoon following the lunch he invited me to yesterday. I quite innocently agreed to go with him, but I don't think he has innocence on his mind!"

"Ohhh," said Jenkins, amused.

"He asked me a lot of questions, first about my job, the museum, and you. Then he wanted to know about my children and my divorce. How did he know I was divorced?"

"What did he ask about me?" Jenkins asked, avoiding her question.

"Nothing important, really. How did I like working for you, about your family, Maureen, general things. He was really much more interested in me, or at least that's how it seemed. I'm sure he's harmless Mitchell, but when the flowers arrived, I thought I'd better say something to you before…well, before…you know."

"Taylor's just really friendly, Ellen. He's harmless and probably flattered you would have lunch with him. Don't worry, just be nice to him." Jenkins rose from the chair but stopped short of leaving and looked back at her with a leering smile on his face, "But remember, Taylor likes to see results when he spends his money."

She looked back at him holding herself as poised as possible. "Go to hell!"

He laughed and left the office.

✻ ✻ ✻

After Labor Day, the construction crew built a wooden fence around the Museum's new downtown site to stockpile equipment. It acted as a signal something was soon to happen and spurred James to almost daily visits with Jenkins. Occasionally he would inquire about Ellen Maxwell, especially on days he didn't find her in her office. Jenkins had other matters on his mind and thought little of the romantic interests of his benefactor. Groundbreaking was only days away, and while all plans seemed to be made, he felt a compulsory need to re-check everything. It was billed as the first museum start since the Civil War in Alabama, and with its radical design and contemporary art collection, Jenkins was beginning to feel an uncontrollable anxiety he couldn't shake, not even when exploring LeAnne's silken body at his office.

Forty-five people were officially invited to the ceremony, mostly politicians. Governor Ford had not decided whether or not he could get away. Officials of federal arts agencies had been invited, as well as local members of the Art Association Jenkins was trying to keep happy. The local media were out in force. He had spent the night before at home. Much of the evening—before, during, and after dinner—Jenkins spent on the telephone. There was much congratulating from people in the city and state. Beau Britian called from New York to offer his assistance in any way. Jenkins remembered later to talk with him about the painting Abram Rubin wanted. While little of the evening was about her, Maureen decided this was not the time to complain. They spent a rather tense time in bed. Tenderness had never been his strong suit, and his time with LeAnne had made him more aggressive. He and Maureen hadn't made love in several weeks, and she knew her husband's needs rarely went unsatisfied longer than two or three days. Never in their marriage had she been as sure of his infidelity as she was now.

Heavy, dark clouds hung over Meriden that important morning. It was unseasonably cool, and the weather forecast was dismal. Jenkins slept soundly, waking at six fifteen. He made his way to the kitchen to heat up coffee from the night before and read the morning's paper. The day's dark clouds had not dispersed by the time he ate lunch in his office. The platform's seating chart for the afternoon was arranged so August Bishop would be seated to his left. It was symbolic, he thought, and hoped his mentor would not choose to cancel at the last moment. They had talked often since the announcement of the James gift, and even though Jenkins declined the proffered position in Birmingham more than once, the old man still talked about it as if his denials were only in jest. The commission was to be seated behind him, and Taylor James would be on his other side. Jenkins had asked Ellen to draw a diagram of the seating, which he studied as he ate his cold burger and fries. Ellen wasn't taking Taylor's attention very well, and Jenkins was becoming increasingly concerned he would make her some proposal that would push her over the edge. He couldn't afford to have James frustrated or angry and thought about asking her to humor the old boy.

By one o'clock Jenkins was at the site, awaiting the activity about to take place. This was the big, first step and he didn't want to falter or seem foolish. He regretted inviting Bishop, knowing he would be more nervous with him there. Just past the site itself Jenkins noticed three state police cars parked in a row. The officers were milling about as he walked toward them.

"Is there something wrong officers? I'm Mitchell Jenkins, director of the museum. May I be of some assistance?"

"No sir. This is standard procedure any time the governor leaves Montgomery for another part of the state."

"He's coming? We weren't officially informed."

The officer rested his hands on his gun belt. "We were told he would be here, sir. The information came from one of his aides. I can call headquarters to see if his car has left."

"No thanks, that won't be necessary."

By one thirty, the refreshment table had been set and the assembling dignitaries were sampling the coffee and sandwiches prior to moving to the platform and their seats. The news of the governor's possible attendance sent Jenkins quickly out for Alka-Seltzer. Taylor James was smiling broadly as he spoke with James Hendricks, deputy director of the

NEA. Jenkins wondered what they were saying. The wind had picked up and with the threat of rain still very real, Jenkins slipped on the black overcoat he felt made him look sinister and walked to the podium to address the press and those who had gathered to witness the symbolic turning of soil.

It did rain later that day. Jenkins gave a speech that was half fund-raising rhetoric, half appreciation. It was uninspired. His voice crackled over the loudspeaker as he introduced the assorted dignitaries present, welcoming all, but particularly those from New York and Washington. The governor never did make it, nor did August Bishop, who telephoned at the last moment to offer his congratulations and regrets. Taylor James rose from his front-row seat and gave a stirring speech about community spirit. As always, he had memorized many statistics pertinent to his subject and concluded by predicting the new building would make a significant mark on art in the South. There was applause afterward followed by the ceremonial digging—an honor shared by Jenkins, the James family, and Rudolph Bates, the newly re-elected chairman of the museum commission. The ceremony concluded with Bates praising the James family for their contribution to the community. Afterward, there was a reception at the James home. The work fence around the site was closed and locked by the contracting crew at the end of the afternoon. The rains did not let up, causing great puddles to form in low pockets around the platform. The colors on the bunting ran together, dripping finally into the red mud, and the three mounds of earth turned over just hours before melted back into the holes.

PART II

"Nobody can write the life of a man, but those who have eat and drunk and lived in social intercourse with him."

SAMUEL JOHNSON

CHAPTER SIXTEEN

The darkness outside the jet's small window reflected against the lights inside so Ted could only see his reflection. Much had happened in the last forty-five days, and traveling always made him philosophical. He didn't know what to expect when the plane landed again, this time in Meriden, Alabama. When he left Cleveland that afternoon, snow was falling in gentle flakes, precluding a blizzard that seemed always to happen on Sundays. He had expected the South to be warm like Miami, where everyone wore shirtsleeves in December, but the temperature in Atlanta when he changed planes was only thirty-seven degrees. *This turtleneck sweater feels good after all!* A recorded chime sounded and he instinctively looked toward the plastic partition that separated classes of comfort.

"This is Captain Elliot speaking." Ted remembered all the jokes he had heard of air travel and recorded pilot messages. "We'll be starting our descent into Meriden and will be on the ground in another twenty minutes. The weather is clear, no clouds and thirty-five degrees. From all of us at Eastern Airlines, we hope you've had an enjoyable…."

Ted had indeed had an enjoyable flight and wished it would never end. Checking the wide nylon seatbelt, he looked out the window again as lights twinkled far off to the right. He let his mind go back to the beginning of this adventure, when the phone in the Osborne apartment rang just before nine, catching him as he was about to leave for the short walk to the Hudson Post Office.

"Hello! Mr. Theodore Martin?" The voice was that of a woman's and sounded far away. "Will you hold please for Mitchell Jenkins?"

Before Ted could answer, the call went into a sort of limbo. He could hear a throbbing sound, but nothing recognizable. He tried to recall who she said he was holding for and didn't know anyone by that name. It was a good two minutes before the phone made a few clicking sounds and a man's voice came on.

"Hello, Mr. Martin? This is Mitchell Jenkins calling from the Meriden Art Museum," the voice said as Ted fumbled for a slip of paper to write on.

Hurriedly he uncapped a pen and wrote "Meriden Art Museum, Mitchell Jenkins." The caller was already into his next sentence as Ted strained to listen, think, and write at the same time.

"I'm calling about the resume you sent regarding your work at the Osborne Gallery. It's very impressive. Tell me something about the collection there and your role as director."

Where to begin! After the episode with Robert Osborne, Ted had decided it was time to prepare for the day when he might get thrown out into the street. That following Monday, when the gallery was closed, he went to the public library and spent the afternoon researching museums in states where he might like to live. The list was an interesting contradiction of localities, either in New England or the South. Over subsequent Mondays he arranged to have a resume printed and addressed one hundred thirty envelopes. He didn't remember the Meriden Museum offhand, but began to answer Jenkin's questions, trying to be as articulate as possible and forgetting the morning's dusting and mopping activities.

"Your resume is a bit unclear as to what kind of position you're seeking. We're looking to fill a new position here requiring someone with both administrative and curatorial experience. This person will be primarily responsible for the museum's collections, organizing temporary exhibitions, and assisting me with administrative duties. I saw you apprenticed at the Philadelphia Museum of Art. That is a very fine institution. What brought you to Hudson?"

"It was a first job. I seemed to be the only one in my graduate program to land any sort of museum position, so I took the offer. It seems experience is the one thing education can't provide." There was a pause in the conversation, and Ted wondered if he had said too much about an old frustration.

"You say you'll furnish references and a portfolio on request. I suppose there would be a sample of your writing as well?"

"Yes, there are all sorts of materials included, yes sir."

"Well, I'm requesting a package of information then. How long will it take to get ready and send? There are a couple other candidates for this position, but I thought I'd try someone from outside the South before making any decisions."

Ted thought quickly now, for while he had sent the resume indicating the availability of additional information about his current position, he had not put any kind of package together.

"I can send those materials out in the morning. Is that soon enough?" Ted asked, not believing what he was offering.

"That would be just fine, Mr. Martin! I've enjoyed talking with you. Goodbye!"

The jet was banked steeply to the right and the lights below grew larger. It was amazing how quickly the plane seemed to descend. In minutes it was only a few feet from the treetops, then with a sudden clunk the jet's metal body was vibrating with the unevenness of the runway and the engines reversed.

Mitchell Jenkins didn't call again, but sent a rather lengthy letter inviting Ted to Meriden to interview for the position of curator and assistant director. Ted immediately wrote back saying he would be delighted to come and received a round-trip ticket for the following Sunday.

The night air was cold as he made his way down the metal steps of the airplane with the other passengers. He followed the line, not knowing what to expect when it stopped. He walked through two sets of glass doors toward a crush of waiting relatives and friends. It seemed he should turn right and follow the cement concourse to the terminal building, but as he started to do so a voice called out from the crowd.

"Ted! Ted Martin."

Ted turned to see a male figure standing in partial shadow. He was in tennis shoes, worn blue jeans, and a heavy navy pea coat. A wisp of blond hair blew across his forehead as Ted realized it was Mitchell Jenkins. While they made introductory small talk, several people greeted Jenkins, asking about the building project. He seemed to know everyone in the crowd as the two men started for the terminal building.

"Did you have a good flight? There's not much to see at night."

Jenkins was much younger than Ted had imagined. "Yes, thank you, the flight was fine. Just one stop in Atlanta. Quite a large airport there, really busy—I was surprised."

They made easy conversation, but Ted felt nervous. He chalked this up to feeling like an outsider at a family reunion and tried his best to take command of the situation and be impressive. The ride into the city of Meriden took twenty minutes. Jenkins apologized for the condition of the car they were riding in, saying it was his wife's. He pointed out landmarks in the city skyline ahead. It was very dark, and Ted couldn't distinguish one light from another, but Jenkins was so earnest in the telling that he paid strict attention.

"The beacon to the left there is on top of the Endicott building downtown. It marks the north end of Main Street, which is anchored to the south by City Hall. Our new construction is only a few blocks from the Endicott building, which should help with our daily attendance. There are twenty-eight thousand people working downtown and they all need someplace to go on their lunch breaks."

Ted nodded in agreement, trying to remember as much as possible about what Jenkins was saying.

"Two large George Rickey sculptures are to be installed on top of that hill." He gestured with his arm to land somewhere off to the right. "They're supposed to mark the entrance to Meriden, like the arch in St. Louis marks the beginning of the West. They were commissioned by the men who had the airport built. The executives at Endicott Industries decided they didn't like driving to and from the Birmingham airport, so they joined up with a couple other fellows to have one built here."

Jenkins pulled the car into the lot of a single-story motel on the outskirts of downtown. It was red brick with white columns with a flashing "Quality Court" sign near the road. Ted looked at his watch and suddenly felt as tired as it indicated he should be.

"You'll have to register, so let's both go in. They're holding a room for you."

A middle-aged man was sitting in a small area behind the registration desk. He rose as the door buzzer sounded.

"Hey, Pete! How's it going tonight?" Jenkins greeted the man in an exuberant country manner—a new experience for Ted. "Pete, this is Ted Martin from Hudson, Ohio. He's the director of an art gallery there and is going to be visiting with us for a day or so. See that he gets whatever he wants, okay?"

The two then joked about local matters and talked about the new museum construction. Ted retrieved his bag from the car, and Jenkins walked him to his room.

"What time do you want to start in the morning?"

Ted couldn't decide how to answer. It was already very early in the morning, and he was tired, but Mitchell Jenkins didn't seem like the sort who arrived at his office at noon.

"How about nine? Shall I get a cab and meet you somewhere?"

"No need, I'll pick you up here."

They shook hands and Jenkins walked back to his wife's car. Ted opened the door to his room, found the light switch, and turned down the heater. He had expected to be met by a middle-aged man in a suit and overcoat who would talk quietly about scholarship and the history of painting as it related to the Meriden collection. He had lived in the Northeast too long and was feeling angry with himself for not relaxing around Jenkins. He called Pete and requested a wake-up call for seven. *Tomorrow I'll be at ease with my surroundings*, he thought, smiling at his poor attempt at resolve.

✲ ✲ ✲

The brightness of morning changed the landscape completely. The quiet highway of the night before was now choked with traffic headed south into downtown. The sky, black the night before, was a royal blue, sporting a great yellow sun. Ted's eyes hurt in the glare, and he realized he hadn't packed sunglasses. The air was still cool, but within an enclosed space the sun provided adequate warmth. Mitchell Jenkins arrived promptly at nine. Gone were the jeans and pea coat of the night before, replaced by a conservative-colored suit and tie, no overcoat even with the morning's chill. Ted tried to recall all the questions he had thought of about the community and the museum.

Jenkins talked slowly and patiently, but with purpose. "Monday mornings are very busy. I hope you don't mind interruptions. There are many things to be done today and, of course, you're part of the list. I want you to meet as many people here as possible to get a good picture of our operation. We'll have lunch with Louis Sterling, one of our commissioners and chair of the personnel committee. The full commission is a relatively small body of people who govern our operation. I'm their employee, and everyone else is employed by me."

As the car headed up a winding drive, Ted got his first look at the museum's current home. It was everything he expected and more. Built originally as a residence at the conclusion of the nineteenth century, it was a juxtaposition of architectural styles. Jenkins stopped the car under an arched and covered side entrance built in the gothic manner. In the shade of the arch the air was still cool, but Ted took several moments to admire the grounds before entering through the double wooden doors. Jenkins strode down the hallway toward what appeared to be a central lobby. Ted wanted to see the gallery spaces and the exhibitions housed within, but he dutifully followed Jenkins as best he could past a receptionist and up a carpeted staircase to the building's second floor.

"You've had quite a few calls this morning, Mitchell," said the receptionist as he climbed the staircase two steps at a time. "LeAnne's got the list."

"Thanks Jenny! This is Ted Martin from Hudson, Ohio."

Jenkins finished the stairs and was walking swiftly away from Ted through an opening he could only assume led to the director's office. He made a brief introduction to someone in his rush, and Ted paused for a moment to say hello. He caught up with Jenkins in a large open room with windows that let in the morning's intense sunlight. The office was well furnished in a contemporary style, its wooden floors highly polished. When Ted entered, he found Jenkins already on the phone, waving him inside. He sat on a black leatherette couch, listening to half of the conversation as Jenkins paced back and forth, sometimes pulling the phone from its place on a low filing cabinet. There seemed to be a problem with an employee who hadn't come into work that morning because of an argument with Jenkins the day before.

"I don't care what she calls herself, she can be queen for all I care. Just get her in here. It's the first week of registration and she needs to be supervising enrollment." The conversation went on a short while longer with Jenkins promising to talk to the woman after she came into work.

"I'll deal with that later," he said to Ted as he returned the telephone to the cabinet's top. "It's a minor problem, the kind you have with artists. I'm sure you've faced similar things in Hudson."

Ted thought about himself alone in the Osborne with all those dead artists and hoped personnel issues were not a large part of the position for which he was interviewing.

The morning was a barrage of facts. Jenkins outlined the history of the museum, its growth and future direction. He talked of local politics, the commission, and the art association. It was a highly detailed conversation, one in which he took Ted immediately into his confidence, relating things that were really not the business of an applicant, even if the position was as his chief assistant. It was a wonderful briefing, leaving Ted feeling as if he had already said yes and moved. He found himself trying to remember everything and remembering nothing. Throughout the morning the telephone interrupted them, shifting Jenkins' mind from one topic to another. But he always managed to know where he had stopped, down to the exact word, as if the interruption never occurred or lasted only a few seconds. His facility at this was impressive, but increased Ted's anxiety about being up to the job. *His gearing ratio is way above where mine is.*

Before leaving for lunch, Jenkins met with two people on his staff—Ellen Maxwell and Stephen Parker—who were collaborating on a script for a children's program and required his opinion to settle a dispute. Parker worked as a graphic designer and audio-visual specialist in a new area of museum communication, combining film, audio, and television in programs designed to fit the needs of the institution.

"There are some problems between Ellen and Stephen," he said as they walked to Parker's studio. "They're always at each other's throats about something. I'm tired of being the referee, but I'm determined to see them working together because they are both very talented."

They found Stephen in a small room crowded with television and electronic equipment. He was tall, pale, thin, and pleasant enough in a hurried sort of way. The production of the video was behind schedule and Parker was quick to put the blame on Maxwell, accusing her of constantly changing the script. Ted's introduction was made but not acknowledged by Parker, who was anxious to get to Jenkins before Maxwell arrived.

"Mitchell, we just can't have these changes and still meet our deadline. I already spend fifteen hours a day here. Just when I get ahead, she comes in and wants things changed. Ellen has no idea how long these things take to put together."

"Stephen, I know this back and forth is difficult for you, but do try to work with her. I'm sure the changes are for the best, but I'll have a talk with her. You know how women are; you should get married if you really want to know."

Parker didn't laugh.

"Have you gotten any figures on that new audio mixer you requested? I know you need it to finish this and other projects. Why don't you go ahead and get the one you want, just make sure its price is mid-range. I'll make the commission understand these are sensitive pieces of equipment, so we can't afford to purchase the very least expensive one."

Parker seemed appeased with this offer and didn't complain further. The sound of footsteps increased in the hall outside the studio.

"Here she comes," Parker said, bracing for the worst. In a moment Ellen Maxwell was standing in the doorway, smiling warmly at Parker and Jenkins. She knew she was late and was letting Parker get in the first licks before making her entrance.

"Hello boys. You must be Ted Martin, the new exhibitionist!"

✵ ✵ ✵

Ted wasn't prepared for lunch at Longleaf Club. It seemed elegance of this kind could still be found in the South, yet his history textbooks had made little reference to this sort of social order after the Civil War. The rooms were richly furnished for its members, who demanded the best in all things. Remembering the television broadcasts of racial unrest, rioting, and marches not all that long ago, he wondered why this part of southern living was never shown, then immediately guessed the answer when greeted by two Black doormen who referred to them as "Sir" and ushered them through a set of interior doors.

"This room is the only one women can use," Jenkins explained with a leering smile of approval. "It's pleasant enough, and since Ellen is with us we can't use the men's-only rooms off to the right."

In a few minutes they were also joined by Maureen Jenkins, who made a solitary entrance down the small flight of steps into the dining room. She was a strikingly beautiful woman, dressed in a pastel sweater and matching skirt. Ted was not the only one watching her. Louis Sterling was already standing by his place at the table as she approached.

"Maureen," he said as she got close enough to hear, "it's so good to see you again. Mitchell doesn't get you out enough. Come sit next to me. You know Ellen, of course, and this is our guest, Ted Martin."

Ted smiled in greeting. Though it was only a week before Christmas, she had a wonderful tan that complimented her hair and blue eyes. Ted made a fool of himself, staring at her as a Black waiter in a starched, white uniform came around to take drink orders. Fortunately, the luncheon was filled with questions about him, a pleasant change that allowed him to assert his abilities and keep his mind off the beautiful wife of Mitchell Jenkins.

The afternoon fled by in the activity of the museum. A special meeting had been called to allow commission members to meet Ted and discuss the potential sale of the old museum property. During the latter part of the meeting, Ted spent some time with Ellen Maxwell, who delighted in showing him around the building. He found this part of the trip quite pleasant, casually meeting other staff members as they passed, or as he walked past their workstations. He could feel the expectation present in their greetings. He had obviously been the subject of discussions before his arrival.

By the time Ellen and Ted returned from their museum tour, the commission's private business was completed and they had adjourned to a reception area. The introductions went quite well. Ted was relieved to find the commissioners enjoyed professions outside the museum world, and there were no Robert Osbornes to be found. Before leaving later that day for the airport, Jenkins took him to the site of the new building. It was a short drive into the downtown area of Meriden. Ted was sure the city had changed quite a bit over the last twenty-five years as the "northern invasion" of people and ideas in the newly prosperous 60s spread south. In their race to keep current and modern, business owners had covered original brick buildings with metal or plastic sidings that now gave Main Street a garish quality. Ted could tell Jenkins was not particularly pleased with the look either and quickly pointed out the entire area was undergoing a complete renovation.

"That's another plus for moving the museum downtown, to benefit from the re-development. In another ten years, Meriden will be a new city."

Jenkins pulled the car off the street and up an earthen ramp to the construction site. Large metal trailers filled with materials were parked around the perimeter; stockpiles of steel pipe were stacked between trees, much like logs are in winter; a large orange crane rose from a mammoth hole that would become the building's lowest level. Workers were placing grids of rebar to support the first stage of concrete. Jenkins and Ted walked to a small trailer serving as the site foreman's office.

"John Browning, the architect, is supposed to meet us here," Jenkins explained. "I asked him to prepare a small set of building plans for you to take back so you can become familiar with the layout and gallery spaces." Jenkins looked over his shoulder at Ted and grinned. "You are coming to work here, aren't you?"

It was to be the only job offer Ted was to receive. He had expected something a bit more formal, but realized later there was little formality with Mitchell Jenkins.

"Yes, absolutely. Thank you!"

They entered the trailer with a breeze blowing papers off the foreman's makeshift desk.

✪ ✪ ✪

On his flight back, Ted tried to remember the names and faces of those he'd met: LeAnne Rickter, Mitchell's secretary; Frances Rivers, business manager; Joe Mullens, building supervisor; Mary Griffin, who ran the art school. It appeared they all enjoyed their work but had a benign rivalry going for Jenkins' attention. He talked with them separately throughout the day, answering questions and giving each the support they needed. It was a contagious form of allegiance that by mid-afternoon Ted found himself catching.

CHAPTER SEVENTEEN

Merton Osborne's two brothers didn't stay idle after their brother sold his interest in the hotel and moved away. They had learned diversification was safer than focusing on one business, especially when that business was running an old hotel in a new era of industrialization.

The oldest brother enjoyed working with his hands in iron and had learned the smithing trade as a young man. He developed a small, steel clasp that could be used to secure an object in place when attached to a rope or cable. During a time when automobile travel was increasingly attractive, the clasps and rope were in high demand from tourists wanting to safely attach their luggage and other objects to the back of their vehicles. Larger clamps were also made for the shipping industry to secure cargo against the rough seas of winter transit. The brothers developed this business into something more profitable than the hotel they decided to sell a year after Merton's return to Hudson. The clamp business was handed down through the family, coming eventually to Robert Osborne, the sole male heir of his generation.

After walking in the bitter cold and snow from the gallery to the clamp factory, Ted made his way down a long hallway filled with objects relating to the Osborne's family history. Robert Osborne sat behind his mahogany desk as Ted entered his office. As always, he was dressed in a black suit and starched white shirt. He had worked all his life, starting as a junior executive and rising through management levels. Ted admired that initiative since Robert knew he would one day run the business, regardless of the amount of time he put into learning it.

As always, when Mrs. Osborne was otherwise occupied, he greeted Ted warmly. Saying he had a Jekyll-and-Hyde personality was melodramatic and oversimplified. Overall he was an extremely affable person, a fact that made Ted's impending resignation harder than if he was constantly in the state he'd been in that rainy evening.

"Ted, come in. Good to see you. Dreadful weather! We'll have a deep snow by afternoon. Lucky you live in the gallery!"

"Mr. Osborne," Ted began with some hesitancy, "I need to talk with you about a decision I made yesterday that will affect both of us."

Robert smiled from his side of the desk. Ted realized his employer had not guessed what he was about to tell him, and worse, would not have any memory of why he had taken this action.

"We both agreed when I came to work for you this would be a stepping-stone position for me. I've enjoyed these last two and a half years, but have decided to move ahead with my career and have taken a job with a museum in Alabama. I'm afraid, sir, I must tender my resignation."

Ted handed him an envelope containing the letter and sat back in the leather chair, readying for an outburst. He remembered Robert's words of anger about throwing him out into the street and felt a combination of vindication and pity. Robert took the letter without opening it and placed it by the telephone to his right.

"Well, I suppose congratulations are in order, Ted. I'm pleased for you and sorry you'll be leaving us. I hope you'll be happy." He paused, looking down at the top of his desk. "How long before you leave?"

"I've given one month's notice, sir, and I'd be happy to assist in the search for my replacement. There are several places where you could begin to…"

Robert eyed Ted across his desk, not angry but firm. "That will not be necessary, but thank you anyway. Mrs. Osborne and I will handle that. I suppose you should be getting back to the gallery now, it's about time to open."

He looked from Ted to the door, making it clear it was time to leave. *He will surely call Mrs. Osborne as I walk out the door, and by the time I arrive back at the gallery, she'll know what I've done.* She would not take the news well, and Ted didn't look forward to her arrival. Perhaps the weather would keep her away.

As he unlocked the gallery entrance and began dry mopping the floors, his mind shifted to the memory of Maureen Jenkins as she entered the dining room at the club. Everyone but Jenkins had greeted her warmly. He may be brilliant, but Ted didn't see him as the kind of man women threw themselves at. There was something about him, however, that made women respond. It was clearly visible in the short time of his visit. Jenkins seemed to not want his wife present at the luncheon. Perhaps he feared she would be a distraction. Louis Sterling certainly found her worthy of a great deal of his attention. The seeming inconsistency about Jenkins' behavior was slightly unsettling, but his wife was certainly an asset.

Mrs. Osborne did not arrive at the gallery the day of his resignation, but was present a day or so later. She was very subdued, disappointed with Ted for "letting her down." His month's notice was cut to two weeks. He was sure she took over his duties, though not every day and not mopping the floors or cleaning the elaborate frames.

Ted packed his car and moved south. Ohio's winter weather followed him, and as hard as it tried, the southern sun couldn't chase the cold winds away. It even snowed a bit that first month, causing school closings and general celebrations to break out all over the city.

An office had been prepared for Ted adjacent to the one Jenkins used. It was the room previously occupied by the new building planning, and drawings and notes could still be found deep within desk drawers. Joe Mullens and his crew re-opened a doorway that had been sealed sometime earlier, creating a door between the offices so they could get back and forth without going into the hallway. While Jenkins was kind and gracious those first months, Ted could tell he was trying to adjust to his being in such close proximity.

Ted's orientation to the museum was supposed to take place the first month. It called for him spending a full week in every department, learning as much as possible about each of them. However, it never got off the ground as projects had been stacked up too long. By February, he was knee deep in all of them. Jenkins had much more going on than any man could care for properly, yet he seemed to thrive on the pressure of deadlines.

The museum had never had a full-time curator, and while that was Ted's official title, he felt uneasy at times with the responsibility it implied. Previously, when desperately needed, Jenkins would hire artist friends to assist him with exhibition installations, but had never had anyone besides a secretary to help with the record-keeping of the art collection. Besides the exhibition of Russell Hall's collection, the museum had not organized many others. He did have an impressive record with local artists though, making him popular with that segment of the community. When Ted wasn't in one of the galleries or at his desk becoming familiar with the museum's holdings, he was with Jenkins, talking over his thoughts and plans for the new building.

While enjoying the attention of his new boss, Ted began to notice the suspicious looks of other staff members. He was already aware of their need for their boss's attention, and he was getting more than his fair share. The situation was compounded by Jenkins' penchant for seeking Ted out, inferring a trust in his counsel that lessened to a degree with the others. Ted was his frequent lunch guest at his club and his home for dinner, arriving well past the normal dinner hour. They would eat alone in the dining room, with Maureen occasionally joining. There was never any discussion about his extra hours—he always arrived at the office early and stayed much later than five. Jenkins was always there ahead of him and stayed later. It was difficult to tell who was trying to impress whom, though his boss clearly had the edge.

Jenkins put their conversations to good use, telling Ted about the people in Meriden who were helpful to the museum, as well as his early struggles to turn the institution into one of note throughout the South. All of Jenkins' talks were orderly, as if he were following an outline, though no notes were ever present. Mixed in with his history lessons were his thoughts on more personal issues—life, women, marriage, and a range of other topics that had nothing to do with the museum or its functioning. Ted would hear him out, figuring with the pressure of his position, Jenkins needed to talk to someone to clear his mind and make room for important matters. By the end of the first spring, Ted was fully committed to both the museum and Jenkins.

✵ ✵ ✵

Though the new museum's opening was a full year away, there was much to do in preparation. Ted's first assignment after acclimating to his new surroundings was to prepare a written history of the Meriden Art Association Jenkins planned to publish. He concluded it was Jenkins' way of helping him learn about the museum's history on his own. It was a profitable exercise, because Ted learned a lot about his boss through the eyes of key figures from the association's past, some of whom were still living in Meriden. Ted made a list of five such early art patrons and artists and set up interviews over a two-week period. Casually he mentioned this to Jenkins, since he would be out of the building conducting the interviews, and was surprised by his request for a list of interviewees. Ted explained the list had been prepared as a result of his own research and that he hoped he hadn't done anything wrong.

"Certainly not, Ted. I'm sorry to have been so abrupt. My only concern was you might potentially be getting incorrect ideas from people you might encounter. The museum has undergone a lot of change in the past few years, and that's created some hard feelings from some of the older members of the association and the artist's group that preceded them. However, from what I see on your list, you have chosen wisely. These folks are still active supporters of our programs and will give a fair and accurate picture of the past and the museum's growth. In fact, I'll call each of them and ask for their complete cooperation. This is an important project to me and to the completion of the new building."

Ted left his office through the common door and sat behind his desk, wondering at the sudden emotional changes Jenkins was capable of. It seemed for a moment his pleasure with his new assistant was going to rapidly come to an end; then, he urged Ted to finish the project because it has real importance. Ted shrugged it off as over-work and began to gather his materials for the interviews. Through the door, he could hear Jenkins talking on the phone in hushed sentences.

Ultimately, all five subjects were filled with praise for the artistic growth in the city and gave Jenkins much, if not all of the credit. Their enthusiasm further justified Ted's opinion of Jenkins and he returned after the first interview with the incident of the morning completely forgotten. It was almost closing time, and he was surprised to learn Jenkins had already left for the day. LeAnne was at his desk straightening papers. She smiled and waved, and Ted stopped on his way to his office.

"Looks like Mitchell left for the day. That's so unlike him. I hope he wasn't ill or there was something wrong at home." The last part of his remark seemed to dampen her smile a bit.

"No, nothing wrong. He just felt like getting away early. He said something about having you around gave him more free time, but don't let it go to your head—he's a terrible kidder!"

Ted thanked her for the reassurance. The late afternoon sun gushed into the office windows, making the white walls glow a beautiful golden color. He placed his legal pad and recorder on a chair facing the desk and walked to the window. The azaleas had recently finished blooming, leaving bright green leaves in place of their white and pink flowers. Joe Mullens or one of his staff had mowed the lawn that afternoon, and the fragrance of the newly cut grass lingered in the air. He opened the window wider and stepped back to the desk. In the center of his ink blotter was an envelope with his name written on it in Mitchell's hand. He slipped it open and retrieved a short note:

Dear Ted,

I know the past weeks have been confusing
for you sometimes, but I wanted you to know how pleased
I am with your work and enthusiasm. I hope you stay
in Meriden a long while and become a real part of our
organization.
You are rapidly becoming irreplaceable around here.
I feel a great deal better since you've come aboard.

Mitchell

Ted decided to keep this note as he had done with his college acceptance letter and the one from graduate school. There were enough reminders of bad things, encouragement was something to be treasured.

✜ ✜ ✜

The following morning, Mitchell and Ted were to travel to Birmingham to meet with August Bishop and staff members of the newly formed Alabama

Arts Commission. Jenkins had recently accepted the presidency of the organization and began his tenure in January. Ted wondered how Mitchell could possibly keep abreast of this activity with the demands of construction in Meriden. But as with his other indulgences, it was a distraction from the worry of his day job and his growing concern of being replaced once the new building came into being. He had begun telling Ted about this concern shortly after he started and was reiterating it again on their way to Birmingham.

"You know Ted, your being here and adapting so quickly to the staff and the institution is a big relief to me. I've been worried about who would run the museum if I were let go or forced to leave for some reason. Statistically, more museum directors are replaced after a new construction project concludes than at any other time. I know there are people who are waiting for just such a scenario with me. It's a comfort to know you can handle things."

Silence was thick in the car as Ted considered these comments. *Surely he's just trying to make me feel wanted in Meriden, but the thought of taking over for him in any near future is not the way to do it.*

"Mitchell, I've only been here a short time, but I certainly don't detect anyone opposing you on the staff or the commission. If they're the only people who can take your job, I think you are safe."

"I appreciate that. Loyalty is the thing I need, what any director needs. But I guarantee there are people who want me to leave Meriden, and I'll have to fight hard to stay after the new building is complete."

It took two hours to make the drive to Birmingham. It was all straight highway, no turns or complications. Mitchell had asked Ted to drive so he could read materials he recently had received from the commission. He sat in the back seat of the car, papers spread everywhere. The trip was pleasant, and Ted didn't mind playing chauffeur. They arrived well before the Arts Commission meeting's start and called on August Bishop. Mitchell had told Ted briefly about working for Bishop and the new construction they had completed prior to his arrival in Meriden. His attitude about Bishop was one of competition blended with respect and a dash of mild suspicion. The "old fox" was how Jenkins referred to his former boss, leading Ted to expect something other than the kindly gentleman who welcomed them into his office. Ted was reminded of his graduate program and museum life at the university in Philadelphia. Dark, secluded chambers were where museum directors lived, contemplating the purchase of beautiful objects as if they were theirs personally. Bishop's office suite was much the same. The large windows overlooking well-maintained gardens were like those Ted had known before. He felt comfortable there with Bishop. Mitchell's attitude changed as soon as they were seated. His amusing irreverence became disciplined admiration. The conversations were of no particular consequence—shop talk between men in the same profession working toward similar goals on different scales—but Mitchell hung on every word, and the "fox" clearly enjoyed the attention.

He was quick to tell Bishop what an asset Ted was becoming and how pleased he was that he'd joined him in Meriden. At the tender age of 24, Ted had come a long way in a profession traditionally limited to the very wealthy or the very bright. He knew he wasn't working in New York, but he still enjoyed the limelight and momentum Mitchell created and was allowing him to share. If there was a price for this celebrity, it had never been mentioned by Jenkins, but Ted would have paid it willingly.

"Well, young man," Bishop said to Ted as an accepted equal, an unexpected turn that both surprised and delighted him. "I suppose your new boss here has told you of our plans for the construction of a whole new museum concept. We're well underway now; the legislature is following the governor's lead and is set to begin the appropriation of massive amounts of funding. It will become a showplace for the South, perhaps even the nation! Have you seen the early architectural renderings, Mitchell?" Jenkins rose to view the renderings Bishop kept on an easel just beyond his chair. "Of course, if you would decide to come back to Birmingham and take this burden off my shoulders, you'd know exactly where we stood." Bishop meant this as a chide as well as a plea. "I've asked him to return, Ted. He claims to have important matters demanding his attention in Meriden, and I'm sure he does. But you seem capable, and he is very confident in your abilities." Then turning to Mitchell again, he said, "You could come now, you know. Ted can handle the building and you'd still be close enough to answer any questions that might arise."

Mitchell was clearly flustered by Bishop's appeal. "I appreciate the kind words, August, but I don't think I'm the man you need, and we've talked about all this before. I'm not a political person, and we both know the director of this complex will need to deal with the legislature and the governor to keep the funding coming. Besides, I'm happy in Meriden and have a building of my own to finish."

"I know all that," Bishop retorted, as if Ted were no longer in the room. "But you would do so well back here. You are well-known and popular among those in office. You could pick right up and be successful with this thing, just as you've been in Meriden. This is where you belong, not down in that country hole, no matter what you think!"

Bishop reined in his frustration and walked across the room to the silver coffee service that had been placed on a low wooden dresser by a large Black man when they first entered. "Forgive me Mitchell, and you too, Ted. I get carried away on this issue and your boss here is bull-headed enough to fight me on it." He turned and addressed Ted as if Mitchell wasn't in the room. "You'd like to be director in Meriden, wouldn't you?"

Ted stammered, not knowing what to say. The subject did seem to reoccur, but was something he never considered. "I certainly would not want to see Mitchell leave Meriden," he said finally. "His are big shoes to fill, and I'm only a size seven."

They all laughed at the joke, and the tension brought about by Bishop's outburst seemed to ease somewhat. He changed the subject to the exhibitions planned for the fall and spring, impressing Ted with the detail he could recall without consulting his staff.

"He does all the planning himself," Jenkins said later. "Always has. He's had a curator for some years. Robert wasn't there today, or I'd have introduced you. He really does little for Bishop, it's always been something of a joke. And Johnnie, the gigantic fellow who brought in the silver tray, installs the exhibitions. I think August just feels he needs someone around with that title." We walked the short distance between the museum and the art commission's office. "Those things Bishop was saying about the state museum and my taking it on shouldn't be taken seriously. I've thought about it many times, but I know I can do more in Meriden than if I were to return here. Plus, I might survive an attempt to be let go after our building is complete, but I would never win that kind of fight here. I'm also not sure I believe in the concept of the complex the governor and Bishop are creating. When, and if, the structures are completed, nobody quite knows what the position of the legislature will be relative to channeling arts funding to other agencies in the state. As of now, the legislature earmarks funds that go to the commission for further distribution in the form of project grants. The commission has a paid staff to administer these funds. They are not their own arts center, but were established as a middleman between the government and arts agencies throughout the state. What I fear may happen after this mega complex is operational is the legislature might stop or at least diminish this funding flow in favor of the monster's operations. Currently it's all an ego thing for the governor who's looking for a legacy after he leaves office next January. After that, who knows what the future holds."

Ted asked if a job description for the director's job had been written and Mitchell said he received a copy from Bishop a full year ago.

"Each agency or branch of what's being called the State Museum will have its own director, who will answer to an overall director, who will answer to the legislature. It's like you and Ellen working in your own areas are responsible to me, then I'm responsible to our museum commission. The only difference is everything's magnified a hundred times. There's a limit to efficiency. The salary is great though and I'm probably crazy not to take it on that count alone." He grinned as they entered an office on the third floor of the new state building.

Ted spent the remainder of the day watching Jenkins in action, organizing and refining seemingly abstract guidelines and procedures for agencies to follow when making their applications. The commission staff enjoyed his directness, though they were led by an equally aggressive administrator. Current grant proposals were read and discussed, amazing Ted at their diversity. Each was judged for their completeness and appeal. Grants were awarded or action was deferred until additional information could be gathered. Nothing was turned down. Through it all, Jenkins seemed to listen when others were noticeably distracted. He would ask appropriate questions of those presenting the applications and would lead constructive discussion.

The day's deliberations concluded after nine o'clock that evening and they rode back to Meriden as they had arrived, Mitchell resting in the back seat, nursing a half pint of Wild Turkey while Ted drove. He had never seen anyone drink from a bottle wrapped in a brown paper bag and somehow found the practice a bit off-putting. He remembered his resolve his first night in Meriden and peeked a look at his boss in the rearview mirror. He was slouched low in the back seat, his tie off and shirt unbuttoned at the collar. His eyes were glazed from the liquor, still he held the bottle's rim close to his mouth and took a long pull, swallowing slowly. His mind was far away, and Ted said nothing, wondering which of the day's experiences were being relived.

CHAPTER EIGHTEEN

"Hey! Let's take old man Pierce's new car for a spin. Come on!"

Jimmy Biggs was crazy for something to do that hot summer night. It had been Wild Turkey then too, and between them they had consumed most of the fifth Biggs had stolen from his father's home. The car was sitting on the street outside the home of Nathan Pierce. It had only arrived in town the day before, and Pierce had driven it abundantly that afternoon, showing it off. Jimmy had seen it when Pierce pulled into the service station for gas.

"Check the tire pressure too, will ya?" Pierce had said. "Careful not to get them dirty with those greasy hands of yours."

Jimmy looked it over from top to bottom. Pierce had bought it in Shreveport and had it delivered. "Why that old man thinks he needs a car like that Mitch, I don't know. We need that car!"

Mitchell was hesitant to steal the car—though he and Biggs seemed to be always in trouble.

"We'll take it late tonight. Your old man ain't gonna know. Hell, Pierce ain't gonna know unless he's recording mileage. We'll bring it back in a couple hours and park it in just the same spot."

They finished the whiskey and Mitchell was finally convinced the night was made for a drive. At two thirty in the morning they crept from behind Mrs. Cassey's wooden garage, crossed the street in front of the Pierce house, and waited for a large cloud to cover the moon and obscure their shadows. The car door was unlocked, and Pierce had made it all too easy by leaving his keys in the ignition. Mitchell slipped behind the wheel, released the brake, and put the transmission into neutral. A quick wave to Jimmy meant it was clear for him to start pushing the car, which moved easily on the level street. After pushing for half a block, Mitchell started the engine and Biggs jumped in beside him, driving off with as little noise as possible.

✦ ✦ ✦

The following weekend was Ted's to work at the museum. He decided to use the time installing a series of prints in a permanent collection gallery on the first floor. The morning was quiet and pleasant. He was the only person in the building beside the phantoms Joe Mullens talked about. The telephone only rang twice. *That is some sort of record,* he thought. During the week it rang with maddening frequency, mostly for Jenkins. Ted had answered the first call that morning on a dead run from the side door. It was ringing when he unlocked the door and he was sure it would stop before he could get to it, but it didn't.

"Meriden Art Museum." It was the standard address he used, though he still caught himself answering as the Osborne Museum on occasion.

"Mitchell?" The voice was sweet, yet had an urgency he didn't quite know how to interpret. "Is that you?"

This had happened before. Even though he didn't have the pronounced southern accent of Mitchell Jenkins, many people mistook Ted's voice for his, usually women.

"I'm sorry, Mr. Jenkins isn't at the museum this morning. This is Ted Martin, may I help you?"

The telephone went dead, which had also happened before, and Ted wondered if he should make a note of the call, but decided that would be useless and a waste of his time. He knew his boss looked at other women and did so in an embarrassingly obvious manner that seemed to be appreciated by the objects of his attention. Mitchell had often talked to him about his life with Maureen. They had separated twice since getting married and there were many other women in between. His frankness on the subject made Ted uncomfortable.

He remembered the first time he had been invited to dinner at their home. Mitchell made a point of talking about how household duties were for the female to handle, opposed to those that were strictly for males. After dinner, Ted absent-mindedly cleared his and Maureen's plates from the table, carrying them into the kitchen.

"Ted," Mitchell said half joking and half serious, "what the hell are you doin'? Southern men don't do that kind of thing."

For several seconds Ted had no idea what he was talking about. Then Mitchell pointed to the dishes in his hands.

"Just trying to help out after that wonderful meal," Ted replied, realizing he was rapidly losing points with his employer.

"I think it's very sweet," Maureen said, kissing him lightly on the cheek. Your mama raised you right!"

Ted laughed and put the plates safely on the counter, then returned to talk with Mitchell while Maureen washed dishes and cleaned up.

Ted heard the staff door slam shut in the light breeze that had joined the morning's sunshine. It was Jenkins's footsteps disguised by tennis shoes. He knew he'd be wearing old jeans with the knees out (before it was a fashion statement), but was not prepared for the dirty white t-shirt, even on a Saturday.

"Hey Ted, what's going on, bud?" He was carrying his brief case and stopped to look at the prints Ted had selected to hang. "Going to install the old Rotan specials? Been a while since I've seen them. Any calls?"

Ted said no, as Mitchell bounded up the stairway toward his office. He wondered what brought him in on such a beautiful morning. One of the phone lines lit on the switchboard. It was Mitchell's extension, and he dropped the question from his mind, returning to the prints he had assembled.

Within the hour, Mitchell returned to the first floor. Ted had finished installing two walls in the gallery and had just returned from a storage area with several more.

"Ted, remind me on Monday to talk to you about the Nathan Logan exhibition we're planning for the opening of the new building. It's about time you were involved. I was just talking to DeBain Howard. I don't think you've had an opportunity to meet him yet. He owns SouthLife Insurance here in Meriden and has had an interest in the museum for several years now. He and his company are going to help underwrite the cost of the exhibition."

Ted was only slightly familiar with the senior Logan's paintings. In fact, when Mitchell had first mentioned a possible exhibition on the telephone while he was still at the Osborne, he thought he was talking about the work of his son, the famous realist. Ted came to find out Nathan had perhaps a better hand, obscured by his son's notoriety. The artist had worked in Vermont most of his life producing soft, colorful paintings of mountain landscapes, many of which had been reproduced on mail-order catalog covers for Abercrombie & Fitch. Most of his paintings had been kept by the family and sold privately after his death. Nathan and his wife raised five children, with only Axel staying in their native Vermont.

"DeBain and Emily Howard purchased their Logan painting at about the same time I opened the Hall-Crowell corporate exhibition at the museum in '68. The purchase was quite coincidental, but that exhibition's opening got them involved in purchasing serious art, and they gave money toward the Endowment funds we received." There was a pause in Mitchell's remembrance as if he had drifted on to another memory. "Anyway, when Taylor gave money for the new building and Laura was elected to the commission, the limelight turned to the James family. It was almost a fatal mistake, and one that was quite unintentional. Suddenly James was doing this and that all over town as he had to purge quite a bit of money before the year ended. I had been bringing the Howards along as contributors and Taylor came in and stole their thunder. It really pissed DeBain off, despite the fact Taylor's gift was in a whole other league. So, I tried to find a way for DeBain to be a part of the activity without getting in Taylor's way, a mission that would be an asset to what Taylor was doing.

"I remembered the Logan painting and how proud they were of it, and, well, things kind of fell into place. I called Howard to ask if he would help me investigate the possibility of an exhibition for the museum's opening, and he was delighted. The problem was dealing with the Logan family. They were planning a major traveling exhibition of Axel's paintings that would open in DC and travel to San Francisco before going on to Japan and Russia. They were not interested in Meriden, Alabama, no matter what we tried. However, they were sympathetic to a friend of the Howards with Logan family connections and wrote to ask if we would be interested in an exhibition of Axel's father's paintings. I said yes, after looking at slides supplied by Logan's New York gallery.

"Now DeBain is talking to his New York dealer about a second Axel Logan painting. He wants me to fly up there with him next week to see it, then we're going to Vermont, where we'll hopefully get a listing of Nathan's paintings the family is willing to lend. The sooner you can take this project from me, the better. You're so easygoing, you'll probably get on very well with them. Besides, you Yankees all talk the same language." He started for the door, talking over his shoulder. "Anyway, I want you completely briefed on this before I leave on Wednesday. Be sure to ask me—it's important."

Wednesday morning, Mitchell asked Ted to drive him to the airport. There had been no time that Monday to talk more about the Logan exhibition, though Ted had tried all day. The morning's staff meeting was abnormally long because of the telephone interruptions that pulled Jenkins away. After that, there was a meeting with the architect about the new building's security, lunch with Taylor James that lasted well after two, then a preview of the video Stephen Parker had completed for Ellen's department. Afterward, Mitchell had calls that needed to be returned, making it five forty-five before Ted was finally able to corner him. LeAnne had just left. There was something puzzling in her manner, as if she were unhappy Ted was still in the building waiting to see Mitchell. She showed him into his office from the public entrance since Ted had been installing new objects in the outer office lobby. Jenkins had fixed himself a scotch and was looking out a window.

"We have trouble getting together for things sometimes, don't we? Well, never mind, we can talk more about old Nathan Logan when I get back from Vermont." He had loosened his tie and sank low in a chair, reminding Ted of the night they returned together from Birmingham.

Once at the airport, Ted stopped the car outside the chain-link fence bordering the airport's FBO entrance. A large blue sign hung over the door of a steel hanger, into which three men in jumpsuits were walking. The sign read SOUTHLIFE. Inside was a large twin-engine airplane, a DC3.

"That's the plane I took last time we flew to New York. It was quite a trip. You should see the size of the bar that thing has on board." Jenkins paused and looked over the field, then pointed to his far left. "That's the plane we'll be taking this time, it's new."

Taxiing not twenty feet from where Ted parked the car was a new, white Lear Jet with the SouthLife logo on its side. One of the pilots retrieved Jenkins' suitcase from the car as a dark green Mercedes drove up the access road. The Howards parked in the company hangar, and emerging quickly without luggage, walked to the plane.

"I guess it's about time to go," Jenkins said a bit under his breath as he walked away. Five people climbed aboard the jet, and Ted walked back behind the fence to watch its take-off. It would be hard to return to the museum after all this excitement. Emily Howard was much prettier than he had imagined from Mitchell's description. She smiled briefly at him as she boarded, taking a seat near the front of the plane. The engines fired and the jet slowly made its way down the cement runway like a sea turtle ambling along a smooth stretch of beach. Within a minute or two it was in the air, its nose pointing vertically toward the clouds ahead, and soon it was little more than a dot in the sky.

✵ ✵ ✵

Louis Sterling was about the museum the following afternoon. He had called a staff meeting, with Ted's permission, to be held in Ellen's office. It concerned Mitchell, though the exact topic would remain a secret until everyone was assembled. There was such speculation! Ted's intercom was constantly buzzing with staff inquiries mainly about Mitchell taking a new position. Ted was in the dark. He had learned of the Birmingham possibility only recently, but it didn't seem Mitchell making that move was much of a possibility. At the appointed hour Ted walked toward Ellen's office with others who seemed to be waiting for a movement to begin. They found Ellen and Sterling sharing coffee and sly laughter upon entering. As chair of the commission's personnel committee, Sterling would be first to know if Mitchell decided to move on. As his assistant, Ted felt the meeting's subject should have been divulged to him, and Sterling's refusal to do so somehow intimated his distrust. Everyone took their seats. Stephen Parker was late and slipped into Ellen's office just in time to hear Sterling's remarks.

"I'm sorry this meeting had to be so secretive, and I hope it hasn't caused too much anxiety." He was looking at Ted. "Tuesday morning I was informed by the Chamber of Commerce and the Meriden Jaycees that they've selected Mitchell to receive this year's Outstanding Young Man award! It's a great honor that will be given to him Saturday night at the Chamber. I wanted you to know first because I was sure you'd be proud of your boss and would want to be part of the reception being planned at the James home."

Sterling paused to gauge the room's mood. While there was general excitement, Ted also detected a slight emotional let-down. They all had different kinds of relationships with Jenkins. They expected him to be offered a better position sooner or later and that he would accept it. That was the nature of the profession. Nonetheless, they were all pleased for him and felt the honor well-deserved if not overdue. They decided to meet as a group Saturday morning at Ellen's home to plan some sort of staff salute to their leader. Afterwards everyone retreated to their respective work areas while Sterling stayed in Ellen's office.

✿ ✿ ✿

DeBain and Emily had gone in separate directions after the afternoon meeting with the Logan family. Howard had given the pilot instructions to return to Meriden with Jenkins, then leave the next morning to pick him up in Boston. As a result, the SouthLife jet landed in Meriden late Friday afternoon with only one passenger aboard. The green Mercedes was waiting as the plane taxied back up the runway and toward the hangar. Mitchell Jenkins climbed down the steps and looked about him as the summer's sun began its slow descent. His single bag was brought around and placed in the backseat of the car. He thanked both pilots and entered the car, motioning the driver to leave. He had enjoyed the private jet trip back to Meriden. There had been no waiting at an airport in New York, no other passengers crawling over him to get their assigned seat, and the drinks were free and plentiful. The Mercedes sped through the afternoon, its air conditioner keeping the interior pleasant. Mitchell Jenkins sat back and enjoyed the scenery, thinking over the last two days in New York and Vermont.

Ted was helping Joe Mullens secure the building when the car rolled into the drive. He recognized it as the Howards' car but didn't expect to see it that afternoon. It looped around the side of the building, stopping at the walkway that led to the front door. Mitchell Jenkins hopped out, grabbing his bag and briefcase. He leaned over to speak to the driver, then watched as he left for the drive back to the airport. The building's front door was locked, and Mitchell had left his keys with Ted, so he went down to open it. "Welcome back," he said, pushing the door open.

"Hey bud," Mitchell responded. "Good to see you."

Ted relocked the door and they headed through the gallery toward the staircase to the second floor. Mitchell was still excited about the private jet ride and being its only passenger. They settled in his office, and he opened his briefcase on a table.

"Here are some things we'll need to start organizing the Logan exhibition. They might as well go to you now." He unfolded several typed lists that accompanied a page or two of his own notes written on an ever-present yellow legal pad. "The current Logans couldn't have been nicer to us. The plane was able to land at a small airfield near their property. The countryside is just beautiful up there. They live in a large, 19th century stone structure that's been updated into this century at some cost, I expect. It's a combination living quarters and gallery for the Logan clan. The north-facing wall of the gallery is glass, providing an incredible view." He shuffled through more paper and exhibition catalogs. "Here's a preliminary listing of paintings by Nathan Logan owned by the family and stored in Vermont. I put checkmarks beside some other ones I saw. I think you should plan to go soon to look them over, as well as others in homes around the area."

Anything else Mitchell might have said after that was lost to the office walls. The sense of excitement Ted felt in making a trip to the Logan compound cascaded through his brain.

"This listing refers to important paintings owned in private and public collections that the Logans think we may be able to borrow. They asked us to furnish them with some sort of semi-official, preliminary listing on letterhead and they would make calls to the owners on our behalf."

They talked for another hour about the paintings Mitchell had seen, most of which had been reproduced in books and periodicals. He then talked about the Axel Logan paintings he had seen that had not yet been released to his gallery. Ted was a bit jealous that he hadn't seen them too, but was excited about making a subsequent trip. He could think of little else but the new building that would thrust Meriden into national prominence, the exhibition that would be wildly popular, and his role in this wonderful enterprise. He felt fortunate Mitchell had selected him for this position. There was nothing his boss could not ask him to do.

The following afternoon Ted joined the rest of the staff at Ellen Maxwell's home. He hadn't been there before and had happily accepted a ride from Mary and David Griffin, who were frequent guests. They talked about the land and Ellen's neighbors during the trip. It seemed family feuds were still quite prevalent in these parts, and they joked about being shot at as they drove past some of the homes. Ellen lived on property her family had owned for generations. It encompassed fifty acres of thick vegetation and sported a lake. She had done much to renovate the structure, including adding a second floor in the original architectural design and a large back deck suspended over a creek. The weather had turned cool and cloudy, which was a welcome relief from the heat that surrounded the city the previous week. The light fog rolling in upon the setting previewed for Ted what a fall afternoon might be like in Alabama.

David and Mary were a bit late leaving the city, so Ted was surprised to find few other people had arrived. It was much lovelier than he had imagined, with the peaceful sounds of fish feeding on the lake's surface. He heard a splash and an odd paddling sound. David had untied one of the two boats at the wooden dock and was rowing across the lake into the fog, now denser than when they'd arrived, singing a sailor's song whose words he couldn't make out. Mary walked over to where Ted was standing.

"He's so funny," she said as her husband faded into the thickening mist. "He can't possibly see where he's going."

Mary seemed different to Ted than when she was at the museum or in the school. It was being out of their workplace, he supposed. There was a freshness about her that was very becoming. She also was not wearing the billowing smocks and sloppy pants that were her usual uniform when weaving or giving instruction. Ted had been sure somewhere underneath all that material was flesh and blood, but he wasn't prepared for the statuesque figure that filled the tight turtleneck sweater and jeans standing before him now. He suspected Jenkins knew this when he hired her to run the school. They talked for a short while about the current semester and the facilities in the new building. Though the space was going to be much larger than the current school building, she wasn't sure she was going to be completely happy in an urban setting. Ted hadn't paid much attention to the school or its relationship to the museum, and Mary's concern surprised him and caused him to think of the architectural drawings he had seen and the school's placement.

"Too bad the school has to move at all," he said. "It's current setting must be so conducive to creativity. With the old museum building empty, the property would make a great four-year art school. Perhaps we ought to mention it to Mitchell."

"He needs to sell the property, Ted. The proceeds will go into the new building fund. Besides, I don't really think Mitchell wants us off by ourselves. I don't know why, but he thinks we'll factionalize and do the museum harm."

David suddenly came out of the fog, bellowing like a horn and startling Ted and Mary. He paddled back to the dock, and they walked along the lake's bank to join him.

"Mary," Ted said as they walked, "I'm sure Mitchell has very good reasons for what he says and does. We can't know them all, but we must trust he has the operation under control and is thinking of what is best for each of our departments."

It was a speech Ted seemed to be making increasingly often, and he was beginning to feel there might be something subliminally consistent with many of the staff's attitudes concerning Mitchell's constant striving to do more. Ted's fervency was inspired by the excitement over the Logan exhibition and the new structure now rising from the ground.

Ellen rang a bell indicating the potluck she and several of the others had prepared was ready to consume. Over dinner, they planned a gag presentation for Jenkins, and after a brief rehearsal headed back to town for the reception at the James home.

✵ ✵ ✵

One of Mitchell's constant strivings included prevailing upon Beau Britian to create a painting to mark the new museum's opening. His paintings were now very expensive, making the gift a substantial contribution as well as a sizable media event. It was another ingredient that would add to the excitement of what they were working toward, with Jenkins masterfully stirring the bubbling pot. Ted's Vermont trip coincided with a New York trip Jenkins needed to make to meet with Britian and view sketches for the painting. Ted was invited to go along, spending two days with Mitchell and Britian before seeing the Logans. Whatever excitement he had felt at the prospect of meeting Axel Logan was almost eclipsed by spending time in Britian's presence. He was perhaps the most important American artist working, with Logan a distant second; one worked in the abstract, the other in stark realism. In a single week, Ted was going to become the envy of his graduate art history classmates!

"We'll be staying in Beau's studio," Mitchell advised as they reviewed plans before leaving Meriden. "It's in kind of a rough part of the city. Beau will meet us there."

"Wasn't a friend of his murdered there recently?" Ted didn't know how else to put the question and could tell by Jenkins' reaction that he was also thinking of the recent death.

"I knew that guy. He took over the room I was using at the studio the last time I was there." Jenkins often talked of mortality, feeling he himself would die young. But the death of Britian's friend was not taken lightly by him, and he knew more about it than Ted had imagined. "He was Korean, and Beau called him "Charlie" because he couldn't pronounce his real name. He was helping with paintings being shipped

186

for an exhibition in Seoul—you might remember it. It took place a year ago, part of a cultural exchange organized by the state department. I met Charlie when I had arrived at the studio. We had dinner with Beau and had planned to go out to some clubs, but I was coming down with a cold or something and decided to leave early. I walked from the restaurant back to the studio. It was only a few blocks but very late. Beau wanted me to take a cab. Anyway, I was into the second block when I noticed two guys walking behind me, keeping an even pace with my progress. I'd walk faster, they would walk faster. At the second corner I ran across the street hoping the traffic would put some distance between us, but it didn't. They caught me in the middle of the next block. They were young, I was surprised. One had a bottle or something and hit me on the head. I was stunned for a second or two and could feel myself falling to the pavement, even though one of them was holding onto my shirt. The shock wore off and I jumped up, punching the other one in the face. I hit him hard, and he fell backwards with a scream. The other guy let go of me for an instant and I was able to run. I turned a corner at the next intersection instead of heading for the studio. After I lost them I circled around to the studio and quickly unlocked the door and bolted it behind me. I was bleeding where I'd been hit. The police came and I filed a report, but we all knew the two assailants would never be found. Charlie was killed unlocking the same door two weeks later. He was stabbed in the throat and back twelve times. Witnesses said the killers were two young men who had been loitering at the corner bus stop." He paused.

"You think they were waiting for you?" It was a terrible question, but Ted knew it had crossed Mitchell's mind too.

"The police do. I received a letter yesterday asking me to come to the city next month and identify one suspect they recently apprehended on a burglary charge. He was wearing a ring that had belonged to Charlie." Jenkins rubbed his nose, then his eyes, as if about to tear them out. "Life's just too short Ted." He cheered up a bit and sat back in his chair. "For instance, marriage should be a renewable contract with a five-year run. That way if you're not happy with it at the end of the contract either party can simply choose not to renew. No divorce, no legal crap, just a simple contractual arrangement. I sure would have dissolved mine!"

Ted was surprised to hear him verbalize that so bluntly.

"She'd be better off without me, and I could do what I wanted with my life. I don't know how property would be worked out, who would get what, but some arrangement would be made, and if you decided to have children another clause could be added." Jenkins made marriage seem like a contemptable institution.

"That would certainly be an interesting departure from 'Til death do us part.' Something to think about I suppose," Ted didn't like talking with him about personal matters since he hadn't known him all that long and, well, they were personal.

"Have your tickets for Vermont?" Mitchell asked, changing the subject almost as a penalty for not being interested in his game. "Beau's sister Colin will meet us at the studio and for dinner tomorrow night. She's young and very accommodating." He looked at Ted for a reaction. "Too accommodating for someone who looks a lot like Beau." He laughed to himself and decided to give Ted another chance. "Last time I was there, she really came on to me. We were alone in the studio; Beau had gone to the country for a few days. She nursed me after my assault until I left. Those last two nights…the first one I was able to put her off, but the second…well, I had no excuses."

Ted decided to seem interested and listened like the good-old-boy he wasn't as he told him of the seduction scene. He attempted to picture Mitchell and Colin in the different rooms of the studio as the sordid details became graphically clear.

"You really ought to write that up and send it off to *Playboy* or something, Mitchell. It's a wonder you two didn't ruin any of Beau's paintings."

"Maybe I should. It surely was out of the ordinary. You should get it on with her, Ted. It would be good for your career to have an affair with the sister of a famous artist. Think of all you could learn about Beau!

Colin acts as his secretary, she must know every important dealer in the city and everything about where Beau's paintings have gone under what circumstances. She'd be a valuable contact. Anyway, you'll be meeting with Logan on Thursday?" He was back to business, although his relationship with Colin sounded like business as well.

"Yes, that's correct. I fly into Manchester Wednesday night from New York and should be met at the airport by his representative, Tate McNeil. I rented a car for the trip."

"How is my friend Tate these days? It's been a while since I've seen him. He helped the Howards with their last Logan purchase. The painting they had seen in New York was sold when they arrived back at Logan's gallery there. Tate found a similar painting at a better price. It's nice to handle transactions like that privately—I've never really trusted New York dealers."

Again, there was a pause in the conversation and Jenkins looked over to where Ted was sitting. His dramatics were beginning to unnerve his assistant, first with his remarks about sex and now this.

"McNeil offered to cut me into that little deal. Always decline those offers, Ted. I asked him to contribute to the museum instead, a much cleaner way to handle things."

It was getting late in the day, and Ted was ready to leave. He had most weekends to himself since moving to Meriden, but several, as this one had been, were spent at the office in preparation for something to come. However, he could tell Jenkins wasn't ready for him to go. It was an unspoken thing that, in part, was Ted's doing, as he wanted to show his commitment to the museum and his boss.

"Is there anything in particular I should know about Beau Britian? I mean other than what any student of art history can read in textbooks?"

Jenkins smiled. He prided his personal friendship with the artist above many other things in his increasingly distinguished career. "Know that he's a Southerner who was forced to leave his native soil because people here were cruel to him, and because there was nothing here to stimulate his artistic callings. Birmingham and August Bishop did more to deprive Alabama of an incredible resource than any state agency or interest group. They ran him off; to survive he fled to New York. He's very bitter about it. It's one of the reasons the painting he's done for the museum is so important. Bishop would kill for an opportunity like that.

"Beau tried to live in Alabama, had a downtown storefront as a studio when I was at the university. Those were some of the best times of my life. People would gather to talk about art and each other's paintings. I was doing some painting myself at the time and received more help there than from any of my instructors. Late at night there would be parties, a lot of sleeping around. You should know Beau likes to sleep around. Maybe you should hook up with him instead of Colin!"

He winked at the suggestion, and Ted laughed nervously. It was a signal that finally his audience was complete for the evening. Ted packed up his materials for the trip and confirmed they would be meeting at his home in the morning. Mitchell had persuaded Maureen to drive them to the airport. As Ted left, Mitchell resumed working at his desk.

CHAPTER NINETEEN

The late summer's afternoon sun smothered most things in Opelousas, Louisiana, and the shallow water of Lake Columbia had not provided much relief to the two swimmers now stretched out on the thin sandy shore. They had chosen a secluded spot to sun in as neither had swimsuits, but the seclusion had not been deep enough for one pair of eyes watching at a distance from behind thick brush.

Jimmy Biggs lay on his back, his left thigh touching that of the other figure who was on his stomach, his arms blocking the sun from his eyes. Maureen Moses couldn't tell from her hiding place who the other figure was, though Biggs did not have many friends. If she could only get a little higher up, in a tree perhaps, or if the other figure would move his arms, she would know who was swimming with Biggs that day.

Her mother had told her not to go to the lake because boys swam there naked, and of course the outing went to the top of her to-do list. It was too much of a temptation. This was the fifth time she had hidden in the brush and only the first time she'd seen anyone. Jimmy sat up, propping his torso with his left elbow. With his right hand he rubbed the skin of the other figure above the swell of his buttocks. Maureen listened to the pounding of her heart as she felt herself become aroused. The other figure stirred. One arm unwrapped from around his face and its hand found Bigg's chest, then slowly worked itself down his torso, falling finally out of her sight. The tension was making her uncomfortable, but she couldn't stop watching as she wondered who Biggs shared such an easy sexual familiarity with. The second figure raised up on his other arm and Maureen gasped, trying to keep silent while turning to run for the road.

✵ ✵ ✵

"Flight 317, Eastern's Whisperjet service from Atlanta is now arriving at gate 43. Departing passengers should be in the terminal in three minutes."

The jet was full for a Sunday morning, though in first-class Mitchell and Ted were very comfortable.

"I'm going to try to change my ticket when we get into the terminal, Ted. I can't believe LeAnne made our reservations in anything but coach! You do what you want though, you've got more flying to do than I do."

He had complained about the seats during the entire trip, though he seemed to enjoy the first-class breakfast and the attention of the flight attendant. It was Ted's first business trip, and he found the accommodations quite perfect. The thought about exchanging his tickets if Mitchell did, but decided to keep them if he didn't. Passengers were walking in every direction inside the Eastern terminal at LaGuardia, and Ted followed Mitchell through the crowds as if they were blockers for an unnamed football team and he was running for endzone. He stopped suddenly at the ticket counter, where was quite a line. "I'll take care of this later," he said, heading toward the escalator.

They took a cab from the airport. The driver sped through the city, under elevated train tracks, down narrow streets with cars parked bumper to bumper along both sides. Traffic seemed heavy for ten in the morning, the city of New York was always busy. After thirty-five minutes the cab stopped at a corner chosen by Jenkins across the street from Britian's studio. Its windows were barred, and spray paint artists had left their marks on its stone façade. They were in a wholly different atmosphere than they had left several hours earlier—harsh, anonymous, fast-paced—it would take Ted years to adjust to, but he found it was a great place to visit.

Except for being on a corner, the studio building resembled others on both sides of the street. By day the neighborhood was very pleasant, a warehouse area taken over by artists because of its large, empty spaces. While most rented, Britian owned his building, a symbol of his affluence. The men crossed the street, each carrying a bag and briefcase, and approached the wood and metal entrance. Ted's mind turned to thoughts of the murdered Korean, who must have also stood there, while Jenkins found his key.

"I hope I can remember which one it is."

A few seconds passed as he fumbled with keys on a metal ring, then a few more passed before Ted realized Mitchell had his own set of keys to Beau Britian's studio! They entered a small space and encountered another locked door.

"This is where Charlie made his mistake," Mitchell said. "He didn't lock the first door after coming through. It would have saved his life."

The second door opened wide into the brightly lit room of Britian's main studio area. Ted felt he had died too—for he was sure he'd arrived in heaven. The immediate space had been gutted of interior walls. Only the supporting columns blocked the long views from any part of the huge room with twenty-foot ceilings and polished hardwood floors. Unsurprisingly, it smelled of oil paint. The windows of the building's two exterior walls had been covered with plywood so light only entered through the top three feet; potted tropical plants sat on shelves and the floor. The heat of the sun through the window tops and the plants made the room seem like a greenhouse. Canvases by Britian were on easels or wrapped in heavy, clear plastic in twelve-foot wooden bins. It was overwhelming for a newcomer, so while Jenkins made himself at home, Ted slowly meandered toward the center of the wonderful room, trying to take it all in.

In a far corner, extending eight feet in two directions, Britian had huge worktables filled with paints, empty coffee cans full of brushes, and reams of watercolor paper—a fully stocked artist's supply shop! Empty canvases were stacked by size two and three deep against white walls, while a large wooden easel built into the middle of one of them held a large painting currently in progress. Ted looked at it for quite a long time, knowing he would likely see it reproduced in an art journal or textbook. He wondered how many others he would recognize. Opposite the studio area was a chef's kitchen with floor-to-ceiling white ceramic tile on its walls. It existed, like the other areas of the huge room, as a place unto itself, as did a living room area with sofas, comfortable leather chairs, and end tables. Ted heard Mitchell's footsteps coming from a room he had yet to see.

"Quite a place, huh? Beau's been here about six years. The room we'll be using is back that way. Take your bag back while I make some calls."

Ted walked back to the entry door where his suitcase stood. The large room led to a smaller room, then a hallway and a bedroom on the first floor. Like most artists of his stature, Britian had traded works with friends, building a collection over the years rivaling that of any museum of contemporary art. The second room, hallway, and bedroom were filled with these paintings and sculptures. Ted looked at everything before finding his way into the bedroom he and Mitchell would share. The room seemed colder than the others, devoid of windows. The ceiling had been replaced with a large skylight the size of the room, its thick glass layers worked into a steel frame rising up from the room's normal height. Ted felt a vibration and the room shook for a second before getting still again. *Surely a subway tunnel isn't underneath this part of the building,* he thought, before a second rumbling proved he was mistaken.

Mitchell was still on the phone when Ted returned to the studio. He was going through his thick, black address book, calling people he hoped to see while in the city. Ted amused himself by looking further about, finding wonderful things the artist had touched. He heard Mitchell finish his calls about the same time the outside doors were being unlocked from the street. In the time it took the second door to open, a rush of several emotions went through Ted. He thought of Charlie and wondered if he should run to the door and hold it shut. Just then it opened with a jerk, letting in the cool air of early winter. A slender young woman dressed in a ski coat, jeans, and sunglasses entered with a smile.

"Hi there, I'm Colin Johnson, and you must be…"

"Ted Martin."

Hearing her voice, Jenkins jumped up from where he was sitting. "Colin!" he said in a loud voice. He held his arms out as if expecting the woman to run to him like separated lovers do in the movies, and she did. They hugged in a long embrace, then he kissed her hard on the mouth. When they unentangled, Colin welcomed Ted with a handshake. This was Beau's sister, who was obviously delighted to see Mitchell, but her reaction to seeing Ted was awkwardly hesitant. *Surely Jenkins had told her I was coming?* The trio talked for a while. Ted mostly listened, since they spoke of other occasions and acquaintances he didn't know. Mitchell finally invited her to lunch, as it was about two. She declined, saying she was late for a party and would see us for dinner that evening. She was gone quickly, but not before kissing Jenkins again. Ted stood watching the door close behind her and Mitchell went back to the phone.

"See what I mean? It's good you're along to protect me."

They left the studio for the midtown museums soon after. Mitchell decided to walk since it was such a fine day. Had he walked at a normal pace it would have been pleasant, but he was a man in a hurry, keeping pace with the bustle around him. His steps were easily two of Ted's, and after thirty blocks he was dragging noticeably behind. Mitchell finally slowed his pace seeing Ted was winded from attempting to keep up. They stopped for lunch a short distance from the Modern, and Ted welcomed the rest.

The remainder of the afternoon was full of museums and a smattering of galleries, more images than anyone could possibly take in. Ted couldn't tell if Jenkins actually looked at the things they saw that day, for he showed no outward emotion. MOMA was jammed with city residents out for a Sunday afternoon. Children in sat in strollers or on the carpeted floors while their moms admired Monets. Students, with heavy sweaters tied around their waists made sketches on small pads using charcoal pencils. Jenkins walked from one gallery to the next, as if searching for something. Ted trailed behind, seeing what he could while trying not to lose sight of his boss. The Whitney and Guggenheim followed, both with special exhibitions reflecting the current tastes of the world art market.

They ended the afternoon in a cozy bar on Fifth Avenue. Mitchell's first scotch was never tasted, but he lingered over the second.

"I love being here. Anything you could possibly want or imagine can be found here. The greatest artists of the world live and work here, and their work can be seen in its great museums. I would live just the way Beau does if I had even a quarter of his talent. People come and go into the life he creates, and he has all the money he needs for whatever he wants. Marelli keeps him in booze, women, men, whatever he wants." He paused as our scantily clad waitress came back to see if he was ready for another. "What do you say Ted, would you join me here if we could figure out some way to live?"

Ted knew that he took Mitchell too literally, but he still stopped to think about the question. His pause broke the spell of the fantasy, and he was sorry he hadn't just played along.

They taxied back to the studio as dusk settled upon the skyscrapers uptown. Ted was cheered by the warmth of the cab until it stopped in front of the studio door and they had to get out. Fortunately, two of the large outdoor lights had been lit by Colin, who slipped in and out of the studio with erratic frequency. Inside, the hospitality of the morning had been replaced with a garish combination of light and shadow.

Jenkins headed for the bar and fixed another scotch, this time on the rocks. "I need a shower before dinner. What time is it anyway?" He never wore a watch but relied on time for everything.

"It's only six thirty. We aren't expected for dinner until nine. Got plenty of time."

He headed for the bathroom, talking over his shoulder. "Sure glad I have you around to keep track of things for me."

Moments later Ted heard the shower water as he settled on a couch to examine his blistered feet. It had been quite a day. After emerging from the shower, Mitchell rummaged through the freezer, finding a bevy of frozen appetizers and putting them in the oven to warm while Ted got cleaned up. He also raided Britian's extensive wine cellar. Finding an excellent vintage champagne, he placed it in a wine chiller and set the timer for ten minutes. By the time Ted joined him again, he had placed four canvases against the longest wall and was seated before them. He was playing museum director and Ted did not wish to disturb him. He uncorked the chilled champagne and poured two glasses.

As Ted approached, Mitchell asked, "Which one do you want? Beau's into some new stuff. I wasn't sure I appreciated this new departure, but after looking at the paintings for a while, I think I've changed my mind."

A buzzer rang from behind in the studio's kitchen. "Must be the snacks," he said, rising from his seat to put them on a white porcelain platter. This domesticity was so unlike the Meriden Jenkins. Ted thought of his disapproval of helping Maureen in the kitchen. Just then, the outside door opened, and Ted hoped it was Colin.

Colin Johnson entered the studio through a sliver of an opening, slamming the inner door shut behind her. It had started to snow, and large flakes swirled around her feet. Gone was the ski jacket and flannel shirt of the morning, replaced with satin and pearls. Despite the change of weather, she only wore a short fur jacket. Her satin blouse was a pastel shade unbuttoned nearly to her waist, exposing her cleavage that was virtually invisible beneath her morning's layers. Her pants were black and tightly fitted about her hips, falling to bell-bottomed legs. She gave Ted a big wave and another embrace for Mitchell, who had finished his kitchen chores and poured her a glass of champagne.

Mitchell had done Colin an injustice with his Meriden description. Walking around the studio, making small talk and telling wonderful stories, Ted found her quite attractive, and Mitchell followed her about the room, playing the victim in her seduction scene. Ted remembered his earlier remark about "protecting him" and watched him slip his arm around her waist as they stood before one of her brother's paintings. *If ever a man did not want protection, it was Mitchell Jenkins.* Ted sat at a wooden table eating the snacks and sipping champagne.

Colin took her guests to an Armenian restaurant across town. They left the studio in the cold darkness of a New York winter night, the wind cutting through clothing and chilling to the bone. Ted had faced plenty of cold in Northeast Ohio, but this was worse than any Lake Erie wind in December. Colin had driven to the studio from her midtown apartment and parked her car at the curb—a rather risky move considering the neighborhood.

"It's silly to have a car here in the city," she was saying, walking in the cold, her blouse still unbuttoned. "But I just fell in love with this one and had to have it. Beau bought it for my birthday last fall. I don't often get a chance to drive and thought since you gentlemen were in town, it would be a good excuse."

Under the neon light of city signage, the car's bright red paint looked magenta, but was still handsome. It was a Volvo P1800 that Jenkins and Ted made a fuss over, walking around admiring the sleekness of its design. The cold seemed invigorating for Colin, perhaps warmed by the excitement she felt at being with Mitchell or the passion she had planned for later. Ted noticed there were only two seats in the car, with a rear compartment meant for luggage but large enough that a person on his side might cram inside. He figured he'd drawn the short straw. As they got in the car, he joked about flipping a coin for the luggage compartment, then readily volunteered, sparing Mitchell's legs from being cramped. Colin drove quickly, taking turns as if she were in a race as he rolled from side to side, hitting his head on the sloped back window, then lurching forward as she made sudden stops. Finally, he laid flat on his back and stared out at the city's tall buildings and the stars now filling the sky.

The party arrived at the restaurant despite Colin's driving and parked on the street a mere block and a half from its entrance. On the walk to the door Colin took Mitchell's arm, squeezing next to him tightly. Inside, the restaurant was lit with candles, and they were escorted to a table by large windows. Colin and Jenkins sat on one side of the table with third-wheel Ted opposite them. Rounds of drinks were ordered; Jenkins had octopus as an appetizer with everyone taking a bite of its thick, chewy meat. The talk was of Beau's work, the painting he had done for the museum, and the building's construction. Ted said little, letting Mitchell outline his plans and the arrangements that would take place in preparation for the opening. Colin was invited to attend, an offer she quickly accepted as she slipped her right hand onto his thigh.

By eleven thirty they had finished eating. Colin had a party she had promised to attend and invited the guys to join her. Mitchell declined for both of them. He didn't look as tired as Ted felt, but he must have been. After trying to make him change his mind, Colin agreed to drop us at the studio and return after the party "to make sure you don't need anything further for a good night's sleep." Ted laid in the trunk again. She dropped them at the same spot their cab had earlier in the day, then she sped off, racing the traffic light ahead.

Mitchell turned to Ted and asked if he wanted to take a walk. "We need some things for breakfast, and there's a deli just up the street."

Ted couldn't imagine anything would be open at that time of night and wasn't excited about walking the streets, but Mitchell insisted. They headed toward Abe's Deli.

"This is where the two thugs mugged me. They caught up with me in this block." He slowed to retrace his movements that night, pulling his coat collar up around his neck. "I slugged one of them about here. He hit his head against that building and then against this light pole. When the other guy let go, I ran down Marshall Street," he pointed, "and around the block, coming out at the studio."

Ted looked up and down the street, wondering how many other similar incidents had occurred there. They made it safely to the deli, which was indeed open, and returned to the studio door carrying two paper bags filled with groceries. Ted faced the street as lookout while Mitchell fished in his pocket for the keys. Once inside, Ted made sure the safety lock was set and breathed a sigh of relief. The studio was warm, and he tried to relax. The champagne was still cool, so he refilled his glass; Mitchell started on Britian's scotch.

"Come on," he said, "I want to show you where Beau keeps most of his personal collection."

They walked across the room to a large wooden door. The subway train rattled the floor again and Ted wondered how close the tunnel was to where they were going. The wooden door opened to a freight elevator that took them down about a floor and a half. The basement had accumulated the dirt of years of inactivity and smelled musty.

"Beau converted three rooms down here for storage. Everything was rebuilt and sealed like a vault. There is, believe it or not, complete temperature and humidity control inside. It cost quite a bit of money."

We stood before a metal door with a combination lock in its center. Jenkins stood for a minute trying to remember the combination, then worked the tumbler twice before it clicked open. Lights came on as they entered, just like a refrigerator. A textbook survey of American art was stored inside, a treasure trove of objects from Duchamp to Dine, Segal to Rauschenberg, Warhol and Lichtenstein. He even kept a room of works he had created but couldn't part with.

"Beau's trying to find his early things and purchase them back from collectors."

A Duane Hanson figure startled Ted as it sat in a corner, reading a book through eyes that seemed real but couldn't see. Scotch in hand, Jenkins began looking through metal racks of stored paintings, leaving his protege to explore. A buzzer sounded somewhere and Mitchell left to discover its source. A telephone was hidden behind an early painting by DeKooning. From his manner the caller must have been Colin. He whispered into the receiver, and Ted left for the last underground room. When he returned, Mitchell told him Colin would be by in an hour or so for "breakfast" if he was up for it. Ted declined, allowing him whatever options he deemed necessary. They returned to the first floor, Ted heading for the bedroom, Mitchell for the main studio and breakfast.

Ted spent a restless night waking every time a train passed below. The twin bed Mitchell was to have used remained untouched. He awoke at seven thirty having gotten to bed at about three, the sky now slate gray through the skylight. The room got brighter and he noticed a silver paper embosser on a tabletop between the two beds. He slipped a page of his notebook between the two silver heads and squeezed against the stiff spring. The resulting mark was like two water drops, one the reverse of the other. He recognized it as the mark of Britian's printer who had recently completed a series of lithographs commissioned by Marelli. Suddenly Ted felt very alone in the vast building but tried not to let the emotion spook him. He showered, dressed, and went into the studio to see if there was any trace of man who hadn't slept in his bed.

There was a note on the wooden table near the kitchen. Mitchell had gone for an early morning walk and made coffee, for which Ted was thankful. He moved around the kitchen finding pans and the food they had purchased the night before. He felt a certain satisfaction cooking breakfast for himself in Beau Britian's studio and wondered who he could call to express his delight. He idly went through a stack of drawings Britian had left on a worktable near the kitchen. If Mitchell had spent the night in the building, he must have used one of the bedrooms on the second floor, where Britian's quarters were located. It was the one place Ted had not been, and now he felt a nagging desire to mount the stairs. If Mitchell had slept there, there was a very good chance Ted wasn't alone in the building after all.

The second floor had been significantly reworked. At the top of the staircase was an open landing, a vestibule leading to a long hall that divided the space into what Ted imagined were two groups of rooms. Two wooden doors were visible on each side of the hallway; the one on the street side had been left open and he quietly walked toward it. Inside was a large chamber, the length of the building with windows overlooking the street below. Colin was sleeping in a king-size bed jutting into the room from the far wall. Though Ted had suspected she might still be there, he was startled and turned to exit.

"Don't run off." Her voice and stopped him in his tracks.

"I did not want to awaken you, I'm sorry."

Except for where the sheet covered her, she was naked and unconcerned Ted was standing in the room.

"I've fixed some breakfast if you're hungry." It was the best he could muster under the circumstances and hoped it didn't sound as awkward as he felt. "I can bring something up if you'd like or…"

"This is what you get for walking into a lady's bedroom."

She sat up, pulling the sheet fully over her. Ted felt the heat in his face, but it broke the ice. He stepped into the room a bit further and apologized again for intruding. "I had a feeling there was someone else in the building. Mitchell went out for a walk. I hope I didn't frighten you coming in like that."

She smiled. "No, I heard you on the steps and could smell the bacon and eggs. If the breakfast invitation is still good, I'll join you in the kitchen in ten minutes."

Ted went back to the kitchen to fry four more eggs, hungry again and pleased to be back in familiar surroundings.

Mitchell returned as the two were finishing. He looked cold but seemed refreshed. "Beau should be here shortly. Is there more coffee?"

Colin said their cook would fix a light lunch in an hour or two. Beau wanted to talk with Mitchell about the painting and have a meal before returning to his studio in the country. He was having the museum's painting framed there, along with several others he had promised Marelli prior to Christmas. It was a busy time for him, Colin explained. He was protective of his art and liked to work when production was coming easily. "He'll work for days straight without sleep when it's going well. I don't know how he does it. I'm sure he'll look awful when he gets here."

While she busied herself around the studio, preparing things for her brother's return, Mitchell went to the first-floor bedroom to change clothes and Ted cleaned up the kitchen, anxiously awaiting the arrival of Britian. Colin transformed the wooden table into a makeshift desk where he could look over his accumulated mail and telephone messages. She answered a loud knock on the door and returned with a delivery of art supplies. It was Monday. Ted enjoyed the easy routine of Britian's studio as it came to life. While the outside door was opened, two young men walked in. They waved casually at Colin and began moving paintings from where Jenkins had placed them the night before back to the stacks on the far wall.

"These paintings ready Colin?" one of the two asked, referring to three large pieces wrapped in heavy plastic sheeting. She said they were, and the men began walking them back out through the door. Ted guessed he would see them next time at the Marelli gallery.

In all the activity, he barely noticed Britian slip in. He would have taken him for one of Marelli's employees had Colin not kissed him on the cheek and ushered him to the table. He sat quietly, reading through black-framed glasses, lighting a cigarette casually with one hand. He wore jeans, old tennis shoes, a flannel shirt, and sweater. There was nothing distinguishing about him. Ted was disappointed. He'd probably dressed this way while a younger man in Birmingham and never changed over the years. If Colin was correct about her brother's work habits and pace, Britian had likely come to the city directly from working on the Meriden painting, not stopping to dress glamourous for New York.

Mitchell came down the hallway and waved at his friend. They seemed glad to see each other, and Ted heard Britian ask if Colin had seen to his needs. Mitchell waved him over as the Marelli drivers finished loading the last painting, and the foursome sat at the table. Britian was pleasant, his quiet manner reassuring. He asked Mitchell for updates about the building and its progress. He knew of the Hall exhibition and asked questions about some of the works that were included.

"Mitchell," he said finally, "the Meriden painting is complete. I would have had it here but decided to leave it at the country studio rather than risk damage. I haven't told Herschel about it and don't plan to until it is shipped out. He wouldn't object, but he'd want to show it off in the gallery first. This way, he'll have to visit your Museum or attend the opening to see it."

Mitchell said Marelli was already on the invitation list and talked about the SouthLife plane that could be sent up to pick up anyone who wanted to come. Britian was intrigued by that, and Ted was amazed. *I wonder when Mitchell and DeBain Howard had worked out that deal?*

The outside door rattled, and Colin rose to open the interior one. There stood a large Black woman in a starched white maid's uniform. Colin gave her a hug and Britian stopped his conversation with Jenkins to say good morning. Mazie, as they called her, had worked for Britian since the days immediately following his discovery by Marelli. She had lived next to the Britian family in rural Alabama, and Beau had sent for her after the death of her youngest boy in the Vietnam War. She had a lifetime job as his cook and housekeeper and kept her own apartment in the city not far from the studio. She walked into the kitchen after asking if the visitors had found everything they needed the night before. It was such a pleasant atmosphere Britian surrounded himself with, and Ted didn't want it to end. He focused his attention to the conversation that turned again to the Meriden painting.

"The painting is a double image, each half mirrored in the other. One side is in color, the other in black and white, and the pigment is very thick."

As he talked, Britian drew a sketch of the painting on a small pad he kept in his pocket. It would be shipped immediately after Christmas, arriving in plenty of time for the pre-opening publicity Jenkins was already deep into planning. Colin busied herself chilling three bottles of Domaine Belle Crozes-Hermitage she had taken from Britian's private stash. The first ready, she uncorked it and served it at the table. It wasn't quite one, and the sun was breaking through heavy gray clouds. Jenkins and Britian were reminiscing about their days in Birmingham. Each had come a long way, and each hoped they still had a way to go. The conversation changed to other things since neither man enjoyed remembering the past that much. Jenkins inquired about the capture of one of the men who had murdered Charlie and had assaulted him earlier. It was a subject that caused Britian visible pain. He drained the wine from his glass, pouring again from the bottle Colin left on the table.

"They found that scum hiding in an alley behind this building." he pointed in the direction of the room where Ted had slept the night before. "He had just robbed the grocer around the block. He knew the police were on his tail and slipped in to wait it out. They got him though, only seventeen! It's a terrible shame." He drank again from his glass, then sat quietly while Mazie began clearing the table for lunch. "Mazie found him the next day, you know. They jumped him, then just walked away. He might have lived had he been found that night. I can't live here anymore, too much violence. I can almost feel the blood run out of my body every time I think of it. You know how that is Mitchell, they were on you too."

CHAPTER TWENTY

The new car sped down the quiet street, turning onto the highway ramp to Shreveport. It was much more powerful than either boy had imagined. They raced ahead into the darkness, screaming out the windows, letting off steam. They drove past the first overpass, ten miles out of Opelousas. Mitchell pulled over so they could change places for the return trip. Jimmy opened the passenger door and ran around the rear of the car while Jenkins slid across the seat.

Jimmy had been talking about Birmingham and the university Mitchell was going to attend. "Mitch, it's just crazy to go off up there and leave your friends behind, even with your scholarship. They just goin' to take it away when you don't make the freshman team."

It was an argument that had gone on between the two all summer. Jimmy put the car into drive and headed back to the city. En route, they decided to stop by the lake for a late-night swim. Jimmy parked the car on the paved road, fearing the dirt road to the lake would leave marks on its finish. The walk was less than half a mile to the spot where they swam, an easy hike for two boys who knew the way. The water was finally cool, and they swam idly.

Heading back to the car afterwards, Biggs again began talking of his friend's move to Birmingham. "I still can't believe you're gonna do it. We're having great times together, always have. I can't let you go up there for basketball and decide to stay there all the time, hell, maybe even go further North!"

"Jimmy, there just ain't much you can do about it. Coach got me that scholarship and I can't let him down. Besides, I won't be there forever — you know I'll come home. By then you'll probably be manager of the filling station, and maybe I can get a coaching job at the high school."

"You can't go Mitchell, I'll talk!" Mitchell stopped on the worn path leading to the paved road ahead. He looked at Jimmy, whose shirt, like his, was wet from the water.

"You do and it'll be the last thing you'll ever say to anyone. That's a promise."

The two eyed each other, then continued walking back to the car in silence. Jimmy pushed Mitchell from the driver's door roughly.

"I'll drive you son-of-a-bitch. And I'm going to tell everyone about us if you go. Your threat doesn't scare me."

In the dim interior light, Mitchell saw Pierce's shiny revolver tucked between the crack of the front seats. The old bastard had always threatened them with the gun. Mitchell climbed in, slamming the passenger door, then quietly reached his left hand between the seats as Biggs turned to his left bring the car onto the road.

✻ ✻ ✻

The jet to Bennington left New York exactly on time, lifting easily into the air amid afternoon traffic at Kennedy International. There were only two other passengers in first class, and Ted was happy to be alone. The New York leg of the trip was complete for him, and Mitchell decided to stay until the week's end. He had an appointment at the local police precinct to identify Charlie's alleged killer and had promised Colin he would drive with her to Britian's country studio while the artist flew to Paris to see a friend get married. How he could work on paintings day and night was a mystery, and as Colin had predicted, he did look haggard. Being reminded of Charlie's death had disturbed him, and Mitchell had been unusually subdued as well. Perhaps he was remembering the attack he managed to repel and wondering yet again if the murderer had meant for it to be him. It was hard to know what Mitchell was thinking when he was silent. Ted tried to second-guess him sometimes but found he was generally wrong.

Colin, Mitchell, and Ted had attended the opening of Dan Flavin's recent sculptures the night before at the Fishback Gallery. It was an interesting affair that included a variety people all walking in a darkened space lit only by the artist's florescent pieces. Colin saw many friends there and introduced Mitchell and Ted as if they were VIPs. Some of them actually knew what a curator was, a nice change from Meriden. The reception lasted until nine thirty, with a private party afterward. They piled into a cab and rode the short distance back toward a studio in another neighborhood of warehouse buildings in the garment district. They stopped in front of a rather run-down looking building with the address they had been given. Colin knew the owner of the apartment and assured the men they were in the right place. After being admitted by a buzzer, the trio climbed three steep flights to the studio apartment of Janice Hopkins and Robert Ewell. Both were artists who worked other jobs in the city. The apartment door was open, and they entered to music and the sound of laughter. There were nearly as many people there as had been at the gallery, some the same, some different, as if each event had its own audience. Early on the three of them got separated, each being dragged off by different groups. It was a highly social gathering, and Ted ended up with a group of young artists who were trying to live in the city. They all sought the same recognition Britian had achieved, but seemed to know those magical days were likely over.

The most heated topic of conversation concerned new residence requirements for artists being imposed by the city. It seemed the recent invasion of the wealthy into the once bohemian enclave was spreading, forcing artists to find new quarters elsewhere.

"It's just crazy," said one man, who was heavily bearded, wearing jeans with gaping holes in the knees, a coarse open shirt, and pea beads around his neck. "We're the ones who revitalized these areas, and now the rich bastards are kicking us out. The fuckin' city passed an ordinance stating people must prove they're bonified artists in order to rent space here. Who's a bonified artist? What's the criteria? Some city asshole is going to set him or herself as a critic? Maybe they'll hire the *Times* critic, give him a title, and we'll meet with him and present slides."

There was general agreement about what the man said. Ted was enjoying their discussion and feared they would be displaced because of the city's ability to make more in property taxes from a trendy set of new residents. But he had to get some rest before traveling to Vermont in the morning. Plus, both Mitchell and Colin were ready to go and were trying to get his attention, so he left his newfound compatriots and headed back to the studio.

✡ ✡ ✡

The flight attendant in first class was a beautiful young woman, tall, blond and smartly dressed. She made the best martini Ted ever had, at least in the air. He was deep in thought about his first professional New York experience when he heard the attendant ask, "Would you like another martini, sir?" She was beautiful, leaning over the empty seat to his left.

"That depends. How soon till we're on the ground?"

She looked at her watch, smiled and replied, "fifteen minutes."

Ted agreed to the second drink and turned back to his thoughts as the plane glided into the coming evening. The lights of Springfield, Massachusetts were off to the right, the wing flaps suddenly pitched toward the earth as the plane began to slow. *Bring on Nathan Logan's paintings and his son's reputation. I'm ready for anything.*

The plane landed roughly in Bennington, and Ted gathered his carry-on to dis-embark. It seemed much darker on the ground than it had been above the gray clouds, and it was cold. There was snow on the ground, which he hadn't seen in over a year. He buttoned his coat and headed for the terminal. Tate McNeil was to meet him there since he hadn't been given directions to the family compound. He smiled, half wondering if he would be taken there blindfolded. Inside, he looked for someone who might be looking for him but found no one. He waited for several minutes as the other passengers dispersed but still no one appeared. He walked over toward the baggage carousel for one last look, then decided to pick up the rental car he had reserved the week before. He had Tate's office number in Boston and decided if he hadn't made contact by the time he picked up the car, he would call. The rental agency had received his reservation, but there was some question as to the size of the car they were going to let him have. After a bit more discussion he was directed to a parking trailer for the keys.

This time, the cold air felt refreshing after the heat of the terminal and the delay with the car, and it was only a short walk to the bright yellow trailer. Ted climbed the three metal stairs and squeezed in. A young man in a pink oxford shirt open at the neck, khaki pants, and Weejens without socks smiled at him from the counter's end. His hair was wet and freshly combed, and he had no coat.

"Ted! Hi there buddy, how was your trip?" He sounded like a preppy Mitchell Jenkins. Ted looked startled and Tate laughed. "Sorry not to have met you inside, but there's too much confusion in places like that and I knew you'd eventually end up here."

He gestured toward the man at the counter. "My friend's here!" Ted was handed a set of car keys. "If you're ready, I'm ready!"

"Aren't you cold?" Ted asked as they walked to the rental car. "Hell no. Besides my car's right here." He gestured at the BMW sedan in bright yellow. "I'll drive up to the intersection," he pointed, "and wait till you get your car going. Then follow me into Woodstock. We're having dinner with some people later on, so I hope you're hungry."

Ted was starved, tired, and getting an early headache from the drinks on the plane. Agreeing to Tate's plan, he walked into the parking lot looking for his rental, which turned out to be a bright red Thunderbird with a white interior. *My, my. It's not what I would have ordered, glad I didn't buy it.* But the car started instantly, and after finding all the appropriate switches, he pulled out and looked for a yellow BMW.

Tate led Ted on a merry chase up the twisting Route 7. The Thunderbird might have been a match for the BMW on a straight road, but through the hills and at night it ran a poor second. Ted managed to keep his taillights in sight most of the way. However, he would have gotten lost at the intersection of Highway 4 without the map provided by the rental agency. Soon they were in Woodstock, stopping before the White River Inn. Ted nosed the T-bird into a space and climbed out.

Tate was already on the sidewalk, grinning. "That certainly is a fancy piece of machinery for a museum curator to have!"

"Yeah, I requested a VW, but they didn't have one in black!" Ted joked back. "So, this is Woodstock," he said, changing the subject. "Home of the Logan painting dynasty."

"I made a reservation for you here. It's the best place in town. Let's go in and get you settled before heading for dinner."

Ted gathered his things and followed Tate up the stairs to the inn's lobby. It was large and warm, with fireplaces at both lobby ends, a blazing fire going in each, drawn by massive stone chimneys. The desk attendant knew Tate by first name, and they talked easily as Ted registered. The counter was larger than most and still smelled of pine. Arrangements were made for his bags to be delivered to his room, permitting them to move on.

"We're going to John Logan's home for drinks. He's the sculptor, Axel's other son. Unfortunately, John's in New York tonight—you'd have enjoyed meeting him. His wife Nancy is here though, and my wife Jill. I thought the four of us would have dinner at the Woodstock Tavern later. It's the only place to go. Hell, even Axel goes there. You can see most anyone in town there."

They climbed into Tate's car and headed down a single-lane road out of town. Ted thought this was likely where the blindfold would be handed to him, but was mistaken. The Logans, like many people in the public eye, enjoyed their privacy. A blindfold would not have been necessary as there were so many turns in the road between the inn and John Logan's home that Ted was quickly turned around. They drove through a narrow opening between two stone pillars marking the entrance to Meadowcroft Farm. The driveway had been cut originally for a carriage and was just wide enough for the BMW. Ted hoped McNeil drove this lane often enough to safely navigate it at his current speed and that no one was coming from the opposite direction.

The embankment on both sides of the driveway finally fell away and, in the distance, Ted could see lights from the farmhouse. "The house was built in 1723 by Jeramiah Tucker, who was given land by the British king's agent in Boston." Tate McNeil talked easily with everyone. His openness was a pleasant change from the intensity of New York. "John and Nancy have had the place for five years. There's a working farm here that Nancy manages, and John has a studio just over the next hill. They have a few cows but predominantly raise sheep."

The men walked along the cobblestones toward a side entrance. The house was stone and stucco, painted white with wonderfully simple carving on the trim where the roof met the vertical walls. The door was wood, arched at the top, and through its small glass window they could see lights inside. Ted had admired John Logan's sculptural work for some time, preferring it in substance to that of his brother's. Neither had any formal training. Just working from within themselves, Axel recorded the landscapes of New England while John modeled figures in bronze. Axel was enjoying the current success of an international exhibition organized by the Museum of Fine Art. The press published many articles about the large attendance at museums in Japan, Russia, and Germany, and Axel's current prices reflected this attraction.

Nancy Logan and Jill McNeil were enjoying the fire in a small sitting room. The two were obviously fast friends, and Ted could hear their laughter over some joke as he and Tate entered the house. Both ladies were lovely in a natural, yet sophisticated way. Jill had shoulder-length blond hair that was striking against her black sweater. Nancy Logan wore a ski sweater with a pattern around the neck and her hair was in a becoming ponytail. She was taller than Jill and thin without being skinny. Jill was pleasantly built in all the right places, an attractive asset to someone like Tate. The house was comfortably furnished with antiques, blond wood railings and window trim, and needlepoint chair cushions. Quilts were everywhere around the sitting room, and wooden eighteenth century toys stood in corners or on shelves. Ted fingered one toy soldier as he took a seat on a heavily tufted couch.

"John collects them," Nancy said softly, sitting next to Ted. "They're quite fascinating, made by craftsmen in the area many years ago. That fellow we think dates back to 1790 and was the work of Hayward Blyth, who traveled through Woodstock between 1785 and 1802."

"I can see where a sculptor would be interested in it. Has John been collecting them long?"

"All his life. Axel collects things like this too. He's a real kid about it. He found this one while walking the countryside. Sometimes he'll trade a small drawing for one or two toys he finds stuck away in a neighbor's barn. They got a good deal from the exchange, but Martha doesn't allow that kind of barter now." She looked around, embarrassed at the freedom of her conversation with me. "John and I don't have that problem yet, though his work is beginning to sell well."

Smiling, she turned to Tate to change the subject. He did so by offering Ted a tour of the farmhouse, taking him past paintings of both father and brother. There were some very important images he'd seen published in journals and magazines. Tate also showed Ted paintings of Nathan's he hadn't seen, but hoped to borrow for the exhibition. They returned to the parlor for a second drink, then headed to the Woodstock Tavern.

The Tavern was old, built of stone, and rose two stories. Inside there was already quite a crowd—young people, maybe college students, dressed sloppily but with the cleanly scrubbed look of money, like they knew they had the world by the ass. Tate carried his bourbon and branch from the farm into the restaurant and finished it as we were shown to a corner table. He was a familiar guest, waving at friends and stopping to talk, while Ted escorted the ladies.

"Do you come here often?" he asked Nancy. "Tate seems to have a lot of friends."

She smiled in a slightly bored way. "When John is in town, we come here all the time. Most of these people are childhood friends of his who grew up here. They left for educations in New England somewhere and returned. Everyone gathers here for partying, especially this time of year when it's nice to be by a fire."

Ted asked if John and Tate had been friends for a long while, knowing Tate had not been raised in this part of the country.

"Not really," she said.

By this time Jill McNeil had turned her attention to the conversation and Ted apologized for talking out of school. They both laughed at this, which embarrassed him further.

"Tate's become part of the family," Nancy explained. "He came to Woodstock ten years ago, while still in college, just before "the event," as it's known here. He came to meet Axel and purchase a watercolor for his mother."

"His family always had money," Jill added. "He had a healthy allowance even as a boy. But instead of spending it on trivial things, he saved it for long periods of time, buying something finally that he could make a profit on later. When he graduated from Vanderbilt, he was buying and selling all sorts of things to college friends and their families. He decided to specialize in art when he purchased a second Logan and resold it for twice what he'd paid. He became a dealer specializing in works by the Logan family and handles major transactions, like Axels European tour."

Tate McNeil found his way to the table as Jill finished filling Ted in on his success in the art world. He was only five years older than Ted, yet possessed a remarkably mature attitude about life, tinged with the recklessness of someone who knew he would never starve.

"That Ricky Moore," he said laughing, "wants me to ask Axel to join in the relay ski race next weekend. That's all I need is for him to get mixed up with those crazies, out in the snow, drinking bourbon to keep warm."

Tate enjoyed his closeness with the celebrity the Logan family provided. Ted was relieved he was on his side when discussing loans for the Meriden exhibition. Dinner was interrupted three times by people coming over to talk with Tate. Though he specialized in Logan artwork, he had begun to diversify his interests to include land in Colorado, condos in Florida, and most recently, diamonds from South Africa. It was a very interesting evening! After an after-dinner drink or two, Ted refused his offer of a ride back to the inn, deciding to walk the quarter mile in the cold, night air. They arranged to meet again in the morning and head to Axel Logan's compound a few miles to the east. Ted waved goodbye to Jill and Nancy and headed for the inn. The sky was filled with stars, as it had been in New York his first night there. He wondered what Mitchell Jenkins was doing and concluded he would probably get into more trouble without Colin than with her.

The desk clerk waved as he passed through the lobby. "Have a good evening?"

"Very nice. Dinner at the Tavern. It was crowded, but pleasant. I think I'll sit by the fire here if you don't mind, warm up a bit."

The clerk smiled as Ted unbuttoned his overcoat, laying it over a thickly stuffed wing-back chair. He watched the flames wrap themselves around freshly worked logs as the air sucked past on its way up the chimney. He watched until he could no longer keep his eyes open.

"Mr. Martin, Mr. Martin."

The voice seemed to come from far away, beyond the darkness that now clouded my mind.

"Mr. Martin."

There it was again.

"I'm happy to meet you, but didn't expect to so early in the day."

Ted opened his eyes to find a red-faced man sitting opposite him on the hearth of the inn's fireplace. His cropped hair was a brown-grey color, his eyes soft blue. He was smoking a short, knurled pipe. On his feet were leather boots up to his knees, heavy trousers and a woolen, salt-and-pepper woven turtleneck.

"Mr. Martin," he said again kindly, "I'm Axel Logan, at your service!"

It was certainly not the way Ted had wanted or intended to meet his artist-of-the-moment. Stealing a look at his watch, he found he had spent the night in the chair, and it was six thirty in the morning. He was stiff and annoyed at himself for not having gone straight to his room the night before. He looked again at Logan, who was still smiling.

"I'm terribly sorry. I don't make a habit of this sort of thing." Ted tried to rise from the chair, succeeding after the second try.

"I do some of my best sleeping in a chair," Logan replied, keeping the mood light.

"It's a great pleasure to meet you. Sorry to seem so befuddled. How did you know I was here? I hope I haven't caused any of you concern by not answering the phone in my room!"

"Please, Mr. Martin. Please relax. Roger the clerk told me you'd spent the night by the hearth when I came in this morning. I go out walking every morning at dawn and come by the inn for breakfast. Will you join me? Breakfasts here are delightful, especially at this early hour before other guests are up and about."

They walked across the lobby floor. Ted again waved at Roger and apologized for any trouble he had caused. They entered the dining room where Axel was warmly greeted by its staff and took a corner table by large windows overlooking a snow-covered valley.

"You should know, Mr. Martin, there are no telephones in the rooms here, only the one in the lobby." He was smiling again.

The joke was on me, and I know he'll tell it often, Ted mused. As he expected, Logan was very curious about plans for the exhibition of his father's work. It was clear he admired his father's painting with more than a casual affection. From what Ted had read about Nathan, his son must have had an exciting childhood, filled with fantasy and adventure in the hills and valleys of rural Vermont. When he wasn't working, Nathan was dreaming up adventures of times gone by that they would recreate. He was a chronicler of the area's lore, specializing in tales of ghosts and goblins, the kind of stuff sure to fire any young imagination. Axel had taken to this life and spent every extra moment in his father's presence, in the studio and the woods. Instead of attending public school, Axel worked with his father, mastering the painter's art and creating astonishingly complete paintings at an early age.

Breakfast was served in abundance. Eggs, potatoes, ham, sausage, Danish, fruit, coffee—it was enough to last the entire day, and it did for Axel, who would leave the inn for his studio. He would work until five before returning to his home for dinner and whatever entertainment there was to be found. Their home was generally full of guests. He clearly delighted in talking with people, but did it on his own terms, keeping security tight.

They parted at the inn's door. He was working on some new things and invited Ted to the studio to see them. "Tate will bring you around later," he said, throwing his coat over his shoulder. "Till then, Mr. Martin!" He waved and was gone.

Ted repaired to his room for a shower and change of clothes. He had not yet gotten to the point in life where meeting famous artists was casually taken. He couldn't help but think about that fellow he used to know who swept gallery floors and cleaned painting frames at the Osborne, and wondered at his current good fortune. If luck was what had propelled him to Meriden, he prayed it would continue.

At nine, Tate McNeil strolled into the lobby, and they were off to look at Nathan Logan paintings scattered around the Woodstock area. He didn't know about the impromptu breakfast meeting, and Ted didn't tell him. The largest concentration of work was at Axel's home, where the men spent most of the afternoon. Everything had to be catalogued, for it was probably the only trip the curator would make to Vermont before the museum opened in February.

Jill McNeil was spending the day shopping with Axel's wife, Martha. Her family summered in Vermont where she and Axel met in 1945. Their love affair was immediate and were married in December of that year. She settled into the Logan style gracefully, supporting her husband's career at every turn. Life hadn't changed much for Axel in the years since, as Martha kept him shielded from the growing business demands of the art world. She handled everything, freeing him to paint and continue living in the manner he had grown accustomed to. Most of his best paintings were held by the family in a trust. Martha and Tate handled Axel's exhibitions, publicity, development of the Logan allure, and recognition. All in all, it was a growing corporate enterprise run from the family compound in Vermont. If Axel knew of the extent of the operation, he gave no outward indication. His was a carefree spirit, allowed to create in an environment that was constantly nurtured.

Martha and Jill returned from shopping in the afternoon. Martha was pleasant enough to Ted, though not with the genuineness of her husband. Jill had briefed her on their dinner the evening before, but Ted sensed she found his presence in her home unsettling. She had several specific questions concerning the exhibition being planned—the number of color reproductions in the catalog, who would write the essays about Nathan and his place in the history of art, how would the objects be shipped, would we carry insurance door-to-door, wasn't Ted awfully young to oversee such an enterprise, and so on.

Ted was sure he hadn't handled her questions in a manner that was as complete as she was accustomed to and ducked her catalog questions, not wanting to admit that the "youngster" standing before her would be the person handling all these things. Martha wasn't dealing with a New York City museum on this one, and Ted was sure it showed. Fortunately, she had put her trust in Tate as her surrogate, and Ted found he covered his trail rather well.

"Ted old boy," Tate said toward late afternoon, "something's come up that requires Jill and me to leave for Boston this evening. I'm afraid we'll be leaving before you finish here and probably won't get back until after you've gone. You'll be here tonight and tomorrow, leaving early Saturday, yes?"

Ted nodded his head.

"Well then, there is plenty of time for you to work, relax, and enjoy the pleasures of the countryside before returning to the sunny south!"

They talked a while longer, then he left to gather Jill and their belongings from John Logan's home. At five, Ted left the storeroom and walked to his car. The surrounding buildings were dark, with no activity to be seen anywhere. There was something almost frightening about being alone in a place where people like the Logans or Britian lived and worked. It was as if you expected to see the shadows of past times come to life, recreating the moments when important paintings were completed. Everything was so very silent. Ted tried to imagine how it had been for Mitchell and the Howards when they visited the summer before. They had stayed with the Logans on some part of the property. There were parties and entertainment commensurate with the status of their guests. Ted preferred the quiet, yet had a very real sense of being watched. *Could Martha Logan be watching me now to make sure I left and that objects in her storeroom were accounted for?* The chill of that thought made him get in the car. He started the engine, backed out of the parking place, and headed down the drive back to the inn.

After leaving the John Logan home and the dinner of the night before, Ted decided it would be good to rest, have dinner in his room, and work on the day's notes and loan documents. He quickly lost interest, his mind drifting to the lightyears of difference between the reality of Meriden and where he had been and what he had experienced over the past week. *Was it possible to become accustomed to the pace and the pressure? The comings and goings, being seen at the proper places with people of the same ilk.* It almost made him nauseous the longer he considered the complexity of Colin and Tate's lives.

The following morning, Ted was up at six, hoping for breakfast with Axel Logan again, but the artist didn't show up. The day was going to be grey and cloudy with a threat of snow toward evening. He had tried to arrange an earlier flight to Alabama but was unable to get anything other than the one he already had booked.

Back in the rental car, Ted went over the map Tate had given him to Axel's studio. It was about a half mile away from the compound and only approached by foot, so he had dressed appropriately. He called before starting out to explain that he was going to the studio as Axel had suggested. A woman answered the phone who he took to be Martha Logan.

"Just one moment," the woman said. "This is not Martha Logan, sir, she is not at home currently. This is the house maid."

Ted was sure it was Martha, for her voice and tone were the same as he had experienced in the storeroom the afternoon before. "Well, please excuse my impertinence. You certainly sound like Mrs. Logan."

"I am certainly not. Is there a message I can relay?"

He paused before giving her the message about walking to the studio and looking at some of Nathan's paintings her husband said he had stored there, then thanked the "maid" and rang off. Standing at the beginning of the studio path, Ted wondered if Martha was watching as he supposed she had been the evening before. He thought about waving to her but decided not to push his luck.

After his father's death, Axel moved from the space he used in two small rooms into the main studio itself. He changed it only slightly, including adding some conveniences his father had thought unnecessary. It was still very much the place where he had grown up. A door key was hung exactly where Tate McNeil told him it would be. A large skylight and north-facing windows filled the room with abundant light even on the cloudiest days. A stone fireplace straddled the center of one of the interior walls. It had been used recently, though not that morning. Again, he wished Axel had been at the inn for breakfast and was further disappointed he wasn't in the studio. He concluded his interrupting the artist's painting time might have kept him away.

It was difficult to begin working without first taking time to explore the building and the many wonderful objects it held. Logan kept a large portion of his toy collection on wooden shelves running against the back wall. Some, Ted was sure, had not been touched in quite a few years. Despite its many wonders, he felt the presence of many specters—perhaps happier spirits than the ones he'd felt the night before at the Logan home.

He followed a hallway leading out of the large space to a doorway that opened to the outside. Two rooms opened off the hallway, built on the back side of the building. Most likely the spaces Axel had used while his father was alive, they were now used for storage, supplies in one and early paintings in the other. Most of the paintings were Nathan's that he had either not finished or was never completely satisfied with. There were quite a few, and while Ted didn't go through them all, he did notice they were inferior to the artist's best work and probably should have been destroyed for the sake of his reputation. He thought of colleagues who would shudder at this notion.

On a large easel in his studio was Axel's current oil painting in process. Ted had been so blinded by his interest in the studio itself he hadn't noticed it or the watercolors laying on a table nearby. Again, he stole another moment from his task to look the paintings over, being careful not to disturb anything. The watercolors seemed to be studies for several parts of the oil, all done rather quickly by their look. Axel worked this way, making the finished painting the culmination of a larger mental process his detractors did not understand. The painting on his easel would be the product of his method. Its image was a dark interior still life, as yet too vague to know much about. *It's better Axel isn't here. I wouldn't be able to view things this way, sidetracked as I'd be by the artist himself.*

Ted easily found the paintings Tate wanted him to see and spent the remainder of the morning working on listing the ones he thought would lend themselves to the exhibition themes he was developing. The time went quickly enough, and by early afternoon he had finished. Before leaving, he took another look around the studio, examining its thick wooden walls, heavily beamed ceilings, and dusty, dark corners filled with history. Axel had done well even in his father's shadow, surpassing the elder Logan's efforts many times over. Ted wondered though how John would fare. Perhaps that was why he had turned to sculpture, making it hard to compare his work to those of his kin.

CHAPTER TWENTY-ONE

After the first of the new year, things developed rapidly as completion of the building drew nearer. Ted was not only concerned with the logistics of the Logan exhibition but also with the museum's collection, much of which was in storage across town. Mitchell had completed the federal purchasing program grant acquiring many objects, mostly by younger artists he hoped would grow in critical acclaim. It was risky purchasing, though the funds went further, and if one's aesthetic judgements were sound, the choices would take care of themselves. He'd taken advice from Britian, as well as from Abram Rubin on the West Coast, so he really wasn't going it alone. Ted had not hazarded an opinion on the works Mitchell purchased as most of them were neatly packed away. Like the public, Ted would wait for his introductions to the pieces.

Everyone on staff was busy, reminding him of an elementary school open house when parents come for a classroom visit. Mitchell was the teacher who promoted the event, steadily increasing the public's interest, as well as the pressure on his charges. Progress was being measured by his mental timeline. The staff all knew their own deadlines, but no one knew exactly how they would all fit together; no one, that is, except Mitchell.

Meanwhile, like all new building projects, this one was running behind. Opening dates had been set and revised three times to the current one of April twenty-fifth. Dates had been promised before, but this one both the architect and contractor said would be it. They would both be proven wrong. Mitchell and Ted would make daily inspections, trying to gauge when one area or another might be ready to begin receiving artwork in a secure and temperature/humidity stable environment. Receipt of the Logan paintings was uppermost in Ted's mind as he wanted to receive them at the museum rather than the storage area.

The building had been designed for maximum efficacy with a minimum of additional staffing. It was full of electronic security gadgetry, maintenance-free machinery, and reusable surfaces that would resist the effects of time and wear. It was also designed in a strong economy, when all materials were plentiful. That began to torment Mitchell, the fear of how the future might shift. Bishop's longevity rule was also becoming a significant worry. He was a believer in predictions and trends, and as clouds began to gather in Washington over fuel costs and the economy, Mitchell listened to the dire predictions proclaiming an end to the abundancy of life enjoyed throughout the 1960s.

The building, like any museum, was a shell in which objects are housed that its constituency wishes to preserve. Meriden's niche was going to be contemporary art, but on a frequent basis a variety of objects might be seen in its temporary galleries as exhibitions come and go. It was incumbent upon its design and functionality that certain standards be maintained, and in these areas Mitchell and John Browning designed for the best and most sophisticated equipment available.

Thanks to the James family, funding for design and construction was plentiful. However, the innovative systems took enormous amounts of power, and while Jenkins had projected their operational costs with the assistance of utility company engineers, no one had foreseen the dramatic escalation of prices, or the country's increased dependence on the oil-producing countries of the Middle East. Mitchell was also concerned with staff. A minimum number in the current building did not equal a minimum number in the new one. He had provided for positions but didn't want to hire until the changeover had occurred. Preferring to live in the structure for a while to gauge where the greatest personnel deficiencies would occur, he created and refined organizational charts, hoping to determine the least amount of manpower needed. He also hoped he could keep a rein on the rest of us as we dispersed into a much larger building.

There were continued conflicts between Stephen Parker and Ellen Maxwell, problems that seemed to Ted to be nurtured by Mitchell to render the most service from both parties. Parker was exactly Ted's age. He was born in Meriden, the only child of genteel but older parents who had raised him in a classical, Southern manner. He was naturally sensitive and drawn at an early age to the visual arts, photography in particular. He was introverted with a strong sense of self. After college, Mitchell had offered him a job as a graphic artist, an area he himself had a natural interest in. Parker excelled in the publications he designed, completely satisfying his boss's own ideas of how something published by the museum ought to look. He also had an interest in film and audio, opening additional options for advertising and educational programming. One such project led to another, and before long he was producing programs of both types for Mitchell and Ellen.

The move of his department into the new structure resulted in an incredible increase of hardware from its former location. For being a support arm for other departments, as Mitchell was quick to call Stephen's department, it was growing precipitously. Jenkins could often be found tucked away in Multimedia with Stephen discussing projects he wanted developed or a media program Stephen himself was wishing to produce.

The conflicts between Stephen and Ellen stemmed from the fact that he didn't wish to be involved for long periods of time in projects for anyone else, even if it directly related to what the entire staff was attempting to accomplish. It seemed clear to everyone but Stephen that if Multimedia was a support operation and not its own programming agency, he should be working with them. If not, he should open his own shop outside the museum's purview. But the situation was confused by Stephen's own creativity and Mitchell's increasing ability to say one thing and mean another. Ted overlooked this tactic, believing as Mitchell often told him that it would do little harm and would ultimately produce excellent results.

"The curatorial function is what is really important here," he would remark, "and you are doing a great job of taking that load off me. Those problems between Ellen and Stephen will work out in time. No need to worry about it."

Thus, Ted would go about his business, trying to be one branch of the operation that would not cause Mitchell concern.

In January, Mitchell had determined that he, Ellen and Ted would attend a regional museum meeting over a long weekend in Atlanta. He felt it would be good for the other two to be introduced to colleagues and to talk up the new museum to their peers. At the last minute, he decided he had to make a trip to New York, leaving Ellen and Ted to make the trip without him. The Logan exhibition was well in hand, and construction crews were finally meeting their scheduled goals, so it looked like an April opening would be achieved. The two set off for Atlanta, giving them time to talk, an opportunity Ellen had been anticipating for some time.

"When your resume arrived, Mitchell was quite taken by it. He needed someone like you to assist him but was reluctant to hire anyone. Your resume came at the exact time he decided to begin the search. He showed it all around, to Louis Sterling of course, and other commission members, but also to me. He was sure you wouldn't come for an interview after talking with you that first time. He said you sounded older on the phone, very mature."

"That's interesting. Perhaps it's because I talk slower than he does. I remember being impressed with his ability to think and talk so quickly. I've noticed he is becoming more and more withdrawn. It seems that as the building nears completion, he's almost afraid to move into it. He refuses to confide in me completely about it, but it's hard not to notice."

"He rarely talks to me about such things anymore. Used to be we would spend time talking about the museum and what it could become, about educating our community, giving students a real outlet to explore their creativity. That was when I first discovered the depths of his interests. He's a very bright fellow for sure. He thinks about everything he does, every action is taken deliberately. One of the results of our discussions was the hiring of Stephen, and Multimedia is the result. Mitchell wanted to add a new aspect to educational approach we offered."

"So, what's behind the conflict between you and Stephen? I really don't understand, especially listening to Stephen talk about it. One of the first things he'll tell you is he doesn't have enough time to do his own programming. Mitchell is the first to deny Multimedia is in the program production business except as it relates to your department or mine."

"You've learned faster than I did." She smiled at him from her end of the car's seat. "It took me two years of this to figure out what was going on between Mitchell, Stephen, and me. It all started out pleasantly enough, all of us trying to figure our roles out and keep it simple without stepping on toes. But I don't think it ever really had a chance of success—there was too much funny stuff going on. Just as he did with you, Mitchell spent a large amount of time with Stephen planning the kinds of things he'd be doing. They would meet together on Saturdays or after work hours. Soon Stephen had ideas of what he would be doing that were different from the ones Mitchell and I had discussed or those the three of us worked through initially. What I don't know though, is if they were different from the ideas Mitchell had all along but didn't tell me. From that time on it became harder and harder to get Stephen enthused about any educational project, even if the three of us had outlined it together. At first, I chalked it up to his creative temperament, but now I'm not sure."

"I truly believe Mitchell wants everyone to work together. I know he puts great confidence in you and Stephen. He does gloss over things sometimes, trying to keep everything light so tempers don't flair, figuring the end result is worth the means to get there." Ted listened to himself saying those words, not realizing the impact they would have later, though Ellen did.

"What I don't understand is why he bothers telling Stephen and me different stories. Why not tell us the same thing, like what he expects the end result to be? He's The Man after all. If he wants to develop Multimedia into something special and independent, why not just say so? I'll live with it, though I don't agree with it. I sometimes think he enjoys the deceit." She looked at Ted as if waiting for a response, then continued before he could disagree. "Really, I do. He'd be the first to deny it, but I think it's some kind of trick he learned from August Bishop. Now there's a master of deceit. Don't let his sweet old man façade fool you, Ted. Mitchell has told me enough about those days for me to piece things together. And what he hasn't told me, Maureen has."

All of this was hard for Ted to hear and absorb. Ellen was not a bitter person. She worked hard and enjoyed her role on the staff and working with Mitchell, though the days of their close collaboration were now rare. If she was telling Ted these things, it was not out of spite but of real concern. Her friendship with Maureen somehow gave an added validity to what she was saying. Ted knew Mitchell and Maureen had problems; Mitchell seemed to go out of his way to make that fact clear. He enjoyed other women frequently, telling Ted enough about his encounters to make him believe in their reality. Certainly, his relationship with Colin was real, and despite his descriptions of her, Ted was sure the sudden trip to New York was to share a weekend together. Ted didn't know if Maureen knew as much about them as he did, but he was sure she suspected. Mitchell often said he only stayed with her because of the children and that he had told her he would be with any woman who offered him the opportunity. Ted surmised there would be a line of men interested in helping Maureen with any sexual urges she was finding difficult to satisfy because of her husband's frequent absences from their home.

"You know Maureen isn't happy," Ellen said, as if coming in on the tail of Ted's thoughts. "She talks about divorcing Mitchell. She's a very intelligent person who isn't given enough credit by that chauvinist she's married to. He's got her believing she could do nothing in the world outside their home; that she couldn't survive without him. She's also concerned about the impact divorce would have on the children. She thinks Mitchell would somehow get custody."

"I had no idea things were that far along. Mitchell is always talking about wanting his freedom. I guess I just don't understand their relationship."

"You know Ted, that's the second time you've admitted you don't understand something since we left Meriden this morning." She laughed lightly. "It's very refreshing. Mitchell is never going to leave Maureen, despite his talk. In the first place, as long as he can keep her fooled into thinking she's unable to make it in the world alone, he can have his life both ways. In the second place, if he left her, there would be no one to take care of him. Can you see Mitchell doing his laundry or cooking dinner?"

Ted considered telling her about the night in Britian's studio when he seemed to enjoy being in the kitchen, but decided not to add fuel to her fire. She was hot enough already.

"Finally, and this is the most important Ted, it would go against the grain of his male being. If he left her, he would be admitting defeat, that he wasn't able to keep her, even if she blamed the divorce on him. Guys like Mitchell can't admit they have problems with their wives. He really believes every marital issue can be worked out in bed. And when you couple that mentality with his competitive nature and unwillingness to lose, it becomes an intolerable situation."

They arrived in Atlanta, found the hotel, and checked into their rooms. Ted fixed himself a stiff scotch from the bar fridge and swallowed it slowly, feeling it move down his throat and burning into his stomach. Ellen had said very good things about Mitchell too, about his capacity to come up with new approaches and his ability to get things accomplished. But her resentments were very real. Ted wondered if he realized how highly she thought of him despite the flaws she also recognized. He was fairly certain at one time or another Ellen had told Mitchell most of what she had told him during the drive. The picture of Mitchell as he had been prior to Ted's arrival was coming better into focus. There was much beneath the first superficial layers of his personality, but there was also a barrier he used to keep anyone from knowing what was going on inside.

They returned to Meriden Sunday afternoon with Ted talking about Ohio and the Osborne Museum. He was pleased not to be thinking about Mitchell for the four-hour trip, and Ellen was in better spirits as well. He didn't tell her Mitchell had called Saturday afternoon from New York. There seemed to be no urgent message, even though they came and got him in the middle of a seminar he was enjoying to take the call. Mitchell was quiet and interested in what was being said about the new museum. He asked if Ellen and Ted were getting better acquainted, teasingly alluded to their travel arrangement, and said he hoped they were staying out of trouble. Ted laughed over the inference, remembering the things Ellen had told him. He wondered if Mitchell had ever tried anything with her. Ted managed to surprise his boss with the news that Taylor James was attending the meeting. Ellen and he, of course, were equally surprised to see him. Ted could almost hear Mitchell's mind turning that news over, wondering what James might be up to.

"He's just chasing after Ellen," he concluded, then instructed me to learn a lot and drive safely back to Meriden.

James' presence at the conference did cause Ted to consider the predictions of replacement Mitchell was so concerned about, but he did seem to spend time around Ellen when at the museum. Ted was sure their relationship was quite casual, at least from her end. James was quick to display an affection for the ladies, and with his money, he could be very persuasive. It was the one thing Ted never asked Ellen about, even though Mitchell teased her about James frequently in his presence.

✵ ✵ ✵

By the end of February 1974, Mitchell and Ted began reporting to work at the construction site rather than at the mansion; the idea being that their presence there might make the construction foreman remember their deadlines. Ted was also there because paintings for the Logan exhibition were beginning to arrive and required safe storage. Even with the implied hazards of a construction site, the new building's temperature and humidity-controlled storage was preferable to the mansion, and the contractor hired a security guard to stay overnight. These were days of getting acquainted with the workings of the building and a feel for its spaces. Ted would often stay in the evenings and arrive before dawn to experience the sun's setting and rising within the galleries. The excitement of these adventures made it impossible for him to be satisfied with his former quiet office or the mansion's comparatively small gallery spaces. He could also feel the slow death of the mansion as they began moving things from it. Mitchell could feel it too, much more profoundly. The contractor's president called a meeting with Mitchell and John Browning to say he doubted the building would be completely finished by the deadline, but that the gallery spaces would. It wasn't a good meeting for any of them, and Ted was happy not to have been included. When he caught up with Mitchell later that day, he looked tired and in need of a shave. His wrinkled clothes were also not his usual style and made it appear he hadn't been home for a while.

CHAPTER TWENTY-TWO

The car went racing down the highway toward Opelousas, with Jimmy Biggs at the wheel and still angry at Mitchell. He was driving recklessly, trying to scare his passenger, who refused to be frightened as he had seen his friend like this before. He couldn't forgive what Jimmy had said back at the lake. Attending the university was his way out of Louisiana—he was taking it and would deal with Biggs any way he had to.

"You motherfucker!" Jimmy screamed suddenly, his eyes wet and his voice filled with frustration. "You can't go. I won't let you make a fool of me and yourself."

He was punching Mitchell with all his might and driving from one side of the road to the other. Mitchell ducked the blows as best he could, feeling Jimmy's anger mount and wishing he would stop the car.

"You're crazy Jimmy. Get this thing back on the road, you're going to kill us both."

Biggs couldn't hear, he was consumed with rage and hatred. Mitchell considered jumping from the car, but it was going too fast. His hand was still on the revolver between the seats. Suddenly, the car came screeching to a stop, and Mitchell was thrown against the dashboard.

Biggs was laughing. "Big man on campus," he shouted, "didn't see that one comin'!" Again, he threw a punch that hit Mitchell squarely in the side, knocking the air out of him. He lunged back in his seat, holding his ribcage with his right hand. In his left was the revolver.

The discharged bullet from the handgun was heard a full mile up the road by the sheriff and Howard Pierce, who was with him as they searched for Pierce's car. It rang loud as magnum rounds do; an almost ear-splitting sound, especially for the two boys in the car. Speeding up the street with the sirens wailing, the stolen car came quickly into view, resting where it had stopped across both lanes in the road. There was no activity inside. Jimmy Biggs was slumped against the driver's door, blood and flesh strewn everywhere from the blast that had turned his head to splinters. The car's engine was still running. The sheriff reached through the blown-out driver's side window and twisted the key off, and the night reclaimed its silence. The gun was securely in Biggs' lifeless hand, too soaked in blood for fingerprints to be taken. There wasn't a trace of anything else in the car, and at that time of night there seemed little point in searching the woods around them. Within an hour the car was towed away and Biggs' body was relocated to the county hospital to be examined before being sent for an autopsy in Shreveport.

✠ ✠ ✠

The installation of the Logan collection began the second week of March. Ted spent most of his time that week with the paintings, checking their physical condition and noting anything that he found. He purposely wanted to begin in the evening so as not to be disturbed by anything or anyone, placing the paintings at locations he had selected for them on paper a month before. If they didn't work per his diagrams, he wanted to be able to move them without being second-guessed by Mitchell, Ellen, or anyone else. Tate McNeil, certainly an "anyone else," called almost daily to check on his progress. In particular, he inquired about the paintings belonging to the Logan family and where they were being placed. He promised to be in Meriden three days before the opening to meet people Mitchell had selected. The Logan name had done much to renew interest in the museum, and it seemed many of the city's wealthy sought to align themselves with that magnetism.

It was three in the morning when Ted decided to stop, but he couldn't bring himself to leave the building or the paintings. While there was a good four weeks until the opening, he was beginning to feel anxious about finishing everything by the deadline. He found a corner in the storage area where packing blankets had been stored and laid among them, falling into a restless sleep. Three hours later he awoke, stiff and a bit dizzy from not having left the museum in over twenty hours. It was near time for the construction crews to begin another day, but at that moment the building was quiet, an eerie sort of noiselessness that bade him to experience the galleries again. Re-entering the Logan gallery, he found everything as he had left it. He walked among the paintings, pretending to see them for the first time, and liked what he saw. He hoped it would pass muster with Mitchell and Tate McNeil.

The last ten days were a strain for the entire staff. There were so few people and so much to be accomplished that assisting someone else on a project was impossible. All the Logan paintings had safely arrived except for one that was slightly damaged through improper packing. It was dispatched with Joe Mullens to the Birmingham Museum for repair by their conservators. Mitchell had done some fancy talking to convince Bishop to rush the job over others, but it was completed on time. The museum's collection was transferred from warehouse storage. It seemed an odd assortment of objects aiming to cover periods of American art history from the Ash Can to the present, with examples of each decade. Ted didn't feel comfortable with some of the objects, though they did indeed come from the time periods Mitchell sought to represent. Then there were the objects he had acquired through the federal grant. Ted wondered if Meriden was ready for the contemporary objects. For Mitchell, each one represented an experience between himself and the artist he remembered in great detail. The collection was a statement he was making about contemporary art, one he might need to defend. That realization brought a new wrinkle to his forehead as he began spacing the objects for installation, constantly referencing the Logan exhibition in terms of which would hold the most public appeal.

Stephen Parker and Ellen Maxwell were busy as well, preparing publications for the opening and programming for the first three months the building would be open. The account of the Art Association's history Ted complied from interviews and written accounts had been turned into one of these programs, planned as an introductory piece to the museum and its inception. The past animosity between these two gifted people were thankfully diffused during this period of high tension and decreasing time. Though Ted tried not to think about it, a resolution of their working relationship was going to be necessary and would require Mitchell to take a stand once and for all. There was sufficient evidence to suggest he had made promises to Parker he couldn't keep. The night before opening, Parker was tight as a drum. He would not talk to anyone, staying in his production center making finishing edits on programs he cared little about but would not show publicly until technically perfect. It was his passion.

By opening night preparations had been completed in all departments. A VIP reception was held, which included commission members, officers of the association, local and regional politicians and corporate heads, as well as the early members of the artists' guild still living. August Bishop did not attend, nor did Beau Britian or any members of the Logan family, just Tate McNeil who, as promised, arrived three days earlier and loved Ted's installation of Nathan Logan's paintings.

Mitchell weathered the stresses of the opening without a single call for his resignation. He was noticeably changed though, working alone in his office with only LeAnne knowing what he was working on. He and Ted no longer shared a common doorway. Ted was given a large office at the end of the suite, which he occupied alone despite there being two desks in it. Ellen Maxwell's new quarters were next to Mitchell's, and LeAnne's were on his other side. Stephen was on a completely different floor. There was much to keep their minds off the anxiety they all felt being in the large, new building that was now their home. It was full of unexpected surprises and issues that seemed best solved by their living within it. Mitchell placed Ted in charge of working some of those out with John Browning, the contractor, and Joe Mullens, though often he would still involve himself in determining the ultimate resolution. Financial matters became his foremost concern.

Rarely did Ted and Mitchell have an opportunity to talk as they had before the move. When they did, Mitchell's tactic had changed. He still wanted to talk, but the conversation's outcome seemed already decided. The meeting would be to persuade his curator to see his point of view on a matter and accept it. Ted didn't understand the depths of this change for several years. Ellen stayed skeptical of Mitchell, which was easily attributed to her additional years working with him. His working relationship with her was perhaps as odd as the one he had with Stephen Parker, though as a woman she was immediately untrustworthy. She was also a bright woman, making matters worse in his judgement. Yet, whenever something he deemed truly important came along, it was Ellen he sought for assistance or advice. Ted had wondered at the time of his interview why she had been invited to the luncheon. During their drive to Atlanta, Ellen explained she had been there to ask questions and help Mitchell make up his mind.

The drama between her and Stephen didn't subside by fall as Mitchell hoped it would. It was quite evident there was no room for Multimedia as an independent video production unit within the museum. Mitchell still tried to mesh the two, going from one to the other as mediator in their disputes. The showdown finally came to a head when Stephen refused to work on an extra educational project Mitchell backed. He was quiet and seemingly at peace with his decision as he walked into Mitchell's office.

"I won't do that program, Mitchell. It's not on my schedule and is only a self-promotion piece for you and Ellen." Stephen didn't care that

Mitchell and Ted were already in a meeting about the next exhibition after Nathan Logan.

Mitchell leaned back in his desk chair, his neck reddening, but his face showing no emotion. "Stephen," he said coldly, "I understand this project is new to you and has not been discussed thoroughly. It is a program both Ellen and I feel is necessary for our future growth and educational goals, as well as being very helpful with future fundraising."

"See, that's the problem, Mitchell. You and Ellen discussed this program. You and I discussed other programs, things more aligned with the direction Multimedia wants to take."

It was the first time Ted had heard him speak of his department in the first person, as if it was a living being with its own goals and interests.

"Stephen," Mitchell started again, attempting a smile, "this is just a short project, something you could do in a week's time. It would really help out and be so easy for you to put together."

"There will always be something that will interfere with the plans Multimedia has. Ellen will have to wait for this new piece of propaganda." With that he turned and left.

Mitchell sat up, his expression not significantly changed, and continued talking to Ted about the next exhibition as if Stephen had not just interrupted. His afternoons for the next five days were spent with Stephen in his production studio. Exactly what was said was unknown, and no one could imagine what the two might have to say that took so much time. Finally, and quite unexpectedly, Stephen's father was called into their meetings, a move Stephen requested, complaining that Mitchell wasn't listening to him or his needs. These meetings covered the better part of an additional two days, culminating late the night of the second day. Ted was already home for the evening when his phone rang.

"Ted, I hate to bother you, but I need a favor." It was Maureen Jenkins, sounding scared and hesitant. "Mitchell hasn't come home yet. I think he's still at the museum talking with the Parkers."

"It's after eleven," Ted said stupidly. "Surely they're not still at it!"

"I don't know. Mitchell was going to stay until it was finished. They won't answer the phone, I've been calling all night. He's been unusually stressed at home this week. His eyes are bloodshot and his face is drawn. Now this thing with Stephen's father…I don't know what to think. It's all so strange. I hate to ask, but I'm really worried. Would you mind going down to the museum and seeing if his car is still there? No need to go in, just look around; it would be a great comfort to me."

"Sure Maureen, I'll leave now and let you know." Ted returned the telephone receiver to its cradle and headed into town.

Maureen tried to relax, but a memory that she kept shut out of her mind was creeping closer into view. She remembered the heat of that other night long ago, the smell of vines and dense vegetation, and her hiding place behind the sandy beach. The memory was clear now—it was too late to stop it. She felt herself fill with the same tension she had known then, watching the water lapping gently around the two naked bodies, the second figure raising up—her mind went blank.

There was a full moon, and it was still quite warm. The streets were deserted, and Ted made good time driving to the museum. *If Mitchell's car is there, should I go in? It will be embarrassing for everyone if I do, especially at this late hour. Mitchell will know I'm checking on him, as will Stephen and his father. However, Maureen wants to know what's going on.* She hadn't said anything specific, but her voice had an unsettled quality. The whole episode was so strange, so drawn out. Ted turned into the lot, noticing how garish the mercury lights made everything. Mitchell usually parked some distance from the building's rear entrance. Ted drove slowly to where he thought his car might be, but it wasn't there or anywhere else in the lot. The correct sequence of ceiling lights inside the lobby were lit, nothing looked amiss. Ted walked around the building's exterior looking for anything that might indicate something was out of the ordinary. Shutting down the exterior security system, he opened the door and entered, locking it behind him. Mitchell's office was empty. Ted called down to the projection booth and there was no answer. He retraced his steps, locked the exterior doors, reset the alarm, and walked back to his car for the five-minute drive to Mitchell's home. *If his car is there, should I stop?* He edged quietly along the street in front of the Jenkins home. Mitchell's car was in the driveway and lights blazed from within the house.

Ted parked and walked up the drive to the side door, which was open. "Anyone home?"

"Ted, is that you?" It was Mitchell's voice. "Hey bud, sorry to make you run around so late at night. Maureen told me she'd called you."

Maureen appeared at the door. Ted was sure the news he'd been summoned to check on Mitchell had not gone over well.

"You must have really had a session with the Parkers tonight. You okay? Anything I can do?"

Mitchell walked to the table that divided their kitchen, pulled out a chair, and gestured for Ted to join him. Maureen was cooking him a steak, even though it was nearing midnight. His scotch had brought some color to his face, though he looked tired.

"Thanks Ted, but it's all over now. Stephen is leaving the museum." It wasn't the outcome he had wanted. "It really is the best thing for him, though I'm sorry it's come to this." He looked down at the woodgrain pattern of the table, his voice subdued and hoarse. "I don't ever want to go through this again."

Maureen finished cooking and placed a plate on the table in front of him. She too looked tired, her eyes red, her skin pale.

"I'm just too soft-hearted," he continued. "A problem like that could have been handled better by someone who didn't consider consequences or personalities. It will be good for Stephen to do something else for a while, to get out of Meriden. I was worried when he asked to have his father present at our meetings, but it worked out for the best. He was much easier to convince than Stephen and actually helped persuade him it was best for him to leave the museum."

Ted couldn't believe Stephen was leaving. *How is a person convinced they should no longer be at a place that was more than work, more like a home?* He sat across from Mitchell as he finished his meal hoping he would say more about the last eight days, but he didn't.

The resignation announcement came a full three days later, though the grapevine had it the morning after the long night's negotiation. Stephen said little, locking himself in his studio to sort out what equipment was his. Mitchell spent the three days finding Stephen another job. It was a strange step for him, and Ted wondered if this was part of the deal between him and the Parkers, or was it to ease his conscience? The announcement was handled like a major media event, with Mitchell personally writing the press release. "Stephen Parker, director of Multimedia at the Meriden Art Museum, has resigned to assume duties with the Atlanta Film Board as associate for video studies. Meriden Museum Director Mitchell Jenkins expressed his deep regret . . .." The release went on to list Stephen's achievements and contributions in a very positive way.

Later that year at the museum's annual meeting, Stephen was given a special award of recognition for his many contributions, and to everyone's surprise, he showed up to accept the accolade. Ted couldn't help but wonder what would happen if he were to leave the museum. Would it cause this much drama? Would Mitchell find him another position? Then he remembered the late night at the Jenkins' kitchen table and his vow to "never to do this again."

Stephen's leaving marked the end of an era. The comfortable pace of work at the old building was gone, everything now was in a much higher gear. The stress of Stephen's dismissal made Jenkins somehow stronger, more assured. He traveled often to Birmingham, working with the arts council and keeping tabs on Bishop and his grand museum complex, filling every waking moment with work. When he and Ted did find time to talk together, there was little of the old familiarity—there was no time for it.

Shortly after Stephen left, Mitchell called Ted into his office for what he assumed to be a routine update on what he was doing curatorially as well as the building's condition and needs. Instead, Ted learned another member of the staff was in jeopardy of losing their job.

"She talks too much. I hear things from the men she dates. We're growing too rapidly to have her talking indiscriminately. She's been unable to keep up with me since the move. I have no justifiable reason to fire her yet – but she's got to go. Don't you agree Ted?"

Ted wondered if the entire staff was being judged. "Gosh, I don't think I can accurately comment of LeAnne's performance. She doesn't talk much to me, but when she does it's never anything indiscreet. You know her better than I do, so you're the best judge."

"Things are getting back to me, details of the operation here that could only come from one source other than me. When she goes out, she talks about what she does, where she works. People want to know what goes on here, things about me." He paused rocking back in his desk chair, his face expressionless. "I'm going to move her to somewhere else in the operation. If she wants to stay, fine. If she wants to go, that's fine too. What do you think?"

"I think if you have reason to believe she's saying things about the museum or you outside of these walls, you should confront her. If she leaves, she can still talk about what goes on. Certainly she knows quite a bit."

"I'll talk to her, you can be sure of that. I'll make it clear that if she decides to leave, she should forget everything about what goes on here. I can make it very difficult for her to get employment in this town. Secretaries are a dime a dozen." He rocked forward, looking at his pristine desktop. "I also haven't decided what to do about Ellen. Stephen shouldn't be the only one to suffer because of their differences. I won't take much more of the 'attitude.' I can cut her off so quickly, it'll make her head spin."

He sat quietly for several moments, then looked up at Ted and asked if there was anything he needed to talk about. Finding nothing, he left. LeAnne Rickter was moved to the art school as its registrar several days later. She and Mitchell talked for several hours in the seclusion of his office the day before she cleaned out her desk. He left immediately afterward and was out of town the day she switched positions, driving to Birmingham for meetings. Though Mary Griffin needed help in the school, LeAnne lasted only five days before finding work at one of the larger banks in another part of the city. Mitchell gave her a glowing reference and an ample send-off at the first staff meeting after she was gone. He even mentioned Stephen again, saying, "it will be difficult to replace two such dedicated employees."

CHAPTER TWENTY-THREE

August Bishop announced his retirement that September, effective the first of the year. It was a shock to most people who knew him, but particularly for Mitchell, who took the news the way one does the passing of a father. The Birmingham Museum project had finally received legislative approval, taking more time than anticipated by Bishop or the governor. Mitchell mentioned several recent instances when Bishop requested he reconsider the position as its director "for the good of the State," but he was still firm in his decision to stay in Meriden. His fears of being dismissed by the commission lessened the longer he held his position. No more did Ted hear about taking over for him. Now Mitchell talked about spending his entire career in Meriden and thought Ted should do the same. Such were the prospects for the future.

After a respectable amount of time had passed, Mitchell began searching for a replacement for Stephen Parker. He toyed with the idea of not filling the position at all for a while, thinking he would work on some of the projects he and Stephen had discussed himself. But the knowledge and skills Stephen possessed as well as the time commitment were more than Mitchell could provide. He hired a replacement for LeAnne Rickter right away. The woman had made a blind employment request months before Mitchell had decided to terminate Rickter, and she must have impressed him, for he called her immediately. Though not qualified for the position in any way, she was hired with a promise to improve her typing and shorthand skills while on the job.

Martha Dyer was tall with short blond hair, trim, and dressed in well-tailored clothing. She was recently divorced and had left her native Arizona to begin a new life. Martha was a quiet person, preferring the seclusion of her office to talking around the coffee maker in the mornings. She was not the sort of woman Mitchell was physically attracted to, though attractive in her own way. She didn't have the build of LeAnne Rickter or the allure of the secretaries Ted was told he had before, so Ted was surprised when she mentioned Mitchell had asked her out for dinner three weeks after her first day.

"Why do things like this always happen to me?" she asked after revealing the proposal. "I don't want to get involved, I'm not sure I trust him. Do you think I'll lose this job over it? He seemed very apologetic after I declined."

To Ted's knowledge, this was the first time Mitchell had ever made a gesture of this nature to a female employee, and while he told Martha it was probably a harmless request, his mind could not quite agree. The refusal didn't jeopardize anything for Martha, who after a few months on the job was well-entrenched in her duties. To her credit she was efficient, highly organized, dependable, and developed the dedicated loyalty to Mitchell that Ted had—and still did to a great degree. She was much closer to Mitchell than the rest of the staff. However, when her title changed from secretary to administrative assistant, there were still some eyebrows raised, particularly among those Mitchell had taken to calling his "senior staff."

With Martha's arrival, he began to take administration much more seriously, and by year's end they had developed detailed files on each employee, kept in a lockable filing cabinet in her office. The files contained every bit of information about a person during their employment, including dated comments from Mitchell on their performance and commitment to the museum. As his second in charge, Ted was told of the files' existence before others, but only shortly before. He was also told about a new employee self-evaluation process Mitchell developed from corporate models, which would be completed on an annual basis. We understood its importance in a corporation, but with so few museum employees it seemed pretentious. Martha oversaw distribution, collection, and analysis with Mitchell.

Senior staff were designated on a new organizational chart by named boxes in a horizontal line under Mitchell's box, with Martha listed in a position just below and to the side of his. Each of the senior staff members, at this point Ellen and Ted, would evaluate those employees to whom they gave direction. Mitchell would rate senior staff and presumably Martha. There was no Multimedia staff on the chart. Instant paranoia broke out when his plan was announced at the Monday staff meeting. No matter how Mitchell tried to sell the new procedure as helpful to him and each of us, there was much dissension over its enactment, especially among people who had been with him the longest.

Joe Mullens, for instance, refused to be part of the process, telling Ted to go ahead and rate him however he wanted. "Mitchell knows that I do my job!"

It was an uncomfortable ten days. The procedure required staff to evaluate themselves from criteria Mitchell developed. Ellen and Ted would evaluate each employee, compare notes with them, and come to an agreement where needed. The revised document would be signed by the employee and returned to Martha, who would set up a short interview with Mitchell for each employee. Mitchell insisted average scores meant people were doing their jobs as described in the newly refined job descriptions he had written. Still, for people like Joe, an average score was hard to swallow. Ted was also chagrined to see Mitchell had not given him a single "Superior" mark, though there were quite a few "Above Average" ones and thankfully no "Below Average" marks.

"Don't be alarmed, Ted. No one should ever get a superior mark. It's something to work toward, a goal."

Ted left his meeting feeling as demoralized as the people who left his office after their own reviews. He expected some of his supervisees would complain about him in retaliation for their average scores and wondered what Mitchell's reaction would be.

Ellen suggested they speak to Louis Sterling about the basic philosophy of the review format and because of his ideological agreement, Ted accompanied her to his office at the *Journal*. As always, Sterling was dressed neatly, sitting in his large office all polished and clean. In his easy manner, he greeted his guests and ushered them to comfortable chairs. Ted and Ellen had told Mitchell they were planning the visit, a move he encouraged as long as he was informed beforehand. He also informed them prior to the meeting that it was Sterling himself who had suggested the evaluation procedure, adding to Ted's discomfort in being there.

"Lou," Ellen began, "Ted and I are not here to complain about anything. We want you to know that at the start."

He smiled through the cloud of cigarette smoke encircling his head.

"But we have doubts about the staff review procedure Mitchell has instituted. Do you know about it?" He nodded his head, and she continued. "We both feel the evaluation technique he's opted to use might do more harm to staff morale than good. Most everyone at the museum works very hard, doing the best they are able. The few who don't know who they are and know everyone else does too. They are people who will leave when something else comes along. It's difficult though for those of us doing what we consider our best work to learn that in the eyes of our supervisor, it's only an average effort."

Sterling said nothing, waiting for Ellen or Ted to continue. Finally, he asked, "Have you talked to Mitchell about your concern?"

The question was directed at Ted. *So much for my plan to let Ellen do all the talking!*

"Yes, I talked to him before the process was implemented. I didn't know anything about it though, until right before Christmas. His reason for introducing it was to conform to standards in the field as well as the for-profit corporate community, but really, there are only seven of us. It's hard to compare someone who hangs pictures, arranges exhibits, and manages our collection to a mid-management bureaucrat, even if the pay scales are the same. By the same token, to subjectively rate someone's job performance on how well they are educating the public seems very one-sided, as no one is seeking reviews from them. I know Mitchell is trying to better manage everything and I appreciate that."

Ted felt as though he had overstepped and decided to answer any further questions with a simple yes or no. James Sterling remained un-moved. Ellen had assured Ted he would have a solution, or at least an explanation for Mitchell's actions, even though Sterling had suggested this particular format. They had come to him for the basic good of the institution and with their employer's knowledge.

"You are both aware, I think, of the rapid growth the museum has undergone in the last year and a half. Mitchell is clearly aware and knows he no longer has a small operation where he can meet with individuals and keep a personal eye on their work and progress. This review proce-dure is one we use here at the paper to gauge the growth of our employ-ees and sort out those who are doing a consistently good job from those who are not. In this way, management can work with those who are not pulling their weight and encourage more productivity if they wish to continue in our employ. Mitchell takes his employees much too person-ally. He wants those who are not working up to their abilities to do bet-ter and is willing to take time from his own busy schedule to help them along. By the same token, if an employee complains he has been passed over for a promotion, or has a complaint about his supervisor, Mitchell has review documents on hand to gauge the employee's history. No one should consider a review of this nature as a bad thing. It's a tool to make Mitchell's job easier."

His explanation was delivered in his usual pleasant style with no hint of irritation. "It's good you both came to discuss this matter with me, because if you agree with what I've said about the process and the reasons for it, you can go back and explain the whys and what-fors to others who might have similar concerns. Ted, I appreciate your point about the differences between art organizations and the business community. I have a very special place in my heart for the artists in Meriden and their needs, though I don't do anything creative myself. But as the museum grows, it's going to become much more like a business. Mitchell has accepted this, and you must too." He paused to grin. "Have you two filled out Mitchell's review?"

Ellen and Ted looked at each other, asking silently if either knew anything about a review for Mitchell Jenkins. Seeing our confused looks, Sterling guessed we had not.

"You should, you know. It's all part of the procedure. Senior staff are permitted to review the performance of those at the top. It helps the manager be more aware his own shortcomings and builds the confidence of folks like you. Your reviews of Mitchell will be reviewed with him, just as yours were, then sent to me. I will review them with him."

✧ ✧ ✧

Mitchell apologized profusely when Ted and Ellen returned from Sterling's office for the "oversight" on his part in the review process. Apparently, he and Sterling had talked. They all laughed over it—Ellen in a way that signaled her disbelief in his story, Ted in a nervous way, indicating he didn't like any of it.

"Martha," Mitchell called to the next office by phone, "please bring in two blank copies of the review form."

Within sixty seconds, Ellen and Ted each had a copy of the review document with Mitchell's name at the top in his own handwriting.

"I think you should take your time with these," he instructed, still treating his review as if it were a humorous exercise. "Compare notes if you like, and we can get together when you're done. Oh, and share them with

Sterling. I'll meet with him after he talks with you about your ratings. And remember, your jobs depend on the outcome!" He winked at us both.

✳ ✳ ✳

August Bishop scheduled his last day at the Birmingham Museum to coincide with the institution's annual meeting on January twenty-fifth. It marked his own twenty-fifth anniversary there, and seemed a fitting time to leave. Orchestrated in true Bishop fashion, it was a highly social event, lavishly held first at the museum, then the spacious accommodations of the Birmingham Society. He had not planned anything so extravagant in several years, feeling the climate wasn't right for these kinds of gatherings, but this was to be different—something to be remembered by his board and invited guests for quite a while. As part of the evening's festivities, Bishop secretly also wanted to introduce his successor. He didn't want this left up to the Board after he was gone. *Boards could take much too long to replace a director, especially when the obvious choice was so clear and close at hand,* he thought. He would not have a search committee formed, advertisements published in trade journals and lengthy interviews conducted with outsiders unfamiliar with the museum or the new museum complex.

The afternoon of the twenty-fifth, Bishop sat in a leather easy chair, looking about his office and remembering his twenty-five years as director. He would leave the South, settling once again in Italy as he had in his youth. He thought of the night ahead, its exhilaration and sadness. Governor Ford would be there to introduce his old friend; there would be applause, an ovation of affection as he walked to the speaker's platform constructed in the largest of the museum's galleries housing his Impressionist collection. He would look over the crowd and see some faces he had known for years, others that were new and young, the sons and daughters of old Birmingham society waiting their turns. He would deliver, in his careful deliberate way, a speech few would ever forget about art, culture, and what it all means to mankind. A moving speech designed to keep his memory alive for years to come. Then Bishop would announce his chosen replacement and Mitchell, who was waiting in the wings, would join him on the platform. The legacy of August Cortland Bishop would live on.

Ted was surprised Mitchell had asked him to go to the Bishop party. It was a very exclusive gathering of Birmingham's elite, with special guests added from throughout the state and region. Maureen was going as well. She had declined to go to most of the museum's recent social functions, and knowing something of their time in Birmingham, it baffled Ted as to why she was now so excited about returning. It had been some time since the three of them had been out together socially. They were always uncomfortable times for Ted, knowing how Mitchell felt about marriage. Over and above that was the pandering way he acted when in a social situation with Maureen. He would become overly kind and gentlemanly, as if he really cared about how she was feeling or what she wanted. To see him in this situation, then to be at their home, an outsider wouldn't believe he was the same man. Mitchell decided they would take two cars, with the two men leaving early Friday morning.

The week before the event, Mitchell went to see Louis Sterling regarding his performance review Ellen and Ted had completed and returned. They had each completed separate forms, comparing scores and consolidating them when they differed. Ted then went to Martha Dyer's office for a third blank review sheet, the one they would present to Sterling. It was a visit like many others. Ted found Martha exuding the confidence of someone feeling well-established within her position knowing she was closer to Mitchell than Ted was, despite his title. While nothing was ever said between them, he was becoming more aware that in his absence, Martha would be able to handle questions of policies he had written better than he could. She knew the detailed background information about an issue, and he knew little or nothing at all. She felt a kind of superiority about this fact, and it showed.

Jenkins had not returned to the museum before five the day he had the appointment with Sterling. In the week that followed he said nothing of the meeting or the review. He had received much higher marks than Ellen or Ted had from him, because somehow the criteria for each question seemed to suit him and his position better than it did to the rest of the staff. Ted and Ellen had given him an average rating in attitude and supervision, and the rest were either superior or above average. Both of the average scores were a result of his inability to relate to other people—staff or the public—after the new building opened.

Ted shivered slightly recalling Martha's smile and haunting comment as he left her office with the blank review form. "Sure am glad it's not me filling that out."

Since she declined his offer for an after-work dinner, she seemed to have the upper hand with him. He listened to her counsel and brought her into most of his meetings. Whatever he found valuable in her, it was stronger than a sexual link and more difficult to explain.

Mitchell was still actively pursuing female company, selecting them now from the docents Ellen had cultivated largely from the ranks of the Junior League and the Woman's Club. His tastes seemed to be changing from the secretaries to wealthy, intelligent, married women with families who were looking for a bit of adventure. The other thing that changed was his pursuits were conducted openly, allowing more than those in his inner circle to draw conclusions. If he were trying to get caught, or at least give Maureen a good idea of what might be going on in his life, he could not have been more open. Martha Dyer knew more than she'd share too, transferring women's telephone calls to Mitchell. She started to recognize their voices, and after a while she would make small talk before transferring the call.

Mitchell said little to Ted the morning before driving to Birmingham, but he seemed to be in good spirits as he stopped to talk with Martha Dyer in the hall. Ted was not looking forward to the drive. Before leaving, he called Ellen to see if Mitchell had talked to her the day before, and if they had, had he mentioned the performance review. She was as animated as usual, saying he had indeed come by her office the day prior and had talked to her for quite some time about everything but the review. It seemed he thought little of it, but she still didn't bring up the subject herself. A few minutes later, Martha rang Ted to say Mitchell was ready to depart and that he should meet him in the parking lot. Based on the business in her voice, Ted assumed she was readying herself to take command of the museum for the afternoon in the absence of its director and his titled assistant.

Mitchell had brought the car to the door, but when Ted arrived, he was seated in the front passenger seat. Ted wondered what papers he would be working on, then saw him sitting with his hands folded on his lap.

Mitchell gave his usual greeting as Ted got behind the wheel. "Hey man! All ready to go? Old Bishop's swan song should be quite an event!" His mood seemed light enough, but his eyes looked cold, and Ted knew from experience he could change the tone of a conversation very quickly.

"How's your morning been?" Ted asked, wondering how many subjects he could bring up to talk about over the next two hours.

"Great, just great. These are the kind of days that make me want to do it all over again!"

This was a commonly used expression with Mitchell that Ted heard him use in both good and bad times. They drove through the city to the highway running northwest. Mitchell said nothing as they drove, just staring in his straightforward way at any woman who passed or was next to them at a traffic light.

"God damn," he exhaled as the light changed. "That was a beautiful piece!" He turned in his seat, continuing to stare at the young woman, who thankfully turned right. He cleared his throat and looked straight ahead through the windshield. Ten minutes later we were on the open road with nothing but trees and farmland to look at. Ted knew if there was something on Mitchell's mind, it would come up soon, and he was not disappointed.

"I had an informative meeting with Louis Sterling last week." It was said with no emotion, just a declaration. Ted couldn't tell if Mitchell wanted him to ask him about it or say nothing. The back of his neck prickled. "We went over the performance review you and Ellen completed, as well as comments you both made to him on your visits. Lou was puzzled by some of those comments and asked me about them. I was puzzled too and thought we might talk through what you and Ellen meant."

Ted knew Mitchell would be able to quote exact passages from the conversations he and Ellen had with Sterling. He tried to remember both meetings, which were days apart.

"I have a copy of the review you gave Sterling." Mitchell reached for his brief case and produced a duplicate of the review, on which he had written questions and made notations. "I asked Lou for a copy, and he saw no reason why I shouldn't have one. What I don't understand is why you and Ellen think I'm only average in attitude and supervision?"

He was looking at the side of Ted's face as he kept his eyes riveted on the road.

"Ted, I think I've always been available to you if you had a question about something. You are welcome in my office anytime. I can't imagine why you gave me an average score when I think we both agree I'm not average."

"As you know," Ted began, "Ellen and I worked through your review together, as we had been instructed. We both completed our own forms then compared them. When something of this nature is done, there are often compromises made when judgements don't coincide. Attitude and supervision were the ones we differed on quite a bit, and after discussing our reasons, we compromised on a rating most consistent with both views."

"That means one of you rated me lower than average in these two areas and the other higher." He glanced down at the definition of "Below Average," and read it out loud to himself: "May be cooperative with supervisor and helpful to others on occasion. In general, however, prefers to be left alone. Tell me Ted, when have I ever been this way with either of you? I won't ask which one of you rated me which way."

"I…don't know, Mitchell. I think we were both thinking in generalities rather than in…"

"You don't know! Can you remember what you said to Sterling when you discussed this part of the review?"

Again, Ted was slow to answer, trying to recall the conversation with Sterling. All he could definitely remember was thinking this review would mean trouble and having a bad feeling in his stomach when they left his office.

"I'll assume from your silence that you don't remember what you said. Let me refresh your memory, Ted. One of you said you felt I was building walls around myself to shut the rest of the staff out. That the reason Martha was working out so well was she kept people from seeing me and that was what I wanted. Don't you remember my saying after the opening week that anyone on staff is welcome in my office when they have a problem? In fact, I said it just the other morning. Of course, if everyone came, I wouldn't have time to do my own work, but for specific problems I always have time. This other thing is also hard for me to understand. Let me read it to you. 'Supervision' as defined on the worksheet is the 'ability to supervise other employees.' However, just below, it is further defined this way: 'Outstanding – someone who demonstrates superior skill in training, developing and utilizing department staff to achieve best possible results; Above Average – someone who is very effective in managing and supervising subordinates. Is proficient in training and developing department staff, recognizing their strengths and weaknesses and guiding them to become more proficient; Average – someone who maintains employee relations. Does adequate job of training and developing department staff. Generally, commands staff loyalty and support.' Now, since you tell me this was a compromise area as well, let me read the criteria for 'Below Average. Record of supervising department staff inconsistently. Leadership qualities below average.'"

He continued to look across the car at Ted, keeping the pressure on. "I suppose you have no real answers for the average rating here either. Sterling indicated you both felt I didn't spend enough time with you, and because my attitude toward you wasn't good enough, my supervision abilities weren't either. Again, Ted, can you give me an instance when I have not helped? You and Ellen must have some examples of when I've failed you. I'd like to know what they were."

Ted remained silent, not being good at arguing and knowing Mitchell could talk through anything he said.

"These reviews are serious, Ted. I have a reason for everything I do or say and for every score I put down. I told Sterling you and Ellen wouldn't take it seriously and not to allow you two to rate me. At least now he knows I was right."

The men drove the remainder of the trip in silence. Mitchell collected his papers and placed them back in his case as they entered the Birmingham city limits. He directed Ted to drive directly to the museum. As soon as the car stopped, Mitchell was out the door, walking into the museum, greeting people he knew, and acting like he'd never been upset. Ted sat in the car alone for several minutes. This was the first time he'd had been on Mitchells bad side, he didn't like it. He tried to remember as much of the conversation as he could to tell Ellen next week, though Mitchell's fury was sure to lose something in the translation. It was the last time he and Ellen were permitted to complete a performance review on Mitchell, while the practice continued annually for the remainder of staff.

✵ ✵ ✵

By the time Ted entered the Birmingham Museum, Mitchell was engaged in deep, loud conversation with people he'd known when he was Bishop's assistant. A small army of people were running about, making final preparations for the evening ahead. Male waiters and bartenders were receiving instructions from a woman who seemed to oversee everything going into the museum's largest gallery, where Bishop's Impressionist paintings hung. Their acquisition was considered one of his greatest achievements. Cases of champagne were wheeled into a bar staging area off another gallery with tables set in various locations for hard liquor and refreshments.

As Ted watched Mitchell loosen up after their ride, it became apparent why he had been invited. Mitchell wanted no part of standing around with Maureen all evening. Ted was there to see to her needs. It wouldn't have been right for her to be alone, and Mitchell was intent on having the freedom to relive his past. He was quite at home in this setting, being treated as a prodigal son returning for his father's blessing. He was into his second scotch when Bishop entered the gallery, having heard of his arrival. Mitchell abruptly left the people he was talking to and greeted his mentor warmly. Ted could only hear their laughter as they talked. Soon they left, Mitchell following Bishop for what Ted suspected was a private conference in the latter's book-lined lair. Watching them, he was again reminded of Bishop offering the state's new museum complex to his boss.

The two men entered Bishop's office through the back door. As always, it smelled of leather, coffee, and the imported French cologne Bishop wore. He looked exceedingly chipper despite his seventy years and a recent bout with intestinal flu. The virus had caused him to lose several pounds, and now the grey suede vest he wore over his crisp white shirt was not nearly as tight. His recently altered tuxedo hung over the door to his private bathroom. It had been a while since the two of them had met in person, but they easily made small talk about the evening ahead, Bishop's retirement plans, and the speech he would give that night.

"I don't have to tell you about the mixed emotions I have today. It's difficult for any man when he's devoted his career to the development of an idea. I've made it a reality for those who have patronized this museum the last twenty-five years. You remember the golden years, but it wasn't always as grand as when you were here or as it is now. I've watched this entity grow in strength and power and have watched you do the same."

There was a pause as Bishop lit a cigar. It was a ritual for him, using only wooden matches. First he would light the tip, burning it without inhaling, then he would inhale slowly, enjoying both the smell and the tobacco's taste.

"You know Mitchell, I've never told you this, but I think you know it anyway—I think of you as a son. It's been wonderful watching your progress since our time together here. We did some good things together, building the new wing for the Impressionist paintings, establishing programming for all those schoolchildren, all the things that make this profession rewarding. When those people from Meriden called me about someone to develop an arts program there, I naturally thought of you. I hated to see you go, the way any father hates to see his son leave to make his way in the world. But I did, knowing you would want to leave here someday to strike out on your own, and it has worked out very well. Neither one of us could have dreamed how your successes would build. Meriden is close to being better than we are. I can say that to you now that I am leaving."

They both smiled, Mitchell denying what he had already told other people privately.

"Soon we'll be building again," Bishop said. "The legislature has approved the final plans for construction, and although there are still a few minor problems to work through, I should think by spring we'll break ground and begin construction shortly thereafter. Governor Ford is here tonight. He's going to introduce me to the audience. He'll probably talk about our accomplishments the past twenty-five years and our future plans, which we'll unveil tonight. Soon Birmingham will move ahead again; ahead of Meriden and everyone else in the South. It would be a shame if you weren't directing those efforts." He looked at Mitchell through his heavy, white eyebrows. "There's nothing left for you to do in Meriden."

Bishop had laid all his cards on the table, though Mitchell suspected the old fox still had one or two tricks up his sleeve. He smiled, wondering how to begin, when Bishop spoke again.

"There are one or two other things I should tell you Mitchell, before you say anything. The first is I have been empowered by the board to name my successor, subject to their approval, without a formal search committee being necessary. I'd like to make the announcement at the end of my remarks tonight. Second, as we've discussed, the future relationship of the legislature to the institution we're building and other state arts organizations has been the subject of some debate. Before he left office, Governor Ford made some progress in this regard which is not generally known, even to the president of the state arts council." He looked pointedly at Jenkins, who was now waiting for the other shoe to drop. "The opinion of the legislature is when the state museum complex is open, the arts commission and the other smaller agencies will be duplicating efforts. So once the new museum is fully operational, the other state-funded agencies should be dissolved. This will channel their funding into the new museum for programming or further dispersal when appropriate. So, you see Mitchell, should you decide not to take the position, you'll be at the mercy of some director of the overall museum complex and the likely executor of the few funds other agencies will be vying for."

The old bastard has sewn this up pretty tightly. Mitchell was angry with himself for not foreseeing something like this. "August you certainly make a convincing argument. I was fully prepared to lecture you about your phone call to Maureen last week. That kind of tactic doesn't work with me, as you well know. You and Ford can't get to me through her."

He paused to gather his thoughts. He never liked being threatened, especially when he felt in a position of strength. The Meriden Museum was now an important location for contemporary art in Alabama. He knew colleagues in the Southeast were envious, and he enjoyed that prestige. If the state museum was constructed, it could certainly diminish the light he was emitting. And if Bishop and Ford were accurate about the legislature's consolidation of funding, it would be the death of many smaller agencies and hurtful to his own. He didn't like centralization, especially when he wasn't in the center, but he didn't want to come back to Birmingham!

"Believe me August, I appreciate the things you've just said about me. My father and I were never close. I left home many times in my younger years. Throughout high school, I practically lived with a friend to get away from him. You were always more than a boss, you were someone I could learn from about things I truly cared about. Leaving Birmingham eight years ago was one of the hardest things I've done so far in my life, but I faced that challenge, worked hard, and have been successful. For twenty-five years, Birmingham has been the top venue for visual art in the state. It's been the place every other agency tries to emulate. It's what I tried to pattern our former venue after. I probably would have been content with that, and even been grateful to come back and take over for you, had it not been for Taylor James. With his money, I constructed my own dream—modern, new, bold—what everyone else in the Southeast now aspires to emulate. Nothing is ever going to take that away from me. My construction in Meriden is not an end, but a beginning. Taylor isn't going to stop spending money. He's a man who likes results, and I intend to lead him there. I will make him interested in filling that building with stunningly beautiful objects of art. He's getting older and he's vain. He'll want a monument to himself, and I'm giving him the opportunity to create one."

Mitchell looked at his mentor to see if he was finally listening. "We both know your groundbreaking is at least a year away. A lot can happen in a year, things can change. The one thing we've never had is a common interest among the museums and their directors. There has never been anything we could all be for...or against. If our colleagues knew what was going to happen to them in two or three years, they wouldn't be as complacent as they are now. Hell, some of those fools think your complex is going to do them some good! Your PR people have done their job. But I will fight this thing, August, and if it means hurting you in the process, I'm afraid I have no choice. I won't let the Meriden Museum get hurt by the dreams of two glory-seeking old men. You've had twenty-five illustrious years, that's enough."

Mitchell rose from his seat and walked toward the door. He turned and saw Bishop sitting unmoved, his cigar gone out.

"I'm sorry August, I came to enjoy your party tonight."

Mitchell closed the door behind him and passed Ted in the corridor without noticing him. His senses were taking him through hallways and galleries, back to where he had left his scotch.

The Retirement Gala was as exciting as Ted thought it would be. He was a sucker for seeing celebrities, and the party was full of them. State politicians of every stripe were gathered for this special event. Assuming his role as escort, Ted stayed close to Maureen while Mitchell made the rounds of the partygoers by himself. By the time speeches were to be delivered, he was holding more liquid than a wet sponge. Ted had only seen him this way one other time—the night they opened the museum in Meriden, when liquor and fatigue had taken him to an almost coma-tose state.

The former governor was still a handsome man, a natural Southern politician. His face was deeply tanned, his white hair closely cropped. He was tall and had taken good care of himself physically. His remarks about Bishop were not quite a eulogy, though they could have been, and he definitely knew how to energize a crowd, building the tone of his words to a high point when talking about the new museum he and his dear friend had worked on together. By the time he completed his remarks before introducing the man of the hour, the audience was ready to crown him emperor. Bishop mounted the platform aware of the audience's anticipation. He waved and smiled with not quite the blatant skill of Ford, but with the quiet dignity of someone who wanted the same goals as a politician without the unpleasant coarseness involved. When he greeted the audience with a gentle smile and "good evening," the applause grew louder, then everyone was standing.

It could easily have been a tearful occasion as Bishop looked drawn and uneasy. He was searching the audience for someone, looking out as far as he could in the dimness until his eyes finally fell upon Mitchell who stood to the far right, opposite of where Maureen and Ted were. Bishop waved to Maureen who enjoyed his recognition. As he held his arms out to quiet the room, which took a few moments to accomplish, he looked at Jenkins again. Finally, everyone took their seats, allowing Bishop to begin his last address as director of the Birmingham Museum of Art.

"I will not take up too much of your time this evening with talk of sad things or times past. We all know what the past has been like and can cherish the events that have made it memorable. Old ideas like old men cannot go on forever. It is the natural cycle of things for change to occur, and if it happens in an orderly way, we can be grateful for it. By next spring the changes Governor Ford has already mentioned will be underway at this site. This building will never be destroyed, though it may not look quite the same in the future as it does tonight. But the spirit of collecting and scholarship started here will live on and in fact, will be better than ever before. This will require new people with fresh ideas. I had a dream that I would be able to stand before you today and welcome the strong new leader who would take the reins and relieve me of all this!" He waved his arms around to audience laughter. "

But I fear this is not to be. There will be some," he turned toward Maureen, who was now staring at her husband, "who will try to keep our progress at bay because of their own fears and inabilities to see the future unfold. We must not let that happen; you must not let them succeed. The State of Alabama has a real chance for exceptional progress in the arts and sciences, progress that will thrust us into the forefront of the public's attention. Each of us must assist in this effort and bring it to fruition. The opposition may be formidable, but together we can overcome it. Our heritage demands that we take this advanced position; I know you will not let me down."

His remarks went on for only a few more minutes. He thanked his board and others in the audience for their support and kindnesses during his tenure. He did not take his eyes off Jenkins though, until his final few words. Jenkins met his stare in his own unflinching manner. Ted knew then their talk had not gone well. He wasn't sure if he was relieved or saddened by the turn of events, but decided not to stay the night in Birmingham as originally planned.

As Bishop's remarks concluded, there was more applause and another standing ovation. Maureen turned from the speaker's platform and asked Ted to walk her into one of the other galleries for a drink and some air. When they were free from the bulk of the other attendees, she spoke to him in a hushed manner.

"I wonder how it would be to attend a function and be able to leave at a respectable time? To do something afterwards with people you liked and return to your home with someone you love. What do you think Ted? How would that be?" He thought a moment before admitting he didn't know. "I'll tell you sometime," she responded finishing her wine, "sometime soon."

CHAPTER TWENTY-FOUR

Mary Griffin had not succeeded in convincing Mitchell Jenkins that the art school would be better off staying at the old site. It wasn't for lack of trying. Mary was a determined woman in most things, a quality Mitchell liked about as much as he liked thinking about how she would look naked. He spoke of that frequently prior to the museum's physical move and fantasized about the different ways she and David had sex. The two had an odd sort of marriage, one that delighted Mitchell. It was plain to all who knew them that David had taken lovers during their years together. It was an easy thing for him to do as he was seen as a ruggedly handsome, brilliant painter. He was irresistible to many of the women who took his classes, young and old alike, and was quite accomplished in caring for the needs of more than one woman at a time—something Mary reluctantly accepted.

Mitchell found it wonderful that David could enjoy the lushness of Mary's ample body while experimenting with the locals who would generally do whatever he told them. Mitchell often hoped that in her frustration, she would turn to him for comfort, and always went out of his way to be available when he suspected David was in the midst of one of his torrid affairs. Despite her outwardly liberal appearance, Mary wouldn't give in, though she probably enjoyed his attention. It was during these times when he would talk to her of the school's growth and potential. David, for all his liberal tendencies, was much more indecisive. He enjoyed the aura of being a painter more than the process. Though he did create wonderful images when he applied himself, it was often difficult for him to get to the easel. It was far easier to be lost within the cerebral confines of philosophy or poetry than it was for him to unleash his own internal furies. The women were emotional outlets, as they were for Mitchell. His furies did sometimes surface, and a canvas was not always available to be vented upon.

A year before the museum's move downtown, Mitchell advised the Griffins they would need to find another place to live other than in the small cottage on the property. They had been living there while they worked at the art school and knew, sooner or later, they would need to find something else. To his credit, Mitchell had not set a rigid timetable, though he had a time in mind. It was several months before they were told they had to move that Mary and Ted had been talking of the school while David paddled around Ellen Maxwell's lake. It wasn't a surprise to Ted to learn the two women confided in each other. It was on one such occasion that Mary disclosed her need to leave David. She didn't go into detail and could barely face the thought of telling him, but her fear of his emotional shifts was forcing her to act.

On a subsequent Saturday morning, Ted arrived at the museum for some work related to the Logan exhibition. As usual, Mitchell was there too. Ted parked near the Griffins' cottage and as he walked toward the staff door he could hear David's voice through the open windows. It was muffled but loud. Mitchell was working at his desk in his usual Saturday attire. Ted noticed the hole in his right pant leg was getting larger as walked past his door and waved. Before long, Mitchell buzzed Ted's phone and asked him to come by. It was his custom to save all his unimportant mail for the end of the week, passing most of it on to Ted when he had looked through it. Ted was sure he was about to receive this accumulation of exhibition announcements, book flyers, and other mis-cellaneous items, and he was not disappointed.

Mitchell was also in the mood to talk to someone and knew Ted would listen. He began telling of his youth, of a close friend he had and their adventures, when they heard a commotion coming from the floor below. It was one of the Griffin children crying uncontrollably and try-ing to get the staff member at the reception desk to come to the cottage. It was something about her mother. As the crying got louder, Mitchell stopped talking and they walked out to the open stairway. By the blood on the young girl's arm, it was apparent something truly frightening had happened. Running over to the cottage they men found Mary lying on the floor, her head the source of a river of blood. The remains of a large, gilded mirror were in shards around her, a small throw rug rumpled at her feet.

"Mama slipped on the rug and fell into the mirror," the child whim-pered. "I heard her scream from my room." The girl stood close to her mother as Ted quickly found a towel to apply to the cut on her head. "Daddy sent me into the museum for help." She looked around her. "I don't know where he is now."

Had this not been such a brutal scene, it might have been the kind of game David played with his daughter. Even now she started laughing, as if it were something like that, while Mitchell covered Mary in a quilt and carried her to his car.

"I'll take her to the hospital. Call over there and tell them I'm on my way and that Mary is bleeding like a son-of-a-bitch. Then try to find David."

The hospital part was easy, finding David was not. The child was correct about her father not being in the cottage. His car was there, as was the old wreck of a motorcycle he sometimes worked on. Ted walked the grounds and through the art school but could find no trace of David Griffin. Finally, he went back to his office to await an update from Mitchell. Within minutes his phone rang, but it wasn't an outside line.

It was David. "Ted, where is Mary? Is she okay?"

There was a childlike innocence in his voice. Ted would come to learn this was a defense he used against misfortune or pain. "Mitchell's taken her to the hospital. Where the hell are you anyway? What happened over there?"

There was silence on the other end. Ted knew David was in the cottage, the school, or some other office within the building. "David, your daughter told us you were in the house when the accident happened. She said her mama tripped and fell into the mirror. When Mitchell and I got there, she was bleeding pretty badly and was unconscious."

"I was out back when she fell. I didn't know 'till I came in and saw the blood and the broken mirror. I was frightened and called the receptionist, and she told me to call you. I'd better get over to the hospital."

"It's probably best if you stay in the cottage with your daughter until we know what's going on. I expect there will be a lot of tests to run on Mary, so you likely couldn't see her now anyway. I'll let you know something when Mitchell calls."

Mary was released from the hospital the following Monday. She had suffered a mild concussion, had a nasty gash above the bridge of her nose, and was black and blue around her right eye. Mitchell took charge of bringing her back from the hospital since David was in a class. He had gone to see her that Sunday. Mary returned to the cottage but didn't venture out for several days. Most of the staff went by to see her that week, and when not in too much pain, she tried to joke about the accident. David seldom mentioned anything about that Saturday. With their small savings, David purchased a piece of property in the country from Louis Sterling, who was anxious to have someone living on the acreage there and sold the property for much less than it was worth.

When the school space within the new building was finally complete, Mary and a few student volunteers moved as much equipment as they could from the old structure. This was several months after her accident, and the physical scars had healed completely. The surgeon was skillful, hiding his sutures in wrinkle lines above her nose and in her eyebrows. She and the children were still living in the cottage while David built a cabin on the country property. As this progressed, we saw less and less of him. When he did come around to teach an occasional class, he was quieter and more sullen than usual. He talked about the beauty of the country and the blight he felt growing in the city. Mary didn't listen, preferring to lose herself in the challenges of the new school space and expanded curricula.

Ted visited them occasionally on weekends. Alabama stays warm through most of November—a boon for a man working alone, building a shelter. The house, like David's paintings, was a striking creation. Though he never studied architecture, his drawings looked complete, and he received some free help from John Browning. The house would rise from a stone foundation into the treetops. Constructed of wood and glass, it would be largely hidden from the valley below. From the materials stockpiled under heavy plastic sheeting, it seemed to Ted that the structure, when complete, would be solid, but he was at a loss as to how one man could move these materials into place.

"It can all be done in time," David assured Ted. His face was tanned, his beard longer and tangled. "It won't be ready by winter, at least not this one. In the meantime, we'll live at what I'm calling the base camp!"

Ted looked in the direction of his nod at a ten-by-ten plastic tent five hundred feet from his construction site. A small metal building was attached to one end of the plastic, resembling the kind of structure a gardener might use to store tools or seeds. The men walked over to it, where Mary stood looking more tired than the week before.

"I like your decorator," Ted said. It was a bad joke.

David gave him a sideways glance as they walked through the plastic part of the structure. David was adapting quite well to this new life as a member of the Alabama branch of Swiss Family Robinson, but Ted couldn't imagine how it might be come winter. While she joked about it, Mary confessed David couldn't understand why she was not happy living "in the camp," surrounded by nature. He wanted her to leave the school, help build the house, and work in their garden, growing all the food they would need. Her refusal to do so made the weekends when she and their daughters would live with him at the camp increasingly difficult. When they left him on Monday mornings for the relative luxury of the cottage Mitchell still allowed her to use, it was a great relief.

Mitchell was dictating correspondence to Martha Dyer when Mary Griffin knocked lightly on his office door. Martha opened the door and offered her a chair across from Mitchell. He spoke briefly to Martha who then left.

"Thanks for coming by, Mary. How are you feeling? I just wanted to tell you how well I think you're handling the transition between the two locations. Classes seem to be in full swing here and I hope your students like being close to the museum again. It's gratifying for me to have such capable people who can take care of any situation. I want you to know you're more than pulling your weight around here."

Mary sat straight in the chair. She smiled at his comments but was sure he would say something about her still being in the cottage.

"You know Mary, it's really none of my business, but you don't look entirely well. Are you working too hard?"

She smiled and wrapped her arms around herself. She didn't need to be reminded she looked tired, but took his remarks as concern. "No, it's not the school, just a lot of things. David's working on the house, as you know, out in the country, and I help him on weekends. It's hard work." Again, she smiled.

"How's that coming? I know it must be difficult for him up there." He didn't wait for her response. "We're very close to selling the old property. I know this is unpleasant news and comes at a bad time, but we've talked about this before. The money from the sale of the old building and surrounding property is critical to paying our first-year expenses." He paused. "I want to help you and David because I know this isn't easy. Could I find you a small apartment here in town perhaps? I'll even help with the rent. It could be our secret from the rest of the staff. You and the girls could live there during the week, and on the weekends…well on the weekends it could be a place where I could go sometimes to get away. While you're with David, I mean." He sat forward in his chair and leaned toward her. "Don't make any snap decisions. Think it over for a few days, and if there's anything else I can do to help, please let me know. I'm a friend."

Mary rose to leave. She was tired, and a bit confused by Mitchell's offer.

"Mary, why don't you take the rest of the day off? Go to the cottage and rest. I'll have Martha look in on the school from time to time this afternoon."

She smiled again at him as she opened the door.

"There may be a realtor out there with a potential buyer when you arrive. Just tell him you live there."

✳ ✳ ✳

Stephen Parker was replaced with two people, a fact that brought him endless joy it was said by those who received occasional letters from him. Mitchell had considered what adjustments should be made within Multimedia, finally deciding the position was too much for one person to handle. He convinced a friend who had moved from Meriden several years before to return for the position of graphic designer. He appeared for work one Monday morning in July quite unannounced, with two cameras around his neck, colored pencils, and other drawing supplies under each arm. He was ushered into Ted's office as Jenkins was out of the building negotiating the sale of the old property.

"Hi there," he said walking in. "They tell me you're in charge."

Martha Dyer was close on his heels, holding a sheath of forms for new employees and directing him to complete them at the empty desk in Ted's office. She then left abruptly.

He bent low over the desk, talking in almost a whisper, as one conspirator to another. "Who was that masked woman?"

"That was Martha Dyer, Mitchell's administrative assistant. Very efficient as you can see. I'm Ted Martin, curator and supposedly assistant director—though don't tell Martha. Mitchell's not here. Was he expecting you?"

"Some things never change. I'm Ray Malone. I'm sure Mitchell hasn't told you anything. I'm starting here today as a graphic designer."

Ray stood up and extended his hand. He wore jeans and an open-necked work shirt, both neatly pressed yet comfortable looking. He was bearded and wore his long hair in a ponytail down his back.

"I was working for Alabama National Bank in Birmingham before coming back down here. Used to work on projects with Mitchell. Glad to be here, the bank thing was a real zoo. You wouldn't believe the things that went on there!" He suddenly looked at the open doorway. "Is she going to come back soon? Am I being timed on finishing these?" He held up the forms.

"Not sure," Ted replied honestly, "but I think you're safe. We've gotten very bureaucratic around here. There are forms for all occasions now. Employment forms seem to be the most common and time-consuming. Be assured, they'll find their way to a folder baring your name, locked away in Martha's office. She keeps everything."

Ted had not meant to talk so much or so honestly with a stranger, but Ray was easy to talk to. Besides, he had started it with the Lone Ranger reference. Ted's phone buzzed—it was Martha.

"Well," Ray said after a few minutes, "I finished them. I left out the part asking how many times a week I have sex and with whom. I'm recently divorced and presume they want this information only if you circle the 'M' for 'marital status.' I'd circle 'FA' if they had it, but they don't. Has Mitchell returned yet? Or can you show me where to put all this stuff? My car is full of things too."

"He's back and wants to see you in his office at the end of the hall. Martha says she'll pick up the forms in there."

The men rose and went for the door. Ray thanked Ted and started to leave.

"Ray," Ted said, feeling embarrassed and out of the social loop. "What is 'FA'?"

"Oh, you know, 'fucking around.'"

Ted smiled and waved as the newest hire knocked on Mitchell's door.

✽ ✽ ✽

For the other half of the media position, Mitchell interviewed and hired a man named Peter Rutledge. The two new hires were like night and day, and Ted wondered if Mitchell knew what he was doing, but he wasn't asked. In fact, Mitchell had made some adjustments to the job description. Rutledge, while able to work with the television and programming equipment Stephen had assembled, would also be handling the museum's public relations duties, a job handled initially by Mitchell himself and most recently by Ellen Maxwell.

"I'm certainly not dissatisfied with the way Ellen has handled PR these last couple years," he explained to Ted when introducing Peter. "However, I think we're reaching a point when that job will be too much for her with everything else she's doing. Peter's been active in that area for some time and will work closely with me and Ellen as he learns our procedures."

Peter Rutledge was tall with a boyish handsomeness. Clean shaven, trimmed hair, deep voiced, crisply dressed in a pin-striped suit, and polite to a fault. Recently graduated from the University of Georgia, he had been recruited by Mitchell through a college art association flier. Rutledge enjoyed the same courting Ted had: lunch at Mitchell's club, interviews with a few members of the commission, and finally informal talks with Ellen, who found his scholarly manner refreshing.

Ellen was working hard to cultivate his interests by making him feel at home in the museum environment. Ted was cautious with most new people he'd meet. Acting like a seasoned news correspondent, Peter asked Ellen for brief descriptions of the people on staff. Ted sat quietly on Ellen's office couch, letting her handle the questions from the new guy. As she had with me, Ellen listed the current cast of characters.

"Mitchell Jenkins is brilliant when he wants to be. I'm sure you'll make your own judgements about him. He tends to think liberally about most social issues, but is careful what he says to whom. And Theodore over there, well, we just don't know about him yet. He's a Yankee you know," she said, grinning.

It was two weeks before Peter was again in Meriden, this time with his young wife, Marsha. They had been married the Christmas before. He seemed devoted to her, setting framed pictures of them around his half of the office. He and Ray shared the space Stephen had had to himself. It was certainly large enough for two people, but it would prove confining for these two. Jenkins had not bothered to introduce them when Peter interviewed, and Malone had become accustomed to having the office the way he wanted it, which generally meant things were everywhere. Their first week together was very productive as they worked to sort through the things Stephen had left behind. Mitchell spent quite a bit of time with Peter, often having extended meetings in his office without Martha present. Peter worked late in the afternoons, often returning after dark and usually seeing Jenkins then too.

Their fidelity caused Ellen to ask Ted, "How's it feel to be replaced?"

Ted hadn't really stopped to think about it, but Mitchell was spending the time he used to spend with him with Peter instead. He didn't know whether to be jealous or relieved, thinking maybe he had gotten to a level of self-reliance in Mitchell's eyes. *I wonder if I'll get better marks in next year's performance review!*

Between the two of them, Malone and Rutledge began bringing Multimedia back to life, though not with Parker's artistry. To Ted's amazement, neither of them had any first-hand experience with the equipment they were now being asked to operate in the production of a full schedule of programming. It wasn't long though before familiar rumbles were being heard by Mitchell, as both men were having problems communicating with Ellen.

This time," Jenkins said to Ted one afternoon, "she's not going to get off so lightly."

It seemed unlikely to Ted that within two months, Peter especially could be having trouble working with Ellen. She was opinionated and often rewrote her own program scripts, but he simply hadn't been on board long enough to feel constrained. He would grumble, using the same words Stephen had to describe the ways she would slow production on anything he and Malone began. Ted wondered if Stephen had left tape recordings of his run-ins with her for future employees—it would have been like him! Either Ellen was what the three of them said, or someone was working against her.

Mitchell was quick to confront her with the accusations. After he and Peter concluded one of their long afternoon sessions, Peter finally emerged from the office, shutting the door behind him. He looked in the direction of Ellen's office, started for it, then changed direction, returning to Multimedia. Mitchell buzzed Martha Dyer, who quickly entered his office holding a folder. He took it from her and emptied it carefully on his desk. He went through its contents rapidly, as if looking for a specific document. Once he found it, he dictated something to Martha, returned the contents to the folder, handed it back to her, then left for Ellen's office.

✵ ✵ ✵

Martha had begun her own undeclared war with Peter Rutledge by the time he had been at the museum for six months. She wasn't happy with the time Mitchell spent with him or with the fact their meetings, more often than not, excluded her. She hid these feelings though—telling Mitchell she found him pompous and a bore, and complaining to Ted about how he would act important and leer at her when Jenkins asked her to leave a meeting. In this personality dispute, as in most, Ted found himself in the middle. Martha treated him as an equal, though he was never quite sure what she might tell Mitchell about him. On Peter Rutledge though, she was very straightforward. As her impatience with him grew, Ted began to wonder if Mitchell was purposely pitting them against each other, as he was sure Mitchell was doing with Peter and Ellen.

Ellen was in tears when Mitchell finished with her that afternoon. "He accused me of deliberately sabotaging Peter, the way I'd done, he said, with Stephen. He said my job was on the line when Stephen left, and now that I was causing trouble for Peter, he didn't know if he could keep me on much longer. Ted, I don't know what he's talking about."

Again, Ted was in the middle. Ordinarily he would have defended Mitchell, but he knew both Ellen and Stephen. The areas of gray in their working relationship far outweighed what appeared black and white on the surface.

✷ ✷ ✷

Morgan James called Ellen to say she had just returned from two months in Spain and asked if could she come by to see everyone. Morgan, Ellen, and Mary Griffin had become like the three musketeers. That her mother was a commissioner and her father the major benefactor behind the museum's construction mattered only peripherally to Morgan; however she was very aware of their power and importance to Mitchell. In her adolescence, Taylor had made provisions for Morgan's future with trusts and other hidden pockets of wealth. When she came of age, she would be a wealthy woman from these sources, quite apart from the bulk of the growing family fortune. Though Ted had not known any heiresses, Morgan seemed better adjusted than most. Her visits were always a welcome diversion.

Mitchell met her at his office door with his arms wide open. "Morgan! Welcome home! I was going to meet your flight with a full brass band, but your mother wouldn't allow it. She said you'd get right back on the plane."

In the new museum's first year, Mitchell began easing Taylor James out of his laboratory more often for exhibition openings, lectures, and other social occasions, and he was starting to enjoy himself at these events. Laura was the perfect commissioner from Mitchell's perspective, relying completely on his judgements in any matter. He never said anything to Ted about his increasing role in the James family, though his curiosity was always high. Taylor's attention to Ellen had increased to an embarrassing point for her and the staff members who knew about his interest in her. He was shockingly open, only half-jokingly inviting her to accompany him to Europe in front of his wife, Mitchell, or anyone else who happened to be within earshot.

Laura tolerated his behavior as she did everything else in their life, concerning herself with the wellbeing of her daughter. "Morgan" had been Laura's family's name, and for her, their daughter represented a link between past and future. The trip to Spain was Morgan's first solo expedition to the old country and a graduation gift from her mother. She had finished at Briarcliff the past spring and was happy for the getaway. She had traveled through Europe with her family many times before and knew how to get around. The best way, of course, was with plenty of money, and she traveled first class all the way.

After talking briefly with Mitchell and complimenting Ted on a recently opened exhibition, Morgan made her way to Ellen. Their laughter was uproarious and easily heard; they were like sisters swapping stories. Mitchell must have heard the laughter too, because he shut his office door.

"This trip was far better than any I've had before, I felt so free and grown up. Really Ellen, you should go over there. It would be good for you to get away." The two had been talking for some time when Morgan confided the secret she had only told her mother. "I met a man in Spain! The most wonderful, kind man. We were introduced at a party. We sort of fell in together, not intending to make anything of it. He was on vacation from the military—he's a captain. He's attached to the personal guard of the prince and is himself titled, and very handsome."

She saw Ellen's concerned expression. She knew Morgan had limited experience with men and distrusted the tall, dark, handsome kind.

"I know what you're thinking. Believe me, I know better than most young women of wealth. This is different though, I know it." She paused. "I'm going back to Spain next month to see Estephen. He's invited me to a royal ball given each year by Prince Carlos. I'll be staying with friends of our family. Strictly honorable intentions—no fooling around!"

Ellen laughed and asked more questions about this Spanish Stephen. Morgan's mother expected sooner or later a situation like this might arise and had prepared herself for it. She advised her daughter not to say any-thing to her father yet and that she would figure out a way for Morgan to get back to Spain.

"Perhaps you could come with me, Ellen. You'd love Spain in the early fall."

It was out of the question for Ellen Maxwell, but a pleasant enough thought. She was sure Taylor would happily pay her way, but was also sure from his previous comments that he would find an excuse to join them there. It was not the kind of situation she was eager to be involved in and asked Morgan, in the most diplomatic way, not to mention the idea to her father.

A letter from Abram Rubin arrived in the morning's mail. Martha received it with other pieces for Mitchell, as was her practice. She would open all of them except those marked PERSONAL, delivering them to him by mid-morning. She also read the letters, sorting them in order of impor-tance, at least as she saw them. Rubin's letter was marked PERSONAL, which annoyed her. Since she typed all Mitchell's letters, she knew what his responses were. It galled her to think the doctor didn't recognize this. She placed his unopened envelope on top of the stack on the right side of Mitchell's desk. He was on the first floor for another "important meeting with Peter." It was after five before Mitchell got around to his mail. He noticed Rubin's letter, but didn't open it, preferring to put it off as long as possible.

He had been able to secure a Britian painting for Rubin a year earlier. At the time it had been an awkward, but ultimately easy thing to do. The painting was a nicely sized oil and mixed media Britian had completed and held out from what was sent to Marelli. He did this from time to time, either wanting the painting for himself or a private sale. Mitchell negotiated for the painting with Britian rather than his dealer after flying to New York. When they came to an agreement on price, he phoned Rubin with the good news and packed the painting himself, sending it out directly from the studio.

Rubin was as delighted with the work when it arrived as he had been with the news of the purchase when Mitchell had called. Britian refused to talk to Rubin, out of a need to feel mysterious more than anything else, and Mitchell said he wasn't in the studio. Britian listened to the conversation on another phone and was delighted with himself when the prank was over. Though Rubin promised the money for the painting would be sent upon its receipt, Britian had to phone twice to ask about the check's arrival, putting Mitchell in an awkward position, a place he didn't enjoy. The money was finally paid a full month later. Rubin explained it had been tied up in a special account and couldn't be released as early as he thought. There were no hard feelings, but Mitchell wasn't anxious to hear from the doctor-turned-art-collector. He reached across his desk for the pale blue envelope, tearing it open with his finger.

Dear Mitchell,

How are things in the South? I know Maureen's
more beautiful by the day; sure would like to show her

around L.A. for a week or two—alone. California itself is beginning to tire me, having problems out here I can't go into now. If anything serious comes of them, might have to get out quick, before legal stuff gets going. It's that bad.

Have had to do strange things for money, government has most of it, particularly out here where socialized medicine is just around the corner. Don't wish to bore you—have many other things to say...

The letter went on to talk about the new galleries springing up on the West Coast and how Rubin had been introduced to many of the younger artists working between Los Angeles and San Francisco. Mitchell kept all correspondence from Rubin in a folder marked "Donors." It, along with others, had been put in Ted's custody. He kept a list of donated works as well as all correspondence from the donors. It was an idea Mitchell got from an article in *Smithsonian Magazine* and had Martha Dyer send Ted a memo about. A copy of Jenkins' response to Rubin was also included in the file. It said little. The two were essentially pen pals writing about each other's fantasies—great scholarly stuff for posterity.

✵ ✵ ✵

"Mitchell?" Martha Dyer called into his office on the intercom. "It's Peter Rutledge on line three, says he must speak with you about an urgent personal matter."

Mitchell was meeting with Ellen and Ted about a video he intended to have made in and around Beau Britian's New York studio. He was working on something else he wouldn't speak about, but Ted could tell he had something up his sleeve. Ellen was asked to research information on Britian while he wrote a script outline. Ted was there out of professional courtesy and because Mitchell knew he would ultimately need his help. He picked up the call without dismissing his visitors.

"Peter, what's happening, man? Are you well?"

Peter's voice was but a whisper on the phone from his apartment across town. It was eleven in the morning and he hadn't called earlier about his absence. Mitchell had asked Martha to telephone him since he was to be in the meeting, but his line was always busy.

"Mitchell, my life has fallen apart. I don't know what to do or where to turn. Its Marsha, she's left me." His office desk was covered with photographs of the two of them. Pictures of them walking hand in hand, pictures in class, in the Georgia cafeteria, all taken by the PR photographer at the university for use in recruitment publications. "She left about an hour ago. This morning she wouldn't talk to me, then said she was leaving, packed a few things, and drove off in her car. I don't know where she's gone or why." His voice wavered as he spoke.

Jenkins looked angrily at Ellen. "Would you both excuse me while I take this call?"

They had no idea what the problem was as Jenkins had said nothing so far in the conversation, but they left him alone.

"Peter, listen to me, man. I know this has hurt you, but you can't trust women. It's the only constant there is besides death and taxes. She'll be back, they never stay away long. If you want my advice, throw her out! If there's another man, don't even talk to her. Do you want me to come over? Or better yet, get yourself out of there, go for a walk or come into work. That'll really throw her if you're not there when she comes back."

There was no response from the other end of the line. Mitchell could hear music in the background.

"Peter, are you still there?"

"Sure. That's her favorite album playing. I've called her parents in Florida, they can't believe it. I just don't think I can come in today, though. Can't face all those photos on my desk and the memories."

"It's OK Peter. Take a day or two, but I think working will help you more than anything else. I've mentioned to you about Maureen and me. Working has helped me through similar situations, when she's gone crazy. I know what I'm talking about!"

"Sure, thanks. I'll be in tomorrow. Thanks for understanding and the advice."

The phone went dead. Jenkins returned his receiver and as he did, Martha Dyer returned hers. Mitchell postponed his prior meeting until further notice, telling Ellen and Ted about his conversation with Peter. They were both shocked by the news. Marsha didn't come around the museum much, and when she did Peter was not with her. She was a slightly built woman whose clothing always looked a size too large. She didn't seem to be a good match for Peter, not clean-cut and squeaky-clean, though pretty in a natural way. She didn't look much like the photographs Peter kept in his office, and Ted wondered what had caused the change.

Peter was at work the following day, looking drawn and as if he had been up all night. He and Mitchell talked most of the morning. Afterwards he went from Ted's office to Ellen's, telling them all that had happened as best he could understand it. He said she had called him the day before. He said her voice had changed from the anger of the morning to indifference, and that she spoke to him in an even fashion with no emotion. She would not be back, that much she had said with purpose. His ways were killing her, and she could no longer live with someone like him. The things she left behind she no longer wanted. In her new life, she could live simpler and happier. She didn't want him to try to find her, though she would still live in Meriden for a while with a friend and would probably see him occasionally about town. She wanted an immediate divorce. Whether losing Marsha was the cause or not, this development in Peter's life became the first of a series of misfortunes that occurred to him during the next year and a half. Ted and Ellen were kept well-informed of his problems by Peter himself, who seemed every week to have something new interfering with his happiness. At one point he appeared to be almost thriving on the misery that followed him like a shadow.

Marsha, it turned out, had left Peter for a rock musician in town who toured with his band through the Southeast. She would soon join them, living in their bus on their concert circuit. Peter divorced her as quickly as the law allowed, still heartsick that she could change so rapidly from the girl he had met in Athens. Jenkins found it unthinkable that a woman should leave her husband, particularly one who had spent as much time thinking of her as Peter had. He was sure that she had been brainwashed by the musician or given drugs that altered her behavior. He would retrace with Rutledge the facts of their short marriage to see if there were clues to what had happened. He was obsessed. As time passed though, Marsha was forgotten, and Rutledge concentrated on coping with the other maladies of his life.

The museum's staff was rapidly becoming a singles club, between Ellen, Ray, and Martha, who were already divorced, Mary Griffin, who wanted to be, and Peter. This did not escape the attention of Mitchell Jenkins who envied them all, except perhaps for Maxwell, and was quick to tell both Rutledge and Malone how lucky they were. He had not altered his own pattern of questionable behavior with women other than Maureen. He had taken a small apartment not far from the museum in a repurposed warehouse building. He said nothing to anyone about it. Martha Dyer was the first to mention the issue to Ted and had even followed him one afternoon to locate it. Though she said she'd not found it, Ted was sure she had a good idea of its location. It would be the type of information he would want discreetly mentioned, hoping it would get back to Maureen. Ted couldn't help but remember her remarks to him at Bishop's retirement gala. Mitchell was perhaps closer than he realized to obtaining his freedom.

Mitchell was now anxious to begin working on the Britian program. Taylor James had promised to finance the effort detailing the life and history of this artist. Mitchell and Martha Dyer had already made a trip to New York to make arrangements. It was the first time he had traveled with a woman from his staff, causing a few eyebrows to be raised. Martha had not changed her mind about her relationship with Jenkins, Ted was sure of it. It would have been too easy for him, had she given in. Once he had her sexually, whatever power or control she had over him would be gone.

When they returned, the logistics of the production had been made with Britian. Martha had kept scrupulous notes as Jenkins and Britian discussed the artist's early years in Alabama. She also devised new procedures for increased efficiency among our small secretarial staff. At the first staff meeting after their return, it was revealed Martha was now a sort of chief of staff for this group, no matter who they worked for. In addition, Martha would now schedule all extra duty hours that might be required of these "support" employees who again, would answer to her directly and not to the people for whom they worked. She would handle all questions and disputes. After that announcement, Jenkins read a list of general procedures, most of which were already being followed, designed to add to Martha's presumed importance.

Mitchell and James discussed the Britian project during the dinner party hosted for Morgan on her return from Spain. The "small dinner party" Laura had alluded to was as grand as the line of cars parked bumper-to-bumper around their property indicated. Mitchell and Maureen arrived slightly later than the stated time for cocktails, a custom he adapted from August Bishop. While Bishop liked to make an entrance, Jenkins arrived fashionably late because he didn't like to stand around waiting for something to begin.

Maureen had been noticeably withdrawn toward him of late. He couldn't remember when he first noticed it, but he liked the change. This night, as with many others when they were out socially, he would leave her sitting on a couch or chair someplace with a scotch and soda while he worked the crowd, moving the conversation inevitably around to the museum. He would see her once, perhaps twice during the evening. Maureen would be social, talking with people she knew.

Tonight, he begrudgingly thought, she looked particularly lovely and wondered how many men in the room had the same kind of licentious thoughts about her as he had for other women. He wanted to tell them she was frigid but enjoyed watching them court her and her feeling of discomfort. They had not had sex since returning from Bishop's retirement party. Martha had made reservations for that night in one of the large hotels in the city. He had expected Maureen to be very sensual that night and planned to have her more than once, but somehow they managed to fight on the way to the hotel and he took a second room, finding someone to share it with after a couple drinks in the bar. It was grounds for divorce in Alabama, which would be awkward right now even if other people in the social spotlight were getting them. He thought about sending her to sex therapy classes if she didn't change her attitude soon and remember why "women were put on Earth."

Taylor James was in the living room talking to Rudolph Bates and Beth Neil. Laura had invited her fellow commissioners, most of whom were scattered throughout the house talking, drinking, or listening to Morgan play the piano in the den. Beth Neil was the "quiet" commissioner, the one who had been appointed because Jenkins needed another woman. She was a personal friend of Laura's and had been suggested to him by her. Beth and her retired husband lived quietly in a nice neighborhood. They were not active socially but were well educated and interested in cultural activities in general. Beth made an excellent commissioner as far as Jenkins was concerned, always siding with the majority on votes and accepting his authority as they all did. Jenkins didn't find the three of them talking together particularly troublesome, but he decided to make it a foursome since he could never count on what James might be saying at any given time.

"...and so, I told George Patrick I'd be willing to serve on their board but knew very little about museums, only about spending money on them!" Bates and Neil laughed politely. James never let anyone forget about the power of his money. "Anyway, we're to meet in Birmingham in a week or so to see what kind of mess they're in and if it can be straightened out. Hello, Mitchell, we've just been talking about this museum complex thing. Mitchell and I have already talked briefly about the concept. In fact, they even offered Mitchell the job as its director, which he turned down. I can't decide if that's a mistake or not. What I haven't told you yet," he turned to face Jenkins, "is that this fellow Patrick called me this afternoon and asked me to serve on their board. It's a state thing, so I can't give them any money, but they think I know about museums. I told them yes but that I'll need to get advice from you. What do you think?"

This was just the kind of proof Jenkins needed to restore confidence in himself and justify the time he had spent with James since he offered to pay for a new museum. *Having him on that board will be a perfect way for me to know what is going on there.*

"Congratulations Taylor, yours is the kind of leadership they'll need in the months ahead. We can talk about it anytime."

Jenkins talked on for several minutes about the state's concept and the view he and other museum directors around the state had about it. His audience of three listened intently. Laura James watched the scene from across the room, remembering other times when Mitchell Jenkins had been in their home, advising on one thing or another. She admired the way he seemed to know about the events and people in the art world that was becoming an ever-increasing part of their lives. He was the kind of man she would have wanted for Morgan and wondered to herself about the Spaniard her daughter had met.Morgan was still playing selections on the piano, radiating happiness from her return to Meriden, which was quite becoming. She had talked with her mother about this man, Estephen, with Taylor safely off in his lab. Laura recognized the excitement in her daughter's voice and face, something she had never known herself. Estephen Coton was a professional soldier. Because of his family name and position in the still courtly society of that country, he had been assigned to a special detail to guard the Prince.

The Coton family could trace its lineage back hundreds of years, its best-known member being a painter of dark still lifes in the seventeenth century. Estephen had shown Morgan several paintings by his ancestor during their month together. She would certainly be allowed to return to Spain and to this young man who'd caught her fancy. Laura knew that to deny her would cause more problems with their daughter than if she went and returned pregnant. Morgan was strong-willed and had inherited her father's temper along with the prospect of his money. Laura and her daughter had not often had differences, something she attributed to her solid management and skillful negotiating techniques. She would have preferred her daughter's first lover to be an American, only because they were less exotic. It would be easier for her to see through someone who did not wear a military uniform or spoke English through a beautifully charming accent. Morgan had never been interested in the local boys, but surely there were men in New York or Boston she might find appealing. The Atlantic Ocean would be a great barrier!

Morgan expected her parents to be skeptical of any man she found attractive, foreign or not. She did not herself know what would become of the relationship but had decided to return to Spain and the invitation in Madrid. Estephen was quiet, polished in a traditional sort of way and very interested in his family, who were now among what was left of the Spanish aristocracy. He enjoyed polo and bull fighting, but Morgan had declined his offer to take her to the latter. He was five years older, never married, and educated throughout Europe. He was a great favorite of her hosts in Spain, who had relayed all his particulars to her following their meeting. Morgan knew Maria was trying to match-make and had permitted it, she supposed, because of the romance of the country. Had her mother tried something like that, she would have rebelled immediately.

Mitchell was in deep conversation with James on the cement terrace by the swimming pool. There they took seats in the cushioned metal chairs facing the pool and the Meriden skyline in the distance. Jenkins and James were still talking about art and museums, with James mostly listening and interjecting opinions about his views of the national economy and how it would affect arts organizations in the future. These chilling reports Jenkins compared in his mind to those of other financial advisors or friends. While James had been a successful businessman and entrepreneur, he had taken some losses due to inconclusive advice, particularly in European ventures. Taylor knew he only knew one thing well but could not help getting involved in other projects that were of interest. Art currently interested him as he reached an age when business was becoming less fun. He was looking for something to move into that would provide him the kind of prestige he required from life as well as satisfaction. He was convinced Mitchell Jenkins was the person who could introduce him to this world.

"This movie you want to make, Mitchell, could it be circulated commercially?"

Jenkins was sure it could but was not aware of the hows of the distribution business. "Artist films are always on educational television, there is a whole class of people out there watching that kind of thing, the people Agnew hated, but they are the ones in control of the country."

"It could be something that this production unit you're always talking to me about could do and maybe make some income?" He had hit on just the approach Jenkins had himself used with Stephen Parker, then with Ray Malone and Peter Rutledge. It was the reason Parker had stayed on as long as he did. Jenkins had not been able to pull it off though until now. He had not had a plan as grand as the one James might be proposing and chided himself for thinking so small. His idea had been to gather a library of these video programs to rent to other museums for a small fee, not to make money but to bring credit to his museum. They talked about the Britian project's projected costs. James was listening, but not as attentively as before. Jenkins had seen this happen on other occasions and knew when to stop and let him alone. He decided to do so now, asking if he would like to return to the party. The older man seemed to awaken from the thoughts he was having, hearing Jenkins' question.

"Wait Mitchell, there's something I need to tell someone else to get another reaction. It's about Morgan."

Jenkins sat back in his chair wondering what he was about to hear about Taylor's only child. She looked and acted fine.

"Morgan's met some son-of-a-bitch in Spain and has fallen for him. Or at least that's the story I got from Henry Tillman, an associate of mine who lives in Madrid." James had twisted his face at the telling of the story, not out of anger, but out of fear. "It seems Tillman and his wife gave a party while Morgan was staying with them. They are very socially connected and invited their usual group of people for drinks. Among them was this young man, a military officer whose family has land and a title. He and Morgan met and hit it off, then spent a good deal of time together while she was there. Don't say anything to Laura or Morgan. They haven't said a word of this to me and are sure I don't know a thing." He smiled at this. "You'd think they'd know they can't fool me!"

Jenkins was amused by the story. He'd have never guessed James was the fatherly type. There was a difference though—this wasn't an ordinary young woman experiencing the world, but one who was wealthy now and would be even more so when her parents were gone.

"Morgan's never really had the chance to meet many men because of the school's she attended and because we've never given her much freedom. She's easy prey for any man, let alone one from "over there" who might want to cash in on a wealthy American. Tillman tells me this guy has invited her to return to Spain next month for some sort of royal function. He says she's accepted. I can't stand in her way; she's got money and is too much like me. She'd go tomorrow if I said anything negative!"

Again, James seemed to slip away into his thoughts, and Jenkins could only assume he was still thinking about his daughter. Jenkins was also silent since he really didn't know what to say.

"Come on Mitchell, let's join the party. Now remember, not a word to Morgan or her mother. I'm sure they will be coming to talk to me soon."

CHAPTER TWENTY-FIVE

Plans for the film production were set. With the help of Ellen Maxwell, Jenkins prepared an outline for a storyboard to follow and selected appropriate locations for filming. Babs Horowitz, who still maintained Jenkins had raped her, was to appear in the production, as was Herschel Marelli, Colin, and several other friends of Beau's who he had promised parts in the film. Jenkins tried to explain to him the difference between "film" and "video" but could not quite make him understand. Film seemed to be used any time a camera of any type was talked about.

Ray Malone and Ted were to drive the museum's van to the city loaded with television gear, cameras, and paintings Ted was returning to lenders from a recent exhibition en route. They were leaving a full four days before being due in New York because of the deliveries, but it was the only way to return works on a non-existent budget for the exhibition Jenkins had organized. Taylor James and Jenkins were to fly up at week's end, when filming would begin. James had asked to be present at the project's beginning, wanting to meet Britian and Babs Horowitz, who he understood from Jenkins might be a great piece of ass. Most of the shooting was to be done over that first weekend when Britian could best spare the time. Then James and Jenkins were to go on to Boston for a museum association conference before returning to Meriden late the following week.

Ray didn't want to go. New York wasn't his favorite place, but Rutledge was having medical issues and his doctor advised against making the trip. "Probably pregnant," Malone jokingly concluded. For Ted, the trip would be an opportunity to see some big museum exhibitions and galleries and gather a few paintings that were being given to the Meriden Museum by artist friends of Britian. These works were scattered throughout the city, so they would be spending quite a bit of time collecting them, with the occasional assistance of Jenkins and Colin Johnson.

The weather, as they moved north, had become unexpectedly cold, causing Malone to complain more than he already was. The first deliveries didn't begin until Philadelphia, three days into the trip during a light blizzard. Ted had not been back to this city since leaving graduate school. He also had never driven a van in the snow before, though he assumed he had more practice at winter driving than Ray, who was raised in Mississippi. He had carried on so much that Ted couldn't tell when he was making jokes or when he was serious. What was serious was the pistol Malone had moved from his suitcase to his briefcase. He had shown it to Ted in Raleigh, North Carolina, and it was the biggest handgun Ted had ever seen.

"There ain't no fuckin' New York screamer gonna mess with this Southern boy."

Ted had ducked as he waved it around the room. It was a 357 western-style revolver with an eight-inch barrel, single action. A cowboy's gun.

"Ray, there's probably not going to be an occasion for you to use that thing just because we're leaving the South!"

"Hell, I carry this in my glove box all the time. You Yankees lead lives that are too sheltered. There's crime everywhere." He was not joking about that.

As they approached Philadelphia, Ted noticed Ray's anxiety level jump. He had an aversion to big cities in general. They spent the better part of that day returning paintings, leaving them with some owners who were happy to have them returned and some who appeared not to care at all. Ray also had a problem with value systems and the collectors who seemed uninterested.

One of the collectors invited them to spend one night in her home. She had been kind enough to extend a personal invitation before they left Meriden. The home was in the country, north of the city of "Brotherly Love" and on the way to New York. The blizzards of the morning and afternoon diminished by four thirty as Ted rolled the van to a stop at a phone booth on the corner of Jones and Third Street in Lambertville, Pa. Finding the number of their host, he called for directions.

The paintings they were returning were done by a Philadelphia-area artist who had come to the attention of the deputy director of the National Endowment for the Arts. He had convinced Mitchell he should organize a major exhibition of the man's work and would see that endowment funding would be made available. Mitchell had called Ted into his office to show him slides of the paintings that had been sent. They were bold, colorful, full-sized portraits of people the artist knew—all people of color with equally colorful backgrounds. The people they had met so far returning paintings were predominately Black young professionals who related to the paintings in a visceral way. So, driving into what looked to be a mostly white community in Northeastern Pennsylvania, Ted was curious to know who among these affluent families would own a large painting of a Black man dressed in a full-length fur coat over a pinstriped, three-piece blue suit.

Ms. Marci Hopkins was pleased to hear the two were so close to her home and were having a successful trip. By her voice there was no way to gauge her age or anything else about her. Instead of directing them—"It's really too difficult for you boys to find it without being led"—she sent them to a nearby Holiday Inn, where they were instructed to find the bar, have drinks on her, and await her arrival.

It was the best news Malone had had all day, and they were soon ensconced on wooden deck chairs in an enclosed bar by an indoor pool, watching bikini-clad young women from a nearby girl's college cavort in the clear water. Ray treated his first imported bottle of beer as if it were water and he had just come out of the Sahara Desert instead of thirty-three-degree weather. He was into his second before asking one of the women why they were there (ladies' night at the bar), and into his third before Ms. Hopkins arrived. When she did, they found her to be a very bubbly white woman who looked as if she had just come from the sportswear department of Lord and Taylor. Ted could not determine her age, though he guessed somewhere under forty-five. She joined the men for a drink before heading to her home in the rolling hills at dusk.

They followed her taillights for twenty minutes through narrow roads and over wooden bridges as if they were going around in circles, though neither Ray nor Ted could remember seeing anything more than once. Finally, they arrived at a large home constructed of rock and glass perched on the top of a hill, looking out over farms resting now in winter. The home was newly built, the lawn still showing tire marks from trucks and some construction debris.

Ms. Hopkins walked out to the van. "I told you it was hard to find. my husband Cole and I moved in three weeks ago. You gentlemen work at an art museum—isn't this place a work of art?" She waved her arm toward the house. It was indeed sculptural, as it sat alone against the darkening sky.

Ray and Ted pulled the large painting from the van's cargo area, taking it to the front door against a stiff wind. On the inside, the house displayed a myriad of balconies, each overlooking a central great room below. It was one of the most beautiful homes Ted had ever been in. Both he and Ray stood for several moments trying to take it all in.

"I once had an art gallery myself," Marci told them as she pointed to where the painting was to be installed. "I kept it open up until about a year ago. Now I work out of the house to connect a collector with something. I don't sell publicly. With Cole's practice expanding, it gives me something to do."

Cole was a doctor, a criminal psychiatrist it turned out, who not only had a private practice in Philadelphia but worked on a retainer for the state. They had been married for fifteen years and had no children. Ray and Ted spent a very enjoyable night in their home, eating and drinking extremely well, talking about the new Meriden Museum as if it were the Metropolitan, and retiring late to private guestrooms before awakening to brisk sunshine the following morning.

When they arrived in New York City, they parked the van in the first lot that would accommodate it in the lunchtime scramble. They had to pay double as the van was wider than most cars and took up two spaces. Then they taxied, carrying as much luggage and equipment as they could to James' Park Avenue apartment. The doorman was not impressed, but the men had a written note introducing them and got in. Taylor and Jenkins would arrive on a night flight from Meriden, so the men had the remainder of the day to do as they pleased.

Jenkins and James arrived by nine fifteen. It was the first time Ted had ever been in close contact with "Uncle Money," as Malone called James. Mitchell wanted to hear about the trip and where they had put the van. The next day they were to move the rest of the equipment to Britian's studio to begin shooting. Mitchell was filled with ideas that night, some of which he shared with Ray and Ted after James retired to the apartment's only bedroom. Ray and Jenkins slept on the pull-out bed, Ted on its cushions on the floor. They had tossed coins to decide, and Mitchell and Ray had lost.

The following day was full of activity. Mitchell was playing director, Ray was the cameraman, and Ted scurried around to set the areas of shooting. Taylor was seated in a corner talking with Babs Horowitz. Mitchell relayed his earlier misadventures with Horowitz in Meriden.

"Babs had a bit of trouble relating to the South when she was down some years ago, but that has all changed. She's working on a new book and wants it published worldwide by someone other than Harry Abrams.

They had a falling-out, I guess. It happens with these people —though I gather she's really pissed."

Ray worked like a demon that day and was as intrigued about being in the studio of a world-famous artist as Ted had been. Ray was the only one with any real experience with filmmaking and most of that had been gained since coming to the museum. Jenkins was following the story he had outlined, while showing off for James, who had agreed to help with this project's distribution and enlarging the Multimedia equipment budget over the following year. Ray was more serious about art and the art world than he'd ever let on. Jenkins gave him the same studio tour that had left Ted starry-eyed. They left the studio that night in a taxi, Jenkins bowing to Ted's wish not to get mugged in the subway. As they entered the cab, Ray remembered he had left a piece of equipment running and asked to borrow Jenkin's key to get back in the studio. As they waited for him to return, Mitchell turned to Ted quite unexpectedly and said, "Ray Malone will always have a job at the museum as long as I'm director!"

It was a proclamation Ted would remember. He and Ray returned to Meriden late the following week, having run what seemed like miles of video tape. Ray's highly prudent philosophy was "Better to have too much than too little. You can always cut!"

Ray and Ted left at six o'clock Thursday morning after taxiing from James' apartment back down to Britian's studio and the service station next door, where they had parked the van. Again, the van was fully loaded with television equipment, luggage, gifted artwork, and a package or two of mementos Ray had collected. The station's owner, a fellow named Alex, and his crew had not yet arrived, though they expected them at any moment. Pulling the van up to one of the pumps in anticipation of their arrival, Ted could feel, then see, two distinct pairs of eyes watching their every move. While the men understood the reason for their presence, the fact that two large dogs thought of them as potential breakfast was unnerving. Ted noticed Ray fiddling with something under his coat for several seconds before realizing it was his gun that he must have tucked under his belt. It was a comical scene that should have been included in the video—two men standing in a deserted service station lot under bright overhead lights with two enormous Dobermans watching them from inside, Ray fiddling with his gun with an eight-inch barrel inside his pants. Ted hoped no one came along and took them by surprise, fearing what Ray might accidentally blow off!

Alex made it to the station by six forty-five. He looked tired without his first cup of coffee to get his body functioning. He waved from his car as he drove onto the lot. "How the hell you boys doin' this fine day?"

Ted could tell by his tone it was not a fine day. "It's much too early to tell," he answered, hoping Alex remembered who they were and that Jenkins had already paid for them being there.

"Mr. Jenkins said you'd be early, but I never guessed it would be before I got to work. Drivin' back, I guess? Wish I was goin' with ya!" He did remember he'd been well paid, and the dogs were pleased to see him, wagging their stubby tails as he unlocked the glass door that had been covered with metal fencing. He came back out with receipts, and Ted placed a large bottle of bourbon in his hand.

"This is a little Christmas present from the three of us. We appreciate you letting us park here."

Alex took it with a smile, thanking Ted and the absent Mitchell Jenkins for the gesture of friendship, and Ted guessed it had just become "a fine day."

Except for being stopped by New Jersey State police on the turnpike, the return trip was uneventful. Ted was driving when the white cruiser pulled alongside and motioned them to pull over.

"Shit Ted, were you speeding?"

Ted was not and couldn't imagine why they'd been stopped. "Ray, I hope that gun of yours is out of sight; they have very strict gun laws in Jersey. We could go to jail!"

The patrolman got out of his car and walked cautiously to the van, circling it before coming to the passenger side window.

"Good morning, you fellows own this van?"

Ted knew the van's paperwork was in the glove box where Ray sat. "Officer," he said, "the van belongs to our employer in Meriden, Alabama. We're with the art museum there and we're returning from several days in New York."

"May I see some identification and registration please?"

Ray fussed with getting the forms together while Ted opened his wallet for his driver's license and museum identification. The whole time, the officer kept his hand on the handle of his gun, looking at them—Ted with a beard, Ray with a beard and ponytail.

"I'm going to need to see what you have back there, if you don't mind."

Ted was sure they had little choice in the matter and got out to meet the officer at the back of the van. A second trooper had pulled up behind them, his lights flashing red and blue against the van's white paint. He raised the van's door, revealing eight large abstract paintings rolled up around carpet tubes, the television equipment, their luggage, and a life-sized sculpture of a hooker made of fiberglass, wearing a very provocative dress exposing her thighs. The officers looked at Ted, then through the van at Ray who had turned around in his seat. They smiled and told Ted he could close the door.

"Sorry to have delayed you, but we've been alerted to be watching for white vans coming from the South carrying contraband cigarettes out of North Carolina. I thought maybe you were one of them heading back south for more."

Ted assured him they were not and climbed thankfully back into the van.

"Did the pig say why he stopped us?" Ray was hot. It came on him suddenly sometimes, left over from marches and protests of another time.

"Cigarettes. He was looking for contraband cigarettes." Ted pulled out heading south again.

"You didn't tell them where I got them hid, did ya?"

"Nah. Do you think we'd be going now if I had?" Ted had learned to get him back at his joking games and Ray smiled.

✳ ✳ ✳

Ted had come to enjoy being at the museum when Jenkins wasn't there. This was a 360-degree change of attitude for him that began after moving to the new building. It had to do with many things, but mostly with feeling comfortable in his own leadership ability in his boss's absence. His own duties, curatorial and keeping tabs on all the building's mechanical functions, kept him out of personnel frays. He often thought Mitchell fostered much of the contention among people on staff, particularly in program areas and administratively. What little he knew or saw of LeAnne Rickter at the old building was nothing like the emerging personality of Martha Dyer. Had Mitchell engendered her "bad cop" personality to allow himself the opposite role?

Martha and Peter apparently had been at each other's throats most of the time the three men had been in New York, each keeping lists of slights they perceived to share upon Mitchell's return. Unfortunately, Ted arrived first, and Peter lost no time in finding him Monday morning.

"She was watching me, checking up the whole time you all were gone." Ted had heard from others that Martha was prone to do this, appointing herself as warden the few times both Mitchell and Ted were gone, when in fact that dubious distinction might better have fallen to Ellen Maxwell. Peter was an easy target for Martha's unhappy nature. She was jealous of the time he spent with Mitchell and was sure he wasn't worth his salary, which she quickly pointed out was more than Ted made.

"Who does she think she is, Ted?" Peter continued. "She's not even part of the 'professional' staff." It was an adjective frequently used by Jenkins and was quickly picked up by both Rutledge and Dyer. "The whole time you were gone, she strutted about as if she were in charge, giving orders, spying on what I was or was not doing. I've said all this to Mitchell before."

Ted's intercom line buzzed. It was Martha. "Ted, would you come to my office, when you're free? I know Peter's in there with you now and I think you should hear my side of the story as long as he's giving you his."

Peter went on for another thirty minutes, occasionally pacing the floor, sometimes sitting with head bowed. He finally left, going as Ted knew he would to some other office to tell the story of his persecution. Ted promised he would find time to talk with Martha without mentioning he'd already been summoned. Martha was dressed in her usual tailored fashion. The curly hair she'd once had was now chopped off in a rather severe cut, making her features sharp and at times unpleasant. If she were trying to look harsh and unfriendly, she could not have chosen a better style. She looked up from her typing as Ted came in, asking him to shut the door.

"I suppose Peter's given you an earful, telling you what a bitch I've been while you and Mitchell were gone."

"Something like that. He says you two had a few run-ins. Nothing too serious from what I gather."

She had been working on financial reports, the papers and forms in neat stacks around her. When she left for the day or went out at lunch, all her work would be put away so nothing could be seen, per the new employee handbook she and Jenkins had written. Martha was increasingly more involved in museum finances since Jenkins had found several minor errors in the bookkeeping of Frances Rivers. After the move, as everything seemed to become more complex, Frances began to fall behind. She was not a professional accountant, and it was becoming increasingly apparent that one was needed. Should anything happen to Jenkins, Martha would be the only person with a clear picture of the museum's financial situation. She and Mitchell worked long and hard on this, transferring knowledge to her instead of to his assistant director.

Mitchell had covered himself on this matter, calling Ted to his office one morning several weeks before leaving for the Britian filming. Ted took his usual seat across from his desk. Mitchell had a hardbound book in his hand, a history of the American art museum surveying the larger institutions and the people who ran them. Ted rarely saw Mitchell with any kind of book. They talked for several minutes about current projects, his work, and finally the book he was still holding.

"This is very interesting reading about the people who run the nation's largest art institutions and their predecessors. I find the way we work is similar in many respects. For instance, I'm a better administrator than anything else I've done in the past. I never handled exhibitions as well as you do Ted, you're one of the best in that department that I've known. I should concentrate on what I do best, which is raising money and running the show here. You, on the other hand, should do our exhibitions, care for the collections, do research, all the things curators are supposed to do. You have much less experience with the things I do, though I must say you stick to a budget well, and that is appreciated!

"Anyhow, what I'm saying, I guess, is that we all have special gifts and should work on perfecting them, allowing other things to be taken on by others. Don't you agree? When you were hired, your job description said curator and assistant director; it was to fill a need that was two-pronged. I knew when we moved we'd need a curator to care for the collection as it grew and to organize and implement exhibitions that would hold the community's interest. I also needed an assistant—someone to help with reports, budgets, staff administration, and the building's needs and operation. We've grown faster than I imagined, and none of us can do all the things we were supposed to do and do them well. You can't be installing an exhibition and writing job descriptions, and you shouldn't be expected to. I was wrong to think I could combine all those functions into one position."

He looked at Ted as if expecting him to agree or not and Ted never was able to think of a response past agreeing with his logic.

"So, Ted, I think you should be our curator only and not worry about the other, because you excel at that. I'll administrate and handle the business functions because I do that best. We each will have people to help us do our jobs, but we all must recognize our strengths and," he paused, "our weaknesses."

Ted left wondering if his title and job description was about to change. It certainly sounded as if it was and, performance reviews aside, he again heard Mitchell express some dissatisfaction with his work. Considering his recent comment about Ray's job security, Ted wondered where he stood. He certainly thought he did a better job than either Ray or Rutledge in Multimedia. He was also hurt that Mitchell had said these things without giving him what he felt was a fair chance to prove himself with administrative duties. His boss did praise him for the part of his job that took more than three quarters of his time. Had he not known Mitchell as well as he did, he might have thanked him for those comments, but Ted knew there was more to his words than there seemed and now, looking at Martha Dyer through the fog of his thoughts, Ted knew where Mitchell's had come from.

She was talking about Rutledge still, about how he thinks he's above the rules and deliberately pays her, and the job she does, no attention. She didn't realize Ted hadn't heard much of her complaining as he had perfected the technique of smiling and looking attentive while his ears were turned off.

"Mitchell asks me to keep an eye on things when he's not in the building and I do that. It's something he's come to rely on. I can't help it if this makes me unpopular with the others; most are slackers anyway who think they can fool us by hiding after doing a bit of work. I don't pretend to see everything that goes on around here, but what I do see goes into reports Mitchell reads and files away in personnel folders. When it comes time for promotions or reviews, the truth will come out." She opened a desk drawer and flipped through several folders until she found the ones she wanted. "I don't know what you'll say to Mitchell when he returns this week, but my reports will be complete and on his desk."

Ellen and Ted often joked about Martha and the notes she kept. Other people on staff also joked about it, particularly Ray, for whom she also had little affection. Ted had never believed her files on everyone existed and couldn't believe Jenkins had instructed her to keep such records. Nonetheless, they were real and in pale blue folders in her right hand.

"May I see them?" Ted asked, wondering how she would respond to the request of her supervisor in Mitchell's absence.

"If you insist, but I will write a memo to the file saying you read them. You are no longer officially assistant director." Ted couldn't tell if she was teasing him or if the title had actually been dropped since his meeting with Jenkins several weeks before.

"I suppose it's not necessary," Ted said. "If you talk to Mitchell today, tell him I'd like to speak with him and will be in my office till five."

She would certainly talk to him that day, for he checked in with her often when away from the museum. Ted sensed the change in her expression from triumph to hostility and was sure a memo would be added to his file. He wasn't as sure that she would let Mitchell talk with him, but spent a good part of the afternoon thinking of what to say if she did.

The morning slipped into afternoon, and Ted had not spoken further to Martha or Mitchell. He decided not to follow up with her but would follow her lead, writing notes about conversations and points of discussion he wanted to confirm with Mitchell—most importantly if his job description had now been amended. Ted was doing just that when he heard loud shouting being answered by equally ugly screaming coming from down the hallway. The first voice was unmistakably Martha's, the second was unintelligible from his office. As it continued, Ted rose and walked down the hall where he found he was not alone in wondering what had happened to make Martha so angry. Whoever it was was feeling the full wrath of emotion that usually stayed tightly wrapped inside her. Ted looked into the lobby and saw Peter Rutledge.

"...you continually disobey the rules that have been set for specific reasons by people who know more about the operation of museums than you ever will."

Peter's face went ashen, then bright red as his own anger came bubbling forth. "You can't tell me what I can or can't do. I work for Mitchell

Jenkins, not you or anyone else in this place. You may think you're somebody special but you're not, you're just support staff!"

"We've told you and all the others the telephone in this area is for incoming calls and is not to be used by staff. How often do you need to hear that, Peter?"

She was gripping the sides of her arms so tight her fingers were white. The remark about being support staff had really gotten to her. The telephone receiver was still cradled on Peter's shoulder, and Ted hoped there was no one still on the other end. He wondered too what other people coming by were thinking as this drama continued to unfold. Frances Rivers looked at him with sad eyes and walked back to her office; Ellen Maxell stood at the far end of the hallway with her mouth wide open.

"There's no excuse for this breach of the rules, Peter, and I will see that the proper actions are taken. Your days of being smug are over. If you think you've had problems with that little wife of yours, you have no idea what's in store for you when Mitchell returns." She left the security center and walked quickly back to her office, slamming the door.

"Shit!" Peter screamed, then let the telephone receiver drop loudly on the countertop.

Ted opened the door and saw the back of his head as he walked out of the lobby. His neck above his shirt collar was scarlet. Peter Rutledge did not return that afternoon, and Martha Dyer left early without saying a word to anyone. Her office was dark when Ted passed it later, the desk neatly cleared as if it had not been used at all that day. He didn't talk with Mitchell that afternoon, though he had given the switchboard operator instructions to transfer any calls from him should he call. Mitchell did call in to speak to Martha and was told she had left for the day and was asked if he would hold to speak to Ted. He declined, saying he would talk to Martha later at her home.

CHAPTER TWENTY-SIX

Taylor James was enjoying the Boston Museum Conference as a board member of the Alabama State Museum, where Mitchell joined him after the video shoot in New York. He had never stopped to consider all museums had directors who answered to the wishes of their boards and that, at occasional gatherings such as this one, he could meet so many of them. In fact, the theme of this meeting dealt with boards and their relationships and responsibilities in today's museums. As a newly elected board member, James felt an immediate association with these people, even though he had not yet attended a meeting.

Jenkins found Taylor's new enthusiasm amusing and made concerted efforts to ensure he was introduced to executive personnel from Southeastern Museum Council institutions. The fact that Martha Dyer was not at the office when he'd called did not bother him at all. He had told her she could keep her own hours in his absence because "you work long enough hours when I'm at the desk." This added to her feeling of superiority over most everyone else employed there, which also didn't bother Jenkins, who felt a certain amount of tension was healthy. Besides, he was quite capable of keeping the rest of the staff in line. A promise here, a promise there—it worked wonders, and he knew it. So, that evening he joined James for dinner and a night on the town. He generally found professional meetings like this a terrible bore. He would listen to the speakers peripherally, but with the rest of his mind he would be thinking of his museum and how it could change to reflect the dreams he carried inside himself.

"Hello Martha! How's it going, kid? Sorry for calling you at home, but I needed to hear everything is going smoothly down there."

She knew he would call eventually, and it didn't surprise her that he called her at home. He did it more often of late, making her feel indispensable. She didn't say anything for a moment, leaving him puzzled over the silence.

"I had a problem today with Peter. He was being his I'm-better-than-everyone-else self, using the receptionist's phone to take a call."

"What was the circumstance?"

"He was leaving the building on some errand when a call for him came through. Joe Mullen called him back in and he reached for the receptionist's receiver. Three other calls came in while he was on that phone, and I finally went out to see why they weren't being answered. There was Peter talking away to someone, seemingly oblivious to everything."

"What happened?"

"I asked him to get off that phone and to use another. I told him the rules applied to everyone and that this was just the reason no one could be allowed to tie up the incoming phone line. He started screaming at me and got ugly, finally slamming the phone down on the counter and walking out the door. Apparently, he didn't come back to work."

"Is that all?"

"Yes."

"Did Ted Martin see it?"

"Yes, I think he was standing in the hallway. Peter had gone to him earlier in the day to vent about how I persecute him and watched him while you all were in New York. Ted came in to talk about it. I think he believes Rutledge, but he never says. He wanted to talk to you if you called in."

"Yes, I know. I haven't talked with him yet."

"It's all in his file for you."

"Okay Martha, keep things rolling. I'm sorry Peter was unkind to you. I'll speak to him when I return. Has Ellen been bothering him?"

"I don't know. She goes down there from time to time to see the video footage Malone shot in New York."

"Okay, try to keep a grip on things. Should I come back early?"

"I don't think so. How's Mr. James?"

"Seems to be enjoying himself quite a bit. He makes me nervous every time he stands up to speak. I wish he were as smooth as Laura. I'm going to his room when we finish. Dinner tonight with some people he's met. See you next Saturday. Can you still come in?"

"Yes."

Mitchell Jenkins considered the conversation and the blowout Martha had with Peter Rutledge, which he had seen coming. Rutledge was young and used to having his way. It was what Jenkins found appealing—his self-confidence. He was sure he could smooth ruffled feathers by talking to him upon his return. Too bad, he thought, walking to the hotel elevators, that their scene had played out in front of other staff. He knew Martha had likely not given a full description of her manner during the confrontation. *I'm sure Peter will do that*, he thought. The elevator stopped on the top floor of the hotel.

Taylor James didn't have a single room like Mitchell did, but rather a suite of rooms, complete with a small balcony overlooking Boston. An attractive blond woman opened the door for Jenkins.

"Oh, I must have the wrong room." He backed up in the hallway, looking at the numbers on the other doors nearby. "Perhaps I got off the elevator on the wrong floor, I wanted Taylor James' suite."

The woman smiled and looked at Jenkins in the hallway. She was under forty, very attractive, and wore a loose floor-length robe with a hood.

"You have the correct suite, Mr. Jenkins. I was just making drinks. Would you care for one?" She opened the door wider, and Jenkins stepped in. Taylor had not said anything about having company when they'd agreed to meet for dinner. "Taylor," she said, "is on the balcony," and pointed the way.

Jenkins smiled at her as they parted, each holding a crystal glass of very expensive scotch. *That old devil,* he thought, walking through the vast living room toward an open French door and the balcony. James was seated in a comfortable chair with a blanket over him, enjoying the last of the afternoon's sunshine. He greeted Jenkins with a smile.

"Did you meet Alexandria?"

"Not formally, though she did let me in just now. Very pretty, I admire your taste."

James smiled. "It's not what you're thinking. I had wanted to bring Ellen Maxwell along for that, but she wouldn't come; she's one hard woman to convince. Alexandria is my daughter from my first marriage." He looked at Jenkins to see if any surprise registered on his face and he wasn't disappointed. For as long as he'd known Mitchell, he had never talked about any children besides Morgan; nor had this first marriage ever been mentioned.

"I had no idea," Jenkins said.

"Few people in Meriden do. Alex lived with us in New York but married an associate of mine three years before we moved South. She never took to Laura and was not the best influence on Morgan when she was a child. Like Morgan, Alex spent much of her adolescence in boarding schools, the best ones of course, but different ones. Holidays were unbearable for us." He wasn't looking at Jenkins as he relayed this history, but followed the sun's golden edge as it moved behind the John Hancock Tower. "Anyway, she married this fellow I had recruited from DuPont. It was a large wedding. Afterward, as they were leaving for a honeymoon in France, she abruptly turned to the assembled guests in the lobby of the Waldorf and publicly denounced me, Laura, and others for defiling the memory of her mother. She carried on for five minutes or so before her new husband came to his senses and led her out of the hotel into a waiting cab. By the time they arrived in Paris it was apparent to him that she didn't care if he lived or died, she had married him only to hurt me. He returned to New York the next day and filed for an annulment. I cabled her telling her not to come back. She lives on a large retainer I send to keep her away."

"And now? How did she know you were in Boston?"

"She called the plant. She was going to New York for a visit, but when she found out I was going to be here, she changed her plans to surprise me. I let her stay in the suite—she is my daughter after all. She got here just an hour or so before you. Life is full of surprises."

It certainly was! Jenkins sat quietly in his chair taking in all he had just heard and trying to decide how this might affect the James family in Meriden.

"Is she staying long?"

"No. A few days to buy some things for a new place she purchased in Italy. She's tired of France. Looks good for forty-one, so life must agree with her." He leaned closer to Jenkins and lowered his voice. "Laura must never know she was here." He leaned back and finished his drink.

"What happened to the fellow she married? Did he continue working for you?"

"That's a separate tragedy Alex caused. He returned to New York and came to see me heartsick, for he really loved her. He left the company because he was too embarrassed by what she said at the wedding. Gregory Clark was his name, a bright young chemist. He had no trouble finding another job with Dow. They put him on a project that used some radioactive materials, and he was accidentally exposed to a massive dose when a co-worker forgot to completely seal the container. He died two years later. It was a ghastly death. He could have been with me now, a full partner in the business. I might have even retired! I'm going to change for our dinner. Alexandria has thankfully declined my invitation for tonight. She'll be gone tomorrow, she just stopped by to pick up her check."

James rose and left for his bedroom. Mitchell followed him after a few moments. Music was coming from the room he had seen Alex enter. He hoped she wouldn't leave it before he and her father did.

When Taylor re-entered the living room he was like another person. He talked in his usual loud voice as if the two of them were alone in the suite. They took the elevator to the hotel lobby, where they decided to walk the five blocks to meet the others James had invited to dinner. They talked of things mentioned that day at the conference. He was interested in the collection Jenkins had developed with the NEA grant and the works Rubin was sending from the West Coast. Then they discussed the work Ellen was doing with school-aged children, then finally Morgan and her impending return to Spain. Alexandria was not mentioned again.

"Morgan finally came to me about her trip to Spain. I'll give her credit—she didn't want Laura telling me first. Morgan's stubborn and takes the bull by the horns as I do. She didn't want to talk about it at first and I tipped my hand too early. Morgan went into a rage, thinking I had spied on her when she was there, not trusting her to take care of herself. I tell you Mitchell, you've never seen anyone angry until you've seen Morgan that way! We went around for about half an hour before I told her quietly that she could certainly return to Spain to see her young man and attend the ball. I know, sounds like a fairy tale! It silenced her immediately. She thought I would disapprove, and I do of course, but can't let her know. Is your daughter like that Mitchell?"

"Too early to tell since she's only nine. I don't know how I would handle a situation like that. Fathers get pretty protective of their female children; I know I will be in a few years."

"What's to protect? You can't be with them twenty-four hours a day. You give them the best breaks, then they've got to handle the rest themselves. Hell, I don't care if Morgan goes to Spain and gets laid by some local aristocrat while enjoying the scenery. It'd do her good if she were the kind of girl who took things in stride. She's not though, that's the problem. She'll get serious if this fellow is attentive and brings her along.

Next thing I know she'll want to marry the guy; that's when it'll get sticky."

Jenkins had already considered this possibility. After the night by the pool at the James home, he had considered every turn Morgan's relationship with the young Estephen Coton might take. She was not a beautiful woman who would be used to having men around her. He'd decided that a person like Coton might have her money on his mind rather than her future with him. Her father's concern for Morgan's future was very real.

"I think there might come a time when you'll have to put your foot down. Morgan could be terribly hurt by someone out to...well, benefit from her name and her fortune. There are men in Meriden she could look toward for companionship from families you know. I don't mean to tell you what to do, but I think I'd investigate this Coton before letting Morgan fly off."

Jenkins stopped talking, hoping James had not taken offense. He looked over at Taylor who was slightly winded from the walk, but not surprised at what he'd heard Jenkins say.

"I appreciate you speaking your mind, Mitchell. We'll talk about it later. Laura is of your opinion, but I lost one daughter by being too forceful, I don't want to lose another."

✵ ✵ ✵

First thing Monday morning after Mitchell's return from Boston, there was a staff meeting. These had grown so large they could no longer be held in Ellen's office as they had been at the old building. They now assembled in the theater of the museum, scattering all about the front half of the space. There was the usual chatter before Jenkins arrived to call the group to order. Peter Rutledge was sitting alone in the first row. He had come in to work the day following the incident with Martha but had stayed to himself in his office writing press releases while Ray worked to make some sense out of the miles of video he had shot in New York. Martha had also come back that next day, being unusually friendly and accommodating to anyone with whom she came in contact. The bad feelings were just under the surface though. Martha was correct when she told Ted many people didn't like her because of the things she did for Mitchell, with or without his direction. Ted had not yet had occasion to speak with him about the incident.

At seven minutes after nine, Mitchell and Martha came into the theater together, each holding a cup of coffee and Mitchell with a tablet in his other hand. They had been together in his office with the door shut for some time according to the sign-in sheet, and they had been in for several hours the Saturday before. Ted wondered if Mitchell had spoken to Rutledge since his return. Martha took a seat in the front row, across the aisle from Rutledge. She did not acknowledge him as she sat down. He glared straight ahead at the floor, his teeth clenched.

"Let's begin," Jenkins announced. "I have only a few things to cover this morning. We're trying to make adjustments in the weekend work schedule that will be fairer to everyone. As it stands now, everyone but Ted and I are on the rotation, making the frequency of duty about once every two months. Ted and I are not on the schedule because, well, he's a friend of mine and I'm the boss!" Laughter. "Seriously, we are not on the schedule because one or both of us are usually already here on weekends. However, I realize we do need more weekend people here to answer the telephone and attend the security stations in the building when we're open. Martha and I are working to make some adjustments here.

"We're also going to advertise a new secretarial position, for the art school and curatorial. I haven't yet had a chance to talk to Ted about his specific needs, but Mary said the school has grown to the point that an extra person is needed. Applications will be handled by Martha, and I hope we can have someone here in a couple of weeks.

"Performance review forms for this year will be given to supervisory staff later today. I would like to have them completed by Friday so I can review them over the weekend. Again, I want to emphasize that there is no reason to fear these reviews, they are only used to measure accomplishments and nothing else. And remember an average score is nothing to be ashamed of. Perhaps," he turned in Martha's direction, "we can find a better word to use than 'average.' It means you're doing your job as outlined. Finally, I'd like to remind all of you to follow the rules concerning the use of public areas and equipment. The receptionist's phone, for instance, is not to be used for conversations by staff other than the receptionist. Please refer to your copy of these guidelines from time to time. Should you need another copy, Martha can get you one. Is there anything anyone has to add to this morning's meeting?" There was silence as the rest of the staff looked from Peter to Martha.

"If not, let's get to work. Ted, I'd like to catch up when you have time today."

"You were supposed to get me my own secretary. I'm not sure half is better than none at all," Ted said to Martha on his way to Mitchell's office.

"Ingrate!" she said with a smile and walked back to her desk.

Mitchell's mail had been neatly arranged on his desk in order of importance according to Martha's criteria. On top of the stack was a letter from Abram Rubin, the envelope marked PERSONAL, as always. They came every couple weeks now and all went into his file; each was of no real consequence, more of a diary of the patron's progress through the art bastions of the West Coast. Ted had not met Rubin but felt he knew him from those letters all typed in a square elite face, single-spaced.

"Sorry to keep you waiting, Ted." Mitchell strolled into his office without a hint of unpleasantness on his face or in his manner. Ted wondered how Rutledge was doing after their conversation. "There are a couple things I wanted to go over this morning. I tried to reach you over the weekend."

Ted looked at him blankly. He had been at his apartment all weekend, leaving only occasionally to run a few errands. He felt guilty now about not being glued to the phone.

"Anything in particular that you wanted?"

"No, nothing like that, just hadn't heard from you since you and Ray left New York and wondered how you made out coming back."

"It was a long drive, but it was uneventful. I believe the video tape arrived undamaged, and certainly the artwork we brought back did. They're in Receiving, have you had a look?"

"Yes, on Saturday. Be sure to get all the letters of gift out as quickly as possible. The documentation is essential since the artists may want to work some sort of tax angle with their dealers."

Mitchell often reminded Ted of matters that were second nature to his job, making him feel important, Ted supposed. Mitchell did it with a smile and all the false sincerity he could muster. He was beginning to remind Ted of Robert Osborne, adding and deleting "employee points", on a weekly or even daily basis.

"How much time do you think you could use secretarial assistance, Ted? I want to get the maximum use of this new person and wonder how many hours you would need her and how many she'd be with Mary in the school?" Ted needed the help, but knew Mary needed it worse, and financial considerations at the time made hiring two people out of the question. They talked about how his needs would likely come in spurts during the year as, to some degree, would Mary's. Ted finally told Jenkins he could use someone when convenient to Mary. Ted knew Mitchell was hoping not to discuss the confrontation of the week before, and had it been anything else, he would have let it pass, but he was interested in Mitchell's opinion of the incident.

"Mitchell, I know you're busy with a lot of things just now, but I would like to talk briefly about the incident with Martha and Peter. I'm sure you know about it and have talked with both parties by now. If it's none of my business, I'll butt out, but I was in charge of things Thursday."

His expression changed only slightly. "It is your business, Ted. I perfectly understand your concern. I've talked to both Peter and Martha about what happened and believe the matter is resolved. Peter was clearly wrong to use the reception phone to take a call. He understands and I'm sure he won't make that mistake again." There was a pause that grew into silence as if to indicate the subject was closed.

"And Martha?"

"Martha did what she was supposed to do under the circumstances. I suppose she acted with more zeal than was required, but the things she told me she said to Peter were accurate. I'm sorry she chose to lecture him about that phone's use in such a public manner, but those are the kinds of things one learns over time. I'm sure she'll be more discreet in the future."

The subject was definitely closed now, but Ted had to ask another question of him. He had to know if he condoned her behavior. "While her reasons for doing what she did might be by the book, she did conduct herself in a manner that lacked a great deal of understanding about personal relationships. She was screaming at Rutledge, Mitchell, not merely talking forcefully, almost hysterical, as if the museum would fall apart if he didn't get off that phone. It was embarrassing for everyone. Staff came out of their offices to see what was going on. Martha might have called me before going on her rampage. She acts as if I'm not able to handle things in your absence, as if there is some unwritten directive between the two of you that allows her to take matters into her own hands." Ted had said more than he intended and could see it in the way Jenkins was straightening in his chair.

"That is certainly not true. Martha takes her position here very seriously. She's highly motivated, loyal, and conscientious. She will make a good administrator someday after she refines her manner a bit. She knows her emotions are sometimes a problem and is working on that. She takes a lot of criticism behind her back from people who cannot know all that goes on here and resent her ties to me. I think we should all give her a chance to bring herself around on this aspect of her very difficult position. You and I have had a conversation about the things each of us do best. If Martha made an error in judgement last week, it was not because she was not aware of the fact, but because of her commitment to the rules I've established. As I've said Ted, I've spoken with her about all these matters and believe she will be able to work to correct any minor deficiencies she might have. She is important to me, and it would be difficult to get along without her. I hope I'll never need to face that situation and that you and everyone else will work with her during this time. Is there anything else Ted?"

There was not, and Ted was excused without knowing the answers to anything. Mitchell stretched in his chair after Ted left, his shadow through the curtain turning away from their conversation and to the morning's mail. The Rubin letter was put aside for a moment while he skimmed through his other correspondence. Finding nothing too urgent, he picked up the letter, slipped a thin ruler under the flap and slit open its side.

Dear Mitchell,

As promised, I am writing again. Hope you
are better than I am. Medicine is not all it's
cracked up to be. Partners and I are having
trouble here that may require drastic action.
I enclosed a clipping from local press for your
understanding of our issues. Grim! May be
bailing out for a while, looking for something
back east, perhaps in home state, if I can
accommodate the cultural shock. Better than
the pokey though.

It went on for another two pages, garbage that amounted to the usual stuff from patron to museum director. Rubin clearly thought he was J. P. Getty or Joseph Hirschhorn. Mitchell didn't read the remainder of the letter right away, but picked up the folded newspaper article that had fallen to his lap instead. Accompanying the article was a picture of Rubin and his partners taken at some charity event. It was a file photo, unrelated to the story or the large black headline that ran across it: "LOCAL DOCTORS INDICTED IN TAX DODGE." The story detailed the misconduct of three of the six physicians in Rubin's practice, saying other irregularities had occurred in addition to those reported by the IRS. Rubin was not mentioned by name but it did say everyone in the practice was being investigated.

Mitchell kept the letter for several months before it found its way into Rubin's folder. Ted read it then, about the time Rubin was coming to the museum for his first visit. Until then, Ted had thought this visit by a collector and sometime benefactor was a casual matter. Mitchell had said only that Rubin was coming, that Ted should make sure the objects he had given were displayed in a gallery, and that the label information was correct. He seemed highly animated about the visit, as he was about most things out of the norm. Still, Ted could tell he wasn't really excited about seeing his old friend. He had started Rubin's foray into the art world, and it had turned out well for the doctor who frequented many galleries on the West Coast and purchased heavily from them. From the art magazines that began to accumulate in Mitchell's office, Ted began to realize the fear of being inadequately informed around his old friend was bothering him more than anything else about the visit. The pupil couldn't know more than the instructor. Ted was surprised by the gallery inspection Mitchell made the afternoon before the "California Dreamer" was to arrive; he had never done anything like that before. Ted assumed everything passed muster as he never heard anything.

Mitchell arrived with his special guest early the following morning. Coffee and Danish were served in his office by Martha Dyer, after which there was a tour of the facility. Abram Rubin was a short, wiry man who dressed casually in the manner of what Ted assumed was standard on the West Coast. He was tanned, with tight curly hair styled in a sort of Italian-looking version of an afro. He wore lightly tinted glasses that seemed too large for his face and talked very rapidly, using his hands to punctuate his sentences.

Mitchell made sure to route the tour past paintings Rubin had given. The two would stop and discuss them, Rubin remembering incidents with the artists, giving each one a unique personality. Ted was introduced while passing the two in the gallery quite by accident and was quickly dispatched on his way while Mitchell finished the tour. The two were together most of the day, Rubin leaving finally in the late afternoon. Jenkins promised to drive him to Birmingham the following day to see the museum and to meet a physician friend of his who was on the hospital's executive staff. By the following February, he was again a resident of Alabama, complaining about the lack of interest the state had for art in general. He spent many of his days off in Meriden visiting with Jenkins. There was the matter of his art collection still on the West Coast that Rubin wanted back with him. Unfortunately, he had no place to store it, and before Ted was consulted, a solution was determined.

An exhibition of the Rubin Collection of Contemporary American Art was to be held at the Museum in early April. Mitchell had reached an agreement that the work would be on a long-term loan to the museum. During this period, the museum would be able to lend objects to other institutions as it saw fit, receiving the appropriate credit in any related publication. In exchange, Rubin would get the exhibition, which did a great deal for his ego, museum storage of any works not exhibited, and insurance coverage, which had become a real financial burden for him. Mitchell had gone to Ted's office with the proposal after he and Rubin had agreed to it the week of his visit. He was told to review it for issues and to respond as soon as possible. Ted didn't know the deal had already been worked out and his involvement at this point was only for the record. The fact that Jenkins had adopted a policy stating the museum would not accept or get involved with loans of artwork for any reason seemed not to matter in his excitement to get the works to Meriden before Rubin had a change of heart.

The years of correspondence had paid off for Mitchell who planned to turn the exhibition into a major event, attracting state and regional publicity at a time when the museum was still riding a wave of popularity in the Southeast and Birmingham was still fooling around with the logistics of their museum project, which was rapidly turning into a nightmare for those connected with it. As Mitchell had predicted, the man who was hired as director of the project was having difficulties with not only state government, but also with statewide museum officials. Jenkins had successfully engineered an informal coalition of his colleagues to study the question of state support of the arts and the role the existing institutions would like to see the state take in helping them, before proceeding in another direction. At the same time, he was advising Taylor James on the questions he had about issues facing the ambitious project. It was an ever-tightening circle for Mitchell, who was playing both sides of the court at the same time. Had Rubin decided to let the state store his collection in facilities at the Birmingham Museum, it might have been just the impetus needed to move it ahead. Mitchell made every possible concession to ensure Rubin didn't change his mind. The exhibition schedule Ted worked from for the year ahead was altered to accommodate the showing, a color catalogue was planned, and the Britian video would premier the night the exhibition opened.

Martha Dyer interviewed potential art school/curatorial applicants that week. There was a steady stream of them, recruited by an advertisement in the local newspaper. Jenkins was not to see any until she had narrowed the field to three; Mary Griffin and Ted were not to see any until Mitchell had narrowed it to two. Martha in a malevolent way found the process utterly enjoyable. It enabled her the first opportunity to be both judge and jury with people she didn't know. She was stern with the applicants during interviews and dressed severely in a style of the time—tailored slacks, jacket, starched pleated shirt and narrow four-in-hand tie. She paced the floor as she administered a typing test, spoke rapidly during their dictation test, and was critical of the "personal appearance" section of their employment applications. By week's end she had selected three applicants for Jenkins to interview, a process he also enjoyed.

The following Monday, each paraded themselves throughout the day in and out of his office, trying hard to impress him any way they could.

His favorite little joke, he told me later, was to ask each of the applicants to take off their clothes in a very straightforward manner. When they would look at him in alarm, he would say, "Well you're here about the modeling position, aren't you? Always breaks the ice Ted, makes them at ease with anything I might say afterward!" Mitchell's two choices were asked to return midweek to meet with Mary and Ted. One woman was his obvious choice, though he didn't mention he had a preference.

"Both girls are extremely well qualified and have experience as well," he told Ted. "One is sexy as hell!"

Friday morning the position was offered to Beth Lawrence, a Meriden native and not the sexy one, which Ted was certain was Martha's work. She was attractive and shy, but with a friendly manner and way of expressing herself. Ted could tell she was not accustomed to the museum's cast of characters or the instant insanity into which she'd been dropped. Martha took immediate charge of her, showing her extra things she would be responsible for in addition to the work she'd been hired to do. Martha was quick to point out she would be working on a probationary schedule for the first three months, "so, for whatever reason, you can leave with a clean record. Should we decide you're not working out, the same is true."

Ted had not heard that clause delivered in such detail to anyone before, though it indeed existed in the personnel manual. No one had ever been asked to leave during or after their probationary period, in fact no one since his coming had been asked to leave at all. Stephen Parker, according to Mitchell, decided to move on to other things by his own choice. For the first time in his career, Ted had someone to type his letters and assist with clerical chores related to exhibitions and the collection. Beth was to work for him in the afternoons and for Mary in the morning. They stuck to that schedule exactly two weeks before Mary asked if Beth could work for her full-time.

"There's just too much work to be done in the school now that we're granting Associate Degrees, and besides, you have an assistant to help with the physical labor in the galleries."

It was difficult to say no to Mary for many reasons. It was her secret, the way she could get things she wanted, her mystique and allure
with men. Beth became acclimated to the museum and the personalities
within it. She was strong-willed and not easily intimidated. It was a
characteristic that would eventually make her an enemy of Martha's, who
for all of Mitchell's promises, never did learn how to control her temper
or develop an easy relationship with those under her supervision.

CHAPTER TWENTY-SEVEN

By Christmas 1976, Morgan James' interest in Estephen Coton had blossomed into something that was more than just casual. She had returned to Spain in the fall and had stayed the month of September, returning in October then back again with her mother in mid-November. The November trip was a signal to Jenkins that things had already progressed too far. Taylor had not asked his opinion again since they had been in Boston. The unexpected meeting with his other daughter, Alex, had done much to sober Taylor to the realities of his own stubborn streak—the very one Morgan had acquired. Mitchell found nothing wrong with expressing his opinions on the subject when the two men were alone; after all, so many of his own plans were based on the continuation of James money coming to the museum; besides his opinion of the bonds of marriage had not changed.

On December 24, Morgan and Estephen arrived in Meriden so Estephen could meet her father and celebrate the holiday. Their arrival was marked by a whirl of social activity during which they were treated as an enchanted princess and prince. Laura and Taylor were very quiet throughout it all, not wanting to spoil their daughter's happiness. It was obvious to everyone Morgan intended on becoming Mrs. Estephen Coton in the new year. Laura found the young man courtly, polished, intelligent, and too eager to please Morgan. Always on guard, she found this last characteristic disturbing, for she feared he had discovered her great wealth and was planning to cash in. While in Spain, she met his family and traveled to the countryside to visit his family estate. This too was a reason for fear, as she was certain his family didn't have the means to keep the home in the condition of its past. Taylor cared little about any interest the man might have in Morgan's wealth. She would always have plenty of money. Should they marry and have it go bad, she would easily be able to buy herself free and begin life again. However, he found Estephen the exact opposite of his own personality, the poet where he was the pragmatist, and Taylor wanted a strong man for his strong daughter. To his way of thinking, the young man didn't understand the business world and would never be able to support himself in the US. His soldier life would not do for his daughter, and living in Spain was out; the country's economy was far too unstable and the potential for revolution far too real.

Mitchell Jenkins, while talking politely to both Morgan and Estephen at parties and during tours of the museum, was convinced the pairing of these two would be a disaster. When the subject of marriage was discussed by James, Jenkins took an adamant stand against it. However, there was little James could do to stop his daughter. Their engagement was announced in February, and they married in Meriden the following Easter. Neither of her parents looked particularly happy in the wedding photographs. The newlyweds spent the spring and summer in Spain, where Estephen resigned his military commission and prepared to move with his bride to Meriden. As Taylor had predicted, the young man didn't know what he would do to earn a living in Alabama, working at projects with Morgan their first year of married life. Laura came to accept her son-in-law's manner and to believe he truly enjoyed making Morgan happy by doting on her in his European way. Mitchell immediately changed his position on the marriage as soon as they were settled in. As he had with

Taylor and Laura beforehand, he worked to interest the newlyweds in the affairs of the museum, enlisting their assistance anytime there seemed to be an appropriate cause.

The Rubin collection's opening was not the kind of event Mitchell needed any assistance in promoting. The works were shipped on an exact schedule by commercial art movers, with Jenkins himself flying out to supervise the crating. A media event was scheduled for their arrival at the museum; Rutledge was instructed to work the press into full coverage even though the insurance providers were largely against it. Video of Jenkins watching the objects being unloaded made the evening news. The opening of the exhibition was the most successful since the Hall-Crowell exhibition almost ten years before. Mitchell's luck was as good as ever, and it seemed in no danger of running out. To cap the evening of the opening, Jenkins, with the assistance of the art association president, awarded Rubin a special citation for his service to the association and museum as a trusted advisor on collection policies. It was a setup everyone recognized but Rubin, who was enjoying his status as the favorite cultural son of Meriden, Alabama.

Mitchell greeted guests in the gallery after the presentation, introducing everyone again to Rubin, who talked about his collecting, the objects on display, and the artists who made them. The following morning Jenkins invited certain members of the local press to come to his office for a feature story about the collection and its importance locally as well as statewide. He quickly linked certain pieces to the museum's own collection of modern art, suggesting the exhibition was further justification for continuing the acquisition policy chartered years before. The articles were timed to appear the next week and would hopefully be picked up by the Associated Press and distributed to other media outlets in the Southeast. Mitchell particularly hoped the Montgomery press would pick up the story as budgeting for the next year approached. The museum was thankfully still receiving the proceeds from the financial arrangement Bishop, then Governor Ford, and the Meriden legislators had worked out to provide annual revenue. As the museum operated with both public and private funding through the art association, Jenkins used the public funding first, which had nicely kept up with the cost of living, while holding on to the private. In years when expenses weren't as great, some of the private funds would be placed in interest-bearing accounts to be used when expenses were higher or when unexpected expenses occurred, such as the Rubin exhibition.

Ted had prepared a breakdown of exhibition expenses for the next budget year to discuss with Mitchell after he finished with the press that day. As was generally the case, the meeting was put off until late in the afternoon when Mitchell could give his time after the museum's close. When Ted entered his office, he found Jenkins and Martha going through the day's mail, Mitchell dictating responses while she gathered the pieces that would be shuttled to Ted. He was in the midst of dictating a letter to Larry Smith, director of the State Arts Commission, and sounded exasperated. This was unusual for him, particularly following the successful exhibition opening the night before and the press briefing, which he generally enjoyed. In his letter, he was discussing the particulars of a grant request submitted to the commission several years earlier. It was from a Meriden sculptor by the name of Roger Blanton. Ted thought he remembered that application from the trip he and Mitchell had made to Birmingham shortly after his arrival. The request was for funding to help Blanton establish a foundry near his home. He intended to teach the "lost wax" technique, but there had been some question as to whether a single artist could qualify for such funding under the commission guidelines.

"...I can see no reason why Mr. Blanton would take such an action against the commission or me. At the time the grant application was denied, Mr. Blanton was invited to resubmit his request under another category of funding. He refused, claiming the commission was never going to assist an individual artist while it took money from them in the form of income taxes and gave it to institutions who, in his opinion, squandered the resources on ineffective projects. He has since repeatedly disrupted scheduled meetings with a litany of verbal insults directed to individual commission members and staff. I sincerely hope this clarifies the matter from the commission's end and that Mr. Blanton will drop his legal claims and intent to pursue court action." With that, Jenkins finished dictating, turning his attention to Ted and the subject of exhibition budgeting.

"Sounds like there's at least one unsatisfied customer," Ted said.

Jenkins smiled, rubbing his hands into his tired eyes and stretching before answering. "It's just old Roger Blanton. I've tried and tried to work with that guy over the years, but nothing seems to satisfy him. He's mad the commission won't grant him money for that request he submitted years ago. I think you were with me when Blanton first submitted the proposal. It was turned down and he's been unhappy ever since."

"Wasn't your fault. As I remember, you tried to persuade him to re-submit under another category."

"I did, but he wouldn't do that because he wanted to make a point about institutions being able to receive larger amounts because of their size and programming scope. He claims I slandered his reputation publicly by calling him 'unprofessional,' when what I believe I said was his manner was unprofessional. Anyway, he sent a registered letter to Larry saying he was preparing legal action against both the commission and me personally." Smith had been the director of the commission since its inception and was a friend of Mitchell's from their university days. Ted couldn't believe Blanton was serious. He didn't come to the museum often, staying on the small farm where he lived and worked as a sculptor. Ted didn't remember Mitchell making any public comment about Blanton or his request during that first reading of his proposal, but did recall his attempt to allow Blanton to re-submit under another funding category. The fact he was now considering a lawsuit against Jenkins seemed preposterous.

"Have you had any recent contact with Blanton, Mitchell? Maybe you could persuade him to give up this notion. Legal matters would be expensive, and he couldn't possibly make that many sales to pay for long proceedings."

Jenkins looked blankly at Ted, still thinking about the letter from Smith and the times he had presided as president of the commission, when Blanton would show up raving. "No, I haven't spoken with Roger in quite some time. I think though it would be best if I didn't talk to him and let the commission handle things. I don't expect anything will come of it, though I'll check my records from those meetings to make sure I'm clear. I just hope Blanton doesn't decide to generate publicity for himself as the poor victim. He has given me problems almost from the beginning of my Meriden tenure. He was very influential in those days with members of the art association and was able to sway the people who ran the museum prior to my coming. I even gave him an exhibition and he had the nerve to come in and re-arrange everything I'd done in the gallery. He wasn't happy with the checklist catalogue or the publicity. A real pain in the ass. He was gunning for me when we announced the move to the new building too. I was sure he would stir up bad press for us because he found accepting Taylor's gift loathsome. And now this! Any attorney's going to tell him to give it up—it's crazy to sue a state agency."

He turned his attention to the budget spreadsheet Ted had prepared and seemed satisfied with it. They talked more often in the weeks that followed, especially about the Blanton situation, which didn't go away as Mitchell had hoped. Blanton's attorney did advise him a suit against the state would be hard to prosecute but that he could bring one against Jenkins as the commission's president when his application was denied and as perpetrator of the libelous comment. The commission secured an attorney for Jenkins as it became increasingly clear Blanton would not back down in his quest to take down its director. It caused Mitchell frequently ugly moods that he would share with Martha Dyer and sometimes with Ted.

Mitchell's attorney called late one spring afternoon to say he had been unable to persuade Blanton, through his attorney, to drop a court action. The opposition was requesting a trial date be set in Meriden for the case *Blanton v. Jenkins, Meriden Museum*. As if things were not bad enough, Blanton somehow managed to involve the museum in the case as well. It was a move that caused Mitchell to sink into even darker moods. He worked steadily with his legal team, going over minutes and records the Arts Commission kept from the time of his presidency. As in all things, Mitchell was determined to win.

From what Ted could tell by reading the transcripts, there was little Blanton could hope to gain from the commission's refusal to act favorably upon his request. The issue seemed to center on whether Jenkins had damaged the artist's reputation with his alleged comment made sometime later. Those remarks were not included in the official transcripts and would be given to the court through sworn evidence brought by witnesses for each side during the trial. It had been rumored that Blanton's attorneys had been investigating Mitchell's character from all angles, particularly his personal life. If they attempted to sling dirt during the proceeding, Ted knew things would get rough. He was surprised to learn the meticulous files Martha kept were much broader than just staff, covering anyone who'd had sustained contact with Jenkins. Ted first saw these files on Mitchell's desk quite accidentally.

"These are helping me cover as many angles as possible, Ted. We don't know yet who Blanton's people intend to call as witnesses, but when we find out, we'll have these notes of meetings and conversations. I've always been a suspicious person and now I'm glad I acted on my feelings. When you're in the public eye as I am, there are people who are always wanting to take shots. We've talked before about the trouble I expected when we moved. Didn't think I'd survive, but somehow I did. This may be that same kind of attempt to get me out of here. I intend to win this little battle with Blanton, and when I do, I'm going to hang his ass on a wall so high it'll take him years to get down. You just can't fool around with people like him. You've got to meet them head on and fight till there's nothing left—and there will be nothing left of Blanton when I'm through. He'll need to move so far into the woods, no one will ever hear from him again."

Roger Blanton had taken on a formidable opponent who would not stop at a simple resolution of the matter in court. Jenkins intended to ruin him.

✧ ✧ ✧

The trial was set for July. By this time both sides had their strategies planned and each knew who the other was going to be calling forth as witnesses. To Ted's chagrin, he was informed by Mitchell's counsel that he would be called as a witness by both sides and likely would undergo heated examination about Jenkin's disinterest in helping Blanton receive his grant. It seemed straightforward enough, but still made him nervous as the trial date approached. The day before his testimony was to be heard, he was asked to attend a meeting with Mitchell's attorney for a briefing on what questions he would likely be asked and a rehearsal of what his responses should be. As nothing else had, this brought the reality of the proceedings home even more.

The trial had attracted a large gallery of interested persons, including many other artists who were attending for the theatrics. Maureen was asked to take a seat immediately behind Mitchell, a ploy to psychologically persuade the jury that Mitchell was a good family man, no matter what anyone might say. His attorneys thought this might become an issue if Blanton's side had difficulty convincing the jury about the libel charge. The first day was background testimony, setting the stage for the fireworks that were to follow the day Ted was called. Blanton and his team entered the courtroom just ahead of the judge, while Mitchell and his team had chosen to sit before the bench as soon as the courtroom had opened. Blanton's principal counsel was a respected older attorney in town, known for his courtroom dramatics. He was going for blood, though out of court he and Jenkins were acquaintances. But now, there were no smiles as he and Blanton sat at the oak table on the room's far side. In another calculated move, Jenkins looked over at the opposition with a smile and a wave that was not acknowledged. The jury noticed it before everyone stood for the entrance of Judge Hugo Clark.

The weight of the proceeding was on the plaintiff, for they had to prove Mitchell had made a libelous statement and that it had damaged the reputation of Roger Blanton. They began their examination of the facts with a review of the artist's career, calling art instructors from the university in Birmingham where Blanton sometimes taught summer courses, local patrons who had commissioned pieces over the years, and even August Bishop, who failed to show up. The courtroom was turned into a lecture hall as the prosecution's expert witnesses gave a brief history of modern art, then a retrospective examination of Blanton's public work. It was truly a spectacle, with the judge leaving the bench—complaining he couldn't see the screen where slides were being shown—for a seat in the gallery. When Bishop didn't appear, the judge was asked for a brief recess so the retired director of the Birmingham Museum might be contacted. It was at that point when Judge Clark recognized the name of the absent party.

"Is that Augie Bishop? Was he a student at Harvard in the 30s? Does anyone know?"

The courtroom was a buzz of conversation as if the question was being pondered by people who couldn't possibly know. However, one person did know; Mitchell Jenkins knew "Augie's" history because it was a subject he'd heard often over the years. Jenkins whispered to his counsel, the two conferred, then his attorney stood to answer Clark's question.

"Your Honor, if you please. My client, Mr. Jenkins, was employed in Birmingham at the museum under Mr. Bishop's direction previous to his coming to Meriden. Mr. Jenkins can confirm that Mr. Bishop did indeed receive his undergraduate degree from Harvard at the time you specified."

"I'll be darned!" the judge exclaimed. "I'm going to issue a bench warrant for his arrest. Perhaps we'll get him down here after all. I've not seen Augie since we were in the same dormitory in '35!"

It turned out the two men had lived across the hallway from each other while undergraduates. His Honor remembered later that Bishop had borrowed a white sweater from him for a date with a girl in Boston and had never returned it, saying he had lent it to his date who had gotten a chill. Bishop was in Europe researching a book he would later publish on paintings of the early Renaissance and never appeared, but the interlude, the bench warrant, and the slides and testimonies from Blanton's witnesses were pure theatrics. Nothing was being taken seriously. It was an event the judge had looked forward to since first learning of the prospect of it six months earlier. He had even read accounts of the historic nineteenth century Whistler/Ruskin libel trial, a fact he admitted during his closing statement to the jury. Blanton took the proceedings seriously, however. He did not move from his stiff, seated position at all that first day. The fact that he was seeking $500,000 in damages was serious too. Mitchell took notes, listening to every word the plaintiff's witnesses said. They were under oath, so whatever they had to say about him would be truthful.

Ted was the first defense witness on the trial's second day. As he had not been present at the Arts Commission meeting when Jenkins was alleged to have made his "unprofessional" remark, his testimony would deal only with the first time Blanton brought his grant request before the commission and Jenkins' attempt to persuade him to change the funding category. Ted heard his name called by the bailiff and rose from his seat to take his place in the witness stand. Mitchell was smiling thinly, his blue eyes cold from the tension. He would be the last to testify and was anxious to be questioned by his counsel as well as Blanton's. Maureen stared blankly ahead. Though she arrived at court both days with Jenkins, Ted had not seen them together for months. She looked tired, unhappy, and apprehensive—all emotions that were quite understandable given the circumstances—yet Ted felt there was something more. He didn't think anymore about it as he sat on the wooden bench next to Judge Clark. The judge smiled warmly as if Ted were there for a social visit. The circus was featuring yet another act!

The defense attorney rose from his chair next to Mitchell. He was a large man who, all the other times Ted had seen him, looked as if he had dressed in fifteen seconds while on his way somewhere. He was now very properly tucked in. As he stepped forward, he casually buttoned his suit coat and begin his examination.

"Would you please state your name and occupation?"

"Theodore Martin. I am curator at the Meriden Art Museum."

"Are you comfortable Mr. Martin?"

Is he crazy? Ted couldn't fathom why he'd asked that question.

"I'm a bit nervous. I don't do this very often."

There was general laughter in the room and among the jury. It was what the attorney must have been after, more levity.

"Mr. Martin, the plaintiff has stated arts organizations like the State Arts Commission, and even the museum here, damage the integrity of the individual artists they should be in the business to serve. I don't wish to begin a discussion of the politics of a museum, but I would like your opinion of Mr. Jenkins' record in dealing with artists in our community and throughout the state, if you can speak to that. Is it not a fact, Mr. Martin, that Mitchell Jenkins, as a past president of the Alabama Artists' Guild, was responsible for three exhibitions by Alabama artists that traveled throughout the state to museums and university galleries? And that Mr. Blanton's work was included in these exhibitions?"

"Yes sir, that is correct."

"And is it not also true, Mr. Martin, that Mr. Jenkins arranged for an exhibition of Mr. Blanton's artwork in a gallery of the former Meriden Museum, shortly after he himself came to Meriden?"

"Yes sir, that is also correct."

"Mr. Martin, have there been other times when Mr. Jenkins has worked to benefit Roger Blanton?"

This question Ted would not have been able to speak to had Jenkins and his legal team not given him a capsulized education on the history of Jenkins' interest in Roger Blanton's sculpture. As it turned out, Mitchell had tried to assist Blanton with major commissions on several occasions during his time at the museum. Each time, Blanton had either not provided the materials necessary to show architects or selection committees, or had told Mitchell he was not interested in pursuing the potential commission for various reasons. Jenkins had recorded each of these occasions and filed them away in the brief he kept on Blanton, secured in Martha Dyer's filing cabinet.

"Yes, there were three other times Mitchell Jenkins tried to further the career of Roger Blanton."

There was an uneasy stirring at Blanton's table as Ted related the incidents in historical order.

"Does it seem to you, Mr. Martin, as curator of a museum, a person knowledgeable in this area and used to dealing with artists of all kinds, that these are the actions of a man who would wish to damage the reputation of an artist?"

"No sir, quite to the contrary."

"Thank you, Mr. Martin." He turned to return to his chair. "Your witness Mr. Prosecutor."

Ted braced for the worst as Blanton's attorney rose. Throughout the trial he had dressed in a black suit, a white starched shirt, and dark tie. His mass of white hair rose from his head like that of an orchestra conductor drawn as a cartoon.

"Mr. Martin," he began slow, his voice soft, "how long have you been employed at the Meriden Museum?"

Ted had not been prepared for such an easy question, and it took several seconds for him to respond. "Three-and-a-half years, sir."

"Thank you. Now during this time, can you recall how many times you've run into Roger Blanton at the museum for any reason at all?"

"I've never seen Mr. Blanton at the museum during that time."

"And why do you suppose that is, Mr. Martin?"

What he was getting at Ted had no idea, but it was not the line of questioning he had been primed for. "Because he lives in the country and finds it difficult to get to town? I'm afraid I have no idea."

Again, polite laughter. Even Judge Clark chuckled before gaveling the court to order. Levity, however, was not what Blanton's attorney had in mind. Ted was sure his subsequent questions were going to be tougher, though he was pleased at his ability to not seem as intimidated as he felt.

"It might interest you to know, Mr. Martin, that Roger Blanton does not come to the museum because in his opinion it does little for artists in the community and is a waste of tax money, which goes to pay your salary. It is this same feeling, Mr. Martin, that caused him to submit a grant for needed funds to the State Arts Commission in a category he suspected would only be used by institutions such as the one you work for. Mr. Martin, you were in attendance in Birmingham when Mr. Blanton's request was first brought before the commission. Is that correct?"

"Yes."

"And at that time, would you please tell us who was president of that body?"

"Mitchell Jenkins."

"The same Mitchell Jenkins who is director of the Meriden Museum of Art?"

"Yes."

"And was he not director of that museum while president of the State Arts Commission?"

"Yes."

"Don't you find that a bit odd, Mr. Martin?"

"That he was president of an arts commission while director of an art museum?" There was laughter. "Mitchell Jenkins is a good man, a valuable asset to the arts in this state."

Without meaning to be funny, Ted was destroying the plaintiff's line of questioning. He looked briefly over at Jenkins who was laughing his loud, nervous laugh. Judge Clark gaveled the audience quiet.

"Mr. Martin, I believe you've failed to understand my question." His voice was rising. "Do you not find it odd that while Mr. Jenkins was director of a museum, one that gets a great deal of publicity, a museum that could easily make or break an artist who lived in its community or even in the state, that he would also be president of an agency that gives away money to artists? Don't you think that might be a bit too much authority for any one person to have?"

It was the first hard question, and one Ted also had thought about during Mitchell's time as president of the commission. "It's an honorary position, I believe, at no salary. It was established so a non-state employee would have oversight. There are other agencies operating in this manner as well. Mr. Jenkins just happened to have been elected president for that year's term."

"Do you think Mitchell Jenkins was elected to that post because of his position here in Meriden at the museum? That his voice and opinions carry more weight because of his position here?"

"No sir, I do not. All members of the commission are employed in some artistic venue. Each member has one vote. I do not believe there was discussion among that body. Mr. Blanton's request was deferred to a later meeting."

"Do you remember the circumstances of Roger Blanton's grant application to this body, Mr. Martin? If so, would you tell us about it?"

Ted tried to pull his thoughts together. He had been on the stand longer than he'd imagined and longer than he'd been told he would be.

"Mr. Blanton's request was one of six that were brought before the commission at their first session in the Spring of 1973. I had just come to the museum and Mitchell had just been appointed as commission president. I went with him to Birmingham to see the museum there and become acquainted with the commission."

"Has the Meriden Museum ever received funding from the State Arts Commission?"

"Yes sir, on several occasions for special projects the museum has undertaken. However, we did not apply for grants during the year Michell Jenkins was president."

"I see. Mr. Martin, do you remember what action was taken on Mr. Blanton's grant at that initial review?"

"Yes, the grant was discussed by Mr. Blanton, then reviewed by members of the commission. The staff there had already reviewed the application and recommended Mr. Blanton re-apply under another category since the one he used was for educational institutions. There was some question as to whether Mr. Blanton himself qualified as an educational institution. The grant was tabled until their next meeting to give Mr. Blanton time to change his application."

"And how was Mr. Blanton informed of the commission's decision at that time?"

"Why, Mitchell Jenkins told him at the meeting."

"Mr. Martin, is it not true that Mr. Blanton was informed of the decision by letter some time after that meeting? And that was the only communication he had with anyone from the time the meeting was adjourned until he heard of the outcome of his request?"

"I can hardly say, sir. I do remember Mitchell talked to Mr. Blanton during the meeting about the difficulty of the guidelines as they were written, and that the two of them talked at some length after the meeting concluded."

"Are you sure of this, Mr. Martin?" The attorney was now speaking in a loud, incredulous voice, as if trying to catch Ted in a lie.

"Yes sir. I heard the comments Mitchell made about changing grant categories during the meeting and saw them talking together afterward. You might want to ask Mr. Blanton what they said to each other because I couldn't hear them."

Blanton's attorney shot a quick look back to his client as if he had not expected Ted's answers to be as they were.

"Mr. Martin, for whom do you work at the museum here?"

"Mitchell Jenkins."

"I have no further questions."

Ted looked around as the buzz of the gallery began again. He hoped he could return to his seat, but noticed Mitchell's attorney rising again and the judge looking at him.

"Your Honor, I have just a few questions for this witness on re-direct. May I do so at this time?" Permission was granted. "Mr. Martin, the plaintiff has chosen to make an issue of your employment at the museum, and since they have, I think we should explore this to a degree. Would you please tell the court what it is you do at the museum?"

There it was again, Ted needing to explain himself to a body of people who really didn't understand what went on inside a museum. Ted remembered his first trip to New York with Mitchell and the knowledgeable understanding of his job.

"I oversee the care of artwork at the museum, including the scope of its collection, recommending works for purchase that will enhance it, seeing that the collection is kept in excellent condition, and displaying select items for the public's enjoyment. I'm also charged with organizing temporary exhibitions of artists or collectors across the country as well as locally and regionally. There are other duties as well, but these seem to take the bulk of my time."

"It's the local exhibitions that most interest me at this time, Mr. Martin. Can you tell me about them?"

"The museum has a long tradition of presenting exhibitions that feature artists who reside in the area. When I came, it was impressed upon me how important these were to furthering the careers of artists in Meriden and Alabama. We plan these presentations throughout each year."

"And do these exhibitions actually assist artists, do you think, Mr. Martin?"

"Yes, I believe they do. It is reflected in the sales recorded from these exhibitions. The artists are promoted and encouraged to continue to explore their interests. It's a good program for all concerned."

"And how many of these exhibitions do you mount in any given year?"

"That varies of course, but I would say we average ten to twelve of these a year, and I have done so for the past three years."

"I see, Mr. Martin. You've been a very cooperative witness and I know you didn't think you were going to be answering questions for as long as you have. However, I do have one more question. Can you tell me how you came to feel so strongly about these local exhibitions the museum provides, especially since opening the new building? It might have been a good excuse to change directions."

"The museum today was brought about through the efforts of Meriden's local artists years ago. Mitchell Jenkins was quick to provide that knowledge to me early on and we, Mitchell and myself, sort of think the program of presenting local and regional artists today is a kind of payback."

"I see...Mitchell Jenkins. No further questions, Your Honor. The witness is excused."

Judge Clark thanked Ted for his time. He was grateful to be able to leave. He hadn't had time to consider whether he had helped Mitchell, though he was smiling as Ted passed by. Maureen was even smiling at him as he quickly looked for his seat at the back of the courtroom. Mitchell's attorney called several other people to the stand before calling Mitchell himself. The other witnesses were asked about Blanton's uncooperative nature and general unpleasant manner. Two were fellow artists from the community, the other the manager of a private art gallery that handled his work. But Mitchell was the star, the person both sides wanted to examine. Ted knew it wouldn't be easy for Blanton's attorney. When summoned, Mitchell stood and walked stiffly to the stand to be sworn in by the bailiff. His attorney rose and walked toward him. Ted sat in silence, as did the whole courtroom, awaiting his first question.

"Mr. Jenkins, much has been said in this case already about a great many things, most of which have no direct bearing on the real question of Mr. Blanton's suit against you. I would like to turn our attention to finding out if libel is really at issue here, or if what we are discussing is a simple matter of pride. I have in my hand a copy of a letter sent to you by Mr. Larry Smith, who as we remember from yesterday's testimony is executive director of the State Arts Commission. It is dated February

1975 and concerns a letter and subsequent conversation he had with Mr. Roger Blanton. Do you recognize the letter?"

"I do."

"Will you tell us, in your own words, what the letter is about?"

"The letter deals with Mr. Smith's learning that Roger Blanton was working to bring a suit against the commission over its refusal to grant him funds for a project he wanted to complete a few years earlier. Mr. Smith wrote to me about it since Mr. Blanton resides in the Meriden area and I was president of the commission at the time Mr. Blanton submitted the request."

Mitchell was measuring every word of his response. There was no sloppy Southern speech now, nothing funny, only the facts as he remembered them. A chill ran down Ted's back as he listened to the cold delivery. Mitchell had wanted this chance to speak on his own behalf, to confront Blanton and his attorney head-on. He was readying himself for that time and he could be deadly skillful.

"Why did the commission not grant Mr. Blanton's request?"

"Roger was applying for funding to establish a small foundry at his home here in Meriden. The project was not going to cost much money but more than was possible to grant under the "individual artist grant" category, so he submitted the request under a category generally reserved for educational institutions."

"Mr. Jenkins, what constitutes an educational institution according to the guidelines of the commission?"

"A non-profit tax status."

"Can artists qualify as a non-profit entity?"

"That's a good question. I'm not sure it's been legally explored, and I don't know of any artist with that kind of classification."

"Does Mr. Blanton qualify as a not-profit institution? Or, to your knowledge, has he ever tried legally to obtain that kind of status?"

"Not to my knowledge."

"How is it then that Mr. Blanton tried to apply for a grant that under the guidelines wasn't available to him?"

"I don't know."

"Did you discuss this matter with him at any time before he received written notification of the commission's decision on his request?"

"Yes, several times. At least twice before the application was actually due."

"During your tenure as director of the museum here, have you had other occasions to meet with Mr. Blanton on professional matters?"

"Many times."

"Is it not a fact that you presented an exhibition of Mr. Blanton's sculpture in 1970?"

"Yes, that is so."

"Can you tell the court about Mr. Blanton's attitude toward you and the museum at that time?"

Jenkins paused and looked hard at Blanton. "I arranged for Roger to have a one-man exhibition of his sculpture at the museum. We talked about it for several months beforehand and I assumed he understood the things we were discussing and where the exhibition would be housed. Roger brought his work to the museum on the appointed day and was surprised to find the gallery I intended to use was not the one he had expected. He stormed into my office demanding an explanation."

"Please continue, Mr. Jenkins."

"All the paperwork I had sent him about the exhibition made note of the gallery area in which his sculpture would be presented. He had even signed one copy of the letter and returned it to the museum as required. I showed it to him. He claimed his signature had been forged and that he had never seen the agreement before. He went to the president of the art association at the time to demand he be better treated. There was much commotion raised, but in the end the association board sided with me, and the exhibition was held in the gallery I had assigned for it."

"How did Mr. Blanton feel about that?"

"He was angry, even said he would withdraw his work, but was finally talked into working with me."

"Was that the only incident you had during this time?"

There was a pause as Jenkins looked again at Blanton as if helpless to continue. Had Jenkins and his attorney rehearsed this scene, it could not have gone better.

"No, it was not."

"Would you care to elaborate?"

"Roger was not happy with anything about the exhibition. He didn't think the opening invitations looked good enough; he didn't like the exhibition's checklist of objects; and finally, he did not like the way in which I placed the objects in the gallery."

"Who places work in a museum's gallery when preparing for an exhibition?"

"Currently Ted Martin does, and he does a great job of it." There was brief laughter. "But at that time, I placed the work myself."

"Did Mr. Blanton know you were personally involved in this matter?"

"Yes, it was in the letter he signed and returned to me."

"You're speaking of the letter on which Mr. Blanton said his signature was forged. What happened then, Mr. Jenkins?"

"Under the circumstances, I allowed him to rearrange the work any way he wished. It's against museum policy, but it was easier than causing another scene."

"Mr. Jenkins, getting back to the letter Larry Smith sent to you concerning Mr. Blanton's suit. Were you surprised by his stated intention?"

"No, I was not."

"Were you surprised at the length of time it took Mr. Blanton to decide to take this action, considering it was two full years since the commission denied his request?"

"Yes, that was somewhat surprising. Like something out of the blue. I cannot account for the delay."

"Mr. Jenkins, can you tell us please where Roger Blanton maintains his studio?"

"In the countryside about thirty-five miles from town. It's an isolated spot, but I would think it's conducive for a working artist."

"Have you ever been there?"

"Yes, twice, when working on his exhibition."

"Do many people go there?"

"I can't say with any accuracy, but I would think not."

"Why is that Mr. Jenkins?"

"I do not believe his studio is open for the public to visit. Roger likes to work alone without interruption."

"Would it be safe to assume then, that Mr. Blanton lives an isolated existence."

"Objection, Your Honor." Blanton's attorney jumped up. "That's putting a judgement in the mouth of the witness."

It was the first time his attorney had interrupted during the two-day proceeding.

"Sustained." Judge Clark had been following everything in silence and now directed his remarks to Jenkins' attorney. "Can you rephrase the question please?"

"Mr. Jenkins, based on your considerable experience, would you say Mr. Blanton's lifestyle is good for his development as an artist?"

"The solitude should be good, enabling him to work without interruption. However, there might be a time when too much isolation would be a handicap. Artists need to talk and interact with each other to see new things and experience new ideas. In that regard, I don't know that Mr. Blanton's isolation would be beneficial."

"At the time of Mr. Blanton's exhibition at the museum and the turmoil caused by his unhappiness with certain aspects of it, was there anyone on the association's board who was aware of the unpleasant nature of the situation and Mr. Blanton's behavior?"

"At the time of that exhibition, Lou Sterling was president of the board. He was directly involved with the complaints Roger registered against me and the museum. They were friends, almost neighbors in fact."

"That would be Louis Sterling, general manager of the *Meriden Journal*?"

"Yes, that is correct."

"And did Mr. Sterling have any comment to you about the circumstances of Mr. Blanton's behavior?"

"He thought it was unfortunate. Lou worked with me very closely on this matter, trying to bring Roger around to the terms of the letter he'd signed. It was not easy for him."

"Was that his only comment, Mr. Jenkins? As you know, I'm prepared to call Mr. Sterling as a witness."

Jenkins paused as if deeply troubled by what his attorney was forcing him to say. "Lou said he thought Roger's attitude was that of a spoiled child." As planned, the statement was met with immediate commotion. Blanton bristled in his chair as his attorney rose to object.

"We can call Mr. Sterling to the stand, Your Honor, to corroborate this statement," Jenkins' attorney said. "However, it is in the deposition that has already been taken of Mr. Sterling and is a matter of record. Just a few more questions Mr. Jenkins, then I will yield the floor. Did you write a response to the letter sent by Mr. Smith, the letter that has already been marked as an exhibit in this case?"

"I did."

"I now show you that letter, also dated February 1975. Do you recognize it?"

Jenkins reached across the witness stand and examined the document he already knew was the letter he'd sent to Smith. It was the letter Ted heard him dictate a year before.

"Yes, this is the letter I sent to Larry Smith."

"Let me read a few paragraphs of the letter so the jury might hear what you actually said, and why Mr. Blanton is bringing this suit. 'At the time that the grant application was denied, Mr. Blanton was invited to resubmit his request under another category. He refused, claiming the commission was not ever going to assist individual artists while it indirectly took money from them in the form of state taxes and gave it to institutions who, in his opinion, squandered the resources on ineffective projects. He repeatedly disrupted subsequent commission meetings with a litany of verbal insults directed at its members and staff—a most unprofessional attitude...' 'Unprofessional attitude' was what you said, Mr. Jenkins. Do you believe that refers at all to Mr. Blanton's performance as an artist?"

"I do not."

"Could you have used any other phrase to explain how you felt about Mr. Blanton's manner, his attitude?"

"I don't understand the question."

"Couldn't you have just as easily said 'a most childish attitude'?"

"Objection, Your Honor." Blanton's attorney was again on his feet, his face red with anger against his white hair. "The defense must refrain from saying things that are not in the witness's own words. That was a deliberate misuse of his power while on the floor."

"Sustained, please try to control yourself!"

Jenkins' attorney glared at his counterpart, then turned back to his table. "I have no more questions, Your Honor," he said, turning away from Jenkins. The point had been made and was now in the minds of the jury. They had played out this bit of drama as planned, and now both Jenkins and his attorney hoped he would make it through the cross-examination to come.

Blanton's attorney rose from his chair for his cross-examination and approached the witness. He walked slowly, in a deliberate manner. Jenkins stiffened on his wooden bench, as if bracing for the worst. All his powers of logic and argument would be trained now on this attorney who would ask questions designed to trip him up, to make him vulnerable.

"Mr. Jenkins, would you please tell the Court approximately how many art museums of importance there are in the state of Alabama?"

"That would be difficult to say. Every director thinks his own museum is important."

"I see, fair enough. Let me rephrase." He took a long look at the jury members. "In your opinion, how many art museums in this state rate regional press coverage and statewide attention. How many have curatorial and educational departments, how many win approval by the American Museum Association?"

Mitchell paused before giving his answer as if weighing the importance of his response. "There are only two in the state that are so approved, the Meriden Museum and the Birmingham Museum."

"I see. Now would you say this distinction would make your museum, the one here in Meriden, a place of importance, a place artists would want to have their artwork shown and recognized by?"

"Yes, I would hope so."

"And you have been director there for how many years?"

"Ten years."

"Let me read for the Court the other areas of artistic endeavors in which Mr. Jenkins has been active in addition to his career as director over the past ten years. Mr. Jenkins has been president of the Alabama Artist's Guild, president of the Alabama Museum's Federation, president of the Alabama State Arts Council, president of the Alabama Arts Commission, and president of the Meriden Arts Council; he has served on advisory boards for the National Endowment for the Arts and the American Association of Museums' review panels; he has been active in the state's artist community, publishing several books about artists here. These are very impressive credentials. Mr. Jenkins, after hearing these offices you've held and after stating you have been director for ten years at one of the two most powerful art museums in the state, could we not conclude that you yourself are a very respected and powerful figure in the Alabama art scene?"

"Yes, I suppose so."

"I would definitely suppose so, Mr. Jenkins. I would further suppose you are probably the most important single art administrator in the state, and as such could wield much authority and make many things go your way if you so choose."

"Objection!" Mitchell's attorney rose. It was sustained.

"Mr. Jenkins, is it not possible that by writing a letter to Mr. Larry Smith, executive director of the State Arts Commission, that you could sway an opinion, particularly on an issue where an artist is concerned?"

"A personal opinion perhaps, nothing more. The commission board members act independently from the staff on grant requests. The staff does not vote. It would be impossible for Mr. Smith to be biased in any way when considering an artist's request."

"But you agree an individual could be persuaded to think one way or another?"

"That is always true, I suppose."

"Then is it not possible, Mr. Jenkins," the attorney turned from Jenkins and addressed the jury, his voice booming in the courtroom, "that your written words to Mr. Smith might also prejudice anyone else who might read the letter after he received it, and that if it was discussed publicly in any manner, Roger Blanton might be wronged by your opinion of him? You are, after all and by your own admission, a significant figure in the art world of this state."

Silence in the courtroom.

"It is only one man's opinion. I'm sure Roger could find any number of people to disagree with it, and the opinion was not about his work, which I highly admire."

"Mr. Jenkins, you are not a naive person. Is it not possible your remarks could find their way to the public out of context, so that 'manner' or 'ability' could be confused or simply not stated at all? That, Mr. Jenkins, is what we are discussing." There was no reply from Mitchell. "I have no further questions."

Jenkins was instructed to step down from the bench. He walked back to the table where Maureen sat impassively behind his attorney. Judge Clark instructed the two attorneys to begin their closing arguments, with the plaintiff to go first. During this time, Jenkins sat stiffly in his chair, eyes straight ahead, as if deep in thought. Ted considered the cross-examination much easier than it might have been and wondered what he could be thinking.

The police arrived early in the morning at the Jenkins home following the death of Jimmy Biggs. Howard Jenkins was taken by surprise as he was leaving for work, the sun just breaking up the darkness.

"Excuse the early interruption Howard, but we're looking for Mitchell. Is he home? There's been some trouble and we would like to ask him a question or two."

Howard Jenkins looked at the officer, a friend of many years, and slowly nodded his head. It was not the first time Mitchell had been asked questions by the police in Opelousas.

"I suppose he's upstairs in his room. I'll get him if you like."

The two officers followed Howard inside and waited for him to return with his son. The house was on a street lined with homes belonging to working-class families. The rooms inside were like most others on the block. The furniture old, yet kept attractive and clean by the constant attention of Howard's wife, Grace. The living room had been repainted the prior spring, a light green color, the windows covered with sheer ruffled draperies. A console television sat in one corner— an RCA with rabbit ears sitting atop the polished wood. On an opposite wall, a small shelf held mementos of their lives, including a trophy Mitchell earned pitching for the baseball team at the military academy he had attended. Framed on the wall and hung next to it was his acceptance letter to the University of Alabama in Birmingham and a letter from the coach saying how pleased he was Mitchell had decided to join the team. The officers noticed it all. In a few moments Howard Jenkins returned to the living room with his son, who he had awakened.

"Mitchell," the officer said, "we'd like to ask you a few questions. Sorry to get you out of bed. Can you tell us where you were at about one thirty this morning?"

Jenkins looked at the policeman as if he were part of the dream he'd been having, then at his father.

"I was asleep in the house."

✵ ✵ ✵

Mitchell's attorney finished his remarks to the jury. They had been solid, retracing the testimony given. It was done in a very slow, deliberate manner, without the dramatics that riddled the remarks of the plaintiff's attorney. When both sides had finished, it was Judge Clark's turn to give his charge to the jury before they left to deliberate over Blanton's complaint.

"Ladies and gentlemen of the jury. You have heard much testimony these past two days in this rather unusual case. The dictionary definition of libel is, and I quote, 'any written or printed statement, not made in the public interest, tending to expose a person to public ridicule or contempt or to injure his reputation in any way.' What you must determine is whether Mr. Mitchell Jenkins intended to expose Mr. Roger Blanton to public ridicule or contempt, and further, if Mr. Jenkins intended to injure the professional reputation of Mr. Blanton in any way in the writing of a letter describing his actions and conduct as unprofessional. If it is your opinion that it was Mr. Jenkins' intent to do this, you must find him guilty of the charge as stated in this case and liable to pay Mr. Blanton damages. If, however, you do not see the case this way, you must return a verdict of not guilty. Let me stress at this time that we are not to examine the reasons for Mr. Jenkins' letter, only the intent of it. If there is reasonable doubt that Mr. Jenkins' intention was to deliberately hurt Mr. Blanton's reputation as an artist, you must return a verdict of not guilty. The bailiff will have copies of what I have just said for your consideration in the jury room; you are now required to go there and reach a conclusion in this case."

Judge Clark rose and the jury filed out of the courtroom. For the first time in two days, Mitchell Jenkins sat back in his chair trying to relax. He turned to his attorney who was smiling. Maureen looked tired and troubled; she rose and walked out of the courtroom. Roger Blanton also rose and turned to look over the spectators who were stirring, stiff from the long afternoon. He talked to supporters who had chosen to sit directly behind him. His testimony the day before had been a rather dry series of answers describing his longstanding concern for proper distribution of funds to agencies. He was asked if he had been unable to sell his work since the commission's refusal to grant his request. His answer was a quiet no. Blanton walked out of the courtroom to the outer hall where reporters waited to talk with him before a verdict was delivered. Several of the younger attorneys on Blanton's side came over to Jenkins, who stayed in his seat. Ted later learned they expressed their regret that the case had come to trial.

The jury stayed out for forty minutes. Ted left the courtroom to telephone the museum and provide an update since Mitchell had made it clear staff were not invited to the courtroom unless they had been called to testify. Ted could tell by the rush of people trying to re-enter the courtroom that something was happening. He quickly got off the phone with Ellen Maxwell and found his seat. Several area artists who had attended the trial feverishly finished pencil sketches, some of which Ted thought might become entries in their next competitive exhibition. Maureen Jenkins walked back to her chair, holding herself as elegantly as ever. She didn't look at Mitchell or anyone else as she took her seat. Ted had not spoken to her at any length since attending the Bishop gala over a year before. The invitations to their home had stopped.

As Judge Clark entered the room, Mitchell turned from his attorney and again assumed his rigid, almost military position. Clark gaveled for the courtroom to quiet, then asked if the jury had reached a verdict, which they had. The bailiff, an older man who sat in a chair outside the jury box, pressed a button that opened the jury room door, and twelve souls re-entered the courtroom. Ted looked at the faces of each of them as they took their seats. There was not a hint of expression from any of them except one, the last woman who gave Jenkins what Ted took to be a smile. It was faint and he didn't think Jenkins saw it, even though he too was watching each juror as if this was a murder trial and he was facing life or death.

"Mr. Foreman," the Judge said in the formal manner of every courtroom drama on television. "Have you and your eleven other members reached a verdict in this case?'

"We have Your Honor."

"Please hand your verdict to the bailiff."

The foreman did so, and the bailiff carried it to the judge, who opened the paper. Mitchell's eyes were intent on Judge Clark, looking for any hint of what might be on the small white page. There was none. Judge Clark handed the slip back to the bailiff, who returned it to the foreman.

"Mr. Foreman, would you please read your verdict to the court?" The tall Black man dressed in a brown suit and striped tie fingered the slip of paper, then slowly retrieved his reading glasses from his jacket pocket. He rested them over the bridge of his nose and read what was on the paper.

"We, the members of the jury in the case Blanton versus Jenkins, after hearing the evidence presented, find the defendant, Mitchell Jenkins, not guilty of the complaint brought forth."

There were other words spoken by the foreman and the judge, but they were not heard as people came forward to congratulate Jenkins on the decision. He immediately shook the hand of his attorney, then turned to Maureen, who had remained seated, and bent over to kiss her. She gave him her cheek, which, in the excitement, went unnoticed.

There was a victory celebration later at the museum. Ted had been asked to leave quickly after the verdict was read, and if it was favorable to set up a full bar for the party. Most everyone on staff who had an opinion on the trial were quietly confident of a positive resolution. Mitchell had not discussed the trial or his preparations for it to any great extent, though Ted was sure Martha was fully up to speed. There wasn't time to give anyone a detailed account of what had taken place, as Ted was sure his boss would arrive as quickly as he could leave the courtroom. He enlisted the aid of Joe Mullens and several others to set up tables in the theater, away from the public's eye. Most of the staff awaited Mitchell's arrival near the entrance he would surely use off the parking area. Ted managed to return there just as Mitchell, Maureen, the legal team, and several commission members entered to applause and cheering. Maureen walked through the lobby as if she were not conscious of the noise. Her eyes caught Ted's for a moment and give him a bewildered look before disappearing down the hallway for the bar. She didn't stay long.

Mitchell Jenkins was surrounded by people as they pressed him to recount what had gone on. Toasts were offered to the law firm, to the commission who had stood behind him, and finally to Mitchell himself for fighting hard to win. The party continued well into the evening. One by one people left until only Mitchell, Martha, and Ted remained. He thanked Ted again for his willingness to testify and for his cool manner on the stand.

"It's what turned the tide for our side, Ted. You broke the ice, made the jury see that we're human and likable. I was worried before you got up there, but afterwards I knew we had them where we wanted them."

In an uncharacteristic move, Mitchell decided to leave the mess until morning, locking the theater doors as the trio walked back to his office.

"That was a hard test for us." Mitchell was talking to no one specifically. "It'll be the first of many from now on. At least we showed them we stand tough under attack and they can't just push us around. I want files begun on everyone who spoke against us today. Our lawyer is providing a transcript of the entire trial. They'll try again, and I want the goods on all of them before they do." He sat back in his desk chair, loosening his tie. The desk was littered with mail and messages. He looked over them before speaking again. "You don't have Roger Blanton scheduled for an exhibition, do you Ted?"

It was an odd question, and Ted couldn't tell if he was kidding or not. He didn't have Blanton scheduled for anything and said so to Jenkins, who was walking back to his desk chair after fixing a scotch.

"Good! I had wanted to be fair to that son-of-a-bitch, but not now, that's over. Keep him off for a couple years, make him think about the fuss he's caused. Besides, if he dares to make an issue of it, you'll be the one on the block—not me!"

They laughed as Ted felt his stomach sink. He did not like his two-day courtroom field trip and felt that he too had been on trial.

"You know Ted, it might be a good idea to institute that exhibition committee we've discussed a couple times. You can manage them if you're reasonably careful and stack the deck. It would be good to get people from the art association involved so if Blanton or any of his ilk complain, it won't look like their not being exhibited is based solely on your judgement. Blanton's attorney was correct, we're an important influence in the state and now that everyone knows it, I want to rub Blanton's nose in it." Mitchell smiled at Martha, who sat across from him. "Right kid?" He addressed the remark to her, and she looked down in her embarrassed way.

"I guess so, if you say that's the way it should to be."

"Right." Mitchell looked across the office at the painting that hung on the opposite wall. "That's the closest I've ever come to being convicted of anything serious, though there have been other attempts. You've just got to be tough and not submit to intimidation. Knock the shit out of the opposition, it's the only way."

Through the gin he had consumed, Ted was feeling hungry. He rose to leave for the night. Martha returned to her own office to finish letters Mitchell had dictated the night of the trial's first day. Ted did admire his devotion to work, but had long since given up trying to match him.

"You leaving Ted?"

"Yes sir, it's been a long day and I need some rest. I hope all this excitement will die down now so we get on with business."

"Don't ever let your guard down, remember that! They'll be gunning for you too now, I guarantee it. The trial established you as a public figure in the community's mind. Be careful."

Ted stopped to consider what Mitchell said, remembering the words he'd spoken when Ted had first come to the museum, about his being forced to leave. He looked pretty secure now.

"Need a ride home Mitchell?" Ted knew Maureen had taken the car when she'd left earlier.

"No thanks. I'm meeting Taylor and Laura at the club. I'll get Martha to drop me there on her way home. Appreciate the offer though! See ya in the morning!"

Ted waved and left. The night's air was cooler than it should have been in July, and the weather warning light atop the Endicott Building blinked off and on. He drove out of the parking lot thinking of Jenkins tucked away in his fortress and wondered what he and Martha might be discussing.

CHAPTER TWENTY-EIGHT

Mitchell Jenkins was greeted as a conquering hero as he entered the lobby of the club. He'd managed to arrive before the Jameses and decided to treat himself to another drink at the elegant bar. There were more handshakes there as the powerful men whom he had come to know well offered their congratulations. Jenkins talked little about the trial itself, only that he was glad it was over and that he felt badly for Roger Blanton who believed he had suffered at Jenkins' hands. He told anyone who asked he hoped Blanton would not harbor hard feelings toward him or the museum and that everyone could again resume the business of bringing high-quality, cultural activities to the city. He was summoned to the James table by a club employee and left the men's only part of the building.

Laura and Taylor were also pleased to greet Jenkins on such a happy occasion. Neither of them had attended the trial, feeling it would be out of place and only add to Blanton's opinion of the wealthy interfering in the art world. They had learned of the outcome from Martha Dyer that afternoon after Ted had returned to the museum.

"Where's Maureen?" Laura asked as Mitchell sat at the round table across from them.

"She was terribly fatigued by the events of the last two days and begged off, wanting to return home. I'm afraid the stresses and worry have been quite a lot for her. But now, it's over! And none of us has to think about any of it again."

"I really don't understand what Roger Blanton was thinking to bring that suit against you in the first place," Laura said. "Is he crazy?"

She looked intently at Jenkins, who was being philosophical now, looking at the starched, white tablecloth as he spoke. "No, not crazy. Misinformed perhaps, and probably out of touch with reality. There is much to his self-isolation getting in the way of his rationality. I was surprised his attorney even took the case. I had a feeling Roger hadn't told them the whole story, and that was confirmed by one of the junior members on his legal team while the jury was out."

"What's going to become of this Blanton fellow?" Taylor asked.

"Nothing. He'll continue to make sculpture, I suppose. There'll be an assessment of the court costs and he'll be liable for the bulk of them, though I may have some as well. I really don't know how he can afford to pay those expenses."

"Will your expenses for this silly thing come out of your pocket, or will the museum cover them? Seems like they should."

"That will need to be discussed by the commission. Had we lost the case, the insurance policy the museum carries on me for just this type of thing would pay the costs and awarded damages."

"I'm quite sure the commission will want to cover these costs," Laura assured him. "Don't give it another thought, Mitchell."

"If they don't, I will," James said to end the conversation.

The three of them stayed at the club until late. Jenkins was beginning to show only the slightest signs of fatigue even though it was well past eleven. They had discussed many things during dinner, much of it family business they felt comfortable discussing in front of Jenkins, the most interesting being Taylor's desire to collect artwork for their Meriden home. He had grown increasingly intrigued since his gift to the museum and began to believe artwork was as good as or better than other investments he made. He wanted Jenkins to assist them in defining areas they should invest in, as well as suggest appropriate galleries and people to call on in New York. Jenkins made a mental note to mark this very special day in his calendar; two wonderful events had occurred: He won the trial and Taylor James had said what he had hoped for since the museum's new building funding was announced. He assured them he would do whatever necessary to advise them in their collecting.

"It will be my pleasure!"

They dropped Jenkins at his home around midnight. Maureen had left lights on for him, but the house was quiet. The yard was littered with toys the children had left out after a day of play. He waved as the Jameses drove off and walked up the sloping driveway. The screen was out of the bottom half of the storm door, the wooden door unlocked. The vestibule light was on, and he remembered Maureen asking him to repaint this area. It was easy to ignore her "honey-do" lists, but now he thought he'd complete the chore over the weekend if she got the paint. It would be a concession. He attributed her moodiness the last several weeks to the trial and hoped now it would change. He turned off the lights as he worked his way through the house to their bedroom. He wanted her tonight; he would take her forcefully if necessary and thought he might enjoy that. The door to their bedroom was closed. He opened it expecting to find Maureen asleep with her reading light on. Instead, she was sitting up in bed.

"Didn't expect to find you up."

He walked across the room, dropping his suit coat on a chair and stepping out of his shoes. She watched as he moved about the bathroom, not saying a word. He knew she wouldn't want to screw around, but that didn't matter tonight. It was the least she could do after not talking to him through the course of the trial and only offering him her cheek to kiss afterward. He stood at the foot of their bed, looking down at her beneath the light-colored sheets.

"Want to make it with a vindicated man?" She looked at him silently as he stood naked before her. "Actually, it really doesn't matter if you want to or not."

"Don't touch me, you bastard." The anger in her voice caught him by surprise. "The only thing I want from you is a divorce. And if you touch me," she picked up the receiver of the phone on her nightstand, "I'll call the police."

Mitchell Jenkins didn't come into the museum the following day. Ted expected he might take a few days off, but when he said he'd been in the night between court appearances, Ted assumed he was mistaken. Martha Dyer called once to see if he knew when Mitchell would be coming in. He hadn't said anything about being out to her. Taylor James called twice and was getting a bit frosty with Martha because she didn't know his whereabouts.

"Do you think I should call the house, Ted?" she'd asked. It was something none of the staff liked to do.

"Sure, why not?" Ted heard her breathing on the other end of the line, and her hesitancy surprised him.

"Would you mind calling?"

Had she suddenly fallen out of favor? "Not at all. Anything specific you want to know from him if he's there?"

"Just let me know when he's coming in."

Ted dialed Mitchell's home number and listened to the phone ring. No answer. Before he tried again ten minutes later, he heard Mitchell's voice as he closed his office door. Only Martha Dyer saw him for the next three days. The rest of the staff knew nothing of what was going on, though obviously there was something afoot. Martha wouldn't talk and would only take messages for him that would be answered by her the next day. According to her, he was taking some time off at a hideaway only she knew of. He did come into the museum at night and sometimes in the early mornings. He would leave Martha messages to relay to the rest of the staff.

Ted wasn't told the cause of Mitchell's current state until later that week. Maureen called to speak with him when neither he nor Martha were in the building and the call was transferred to Ted. He was surprised to learn she had acted on the veiled threat she'd made at Bishop's retirement party, and further surprised to learn Jenkins had taken the news so hard. It was what he'd alluded to wanting since Ted arrived in Meriden. He would have thought the prospect of being a "free man" would have been great news. It was not! Maureen told Ted of the scene in their bedroom the night following his courtroom triumph and how it turned into ugly threats from each of them. Jenkins didn't even spend the remainder of the night at their home, grabbing handfuls of his clothing as he went. She had not heard from him since.

The morning of the fourth day, Mitchell was in his office looking and acting like business-as-usual. Before Ted had a chance to sit at his desk, Mitchell called him into his office. Ted walked the thirty feet between their offices very slowly, not knowing what to expect. Mitchell was alone when he entered.

"Hey there, Ted. Sit down." He was in shirt sleeves, his tie askew, the draperies closed, the only light coming from the ceiling spotlights. "Maureen is planning to divorce me. It caught me by surprise, but I'll recover. The last few days I've been trying to find a place to live until I can sit down with an attorney to understand my options. I just wanted you to know because I'll be in and out a lot over the next week or so and you'll be running the show." He sat expressionless, but with a manner different from the one Ted knew so well.

"Mitchell, is there anything I can do?"

He smiled in a bittersweet way. "No, Ted. This is just another battle I must win...and I will, you can be sure of that. If she's going to fight me, I'll fight back. It won't be pleasant for her."

With that Ted excused himself and went back to his office. He buzzed Martha to ask about Mitchell's schedule for the day and if there was anything of importance he should be aware of. She was unusually quiet in her answer.

"I'll come up and talk with you, Ted. Did he tell you what's going on?" Ted answered he had. "I can't believe he's taking this so hard." It was the first time Ted thought Martha had been honest. She arrived just before noon and took a chair opposite his. "Mitchell has gone for the day.

I don't think he'll call or be in again. Nothing is getting done at the opposite end of the hallway. He was to see Abram Rubin this afternoon and I haven't been able to get him on the phone to cancel. Would you be able to see him at two? I don't know what he wants. Rubin doesn't know about any of this, and Mitchell doesn't want anyone to know unless he tells them personally. Just make up some excuse for his absence. How much did he tell you?"

Ted looked at her blankly. How much was there to tell? "Just the facts of it. I suppose it would be a shock getting it the way he did, but I'm sure he must have thought about the possibility of her wanting out. He surely talked to me enough about his wanting out. Do you know where he's living?" Ted had not considered Mitchell living anywhere but where he had since he'd known him.

"At the East Side Arms." She said it without a smile or any other show of emotion. The Arms was an older, multi-level apartment building in the center of downtown, within walking distance of the museum. Built in the early fifties, it was originally a luxury dwelling in keeping with the modern look of the times. Over the twenty years since its construction, however, it had become a haven for prostitution, drugs and occasional violence. He had taken a studio apartment on the seventh floor.

"Why there, of all places? There are plenty of apartment complexes around Meriden that are better. Is he trying to get himself killed?"

"He says it's convenient to the museum and the rent is low."

It was all she would say and probably all she knew about why Jenkins had chosen to exile himself in such shabby quarters. Ted knew something of his financial position through keeping his ears open around him for the years he had been at the museum. His salary was more than adequate to support his family. The payment on his home was minimal; he had no car payments, and except for his children's educations, there was very little else that presented a financial responsibility of any size. Mitchell could have lived anywhere he'd wanted; his reason for choosing the Arms had nothing to do with a shortage of money.

Abram Rubin was his old self, hot to tell anybody about his West Coast artist friends and trying to pick up any of the secretaries he passed by. He had learned that Martha Dyer grew up in the West and tried unsuccessfully to strike up a friendship with her that was more than professional. He wasn't too disappointed to learn Jenkins wasn't at the museum. Martha had covered by saying he was taking time off after the stress of the trial. Rubin made small talk with her for almost an hour before turning his attention to Ted. Jenkins had asked Rubin to gather documentation to substantiate the insurance values he had placed on the objects in his collection that the museum was now responsible for. The loan agreement he and Jenkins had agreed to now seemed too complicated and not the sort of document an "old friend" would design. Rubin wanted a simple gentlemen's agreement, but Jenkins insisted on the other.

"The second something happens to one of those paintings, or there is a question as to the rights of the museum to use them in some manner, Rubin will be all over us unless we have some protection," Jenkins had said.

Rubin had chosen to live in Birmingham after his West Coast practice fell through, joining a medical practice there. It seemed to Ted his adult life had been spent trying to make himself over. The art collection was just such a ploy, and the affluence of his California practice made it easy to nurture. Moving back was as much a shock to his personality as it was to his purse. He no longer could make purchases with the free-wheeling nature that had gained him access to the gallery community in Los Angeles.

"Ted," he said while reading through the second page of the agreement, "I can appreciate the need for the museum to be covered if something should happen to pieces in the collection, but does Mitchell really think all these clauses are necessary?" He had gotten over his reluctance to speak to Ted but only because Jenkins had forced the two of them together at social events. He knew that if Jenkins was in the building, Rubin would not be with him now.

"Mitchell felt it's good for both you and the museum to be as careful as possible in the handling of your collection for the term of the loan. We attempted to list as many possible areas of concern as we could think of. As you will see it covers not only physical liability but also reproduction rights, requests from other institutions for loans, future additions you might make, and details you and Mitchell have discussed about your continued support of the Museum."

It really was quite a document engineered by a master technician. Not only did it specify that Rubin would make annual gifts of his collection or a cash donation to the museum, it also allowed for the use of any part of the collection for any purpose the museum might have. Rubin asked one or two more questions, signed the document, then proceeded to fill the afternoon with stories about his California adventures. The remainder of Ted's week was spent trying to determine what Mitchell had meant to decide on various small issues that needed closure. He was in and out at odd times of the day and night, still meeting only with Martha, who would pass along his directives.

By Tuesday of the next week, Ted had still not seen Jenkins, but had heard through the grapevine he was acting irrationally—fighting with Maureen and attempting to find "the meanest divorce attorney in town." That afternoon Maureen called asking for Ted specifically.

"Have you seen Mitchell yet this afternoon? Is he there now?" Ted confirmed he was not. "Well, he left here several minutes ago and is mad as hell. I just wanted to warn you all to stay out of his way if he comes in."

"Are you all right? He didn't..."

"No, nothing like that, just verbal abuse. He won't accept the fact that I will not take him back and plan to go through with the divorce. We've been separated three times in the twenty years we've been married, each time getting back together for the kids or for appearances. This time, there's no going back. It's over for me. He won't be reasonable about any of it. Anyway, if he comes in, watch out. I'm sure he'd like to get his hands on somebody."

Ted thanked her for the warning and alerted both Martha and Ellen, but Mitchell didn't come to the museum. Ted worked until six that evening and asked the night security officer if Jenkins came in while he was on duty. He did, Ted was told, though not the last two nights the guard had worked. Ted's home phone rang at ten thirty-five; it was Maureen.

"I'm so scared, Ted. I don't know what to do!"

There was real fear in her voice, and Ted thought immediately of Mitchell. "What's happened? You alright?"

"It's Mitchell again, he just left. We had another terrible argument, I had to send the children to a neighbor because I was afraid of what he might do. He's threatened to kill himself tonight if I don't take him back. I think he really means it."She paused, and Ted remembered the times Mitchell had talked to him of dying and hoping he could pick his own way and time because he wanted to savor the experience. They were grim dialogues coming from a man who prided himself on his physical appearance.

"Did he say anything about where he might be going? Did he say how he'd do...I mean did he indicate the way? People who talk about suicide usually don't really want to go through with it."

"He said there were several ways. He talked about running the car into a bridge or overpass abutment. But you know he lives on the seventh floor. He might try anything. And Ted, you know he owns a gun."

Ted did know about the gun, as Mitchell had taken considerable pride in showing it to him. It was a snub-nosed 38, Smith and Wesson. He kept it in a cabinet beside his office desk, saying he'd bought it for protection.

"Have you called the police, Maureen?"

"I've been afraid to. It would create such attention, but really, I don't know what to do. I'm in no state to make decisions, that's why I called you."

"I'll call them, then head down to the museum to see if his car is there. You stay put and don't let anyone in. I'll have a patrolman sent over in case Mitchell decides to come back."

"Call me from the museum Ted, I want to know if he's there."

The conversation with the police was very unpleasant, not because of anything the police said or indicated, but because it was hard for Ted to tell anyone what was going on with Mitchell. They were somehow reassuring with their almost casual attitude to the threat of a suicide, though it did little to calm Ted's nerves. He described Mitchell's car and gave his address at the East Side Arms. He didn't say anything about Mitchell's revolver.

Once again, Ted left late at night for the museum after a phone call from Maureen Jenkins—the last time being when Mitchell and the Parkers had been deep in negotiation about who knows what. The conclusion of that night's search had a positive outcome, and Ted hoped this one would as well. Yet he was feeling the same dread he had before. He had asked for a police officer to meet him at the museum. From the parking lot, he could see lights shining in windows of the Arms building and wondered if Mitchell's was among them. Then he saw his car parked close to the museum with a patrol car pulled alongside and officers inspecting it.

"This his car?" one of them asked, assuming he was Ted Martin.

"Yes, that's it. Anything inside?"

There was nothing out of the ordinary. It was parked as if nothing was amiss. In fact, he had it washed, and the interior had been cleaned since Ted saw it last. He followed the officer's flashlight as it lit the interior, fearing he would see Mitchell's slumped body on the floor; but there was nothing.

"You have a key to get in this place? We'd better see if he's inside."

Ted pulled a wad of keys from his trouser pocket, turned off the door alarm, and they went in.

"This man Jenkins, does he own a gun?"

Ted remembered not having mentioned that fact when he called from home. "Yes, he does. Sorry, I meant to mention that earlier. A 38 he bought about a year ago. He keeps it in his office."

The officers shook their head at this. As they entered and Ted locked the heavy door behind them, he noticed they had unhooked the straps of their gun holsters, a sign he didn't like, and one that made him wary going into Mitchell's office. There were no lights on as he unlocked the door to the office suite. Mitchell generally made it a practice to leave his office spotlights on to light the interior at night. Now the glare from the hallway lights into his office, which was open, made it impossible to see inside. He wanted to see in just a bit so as not be horrified by what might be there. With the two policemen, one in front and one behind, Ted flipped on the lights. There was nothing amiss and no Mitchell Jenkins. His desk was dusted, clear of paper, and the ash tray was as clean as if it never had been used. As the officers poked around, Ted went to where the gun was kept and opened the cabinet, hoping to find it inside. It was not. His phone was now ringing, the clear, plastic button flashing wildly. It was Maureen.

"The car is here," Ted informed her, "but little else. His office is very clean and tidy as if someone was here recently. I don't remember it looking this way when I left earlier, but I really didn't inspect it on my way out. The gun's not here."

Maureen had not heard from him, and her voice was still fearful. As they hung up, another line was flashing and Ted picked it up.

"Meriden Museum of Art," he said out of habit and without deference to the hour or the circumstance of him being there.

"Ted Martin, please. This is Lieutenant Inspector Cain calling, Meriden City Police." Ted's heart stopped for a second, then he managed to say hello. "We're over here at the East Side. The manager says he saw Jenkins going up to the seventh floor of the building just, oh, a half an hour ago, and that he's not left the building since then. We're going up now and wanted you to be aware in case there's any trouble."

"He has a gun," Ted blurted out, not wanting to forget. "It's usually here in his office, but it's not."

"Ok. Thanks for the information. You going to be there for a while?"

"Yes, I suppose so, unless it would be better for me to come there."

"No, stay where you are. I'll get back to you."

Ted told the two officers what the inspector had said. A similar account had been relayed to them over the radios they wore. They indicated they would rather wait outside, and Ted let them out of the building, returning to Jenkin's office for a call from Inspector Cain. Sitting at the desk, Ted imagined every possible scenario for the outcome of the story, while asking himself if it were really happening.

✵ ✵ ✵

Mitchell Jenkins sat quietly in the living room of his parent's house answering questions from the sheriff. He hadn't mentioned anything about Jimmy Biggs or the Pierce automobile. He was determined not to volunteer any information. Though scared, it was not the first time he'd been questioned by authorities for offenses ranging from shoplifting to assault. His familiarity with the law gave him a sort of confidence now, even though the stakes were much greater.

"You were here asleep. Is that correct? Is that what you said?"

There was no emotion in the sheriff's voice; he had been up most of the night searching for Harold Pierce's car. He pulled a straight-backed, wooden chair close to Mitchell and straddled it, resting his arms on its back. His face was only inches from the teen, and he spoke softly.

"Mitchell, your buddy Jimmy Biggs apparently committed suicide last night after stealing Harold Pierce's new car. We found him and the car, his body still warm, his brains sprayed all over the interior of that fine, new automobile. Pierce's gun was tucked in his hand and coated with blood." He looked at Jenkins as the young man covered his mouth, imaging the scene the sheriff had described. "What I want to know is if you were there."

Mitchell's father interrupted the questioning. "You got any proof my son was there, or are you trying to scare him into sayin' somethin' that ain't true? You got something to say, be quick about it or get out. There's a lot of you people who want him to get kicked around like he used to around here. Mitchell's getting out of this town, goin' away to college and makin' something of himself."

"Hold on now Howard, I ain't here to cause any problems or to scare Mitchell. But," he again looked at Jenkins, "we've got reason to believe your son here lied about being asleep in this house at 1:30 this morning."

"Just because he and Biggs are friends, that ain't enough for you to assume..."

"We've got a witness who saw Biggs and somebody else run from behind her wooden garage and get into Pierce's car. Somebody who watched as Biggs pushed the car down the street and away from the house so they could start the engine without alerting Pierce."

"Is Mitchell being accused, then?" He looked at his son who still had not said anything, but sat as if overwhelmed by the proceedings. Howard Jenkins knew Mitchell very well could have been with Biggs last night, he could have stolen the car and he could know about his friend's death. He would not say anything though.

"No." The sheriff looked Mitchell in the eye. He smelled of sweat and cigarettes but still put his face up to that of the young man. "Because our witness couldn't make out the identity of the other person with Biggs. She didn't see him clearly."

✳ ✳ ✳

It was twenty minutes more before Inspector Cain called back. His voice was still calm, detached, yet with a questioning quality that disturbed Ted. "Mr. Martin, we've found your boss. He's in his apartment having coffee. He acted very surprised when we knocked on the door."

Ted tried to visualize Jenkins in the small apartment having coffee at almost midnight. "Is he okay? Did he act funny? It was his wife who told me of his suicide threat."

"He seemed perfectly fine, asked if he could help us, totally oblivious to what was going on. We told him about his wife's call to you and that she was concerned for his life and that you had called the police. He acknowledged he had seen his wife earlier and that they were separated, but said he left their home in a good frame of mind and that he really couldn't understand where she would get such an idea."

"I see. Well, thank you Inspector, I'm sorry to have caused you this trouble. I really don't know what to think about any of it."

"That's quite alright, Mr. Martin, you did the right thing. Mr. Jenkins did ask where you were, as if he might try to call."

"Okay, thanks again."

Sitting in Mitchell's office, Ted wondered if he should call Maureen to tell her Mitchell was safely tucked away in his apartment drinking coffee. He felt used by both Maureen and Mitchell. He then remembered the inspector saying Mitchell might call, or he might decide to walk on over. Ted was suddenly afraid of him for involving the police. He quickly left the office, locking every door behind him. He looked out the lobby window at his car parked only a few feet away. The police car was gone and he saw no movement. He unlocked the outside door, re-locked it, and secured it with the electronic alarm. There was no one in sight, yet he felt he was being watched as he walked to his car, got in, and drove away.

The following morning Jenkins came in late, but during normal hours. Ted could hear him talking to members of the staff. There was nothing strange in his voice, no hint of his relationship with Maureen and especially no hint of his actions the night before. Ted listened as his office door shut softly, the way it had in days past, then buzzed Martha's office line. It rang for quite a while before the receptionist picked up and asked what he wanted.

"Is Martha about somewhere?"

She paused for several seconds before answering. "She's in with Mitchell, I can see them through his curtain."

Ted thanked her and returned to his work, wondering how long it would take Jenkins to come in or buzz his line. The fear of the night before had turned into anxiety. He hadn't spoken to Maureen yet this morning but had called her from home the night before. She was relieved her husband was not dead, but the same fear Ted felt was in her voice. She was thinking about late night visits and she, better than anyone, knew the extent of his temper.

Mitchell didn't come near Ted until the very end of the day as he was leaving to have dinner with Louis Sterling. Maureen had called Sterling the night before too, and the dinner was to judge Mitchell's mental well-being.

Mitchell stuck his head into Ted's office but didn't come in. "Hey there, Bud, how's things with you?" Ted looked at him blankly. "Sorry to get you out of bed last night. It was really nothing, just Maureen over-reacting. I do appreciate it though." He paused, expecting Ted to say something. He did not, only smiled at him from the relative safety of his desk fifteen feet away. "See you in the morning, okay?"

And with that he was gone. Nothing more was ever said of the incident. From that day on though, he was on the offensive about the subject of his pending divorce. He would tell anyone about it quite freely, gathering their support and sympathy.

Sterling's verdict was that Mitchell seemed perfectly rational, in reasonably good spirits, and Maureen must have been mistaken in her interpretation of Mitchell's remarks the evening before. As far as he was concerned Mitchell was in the clear and Maureen was starting a less-than-lady-like campaign to discredit her husband. Ted didn't believe Maureen had lied, nor did Ellen Maxwell, the only person to whom he'd confided in about the episode. She was as appalled as he was about Sterling's conclusions, crediting it to Mitchell's ability to distort events and influence people. Taylor and Laura James were saddened that Maureen would treat her talented husband in such a way. Taylor even remarked to Sterling that she was an ingrate to throw away all Jenkins had given her. Upon learning he was living in the East Side Arms, they offered Mitchell their home through the coming autumn as they were to be in Europe. Mitchell quickly accepted and spent September and October in comfort. Even after they returned, he was a frequent guest, using the time to further indoctrinate Taylor to the museum as well as provide him updates from colleagues around the state on the Birmingham complex.

Strengthened by this support, Jenkins quickly began recovering from his earlier anguish. He talked openly about the divorce and her charges (mental cruelty). He also developed a fervent interest in religion, joining the same imposing Methodist church where both James and Sterling belonged. However, his newfound faith did not convince him to turn the other cheek. His vow to obtain the meanest lawyer he could find was not idly made. In his usual calculated way, he smiled and projected a sympathetic attitude when at meetings with Maureen and her counsel, then found ways to damage her reputation when he was not. His justification for this was self-preservation. The financial agreement he engineered was, like the Rubin loan agreement, a master stroke. He counted on Maureen's beauty to attract men to her as soon as the ink on the divorce papers was dry. The clause that had been most important to him was if she remarried, all alimony payments would stop, and she stayed single exactly six months after the agreement was final.

Mitchell and Ted were to drive to Birmingham for a meeting of museum professionals from across the state. Mitchell arrived on time to pick Ted up for the trip, but when Ted approached the car, Mitchell continued writing on something, instead of greeting him in his usual verbose way. It was his daily planner.

"What's up?" Ted asked.

He hadn't noticed Ted had opened the passenger door and was sitting beside him. Finally, he looked over triumphantly. "Maureen tells me she's getting married in April. I was just checking the dates." He started writing again, ignoring Ted until he was finished. "It means I only need to make two more alimony payments. I'm going to save a bunch of money."

Mitchell put the car in gear and they headed north. The smile didn't leave his face the entire time, though they talked of other things. Along with his religious pursuits, the divorce also caused Jenkins to take an interest in his children. In the years Ted had worked with him, he never mentioned them except on their birthdays or at Christmas when he generally bought out the toy departments of local stores, purchasing gifts he knew Maureen wouldn't approve of. If it was an attempt to win them over and take them from their mother, it was working. His son declared an interest in living with his father by the summer after Maureen's wedding. While that was the response Jenkins wanted, the reality was not. He played a careful game, taking his son's love without the constant responsibility.

His interest in women didn't diminish. He would talk about how difficult it was to be dating at his age and the differences between the morals of women now and when he was younger. His painfully shy routine was difficult for Ted to understand, knowing as he did how forward Mitchell had been with women when he was married. This was part of the new Mitchell Jenkins, one that seemed to evolve in other areas while remaining at the core as he had always been. Ted no longer saw him socially; he traveled alone on business and was entertained by the Jameses, the Sterlings and other people of substance. Martha Dyer became his supreme confidante, knowing more about Mitchell and his activities, including the extra-curricular ones, than any other person. The burden of this knowledge caused her to become more secretive and protective. She was, in all respects except title, his assistant director, and she took pains to let staff know it without ever saying as much. Mitchell just let it happen. The lives of his senior staff now became an obsession to him, as if each of them were expected to measure up to the growth he had achieved in his own vision of his role. They were all suspect until they could prove their loyalty; only by this time they had lived and worked with Mitchell Jenkins too long.

PART III

"Fool!" said my muse to me,
"Look into thy heart, and write."

SIR PHILIP SIDNEY

CHAPTER TWENTY-NINE

David Griffin worked to ready the new house for some kind of occupancy by spring of 1977. His self-imposed exile to the property he had purchased only worsened his frustrations about life and his new role. Born into the upper middle class of Mobile, David spent his youth and adolescence quite aware of the expectations his parents had for his future. The fact that he was drawn to painting did not sit well with them, particularly his father who, as a successful shipping broker, wanted David to have an interest in his business and to take it over eventually. He was sent off to the University of Georgia enrolled in the business program, but gravitated to fine art under the watchful eye of Lamar Dodd. College was a life-giving source for David, who could now express his own interests out from under the crushing burden of family responsibility. He became entrenched in the university environment, allowing art and related disciplines of literature and language to create a new world of ideas.

Relations with his father strained, but the self-confidence he felt in gaining knowledge replaced family ties. The threat of cutting off his college funding ceased when he demonstrated his ability to succeed in the art world by earning a solo exhibition in the university gallery his junior year. By the conclusion of his senior year, a liberal arts education had prepared David not for business, but for teaching or working seriously as a painter. His dream was to travel to New York and work at odd jobs until he could save money for a European trip, but it was only partially fulfilled.

During his senior year, he began dating Mary Hollis, a fellow art student who he knew but never thought of romantically or sexually. It was a revelation to him that she was as liberal physically as he thought he was. Other women talked about the kinds of sex acts they thought men would enjoy; Mary was quite willing to try them. Their relationship was a torrid one, ending in marriage shortly after their graduation. David didn't want the marriage, but his parents insisted on it, not being able to face their friends with a son who was a painter and living out-of-wedlock with a woman. Both David and Mary were awarded scholarships to graduate school and settled into an apartment in Athens. Their time there was put to good use, and after their second graduate year they planned a very successful exhibition together. Seen by Jenkins, who at the time was searching for artwork to purchase, one of David's paintings was added to the museum's collection. Additionally, both David and Mary were hired to teach at the museum's school. Mitchell spent as much time with Griffin as his schedule would allow, but the confines of life in the small town quickly soured for David, a condition Jenkins could do little about. The positive side of the job had much to offer Griffin, who was serious about his art and unable to face the real world. Besides his teaching assignments there was very little that was required of him; it was a wonderful shelter. On their combined salaries, he and Mary could live quite comfortably in the rent-free cottage on the property. The impending birth of a second child added to the confinement David felt, and he was prone to dark periods when neither his work nor their marriage went well.

Eviction from the cottage signaled the beginning of his most prolonged dark period. Already no longer interested in or happy with teaching, his desire to paint ceased as well. Jenkins, who had originally hoped

David would take over the school's responsibilities, was rapidly losing faith. When David announced he was no longer interested in teaching, Mitchell was in the unpleasant position of deciding if Mary's abilities were enough to transfer that position to her and pay David a small stipend as an artist-in-residence. Without the stipend it would be difficult for the two of them and their young children to scrape by. Jenkins was not initially of the mind to give David anything, angered over the painter's attitude. However, Mary did do an adequate job as a teacher, and he knew it would be difficult to replace either of them on the small amount of money he offered. An agreement was reached allowing David to stay on the school's staff at a cut in pay. He would teach three courses a year, plus consult with Ellen Maxwell on educational projects and public demonstrations by practicing artists. The remainder of his time could be used however he chose.

Reluctantly, Jenkins offered Mary the position of school director. To his surprise, Mary worked hard, broadening many programs that had fallen behind through lack of attention. David never lost interest in Mary from a physical standpoint and never took her seriously as an artist. She was the stability he needed, but he was rarely completely satisfied with her. His own attitude toward marriage was much the same as Mitchell's. There were many other women in his life, beginning in graduate school. Mary knew about several of them and chose not to make it an issue. It wasn't that she didn't care about David being with other women, but confronting him would bring out the accumulated rage of his frustrations. She had learned early on not to disturb the temperamental artist. She endured the hard times of their life, forgetting them when possible and allowing David as much freedom as he needed.

Ellen Maxwell was the first to tell Ted of the renewed problems Mary and David were having in their marriage. His insistence that Mary leave her job and join him in the country was rooted in his belief that Jenkins and the museum were corrupt, and that Mary used the time away from him to see other men. At times David's biggest fan, Ellen now was more sympathetic to Mary and angry with David's inability to cope with life.

Mary said nothing to Ted until coming into the museum one morning sporting dark sunglasses. David had been in an ugly mood the evening before and lashed out. In an emotional account, she told Ted of the times he'd beaten her and how, on that Saturday morning at the cottage, she had not tripped on the carpet, but had been thrown by David into the large gilt mirror on the landing.

"I'm afraid to go home and afraid not to. If he knew I was telling you these things, he'd probably kill me. He thinks we're lovers anyway!"

Of all the things Ted had heard that morning, this was the most unbelievable. Not because Mary was unattractive, but because it could not have been further from the truth. David's isolation was turning him against everyone he knew.

"You might consider taking an apartment in town, Mary. You can't go on taking this abuse."

She looked at Ted through her smashed right eye hidden behind the glasses.

"I've thought about it but haven't been able to bring myself to do it. I've also thought about leaving David—my parents have told me to do it many times, and even his parents agree. I can't though, he'd kill me or himself." She paused. "I don't know which would be worse. Ever since we bought that land, David's been like this. Mitchell offered to help me find an apartment in town before he and Maureen were divorced. I guess I should've done it and ended it once and for all."

It took most of the morning before she could concentrate on her work, and by late afternoon she was scared again, anticipating what kind of mood David might be in when she returned that evening.

For the next several mornings, Mary arrived at the museum un-bruised, at least as far as anyone else could tell, but she was increasingly strained and tired. David had changed his tactic a bit; instead of hitting, he would keep her up most of the night, talking about what he considered their marital problems and what he would like to do about them. One night's discussion flowed into another, as if the daytime break didn't occur.

"Beatings," Mary said reluctantly, "would almost be better."

That Friday, Mary's car was parked at the museum very early in the morning. It was not like her to arrive early. Joe Mullens greeted Ted at the door and said Mary's car was there when he'd arrived at seven, but that she would not answer his knocks on her office door. Although he had a master key for all doors in the museum, he didn't enter, thinking she might be asleep. Joe seemed to know something about everything that went on at the museum, though he generally was not completely accurate. He also said Mitchell had been to the museum early and had talked with Mary before leaving half an hour ago. Ted sat at his desk and began working on loan agreements for a new exhibition. He wondered about Mary's early morning arrival and where her daughters were at this hour. Joe hadn't mentioned them being here. Then his phone's intercom began flashing.

Mary sat on the small couch in her office, her clothing wrinkled from sleeping in them. The room was dark, but she asked Ted not to turn on the overhead lighting. He asked if she'd eaten anything lately, and she said she wasn't hungry. She looked at him blearily, not speaking for a couple minutes.

"He almost killed me last night." Her voice was hoarse from crying. "He flew into a rage, talking about how I no longer cared about anything except the school. He denounced everything we ever did together, called me a whore. It was terrible, Ted, a nightmare."

She stopped talking and went into a sort of trance as if seeing it all again in her mind. Ted watched her face change as the pain welled up inside her and came bursting forth. She gasped, holding her breath for what seemed longer than reasonable, then finally buried her head in her arms and sobbed.

"He threw me against a wall and held me there. I said nothing, stunned by the fear of dying and by the look of pleasure in his face. Then without a word, he drew a knife from somewhere close by. It was a hunting knife, one with a heavy handle and a blade he was constantly sharpening. He brought the blade to my throat—here, right under my chin—and began pushing it in. I thought I was about to die and shut my eyes." She blinked, as if awakening from a dream. "I don't know how long he held me there, but he finally let go, and when his back was turned I ran out and drove here. He didn't try to stop me."

"Where were the children? David surely didn't do this with them there."

"They were spending the night in town with friends...though they have seen him hit me. They think it's part of a game we're playing."

"Have you spoken to anyone else since last night? Anyone else know what David tried to do?"

"I saw Mitchell briefly this morning. I spent the night in my car, because I couldn't find my keys to the building. They must be at the country house. He let me in, and I told him I'd talk with him later in the day, after I'd rested."

"What time was that?"

"I don't know, it was early; the sun had just come up. I was sure David would try to find me in the night, break the car windows and use the knife again."

Ted told her to lay down on the couch and sleep as long as she could. Beth Lawrence agreed to keep people from bothering her. Even though she was harassed by Martha Dyer, Beth was loyal to Mary and strangely enough to Ted. She asked no questions of him, though he was pretty sure she and Mary talked about David and the problems the two were having. That night Mary stayed in Beth's small apartment.

✵ ✵ ✵

Mitchell Jenkins drove out of Meriden toward the vast, rural stretches of southern Alabama. He knew the road well as he had purchased property from Louis Sterling that lay to the east of the highway, near the Black River. It was a ten-acre plot near the acreage Sterling had sold to David and Mary Griffin. Often when he and Sterling would walk the property, they would find themselves at the Griffin homesite and would spend time with David and Mary as they worked on the early stages of construction. Jenkins had not been to the site since they had started living in the structure now near completion. Jenkins left the highway and drove down an unmarked secondary road and across an old wooden bridge, stopping finally at the foot of a hill where a badly eroded dirt driveway led to the structure. He didn't try to drive the car any further, deciding the morning was pleasant and he needed the exercise. He could hear the whine of a power saw in the distance.

"Hey there David!" he shouted catching the worker's attention as he waved his arms back and forth. "It's lookin' pretty good; you should be very proud."

David Griffin waved back at Jenkins and stopped cutting plywood to greet his visitor. "What brings you up here so early? It's not a Saturday, is it?"

Jenkins smiled as he walked closer. "No, it isn't Saturday, and you wouldn't believe me if I said I was just in the neighborhood."

"Seen Mary this morning?" David asked. "She didn't come home last night. I've got no phone up here, didn't know where to call anyway."

"She was at the museum when I arrived this morning. Said she'd forgotten her keys and thought she might have left them here. We didn't talk long; she was tired and wanted to nap for a while in her office."

"Well, then you know as much about her night as I do. Sorry I can't offer you coffee or something for breakfast, but it's still a bit primitive up here. Might be different if Mary would just live here." He looked at Jenkins harshly through the mass of unkempt hair covering his face. "You gave her that job, it's what has caused the problems between us." It was unlike David to speak his true feelings. "Her place is with me out here."

Jenkins looked at David's tanned and muscled body. He had gone there to talk, not seek a confrontation. The artist reminded Jenkins of a suntanned youth from his past, but the memory faded as David spoke again.

"Mitchell I really must be getting back to work. My payment is in a day's labor, not by the hour." He turned and walked a few steps back to his sawing while Jenkins stood among the weeds and wildflowers that managed to grow even among the debris of construction.

"Anything you want me to tell Mary when I get back to town?"

David turned from his saw. "She knows what I expect of her and what she needs to do about it."

Jenkins watched as the saw again sprang to life. The blade ripped through the wood, sending splinters and sawdust everywhere. He turned and walked back down the hill to his car. From a distance he noticed a Jeep coming down the road he had traveled earlier. It was moving swiftly on the dirt and gravel, much quicker than was safe, he thought. It slowed as it approached Jenkins, then spurted ahead, turning up the washed-out path. The driver was blond and dressed to reveal as much of her splendid body as possible. He knew the figure and face, though he never had occasion to get close to either. The driver was the former wife of two men in Meriden who had stayed with each only as long as it was profitable both financially and physically. Jill Robinson waved as she passed by. Thirty feet of ground separated them, but Jenkins could still see her blouse tied loosely just below her breasts and her long, bare legs through the Jeep's missing passenger door. She had been a student of David's when he was teaching, and it was rumored a lover as well. He wondered just how much work David would get done today!

✲ ✲ ✲

Mary stayed in her office into the afternoon. Ted retrieved the morning's paper from Joe, who always kept it for himself to clip coupons, and read through apartment listings for Mary to consider. He felt odd doing it because she was so hesitant about leaving David. Considering recent events, Ted couldn't understand her reluctance; it was almost as if she was attracted to his physical abuse.

Mitchell returned to the museum just before noon. He called Martha into his office and the two stayed sequestered for an hour or so. He was dictating something; Ted could see her taking notes. Mitchell left afterward and walked to the school, where Mary's door was still closed and Beth was standing guard. Jenkins exchanged a few words with Beth before leaving. There wasn't much small talk between the two of them. Most of the other women would talk and laugh with him, providing ample opportunity to tease and joke. But he was unable to get close to Beth, which caused a certain amount of resentment on his part, Ted was sure. This feeling was fed by Martha who didn't have much luck controlling what Beth would do for her and would delight in finding fault with her performance. There always had to be a "goat" for Martha, and Beth had more than her share of occupying that position. Martha had succeeded in running off a receptionist and had played a major role in Peter Rutledge's announcement of his resignation the month before. Beth, Ray Malone, Frances Rivers and Joe were on her list for removal next; Ellen, Mary and Ted were sure they would find their names there at some point as well.

Mitchell left word with Beth that he wanted to see Mary that day when most convenient, and on her way to his office she passed by Ted's open door. Mary didn't say a word to him or anyone else.

"Feeling any better? Were you able to sleep at all?" Jenkins asked as he rose to shut his office door.

"Still sleepy, I'm afraid. I would like to take a bit of time off in a day or so, as soon as I can make sure the school is in shape for that. We're mid-semester, so it's a good time."

"Sure, we can arrange that," Jenkins assured her. "I like to be able to help our folks here when they need it. Do you think you'll begin tomorrow?"

"Perhaps, I don't know quite."

"I'll tell Martha. Just let her know when you decide to take off. We'll get you some vacation pay as well."

Mary smiled weakly. Mitchell was talking fast, and it made her nervous. "I went up to see David this morning after letting you in. I thought there might be something I could do to help. He seems to think you'd be better off living there with him full-time, giving up your job. I don't know how he expects you to live without an income, but I suppose he has that worked out too."

"He doesn't," she said almost to herself. "Did he say anything about me, about last night?"

Mitchell wondered what exactly had happened between them the night before. "He said only that you should go home. He was working on the house and wasn't terribly friendly. Jill Robinson drove up as I was leaving. Does she visit you all often?"

Mary looked over at Jenkins, who knew he'd struck a nerve. "Only when I'm not home. She's David's friend. Hope he treats her better than he does me."

"What happened up there last night?"

"Nothing unusual, just the same kind of aggression I've grown too accustomed to. David really doesn't mean any of it, he just gets carried away. If I leave for a while, maybe things'll get better between us."

"I hope so. Do you need a place to stay tonight? I have an extra bedroom at my new apartment. I've moved out of the Arms and have a real place now."

She looked at him not knowing what to say or do. She didn't yet know of Beth's offer since they didn't talk past the request to be in Mitchell's office. She wasn't foolish though, she knew Mitchell's history and his interest in her.

"I'll let you know. I haven't made up my mind about anything." She rose to leave and walked to his office door, then turned. "Thanks for the offer though."

It was typical of Mitchell to make someone believe the best about him even while knowing the worst or at least suspecting it. Of the three,

Mary would be the easiest for him to catch in this cycle. She would always believe the best, hoping the other would go away. He dictated the
morning's conversation with David Griffin to Martha and would record
the conversation with Mary later in the evening.

CHAPTER THIRTY

Peter Rutledge, who had talked about having other job interviews, left the museum's employ by summer, and Martha Dyer took a temporarily passive role in office politics. It was her custom to do so after every skirmish of which she was a part. The resignation, however, left Multimedia in an unsettling position. Though Malone and Rutledge had been hired as equals, Rutledge was the designated department head. While Malone, in the words of Jenkins, "would never need a job as long as I'm around," he was not trusted enough by Mitchell to assume the position Rutledge vacated. This added to the irritants Ray found working at the museum, for he was expected to perform the duties of a department head without being given the recognition.

To assist Malone, Jenkins elevated an existing employee, Lewis Jeffers, who was originally hired in mechanical maintenance. Jeffers had impressed Jenkins with his technical aptitude and interest in the functioning of Multimedia. He had been at the museum through both the Parker and Rutledge eras but had no audio-visual training. Since Parker's exit, none of Jenkins' replacements had any training except for Malone, who was an excellent photographer. Jenkins again began spending increasing amounts of time there, promising new equipment and a freedom of pro-gramming that he could never deliver. For Ellen, it was a repeat of the same frustrations. She hadn't been able to work smoothly with Parker because of what he'd been promised by Jenkins. Rutledge's angst with life, the museum, Martha, and Jenkins had been much the same; and now poor Ray, the consummate team player in every way, was asked to work with Jeffers, who was quickly morphing into an artist with a capital "A," temperamental and aloof.

The issues Ellen faced before were now compounded by Jenkins making her director of Multimedia as well as Education instead of giving that promotion to Malone. His reasoning could be interpreted in several ways—a characteristic that usually gave him an out and was, Ted started to believe, calculated to cause as much confusion as possible. On one hand, the decision to re-define the role of Multimedia to make it a direct adjunct of the museum's education initiatives was in line with his avowed definition of the department from its beginning. The step then could be seen by some as a reaffirmation of his original concept. It also could be interpreted as a test of Maxwell's ability to do the things she'd talked about in museum education while directing several people in meeting a pre-scheduled deadline. Jenkins hadn't forgotten what he considered her part in Parker's decision to leave. Rutledge's difficulties dealing with her only added fuel to his latent hostility. Should pressures and personalities begin to flair under the new arrangement, it would put Ellen in the hot seat and perhaps give Jenkins reason to relieve her of all her museum duties.

✧ ✧ ✧

Taylor James enjoyed the attention he received from being involved with the state's building project almost as much as he enjoyed working in his Meriden lab. The overall concept of the museum plan was one in which he found agreement, much to Jenkins' displeasure. There were no direct ties between the State Museum Commission and the state legislature yet; funding levels had not been settled. Jenkins' opinion on this subject was that the commission and its funding, would eventually be cut loose by the legislature after it proved too much to administer. Laura James continued to serve on the Meriden Museum Commission through the end of 1976 while other members of the original group found their staggered terms about to expire. Those who wanted to continue were given special permission to serve a second term for the length of their original one. Jenkins was careful to keep as many of these people as he could, complaining to Ted about the difficulty he would face should he have to "train" a large group of new commissioners after doing so well with the original group. He was particularly careful to keep Laura from assuming the chairmanship, fearing the community's assumption that a complete takeover of the art scene had been accomplished by the wealthy family. For the chairmanship he would tap male members like Rudolph Bates or Louis Sterling, who were now part of the community's old guard. At the same time, Jenkins appointed members of the city's corporate community to terms on the Art Association Board and worked them into officer roles.

Mary Griffin took her week off and went away with her children to her parent's summer cottage on Bankhead Lake. She returned with little more resolve about things in her life than half a decision to leave David and found, after a short time, a five-room house in the city. Dialogues between the two went on for several months, David coming from the country to visit, staying sometimes for several days. Jenkins continued to exert pressure on Mary to accompany him in social situations, though always giving her enough room to maneuver. Ellen tried with exasperating regularity to mold something out of Multimedia. Between Ray, who believed all publications could be put off until the last minute, and Lewis, a consummate perfectionist with anything he touched, she met with little success. Through this period Jenkins made sure to pay attention only when things got significantly out of hand, finding fault with Ellen first, then with "the boys," as she called them. Added to this was the continuing bombardment other staff were feeling at the hands of Martha Dyer and the increasing number of activities being held at the museum. From a distance there was a business-as-usual attitude in place, but most staff were more drained from ducking internal issues than from working on the needs of the institution.

The environment could have not been more intense when Jenkins announced to Ted, the day prior to it being made public, that Taylor James was selling his business and patents to Dow Chemical for an estimated thirty-five million dollars. Jenkins had learned of this seemingly seismic change to Meriden and the museum the evening before and wasn't sure what impact the news would have on either entity. As far as he knew, James planned to retire in Meriden but would not elaborate. There was, of course, much excitement at the plant as news of the sale leaked that afternoon. James had brought many scientists and technicians to Meriden over the years. Those people, many of whom patronized the museum, were now wondering what would happen as Dow took over. Many felt they would lose their positions and be forced to move elsewhere, even though James, in his remarks the following day, indicated no positions would be lost because of the sale and Dow had agreed to retain the scientific culture he had already established.

Jenkins felt the sale would relieve James of enormous amounts of pressure that fatigued "the anonymous benefactor," as he'd become known to all by Ray Malone. He mentioned how James seemed to tire easier than before and complained about feeling winded after the briefest exercise. The intended goal of his new life was to act as an advisor to Dow, participate in community activities, and devote time to his honorary positions. One of these, of course, was the state museum. The other, Jenkins hoped, would be his museum, which James had already put time, effort, and money into. Because of his family-like ties to James, Jenkins was kept abreast of all activities surrounding the sale. He marveled at the speed and efficiency of the corporate lawyers, how they could make something so complicated seem easy. He counseled Laura, who feared the inactivity of life without the business world be hard on her husband. She felt her position on the commission might be a hinderance to Taylor's involvement on the state museum board and offered to resign if Jenkins thought it wise. Her offer, of course, was quickly rejected, with Jenkins promising to work with Taylor, allowing him to participate in the museum's many activities and educating him to the complexities of the art world and the role Meriden could play in it.

In January 1977, the sale was finalized at Dow Corporate Headquarters in New York. Taylor flew there two days earlier, wanting to relax, go over the paperwork again with his lawyers, and see friends. Laura was to meet him at week's end, then continue to Spain, where Morgan and Estephen were living against her father's wishes. Taylor spent time the Sunday before with Jenkins and a small group of male friends who had dropped by his home after church. Mitchell continued to attend most Sundays and participated in study groups throughout the week, though he was beginning to tire of it all. It was an important part of his overall scheme to be thought well of in proper social circles. James was quieter than usual that afternoon but with the signing of the sale's documents imminent, Jenkins thought little of it. Laura had said nothing to him to indicate there was any problem with Taylor other than the usual ailments of a sixty-nine-year-old man. He was a little paler than usual, but it was winter.

"The trip to Europe will be good for him," she told concerned friends, "and when we return there will be plenty of things in Meriden to keep him busy."

The meetings with the lawyers went smoothly. James seemed to have little interest in the details of the sale. He complained of being worn out walking from his suite at the Stanhope to the Dow offices. He dined with friends that evening but ate little. He returned to his hotel and collapsed. Just after 1:00 a.m. the telephone rang in Mitchell's apartment. He had just arrived after an evening of dining and smooth talk with a female ceramist who had caught his eye and was in his shower "freshening up," when he took the call. He was surprised and angry at the lateness of the call and was sure the police would be on the other end saying the museum's alarm was going off. He wondered why they hadn't called Ted first, per the scheduled procedures.

"Hello?"

There was a pause at the other end. "Mitchell? This is Laura. I'm sorry to call you so late, but it's an emergency and I didn't know who else to call."

There was another pause as Jenkins tried to change his frame of mind; the joint he had shared with his lovely potter clouded his thinking.

"Laura, what happened? Are you at home?"

The water shut off in the bathroom and suddenly Jenkins remembered he wasn't alone. He would need to be attentive but quick with Laura so he could get to another phone. By the sound of Laura's voice, he knew the call was important.

"Taylor's had a heart attack in New York. I don't know much except it happened tonight and he was with some people when it happened. He's in Bellevue now and his doctor is looking after him, but there has been no word of his condition. I'm leaving in the morning to be with him but wanted you to know before I left. I wish I had more information."

Now the pause was on Jenkins' side of the telephone. The bathroom door opened, and his naked visitor pranced across the shag carpeting to the side of the bed. He covered the receiver with his hand and told her in a hushed, hard tone to be quiet. The coldness of his manner was in sharp contrast to his advances during the evening and his promises of what she could expect later that night. The girl covered herself with the bedsheet and sat quietly as Jenkins continued his conversation. Though he was only a few feet from her, she could not clearly hear his replies.

"Please don't apologize for the late hour. I was already awake, just doing a little reading. Are you going up alone? I think I should go with you, particularly with Morgan out of the country. What time is your flight?"

"I couldn't ask you to go, Mitchell. You just can't pick up like that…"

"No, I insist. You shouldn't be alone. If Taylor is better in a few days, then I'll return. In the meantime, there's always something for me to do in the city."

There was silence as she considered his offer. "Well, the plane is at seven. I suppose I'll see you then. Perhaps I'll have more news."

"Laura, shall I come over tonight? Are you going to be okay there by yourself?"

She answered that she would and had plenty to do before leaving in a few hours.

"Then I'll pick you up at six. There's no need for you to leave your car at the airport. I can get Ted to pick up my car and drive it back to the museum tomorrow sometime."

She agreed, thanked him again for his concern, and hung up, leaving Jenkins to deal with the young woman now asleep in his bed.

There was much for Mitchell to think about that night and little time in which to take care of all the details that might prevent him from going to New York. He remembered how Taylor had appeared out of breath or tired, wondering if he had felt this coming on and if it were the real reason for the sale of the company. His mind then switched to Taylor's will and if the museum was included. He felt the institution was entitled to something. He had endured the chemist's peculiar personality a long while. There was no time to call Martha Dyer before the flight; he would call her from New York and have her take care of anything he'd left unfinished. He hadn't been in New York for a year. Colin no longer worked for her brother and had, in fact, left the city. The two had taken to arguing Britian had told him, and had mutually agreed it would be best if they parted. He was living in the country exclusively now, sub-leasing the downtown studio space to several other artists. Jenkins doubted he would see Britian this trip and resolved to stick close to Laura and the drama playing out with Taylor in Bellevue.

He arrived at the James home just a few moments before six. He'd awakened the young woman who'd been with him at four thirty, taking her to her own apartment for the remainder of the night. She hadn't understood much of what Jenkins said to her as she walked sleepily to his car. He didn't bother to dress her—it was still very dark, and she was able to navigate well enough to get into her apartment without his assistance. He felt an empty revulsion as she left him, wishing he hadn't asked her out in the first place, yet knowing he would do it again sometime in the future. He then drove to an all-night restaurant where he could get a large breakfast before leaving. He sat in a corner booth and a young woman came to take his order of eggs, ham, and grits. He tried to imagine how it would be when he and Laura got to the hospital in a few hours. Taylor would be in intensive care, tubes streaming from his body assisting him with the functions of his fragile mortality. He wondered how Laura would hold up seeing him that way. Death didn't frighten Jenkins, but he thought it would frighten Taylor.

There were a few lights on inside the James house. Jenkins could see Anne's black face in one of the kitchen windows. "Good help, sure a blessin'," he said to himself getting out of the car. He knew he would need to be concerned and polite throughout the day and wanted to vent as much steam as possible beforehand. As his car door shut, he looked to the kitchen window again, but Anne was gone. Laura kept flowering plants in the garden across from where he stood so visitors could look at something beautiful while they waited for the door to open. The year they moved in, she planted hundreds of spring flowers in that garden, enlisting people from the lab to help with the project. When she finished it began to rain, then storm, then hail. In a matter of moments, everything she had done that day was ruined. Not being particularly superstitious, she didn't take it as a sign of bad things to come in her new Meriden life. Instead, she had the garden completely plowed under and started again. It was winter now and nothing was growing, but she might need to think about starting over again if Taylor died. Jenkins decided to stay by her as long as necessary.

The door behind him swung open and Laura stood with a small suitcase ready to go. "Sorry to keep you waiting, Mitchell. I didn't see you come up the path and thought you were still in the car. I guess I'm ready to go."

Jenkins reached for her bag. She was dressed warmly but plainly despite her wealth. "Any news?" he asked.

"Only that he spent a stable night. They are moving him this morning out of the ICU and to New York City Hospital if everything continues to look good. We're to meet with the doctors there."

She looked tired, drawn. Within thirty minutes they were in the airplane that would take them to Taylor's side. Jenkins had found it easy to secure a seat since Laura flew first class and this section was always empty. Laura hadn't spoken since they found their seats, and Jenkins took the opportunity to rest, as the night before began catching up with him. He reached into his upper right vest pocket and casually fingered the three loose pills held within it. He asked the stewardess for a glass of water and when she brought it, he covertly slipped one of the pills into his mouth and swallowed without Laura noticing. The plane taxied the runway. He felt the pill take hold, loosening his body, and closed his eyes. The plane was now moving swiftly down the long runway, its engines lifting the silver tube into the air.

✳ ✳ ✳

Mitchell's father sat down on a wooden chair in the far corner of the living room, considering the possibility his son hadn't been sleeping in his room all night and could very well know something about Jimmy's death. The two had been nothing but trouble for each other since they started hanging out several years before. And now this, a week before Mitchell was leaving for the University of Birmingham. Howard Jenkins decided to keep quiet, to let the officers handle matters in their own way. He knew if Mitchell had been involved in Jimmy's death, he wouldn't allow himself to be exposed by the likes of these country policemen. "Mitchell," the sheriff said, "we'd like you to come with us and give a statement on your whereabouts last night. It's purely routine."

"Sure," he answered slowly. "I just can't believe what you've told me about Jimmy. Stealing the car, that's something Jimmy might do, but he'd have returned it to old man Pierce. He wouldn't have done it any harm. Where's the body?"

There was no remorse in the sheriff's voice. "Get dressed, Mitchell, I'd like to go now. We won't keep you long."

Jenkins left to go back to his room and dress. He did this quickly because he was nervous. The killing of his friend was not something he'd planned, but there was little choice. He was in the clear so far, and to stay that way he would charge ahead and take the investigation as it came. He heard his mother coming from her room, calling his name. "Damn," he said under his breath.

"Mitchell?" She opened the door to his room. "What's going on? There's a police car outside and your father's car is still in the drive. Why didn't someone wake me?"

His parents had gone through a lot with their son. He had been at odds with them since childhood. Nothing he did ever really satisfied them and nothing they did was good enough. He had hoped to slip quietly out of the city for college and never return, finding excuses not to visit during holidays.

"It's okay!" he had not meant to raise his voice. "There's been some trouble and the police think I might be able to help, but there's nothing to worry about."

"What kind of trouble, what do you mean?"

She would never believe him. Mitchell looked at his mother standing before him in a blue robe and fuzzy slippers. He guessed he had always been ashamed of his parents and couldn't bear to look in her face now.

"Mother, I said it was nothing, believe me. I've got to go to the station for a few things, that's all. Be back before lunch."

He hurried past her to the living room. The police left with Mitchell, with his father close behind. Mitchell got into the cruiser. It was the same one that had been at the accident the night before. He looked back at the house, through the window where his mother was watching from her upstairs bedroom. He turned and stared ahead as the cruiser rolled down the quiet street.

✦ ✦ ✦

"Mitchell, wake up. We're almost in New York," Laura said.

His dreams vanished as the smell of coffee brought him around. He smiled at Laura then felt the wetness of his shirt against his back as he sat up in the padded seat.

"Hope I didn't snore. Flying always puts me to sleep."

He was embarrassed he had let his guard down in front of Laura. The dream of Jimmy Biggs' death had unsettled him, but he had overcome the fear of it then and would quickly do so again. There were other problems to face now. The plane made its final approach over the East River before bumping solidly on the concrete runway. In another forty minutes he and Laura were in a cab headed for New York Hospital. It was cold outside, but Jenkins could already feel the vitality of being there, so much to think about, so much to see and experience. He recalled when he and Rubin had gone there together. He had not especially enjoyed being with Rubin, but at least he was more daring than Ted Martin had been when they were there together. *Martin would never be a museum director*, he thought to himself as the taxi sped down Roosevelt Drive. *He doesn't enjoy the more explicit forms of art enough and certainly won't seek out new talent.* He glanced over at Laura who, now that they had arrived in the city, looked more anxious. They arrived at the hospital well before visiting hours, but she had arranged an appointment with Taylors' doctor for a full briefing of his condition and prospects.

The hospital complex was huge and smelled like every other hospital Jenkins had ever been in. He escorted Laura to the information desk where she asked for Dr. Jacobs' office. They were directed to elevators in the building's center and headed for an office on the eighth floor. Jenkins waited as Laura went in to see Sam Jacobs, who had been their family physician during the years they had lived in the city. After a few minutes of waiting, Jenkins walked down a long corridor, found a pay telephone not in use, and dialed the museum's number.

"Meriden Art Museum." It was Joe Mullens' voice. He was punctual as ever, arriving first every morning for the last eight years by seven.

"Joe, it's Mitchell. Is Martha there? I'm calling long distance."

"She just came in, Mitchell. I'll get her on the line."

Joe had not yet mastered the five-line telephone system, so rather than risk cutting Jenkins off, he laid the receiver down on the desktop. Jenkins could hear the squeak of the security door open, then close behind Mullens. Martha was on the line almost instantly.

"Mitchell, where are you? Joe said you were calling long distance."

"I'm in New York, with Laura James. I can't talk long because I'm waiting for her now. Taylor had a heart attack last night. I guess it's pretty bad, though I've not heard anything directly. Anyway, I'm going to stay up here until we know his condition and prognosis."

"Oh, that's terrible! How's Laura holding up?"

"She's stoic now, but I'll keep you posted. Use your discretion about this—I don't know who Laura has told. Is there anything on my calendar I can do from up here?" He waited as she checked the long schedule that was kept by her phone. There was not. "Okay then, I'll get back to you when I know something."

He walked back down the hallway, revisiting all the sexual encounters he had imagined with Martha Dyer. She was much too close to him to allow involvement, but the thoughts of being with her provided him more than occasional stimulation. Laura had not come out of the doctor's office. He took a seat in the glass-walled waiting area and thought about Taylor. He too had known many women, even some in Meriden. Jenkins knew about some of them, guessed at others. He had wanted Ellen Maxwell and made a fool of himself trying to persuade her to comply. She had been onto him from the start and, because he was so obvious, discounted the true intent of his attentions. She had traveled occasionally with both Taylor and Laura quite innocently. Taylor spent money on her freely, but always in Laura's presence. Laura knew what was going on in his mind; she had to know. The thought of Ellen being with a man intrigued Jenkins. It was not that she was unattractive, quite the contrary. In her modest, provocative way she was very seductive. She could turn it on and off.

The door to Dr. Jacobs' office opened and Laura stepped out followed by an older man wearing a white lab coat. Sam Jacobs, Jenkins was to learn later, was one of the finest physicians in the city. He had treated the James family for all sorts of ailments over the years, however, Taylor's heart issues this time was his specialty. Laura saw Jenkins awaiting her return and waved. Introductions were made, and the three of them walked back down the hallway toward the elevator.

"Taylor's had a restful night, Mr. Jenkins, which was the only way we would have moved him from Bellevue. But he is still in critical condition. It will be touch-and-go for the next forty-eight hours. His attack was really no different than most, just larger and more prolonged. He's a determined old buzzard though, and if he wants to pull through, he will. I expect it will take some time, though. It's good Laura is here, and it was very kind of you to accompany her." Laura smiled at Jenkins. "I'm taking Laura to see him now. I'm afraid I can allow only one visitor at a time."

"Sure, I understand. Laura, is there anything I can do for you, perhaps take your bag over to the hotel?"

She indicated that service would be of great benefit, and Jenkins assured her it was no trouble. Taylor's suite was very large, and Laura invited Mitchell to use one of the bedrooms if he cared to. Jenkins declined, preferring a small room at the Taft. It would be easier for him to come and go that way without disturbing her, and Morgan and Estephen would be arriving the following morning. He promised to keep in touch with Laura throughout the day, and Dr. Jacobs got him the phone number of Taylor's room. They planned to meet for dinner that evening, and he left to deliver her suitcase to the Stanhope. He was glad to be out of the hospital and on his own. It was still early in the morning and there was much to see before regrouping and hearing the latest on Taylor's condition.

He taxied to the Stanhope, where he gave the doorman five dollars for seeing that Mrs. James' luggage was safely placed in the suite. Taylor's heart attack had caused a great deal of commotion at the quiet, elegant hotel. Everyone on staff now knew who Mr. James was and were anxious to see to the needs of his wife. Jenkins then went to the Taft and registered for a single room. There were plenty to be had on a weekday in January. His was clean enough with a view of the rooftop of the Winter Palace. Opening his suitcase on the bed, he extracted his black phone book and a pint of Wild Turkey. He paged through his book, finding numbers he should call for the museum and for himself. He set appointments at several of the major galleries dealing in American art and remembered once telling DeBain Howard how he didn't trust New York art dealers; that time seemed so long ago. There were only two or three dealers in the entire country he knew on a first-name basis. Most had little time for someone who couldn't freely spend money. Except for Tate McNeil, who Jenkins didn't really take seriously, only Herschel Marelli and Jack Grossman of Bookbinder's were of any interest to him. Both men managed or owned big, important galleries, ones museum directors would frequent. Jenkins never took the time to meet any others. It was a nagging deficit in his background that surfaced only occasionally, when someone from Meriden would want information or was trying to locate objects by a specific artist.

He would take Laura to some galleries if and when Taylor improved; it would be good for her to get out of the hospital, and she might even buy something. Her artistic interests didn't exactly coincide with what the museum collected, but he could take her to galleries where she would see things of interest to her, and perhaps she would eventually begin to appreciate other things as well. He often plotted the tactics he would use on her and Taylor both, given the opportunity.

Turning again to his address book, he began looking for a local number written on an otherwise blank page. Taylor had given it to him once, telling him to use it whenever he wanted. He was to mention Taylor's name to the woman who answered. The number was unlisted, yet well-known by politicians, financial experts, and businessmen with only wealth and discretion in common. The conversation was brief but to the point. He would be expected at an expensive apartment on Park Avenue between ten and eleven that evening, and Mr. James' account would be charged. Taylor, he thought, wouldn't mind. The hospital lingered in his memory; he did not wish to go back and see James asleep with tubes and equipment strapped to his body.

✤ ✤ ✤

The sheriff's cruiser turned left instead of right at the intersection of Corporation and Broad. Mitchell was confused, but determined not to say anything to the officers in the front seat; he would let them play out this scene. The car headed out of town on the same road he and Jimmy had taken the night before. It looked different in the daylight. In a few moments they would be passing the hospital. Jenkins felt his stomach tighten as the cruiser slowed and turned into the hospital's driveway. It didn't look particularly busy this morning, and Mitchell wondered if Jimmy Biggs was inside. He followed the two policemen through the emergency room and past an attendant who waved at the officers. Jenkins said nothing until they came to two heavy metal doors without the usual small, chicken wire-and-glass windows.

"What's going on?" he asked.

The plaques on the door said NO ADMITTANCE and AUTHORIZED PERSONNEL ONLY. The sheriff swung the right door open and his deputy pushed Mitchell through. It was the first time they had been at all rough with him. The teen stiffened when he saw a body covered by a white sheet on a table in the room's center. He could tell it was Jimmy and balked slightly as the deputy pushed him again.

"We wanted you to see Jimmy again, Mitchell." The sheriff was now show-ing the fatigue the night before had caused. "He was your friend after all. We thought you might want to say good-by." The Sheriff walked the long way around the table placing his large hands on the covered body's stomach. "Jimmy Biggs ain't no account to us. He was only trouble, better dead than alive. One less fuck-ing delinquent to worry about. I used to think you was just the same, Mitchell. But that was before you managed to get that big scholarship for college. You're a

good ball player, no doubt about that, but not that much better than others on the team—just smarter. Yep , you're a smart boy Mitchell, that's why I figured you'd know more about Jimmy's death than anyone else." His hands were still on the body. "Not that it really matters, as I say."

The deputy had worked Mitchell closer to the corpse and he was surprised he could see no blood. It was cold in the room, ice cold.

"I suppose Jimmy never felt anything, died instantly. Strange way to commit suicide though, right there in the middle of the road. We're sending the body off for analysis in case there was something more wrong with Jimmy than just being a dumb bastard…but you wouldn't know, would you Mitchell?"

The body was between Mitchell and the sheriff now. Jimmy had been a friend, no matter how it ended between them; there was no need for him to be talked about in such a manner.

"Just thought you'd want to say goodbye to your old buddy." With his right hand, the sheriff whisked the sheet off the body and Jenkins looked at what was left of his friend. "Few people can imagine what a 357 shell does to a human head at close range, Mitchell. Why, there wasn't enough of Jimmy's head left to look at, we had to scrape what you see here off the car."

Mitchell could feel his stomach turn, he wanted to throw up but there was no place to be sick in. He moved to the right to get away from the sight of his friend, but the hands of the deputy were on him, holding him in front of the mass of shredded flesh. Mitchell couldn't hold his sickness any longer, yet the grip of the deputy did not let up. He felt his stomach heave and tasted the liquid that was contained in his mouth. It spewed across the porcelain tabletop.

"Careful there Mitchell, we don't want to get your mess mixed up with the corpse here, took too long to get that straight."

The deputy released his grip and Mitchell fell to the floor.

"Get 'em outta here," the sheriff said. "I think he's ready to play baseball now."

✿ ✿ ✿

The telephone was ringing. The mosaic pattern of the morgue's tile floor disappeared from Mitchell's mind. He looked around and swallowed another pull of Wild Turkey before answering. The scene had long since stopped giving him nightmares; he thought of it matter-of-factly, the way he had come to see many things in his life. It was Morgan James calling from the Stanhope. "We didn't expect to get in until tomorrow, but Estephen managed to finish early, and we came straight here. Mother said you might be at the Taft, I just talked with her. Daddy's awake and talking but very weak. I can't believe you came up with her like that, it was really very kind."

Mitchell was glad it was Morgan who'd called and not her mother. He would not need to say much to the younger woman, for she had a habit of talking for both sides in a conversation.

"I'm glad Taylor is feeling like company, it's a good sign." Jenkins didn't really believe in signs, he was only making small talk. "You're probably going to the hospital then? Or is it too soon for that much company?"

"Mother thinks it best if I don't go until tomorrow, though Daddy knows we're in town. I'm so glad Estephen is here too, it's good to have someone to lean on at times like this."

Mitchell didn't respond. He had worked hard to stop that marriage but failed. While he had gone out of his way to be cordial to Estephen Coton, he didn't like him. He was too quiet, too careful, too slick and continental for his tastes. *Surely*, he thought often, *there are other people who can see this fellow is only after her money.*

"We'll all be having dinner tonight then? I'll look forward to seeing you and Estephen again. Are you going back to Spain after this business is concluded?" He knew she was happier there than anyplace else.

"Not for a while." Morgan's voice took on a noticeably quiet tone. "Mother wants us in Meriden to help with Daddy's recovery."

"Well, that's good news. It's always a pleasure having you here. Listen, I was just on my way to visit a few galleries, why don't you both meet me?"

Mitchell was relieved when she declined his invitation because he wanted to go alone. They concluded their conversation and he returned to the bottle of liquor. He counted on Estephen to keep Morgan occupied in their marriage while he maneuvered Taylor and Laura into becoming interested in art. He had introduced the "collecting disease" to Abram Rubin and knew it worked. With the Jameses, real money could be spent, making the benefit to all concerned much higher. He rolled over on the bed and looked out the window at steam rising from buildings clustered below him. He held the bottle up to his mouth, keeping it there without allowing anything to enter, feeling the lingering memory of Jimmy's death, Taylor's heart attack, and the short conversation with Morgan drift from his mind. He tilted the bottle then swallowed, tightening his face as his throat burned. *It's been worth it, Jimmy. You'd have never understood.*

CHAPTER THIRTY-ONE

The days passed quickly for Mitchell in New York, more slowly for everyone back in Meriden waiting to hear from him. Taylor's heart attack was on the minds of many people of course, but there were other matters that needed Mitchell's attention too, and when he was out of town, everything stopped. When Ted knew he would be gone for a period of a few days, it would be easy to check with him when occasions arose. But with trips like this, the entire organization would just coast until he could be reached or decided to call in. Ted would only get to speak to him if Martha wasn't in the building. It was another minor aggravation for the staff, particularly after Mitchell would announce a crackdown on absences during business hours. Martha, it seemed, was given special dispensations in that regard. When Mitchell was gone and Martha opted not to come in, the administration would be completely shut down since Ted was kept in the dark about most things. Ted once asked Mitchell about this and was told she worked from home sometimes because it was less distracting. She was always doing something for the museum though, regardless of where she was—Mitchell's attitude was clear about that.

The word on Taylor was he was doing well, or at least as well as he could, and making a slow recovery. Martha decided to tell Ted about Taylor the day after Jenkins' call from New York. He was summoned to her office for the short briefing on their benefactor's status and Mitchell's absence.

"You mean Mitchell's in New York?" Ted couldn't believe he would up and go that quickly after setting up a meeting with Abram Rubin for that afternoon. The two had grown testy toward one another. He frequently didn't return Rubin's telephone calls or letters and had even instructed Ted to ask him to remove paintings from the safety of the storage area. Martha Dyer was unconcerned. She looked at Ted coolly from her tufted desk chair, a copy of the one Mitchell used. That Ted had not known of Mitchell's absence also did not seem to concern her. "Really Ted, as long as I know what's going on with Mitchell, you needn't become involved."

Ted didn't need to remind her his title hadn't changed, she knew what he was thinking and spoke before he could.

"We all know who's in charge here, and I've got everything under control."

Ted had lost count of the number of times she had made that boast. After the first time, he stopped responding. Besides, she was right. The long string of people who had left the museum's employ since she had come bore testament to that fact. Ted still didn't understand what power she had over Mitchell, but he allowed her free rein. Only Martha could do things without asking and get away with it.

Taylor continued to recover, and by the end of his tenth day Dr. Jacobs decided to give him a pacemaker. His estimation of James as a "tough old buzzard" seemed apt enough. At the conclusion of the fourth week, he was sitting up in bed and moving around his room with the assistance of Laura and a nurse who had been hired to stay with him full-time. Jenkins found it interesting that the woman was young and beautiful and wondered just how sick Taylor really was. Jenkins became increasingly close to Laura. He learned quickly that the time he had previously spent with Taylor might have been better used on his wife. When Morgan relieved her mother at her father's bedside, Laura and Mitchell would visit museums and galleries, always after a call from Mitchell to the galleries to ensure someone of importance would be there to greet them. Laura seemed to enjoy this attention and the break from the hospital grind.

As they talked of the artwork they would see at the galleries, Laura gradually became attracted to it. Morgan didn't seem to sense anything out of the ordinary happening between her mother and Mitchell. He would leave their suite by nine each night and make his usual rounds of 42nd Street, alive with perversity and titillation. Since his first trip with Rubin, the good doctor had kept Jenkins' penicillin prescription filled to protect against any unforeseen infection. It wasn't the only drug Rubin had prescribed for him, which proved to be a reason for keeping the doctor around. Mitchell's drug use had started at the university, where he was given a variety of substances for baseball-related pain. He had been able to deal with it until his senior year, when he was hit in the face by a line drive that knocked him out. He was self-conscious about taking pain medications, feeling it a sign of weakness. Rubin's drugs, however, were for entirely different purposes and made him feel invincible.

Jenkins returned to Meriden ten days later on an evening flight that also brought Morgan and Estephen Coton. Taylor James was making a strong recovery now, seeing friends in his room and giving Laura freedom to be on her own. They planned to stay in New York until he was stronger. After leaving the hospital, they would take up residence at the Stanhope until Jacobs was sure the pacemaker was functioning perfectly and James learned the new limits of his capabilities.

Jenkins had succeeded in infecting Laura with a curiosity about post-World War II painters. He made contact again with Jack Grossman of Bookbinder's and left Laura in his capable hands. Jenkins knew she would take Taylor to see these paintings once he was strong enough, and if intrigued, he would be inclined to possess them. There was nothing further Mitchell could do there and could no longer justify spending time away from the museum. He could always return if they had some need or James became interested in making a purchase.

Morgan returned to Meriden to look after her parent's home and find larger quarters there for herself and Estephen. She enjoyed living in Europe but was aware of the instability. Estephen was not anxious to stay there either, citing the many opportunities available in the US. He had resigned his military commission and was trying to decide what he might do to earn a living. The fact his bride was a wealthy woman was never discussed with the outside world. In fact, it was treated by both of them as if it weren't true. Their first year in Meriden would be spent seeking employment consistent with their status in the community.

Mitchell returned a hero of sorts, having proved himself to be the concerned Christian, ministering to the needs of a friend. The fact the friend was a major patron of the museum seemed to escape many. Morgan visited the museum on a regular basis, assisting as she could with small projects Mitchell would devise for her. The operation of the museum was up to speed a few days after his return. All the normal functions of each department were being carried out to the indifferent satisfaction of its director. Ellen Maxwell was trying to come to terms with the Multimedia crew, Mary Griffin had not taken legal action of any kind against David, and the art school's enrollment grew nicely through the work of many temporary instructors hired each semester.

Jenkins finally decided Frances Rivers had reached a level of incompetency he could no longer allow. Surprisingly, instead of easing her responsibilities or suggesting the museum consult an accounting firm, he came down hard on her, negating the years of service she had given. His original thought was to let her go unceremoniously and find a replacement. Ted was sure Martha had encouraged this action, for she and Frances were often at odds and the bookkeeper was definitely on her "kill" list. As his plan began to unfold, both Ellen and Ted tried to discourage what was an incredible miscarriage of her loyalty, but it was the friendship between Frances and Morgan that caused him to decide on an alternative. Frances was to be put into another area of the museum's operation, someplace where she would be equally inept. The tactic's only purpose was to prove to anyone who might object to her dismissal that the action was well-taken. Frances was sent to operate a satellite gallery the museum had opened the previous summer at the other end of town. The project itself was started as inexpensively as possible to accommodate the wishes of several women's organizations that contributed heavily to the museum's general fund. While easy to talk to, Frances had never worked with the public and, what was worse, had no marketing background, no sense of display or promotion. She was doomed.

Ray Malone was on his way out too. Nothing had gone well in Multimedia since Stephen Parker had left years earlier, and hostilities in the projection booth were growing worse than they had been before the meetings between Mitchell and the Parkers. The remark Mitchell had made to Ted concerning Malone's future employment was forgotten as he and Martha squared off against his former friend. His file was hastily thickened, ammunition for the deed Jenkins would eventually ask Ellen to undertake. He took great pains to see she understood her responsibility as a supervisor, including handling the unpleasant tasks. These were the ones Mitchell wasn't interested in performing because they spoiled his image as an all-around good guy. It put pressure on Ellen, who took the position she would only fire those employees she had hired. Responsibility was hers only if given completely—a condition to which Jenkins did not subscribe. This caused a great deal of strain between the two and rekindled the hard feelings Jenkins had toward her after Parker left. He called her a "troublemaker," convinced the problems those staff members had with the museum were directly rooted in Ellen's inability to get along with others. He was quick to speak of those feelings when asked about Multimedia.

Mitchell thought of Louis Sterling as a natural ally, but as a friend of Ellen's, statements she was working to undermine the museum caused

Louis to question Mitchell's remarks. Through his silence though, Sterling agreed without actually taking a stand. As chair of the commission's personnel committee, his "agreement" on this issue was critical to Jenkins' overall plan for absolute control. He felt the days he would remain untouched by criticism were drawing to a close.

His concerns about Ellen were the subject one evening at a large cocktail party hosted at the home of Mr. and Mrs. Rudolph Bates, the occasion being the return to Meriden of Morgan and Estephen Coton. Bates, nearing retirement from Hall Crowell, and Chairman of the Meriden Museum Commission, purchased a vast section of wooded property on Martin Lake and built an exclusive home there, which they used on weekends. The weather had turned warm, spreading the guests not only through the house, but over the grounds. Mitchell arrived with a date and didn't see his former wife with her new husband right away, but he knew they had accepted an invitation. He was concerning himself only with talking to Sterling about Ellen's inabilities and irritating nature. He was laying the groundwork for how he would deal with her should it become necessary.

Morgan and Estephen were being warmly re-greeted by Meriden society. Coming and going as they did, it was difficult for them to be acclimated into the proper circles that made up Meriden's social register. News that they planned to settle in the city was received with the coy warmness that runs through any group of elevated egos. Had the city been Birmingham, with its old history, the scene would have been different. In Meriden, newcomers had succeeded in removing the old guard and replacing them with people who, because of their economic position, had status in the community. Relative social positions rose and fell, depending on transfers, promotion, and the ability to cope with a corporate body—not blood, birth, or bondage. It was a key to the city's success and growth. Left to old money to build a similar institution, little would have happened. It was the reason the Birmingham Museum faltered after the retirement of August Bishop. The new director was unable to maintain the power structure Bishop had built and cultivated at the cost of not having a more diversified following.

Morgan was also at a disadvantage because of her travel with Estephen. The courtly life she enjoyed in Spain couldn't be duplicated in Alabama. The closest thing to what she and her husband had known in Europe was a mobile social order trying to warm up to them without risking their own positions changing. Morgan was hard to deny though. Since the sale of her father's company, there were few people in the city who didn't know the name James meant money. Having spent most of her life out of the city, she had few firm commitments to anything in Meriden and knew few people with whom she could confide. For this education she turned to her parents and adopted many of their attitudes about who was and wasn't acceptable. The museum and Mitchell of course, were high on her parents' list of acceptability, and conversely, the people or things he didn't like were not. The notable exception to this was the new museum in Birmingham that Taylor wouldn't abandon as easily as Mitchell wanted. Maureen Jenkins was apparently an exception too. Mitchell had constructed a thick file on her, giving the Jameses a picture of a woman who didn't understand his position or importance in the community. The fact that she'd been invited to the Bates party indicated this view was not universally held. Besides, she had remarried a senior executive of the Endicott Corporation, which the local population held in esteem. Morgan, however, was most distressed by her appearance and had taken pains to warn Jenkins early on that he should expect to see her there.

Maureen had accepted the invitation knowing full well Mitchell would probably be there. She had ceased going to museum functions and felt because of the divorce, a part of Meriden society had been closed to her. It wasn't missing it as much as her desire to stand up to social pressure and Jenkins that gave her the courage to attend. She could not forgive Louis Sterling for doubting Jenkins had threatened to kill himself that night simply because Mitchell appeared rational the day after the incident. She knew too well the game Mitchell was playing to stay on top. It had been his pattern throughout their lives. The party at the Bates home would not be a forum for confrontation with him. She wanted only to arrive with her new husband, see friends and leave. Her appearance would be enough.

The evening proceeded very smoothly. Jenkins did his best to stay out of Maureen's way, choosing a room out of the main traffic pattern to have his discussion with Sterling and to greet other people who wanted to speak to him. Being a friend of the museum director was becoming a status symbol. He was too busy with his own affairs to notice Morgan entering one of the larger bathrooms assigned to female guests. She left Estephen talking with a group of older ladies who were enthralled with his accent and manner. She waited several minutes before going in, locking the door behind her. Alone, at a dressing table, she found Maureen Jenkins-Anders combing her deep brown hair, which she wore longer since the divorce. Maureen smiled when she saw the younger woman. Morgan was pleasant, smiling falsely. She hadn't planned to meet with Maureen in this way and didn't know now what to say. She knew it was probably not in the best of taste and that she would likely live to regret being there, but it was too late to turn and leave. "Hi Maureen. I just wanted to ask if you were happy in your new life? You must know Mitchell had a rough time adjusting and has succeeded remarkably in bouncing back from what was . . . well, an unsuspected blow."

It was just this kind of attitude Maureen knew Jenkins had spread and that she was unable to combat. "I'm doing well, thank you." She realized now it would be impossible to ever again associate with this group of people—Mitchell's group. "I'm so happy you and Estephen are moving back to Alabama. I know it will make your parents very pleased as well."

It had been meant as a way of making conversation, a way of avoiding unpleasantness, but Morgan flinched at the mention of her parents by a person who she knew they cared little for.

"Don't speak of my parents. You don't care about them, or about anyone else. If you did, you'd never have left Mitchell and made him suffer like he did. My parents told me how you caused him such pain. He deserves much better than you and with luck will find someone who is appreciative of what he has done in this community and for its people. He is someone who cares for people, who is honest and compassionate, he..."

"Forgive me," Maureen started, regaining her composure, "but Mitchell has you just where he wants you. You see my dear, Mitchell does nothing without a reason. He may seem honest and open on the outside, but inside, he calculates every move he makes. Nothing is done if it won't benefit him either in the short run or long run."

"How dare you speak of him that way! What right do you have to say those things after what you did?"

"I'm sorry to upset you, but I know him better than anyone. I was his wife for thirteen years and knew him most of his life before that. There are things I know about Mitchell no one on earth knows—certainly not you, a rich brat unable to stay in one spot long enough to know anything. I'll tell you something Morgan, Mitchell may seem like Mr. Wonderful to you and your parents, but he's using you for everything he can possibly get. He went to New York with your mother to align himself with her for his future needs; he'd be better off if your father never recovered. Don't you see? Why do you think your mother's on the commission and was reappointed after her term expired? He doesn't miss any opportunities, believe me. I can't possibly begin to know what he has told you and everyone else in Meriden about me and our marriage. But whatever it is, I'm reasonably sure it's not accurate. Accuracy would undo the layers of lies he has told to keep his interest group happy. But I can see you don't understand any of this."

Maureen rose to leave the bathroom, having been gone from the party and her new husband too long. She walked past Morgan, who was visually shaken, then paused. "Oh, There's something else you should know about Mitchell Jenkins, something that affects you directly. He opposed your marriage to Estephen. In fact, more than opposed it. He tried to stop it, spent a lot of time trying to convince your father a relationship with Estephen wasn't in your best interest. He failed in that battle, so I guess there's one person who won a confrontation with him. You didn't even know battle lines had been drawn."

"I don't believe a word of that."

"No, I didn't expect you would. But ask your father sometime when he is fully recovered. I'm sure he'll tell you the truth. He was afraid of losing you and didn't take Mitchell's advice. Ask him, then think about what I've just said. Goodbye Morgan."

Maureen was out the door. She found her husband and asked if they could leave, a request he was only too happy to grant. Morgan stayed in the bathroom for another five minutes before returning to Estephen's side. No one had noticed the two women had been absent or that Morgan now had a decidedly worried look on her face. She took Estephen's arm and stayed close to him the remainder of the evening. She would certainly not change her opinions about Mitchell because of what Maureen had said, at least not until she had the opportunity to check further. If she had lied, she would pay dearly. If, on the other hand, what she said was true...

✵ ✵ ✵

Taylor and Laura James returned to Meriden one month later. The expense of the private room, nurses, and their suite at the Stanhope were covered by Taylor as if they were nothing more than a weekend in the country. He made an astounding recovery, surprising even his doctor. By the time of their return, he was as active as ever. He did, however, seem to have an understanding of his own mortality and an interest in preserving it as long as possible. Laura had made several purchases for their Meriden home from galleries Mitchell had recommended, and Taylor had started taking an interest in the New York art community, especially being introduced to gallery owners or senior dealers and the response someone of his wealth received. He felt it gave him an edge in meetings or conversation with other members of the Birmingham project. Knowing the "lions" of the art world on a first-name basis was exactly the kind of relationship Jenkins wanted for him. Taylor was going to have another significant financial problem at tax time and his advisors listed the benefits of converting cash to artwork that would increase in value if he chose well. Jenkins was also quick to point out the importance of being able to donate works at their fair market values to suitable institutions.

✵ ✵ ✵

Mitchell felt he had met his obligation to Ray Malone by telling him confidentially Ellen was recommending he be discharged because of his poor attitude and inability to meet schedules and deadlines. He made it clear there was little he could do about the action, as it wasn't the first time such an accusation had been made and because the charges were documented by Ellen, who also "kept lengthy files on her employees." Mitchell said he would put her off as long as he could, but advised him to begin looking around for something new. He was much luckier dealing with Frances Rivers, whose husband received a transfer notice quite unexpectedly, forcing them to move back to North Carolina.

Morgan and Estephen had lived in the James home until her parents' return, after which she bought a rambling New England style home near the country club in a wealthy section of the city. She spent less time at the museum, working instead on helping her husband find a profession that utilized the many foreign languages he could speak. She didn't forget the things Maureen had told her about Mitchell's involvement in her marriage and planned to diplomatically ask her father about them at the first opportunity.

Mitchell enjoyed the progress he perceived himself to be making in both his public and private lives. He and Martha continued to keep close company, charting the course the museum would take, including the futures of those within its walls. Publicly the museum continued to function with a high degree of professionalism, reflecting well on Jenkins as the leader of his small, but dedicated staff. The Jameses were gamely assimilating themselves to the excitement of owning increasingly important works of art, and they began to seriously consider building a private collection for their home.

Ted had spent his first years in Meriden defending Mitchell and all he did with the utmost vigor. He was a role model to Ted in many respects—successful, bright, able to make things happen and to take risks that always turned out positive. During the brief period before the move, there were many reminders of his infallibility and the importance of total loyalty. His control stemmed from his having more information available to him on most any subject than any other member of the staff. While he was able to maintain that edge, his ability to inspire was strong. Mitchell was open with Ted, giving more insight into his thoughts and the issues he might face at the museum than he relayed to others. In this manner he was able to keep his curator content and unaware he too was being used. It was much the same tactic he used with others he wanted to impress. Keeping Ted content was easier than letting him discover things for himself and become a possible irritant, because it would be difficult for Mitchell to rid himself of his curator should he decide it was necessary. Through Ted's first four years, he was a model employee. Deadlines were always met, exhibitions planned and installed to their best advantage. Ted's track record with artists was exceptional; he gave them no trouble and had no enemies. Those accomplishments continued to only provide "average" scores on his review. Where Ted was most valuable to Mitchell was in the area of loyalty and his ability to work well with all segments of the staff. It was easy for Mitchell to ask him to talk with a particular member who seemed to be having a problem and relay the information. What Ted didn't know until late in the game was Mitchell would ultimately use this information against the individual in question. His remarks, thoughts, and counsel became Mitchell's greatest weapon.

Until the fall of 1977, the file on Theodore Martin contained only good things—his outstanding attendance record of only three sick days in four years, a list of exhibitions he had planned and organized, a copy of the letter Mitchell sent him after the libel hearing concluded, thanking him for his testimony—nothing that would stand in the way of pay increases that came regularly. Ted watched Mitchell in all kinds of circumstances, dealing with both professional and personal matters. He measured himself using his boss as a yardstick, concluding he was doing a given task adequately, but never quite achieving his overall level of proficiency. Ted was resigned to accepting Mitchell's opinion of his administrative abilities; certainly his other duties were done to his satisfaction. The only other way Ted felt he was a disappointment to Mitchell was in his aversion to sharing the more sordid pleasures while traveling with him to cities where sexual gratification walked the streets or lurked in dark bars. He knew every time they traveled together this urge would be one of the first things Mitchell would concern himself with. Ted also suspected Mitchell thought it would be more fun if someone else tagged along. Ted's reluctance and final refusal to be that person probably seemed like a rebuff of his actions by someone he considered inferior.

✵ ✵ ✵

Ray Malone quickly found other employment with an advertising firm in the city. Since Ellen refused to fire Malone outright, Mitchell was convinced she wasn't capable of supervising other staff. It added to his desire to discredit her in the eyes of people like Louis Sterling and anyone else whenever a conversation went in her direction. What was worse, he would drag others into the conversation, interrogating with his yes-or-no answer technique that was so deadly. Ellen would not lay low and take criticism she felt unjust, she would argue with him instead. Because her vocabulary was larger than his, it allowed her to say things in response he didn't always understand. Out of what they felt was a necessity, Ellen, Mary and Ted banded together, at first informally, to discuss actions Mitchell would take regarding the museum and the people within it.

Beth Lawrence was another casualty, joining the ranks of Peter Rutledge, Frances Rivers, Ray Malone, a receptionist, and two janitors, all who had been fired because Martha Dyer didn't like them. The noose often seemed to be tightening around the necks of Ellen and Mary as well. Martha had confrontations with each of them and Jenkins would take her side. It became increasingly important to be careful about every aspect of one's job, so as not to become trapped by something unforeseen. Curveballs were thrown fast and often.

✵ ✵ ✵

Mitchell Jenkins was helped into the sheriff's cruiser. He was soaking wet from sweat and his own vomit, hardly able to think about what he must do and say to avoid whatever action would be taken in the investigation of Jimmy's death. He was still to be questioned by authorities and knew the sheriff would make that as difficult as possible. The scene at the hospital only proved he needed to be more careful and on guard. Within minutes the car stopped in front of the municipal building that housed the sheriff's office and jail. He was seated in a room where additional questioning would occur. He knew that while he was alone in the room, he was being watched through a mirrored window. He sat quietly, feeling their eyes run over him. Their underestimation of his intelligence helped him pull himself together after the hospital. Still, seeing Jimmy on that slab had caused him to panic. He began breathing slowly, deep into his lungs, just as he had done so often in other bad situations. They gave him a clean shirt and pants to wear.

In due course, the sheriff entered the room and began the questioning that Jenkins knew was coming.

"Okay Mitchell, I'm tired and I want straight answers from you. Were you with Jimmy Biggs at all last night?"

Jimmy's death did mean something to the sheriff after all; the speech at the hospital was to make Mitchell angry and slip.

"Only for an hour or so, I guess between eight and nine. After that we split up."

"Where'd you go?"

Jenkins looked at the man sitting across from him. He was too heavy and had lived in this city all his life. He had the look of his father and other men in Opelousas. There was something about them that reflected the oppressive heat, poverty, and isolation. It was a look Mitchell didn't want for himself. The Sheriff was elected to his position and had kept it for years because he never faced any opposition; no one else wanted the job. Though he was married, he kept company with a black woman who lived just outside the city. He felt the night gave him cover for his visits, a privacy he somehow found necessary due to his vanity. They weren't always alone though; Jenkins and Biggs often watched them through a hole in the roof covered loosely by a flap of tar paper that could easily be removed. The bed was conveniently located just below.

"Look Sheriff, I'd rather not answer that. We all have secrets about where we go at night, after dark." He watched as the older man's eyes widened, then glared back at him. "I wasn't with Jimmy after nine and can prove it if I have to, but would rather not because of another party involved."

He relaxed now because he had someone who would say anything he told her to; someone whose word the sheriff wouldn't question because of what might happen if his relationship to her were brought into the open. Mitchell Jenkins knew he was safe and would get through the remainder of the questioning.

✵ ✵ ✵

With her father's recuperation progressing, Morgan decided she had to know if what Maureen told her at the Bates' party was true. It would not be an easy question to pose, for she knew how deeply his friendship had become with Mitchell. But she couldn't bring herself to act in a friendly manner toward Mitchell with this doubt in her mind, and she was becoming increasingly anxious at his ability and willingness to spend her parent's money. The life she'd led in her parents' home had been comfortable, but tinged with frugality, so the sums now being spent for artwork seemed to her an exaggerated splurge. No two people needed to be surrounded by the quantities of objects arriving every week to their Meriden home. Since her marriage, her father hadn't talked to her about Estephen and what he would do for a living once they settled in Alabama. She knew of his personal opposition to the marriage, even though he said little to her. But Mitchell Jenkins had no business expressing an opinion one way or another; it was one area of her life in which she would tolerate no interference regardless of how grateful she felt toward Jenkins for bringing her mother to New York.

She found her father alone in his study. It overlooked the pool and the spacious concrete patio area attached to a landscaped pathway to a private tennis court. She didn't know exactly how she would bring the topic up, but she was determined. Taylor smiled as she entered. Though he was never overly emotional, she knew there was little he wouldn't do for her. Since the heart attack his hair had gotten grayer around his temples, but she thought he still didn't look his age. As soon as Dr. Jacobs was confident her father's pacemaker was working properly, her parents were going to vacation in the Caribbean, where he could exercise and get a tan. Morgan knew they had invited Jenkins to go along for all or a portion of the trip and that he was undecided, citing personnel problems at the museum as the major obstacle.

"Have you heard from Mitchell if he's going south with you and Mother?"

"No, though I'm sure he'd like to. There are a couple things at the museum he feels may become real problems if he doesn't deal with them, so he's hesitant to be away for any length of time."

"Oh. I thought Mitchell always had everything there under control. The only troubles he told me about are financial."

Taylor put down the book he'd been reading and looked at his daughter. "I'm sure he has plenty of those, but these are with people who work there. I'm sure he'll work them out."

"Is it still Ellen?"

This caused her father to shift in his chair. Morgan had been at college and flying around the world during much of the time he had spent trying to convince Ellen she could do better for herself by letting him into her life. He didn't know how much his daughter knew, and as Ellen would have little to do with him, his own attitude toward her had changed considerably.

"I'm reasonably sure Ellen is part of the mix, but I think it's deeper than that. Even Ted Martin, who I always considered harmless, is causing him concern. I think Mitchell has given some of those people too much responsibility too quickly, but I really don't know much about it. It's your mother who's the commissioner."

"Mitchell seems to have his share of problems with people in his life."

"I don't know what you mean."

"I talked to his ex-wife recently. She told me things about Mitchell, and while I don't want to believe them, they hit close to home."

"Morgan, listen, you can't believe anything that woman says. The things Mitchell has told me about her make me think she is incapable of any sensible behavior. She hates Mitchell and would say anything about him."

"Her remarks weren't about Mitchell as much as they were about Estephen, and I need to know if what she said was true. She told me Mitchell opposed our marriage and tried to convince you to stop it."

Taylor sat still for a moment before raising in his leather chair. He would not lie to his daughter about Jenkins suggesting he stop the marriage. Besides, it didn't matter now; the wedding was over, and she appeared happy.

"It's true, though I'm sure she blew it out of proportion. Mitchell did feel..."

"It's true? Mitchell Jenkins tried to get you to stop my marriage? He came here to this house to discuss something that was no concern of his, something that's a family matter?"

"Now, don't jump into one of your rages. Mitchell was and is concerned about you and…"

"Mitchell Jenkins is only concerned about money—your money. He has always been concerned with your money, ever since you sent him that first check to shut me up. He played me, trying to find out about you and what you did for a living that enabled you to send a $10,000 check to him out of the blue. Until he got where he wanted to be with you and Mother, he made me think I was important to the success of the museum—and I guess I was! I delivered you and Mother to him on a silver platter."

"I hardly think anyone delivered your mother and me anywhere. You're becoming hysterical."

"Really? You think so? Mitchell doesn't do anything without a calculated reason; I've been around him enough to know that. In his world nothing is ever left to chance. That's how I know if he talked to you about Estephen and me, it wasn't idle chatter. It was something he thought about for a long time, and it scared him because it wasn't in his plan for you and Mother."

"You're way off base here, Morgan. It doesn't matter what Mitchell may or may not have been feeling about you and Estephen. He may have had doubts and it may not have been his business, but he spoke to me as a friend, and I appreciate that. You know I had doubts about your marriage and might have said something more about it had your mother not kept me from doing so. But it's water under the bridge. Your husband has worked out fine. He's very good to you, makes you happier than I've ever known you, and he doesn't get in my way. If he had, I'd have crushed him like a bug. Nobody uses me without my permission, not even Mitchell Jenkins. Sure, he wants me to buy art—anyone would want me to spend money for them given the opportunity. I'm enjoying myself spending money where it will do some eventual good."

"Some good for who, Daddy?" His tone had raised her own temper, which he had always said was a carbon copy of his own. "You really think you're spending money for the common good? I was in New York when Mitchell started taking Mother around to visit art galleries, introducing her to dealers who could charm the eyes out of a snake."

With that she stormed out of the room. She hadn't felt this much rage in her life. Mitchell Jenkins could not be trusted, but she had no way to convince her parents of that. She wondered what he had told them about Maureen and other things, how many of them were true. He had become very close to her parents and would be difficult to guard against.

CHAPTER THIRTY-TWO

Ted walked back to his office still hearing Mitchell's words about how Beth Lawrence had done such a poor job working in the art school and how even Mary Griffin had complained to him about her.

"I wasn't going to act on the things Mary said to me, but it finally became evident Mary couldn't deal with it, so I had to take the matter into my own hands. At least Mary had the gumption to tell Beth she would need to look for work somewhere else, unlike Ellen with Ray."

Ted couldn't believe Mary had said anything negative about Beth since that first session with Mitchell months earlier. Somebody was lying. He was well aware of how his boss worked these kinds of things—setting someone up for a conversation destined to do somebody else in—yet for some reason Ted also didn't believe Mary was entirely innocent in the matter. *Could she have stopped it?*

Ted's intercom line buzzed. It was Mitchell. "Martha tells me you have the safe room keys. I've been looking for them all afternoon, afraid I'd lost them. May I have them back?"

The keys to which he referred gave access to a small, private room in the museum's storage area where small, valuable items in the collection were kept. Jenkins also used the room to stash personal things he wanted to remain secret. He had installed a special cabinet in the space and had the key to it on the same ring with the key to the room itself. These were all stored in Martha's desk, which was locked at all times. Ted was the only other person besides Mitchell allowed to access the room, and he had been given the keys by Martha the morning before to retrieve some objects he planned to display and returned them to her prior to leaving for the day.

"I don't have the keys, I returned them to Martha ."

Mitchell checked with her again and called Ted a few minutes later. "Martha doesn't have them and says she doesn't remember you returning them to her."

Ted tried to remember as much about the afternoon before as he could, knowing he had returned the keys to her office. "Mitchell, I don't know what to say, one of us is mistaken. I borrowed the keys from Martha yesterday morning to get the Bronson glass piece and the silver cup by Mario Davis for installation in the permanent collection gallery. I retrieved them from the safe room, locked the door, and carried the pieces with me to Martha's office so I could return the keys. She wasn't in her office and her desk was locked. I sealed the keys in an envelope, wrote her name on the front and placed the envelope in the center of her desk, locking her office door behind me. I don't know what she did with the envelope when she entered her office. It was clearly marked so no one would think it was trash."

Ted could hear Mitchell breathing heavily on the other end and knew he didn't believe him.

"I'll get back to you on this."

Ted didn't like Mitchell's tone or the idea he believed Martha's story about the keys over his. She had obviously misplaced them. That was the best explanation. The alternative left an empty feeling inside of Ted. He tried to think of ways he could check Martha's desk to see if she was trying to make him look bad by lying.

Mitchell called Ted again mid-afternoon. "Ted, I'm calling from the storage room. The door to the safe room is open and everything is gone.

I've decided to run away to Mexico with the stolen loot." He started chuckling the way a child might when caught in a lie.

"That's not funny, Mitchell!"

He was laughing now, but with the same nervousness. "I know, bad joke. I'm really in Martha's office and guess what? We found the keys just as you had described. As far as I can determine the envelope must have fallen into an open drawer between the drawer and the inner wall of her desk. Fluke thing! I just wanted you to know we found them."

It was Ted's turn to speak, but he didn't know how to respond. The rage he felt hardly seemed appropriate to vent. The "key issue" could have been a fluke of course, but how did the envelope get from the middle of her desk into a drawer if she hadn't put it there? Was it part of a plot to make him look bad? Mitchell probably took her desk apart and Ted smiled at the thought of that.

"I'm glad you found them, Mitchell, and sorry my word for their being returned wasn't enough." Ted knew his back would stiffen at that, but he wanted him to know how he was feeling.

"I'm sorry about that. But Martha wasn't in her office when you returned the keys and accidentally let the envelope fall into that drawer. She really didn't think you had returned them. It wasn't your word against hers. I never thought you'd take this so personally."

The conversation ended on that note. Later that afternoon Martha went to Ted's office and apologized for having caused conflict between him and Mitchell. It had all been a bad set of coincidences, she'd said. Work went smoothly for the next several weeks, but the key incident would require time to pass. Ted told both Ellen and Mary about what had happened and his growing paranoia. They thought he should talk to Lou Sterling about it, but Ted never completely trusted him. He also didn't want to put Mitchell on the defensive, and Ted knew going to Sterling was a signal he didn't want to send.

✤ ✤ ✤

Taylor James began buying artwork compulsively, much to everyone's surprise but Mitchell's. His tastes were eclectic, though Laura and Mitchell guided him. Bookbinder's became a constant stopping place for the Jameses when in New York, and Jack Grossman went above and beyond for his "special Alabama clients," showing them things he kept in the back room of the gallery on 54th Street. Prices did not seem to matter to Taylor, who delighted in purchasing things he knew neither Mitchell nor Laura expected him to. Wooden crates arrived frequently at the museum. Jenkins opened them, examined the object, dictated a condition report to Martha, and personally delivered the piece to its owners. All the works were by American artists from other time periods. The notable exception to his pattern was a landscape watercolor by Axel Logan, purchased because it was reasonably priced and for the Logan name. It didn't relate to anything he had previously purchased.

In his first year of collecting, he spent two hundred thousand dollars, mostly at Bookbinder's, for an assortment of objects Mitchell recommended. The paintings were installed in the James home with the objects they replaced going to the museum as gifts. Word of Taylor's collecting ferocity drew interest in New York and Meriden. Abram Rubin had collected, but few people knew about it until the exhibition Jenkins arranged. Because of its contemporary direction by California artists mostly unknown in the South, it caused little excitement. But the James collection was handled differently. As each object came to the museum, a release written by Jenkins was issued to the press. Works were taken on loan, a practice that had long been against the commission's wishes, and hung predominantly in a gallery. Impressive gifts were given to the museum by Bookbinder's and other New York galleries at year's end in the James name, pleasing both Mitchell and his "anonymous benefactor."

Laura said little about her husband's artistic spending. She never said much publicly about anything Taylor did, being an intensely private woman who worked her influence quietly. Laura's fondness for Mitchell grew enormously after her husband's heart attack, and Taylor's eagerness to purchase artwork for a "James Collection" was seen by her as a reward for Jenkins' kindness during his illness. She wanted to ensure Mitchell Jenkins would succeed at the museum and that the institution would grow into something of major proportions.

Morgan Coton said nothing about her father's art collecting. Blood might be thicker than water, but Mitchell had caused that adage to be severely tried. She and her father had additional words about Jenkins' attempted interference in her marriage. Taylor held the family position firmly in Mitchell's court but was unable to stop his daughter from seething every time Jenkins was in her presence. That caused difficult moments for them as he appeared seemingly everywhere the family did, like an unofficial second child—the son they never had. It was a position Mitchell realized could backfire if not constantly tended, but the rewards were worth the risk. The dangers of aligning the museum too closely with one wealthy and powerful individual were many. The museum world was full of institutions dominated by private money, with most finally succumbing to this influence in unfortunate ways. Mitchell was convinced that through his constant attention Taylor would break that mold. He promoted his patron's interest in building a personal collection and talked up the possibilities of the collection the museum would eventually own, but "eventually" seemed far away compared to what needed to be accomplished in the present. Mitchell talked about future gains from spending time with Taylor now, and clearly he was fantasizing about a James wing being added to the museum or even a separate James Museum. Without asking Ted outright to steer clear, Jenkins firmly relayed he had Taylor under control.

The state's museum project was floundering in the legislative quagmires as Mitchell had predicted. Since its formal announcement by Bishop, three directors had come and gone due to the conflicts and frustrations. The current governor wasn't on the same page Governor Ford had been. Spending state funds for a museum was not his priority. Mitchell still viewed Taylor's involvement there as a mixed blessing. It allowed him to burn excess energy that might have otherwise been directed at Meriden, but it also allowed him to begin thinking of himself as an authority on museum operations—an unfortunate result that would almost certainly affect the Meriden Museum. Taylor was very aware of Jenkins' opposition to the state institution, a position that caused occasional jibes from James as his interests in the project grew.

To ensure everything at the museum ran to his satisfaction, Mitchell and Martha once again revised the personnel chart. Ellen, Mary, and Ted had been grouped together on the last chart as heads of specific departments, but now it seemed their working together at this level threatened Mitchell's sense of self-preservation.

"The three of you," he had told Ted eighteen months before, "should function independently of me on a day-to-day basis, scheduling programs in your areas of responsibility that complement each other, producing a complete package of activities for the public to enjoy. As I need to be spending more time out of the museum raising funds, visiting foundation chairmen, et cetera, you three will need to take on the responsibility of running the operation. I need that support from you as I promote the museum outside its walls."

In truth though, Jenkins really didn't want to play the role of museum director as defined by any number of professional publications; he didn't want a strong and capable staff that carried out programing mutually decided upon. What he did want was to direct every move made by his employees. He was developing an increasing feeling of inadequacy from dealing with the kind of people the growth of the museum was now attracting. He was a "builder," one of three categories of directors he often talked about; the other two categories being "shapers" and "scholars." These categories ran in sequence, according to Jenkins—one replacing the next as a museum grew. He knew which category he fell into and was worried someone might decide the time had come for the second type to take over, so Jenkins decided he needed to appoint a strong hand to deal with a future he felt was sure to occur if his department heads were left to work together largely unattended.

The person who would work as his surrogate was, of course, Martha Dyer, for whom he created a new title—chief of staff. He then divided the responsibilities of the existing departments, making each staff member more isolated. The plan was not revealed to the staff at the same time nor in total. As had become a habit, he made rounds to each person's office individually, explaining what he had in mind in this new order. Each version, they would come to find later, was slightly different, with Ted's being perhaps the most complete.

Mitchell entered Ted's office without calling ahead, oblivious to the work his curator might be doing or to any appointments he might need to make. Nothing was ever as important as Mitchell's business, and Ted had spoiled him over the years by dropping whatever he was doing in order to accommodate his schedule. Ted had begun to notice a chilling attitude toward him from some of the commission's membership, and Taylor James would often walk past him in a gallery as if he weren't there. Ted had asked Mitchell about this to determine what he had done to offend him. Mitchell's answer was always the same: "That's just the way he is, don't let it bother you." But just as Ted was sure Mitchell had discredited Maureen with the Jameses and Louis Sterling during their divorce, he knew his boss was capable of doing the same with him, and Mitchell's unannounced appearance was a foreboding sign.

"Hi there, Ted. Everything going well?"

Ted nodded and waited for him to speak again.

"You have a moment to talk? Let's go down to the board room so we won't be disturbed."

This was a sure sign things were not going to be to Ted's liking. He tried to remember if he had done anything wrong or missed something related to his job, but nothing came to mind.

"We've talked before about the polarity I feel exists between members of the staff who should always be working toward the same end, like players on a sporting team, working for a common goal. I've tried to work with everyone but haven't succeeded because I'm being fought every step of the way by certain people who want to hurt the museum. They spread their poison as far as possible, infecting good people who come in, turning them against our goals very quickly. And Ted, I think you know the people I'm referring to. Ellen (in Ellen's version of this conversation it was Ted, and in Mary's it was Ellen) continues to cause problems that undermine the museum. I'm not going to put up with this anymore. I'm going to crush this resistance as hard as I can.

"There are two camps of employees here when there can only be one. The first of these is out to assist me in worthwhile projects, while the second seems to be against everything I'm trying to accomplish. I think you're in the first camp, for which I am grateful. You work hard, put in long hours, and our exhibitions show that commitment. The collection has grown remarkably, and I know your record-keeping on each piece is up-to-date and exacting. Absolutely no complaint from me. But, to streamline our operation, I'm thinking when you have a question or a need, you can go directly to our new chief of staff, who will be Martha. If she can't help, she'll get with me and have an answer for you by the end of the workday. It's just an idea, but what do you think?"

Ted looked at the paper containing his new staff chart as Mitchell penciled Martha's name into a box directly below his own. It confirmed exactly what had gone on since she started working for him but had never been put into writing. His comment about Ted not being "capable of administrating" crashed through his memory. Ellen, Mary, and Ted were now being asked, or told, to report to a person who was becoming Mitchell's alter ego with little professional background. What could Ted say?

"Has the commission seen this? Has it been approved?" It was all Ted could think of and immediately put Mitchell on his guard.

"No, I've only shown it to Martha. I'll not bring it to the commission until we've all had a chance to discuss it. Then I'll speak to Sterling first to get his reaction. But something along these lines has been brewing in the minds of the commissioners for some time; they think I spend too much of my time coddling you all, and I must agree!"

Ted sat still for several more unbearable moments listening only to the air pass through the ceiling vents. Mitchell, hands folded in front of him, waited for his reaction. Ted wondered if he was the first department head to see this new chart and concluded he probably was. Ellen would have alerted him immediately had she seen it, and Mary was busy in class. Ted felt betrayed. His loyalty to Mitchell may have been damaged in the years he'd been there, but never his loyalty to the museum. Mitchell's judgement on this was impaired and he had no idea. Worst of all, there was no way to fight him. Soon he would be telling Ted, as he had done to Ray, that he knew he wasn't happy here and should perhaps look for something else to do. Ted looked over to where Mitchell was sitting, his hands still folded almost as if in prayer. Ted knew this chart was the product of Mitchell's paranoid thinking, and that he likely had developed a back-up argument to justify whatever Ted, Ellen, or Mary might say.

"Well," Ted said finally, "I'm sure you've given this considerable thought, but I personally believe you have the wrong impression about the things Ellen, Mary, and I have done in the name of what we believe to be the good of the museum. You may very well need an assistant director, but Martha is not the person who should hold that position. You've made it clear I'm not that person either. That may be, but whoever is put in that slot should have some experience in the running of museums and be able to relate well to people. Martha has neither of these." Mitchell didn't like criticism of Martha Dyer, but for once he was going to know what Ted thought and not what he wanted to hear. "Martha hasn't been able to relate in any meaningful way to anyone here, and it's time you faced up to that. I'm not saying she's totally to blame for everything that's gone on in the past, but she does have a very unpleasant way of making people feel less than useful. She has said things to people that shouldn't be said to anyone in a work environment."

"She's able to work with Mary."

"Anyone could work with Mary. She's the kind of person who takes quite a lot of punishment before striking back—she's married to Jekyll and Hyde! I'm a lot like that too. Martha's careful around us, working her mischief only when she thinks she can make us look our worst in your eyes. The key incident is an example of that, in my opinion. We'll never know if that was done deliberately or not, but the attitude you took tells me if it was deliberate on her part, she achieved the desired effect, even though it wasn't completely successful since the key was found. I've done a good job for you over the years. Ellen and Mary have as well. We do not need to be channeled through a person who has no idea what we do and what's needed to be successful. Mitchell, you don't need to be isolated from the three of us, we're not your enemies! I don't like being demoted without cause."

"Well, as I said Ted, this plan is for discussion only. No need to get upset. Let me talk with the others, and perhaps we can all talk together before taking it any further. You shouldn't see this as a demotion, it's only an administrative reordering." He paused. "I suppose you need to get back to your office now."

Ted walked past Ellen's office and looked inside. She wasn't there, which was just as well; Ted didn't want Mitchell to see him talking with her at the conclusion of their meeting. He knew they would likely talk soon enough. Mitchell was unable to get around to meeting with Ellen and Mary until late the following day. Ted said nothing to either of them until Ellen called to ask if Mitchell had spoken with him.

"He apparently came into my office this afternoon when I was at lunch and left a paper on my desk. I had no idea what it meant. It was obviously one of his "tree of life" diagrams, but there were boxes drawn that I didn't understand."

"You found it on your desk?" Ted couldn't believe Mitchell would be that cavalier.

"He put it there deliberately, I'm sure. It was like a warning, something for me to think about without his telling me what exactly it meant. I took it into his office, but he wasn't in. I asked Martha about it and she played dumb, but agreed it was probably his."

"I see." Martha was lying of course, but Ted didn't want to alert Ellen to it.

"Then about half an hour ago, he comes waltzing into my office, smiling and pleasant as can be, with the paper in his pocket. He tells me of his concerns about the museum and staff. How there are camps of discontent spreading poison." She laughed. "I didn't realize the things I say mattered to anyone as much as he seemed to think they do. What do you make of it?"

"My hunch is he's trying to surround himself with people who agree with anything he says. There's Martha, Robert Evans, the new book-keeper, Joe Mullens, and he says the remainder of the staff, with the exception of you, me, and Mary, and he's not terribly concerned about her. I'm not sure about Mary after what she did to Beth Lawrence. Sometimes I wonder whose side she's on."

There was silence as Ellen considered what Ted said. He knew she and Mary were quite close and that his questioning her motives might cause a reaction. But it didn't, so he continued. "Maybe we ought to get together and talk before he takes this thing any further."

"I agree. He's determined to push this through as a buffer between us and him. He told me we were working against the museum, and I can't understand why. You know he's now considering hiring someone for Ray's position that I thought he was going to abolish. Some young, male hotshot came in on Monday. Claims he heard about the opening through the grapevine and wanted to discuss it with Mitchell. Of course Mitchell was very impressed with the young man's ability to express himself and is now attempting to find out more about him. It's going to be Stephen Parker all over again, I guarantee it."

She was correct, it was another habit of Mitchell's—hiring people into that position to whom he promised much then watching them battle Ellen or anyone else who might derail the development of Multimedia into what Jenkins and Parker had planned originally.

"I think we should meet tonight with Mary, but not here at the museum. Mitchell can't know we're actually going to do what he accuses us of!"

Ellen and Ted decided to use a small apartment that belonged to a friend of Ellen's. It was vacant and she had a key. They parked their cars at different points around Meriden and had Ellen pick them up since it seemed there should only be one car in front of the apartment. Desperate times seemed to be calling for desperate measures.

Each of the three had their own stories to tell about Mitchell and the things he had said or done. It was certain he was capable of using anything that looked the least bit harmful to him to their disadvantage. They felt there were already members of the board and commission who acted indifferent to them or were downright unpleasant. They agreed his elevation of Martha was out of the question and that it was time to take a stand, even if there was nothing to be achieved by it except peace of mind—and possibly losing their jobs. They would ask for a private meeting with Mitchell, without Martha present. It wasn't a particularly pleasant evening, and one Ted was not proud of. The three of them had never met before as conspirators to stand united against something Mitchell wanted to happen. Before that night, the "camps of resistance" he spoke of were only fictional apparitions he alone lived with. Ted worried for the future. It would be very difficult for him to dismiss Ellen, for she had many influential friends in Meriden who would cause him more embarrassment than the action would merit. He would not dismiss Mary because he still hoped to get her into his bed. But he could dismiss Ted easily enough.

✳ ✳ ✳

The autopsy of Jimmy Biggs' body showed nothing unexpected. There was alcohol in the bloodstream, enough to cause drunkenness leading to suicide if someone was so prone. They also found sand under his nails which, with the damp clothing he wore, indicated to the sheriff he had been at the lake shortly before death. This led to an investigation of the lake and the surrounding shore, but nothing was found to indicate another direction in the case. There were tire tracks belonging to the stolen car, but because it had rained the night following the questioning of Mitchell Jenkins, any other human impressions had been erased.

The funeral took place a week later. Without telling his parents, or anyone else, Mitchell thumbed back to Opelousas, keeping a good distance from the grave-side ceremony. There were few people in attendance. Howie Clark, who owned the filling station where Jimmy worked, stood looking at the casket as it sat beside the open hole. He had driven the station wrecker that now was parked under the shade of a tree. Two or three other members of the "old crowd" were there as well. Preacher Thomas was gesturing, saying something Mitchell couldn't hear from his hiding place. None of the faces displayed any emotion. He had little emotion either, only a desire to be gone before anyone saw him.

CHAPTER THIRTY-THREE

Martha was unsure of Mitchell's schedule when Ted called to ask for an appointment the following day. He had chosen to take the morning off—another example of how he seemed to know when something unusual might happen. Ted knew she would be in contact with him that morning if she hadn't been already. Finally, she admitted he had an hour open at three and could possibly see them then. Ted took the opening and thanked her as politely as possible.

Mary was upset by the prospect of confronting Mitchell, though Ellen and Ted were attempting to act calm. Mary was to read a statement they'd written because, as she appeared to be in his good graces, he might take it better. In the heat of the discussion the night before, she had readily agreed to this, but the light of day caused her to waver. As three o'clock grew nearer, all three were wondering if they were pursuing the proper course. Mitchell didn't come into the museum until two. When Martha called Ted to confirm the meeting, her voice was cool, detached, and unemotional. Nothing Ted had been through before with Mitchell could give any possible glimpse into what they might expect now. He was relying on Ellen to lead the charge, but even she couldn't match Mitchell when he was on the defensive.

They met in the board room. Mitchell made sure he was the first person there and took the seat at the head of the long table. He was wearing a navy, pinstriped three-piece suit with a white shirt and striped tie. He was very jovial, not at all like someone harboring emotional strains capable of impairing judgement. Before him on the table was a yellow legal pad and two sharpened pencils. He checked his watch as Ted entered, followed momentarily by Ellen and Mary, each trying to act as if this were a friendly gathering. The seats the trio selected for themselves mirrored their individual notions of their approximate distance from the ideal position Mitchell thought he represented. Ellen and Mary were on one side, Ted on the other; the three were centered at the table's middle. His manner was controlled. There was a brief silence in the room as Mitchell looked down the table at them.

"Ted," he said, "would you please close the door?"

Ted did so too quickly, revealing his nervousness and causing Ellen to laugh.

"Martha tells me you expressly asked she not attend this meeting. Since she usually accompanies me to all meetings when museum business is being discussed, I must assume this meeting is about her. Is that accurate?"

His tone turned cold and caused the others to wish they were somewhere else, anywhere else. Ted looked at Ellen in the silence, and Mary stared down at her folded hands.

"Martha is part of it," Ted heard himself say as if from a long way away. After each word, he wondered how he would proceed, where the sentences would come from. "Actually Mitchell, there are several topics we wanted to meet about today," Ted said, trying to include "we" as many times as possible to make sure Mitchell understood they were a unified group. "We felt obliged to discuss some mutual areas of concern in light of the new reorganization you've outlined to each of us. But first we thought we'd read a statement expressing our feelings about the direction in which the museum seems to be moving."

The three had agreed to only read the statement and not answer any questions Mitchell might raise, knowing it was impossible for any of them to successfully debate him. Unity seemed their only defense and their only strength in trying to keep our jobs.

"Mary has the statement, Mitchell," Ellen said, "and will read it now, if she may."

Jenkins drew his brows together, knowing this very sight would scare Mary enough to make her mumble the words. She produced the scrap of paper on which she had written their remarks from the pocket of her jeans. It was folded into a tiny square, a presentation in marked contrast to the one Mitchell would have made. To anyone entering the room now, appraised only that there were two groups of opinions represented by the people seated around the table, Mitchell's leadership, command and sanity would not be questioned. It was how he was able to fool so many people.

Mary looked up finally at Jenkins, then at Ellen and began to read.

> It is with the utmost concern for the welfare
> of the Meriden Art Museum that we feel compelled
> to take a stand against the subversive nature of
> comments and criticisms emanating from the
> administrative branch of this institution. We feel
> the information from which these comments
> originate is inaccurate and intended to discredit staff
> so that divisive gaps appear and become broadened.
> It is further our conclusion that these subliminal
> attacks have ripened at times to irrevocable
> proportions and have directly caused the dismissal
> of members of the museum's staff who did little
> more than try to resist the humiliating type of
> pressure exerted by the perpetrators of innuendo.

We feel for the good of the institution this kind of
atmosphere must be replaced with one in which
the creative purposes of the museum can again be
served. We hope you will understand our sincerity
in bringing these comments before you. We wish only
to be allowed to carry out our work in an enriched
environment, instead of the one in which we now
occupy.

Mary Griffin
Ted Martin
Ellen Maxwell
December 1978

"We also want you to like us again."

It was her own remark at the end, designed to cover the immense
sense of horror she was feeling for being the one who read the statement. It caused a second of short laughter from Ted and Ellen. Mitchell
remained unmoved. Throughout the reading he had looked hard at each
of them, glaring at the opponents he felt he was facing.

"This is a reaction against what I came to talk to you about yesterday?" he asked. "Something that I said was only a proposal to be discussed between us? This is exactly the problem I have with you three,
you don't listen to what I say, you don't allow me the time to discuss
options. Can you give me concrete examples of the things you stated?
Can you prove any of it?"

It was just the sort of remark they thought he would make, though they
hoped he wouldn't. To argue would prove pointless. They had decided the
night before only to read the statement again if asked questions, but knew
this technique of passive resistance would only serve to aggravate him further. There was no alternative way to handle his unpleasant attitude. Ted
held his breath, wondering if Ellen would prompt Mary to read the statement again as they had discussed, for she would not do so if left to herself.

Instead, Ellen spoke out. "Mitchell, we do understand that what you talked to us about was only a proposal. This has much deeper roots; it's a reaction against being thought of as problem employees when the problem that does exist, exists somewhere else and with someone else."

"So, you're saying the problems here lay with Martha and me. We're the ones causing the frustrations and bad feelings; we're the ones creating the opposing camps!" A hint of exasperation crept into his voice.

"Just Martha." It was Mary this time. She had taken a remarkable turnabout in attitude from the one she projected when reading our statement. What she had said though was only partially true, for Ted believed it was both of them acting together. Ellen thought so too but wouldn't admit it.

"Martha Dyer is one of the hardest working members of this staff. She has come to learn it is lonely at the top, to be the one that dishes out the bad as well as the good. She is my ablest employee."

There was genuine emotion in his voice as he talked about her. It was an embodiment of the same blind loyalty she gave him, now in reverse. For Mitchell, the possibility that Martha was a major hindrance to the unity of his staff and his own relationships to those who worked for him was impossible. Ted watched in disbelief as he became visibly angry at the charge Mary had leveled and the other two agreed with.

"I have never taken ultimatums well. This statement you have written is nothing but an ultimatum that I fire Martha or suffer the consequences from the three of you."

They watched him as he spoke, then fearfully, looked across the table at each other, wondering how to calm him down.

"I could fire Martha, even though I feel it would be a terrible injustice and wouldn't solve the problems we're having. But the consequence of my action would be very hard for the three of you to live with." He paused and looked down at his yellow tablet. "I would like to think this statement and your opinions reflect what you think serves the best interests of the museum. As I said to each of you yesterday, I take some of the blame for the fact we've grown apart. But I don't believe the action you're trying to force upon me is in anyone's best interests. Martha is not the only one with a blotch or two on their record. You all need to realize your employment here depends upon my goodwill and my knowing you are working in your assigned areas of professional responsibility. This is a benevolent dictatorship, and if you persist in sticking your noses where they don't belong, they can be cut off! Is that what you want? I can become very ugly if forced to."

"Mitchell." Ted was speaking again, but this time from a growing rage. "The fact is Martha has a much more dramatic impact on the people who work here and on staff attitudes than you know. Do the commissioners know of Martha's "problems" as you say they do about Ellen's or mine? Do they know about the vault key "disappearance" and how her word for its whereabouts was wrong but still taken by you over mine?" Ted couldn't leave the room without confronting Mitchell on this at least. It was obvious they hadn't made a productive impact on him so far. "I don't know if Martha was consciously trying to make trouble for me or not, but I do know I felt threatened by her and by you when the keys couldn't be found and I realized you believed I had kept them."

"I never believed you kept them—perhaps misplaced them. There were no witnesses to you bringing them back. You said yourself Martha was not in her office when you placed them in an envelope and put them on her desk. I felt I had to keep asking you about it, in case you were mistaken."

"Yes, in case it was my mistake and not Martha's."

"She admitted she had been in error and even went to your office to apologize personally. I thought that was very good of her."

At least Ted had managed a draw over this. Mitchell had not made him look too bad, but the points of the confrontation were made.

"I would suggest, in light of the fact this statement was made by you all as a constructive message, you allow me to have, say a month to work on helping Martha modify her personality. After that time, we'll meet again. If there is no change, I shall re-evaluate my position on her importance to me. If we feel the climate here has improved, I will over-look what has transpired here, and we will begin to move forward to-gether. Can you give me that much leeway?"

Ted felt like a fool, wanting to believe Mitchell and doubting his words even as he spoke them. Ellen said she thought she could live with that position; Mary and Ted nodded their heads in agreement. Ted won-dered what Ellen and Mary had thought of all that had transpired and what Mitchell would say to Martha when they met afterward. He had kept Mary's copy of the statement, and by evening Ted was sure it would be in each of their personnel files as well as in the hands of Louis Sterling as proof of the things Mitchell had alleged about them.

Later, Ted called Ellen's office. "What did you think?"

"I think we should talk with someone else. Perhaps Louis Sterling or Rudolph Bates."

"Bates doesn't know anything about what goes on here. He doesn't even know my name. And I don't know why you continue to put so much faith in Sterling. You remember his reaction to Mitchell's suicide attempt. What makes you think he'd have a different reaction to any of this? No matter what we might tell him, Mitchell will convince him we're insurgents and should be replaced."

"Hold on now. I remember what he said about Maureen, but I think we can count on him in this matter. I just finished speaking to him and he tells me Mitchell has talked to the commission about us and that he, for one, finds what he is saying difficult to believe. He says Laura James thinks this way too."

"Ellen, I don't think it's wise to involve Laura. Particularly with your trying to keep Taylor at bay. I think she is devoted to Mitchell and won't do anything to jeopardize that relationship. Besides, she isn't on the per-sonnel committee. Aside from that, I still don't trust Louis Sterling."

"He's agreed to meet with me this afternoon. I intend to show him my copy of our statement and to talk frankly about Mitchell's attitude toward it and Martha Dyer. I wish I could understand that relationship.

I wish it was merely sexual. I could understand that. But it's not. It's something else, and whatever it is, it's sick."

Ted was quite sure it wasn't about sex, though Martha was unhappy in her relationship with the man she was dating. Her first marriage had ended badly. She too blamed her former partner for their breakup, much like Mitchell did with Maureen.

"You can be sure Mitchell will be talking to Sterling as well tonight," Ted said.

"He already has an appointment, according to Sterling. Mitchell called this morning after hearing from Martha about our meeting request. They're to have dinner together. That's why I think it's a hopeful sign that Lou agreed to meet with me first."

"Either that, or it'll be the end of everything. Are you telling Mitchell you're going to see Sterling?" She said she was not. "Well, I hope he doesn't find out from one of his sources."

"I think you should come too."

Ted declined, saying he'd had more than his share of intrigue for one day. They hung up and Ellen left for Sterling's office. Sterling offered to preside over the meeting Mitchell had set for a month hence to discuss changes that might have occurred with Martha and to help deal with any changes that might still need to be made. According to Ellen, who talked with him again after his dinner with Mitchell, their boss had resisted the commissioner's offer but ultimately couldn't turn him down due to Sterling's insistence. That was the promise he had made to Ellen, and he had kept it as far as she could tell.

Ted, Ellen, and Mary's relationships with Martha over the next month were icy at best. Martha wouldn't look any of them in the eye and would only relay the shortest of messages when forced to. It was clear Mitchell was preparing for the meeting Sterling would moderate by attempting to build some rapport with each of them. He would want Sterling to know he had tried to talk to them individually, so if progress wasn't made it would look all the worse for them.

Ted could not help but remember the measured footsteps of Robert Osborne as Mitchell walked into his office or a gallery where he'd be working. Never certain of what he would say, the sound would make Ted cringe as he tried to pretend his life and position were as they were five years earlier. For the next several days following the meeting with him, Mitchell visited regularly to chat about plans or concerns Ted might have with his museum duties. During these visits Mitchell would be overly kind and friendly, as if the meeting with his three department heads had never taken place or the new personnel chart had never been drawn. He would enter Ted's office, greet his new registrar, Janet, as if she were a centerfold from a men's magazine, then pull up a chair. They were short visits that, while nerve-wracking, were easier for Ted to tolerate than when he'd ask anyone else in the room if they'd mind leaving for thirty minutes or so. Worse yet were his summons to the board room, where Mitchell would face Ted from the table's head. Since his divorce, he seldom talked about his sex life or views on marriage as he had done years before. He did keep his practice of telling off-color jokes generally about homosexuality or people with disabilities to break the ice in various situations. Ted had difficulty reconciling this sick humor with Mitchell's newfound religion or his desire to maintain a proper image for the museum.

Halfway through the 30-day grace period he'd requested, Mitchell asked Ted to join him in the board room. When Ted arrived, he found Mitchell sitting with his back to the door at the table's middle, reading a catalog of some kind. He was making notes from its pages as he asked Ted to sit next to him after closing the door. It was a catalog from an exhibition by Axel Logan in San Francisco the year before. It had caused a great deal of public interest throughout California. His artistic following was growing, and the exhibition was also scheduled to travel to Chicago and New York. Ted hadn't thought about Axel in some time and fondly remembered their meeting at the lodge in Woodstock. Mitchell flipped through the catalog, making comments about the paintings as he turned the pages, each being more complimentary than the last, concluding

Logan would stand with Beau Britian as one of the giants of this century's visual artists.

Ted said very little, letting him talk about Logan in his abstract way, noting aspects of the works most intriguing to him. Mitchell wasn't an art historian or scholar. He had no particular field of interest, except for Britian's works, and tended to be enthusiastic about whatever was being presented in one of the galleries at any time. This wasn't his fault exactly; in fact, he prided himself on being more of a businessman than a museum director. As he was fighting now for absolute control of his staff, he was also more concerned than he had been in some time about his longevity, especially if Louis Sterling found any validity in the charges Ellen, Mary, and Ted had leveled. His occasional meetings with Ted to discuss artwork was how he tried to compensate for his lack of scholarly credentials. Ted had read the catalog prior to Mitchell's review of it and knew the things he was saying about Logan's paintings were in the text written by the organizing museum's curator. Mitchell's memory of the text astounded Ted as he relayed what he'd read with the conviction of its author.

Finally Mitchell stopped considering the catalog and turned to Ted. "A museum that owned or controlled these paintings would need to turn people away; it would put the institution on the map."

Ted had to agree with that assessment.

Since the completion of construction, Mitchell had become increasingly restless, a fact Ted was sure contributed to his increased paranoia about those around him. As in most cases, it was easier to find money for construction than the acquisition of artwork. Mitchell had hoped the completion of the first would bring on the other, and it had up to a point, but Jenkins knew the reputation he amassed for the museum was becoming a bit stagnant. He had been unable to create a major collection for the museum, and there was no need for any further construction. As a "builder," his days might be numbered, especially if the commission felt there was more than a modest amount of internal dissent.

"Ted," he inquired, setting the Logan catalog aside, "if you had all the money in the world to purchase artwork for the museum, what would you buy?"

Ted didn't enjoy hypothetical questions with Mitchell because he knew he already had its answer in mind. Over the years they had played this game, and each time Mitchell's answer would be different depending on the kind of proposal he wanted to make to a collector or granting agency. The last time they played this game, the answer he was looking for was to purchase a diverse number of works from contemporary artists he thought appropriate, as he'd done with the NEA funding. As he was looking at the works of a specific artist, Ted suspected he had changed his mind and decided to play along. Even now, he found himself wanting to be counted among Mitchell's friends.

"I suppose I'd try to build an important collection of some kind. Works that could only be seen at this institution, by a critically recognized artist or group of artists like Abstract Expressionists or members of the Ash Can school." It was of course, a complete turnabout from what Ted might have said had Mitchell not been perusing a Logan catalog.

"You mentioned two divergent and historically important schools of American painting. August Bishop went after history in his collection of French Impressionists; it gave his museum something unique but also dated it and eliminated a certain segment of his potential audience. It was certainly why Britian went to New York, or at least contributed to it. You've done quite a lot for the contemporary artists here and I think that's the course we should continue going forward."

Mitchell had a knack of bringing one to a decision he had already made. He had set the collection and exhibition goals long before Ted arrived. "If we had a collection of Beau's works that traced his artistic career from Alabama to the present, it would be unlike any in the country or even the world. He doesn't exhibit as much as an artist like Logan, so I think a collection of this nature would have a real impact. On the other hand, it might be interesting to only a small percentage of the people living in or around Meriden."

He was definitely leading up to something. It was almost time for the annual state budget hearings that produced the largest portion of the museum's revenue. The amount had been consistent since Bishop had worked to establish it six years earlier.

"A collection of paintings by an artist like Logan, for instance, would have incredible public interest here while also being something that would put the museum in the league with those in New York." He sat back and flipped through the catalog again.

"Any particular reason why you're looking at that catalog?" Ted asked. "Is old Tate McNeil trying to promote an exhibition for another member of that family?"

Mitchell smiled thinly. "No, though this second catalog did come from Tate."

The publication to which he referred was newer than the first and was from an unnamed private collection that Ted suspected McNeil had a hand in developing. Our meeting ended when Martha opened the door and announced a call from Taylor James that Mitchell had been waiting on. The Jameses were traveling through Asia, and Ted was surprised Taylor would call Mitchell from the other side of the world. Martha's appearance was brief, as if the room were filled with lepers. She was acting martyred by the department heads' statement and whatever Mitchell had told her about their meeting with him. Seeing her immediately brought Ted back to reality. Jenkins thanked him for talking, then excused himself for the call.

Three days after the appointed date for the meeting with Louis Sterling, it was finally called to order. The delay was caused by an apologetic Mitchell, citing pressing matters of which he was not at liberty to discuss as the reason. Ted had not talked to Sterling since Ellen and he had gone to his office to discuss the performance reviews Jenkins instituted two years before. Ted would see Sterling casually at the museum for one event or another but never had the occasion to talk with him about his role there or anything else. Ted was always surprised at Ellen's insistence on consulting him when there was something she felt Jenkins was incapable of handling. Ted credited her belief in him to their longstanding friendship but found it difficult to talk with him at all, and certainly not with the candor of Ellen's conversations with him.

Sterling arrived at the appointed time that morning. It was not the best time for him to be away from his office, but he wanted to settle things at the museum. Mitchell and Martha had been in Mitchell's office from the time Ted arrived until the meeting was to begin. As specified in an agenda sent in advance from Sterling's office, the meeting would last the entire day, with a "working lunch" to be held in another part of the building to provide a change of scenery. Louis Sterling was a believer in creating appropriate atmospheres for his employees and regularly changed the décor of the management offices at the paper. He also believed in group therapy sessions and staff retreats in the country to free and open their minds. Though Ted had never attended a meeting Sterling conducted, he expected it would be run efficiently and without the tension of those held by Mitchell. Sterling had met with Ellen Maxwell before things were to get underway. Ted didn't know what it was about, but expected it was nothing more than a friendly visit, which he did with her whenever in the building.

Everyone assembled in the board room, Sterling taking Mitchell's usual seat at the head of the table. Ellen, Mary, and Ted spread themselves around the table as they had done earlier. Mitchell was absent from the session. Sterling made a clever remark about having the correct time for the meeting, and at that moment Mitchell arrived, followed closely by Martha Dyer. They took seats next to one another after he closed the door.

"I've asked Martha to join us," Mitchell said, "as she is the person being discussed. I thought she should be allowed to hear what's being said about her and answer if she wishes."

No one had expected this turn of events. Mitchell's tone was again harsh, as it had been a month earlier. Martha sat motionless near the head of the table, dressed in white, her hair recently done, everything about her appearance pristine. She didn't look the part of the monster the three staff members felt she was. Mitchell glared at her accusers, waiting for an objection to Martha's being there. If Sterling knew Martha would be present, he hadn't let on and didn't object.

"I didn't think Martha would be included in this meeting, Mitchell." Ellen was indignant he hadn't told anyone beforehand. "It makes things very awkward, don't you think?"

"If you believe what you say, it shouldn't matter one bit. If you don't mean any of it, then we get to see that too—finally!"

Sterling didn't look surprised. The three staff members were being set up by Mitchell, and perhaps Sterling too, regardless of what Ellen said about him.

"I think we should begin now, if we're all agreed," Sterling said. "I have seen the statement issued by Ellen, Ted, and Mary concerning their feelings of frustration caused primarily, Mitchell, by their relative distance from you as the museum's director. This is a condition that could well have been predicted as the museum grew and as the demands of positions have evolved. Ellen, you can remember when the museum was small and communications were easy between you and Mitchell. Mitchell I'm sure remembers that time too. But the rest of you don't and have had to live with the unusually swift growth of this institution during your time here. I've had similar organizational difficulties at the newspaper. Some have worked out successfully, some have not. We have reorganized and are trying to work in groups to achieve the goals needed on the management level.

"I understand Mitchell's need to have a management committee or team to free up his time to seek new avenues of interest in the museum. However, when this reordering creates a problem for the people responsible for the museum's functioning, it may be time to rethink its structure."

Just as Ted had thought, Sterling was taking the road's middle, encouraging Mitchell while slapping his knuckles. Mitchell had not looked up from a spot on the table he'd chosen to stare at through Sterling's opening remarks. Martha hadn't moved either, the two of them sitting like the lion statues flanking the entrance to the Art Institute in Chicago Ted had seen so often—the Guardians of the Muses.

"It's very difficult," Sterling began again, "for anyone to operate an organization if he feels those people in key positions are deliberately attempting to undermine his progress. I think we would all agree to this. Since Mitchell began keeping records on employees here, we've noticed that certain people have been less than cooperative in keeping to the guidelines set by the director or his department heads. Fortunately," he looked between Ellen, Mary, and Ted, "none of those people are currently in this room or currently on the payroll. It hasn't been easy for Mitchell to let some of these people go, though he knew it was for the good of the museum. With the governmental safeguards for employees currently in effect, it's also entirely possible for an employee who is let go to begin grievance proceedings against the employer. This is very difficult to wade through, and something to be avoided if at all possible. This is why the annual employee reviews are so important. Normally..."

Sterling went on for some time, explaining certain principles of employee management that were probable reasons for Mitchell's reliance on the impersonality, increased bureaucracy, and red tape that marked the move into the new building. Sterling mostly agreed with the procedures, providing little relief from the anxiety Ted was feeling. He was waiting for the background briefing to be over to see what kind of defense Mitchell was going to use to justify the things that had been going on for the last several years. It seemed that his department heads' personalities were blended together in his mind, tempered by what he felt were the outstanding limitations of each individual. Ellen's was her interpretation of what the museum was about, based on documents Jenkins himself had written. Her only fault in this was she believed in them. Ted too believed in them, though in the beginning of his employment he saw many more sides to the issues than he did now. They were, of course, the sides Mitchell wanted him to see and understand. Ted remembered

Maureen's divorce was granted on the grounds of mental cruelty. Given that knowledge and the issues they were facing now, how could Sterling help but agree there were inconsistencies in what Mitchell had told him about camps of dissent.

"In regards to this organizational chart you've formulated Mitchell, is it still your intention to create this new position?"

It was the first time a direct question had been asked by Sterling, and it seemed to catch everyone else by surprise. The chart he had pulled from a notebook on his lap was a finished version of the one Mitchell had carried in his pocket when he met with Ted, who hadn't seen it since. Mitchell answered positively.

"And do you still plan to name Martha as chief of staff?"

"Yes sir," he answered. "As we've discussed, I believe she is the most qualified of the current staff to handle the position. However, I'm subject to you or the commission's veto."

His ability to appear humble in front of the commission or people like Taylor James was so very similar to a parent/child relationship. Ted had listened to parts of meetings when Mitchell seemed to be someone other than the strong, decisive person he was when dealing with those in less important stations.

"That very well may be, Mitchell, but I believe under the circumstances you might prefer to do this another way. It's important that whoever holds this position has your staff's support." He turned his attention now to the others in the room. "For many years now, the commission's been after Mitchell to hire an assistant director, someone who could take some administrative burdens off his shoulders. This would be a new position, one Mitchell has been reluctant to fill out of deference to your feelings, Ted. But the time has come."

Mitchell nodded his head in agreement and wrote something down on his yellow tablet.

"Ted, I think you should know the commission's decision in this regard is not a reflection on the job you do here, but is based on data Mitchell prepared and our own observations. You do a remarkable job with curatorial matters but are not as ...administratively oriented as this new position demands. In fact, there is no one currently employed here, in my opinion, who qualifies for this position. I think this is a top priority and I will make a recommendation to the commission that the position be filled within the next six months."

"Yes sir," Jenkins said again, acting as if the burden of this decision had been taken from him. He looked at Ted. "If that is your recommendation, I shall work toward that schedule."

"I think the other two positions you're considering need some further consideration as well, Mitchell. I believe they are certainly worthy of implementing, assuming everyone understands their exact purpose. Perhaps you could recap how you envision them."

Mitchell began discussing his "group leader" concept and how it might work. Ted noticed he'd changed it from an earlier version, removing Martha Dyer as the person the group leaders would meet with and inserting himself as the individual who would meet with the two people directly responsible for curatorial and educational programming and the physical plant. Sterling listened and agreed with the concept. Ted agreed with it in theory as well, but didn't think it was needed, at least not in Meriden. Mitchell concluded his remarks by assuring Sterling this step was vitally needed, even with the addition of an assistant director, and that he'd intended to discuss the concept fully in just such a meeting. In reality, Ted knew Mitchell found his being subject to this kind of scrutiny by a commissioner, to say nothing of his staff, intolerable. As intolerable as Ellen, Mary, and Ted had found his conduct in the first place.

"Is there anything anyone would like to add to this?" Sterling asked. "A question perhaps?"

He looked at Ellen. Things were about to get complicated as Sterling yielded the floor to a leader of the "opposition."

"I'd like to know why Mitchell thinks these positions couldn't be filled, if they must be at all, by people who already have some experience at the museum. People who know how our programs work and can anticipate their needs."

Jenkins sat back in his chair for the first time. Martha still didn't move. In the month between these meetings, Mitchell had continued to discuss Ray Malone's position with the young man who had interviewed for the job. George Whitmire was a photographer from New Orleans who, at the age of thirty-three, ended up in Meriden because he admired the countryside and was working on a freelance basis with two of the larger manufacturers in town. Like Mitchell, he had a thick Southern accent and was prone to an overpowering confidence in himself. Ted had only met him once, when the two of them had returned from a luncheon meeting to "further explore the possibilities of his employment," and was not impressed. Ted could see the same coalition forming between Mitchell and Whitmire that had formed between his boss and every other Multimedia person the museum had hired. Ellen had predicted it accurately. Ted was sure Whitmire would be hired and the confrontations between Ellen and the new Multimedia Director would take up where the others left off.

"In the first place," said Jenkins, "I still believe resistance to the goals of the museum exists, even though I continue to make every effort to commit myself to its elimination. I'm tired of dealing with it though, and I'm determined to be on the winning side of the situation. These group leaders would be people who can work with me, not to my detriment, and would be people with leadership potential."

"But I think there are people here who could work with you if left alone to do so," Ellen countered. "The difficulties we have aren't created by only one person, Mitchell, they're the result of diverging points of view."

He was unmoved and continued with his defense. "Mary could possibly be considered for one of these new positions, I suppose, in place of the Multimedia director. But her area of concern, while important to the overall success of the museum, is in its own way separate from what you and Ted do. The Multimedia director would be someone who coordinates work between the art school and the educational departments, and in fact, does work for curatorial as well. Because of his position, he knows what is going on in all three areas of our operation at the same time."

"I agree Mary would be a good candidate for the position," Ellen said, "but are there no others?"

"No."

At this point Louis Sterling rejoined the conversation. "I would think either Ellen or Ted might also be given some consideration, Mitchell. They have been department heads for quite some time and must know something about what goes on here. Your point about the Multimedia director is well taken, but so is Ellen's comment about organizational history."

Jenkins was glaring again. "Perhaps Ted, but Ellen is too isolated to handle the assignment the way I believe it should be done. Besides, she doesn't lead well. It is no reflection on her. She does a remarkable job with the volunteers, however, some people have difficulty relating to equals."

"I'm not sure this is the time to discuss individual strengths or weaknesses, but I do think both Ellen and Ted ought to be discussed for these positions as well as Robert Evans and whomever you hire in Multimedia. I will also make this recommendation at the next commission meeting. You plan to go over this reorganization with them at that time?"

"Yes sir."

The meeting went on for the remainder of the day, with lunch served in the theater, where the mood seemed to lighten. As Ellen had hinted, Sterling was on their side in thinking Mitchell was going too far in singling them out as problems. Ted was sure nothing said that day would have any meaningful impact on Mitchell; this meeting would only serve to slow his progress. By afternoon decisions were being made about the group leader positions, the chief of staff position being effectively blocked. Jenkins discussed the people being considered for the positions, watching for reactions from Sterling as he talked. It became clear Sterling was not going to allow him to place people into these slots who had no experience dealing with the workings of a museum, yet Jenkins was not going to be happy with any of his current department heads serving there. Ellen and Ted said little during the afternoon, but watched as Mitchell tried to decide who he could work with over the short run. Whoever he chose from the ranks of the "enemy camp" would be the one singled out to discredit. As the conversation concluded it looked like Robert Evans, the new bookkeeper who Jenkins chose to replace Frances, would be assigned to watch over the building's functions, which Ted had been doing as part of curatorial, and Ted would watch over Ellen and Mary. Oddly enough, it was similar to a plan Ted had once outlined to Mitchell before the move from the old building, when he thought he might be of some use to Mitchell in dealing with the struggles between Ellen and Stephen Parker. Ted was now the logical choice, as all museum programs were developed around the exhibitions or permanent collections.

"Ted would really be perfect for this!" Jenkins exclaimed. "I can't imagine why I didn't think of it before. I guess I was drawing lines between his department and these other two and not seeing them in a circular fashion. Plus, he's had administrative experience!"

Jenkins thanked Louis Sterling for taking time out of his schedule to moderate the day's meeting, then hurriedly adjourned it. Ellen and Mary were quite pleased with the way the day had turned out. Ted sat quietly, thinking of the turnabout in Mitchell's attitude regarding him and his abilities to make an effective administrator. Ted had seen several changes in his personality in his time, but never one so dramatic. A day earlier Ted was part of the enemy camp, attempting to harm the museum. Perhaps Mitchell thought he could keep better tabs on him and once again fill his head with ideas to his benefit. A year earlier that might have worked. While everyone else in the room was feeling good about what had transpired, Ted was feeling very uncomfortable.

Promising to meet early the next morning with Jenkins and Evans, Ted left the room. As he did, he heard Sterling and Mitchell making dinner plans that evening. It was after the two men met following the suicide episode that Sterling had completely changed his opinion of Maureen. Instead of walking immediately back to his office, Ted took a detour through the collection galleries he had recently redesigned and was pleased with how they had turned out. He especially enjoyed the smaller, more intimate spaces where a visitor could experience an object closely, without the impersonality of some of the larger galleries. He was enjoying a seascape painting when he heard footsteps from behind. He turned to see Louis Sterling a few feet away, the troubled look of the morning completely erased from his face.

"Ted, I just wanted to thank you for being completely honest in the meeting today. I think things will work out now. Mitchell has just been feeling the weight of his responsibilities and frustration about a lot of things. I know he has complete confidence in you as do I and the rest of the commissioners, and if things don't get better here, I want you to let me know personally."

Ted felt a bit overwhelmed by this gesture, but his uneasiness didn't go away. "Thank you, Lou. I appreciate what you just said and sincerely hope things can be smoothed out. The actions Ellen, Mary, and I took were truly for the good of the museum. I'm still not sure Mitchell completely believes that."

"You just keep working hard and, as I said, let me know if things don't get better."

With that he shook Ted's hand and left him and the seascape, heading for an exit door.

CHAPTER THIRTY-FOUR

There had been a time when nothing would have pulled Ted from the museum after the workday's end and when he would skip breakfast to get there in the morning. He remembered those times now with sadness and contempt as he thought of the way Mitchell had turned on him just as he had Ray Malone and Frances Rivers. Ted believed he was falling into a routine with temporary exhibitions. He could tell the months of the year by what was installed in the galleries. Spontaneity didn't often occur—it was just the nature of things, because exhibition schedules had to be made into the future.

Over the six years he had worked for Mitchell, Ted knew of at least five museums Mitchell was asked to direct all over the country. He could have taken any of them, but always decided to remain in Meriden. There was something that held him there, even after the divorce. Originally, Ted thought he was afraid of being uncomfortable in a new surrounding, that a larger museum might swallow him up, turning his current winning career sour. But Mitchell had enlarged the Meriden Museum's budget into one bigger than all others statewide and many in the South. Ted knew he'd stayed during the construction period to see the building completed, but now construction was long over, and he was still turning down job offers. When Mitchell mentioned potential changes to Ted, he would say he was staying in Meriden "where I can do the most good." The question was, the most good for whom? His scheduling of new, sometimes questionably related projects for the museum to undertake was an outgrowth of his fear he would suddenly be caught there with nothing to do. Since the move, they had worked to stage large, impressive exhibitions to capture the attention of the city. Many of these had been spectacular, creating regional and even some national attention—all to the credit of Mitchell Jenkins. These projects helped him fill the creative void once construction was completed and gave him much to talk about to commissioners and at Art Association annual meetings.

The following morning, Ted arrived early for the first daily meeting of the new Executive Council. Robert Evans, a rather quiet man, arrived a few moments before Ted and took a chair in Jenkins's office. Jenkins, already in shirt sleeves, had been at the museum since six according to the log and had prepared several sheets of charts and graphs, including the new personnel chart with all the blank boxes filled with staff names. Department chief status was to be maintained, so while Ted was the group leader for the education group, he was also the department chief of curatorial services. The chart had been changed from the one Mitchell had shown Ted, Ellen, Mary, and Sterling the day before. Ted decided to say nothing until Mitchell had explained everything. He was keenly aware of Mitchell's sensitivity to criticism and didn't want to be the uncooperative member of this threesome.

"The first thing I want to discuss is this organizational chart. You will note the 'Chief of Staff' box that appeared under my box in the last chart is no longer present. As of yesterday, that position—or proposed position—is no longer valid." He looked at Ted as if in accusation. "At some point soon though, I will be employing an assistant director, and a new box will be inserted directly under my own. All lines of authority that now go directly to me will be channeled through that position first. As it stands now though, the group leader positions are below me, but higher than department chiefs, which I will discuss in a few moments. These group leaders, as I've said before, will be responsible for meeting with department chiefs in each of the designated areas to discuss on a weekly or bi-weekly basis the progress of each department, as well as any problems in specific areas. Department chiefs will be informed they should no longer come directly to me with concerns but to one of you first. Only if it is your opinion that I need to intercede will I do so. This will free a great deal of my time to do other things of more benefit to the museum.

"The three of us will meet every morning for a while to discuss things going on in the departments. I expect you to give me a brief, concise breakdown of these problems and possible courses of action. Then I will decide if they should be carried out based on the overall view of the museum's operation and my plans for where the institution is to be going in the months and years ahead. All decisions relating to personnel will be up to you, including the hiring and firing of individuals in the departments you represent. I expect you to fire someone only after discussing the action with me. I expect that as we begin there'll be mistakes, but we'll try to keep them to a minimum."

He paused to ask if there were questions concerning their roles. Ted couldn't help but think if he could bring himself to trust Mitchell again, this new plan might actually work. Unfortunately, he knew Mitchell was very good at setting up guidelines, but found it difficult to follow them. It would be next to impossible for him to keep out of the affairs of individual departments and staff members. So while it sounded good, the group leaders were to be nothing more than his puppets.

"Now, on the next level we have the department chiefs, who are responsible for the individuals in each department and for the daily implementation of the year's planning. Ted, you're still responsible for curatorial and security activities, but Robert will take over building needs and maintenance. Joe Mullens is nearing retirement age and we should look toward his replacement now rather than later. His assistant seems to be capable and is likely interested in taking Joe's position when the time comes. I haven't discussed the timing of Joe's retirement with him, but I expect it will occur early in the new year. So, to stem a potential gap there, his assistant, Tom, should be trained in every aspect of the position. I'll count on you, Robert, to bring that about. In security, I'm moving the receptionist from the main entry to another area we will discuss in a moment. Otherwise, security stays about the same, and Ted, you will continue to work with the head guard to see that schedules are maintained for regular hours and all special events."

The disparity between what Robert was being asked to do and what Ted would soon be doing as group leader of educational services was vast. If he couldn't handle these areas effectively, Mitchell would have good reason to let him go. *Was that why he had readily agreed to place me here?* Ted wondered.

"Ellen will continue as department chief for her area and Multimedia as it stands now. However, I'm very close to hiring George Whitmire and I'm thinking about elevating this position to full departmental chief status. We'll discuss it within the next few days, but I plan to make that decision by the week's end."

Ted thought about asking if, as the group leader for educational services, he should be consulted before the Multimedia position was filled and would have had Mitchell not moved directly on to the art school.

"Mary will continue at the school as things seem to be running well there. I think JoAnne is working out very well as the school's registrar. In fact she's the best registrar the school's had. don't you think so Ted?"

It was a dig that Ted ignored.

"The other box on this level is a new position I'm creating today and reinforces what has gone on here for some time now. Martha Dyer will be moved to department chief status and will continue to oversee all secretarial positions. I believe this upgrade of her status will only stream-line our operation and give no doubt as to where lines of authority are drawn. I plan to meet with all secretarial staff tomorrow to discuss this thoroughly with them. I want no misunderstandings here. Also, Ted, I'm placing the receptionist position under Martha's purview as well. She will be responsible for seeing that this person is at her station and hiring and training weekend attendants."

This was a new wrinkle, one that had not been discussed the day before with Sterling and the group, but likely had come about as a result of Mitchell's not being able to establish the chief of staff position for Martha.

"I know this wasn't discussed yesterday," he said. "I just forgot. But I've spoken with Sterling about it, and he fully agrees."

He looked at Ted as he said this, certain he would be the one to oppose it. It occurred to Ted then that throughout the entire meeting, Mitchell had been looking at him. Evans had chosen a chair to Mitchell's extreme right, out of his direct vision. Ted was on the opposite side of the desk. *He isn't having a meeting with two people, just with me,* Ted realized.

"There's one other thing. Beginning tomorrow, I'll ask Martha to join our meetings to take notes and help me remember the things we discuss. I hope neither of you will have an objection to this."

Evans was quick to say he did not. Ted remained silent, feeling Martha's presence would violate any confidence they might want to place in Mitchell. She would be attuned to everything that went on, though the organizational chart would not indicate it. The remainder of the morning's meeting was taken care of very quickly. Mitchell adjourned it, then asked Ted to stay for a moment. Evans jumped up from his chair and hurried out the door, closing it behind him.

"Ted, I wanted you to know that Sterling and I had a very good meeting last night and discussed in detail some of the things that were touched on during the meeting yesterday—I mean the real underlying causes for staff discontent here. He agrees with me on the basic issue of this undercurrent that our growth has created. It's impossible for me to be with each of you every minute of the day like I could in the old building, and even here up until a year or two ago. My hope is that this reorganization will take some of the daily burdens off me so I will again have a chance to meet with you, Ellen, and Mary on a personal level, so we'll all feel like part of the program again."

There was such sincerity in his voice and manner that it was hard for Ted, even in his most cynical moments, to disbelieve him. Ted wondered if they really wanted him close, if they weren't better off with him at a distance. Getting back to his pre-construction manner would provide him a greater opportunity to meddle in things, which was what he'd said he wished to avoid and why he'd designed this whole new staff structure. Ted was convinced Mitchell thrived on adversity he could control.

"I hope you approve of the things we covered today regarding the organization chart."

"Actually Mitchell, I did have one question about the chart." Ted had debated talking at all, but in light of Mitchell's sincere smile, he decided to give it a try. "I'm a bit concerned about your decision to make Martha a department chief. I assume that a rise in her employment status will be reflected in her paycheck as well."

He looked at Ted sideways for a moment, then returned the smile to his face. "That's correct."

"Well, it's just that there have been many employees in my areas of operation who didn't receive any increase in July, and I think that might create some hard feelings."

"Is that your only concern?"

"No, it's not. Yesterday you seemed determined to make her your chief of staff, a position I never really understood, but one that would have made her, in effect, an assistant director. It was decided that wasn't in the best interest of the museum and that a real assistant should be found."

"What's your point Ted?"

Ted thought rapidly about how to express himself without putting his head in a noose. "I don't want this new effort to fail, and I think promoting Martha to department chief level might cause additional tension. The secretaries, for instance, may not like it. Some of them have been with us longer than Martha and might think they should have a crack at the position because of their seniority. Then there is the psychological problem of having Martha on a level with Ellen, Mary, and myself when, as you will remember from the statement we presented, it is in Martha that we think much of our problems exist."

"And you think the three of you may have problems coping with this? You don't see Martha as an equal? You think you're better than she is?"

"No, it's not that at all. I was thinking of what Martha might think at suddenly being placed in this position. I'm concerned for her psychological well-being."

"As I said Ted, I discussed this with Sterling, and he sees no reason why Martha shouldn't be given this position. If there's going to be a problem about it, as I told him last night, it will come from one of the three of you. And if it does, I'll hold you directly responsible, Mr. Group Leader. Do you understand? I won't have her humiliated by you, Ellen, or anybody else anymore."

The anger of a month earlier had not passed, only subsided. Ted knew Ellen and Mary wouldn't like Martha in this new position, not because they were jealous, as Mitchell thought, but because it once again put her in the middle of all interaction with him as it had before. What he'd done was merely shuffle the deck. Martha was still to be as influential as ever in his decision-making, perhaps more so now. If Sterling had agreed to this, the remarks he made yesterday had now fallen flat.

Mitchell's phone rang. "Good morning, Martha. How are you doing out there?"

Ted decided this would be a good time to leave and started to raise from his chair.

"Hold on a minute," Mitchell told Martha, then turned to Ted. "Sit still, Ted, it's okay. Martha, would you bring those papers we were working on last night and join Ted and me?"

He hung the phone up and turned again to Ted. The office door opened, and Martha stepped inside. She smiled broadly, handed Mitchell a third cup of coffee and several folders of papers, and readied her notebook and pen for dictation. She spoke to Ted as if her silence of the past few weeks had never occurred. The two of them had obviously decided they would appear to be cooperative so if there was any staff frustration, they would be in the clear.

"Ted, you will recall several days ago we were talking about the museum's collection. I was paging through an exhibition catalog from Tate McNeil of Axel Logan's paintings."

Ted remembered the meeting well and acknowledged it.

"Here's the catalog. Take another look. I said a museum that owned these things would need to turn people away. Do you still agree with me about that?"

Ted paged through the catalog, trying to remember what Mitchell had said about the Logan paintings. He was about to put Ted on the spot about what he thought of them for some reason. Ted noticed some of the images bore the check of a red pen.

"They are certainly very popular, as these exhibitions he's having make clear. The entire town of Woodstock is devoted to him. According to McNeil, people flock there in the summer in the hopes of seeing him. He's kind of a cult figure, like Warhol, but with another sect of followers."

"Exactly. His followers are everyday people, the people who make up Nixon's silent majority, the kind of people who work, pay taxes, and live here in Meriden."

"I suppose so."

"What would you think if some of those paintings were here? Could you create a special gallery for them, something in keeping with their character?

"How many of them?"

"Oh, maybe forty, as a permanent part of the collection."

The look in his eye was serious. A collection of this nature would have enormous implications for the museum and for the other things seen in its galleries. Ted had just completed a very successful installation of works for the major gallery spaces and didn't relish the thought of ripping it all out, even for forty Logan paintings. Mitchell was looking through several other folders as Ted thought about how to respond.

"These folders contain comments, essays if you like, written by some of the foremost critics and museum directors of our time—a tribute to Logan's ability as an artist and his importance. I know he has a lot of detractors, but I'd be willing to use these as a basis for defending his artistic talent." He lifted the folders as a gesture of their importance. "Well Ted, could you mount a gallery with these things in them or not?"

"Certainly, but I'd want to know exactly what is being considered and how a collection like this would affect the other objects we own and exhibit."

"You're a good curator Ted, cautious, very cautious. Sometimes directors must act without time for careful consideration, and this is one of those times. Tate McNeil told me the Logan family is willing to sell forty important paintings from their collection of Axel's works because they need cash for some project. He's been instructed to sell them off and thought rather than doing so individually over time, he might be able to find an institution to purchase them as a collection. He could give a better price for a collection, much less than their total values if sold individually."

It was just the way Mitchell had come to think about artwork, in terms of lots, precipitated by Taylor James' wholesale purchasing from Bookbinder's.

"He's approached only two institutions in the country and selected Meriden to talk with first. What do you think about that?"

The art world is a very small place, particularly among dealers. The word that a nobody from Alabama is spending big bucks in New York would travel fast. Ted imagined McNeil's surprise when he learned the nobody was Taylor James, who he had met when the museum opened. It must have sent his heart fluttering.

"I'd say Tate must know something I don't if he thinks we could come up with the kind of money it would take to make a purchase of this size." Jenkins smirked. Ted was afraid he was about to say James had agreed to purchase the collection. "What would you say if I told you Taylor is thinking very hard about purchasing the collection for Meriden?"

An hour later Ted left Mitchell's office. It seemed he had convinced Taylor to consider purchasing the Logan paintings by telling him it would place him among the most important collectors of the twentieth century. Until he'd told Ted of the possible purchase, Martha was the only staff member to know. She, Mitchell and Tate McNeil had prepared a package of materials designed to sell Taylor on the idea of spending up to six million dollars for the paintings. Mitchell had put a call through to Taylor in Asia, finding him in Formosa just prior to entering China. During their conversation, Jenkins planted the seeds of the proposition. Within a few days, he had called back asking when he and Laura might see the paintings, and a time was arranged for a flight to Woodstock upon their return. Mitchell would meet them in New York, and they would journey with Tate to Woodstock. Everything was to take place in a thick blanket of secrecy, so if the collection wasn't purchased there would be no bad publicity for the Jameses or Logans. Ted was asked to begin designing a preliminary gallery installation based on the paintings in the catalog checked with red ink. Jenkins wanted the drawings for the trip, to show Taylor how they might look and increase his interest. Ted was not to tell anyone about the possibility.

Jenkins was completely convinced of the importance of the collection and its impact on the museum and the city. Ted had never seen him so animated about anything. The Logan paintings were completely oppo-site of what they had once decided the museum's collection policy should be. However, turnabouts were becoming the norm rather than the excep-tion as illustrated by Mitchell's newly found confidence in Ted's abilities. Had there been time to discuss the merits of such a purchase compared to the problems it might cause, Ted wondered if Mitchell's enthusiasm would be so great. Ted would have preferred to stay with the collection policy they had approved and seen where Taylor's six million would have taken them. For that kind of money, the museum could have collected paintings by Britian and other stars of the late twentieth century, but now there was no time and no discussion.

In the excitement of the morning's session, Martha's department chief position went quite unnoticed until mid-afternoon when Ellen called Ted frantic. Copies of the new "tree" had been issued and Ellen received hers. During the group meeting with Sterling, it was pointed out that Martha, more than occasionally, overstepped her boundaries in personnel and other matters. According to Martha, she was completely within her boundaries of authority as Jenkins' designated administrator. However, that position had never been clearly defined. Copies of her job description were distributed by Jenkins and reviewed point by point. Throughout this agonizing process, Martha remained silent. It became obvious there were plenty of vague areas subject to interpretation from differing points of view. For Martha it was a green light to do things as she saw fit, keeping what she assumed to be Mitchell's best interests always in the forefront of her mind.

After much discussion, Sterling decided it might be wise to amend several of the entries to make them more specific. He also talked about titles and that perhaps secretaries shouldn't be called by that rather old-fashioned term, but something more current. That accomplished, the meeting moved on to other concerns before Evans and Ted were confirmed as group leaders. Jenkins immediately started rewriting Martha's job description and gave it to Sterling, pronouncing his personal endorsement. Sterling also praised her abilities, and attempting to keep everything light, cited several funny incidents that had occurred in the past with his administrative assistant. It wasn't really amusing, and through it all, Martha never moved. Ted had to admit feeling sorry for her as he and Ellen took her former job description apart. Ted knew he shouldn't feel that way after the role she played in the elimination of former employees. Finally, when read aloud, it was the way it should have been written in the first place, and Sterling proclaimed there should no longer be any question about Martha's position or the lines of authority. Ellen remembered all of this too and couldn't believe Jenkins had moved her into a position where she would have equal status with her, Ted, and Mary.

"What was that all about yesterday then?" she asked. "What did he say to you about it this morning?"

"He said it was only a complete clarification of duties and that Martha had already been coordinating secretarial, I mean assistant help. He's also taken the receptionist and weekend security people away from building security and given that responsibility to Martha."

Ellen was helping Ted find a new person to take on the weekend receptionist position as the woman who had been working it for several years had been moved by Mitchell to the satellite gallery as a replacement for Frances Rivers. The 'advancement,' as he was calling the move, was given on the grounds of her deserving nature and commitment to doing a good job. However, rumor was the young woman in question had finally accepted his dinner invitation and was occupied the entire night. The promotion came shortly after that.

"Ted," Mitchell had said, "find another female for the weekend receptionist position, preferably a minority. That'll make us look good!"

Ted had chosen a former student of the school who was bright, attractive, and Hispanic. Jenkins might have preferred an African American, but after talking with her at length, Ted recommended her for the position. After meeting with her himself, Mitchell hired her and she began immediately. As it happened, Martha was away that week, taking a spur-of-the-moment vacation Mitchell authorized, even though it clearly stated in the employment manual that three weeks' advance notice was to be given. She was most upset upon her return to find a replacement had been hired without her consent, and life for the new employee took an unpleasant turn.

"You know Martha has Sofia under her thumb," Ellen said. "I'll bet she doesn't last till spring."

"You're close to that workstation, listen to what Martha says to her. If she really gives the girl a hard time, we can take notes and present them to Mitchell to prove Martha won't change."

"Mitchell? Hell, we'll present it to Sterling! In fact, why don't you call Louis and ask him about this whole Martha promotion situation? I'd feel better if I was certain he knew, because I don't really think he does."

"Why don't you call him?" Ted countered. "He's your friend. If I call it'll be awkward since we don't know what Mitchell has told him about me lately. Besides, Mitchell made it very clear to me this morning that life would be bad for anyone who objects to her elevation. I don't trust Sterling—don't know what it is. He was good at the meeting yesterday, just as you said he'd be, but things get back to Mitchell too easily; it's like the walls have ears, or someone we confide in is talking."

"You're imagining things, Ted. Sterling and I go back a long way. He can keep confidence even with Mitchell Jenkins. Go ahead and call him, we've got to know if he approved Martha's promotion. I suppose she's getting more money too!"

They talked a few more moments then hung up. Ted didn't want to call Sterling and decided to put it off as long as possible. There were only a few days until Jenkins would be leaving for New York on the Logan project and there were still many drawings to prepare. *It's just like him to think up some big project to distill other simmering issues.* Ted decided the only place he could work on the drawings in privacy was in the collection storage room. To get there, he would need the special keys Martha kept. Ted remembered that incident as if it had happened yesterday. She happily handed him the keys when he arrived at her office.

"Is Mitchell in?" Ted asked, noticing his door was shut and his line was lit on her phone.

"Yes, he's on the phone with Louis Sterling, I think. He's telling Sterling about our little secret. He's very excited."

"I suppose he would be. Thanks for the key. I should be down there the rest of the afternoon."

Telling her where he would be wasn't necessary, but if the offices did have ears, Ted wanted it on record that he intended to return the key prior to leaving. Mitchell called him twice that afternoon, the second time informing him his timetable had moved up and he was leaving for New York Saturday afternoon instead of Sunday night. He wondered if Ted could have the drawings ready. They talked for a short time about them, and Ted concluded they could be finished Saturday morning if he gave them his full attention between now and then.

Ellen called Ted around four. "Where are you? I've been looking all over the building!"

"I'm just straightening some things in storage for our next exhibition." He hated to lie but had little choice. He understood Taylor wanting secrecy.

"Well, I won't keep you from such important work," she said, sneering through her voice, "but I wanted to know if you'd called Sterling yet."

"I did, but he wasn't in the office." Another lie. *Mitchell will have me saying untrue things about Ellen next.* "Listen, I'll call him back and let you know."

Ted still didn't want to call Sterling, but his lying made him feel almost bad enough to overcome his anxiety. He called and Sterling's assistant, Alice, answered.

"Good afternoon, this is Ted Martin at the art museum. Is Mr. Sterling available please?"

The voice on the other end politely confirmed he was, and Sterling came on the line.

"Hello Ted, how are things going over there?"

They talked about a few small matters before Ted got up the nerve to ask about Martha's position change. Sterling didn't mention the possible Logan purchase, and Ted didn't tip his hand. He was sure Jenkins had sworn Sterling to silence too and hadn't mentioned his curator was part of the inner circle.

"Lou, I was really calling to ask you about something that happened at this morning's meeting. Have you seen the new organizational chart?"

"Yes, Mitchell gave me a copy last night at dinner."

"And it looks good to you?"

"Yes, I thought it was pretty much what we had discussed yesterday. What are you getting at, Ted?"

Ted could tell by his tone that Sterling was wondering if perhaps he really was the problem Jenkins had mentioned. Taking a deep breath, Ted got to the point with concern in his voice.

"It seems Mitchell has promoted Martha to the level of department chief, giving her several new responsibilities. Considering the conversations at yesterday's meetings, I didn't expect he would move her in this direction. I thought she would take a less dominant role. I've been sort of isolated over here today and haven't had an opportunity to speak with anyone else, but I'm concerned there might be others who share my confusion."

"Did Mitchell not explain to you why he's moving Martha in this way?"

"He indicated it would streamline the operation here, since she was responsible for secretarial support it would make the lines of authority and communication clear."

"Well, there you have it, Ted. Sounds clear to me! Try not to make a mountain out of it. Mitchell is trying to cope with things as best he can. It would be foolish for you to cause a commotion over a little thing like this."

"Yes, I suppose so, only I worry it might do more harm than good right now. Feelings being what they are among the staff. It goes much deeper than just Ellen, Mary, and me, you know. Martha really doesn't have many friends here."

"I'll take all this under advisement, Ted. For now, try to roll with what Mitchell is proposing. He too has a good grip on the politics over there."

Sterling hung up, and Ted felt foolish. It had gone as badly as he had feared, with Sterling thinking he was purposely working to Mitchell's detriment by continuing to be at odds with what he was proposing with Martha. Ted didn't want to bring Ellen into the conversation with Sterling, though he now wanted to tell her about the trouble she may have caused him.

"Sterling knows about it, Ellen. He thinks we should allow Mitchell this considering what happened yesterday and roll with it."

"I hope Martha can roll with it. He really didn't seem concerned?"

"No, but perhaps I didn't put it to him in the best way. You should talk with him, just not anytime soon. I think he suspects I'm trying to cause waves, no point in sticking your neck out as well."

She agreed and they finished their conversation. Ted completed the drawing he was working on, and as it was time for security to begin closing the building, left the storage area to return the key to Martha. As he passed by Mitchell's office, Ted heard him call his name. He answered instinctively and poked his head in the room.

"Got a minute? I need to talk with you."

Ted entered the room and sat down in the chair Mitchell indicated.

"What the fuck is the big idea of trying to start problems with the Dyer promotion? I thought I made it very clear this didn't concern anyone but her, the secretarial pool, and me. It hasn't been twelve hours and you're stirring the pot! You're walking on thin ice and you're about to fall in. I can make life very difficult for you and anyone else around here who refuses to meet me halfway, and if you persist on this course, you're going to find out what I'm saying is true."

"Look Mitchell, I'm sorry if I acted indiscreetly, but the charts were only passed out by Martha this morning. I'm supposed to talk with other department chiefs, and I waited until they called me. I knew Ellen would be upset."

Ted wondered how Jenkins knew about their conversation. Perhaps the walls were bugged after all, something they joked about often.

"Hell! I don't give a damn what you and Ellen talk about. I'll deal with her soon enough. I just got off the phone with Sterling who gave me hell for not properly explaining my position about Martha to you in this morning's meeting. I told him I did explain it and that you had voiced only moderate concern. Are you telling me your concern has gotten worse throughout the day?"

It hadn't taken Sterling five minutes to call Jenkins and relay to him the entire conversation. Ted now knew Sterling was not to be trusted, despite what Ellen thought of him. How many things had she told him over the years that had come right back to Jenkins and had gone into her file?

"I meant no disrespect to you in calling Sterling. I just wanted to hear from him that he knew about her new title. It still seems a bit inconceivable to me considering how her job description was rewritten yesterday."

"You think I lied to you? I told you Sterling had seen the chart. This is just the kind of attitude that causes problems around here. I'm glad you called Sterling, because now he knows I don't make this stuff up! Now he knows how it is dealing with you and Ellen. I want you out of my office now!"

Ted left feeling he had betrayed Mitchell, but that he had done so out of true feelings about his conduct. Ted had played into his hands and assumed a new round of persecution would take place on all fronts. There was no point in talking any further with Ellen, so Ted left the building, knowing Jenkins was thinking about him even then.

CHAPTER THIRTY-FIVE

Mitchell left for New York, the gallery drawings in a folder under his arm. Ted had finished them early that Saturday morning and had left them on his desk in what he considered to be a neat presentation, one that Taylor would be sure to like. Martha was in the building, trading Saturday for the following Monday to complete several projects Mitchell wanted finished prior to leaving. She was also to take him to the airport, rather than Ted. Mitchell was meeting Tate McNeil in New York to review their strategy for Taylor and Laura the following day. He hadn't said anything more to Ted about his conversation with Louis Sterling. As was often the case, Mitchell acted as if nothing at all had happened, and for the first time Ted found this a relief. He did not delude himself into thinking he was forgiven, only momentarily pardoned.

Their schedule was very tight and still secretive. McNeil had arranged for the four of them to drive to Woodstock on Monday afternoon, have dinner with the Logans, and view the paintings the following day. Even though McNeil was representing Logan in this action, Jenkins had been told the artist would have several tax lawyers on hand and that the Jameses might want to do the same. Taylor had laughed at the prospect but asked Jenkins to consider every angle of the sale and to watch McNeil, who he thought might try to pull something over on him if he decided to make an offer. McNeil had mentioned that while Logan needed the money, he would not sell the paintings to Taylor if he didn't like him personally. Jenkins told Ted he was concerned Taylor might say something to antagonize the artist and asked him for an assessment of Axel from their earlier chance meeting in Woodstock. Jenkins was aware Martha Logan might also be the problem and counted on Laura's gentle way to offset her husband's often brusque personality. What surprised Ted was that if the offer was accepted, the paperwork would be signed Thursday and the paintings shipped early the following month. He never dreamed things would move that quickly and suggested to Mitchell that he should examine the works prior to the sale. Mitchell took a dim view of this, saying McNeil had arranged for an independent conservator to examine the paintings and would provide a complete condition report to Taylor. He reminded Ted the paintings were to be the property of Taylor and Laura, not the museum.

"Besides," he said, "I'll be there to look them over."

Ted let that remark pass, not wanting to cause any further friction. He still didn't understand the rush to get them to Alabama. The museum was equipped to handle something as valuable as six million dollars' worth of new artwork, but as far as he knew insurance hadn't been discussed, or the method of transportation. Mitchell was moving rapidly and didn't want to be bothered by these details. There might have been a time, Ted thought, when he would have moved rapidly along with him.

Mitchell told Ted Martha would know his schedule and when he hoped to call back. Under no circumstance was Ted to try to contact him or to talk to anyone about his trip. As far as the staff was concerned, he was taking a few days to unwind after the rigors of the recent meetings with Sterling and to organize his thoughts in relation to the new working atmosphere he hoped to foster. In this regard, he planned a series of three day-long retreats to be held with senior staff upon his return from Vermont. The sessions were to discuss the museum and its future. He invited several people in addition to the department heads, including the museum's public information officer and the Art Association's membership secretary. He told Ted about a lodge that could be rented for the sessions.

"It's out in the country, a very pleasant place. Perhaps we could all stay out there for a few days, uninterrupted. See about it, Ted. I'll call you from New York."

It was still daylight when his plane landed at JFK in New York. Jenkins didn't fly first class this time, but remembered the trip he'd made to the city with Laura James. Much had changed since that time. He hurried from his seat to the front of the plane to disembark. He didn't like crowds, preferring to be in the terminal moving toward the luggage carousel and the taxis beyond. As before, he had made himself a reservation at the Taft, and the Jameses would again be staying at the Stanhope. Tate McNeil would arrive early the next morning and meet him for breakfast. Mitchell arrived at his hotel, checked in, and deposited his luggage on the bed. The window's view was much the same as the one he had the last time he stayed there. It was a bit warmer now, for which he was grateful, and he decided to have a few drinks in the lobby bar before finding somewhere to have dinner. The night would be his, and the anticipation made him thirsty. He was drinking martinis this trip!

The small bar was crowded even though there was no entertainment. The people there weren't New York visitors, but locals out for a night on the town, finding this a comfortable place to be for a couple hours before going out again. He was able to get a small table by one of the large windows facing 57th Street when the couple using it decided it was their turn to take the plunge back onto the pavement. She was an attractive woman with nice features, the man undistinguished.

Within a few moments a waitress was at his side. "You don't look like a New Yorker," she said.

Jenkins looked at her. She looked cheap, which excited him. Middle-aged, nice legs, though not the type he wanted for the night.

"You're right darlin'. I'm not from the Big Apple, but I get up this way every now and then."

"You're Southern," she said, smiling at him through orange lips. "I can tell by the way you talk. Where you from, Sugar?" He looked up at her again and wrinkled his forehead, as if he had only now seen the woman and had discovered her to be hideous.

"Alabama, deep in the heart of Dixie. I'll have a double vodka martini with a twist."

She smiled and took the order to the bar. He returned to watching people as they walked by. It was dark and reflections of the drinkers inside added to the confusion of the bustle on the street.

✵ ✵ ✵

Jenkins arrived at McNeil's hotel early the next morning and called up to his room. The voice that answered sounded tired and a bit nervous.

"Go on into the dining room and order breakfast," McNeil said. "I need a shower but will be down shortly."

Jenkins wondered what was causing the tense tone in McNeil's voice. Perhaps the artist was having second thoughts about the sale. If so, McNeil would need to do a lot of explaining. Jenkins wouldn't take any of the blame for getting his Meriden patrons excited about this meeting only to have it dashed by the whims of an artist. He walked into the restaurant. It was a far cry from what was at the Taft. It was what McNeil would pick, but Jenkins felt uncomfortable. Though it was a Sunday morning, there were people there already looking polished and over-dressed—the women expensive and tight-assed. He was shown to a table where he could watch for McNeil, and the waiter brought coffee.

"I don't suppose you have grits?" he asked.

The waiter looked at him quizzically, then politely said they did not.

Tate McNeil entered the dining room carrying a soft leather brief-case and several large folders. His hair was combed and still wet from the shower. He wasn't wearing a tie, but did have on a tweed jacket, his starched shirt open to the second button.

"Sorry to keep you waiting. Have you ordered?"

Jenkins nodded and waved the waiter over as McNeil sat. The dealer made several remarks about the weather, which had turned cloudy and gray. His tone was still strained and made Jenkins uneasy.

"You always this tense when you sell a few pictures? You Yankees need to lighten up a bit—tension's not good for the mind." Jenkins smiled as McNeil downed the freshly squeezed orange juice that had been brought to him.

"You know I ain't no Yankee, I just look that way. It's the air up here."

"And I thought it was the women!" Jenkins smiled again. "Taylor and Laura are due in at noon. They'll be at the Stanhope and expect to see us by two. Though their daughter and son-in-law went to Asia with them, I asked Taylor to make up some excuse for staying in the city for a few days and send them home."

McNeil was listening as Jenkins talked, pushing the folders he had laid on the table aside. "They could have come too, Mitchell. They're family, and the Logans wouldn't have minded."

"I thought it was best to leave them out of this for the time being, and so did Taylor. The one thing you're going to learn about him is once he's made up his mind on something, nothing's going to change it. Their daughter Morgan is pretty headstrong herself and with this being as delicate as it is..."

"You think she'll object to him spending six million bucks that might have come to her?"

"It will still be hers, even if the money is spent. The paintings, if things go through, will be in Taylor and Laura's name for now, then in their heir's name afterward. He's playing this very conservatively, enjoying the power of owning such a collection. He likes converting dollars into objects, especially objects with good investment potential."

"Until Logan dies. When he goes there's going to be a lot of scrambling in that community, and if things aren't handled correctly there could be a lot of paintings on the market at once. I don't have to tell you what that would do to the price of Logan's paintings. I'm hoping the old boy hangs in there for a few more years, at least until this deal is done and there's some distance behind it."

Breakfast was served by the waiter and an assistant. The dishes filled the small table, so McNeil had to move his folders.

"What is all that stuff?" Jenkins nodded at the folders now on the floor under their table.

"I'll show you after we've eaten. It's information on Logan I've compiled for the Jameses. Factual stuff about the prices of paintings, exhibitions in the works, and other collections. Trying to put my best foot forward. This could be the single most important sale of the century, Mitchell, or at least the largest. What are you going to do with your cut?"

Mitchell stopped chewing and looked sternly at McNeil. "I don't want you to ever mention that again. After the transaction is done, I want it forgotten."

"Hey, don't get upset, I'm with you on that. But you're not the first museum director who's ever taken a percentage of a sale. It happens all the time."

"Used to happen all the time! The museum business has gotten very uptight about policing itself. It's the fuckin' curators who are doing it, bunch of moral sons-of-bitches. They say it's unethical for someone in the public trust to take money of this kind. I've got my image to think about, and the museum's. Jesus, I've got enough problems down there now without this coming to light. My fuckin' staff would be all over me. I'm sure Morgan would have something to say about it, and shit—I don't know what Taylor would think!" He paused for a moment. "Though I could probably convince him it was okay. Anyway, I'd like to slip this by

Uncle Sam. Taylor's taught me a lot about foreign accounts, and I expect to be using his agent in the next few days."

McNeil laughed. "Well, I'll send you the money in cash then, if that's your plan. They'd trace my check. Perhaps we can work it out so you never actually handle the money—it could go straight to Switzerland! I have connections too, you know."

"No, I want to actually touch it, like in the movies. It'll be in a suit-case, right?"

"In one of these." McNeil pointed to the leather case on the chair next to him. "I'll put it in one of these since the sides expand!" They laughed again. "You're not planning to tell Taylor about the money then? It might be smarter to alert them in case it gets out. That way they could say they gave it to you as a fee. They've made a point of saying the collection belongs to them and not the museum. The paintings are going to end up in the museum sometime, aren't they? It's a thing with Logan that they be in a public place."

"Yep, going to go in one of the front galleries. Ted Martin's made some drawings. I have them over at the Taft."

"Martin knows?"

"I had to tell him to get the drawings, besides telling him is part of something else I've got going on down there. He won't say anything, even though I'm going to make it difficult for him to keep the knowl-edge to himself. It's staff stuff, part of the reason I can't let anyone know about the money. But you have a point about Taylor. I'll feel him out."

"It seems everybody has staff problems. Ted playing the moral curator?"

"He's gotten himself mixed up with two other staff members who are beginning to dislike the divide between themselves and those of us who run the show. So, the three of them are constantly thinking they're be-ing controlled and watched. Ted's about due for a change of scenery." He looked at McNeil to see if there was a change in his expression. "These guys come and go, the the director just needs to weather them out. Ted's been more than useful, but after a while people don't want to follow the way they used to. Then it's time to make a change. Tough to do when he works so hard though!"

They left the dining room together and went up to McNeil's suite to go over the material he had prepared for later in the day.

Jenkins and McNeil performed as well as any other song and dance team in the Northeast that season, and Taylor and Laura were as excited about traveling to Woodstock as they had been about traveling to China. The prospect of purchasing the collection was even more intriguing to Taylor now than before. Jack Grossman had done his job well but wasn't in the picture—only McNeil and Jenkins. And because Jenkins was involved, James felt even more confident about the transaction. The four of them left the following morning. McNeil had rented a large Mercedes sedan for the trip that would take two hours in traffic. Jenkins felt a bit uneasy, not knowing what to expect when they arrived, even though McNeil had assured him he had spoken to Martha Logan the night before and everything was set. Axel had just completed a major painting and was in a wonderful frame of mind.

Tate and Taylor had taken the front seats of the car, leaving Mitchell to ride with Laura in the back. She was quiet as usual, but happy to see Jenkins and excited about the trip. He hadn't spoken to her about the events that had occurred with the staff while she and Taylor were away, but wanted to before returning to Meriden. He didn't want her surprised by Sterling's report at the commission meeting.

"Sure will be good to have you and Taylor back in Meriden. The community needs your stability and I need your trusted counsel on museum matters."

She looked at him and smiled. Since the heart attack, Laura had come to think of Mitchell as part of their family, and these words were just the kind of greeting she expected after a long absence.

"Everything well at the museum? In all the excitement I forgot to inquire."

Jenkins suddenly looked pensive, talking just above a whisper. "Oh, there have been some personnel things. Ted Martin and Ellen Maxwell stirring things up again. This time they went to Sterling and got him involved. But I think things are on the mend now. I've reorganized the whole staff, subject to commission approval, and hope it will alleviate the problem. I don't know about Ted though; he's been something of a disappointment to me lately."

Laura looked troubled and echoed Mitchell's hushed tone. "I don't understand, after all you've done for that young man." She paused. "It's really too much, Mitchell. You shouldn't have to deal with that kind of insubordination."

"Well, he's been a good employee on most counts, and I want to be fair, to give him the benefit of the doubt. I believe we should try to go the extra mile when possible."

"I think you're being entirely too tolerant, especially if he's infecting others like Ellen, though I know you've had problems with her before. I just don't understand why they don't want to cooperate with you and help build the museum. Does Ted know about the Logan collection?"

"Yes, I told him before leaving. I'm sure he'll keep my confidence about it."

"Was he excited about having the works in the museum's collection?"

"I couldn't tell. It's a lot of news to be told at once, but he seemed enthused when I showed him the drawings of the gallery installation I'd made—the ones I showed to you and Taylor last night. Ted's a funny man. I'm sure he understands the importance of this purchase even if he doesn't act like he's delighted. He worries too much about details and not the bigger picture of what the museum will be like once the paintings are exhibited."

"If he's going to be ungrateful, I think you ought to encourage him to move on. Taylor and I both feel if the paintings are purchased and the announcement is made, Meriden should turn out to show some support for you. If they don't, we can place the collection elsewhere, and I intend to explain that if the gift is questioned. But don't worry," she said reassuringly, "we don't intend to take it anywhere else, as long as you're in charge of the museum. Few people realize how much you've done for that city, and you certainly aren't getting rich on the salary you're paid."

"Money's not everything Laura. It helps just knowing you're aware of the problems. The commission is the better for it, believe me!"

They arrived in Woodstock in time for lunch at the inn. Laura took time to freshen up for the afternoon's meeting. Tate had reserved rooms for the group, but hoped the negotiations would go well enough to persuade the Logans to let their guests stay with them. He reasoned if the Jameses felt they were friends of the artist and his wife, it would be more conducive to the completion of the sale. During lunch, Taylor said very little after he and Tate had talked throughout the drive from New York. Jenkins was amazed at how good he looked after the trip through Asia. The heart attack seemed to have left him almost in better shape than before.

As they were finishing the meal with coffee, Taylor finally spoke. "I hear this fellow Logan has a real shrew for a wife. Is that right?"

Jenkins felt his lunch churn as McNeil looked across the table at him in alarm.

"Taylor!" Laura exclaimed. "What a terrible thing to say. Please don't embarrass me in front of Mitchell and Mr. McNeil! Where did you hear a thing like that anyway?"

"I don't know, from Grossman or someone like that. I don't intend to ruffle her feathers, but I want to know if she rules the roost over there, like I heard."

McNeil was quick on his feet and took over the conversation. "I think it's fair to say she's careful with her husband's talent. Axel has always been very free with it himself, talking to people and doing whatever he can to help folks out. It was his father's way, and here in Woodstock he's insulated from the rest of the world that may be out to take advantage of him. Martha protects his interests, just as Laura would if you were hurt, or perhaps as she did while you were in hospital."

Jenkins smiled to himself at McNeil's trial by fire, remembering his own run-ins with Taylor over the museum project.

"She's above all a lovely woman and will be delighted to meet you and Laura."

"I'm sure she is," Laura replied. "My husband sometimes likes to get reactions out of people, particularly ones he doesn't know well. I hope you will excuse him."

Taylor laughed. "Listen Tate, you have nothing to worry about from me. I intend to be a perfect gentleman the remainder of the afternoon. But you know, you and Mitchell are asking me to spend a significant bit of money and I want to know something about the people I'm dealing with. You've been very good about detailing the life of the artist but have said nothing about his wife. Jack Grossman told me she wears the pants in that family, and I wanted to know."

"Grossman doesn't know you're here today, does he?" McNeil sounded worried and tense again.

"Of course not! What do you take me for? The art community isn't so much different than the scientific community as far as secrets are concerned. Grossman would probably want to talk me out of this thing if he knew. Or be part of it in some fashion. You just can't be too careful is all. Right, Mitchell?"

Jenkins smiled at Taylor from his seat next to Laura on the opposite side of the table. He enjoyed knowing Taylor was going to make a game of the purchase of the Logan paintings, much as he had giving him the original ten grand to keep his daughter quiet. He wouldn't be fooled by McNeil's smooth talk or the intensity of being near the famous artist; he would make his deal for the paintings and add Logan to the list of names he enjoyed dropping in social conversation.

"Absolutely right, Taylor," Jenkins agreed. "You can never be too careful about anything. This is a historic moment; if the paintings are purchased it will represent the largest single sale for a collection this decade—perhaps even this century. It'll mean a lot to you as the collector who brought it about, and it will mean a lot to Meriden and the museum when the transaction is announced. We'll need to rethink everything we do there, from educational programs to security. Our attendance figures are going to increase dramatically too, and you and Laura, as you have been in the past, will be the major reason for these changes. So no, we can't be too careful." He looked over at McNeil who was recovering from Taylor's barrage. "The Logans should also be very grateful to you for keeping the collection together. Tate will tell you that. They need to sell these paintings, yet want to keep the prices of others on the market as high as possible. What do you think would happen to those prices if this collection was suddenly on the market as individual pieces? The Logans are going to be interested in working with you any way they can. I don't think Mrs. Logan is going to stand in the way of the sale or cause any problems whatsoever."

Again, Jenkins looked over at McNeil, who backed his statements with assurances that the Logans were most interested in seeing things run smoothly. They again climbed into the Mercedes for the short ride to the Logan compound. McNeil checked his watch to make sure they wouldn't be too early, but everything was on schedule.

The sun brightly blazed over the winter landscape. Last vestiges of a snow could be seen lingering in the shadows of trees in the valley below them as they traveled down the narrow country road. Laura remarked repeatedly to Mitchell about how lovely the countryside looked even in winter, and about the views she was sure would be included in future Logan paintings. Mitchell responded, though his mind was on the negotiations that would soon take place. He had promised Taylor the collection could be had for six million and hoped that figure was still accurate. It was, as Taylor had said at lunch, a lot of money. It would be hard to ask him to spend more if the artist or his wife decided the price should be higher. The car rode past stone gates leading to the forest surrounding the Logan home and Axel's studio beyond, then stopped in the small parking area adjacent to the door of the main building. Leading the way, McNeil opened the door and they stepped inside. The room they entered was huge, with rough-cut wooden beams overhead, walls of stone, and oak floors polished to a lush shine that reflected a roaring fire. McNeil bade them over to the fireplace to erase the chill from their short walk.

"I'll find Martha," he said, rubbing his hands together. "She's likely in the kitchen making something warm to drink."

Mitchell stepped across the room to look at the paintings hung on the stone walls. They were some of Logan's finest, most popular paintings, and they seemed to take on a new life when seen in person. Laura was struck by them too and followed him across the room, leaving her husband with his back to the flames, becoming slightly irritated the artist wasn't there to greet him. McNeil re-entered the room holding a large wooden tray with a steaming pitcher and cups.

Martha Logan was walking next to him, smiling at her guests as she entered, gesturing to the tray Tate carried. "I'm so sorry not to have had this ready when you came in. I'm Martha Logan and you must be Taylor James." She walked past McNeil to Taylor standing by the fireplace. "Welcome to Woodstock and to our home. Both Axel and I are so pleased that you and Mrs. James could come to see us."

Martha Logan was a tall woman, casually dressed in slacks and a sweater. She was older than Mitchell had thought but seemed outwardly genuine in greeting them.

She turned to Laura and Mitchell. "Won't you have some cider, Mrs. James? And you too, Mr. Jenkins. Tate has told me so much about your progress in Meriden since the opening of your building and the exhibition of Nathan's work there. Axel and I still talk about it."

Jenkins took a cup of cider. It was hot, and he blew at the top of the cup. "You're very kind to remember that," he said. "We certainly enjoyed having those paintings in Alabama and still have visitors coming by in hopes of seeing them, even now."

Jenkins began feeling uncomfortable. It had been over five years since that exhibition, and though his memory was generally very good, Ted Martin had handled much of its details. He hoped he wouldn't be asked too much about it now.

"Axel feels such a debt to his father. He is very proud of that exhibition and so enjoyed meeting that nice young man who came up with Tate before it opened. I can't seem to remember his name, Mr...."

"Martin," Jenkins offered. "He enjoyed your hospitality and talks of it often."

"He's still working for you then?"

"Yes."

She could tell from his curt answer that Mitchell didn't want to elaborate about his curator and changed the topic to one she felt he might be more interested in. "Axel should be along very shortly; he's in the studio. Tate may have told you he just finished a rather large new canvas, and he's been like a child with it. Goes down to look it over every day. He wants you to see it before you leave. It's being sent, along with some other things, to an exhibition in Monaco as a special favor to the prince. We're getting rather tired of doing all these exhibitions and hope to relax a while, especially if Mr. and Mrs. James are interested in the paintings."

Two cars pulled up, parking beside the Mercedes. Four well-tailored men got out, each carrying a briefcase and heading for the same entrance McNeil used. They were greeted warmly, smiling at McNeil, then were introduced to Jenkins and the Jameses. They were the lawyers and businesspeople the Logan family used to manage their trust funds benefiting a dozen different projects in and around Woodstock. They were invited, McNeil had told Jenkins earlier, to help with the paperwork for the sale of the paintings. He hadn't expected them until the following day, and their presence would be hard to explain to Taylor, who was under the impression that the afternoon's meeting was more social than business.

"We're taking a final inventory of the paintings, and these gentlemen have come over to finish," Martha explained. "Sorry to mix business with pleasure like this, but their being here shouldn't interfere with our getting to know one another. They'll be working in the storeroom."

She led the four out of the living area and through the door she and Tate had used when they entered with the cider. When they were gone, McNeil turned to Taylor with an apologetic grin on his face.

"Sorry about that, I had no way of knowing she would have her people here today. I hope it doesn't make you nervous, they really are just working on an inventory and developing tax angles for the money should you decide to purchase the paintings."

Taylor said nothing but looked crossly at Mitchell. "Looks like the old hustle to me," he said finally. "Sure she's not up to something? I remember that little speech you made at lunch, McNeil. Two old Scots like us should be square with each other."

Tate ensured everyone the Logans were anxious to settle the sale with a minimum of business. "You heard what she said, they're tired and want to relax. The sale will help them do just that while still moving forward with their pet projects."

He went silent as the door opened again and Axel Logan entered, followed by Martha. He was wearing outdoor walking clothes that looked to be made of leather. His hair was blown around his head, and his cheeks were a rosy color from being outside. He fit the image they all had of him.

"Well, hello everyone. Sorry if I've not been the proper host, but you see, there are some good things going on in the studio and it's hard to get free." He crossed the room in long strides, holding his hand out in greeting to Taylor, Laura, and Mitchell. "It's my pleasure to meet you all, I hope Tate has taken care of your needs."

Axel Logan was quite charming and immediately took command of the afternoon and evening. His way was warm and natural, and it was easy for Mitchell to understand how he drew people to him. Even Taylor seemed to let his guard down in his presence, the two of them talking in a corner of the room that gradually filled with people Axel had invited over for drinks. By dinner, there were twenty people seated around a long table in another room, reminiscent of something out of the Middle Ages, with Logan seated at the head of the table as a king would be. The evening slipped by, with everyone except Laura and Martha drinking too much. Taylor and Axel were the worst, seemingly trying to out-drink each other.

Over the protests of their host, the guests opted to spend the night back at the lodge and left with McNeil at the wheel of the Mercedes shortly before midnight. They were to meet again for brunch the following morning and to view the paintings. Mitchell was pleased with the friendship Axel and Taylor had made. The impact to Meriden of the sale of these paintings was incalculable, and as the person who made it happen, he would be untouchable! It was what Bishop had done all those years before. No longer would he need to fear Ellen Maxwell or Ted Martin—they would be expendable.

✳ ✳ ✳

The lobby of the lodge was warm and friendly as they entered and waved to the night clerk. Taylor wanted a nightcap and asked Mitchell to join him. They bid goodnight to Laura and Tate and took facing chairs near the fire in the vast lobby. The clerk brought brandy and Taylor began talking.

"How do you read it, Mitchell? I like Logan but can't cotton up to the wife. I think she's sizing me up, trying to decide if I'm good enough to own those paintings."

Mitchell was caught off-guard and stalled a moment before responding. "I wouldn't let her worry you, Taylor. She may be the boss of their family, but she has to be influenced by what Logan thinks and says. I don't think she's going to cause any problems."

"No, I don't think she's capable of that, but just to be sure, I want you to have a talk with McNeil before we go over there tomorrow. I don't want any problems, especially with those business types in the back room. Never could trust that crowd, even in the sciences."

Jenkins agreed to talk to McNeil.

"The paintings on their walls, are they the ones we're getting?"

"Some of them are. I was surprised to see them there. I thought they'd all have been in storage for inspection tomorrow."

"Did you like them? I mean were they good? Worth the money?"

"Oh, yes. I liked them very much. They are some of the most important work Axel has done. They would really put Meriden on the map. Scholars from across the world will come to study them, especially after Axel's dead."

The reference to that eventuality didn't sit well with Taylor, and Jenkins was sorry he'd said it.

"He looked pretty hale and hearty to me tonight," Taylor replied. "I don't know why you and McNeil keep mentioning his death. Believe me, it comes soon enough!" He paused to finish his drink, staring into the fireplace. "I've decided to buy the paintings if the price is as McNeil has quoted. Tell him not to fuck up tomorrow. He gets a healthy chunk of this, I suppose."

He looked over at Jenkins who was nursing his brandy.

"Yes, ten percent of the gross sale."

"Not a bad night's work. I think you should wake that son-of-a-bitch now for that kind of money. Make sure nothing goes wrong. I want them for Meriden, and I want Jack Grossman to know I'm capable of making decisions without him. I like the guy, but it's time he knew that I ain't no sucker."

Taylor rose to leave, patting Jenkins on the shoulder as he walked past.

Mitchell was glad for the opportunity to be alone. He hadn't wanted to say anything to Taylor, but he didn't like the way the four suits had been working all evening on the paperwork for the sale. He hadn't had time to talk to McNeil about it, but now thought he would. Taylor was right, for $6,000,000 McNeil could lose some sleep. His door was open as Jenkins approached.

"Come on in, Mitchell, I've been expecting you." Tate McNeil was seated in an overstuffed chair with his feet propped on a matching otto-man. He was sipping bourbon and water in a tall glass with ice. "You and Taylor have a nice chat? I suppose the old boy wants the paintings and told you to tell me nothing should go wrong tomorrow. No surprises! Well, I'm going to do my best, don't you worry."

Jenkins took a seat on a corner of the bed, opposite McNeil. "Hell, Tate, your best just isn't good enough. You've got to be absolutely sure. Taylor is willing to spend the money, but you saw those accountants. What's their take in this thing? How many people does old Axel support with this sale anyway? Those boys looked hungry to me, and Martha looked like she was sizing us up to see just how much Taylor could afford. I think they're going to try to slip one past us tomorrow. I need to make sure that doesn't happen."

"Already got the money spent, is that it?"

Jenkins glared. "I told you I don't want that discussed. There is more to this than the money. Just don't let us down tomorrow, old buddy boy." He rose and walked to the door. "I may have been born in the south, but I'm not slow. The James family means a lot to Meriden, to the museum, and practically everything now to me."

✳ ✳ ✳

The Arcade Theatre was one of the premier movie houses in the South in the 1930s. Built by the Fox chain, the Arcade's mirrored lobby came to symbolize the beginning of the modern era of American life. Meriden families visited weekly as the biggest Hollywood pictures were shown, consuming nickel bags of popcorn and Coke in cold glass bottles. By the mid-60s, the southern end of the city where the Arcade had been built was in the early stages of decay. No one of prominence went anymore, and the films it showed were called "art" pieces, catering to adolescent boys looking for voyeuristic thrills and old men for whom the films represented the only sexual stimulus left to them. The mirrored panels in the lobby had long since cracked or fallen off entirely, the metal sculptures defaced, the air stale with the smell of sweat and old wood. Two figures sat in the back row of seats one spring morning in 1970. They watched a French film starring the celebrated mime, Henri Peraeux. It had been banned in several cities when it first appeared in 1965 because of its subject—the strong, emotional attachment between two young men—but had by the early 70s been acclaimed a classic. Only a small advertisement had been placed for the film by the theater's management since it was not their standard fare, but rather something of interest to a segment of the community that was not mentioned socially. The two patrons in the back row were the only people in the audience that afternoon—a normal attendance for the first matinee on a weekday morning. One of the men had left his office, telling his assistant he would be out for several hours and would check in later. It was easy for him to get away, he was the boss. The other man had to make up a more complicated excuse for his absence. He told his young secretary he would be driving to Birmingham for the afternoon to attend an important meeting at the museum there. He wouldn't be back until the following day, and she was to take messages for him if there were any calls.

✵ ✵ ✵

The telephone beside his bed was ringing; they had only been installed in the lodge's rooms the year before. Mitchell heard the sound as if it were far away, a disturbing noise breaking through the layers of his unconsciousness brought on by the three capsules he had taken late the night before. The ringing didn't stop and seemed to get louder. His hand reacted by reaching out as he was jolted back to consciousness.

"Hello." His voice was thick, but audible.

"Mitchell! It's Tate. I'm sorry about the time but we've got to talk. It's important."

"It's fucking five thirty in the morning Tate," Mitchell cursed as the digital clock on the nightstand flipped to 5:31. "What could be so fucking important? I didn't get to sleep until two."

"I'm really sorry, but Bob Warder just called. He's one of those guys we saw yesterday. One of the accountants, remember?"

"Yeah, so what's he doing up at this time of day?"

"Martha had them up all night working on the figures for the sale. That's why he called. It's running into a little more money than we thought. Martha's given them new figures on the paintings' values."

"Shit! Listen Tate, that's not going to go down well with Taylor. You'd better get over here right now."

Mitchell slammed the receiver down and swung his legs out of the bed. The narrow shaft of light coming from the bathroom caught him in the eye and he blinked as he considered what McNeil just told him. He walked the few steps to the bathroom and opened small tan toiletry bag. Groping through the contents, he found the brown, plastic bottle that contained what Abram Rubin called "wake-up pills, guaranteed to get you going in a hurry," and from experience Jenkins knew they would. He swallowed two and returned to his room, finding his pants heaped over a chair. There were footsteps in the hallway, then a quiet knock. Tate McNeil entered quickly when the door opened. He looked worried, his hair uncombed.

"Ok, here's the thing. Martha went into the room where they were still working last night after we left. She had a sheet of new valuations for the paintings supposedly based on Axel's New York gallery."

"Is she on the level?"

"She is apparently about the prices. I don't know about the telephone call. Anyway, it threw everything off and caused them to be up most of the night refiguring. It comes to a million more than what was originally quoted. Bob told me she feels terrible about the difference but feels compelled to get the best price she can for the paintings. They want to slow their lives down for a while."

"Have you talked to her?"

"Phone must be off the hook. All I got was a busy signal."

"I'll bet! Listen Tate, we aren't going to be suckered into spending more money. It was the last thing Taylor said to me last night before I came to see you. He wants to buy the paintings at the price originally specified. No more. Doesn't she realize the importance of somebody buying the entire collection? Does she think the Met would stand for this? I think you better get out there right now and talk to her. Does Axel know about all this? I'm not saying anything to Taylor until you call back and fill me in on what's going on. I'd go myself but I'm afraid of what I might say to her."

"Okay, okay, try to calm down. I'll go out there now and see what I can do. You and the Jameses aren't due there until eleven, which gives me a bit of time. I'll send a car for you thirty minutes before."

"But call me before then. I want to know exactly what's going on. You understand?"

McNeil nodded and left the room as quietly as he had entered.

Mitchell paced across the floor to a shaded window and peeked out at the early morning, dark and overcast. "Shit." He reached for the bottle at his bedside and emptied what little remained. "Shit!"

✲ ✲ ✲

The intercom button on Ted's phone lit up. It was surprisingly early for him to be receiving any calls, but the outside line was flashing wildly as he picked up the receiver.

"It's Mitchell on the line for you," Joe Mullens said at the switch-board. "He's calling from Vermont."

Ted paused a moment before connecting. It wasn't like Mitchell to call him when he was away, and especially odd considering the nature of this trip. He had worked at being extra friendly since telling Ted of the potential Logan deal, which served to unnerve him further.

"Mitchell? How are you? How's it going up there?"

Mitchell's voice sounded rough and tired. Ted had heard it this way one other time, right after the suicide threat when he had called to make small talk about Ted's loyalty to him, and how much it was appreciated.

"I'm doin' the best I can, Bud. But things with the project are not good. I can't talk now, but it doesn't look like it's going to happen, too many last-minute complications. Listen, I want you to do me a favor. Martha isn't there yet, but when she comes in, I want you to tell her to take the project files to the storage room and lock them away. I want you to take any notes or drawings you might still have for the installation and shred them. Taylor is not going to be happy with the current developments here, and I don't want him ever to know how much planning we already did on this. Okay?"

"Sure Mitchell, we can do those things first thing when Martha comes in. Sorry we didn't succeed, I know you were excited about it."

"Well, there's still a chance, but not a big one. I'm not optimistic about any of it. I'll talk to you about it when I get back in a day or so. Take care of those things, Ted."

The phone went dead. Ted wondered if he was calling from the booth at the lodge and again thought of his chance meeting with Axel Logan and their breakfast together. Ted had mixed emotions about the sale and what it would mean to the museum, so the news things weren't going well didn't sadden him greatly. Taylor had become a steadily tightening noose around Mitchell's neck, and owning the Logan paintings, Ted thought, might kick the stool out from under him. No one could spend millions in this way and have it not affect them, and despite Mitchell's denials, he knew it too. Since the issuance of the statement about Martha Dyer and the condition of the staff, they had been forbidden by Mitchell to talk to any outsider, excluding Louis Sterling, who had now become part of the conspiracy. Mitchell didn't want anyone talking to Taylor about anything, describing his personality as volatile and unpredictable; he could well be one of the forces to relieve Mitchell of his job, despite the obvious ties he had established with Laura. Ted wondered how deeply Mitchell felt he would be blamed if the paintings were not secured. The tension in his voice was not a good sign. Ted called Martha and advised her of Mitchell's request. She said she would take care of the files and hung up. Ted gathered the extra drawings he had kept on the installation of the paintings and took them to the paper shredder on the other side of the building. In seconds they were thin strands of trash, their original contents illegible.

✤ ✤ ✤

"Good morning, Mitchell!" Taylor was chipper despite the heavy gray clouds of the morning. "You look like you didn't sleep well. I think this trip is taking a toll on you."

He was correct, but didn't know how accurate his assessment was. The earliest reports from McNeil weren't good. He hadn't seen Martha Logan, who had gone to bed complaining of a severe headache and asked not to be disturbed until shortly before brunch. Bob Warder was sympathetic, but neither he nor any of the other men could lower the values to their originally stated levels. They were at an impasse until McNeil could get to Martha, which was what he told Jenkins when he called.

"I haven't had a good night," Mitchell replied. "Is Laura going to join us for coffee?"

"No, she's having it in the room. We can have some though, and a bit of breakfast if you'd like." Taylor led Jenkins into the restaurant where other early risers had assembled. "McNeil up yet? Did you two have a little chat last night?"

Jenkins smiled tightly. "The answer is yes on both counts." He couldn't make up his mind how to tell Taylor about the situation. "Tate was up early and went over to the compound to talk with those four fellows who were working on the valuations last evening. He called a little while ago to say he's sending a car over for us."

Taylor fingered the leather buttons on his suede coat, not looking Mitchell in the eye. "Are there problems?" he asked, his voice low.

"There is a new wrinkle, but Tate's working on it and hopes to have things ironed out by the time we get there. They're having trouble coming up with the figures on the paintings, but I'm sure he'll get things under control."

Taylor was still playing with the buttons. There was no change of emotion on his face or tone of his voice when he spoke. "They trying to shake me down? Get more money after they've seen me? I expected something like this. Old Logan, he doesn't know from day to day about money, leaves it to that bitch he married and her accountants and lawyers. I'll bet she'd like to retire for a while, and on the money from this sale, she can do it in style."

"Oh, I don't think it's anything like that, Taylor. Just some fuck-up with accounting. Tate's assured me it can be fixed. Really, he just left an hour ago and I've talked with him already. There's nothing to sweat about."

Taylor didn't look convinced. He sat back in his chair as the waitress refilled his cup and spoke as she walked away. "Laura and I have given this matter much thought over the past week, or however long ago it was that you called us overseas. The more she thought about it, the more she was convinced that buying those pictures for Meriden would be a grand thing. But do you know why it would be such a fine thing, Mitchell?"

Jenkins looked blankly at James who did not give him time to answer.

"Because it would secure your position as director of the museum, practically for all time, and that's what she wants. Laura is a very quiet woman, never says much, but I've come to trust her judgement and to listen to her when she does speak. She seems to think you are in some trouble there with the staff and sees this purchase as something that will put you above any petty business that might do you harm. We're both grateful for your kindness to our family when I was sick and want to see you succeed in Meriden, because it's important that someone strong be there. It would disappoint her greatly if after coming this far with the painting thing we didn't get them. If there is still a problem when we get there this morning, Mitchell, I want you to let me handle it. Just stay in the background. I'm much more accustomed to working with people like this because I've had to do it all my life. Okay?"

He looked at Jenkins almost as a father to a son.

"Absolutely Taylor, as you wish."

The words had been at once comforting and frightening to Mitchell. Taylor found it too easy to ask him to take a back seat in these negotiations; Mitchell wasn't used to doing that and didn't want it to become a precedent. If the sale went through, and millions of dollars were spent, it would be very difficult for him to ask Taylor to stay out of his museum politics.

At ten thirty the dark Mercedes pulled up to the front of the lodge. The sun poked in and out of the low clouds, causing strange casts over the landscape. Tate McNeil hadn't called back, and Mitchell was worried. Taylor led Laura to the car where Mitchell was waiting. He wasn't wearing a topcoat, but Laura was bundled up and smiling as they walked to the driveway. Taylor was carrying a leather case larger than his usual briefcase with two gold combination locks on either side of the handle. He wouldn't let Jenkins take it as he entered the car, sitting with Laura in the back seat this trip. They proceeded down the drive to the narrow highway that would take them to the Logan home. Though he had taken Alka-Seltzer after breakfast with Taylor, Mitchell still had terrible anxiety. The driver pulled the car into the same space McNeil had used the afternoon before and they all got out. Tate was at the door trying to look cheerful, but Mitchell could tell the tension was still with him.

"Hope you all had a restful night."

He stepped out of the doorway to shake Taylor's hand. He was still holding the case, which Jenkins had forgotten about during the drive.

"Got a good breakfast here for you. I'm starving myself," McNeil said.

Jenkins looked at him as he said it and wondered how he could be thinking about food. They again walked into the large room. The paintings had been hung or placed on easels for everyone's inspection. Seeing them all in one place was striking, even to Mitchell who stopped, despite his eagerness to get McNeil aside, to view them. Taylor did not stop; he walked across the room, as if wearing blinders, to a small wooden table that stood against one of the outside walls. He removed a ceramic bowl that sat on it and placed his briefcase there on its side. It was the first time he let go of it since leaving the lodge.

McNeil had taken Laura around to show her the paintings. It wasn't what Jenkins had wanted but, under the circumstances, could not stop. Had the problem with their valuations not come up, it would have been exactly the thing he would have wanted McNeil to do. Axel Logan came into the room and greeted Taylor warmly. The two of them talked by a large window overlooking the mountains and seemed oblivious to the fact there might be very sharp words spoken between Taylor and the lawyers shortly. Jenkins was the only one of the group to appear nervous. Martha Logan entered and summoned her guests into the dining room. Jenkins could feel his stomach churn as she took Laura by the arm to escort her.

"Tate," Mitchell said, "would you show me where the bathroom is, I'm afraid I'm lost."

McNeil walked across the floor to lead him out of the room, down the hallway, and past the storage room's entrance.

"What's going on? You're acting as if everything's in the bag."

McNeil looked at Jenkins as if for the first time. "It's part of the act. You've got to become adjusted to this when you play for big stakes."

"Listen Tate." Mitchell grabbed him by his right arm and threw him against one of the hallway walls, pinning him there with his body. "This is more than big stakes. Taylor knows. I tried to make it seem less than it really is, but he knows and is prepared to deal with the lawyers and anybody else who attempts to fuck him. I'm counting on you to tell me now that he won't have to do that. That you've straightened things out."

"Take it easy Mitchell." The grip on his arm had not loosened. "I'll tell you where we stand if you let go of me."

Mitchell stepped back, allowing McNeil to straighten himself. "I talked to Martha for about forty-five minutes this morning, right before you got here. She says she wasn't aware I had quoted any price to you and Taylor, though I can't believe she's really that naive. Anyway, she doesn't know what to do, as she claims the new prices were called in from New

York last night and the accountants have already figured them in. We decided we'd just level with Taylor and see what he says. I put the paintings out for him to view, figuring he'd want them after he saw them, but I don't think he's looked at them since arriving."

"Hell, he doesn't care what they look like, only what they will do or mean to someone else. I don't know what he'll say when this all hits the fan, but he can be pretty cutting when he wants to be. I hope you get out of this alive."

Jenkins turned and walked back down the hallway toward the dining room, leaving McNeil alone in the hall. After eating, they adjourned back into the large room where the accountants of the Logan business empire were seated around a low coffee table littered with paper.

"Mr. James, my name is Robert Warder. I'm the business manager for the Logans. And these gentlemen," he gestured to the other three men seated around him, "are my associates. Martha Logan asked us to draw up the paperwork for the proposed sale to you of thirty-eight oil and watercolor paintings by Axel Logan, executed between 1956 and 1977. The paintings have been widely exhibited over this period and are currently the property of the artist."

Taylor was sitting in a rocking chair facing the accountants with Mitchell and Laura sitting on a small couch by the fireplace. Tate McNeil was standing by another large window near two identical wing-backed chairs, in which Axel and Martha Logan were seated. Robert Warder talked on for several moments about the paintings to be sold before Taylor cut him short.

"Cut the crap Warder. I've been told everything about the paintings and about where they've been exhibited and what Axel was thinking when he painted them." He looked over to Logan as if to ask his pardon. Laura stiffened in her seat and Mitchell began to feel his back sweat. "The thing I've not been told is how much these things are going to cost me today. I was told a figure by Mr. McNeil a week ago in New York, but what I want to know is what they're going to cost me now."

Warder sat back in his chair and looked, as did the other three men, at Taylor. They weren't accustomed to being talked to in this manner. It took Warder several moments to respond.

"Well, the figure we have arrived at, based upon the current gallery values, is seven and a half million dollars. Allowing for a museum discount, it comes to seven even."

"That's a million more than I was told by Mr. McNeil. He ought to know what the prices are."

Warder sat up in his chair. "Mr. McNeil is a representative of Axel Logan's, but he is not directly in the daily marketplace. These figures arrived only last night..."

"Please, I don't want to hear about what came about last night. I was at a meeting with Axel's representatives in New York with Tate and Mitchell. Can I not assume the figure Tate came up with was accurate as of just a few days ago?"

"Mr. James," Martha interjected, "we have not meant to upset you, but are just trying to get everything in order. If Tate mentioned a figure to you, it was without my knowledge or that of my husband's. I think we can negotiate something fair to all of us."

Taylor looked at her as she spoke, his back of his neck turning a deep red. "I think we can too, Martha. I really do. As a matter of fact, before we negotiate any further, I want you to see some of my artwork."

He turned to the leather case on the table and quickly worked the combination on each latch. In an instant they clicked, and the hasps sprung open. He turned again to her, standing to one side of the small table. He lifted the lid of the case. Lined neatly inside were rows of $5,000 dollar bills in small stacks with paper strips wrapped around their middles.

"Ever seen six million dollars in cash before? Well this is what it looks like," he said, mimicking the tone of her lawyer. "And it can be yours, if the price is right!"

The money acted as a magnet, bringing people up from their chairs around the room. Mitchell stumbled slightly as he rose to look at the contents of the leather case. He couldn't believe James had the money with him all along.

"I stopped in Switzerland on my way to New York and picked this up, just in case I liked the paintings. There are many advantages, Axel, in dealing with cash, which I'm sure Mr. Warder here will be happy to explain to you. If it were me, I'd take the money and spare us from dancing around."

"You have taken us by surprise," Martha Logan said as she turned and looked at her husband. "I'm pleased you like the paintings well enough to offer us a settlement in this fashion, but I think Axel and I ought to talk it over. May we call you later in the day, at the lodge perhaps?"

"Sure Martha, we aren't due to leave Woodstock until late this afternoon. I'd like to have some sort of answer by then." James bent over the leather case and shut the lid, pushing the clasps in firmly. "It really is all there, in case you were wondering. Come on Laura, Mitchell, let's give these good people some time alone."

The mood of the passengers on the small shuttle to New York that evening was highly animated. Tate McNeil had arrived at the lodge shortly after two that afternoon with the sale contracts under his arm and appeared slightly nervous about carrying six million dollars back to the Logans. Mitchell sensed the dealer's anxiety and quickly pointed out how it was to play for high stakes. The Logan lawyers had at first been taken aback by Taylor's attitude and abrupt manner, but after discussing the tax advantages of accepting cash, they decided the artist should take it.

"They said the only way you might have done better, Mr. James," Tate relayed, "was to have brought gold."

The papers were signed immediately, and Taylor turned over the leather case. Now, as the plane circled LaGuardia, he enjoyed his triumph over the lawyers and his new status as major art collector. "I want these transactions kept secret, Mitchell. I instructed McNeil this was to be the case as well and he agreed. Nothing can be said to anyone. When the announcement is made, I want it to be big."

✿ ✿ ✿

Mitchell arrived at the museum late the following day. Ted was surprised to see him when he walked past his office on his way to the board room.

"Ted, can I see you for a moment?"

There was that question again, but this time Ted was sure it had to do with the secret project and not his allegiances. He rose to follow Mitchell down the hall, sensing his relief and air of triumph.

"You can't believe what a wild couple of days I had up there with Taylor," he said as he closed the door. "He's really something. He's going to make me old way before my time."

"It went well then?" Ted could tell Mitchell was anxious to tell him the story of his adventure and that the outcome did indeed come out favorably.

"It was touch and go, but the paintings now belong to Taylor and Laura. I'll tell you about it, but first I must know when they can be installed. It's important that they go up as soon as possible."

Ted looked at the pleased expression on Mitchell's face and wondered how to answer him. He was sitting on a bomb and wanted off before he got hurt. Ted knew summer wasn't the best time for the unveiling of a major collection like this one. Fall would be better, but he knew his boss would never stand for a delay of that length.

"When will the collection arrive?"

"In three weeks."

Ted had hoped the delivery would be pushed back from the time Mitchell had told him earlier. "They must have been packed and ready, a collection with nowhere to go! They are coming commercially?"

"That hasn't been worked out yet. Taylor wants them here as soon as possible, and Tate assured me there would be no problem getting them right down. He's in charge of that detail."

"I guess he can afford to take care of that on what he made off Taylor. Did quite well, I expect—probably can take the rest of the year off."

Mitchell said nothing. It would have normally been a topic he would have been delighted to joke about, and Ted found his silence a bid odd.

"Does Taylor want them installed immediately? Are you under pressure?"

"Yes, though I can stall him a little while. The sale is to be announced in Woodstock and Meriden next Monday at two in the afternoon, eastern time. It will miss the papers but get television coverage locally and nationally. Sterling will be unhappy, but it's the way Taylor wants it played. He would like to be able to announce the date the paintings will be on view at that time. You haven't answered my question yet, Ted." He was smiling as he said it, but Ted knew his posturing time was at an end.

"We're very heavily committed with temporary exhibitions until summer Mitchell, and really a collection of this magnitude should be installed with more than usual care and thought. Taylor's going to want them up for a while—probably forever—and we can't just give up one of the temporary exhibition galleries; there are too many exhibitions that have been on the schedule for at least a year. That brings us to the summer slump. Everyone is out of town, and we don't get a lot of tourists. The best time to work the paintings into something of major proportion would be the fall, but I'm sure he won't want to wait that long."

"You're absolutely fucking correct! He's not going to give us that kind of time; he's liable to take the collection somewhere else—like Birmingham. They'd drop whatever they had to for such an opportunity!"

"No place is going to be able to drop everything to accommodate his agenda. Surely Taylor can understand..."

"Taylor isn't going to understand anything except seeing those pictures up and our collective gratitude for purchasing them."

"Perhaps if I went to him officially and tried to explain..."

"Nobody talks to him except me. I've made that clear, or at least I thought I had. You and Ellen don't seem to listen to me sometimes. Nobody talks to Taylor James." His clenched hands rested on the table before him, his eyes were bloodshot. He reached into a vest pocket for something, then put it in his mouth. "You haven't said anything to any-one have you?"

Ted had not and told him so, though he knew news like this was going to affect everyone on staff.

"Think I'm going to have a problem with the staff when they find out?" he asked. "Anyone hate Axel Logan's work?"

"When are you going to tell them?"

"Not until just before the press conference, like everybody else. It's the way Taylor wants it."

"They have a right to know, at least Ellen and Mary. This is going to change everything Ellen is working on now; it shouldn't be dropped on her out of the blue."

"Have you arranged for the retreat? Is that lined up?"

Ted had gone ahead with this, though he was personally opposed to the idea of being cooped up with Jenkins and the others for an extended period. Large meetings were generally unproductive, he'd found, and he didn't think being in the woods together was going to be any different. However, as Mitchell had instructed, he had made the arrangements. The sessions were to be held over the approaching weekend, and most everyone had gone to considerable effort to change their personal plans to attend.

"Perhaps we can begin thinking about some of this at that time. Now, start thinking about the exhibition schedule and what can be cut or postponed to make room for Axel Logan, but don't make any calls or take any action until after next Monday."

CHAPTER THIRTY-SIX

The following Saturday morning the staff arrived at a secluded cabin in the country for their series of meetings on the state of the Meriden Museum of Art. As Jenkins had described, the place was very comfortable. They lit a fire in the large open fireplace, made coffee, and put out breakfast rolls before sitting around a large wooden table for what promised to be a long day. Martha Dyer had been asked to attend and sat with Jenkins at the table's head, by the fire. She provided everyone with a color-coded folder containing materials relevant to the meeting's stated purpose. Everyone was asked to speak openly about individual problems in their departments.

It wasn't until after lunch that Mitchell spoke at length for the first time.

"I'm anxious to ask you all some questions based on what we've already heard and discussed about the museum and what we see in its future. I'm going to offer a series of possibilities and get your individual reactions. It's kind of a game! Suppose for the sake of discussion, you were me and suddenly had all the money in the world with which to build an art collection. What would you choose to do with it?"

He gave everyone a few moments to think, then started with Ellen. His question struck a nerve within Ted. The parallel between it and what already had occurred was too close and very calculated.

"I don't know," Ellen said. "What specifically I would purchase? It would be something that could easily be worked into a series of educational programs. Something with real appeal, not like some of those contemporary things old Martin here finds to install!" The cool in her voice was only meant as a tease and Ted knew it; they often bantered this way. "Based on our stated goals and purpose, I guess it would be something that fit into those criteria."

Jenkins took notes about what she said. "And, if you had all the money in the world, I suppose your collection would be something unique, something that only could be seen in Meriden and no place else. Right?"

She agreed and he wrote it down.

"Anything else?"

"No, I guess not. My concern would be for the collection's content, how easily it could be discussed, and how it would be relayed to our visitors."

Mary Griffin was next. She agreed with the things Ellen had said but had a definite bias as to what her collection would be. "I would collect weavings, textiles, and related craft forms. It would be unique and exciting with wide appeal to people living in Meriden and the South—especially with students in our school. A collection of this nature has never been brought together by a museum in this region and wouldn't take all the money in the world to gather."

Mary enjoyed games, and Mitchell, when he seemed playful. The conflicts of the recent past seemed forgotten by them now as she played along and right into his hands.

"Would they be contemporary crafts, or more of a historical overview?" he asked for the sake of the question. The outcome was already decided.

As he continued asking the rest of the staff, Ted marveled at his ability to lead his sheep right to the place he wanted them. Martha Dyer was excluded, presumably because she was an administrator, and to the surprise of Ellen and Mary, Ted was too.

"Ted's too close to these sorts of considerations," Mitchell explained. "Besides, we've all read the paper he wrote detailing the collection's growth and priorities."

Ted was embarrassed because he knew the answer to this game. Before the Logan purchase it had been only Mitchell who played games with the museum's staff, now he had drawn Ted down the rabbit hole. There had been a time when Ted would have enjoyed Mitchell's confidence to the exclusion of the others, but not anymore. It left him sickened and desiring to get away from Mitchell and the museum.

"Now, let me review what you all have said and perhaps add some of my own ideas to see what you think of them. You all said you would establish a collection that suited the existing goals of the museum based on established statements of purpose and objectives. You would want something with mass appeal to our area, our state and the Southeast, and, if possible, something that would create national interest. A collection that was unique, with thematic content so we could talk constructively about it, something that could only be seen at our museum. I agree with all those points, but want to offer some of my own. The collection should be contemporary but try to bridge gaps between generations with universal appeal. It should be something easily merchandized to the public. I know this sounds like bastardization to most of you, but we need to think about our finances. There's plenty of precedent for this—just look at the Tut exhibition and all that was sold in relation to it. The collection should also be one that could be added to in the future so additional interest can be generated over time. What do you all think of my additions?"

There was general agreement; he was doing quite a job on them. Ted excused himself from the room, but Mitchell's look made him return quickly.

"Considering all these criteria," he continued, "it seems to me there are two avenues we could follow in terms of what we might collect. Mary mentioned a collection of diverse, yet related things that would satisfy many of the points we have made and agreed on. However, it would be hard to merchandise a collection like this, and that's important. Would it have massive appeal to people in our area? Probably some appeal, but not quite as much as other things. It certainly wouldn't bring people from out of state to visit like some other collections would. Remember, we have all the money in the world to work with. Another response might be to get something like the Tut exhibition, something historically significant, yet with a certain drama that appeals to the imagination. This would be difficult to do within the stated goals of the museum and our collection's policy, though it would satisfy other requirements. These stated goals might need reviewing and changed. However, I think we might satisfy all the requirements for our imaginary collection if we decided to collect the work of a single artist, or even a group of artists."

He looked at the faces around the table to gauge a reaction. His staff was saying nothing, listening to his arguments and suggestions, still playing the game. "Ted, who would you say the single most important contemporary American artist still living today might be?"

Ted looked at him in disbelief. Mitchell hadn't spoken to him before everyone had gathered, so he didn't know how Mitchell wanted him to answer. Ted wasn't going to say Axel Logan even if it was the right answer.

"Beau Britian." Ted bit his tongue after saying it, as he realized what Mitchell was up to.

"That's a good answer. Beau is certainly up there in the top two or three. He's a friend of mine, has been generous to the museum, and is a native of the state. A retrospective collection of his works would be very impressive and would bring many people into the museum. Reproductions could be sold, generating a revenue stream, and pieces could be added in the future. That would be a good choice." He paused. "But do you think Beau's work would be accepted by people in Meriden or Alabama, even though he was born here? Would it be difficult for Ellen to train docents to talk about his work? It sometimes gets very cerebral. I don't know, these might be difficulties. There are other artists who could be collected. Ellen, any thoughts?"

"I don't keep track of these things like you and Ted do," she began, "but what about someone like Axel Logan? He's certainly important in contemporary art, has wide appeal, and since we have all the money in the world, with a collection of his paintings the museum would probably be filled."

"That's another good choice! Logan's paintings would certainly have broad, popular appeal, could be merchandized and added to, suits our existing goals as an institution, fits into our collection philosophy, would have educational content, and would be unique." He looked around him again before continuing. "I'm sure there are other artists also who would be equally good in a situation like this one."

"Do you have something to tell us, Mitchell? This line of thinking is very interesting, and I'm excited." Ellen was thinking after all, but wouldn't be told the truth even after hitting it squarely on the head.

"No, this was just an exercise. I'm trying to get us all on the same wavelength. I want our common goals to be the same, so when we leave here tomorrow afternoon, we can go back to the museum working together, without secrets from one another."

Ted couldn't bring himself to look at Mitchell. Martha Dyer was smiling to herself as a conspirator would. They talked on for several more hours before breaking for the first day. Ellen read a paper concerning the future of her department and the new programs she wanted to begin. Her concern was shifting from students to adults, and the Logan collection hypothesis, Jenkins was quick to point out, was equally suited to either market.

Mitchell's original idea was to have everyone sleep at the cabin, talking into the night and breakfasting together the following morning before resuming at noon. To no one's surprise, that idea was voted down. Mitchell was the only one staying the night and as he stoked the fire, Ted talked briefly to him about the placement of the collection that so conveniently met the staff's requirements.

"There's only one place the paintings can go for a prolonged period, and that's in the collection gallery. I hesitate to do it because of the recent installation there. I think it looks very good and works well with Ellen's programs. But it is the only area that we can control without changing anything on the schedule. What do you think?"

"It's what I've been thinking all along." He was talking in a low tone, so the few stragglers wouldn't overhear. "It could go there almost immediately, which would take a lot of pressure off me as far as Taylor is concerned. How quickly could it be converted to the drawings you gave me?"

Ted still didn't want to move without further planning for the Logan collection. He didn't know the exact price paid but knew it would have been considerable and that the paintings merited more than a causal installation.

"I don't think it should be a question of how quickly, Mitchell. There are things we should do to ensure the safety of the paintings. A complete examination should be made of each one. Some sort of publication will need to be printed, and that will take a bit of time."

"Not some kind of publication, Ted. *The* publication! It will have to be something special. That's why I wanted George here, to get a feel for what our future might be. He's a good designer and will be an asset to the museum."

Whitmire had been hired only a month before but already was in Mitchell's pocket in the tradition of Stephen Parker and Peter Rutledge. The difference was that he was much more outspoken, a characteristic Ted wasn't overly fond of.

"But that will take more time than we have," Mitchell continued. "Taylor is hot to have things underway. Something simple can be developed to serve the immediate need. How soon can the gallery changes be made?"

"How soon do you need it?"

"By the anniversary of the building's opening in the spring. I need it by then."

Ted couldn't believe Mitchell was giving him a month when he was thinking six. "I suppose it can be done, but that really doesn't give much time to do it right. Since we've been in the building, we've had to rush doing everything. It's been five years; I'd hoped to be more civilized with this."

"Can't be helped Ted, believe me. You and your people will just need to get in there and do it. We can hire outside labor if you want, but the job must be done."

Ted declined outside labor; with objects of this value, it wouldn't pay to have people around who weren't careful.

"Besides, said Jenkins, this will only be a temporary thing until we can free up the exhibition schedule and move the paintings into those galleries. You know, with all the things Taylor has been collecting, I wouldn't be surprised if he opts to build an addition onto the museum—the James Wing. He's very interested in keeping his collection together after he's gone. I've been talking to him about it."

Nothing surprised Ted about Mitchell anymore. He smiled at the suggestion of the James Wing, knowing it was probably already in the works. "What does Morgan think about all this? Wouldn't she want the paintings if her parents were no longer living?"

Mitchell leaned in close to whisper, leading Ted deeper into the conspiracy. "She doesn't know about any of it yet. Taylor isn't going to tell her until the morning of the press conference. He wants to surprise her!"

"I see. I'm sure it will!"

"I'm sure she'll take it well. Her father is a hard man to contradict, and his motives for purchasing the paintings are good. She's supported his contributions before. Honestly, I'm surprised he hasn't put restrictions on how the paintings should be installed. I think Laura is keeping a tight rein on him. We're lucky to have her on our side."

Ted wasn't surprised by this. Taylor had no idea what to do with the paintings after the sale and would certainly want the museum to deal with them. The fire was casting long shadows in the room as darkness fell around the two men. Mitchell looked satisfied that the day's discussions were going well for him.

"Sure you won't stay the night, Ted? I brought a couple of steaks and there's plenty of gin."

"No thanks. I have some things to do in town tonight. I'll see you in the morning. You going to be okay here by yourself?"

Mitchell smiled and looked out across the room. "Sure, I'll be just fine, besides I won't be alone. Lou Sterling is coming out. I told him about the collection, and we're going to strategize over the commission's reaction. His wife's away, so he's got a free evening. See you in the morning."

Ted left the cabin just before it became too dark to find his way back to his car. He had been surprised at first to learn Sterling had been told before Rudolph Bates, but considering their long friendship he supposed it was natural enough. He still did not trust Sterling completely.

✵ ✵ ✵

A telephone rang somewhere in the cabin, interrupting Jenkins and Sterling as they joked in the large central room. Jenkins had made a large pitcher of martinis and they had already enjoyed half of it.

"I didn't know this place had a phone," he said to Sterling, who also looked surprised by the sound. "I guess we should answer it if we can find it." The two went from room to room, getting closer to the steady ringing. Finally, in the third of the six bedrooms, they found it still ringing, and Jenkins picked it up.

"Meriden Bar and Grill," he said in a comical voice he used to imitate a Black man. "What's u want, boss?"

There was a brief silence on the other end. "Hello, I'm calling for Mitchell Jenkins. Is he there?"

"Who? Look boss, I got a room full of people here. Houz I 'posed to know if a Mickey Jenkins here?"

"Is this a restaurant? I was told it was a private residence and that Mr. Jenkins would be there this evening."

"Hey, listen. Weez got a private party here tonight, see. And them's people in the big room all naked and foolin' around, you dig? If Massa Jenkins in there he sure not goin' ta want me interferin.' Besides Tate," his voice changed back to normal, "if I was here, I wouldn't want anyone to know. How you doing?" He laughed. "Been thinking about you a lot these days."

"Thought I had the wrong number, Mitchell! Good joke. You're a hard man to track down. Why not leave numbers where you can be reached with your personal answering service? That poor girl went through hell trying to find you. I told her I was an attorney representing the estate of a great uncle of yours and had to get in touch with you this evening to discuss your inheritance. I told her after nine o'clock the money would revert back to the estate. That really got her cooking!" The two men laughed, and McNeil continued. "Listen, I hope I haven't caught you at a bad time. I called to let you know a courier from my office should be in Meriden tomorrow night with a package for you. Something small but valuable. I'd have gone ahead and sent it to your Swiss account, but remembered you wanted to look at the cash, so I'm sending it this way! The fellow will bring it wherever you say. He has your description and will be armed, so don't try any of your stupid-ass imitations on him; he's not easily entertained. Where do you want the delivery?"

Jenkins held the receiver close to his ear. Sterling was in the room and was not to hear any of this. "How about the museum? I could meet him there. What time do you think he should arrive?"

"Someone there, huh?"

"Right."

"He can be there at seven tomorrow evening. Is that going to be okay?"

"Sure, absolutely. Has James seen those documents, perhaps at your place?" Jenkins trying to make the call sound like anything other than what it was.

"No, you won't know this fellow, but he'll know you. Just be there at seven and he'll give you the package. It'll be in a leather case. How you get it to Switzerland, or wherever, is up to you. But if you need help, let me know."

"Sure thing, Tate, I appreciate your efforts. Be looking for it tomorrow. Goodnight."

Sterling had wandered over to the window that overlooked a creek.

"That was Tate McNeil," Jenkins said. "Some documents are arriving tomorrow that I need to accept in person. Things are really getting exciting now!"

The two walked back into the cabin's main room and continued drinking.

The following day's staff discussions brought more of the same kind of manipulation; Jenkins would not let the Logan idea fade away. He delighted in piquing everyone's interests, then denying everything. Lou Sterling stayed for the afternoon, "observing us at our best," according to Jenkins. George Whitmire was the star of the second session, talking in detail about museum publications, analyzing their faults and making suggestions for improvements. When he finished, Jenkins played a game similar to the one of the day before. This time the topic was exhibition publications, using the hypothetical Logan collection as a subject. The discussion went on to all manner of promotional gimmickry, and the longer Whitmire talked, the more distasteful he became. Ted's headache returned the moment he began and got progressively worse throughout the afternoon. By five that evening he was one of the first ones out. Mitchell had succeeded in convincing everyone he should actively begin to pursue a collection for the museum like the one discussed.

"It is now time," he said, "that we shift our priorities! We have the building, thanks to Taylor and Laura James, now it's time to put something worthwhile inside it."

The current collections seemed no longer significant, though they had built countless educational programs around them. Ellen got caught up in the excitement of new possibilities and seemed ready to scrap what she'd already put together to support a bold new collection of art. Tomorrow would be that time, with everything else taking a back seat. Ted wondered if he could live with that change. Ted drove back to Meriden slowly. There was going to be a pleasant winter sunset, but he had too much on his mind to enjoy it. Mitchell had met with him earlier in the day about the press announcement at the museum at two on Monday, a day they were generally closed to make changes in galleries and other public spaces. Jenkins and Sterling had called media outlets in Birmingham and as far away as Atlanta. Surprisingly, most agreed to send reporters even on short notice. The event would occur in the museum's theater, with the staff assembled at eleven to receive the news, followed by remarks from Taylor James. Commission members would also learn the news at that time. Ted was to stand guard at the theater's entry against journalists who might try to weasel their way in.

Jenkins didn't think staff members who had attended the meetings of the past weekend would feel they had been used. His view was characteristically hard-boiled. "Not if they're smart they won't! This is a momentous occasion. They can be made to understand the pressure I've been under, and besides, they've already agreed to why decisions were made."

On his return from the lodge, Ted decided to stop at the museum to finish some work he started Friday afternoon in the storage area. Needing some fresh air, he parked on a residential street and walked over. The mercury lights in the parking lot were just coming on, blinking against a purple sky. He let himself in and locked the heavy door behind him. Everything appeared tidy, and the guards had locked every door, including those that led through a labyrinth of hallways to his destination. It was just six o'clock, and by seven thirty Ted had finished moving objects for a special exhibition into a holding area where his assistant could get them the following morning to begin their installation. He retraced his path back the way he'd come, locking doors, walking down dark corridors. The lobby was still quiet, and there were no cars in the lot outside. He went to the office complex door and found it unlocked. *Did I forget to relock it when I came from my office earlier in the evening? Perhaps.* He was glad he'd decided to go back, mainly so Joe Mullens wouldn't find the door unlocked in the morning. He would have told Ted about it for days.

Ted walked up the office hallway and thought he heard muffled voices coming from the other end. As he entered his office, he heard them again. All the doors were shut, the corridor lights off. Surely if one of the staff were here something would be on, but except for the unlocked door, nothing was amiss. Ted slipped off his shoes and walked carefully back down the hallway. The carpeting the architects had chosen was thick, making his approach completely silent. There was a shuffling noise, then a voice he didn't recognize came from Mitchell's office. Ted wished Mitchell were still in his prior space so he could see in through the glass, but now there was no way he could determine who was inside without entering. The unfamiliar voice was deep, talking in a monotone, very factual and without expression. Ted was at a loss about what to do. There might not be time to call the police. *What if the intruder is a reporter trying to discover what the morning's events are about?* There was a sound of paper being shuffled as his hand went for the doorknob. He twisted it slowly; it wasn't locked. He pushed the door open in one quick motion.

Mitchell sat at his desk, his faced washed in the light from the floor lamp at his side. A very large, blond man was seated across from him. His right hand moved to his jacket and came back holding a very large silver colored gun, which he pointed at Ted's head.

"Don't shoot please, I work here," Ted said stupidly.

The man looked quickly at Mitchell, whose face had turned white at the sight of his curator. He nodded to the large man, who eased the gun's hammer back down with his thumb. On the desk to Mitchell's left was an open case containing more cash than Ted had ever seen.

"Please forgive me," Ted blurted. "I was working in storage, you must have come in while I was there. I was just leaving when I heard you talking and came to investigate. I thought someone had gotten in and was snooping around your office, Mitchell. I had no idea it was you as your car's not outside and no lights were on."

Mitchell quickly shut the lid on the case with his left hand and asked the man to put his gun away.

"You took us by surprise, Ted. We were just transacting a bit of business here concerning Mr. James' purchase." He motioned to the case. "This is the last payment that goes to Logan." He opened the case again. "Ever see so much money?" He couldn't help showing it off, and Ted was in no condition to think any differently. "This gentleman works for Tate and is going to take the money to him—that's why he's armed. You're lucky to still be standing there."

Ted nodded to the man and hoped he hadn't wet himself; he was too nervous to look. "Again, please forgive me for busting in. I'll call the police next time."

"It's okay, don't worry. You did what you thought was right under the circumstances. I appreciate that, but you might have been hurt if someone else had been in here. Listen, go home and have a drink. We've got a big day tomorrow and I'm counting on you. I'll lock up everything when we leave."

Ted was glad for the easy dismissal and left the two men, shutting the door as he left. Before he could think about anything again, he was out of the building, heading for his car. He looked back only once and thought he could see Mitchell watching him from the window. He turned away, not wanting verification.

Ted was still rattled when he got to his apartment and downed a scotch. It took another before the shock of the gun wore off and he began to think about what Jenkins had told him. It was definitely a case full of money on his desk, that much was certain. He had relayed the Woodstock story to Ted, and the office transaction sort of fit if Taylor had needed to make an additional cash payment. But he remembered Mitchell saying Taylor had paid for the collection in full. It was the reason he'd paid in cash—to make a statement. Ted didn't know how much money was in the case this evening; it was dark, and a shadow fell over that part of the desk, but it was considerable. He thought about it the remainder of the night but couldn't come up with any other scenario than the one Mitchell had given, leaving Ted to wonder what he'd say to him about it the following day.

CHAPTER THIRTY-SEVEN

Mitchell was at the museum by the time Ted arrived at eight thirty the next morning, as was Martha. She had taped memos to all office doors announcing an important staff meeting in the theater at eleven. Ted buzzed Mitchell's office and asked if there were anything he wanted him to do prior to the meeting. Mitchell was polite and friendly but said there was not.

"Taylor and Laura will be arriving about ten thirty. You might watch out for them if I'm busy in here. Tate McNeil got in last night; he wanted to be here for the announcement instead of Woodstock."

"What about the man I met last night? I thought he was going to Tate's."

"There was a change of plans; he went directly to Woodstock with the package. You haven't told anyone about that, have you?"

"No, of course not. After what happened, I wanted to forget all about it."

"Good. It's important no one knows. Taylor wants it that way. He's afraid of people thinking he spent too much money. You know how he can be."

Ted didn't really know since neither of the Jameses were overly friendly toward him.

"See you around ten thirty!"

Ted sat back in his chair remembering the case full of money and the barrel of the gun pointed at his head. Life had certainly gotten dramatic since Mitchell's return from Woodstock. He was still deep in thought when his phone rang again.

"OK, Mr. Answer Man, what's going on at eleven? What's so important?" It was Ellen.

"Your guess is as good as mine! I had one of those memos on my door too." Ted hated the deception, but it was only for a little while longer.

"Don't give me that, you lying Yankee. I know there's something funny going on here and I know that you probably know about it. Mitchell is quite capable of a lot of things, but keeping a secret isn't one of them. He would turn to you if he thought he needed to. Now level with me!"

"Listen Ellen, you know Mitchell and I don't see eye to eye on things like we used to. He generally turns to you when he's in a pinch about something. Like when that ambassador came into the building with that woman's committee from Birmingham. We were all in the room together, but it was you he wanted with him to show the man around."

"That's exactly my point, he'll use any of us when he has to, even if we've just been fighting with him."

There was little point in keeping it from her any longer. She'd know everything in a couple hours. "Meet me in the big gallery in five minutes. Try to be nonchalant, as if our being there is accidental." Ted hung up, not giving her the opportunity to argue. If she wanted to know, it would be on his terms. He talked briefly to his secretary who came in as he hung up the phone and made an excuse for going to the gallery.

"Okay, so what's so damn sinister that we can't talk on the phone?" Ellen joked when Ted arrived.

"Walk over this way some," Ted said, "there's a TV camera above where you're standing. I don't want to be in its view if Joe decides to turn them on early and survey the building. Mitchell might walk past one of the monitors and see us."

She moved to where she wouldn't be seen, her expression changing as she realized Ted was serious.

"The past weekend wasn't just a forum for Mitchell to talk philosophy with us all, he was up to something very specific and wanted to get you and everyone else in tune with what's about to happen. He's been using me for the past couple of weeks, pitting me emotionally against you and everyone else because of the news he's going to announce at eleven."

"Ted, you're not making sense! Slow down, tell me what's going on."

"He's about to announce that James just purchased your dream art collection. The very one he led you to talk about on Saturday. Oh, there was a chance you or Mary wouldn't say what he wanted you to, but he took the gamble and won. He led you right to it."

"Logan? He bought Logan paintings?"

"Forty. Forty important Logan paintings. They will turn this place all around. All those criteria for collections he talked about were to get everyone at the cabin to come around to what's about to happen. At eleven, he's going to tell the staff and the commission; at two, there will be a press briefing held simultaneously with one in Woodstock to announce the sale. Taylor James will be famous, as will the museum, mobbed with tourists who will want to see some of Logan's most important paintings—at a cost of millions!"

The look on her face changed again, from concern to disbelief. "All those things he said had already happened? The game had already been played, he just wanted the players to agree to the rules? I can't believe he would do that to us, not after those meetings with Sterling. What was all that about?"

"He was acting, just like always. Mitchell's got it made now. Like August Bishop, nothing can not touch him here, no amount of internal controversy will convince the commission to question his conduct or discipline him. Don't you see? He can treat us any way he wants. If we complain, we'll be out; just that simple."

"How long have you known?"

"You remember when he took the vacation to Vermont? It wasn't a vacation at all. He was meeting the Jameses and Logan's dealer, who happens to be in town today. They were negotiating the sale. Then they went to Woodstock to clinch the deal. James paid cash." Ted hadn't meant to say that but could not help himself.

"How much was the purchase?"

"Several million dollars, I expect. Mitchell hasn't told me an exact figure, but there was a final payment made last night. It was in cash too, I saw it."

Ted told Ellen about the meeting between Mitchell and the courier and how he had walked in on them thinking they were burglars. It was just then that it first hit Ted that Mitchell might not have told him the truth about the money and the circumstances of his presence at the museum the night before.

"You can't say anything to Mary or anyone else about this. And you must act surprised, excited, enthused, or however you want to express delight when he tells us all about this at eleven. I don't know how much longer I'll be here, but if he thought I talked to you, I'm sure I'd be out immediately."

Ted didn't attend the meeting at eleven. He couldn't pretend to show excitement about the news, and he didn't want anyone to know he was aware of the plan all along — or almost all along. Taylor and Laura showed up on time and were directed into Mitchell's office by Martha. The four of them sat for some time before emerging to meet Tate McNeil in the lobby. Ellen told Ted later that Taylor did most of the talking at the meeting with staff and the commission. He was very pleased with himself, particularly in warming them up for the announcement itself. There were rounds of applause as Taylor took his bows, then a luncheon for the commission, where the story of the Woodstock trip was told.

Reporters began to arrive at one thirty, and Ted took his station in front of the theater door. Jenkins, McNeil, and the Jameses were still inside talking with Rudolph Bates and other commissioners about the long-range effects of the collection on the museum. The reporters wanted to know what was going on and peppered Ted with questions, hoping for a scoop.

"Is it true," asked one from Meriden, "that Mitchell Jenkins is going to announce his resignation?"

Ted looked at the reporter for a moment, then laughed nervously. "No, that is not true, to the best of my knowledge."

The crowd grew as the time got closer. At exactly two o'clock the doors opened and the announcement was made. The following morning the story made the national news. Tom Brokaw broke the story on the *Today Show*, the *New York Times* called it the sale of the century. "Meriden where?" was being asked frequently, and in the jubilation that followed, Ted decided to request a three-month leave of absence after the Logan installation was complete. He thought if he got away for a while, perhaps things would change. He was kidding himself and he knew it.

In the confusion of the next few weeks, all the personnel discussions that had taken place prior to the Logan announcement were largely abandoned. Louis Sterling was to have met with the staff again to see if tensions had eased, but that did not occur. Mitchell was in the limelight as the young museum director responsible for this incredible coup for the South and a virtually unknown museum. The museum wasn't entirely unknown of course; there had been recognition of programs they had pioneered, like the Britian film, but Logan indeed put them on the map.

While most of the staff were trying to adjust to the quickened pace of schedules and deadlines that had to be changed or scrapped, Martha Dyer took the opportunity to return to her familiar position of staff antagonist by making a barrage of small, but potent negative salvos at Joe Mullens. She felt he was too old to oversee building maintenance and security when a collection like the Logan one was involved.

"He simply cannot handle the duties anymore and should be retired. It will be ridiculous to have that old man up there with six million dollar's worth of paintings on the walls."

That was the first time Ted heard an exact dollar figure mentioned. In her zeal, she had probably said something Mitchell wanted kept secret. Joe was a proud old man. He had served Mitchell for ten years without missing more than five days over that time for any reason. He was the first person to arrive in the mornings and the last to leave. He had his problems with change and the museum's growth but was consistent and trustworthy. Unfortunately, he was now the target of Martha Dyer. It wouldn't take him long to get angered by her tactics. He didn't take criticism well from any quarter and would not admit his own limitations.

"Joe resigned this morning." Jenkins had called Ted into his office between phone interviews with *The Washington Post* and the *Atlanta Constitution*. In the years Ted had been there, Joe had resigned at least three other times, usually when mad or hurt by something he didn't like. He had always come back after a day or two at Mitchell's request, finding his kind of service was hard to replace.

"I'm not going to wait for him to get over his snit this time. I've instructed Robert Evans to send him a severance check immediately with a letter he can sign and return confirming his verbal comments to me this morning. I want you to find a replacement for him immediately. With the Logans coming, we can't be too careful. His leaving is very timely actually, I was thinking about replacing him anyway."

Joe and Ted had had their ups and downs, but after ten years of service a proud old man should be treated better, and he told Mitchell so.

"Ted, I appreciate your feelings, but the man quit. You know as well as I do he's done it before, and I've always crawled back to him."

"I don't think you crawled. For all his faults, we know Joe is a good employee..."

"Yes, but it's about time he retired. With this collection, security is going to be more important than ever. Joe wouldn't fit into what needs to be done. This is the best way really; he feels self-righteously justified in his actions. Robert can pay him and it will be over. This is very clean."

"I think your next appointment is waiting in the lobby, should I show him in as I leave?"

"Thanks Ted, that will save Martha from doing it. I know you feel bad about Joe, but things will work out. Look at this place already — you'd hardly know it was the same!"

A reporter from Montgomery was only too glad to be shown into Mitchell's office. Ted couldn't get his mind off Joe Mullens—not for Joe's sake but for his own. Martha was in her office when Ted passed.

"Joe's gone," he said. "I suppose you know." He wasn't in the mood to play games with her. "Mitchell's going to send him a check and a resignation letter."

"Mitchell did what was necessary. Joe quit on his own."

"You had nothing to do with it? He just picked today to leave. You're getting much better at all this, Martha."

Ted continued up the hallway toward Ellen's office. He was convinced things were again progressing in the old way. The announcement of the Logan paintings had had its effect on Mitchell, and by association, on Martha. Ellen was at her desk, the door of her office partially closed.

"You know that Joe resigned?"

"I was there when it happened," she said. "I saw the whole thing."

Ted shut and locked her office door. "What happened? All I know is Mitchell isn't going to get him back and Martha is gloating."

"I don't know what to think about any of it. Everything happened so fast. You know Martha has been giving him a hard time for the last week about all manner of small things that he just does. He's always done his job in the same way but now they weren't correct, and she took it upon herself to straighten him out. This morning she came in early. Joe was at the security desk reading the paper and talking to me. She came to the door and told him he shouldn't be reading the paper, he should be making rounds of the building. Joe just sat there not knowing what to say. She was in an ugly mood and told him about the importance of the Logan paintings and that he was going to have to change his manner as soon as they arrived. There was real anger in her voice, Ted. I was shocked. Then she grabbed the paper out of his hands and said she was going to speak to Mitchell as soon as he came in. I could see the look of hurt and anger in Joe's face as she stormed away. She never did speak to me. Next thing I knew Joe was walking out behind her. Martha didn't know Mitchell was already in his office because Joe had taken his car to be serviced earlier. Joe walked into Mitchell's office, laid his keys on his desk and said he was leaving. He said he'd taken all the guff from Martha he was going to and left. He got his hat and coat and walked out of the building. Martha heard Mitchell's door slam as Joe left and a moment or two later went into his office until just before his first interview of the day. Now you tell me he's sending Joe a resignation letter. I guess Martha got her way."

"Remind you of anyone? Peter Rutledge perhaps? How can Mitchell condone her actions, especially after our meetings with your buddy Sterling? You know, he and Sterling were together that night at the cabin between sessions. There's no telling what they discussed or what Jenkins convinced him of."

Ted stopped short, thinking about what he had just said about Mitchell and Sterling. The thought of their association in the sexual context his wording had implied had never entered his mind. "I'd be willing to bet Mitchell persuaded Sterling to give him full power to deal with things here, just like before. You know, something like martial law! It's business as usual."

"We need to talk to someone on the commission about this. Martha was clearly overstepping herself. We have her dead to rights!"

"Who do you suggest? Lou Sterling? Laura James? There's no way we can get at Martha, Mitchell's made that abundantly clear. He's invincible now, and so is she. We either take it or leave."

Ellen didn't like talk like this. "No, I think we should see Rudolph Bates. He would listen and could stand up to Mitchell if he had to."

"He doesn't know who we even are, Ellen. He's probably a very good man, but would he believe the things we'd say about Mitchell? He's been on the commission since its inception and been its chairman for the last two years. He's heard nothing but good things. Besides, Mitchell would get to him first."

"We won't tell Mitchell until immediately before the meeting with Bates."

"Mitchell will have our asses! We'll be lined up right behind old Joe, headed out the door."

"Will you talk to Bates, Ted?" She was pushing him again out on a limb.

"I think we all should talk with him—you, me, and Mary. We should go separately and each of us should give our sides of the museum's problems. I think Sterling should be out of this completely, which is going to be difficult because of his position, but he tells Mitchell everything, even when he's told things in confidence."

Ellen reluctantly agreed, Sterling could not be trusted.

"You call Bates, Ellen. Get the meetings set after getting Mary on board."

"You'll stay then?"

Ted was tired of secrets, and Ellen was a friend. He wanted her to know now that he was sure what his plans were. "No. Regardless of the outcome of the meetings with Bates, I'm leaving. I've asked Mitchell for a three-month leave after the Logan paintings are installed. You should get out too—you and Mary both."

Mary Griffin actually made the arrangements with Bates. She was the one Jenkins would least suspect. He was surprisingly receptive to meeting with them, as if he knew about the actual tensions that had arisen, not the watered-down versions Sterling gave at commission meetings. As planned, Jenkins was told of the meetings after they were set with Bates, who invited him to meet about the internal problems. Mitchell asked if Martha Dyer could meet with Bates as well.

The meetings were to take place at Bates' suite of offices at Hall-Crowell and would be conducted on a one-a-day basis for a week. Ellen was to go first. The interviews also included Robert Evans and George Whitmire, two names Jenkins suggested at the last minute. He had declared war and was going into it with as much support as possible. Evans wouldn't take sides; he would make allowances for Jenkins he figured any chief executive should have in difficult circumstances. George Whitmire was another story. He had replaced Ted as Mitchell's resident "yes man." On staff only a short time, he presumed to have an opinion on everything, generally in line with Mitchell's.

Ellen's session was scheduled for two, and as the hours passed and she didn't return to the museum, Mary and Ted grew more anxious for her impression and Bates' reactions. Mitchell was again avoiding the three of them, and when he had no choice, he was very cold. He was never impolite, but the emotional exuberance he'd displayed leading up to the Logan announcement was gone. During Ellen's meeting with Bates, he stayed out of the building, his whereabouts known only to Martha. The tension was as intense as it had been during that early meeting when Mary had read their statement about conditions there. She was to present Bates with that statement during her meeting the following day. Ted would be the last of the three to meet with Bates.

When Ellen returned to the museum at six that evening, Ted was the only one in the building. She saw his office lights on and came in, looking very tired but pleased. "Rudolph listened to every word I had to say, and I said everything, regardless of who I hurt. He is a real gentleman. He treated me with respect and was saddened to know many of us were unhappy with things here..."

"But what did he say about the things you told him?" Ted was anxious to get to the heart of her meeting.

"Nothing. He took notes but made no comments. I think he intends to do that with all of us, make notes and get a general sense of how we feel things are. Then, I suspect he'll draw his conclusions and perhaps recommendations. He's an honest man, Ted. I think we can trust him."

"You were over there for four hours; he must be a patient listener."

"He is, very calm and intent. I discussed everything with him from the time Martha joined the staff. Every person she had fired, every note and file she keeps on all of us at Mitchell's request, and the dismissal of Joe. He was very interested in that." She lit a cigarette, blowing the smoke high into the air. "What went on here this afternoon?"

"Nothing much. Mitchell left before noon and didn't come back. He talked briefly to me about the meeting schedule with Bates. He says he thinks it's a good thing, will finally clear the air. I think he's raging inside and scared. He said when all this was over, he was going to take a long vacation, maybe Europe. He also said he was going to buy an expensive car over there and have it shipped back. Sounds like he's blowing smoke to me. He hasn't taken a vacation since he's been here."

"Maybe, but you know, I can't help but think he'll do it."

Ted changed the subject. "I can't get that case full of money out of my mind. If he was telling the truth about a final payment to Logan, why wasn't his car in the parking lot? Why were things so secretive in the office?"

"Your car wasn't in the lot either. Maybe he decided he needed the walk as you did."

"Carrying a suitcase full of money that Taylor had given him? That other guy had a gun for protection. You think Mitchell would just be walking around with that much cash?"

"Well, what else? Mitchell isn't always completely logical, but there must be an explanation."

She had finished her smoke and the wine Ted had given her when she'd come in. He filled her glass again. He had come up with a second theory about that night, the money, and the mystery man with the gun – and he wanted her properly braced before telling it.

"There's always an explanation, Ellen, and things aren't always as they seem. Suppose," Ted watched her closely, "the fellow with the gun was indeed a courier for Tate McNeil. That much of the story could be correct. But what if the money wasn't going to Logan in Woodstock, but was coming to Meriden—to Mitchell?"

"I don't understand. Why would it be coming to Mitchell? Did Taylor pay too much for the paintings?"

"Listen to me for a moment, and don't think. Tate McNeil's usual commission on the sale of a Logan painting is ten percent. He sells maybe ten paintings a year and makes a good living. But if he sold this collection, he could quit for a year or work at his usual pace and be way ahead of the game. He would want to sell these paintings for the commission he'd receive. What if he offered Mitchell some money for bringing Taylor along? What if that money on Mitchell's desk was a payoff from McNeil, his cut for helping persuade Taylor and Laura to make that purchase?"

The full force of what Ted just said hit Ellen like a slap. "No, Mitchell wouldn't do that...would he? It sounds illegal."

"It's not illegal because the paintings don't belong to the museum, yet. It's unethical as hell by museum standards, but he can't be hurt by that unless the commission gets wind of it, and then only if it's true. I may be way off-base, but if he goes out and starts buying a lot of things, we'll know something's up. Plus, it was cash! It's easy not to report cash to the IRS, and that is illegal."

They talked for another hour about Ted's theory, trying to come up with some way they could be certain about the money. Ellen wasn't totally convinced, but distrusted Mitchell enough to consider it a possibility.

"McNeil was here the next day, though. Why not bring the money with him then?"

"That would be the last thing he would do, or Mitchell would want. It would be much too public. I think this is something to consider. Keep my theory to yourself please, okay?"

The following afternoon Mary Griffin went to see Bates. She didn't return to the museum afterward, so it was the following day before Ted and Ellen were able to hear her say many of the same things Ellen had about her time with him. Ted's session was to be that afternoon, but at nine thirty he received a call from Bates asking if he could come for lunch. Ted agreed and spent six hours with him, the longest session of all.

Rudolph Bates was a large, imposing man. His graying hair was worn thick in the back which, along with the charcoal suit he was wearing, made him look a bit like a fiery Southern preacher. Bates welcomed Ted warmly into his suite of large, airy offices. A glass-topped table was set formally for lunch, and as Ted sat down on a leather couch, an employee brought in a cart holding metal dome-covered plates. They were served, then left alone as Bates began the discussion.

"Ted, I've had conversations with two of your colleagues over the last couple days that concern me very much. These meetings, as you know, are allowing me to gather information concerning issues that may not be reflected in Mitchell's reports to the commission. The other commissioners and I are aware that things were not 100% at the time of Peter Rutledge's leaving. That was something Mitchell worked hard to avoid. But we thought, and were led to believe, things had evened out since then. It appears now we were mistaken in that assumption. Lou Sterling brought us up to date on some of this, but what he told us doesn't completely jive with what Ellen and Mary have said, and I'm hoping you will be able to help me sort through some of this and get an accurate picture. That's why I asked you here earlier than the others, because I think it will take some time."

There was a tablet by his place at the table just as Ellen had described, with many pages turned over its top; he was indeed taking notes. Ted felt confident for the first time.

"What I'd like you to do, is to give me an overview of the museum and Mitchell in particular. You came to Meriden just before the move to the new building, so you don't have a deep history to dwell on or affect your view of things as they've developed. If you don't mind, I will make notes to help me sort things out."

Ted tried to remember everything about his coming to Meriden and how Jenkins acted toward him and others. For the next five hours he talked about the history of the museum between the years 1973 and 1978, conversations about people, places, and events he and Mitchell had shared. It was a painfully honest exercise, during which he began to draw his own conclusions about Jenkins' character in the position of the museum's director. Bates listened, saying little about the content of his memories or if they related to anything that had been said before.

"Is it difficult," Bates asked finally, "for Mitchell to relinquish authority to anyone on the staff beside Martha Dyer, who you've said seems to have some sort of hold over him?"

"I know that sounds unbelievable," Ted said, "but I believe it to be true. For the most part, their professional relationship is private, but I can tell she buoys him, giving him extra confidence. She tends to cut him off from the rest of us, acting as a filter that determines who will get to see him, and only if she's interviewed them first. He's the 'star' of the team, especially now."

"Are you referring to the Logan collection and the publicity it's generated for the museum and for him?" Ted confirmed he was. "You've got to admit it took a lot of work on his part to pull it off. It will put the Meriden Museum squarely in the public's eye. Most directors would receive support from their boards and probably provide him a raise in pay."

Ted leaned up from the couch he'd returned to after lunch. Bates' mention of a raise in Mitchell's salary intrigued him. He wondered how much Bates knew about the Logan purchase. He wondered too if the commissioner knew about the alleged "final payoff" to Logan. The thought that this was all an elaborate trap set by Mitchell Jenkins caught hold of Ted, and the innocent-sounding remark Bates had made now took on an ominous tone.

"I suppose you're correct about that," Ted ventured. "I'm sure there aren't many members of either the board or the commission who are in much of a hurry to find fault with Mitchell. As for the raise, what Mitchell accomplished with the Jameses and the Logan collection is just part of what he is paid to do. It seems that he's already received that money and should not expect any more."

Ted could tell he had taken Bates by surprise. He looked at him intently, his heavy eyebrows almost forming a "V" on his forehead.

"I agree with you, Ted, it is part of his job."

Bates fell silent. Ted decided he'd been too suspicious of him. Bates was just trying to draw him out with his comments, to see what he would say.

"Is there anything else you want to tell me Ted? It's getting late, but I want to make sure everyone I talk with has an opportunity to speak freely. Nothing you or anybody else has said to me will leave this room, and nothing will get back to Mitchell."

Ted remembered the episode at the museum when he'd almost been shot and had seen the suitcase full of money. Mitchell had explained it all away, just as naturally as could be. Maybe it was the truth, but as Ellen had reminded Ted, McNeil was there the very next day—so why the courier? He concluded by saying he believed Mitchell needed to be placed on a forced vacation and that he might even need psychiatric help. Strong words, but Ted meant them. Bates was tired. He sat in silence after Ted's final comments, rubbing his forehead and then his eyes.

"I want to thank you for your honest, direct answers and narrative. I was correct when I thought your meeting might last longer than the others." He looked at the clock on his desk. "I don't know what will come of all this after I talk to everyone on my list, including Mitchell. I want you and the others to know I will take all of what you've told me into account and will present the information to the commission at a special executive session next week. The director of the museum must have the support of his staff or nothing will work properly. It is much the same in business."

The men rose and shook hands. Ted believed Rudolph Bates would think clearly and honestly about what they all had said. He also knew Mitchell Jenkins could convince anyone of just about anything. That he was the last person on Bates' agenda was very worrisome. The gloves were off, and if Mitchell survived this, none of them were secure in their futures in Meriden, or anyplace else if they stayed in this profession. Mitchell Jenkins could prove to have a very long reach.

The meetings with Robert Evans and George Whitmire were short, with both men arriving back at the museum within two hours after they'd left. Bates had instructed his secretary to schedule both for the same day, and Ted hoped from that he knew they would have little of real importance to add. Martha's interview, on the other hand, went a full four hours. Ellen and Ted spent that evening speculating what Martha's responses were to Bates' very pointed questions. There was no way, of course, they would ever know. Bates wasn't talking with anyone after they had their time with him. Ted's guess was Mitchell had thoroughly coached her, the way his attorney had done with him at the time of the libel trial. Mitchell wouldn't want anything left to chance in her interview.

Since originally telling her about it, Ted had remembered other times when Jenkins had been impatient for Taylor to purchase works from galleries—things Taylor didn't need in view of what he already had purchased for his home. Jenkins explained this away as a collector gone wild, but now Ted wondered if it was James or Jenkins who had gone wild. It would benefit him to push his museum patron if there were something coming back to him...still, there was no part of any of it Ted could prove.

The following Monday Mitchell was to meet with Rudolph Bates. Both had scheduled the entire day for their discussion, and Mitchell didn't come into the museum first as he often did when he had a day-long session somewhere else. There was an unnerving quiet throughout the building as Ted, Ellen, and Mary wondered what was going on at Hall-Crowell. Something important was going on that would affect all of them, but the world was just moving on in spite of it.

At four thirty, Bates placed a call to Mary from his private office. It seemed his meeting with Mitchell was going to go on for a second whole day and he wondered if it would be acceptable to Mary, Ellen, and Ted if Louis Sterling sat in. Mitchell had requested it and Mary agreed. There was not much else she could do. Ellen had already gone home for the day, Ted was somewhere in the building, and Bates seemed in a hurry to have a response. Had they opposed Sterling's presence, it would have seemed they were out to get Mitchell. They didn't want to hurt anyone, they just wanted the behavior of Martha Dyer to be recognized as toxic.

When Mary told Ted Mitchell's meeting was going a second day, he was shocked. It was a bad sign, because all Mitchell needed to concoct a story was time. Ted's heart sank at the thought of the eloquent things he would be saying to Bates about his job and its problems. Ted called Ellen that night and she agreed. The only way they could possibly stop him was proving he did accept money from Tate McNeil over the Logan sale, but that was impossible. Ted said if Mitchell pulled this one off and if the commission bought it, he would be once again in full control. Ellen argued that point with him, thinking the commission would be watching Mitchell closely even if he did come out on top; but she still didn't understand his power.

The second day of Jenkins' interview the atmosphere at the museum was much the same as the day before. Martha would call Bates' office from time to time with messages she thought Mitchell should have. Ted was sure it was a tactic they had discussed at some point to make him seem indispensable. Her spirits were very high that day, as if the outcome was already assured. Joe Mullens was long forgotten by Martha. The newspaper advertisement Ted placed for his replacement resulted in twenty-two applications that on Mitchell's explicit instructions Ted was to review with Robert Evans. At five that evening Ted began gathering his things to leave for the day. He was almost out the door when his phone rang.

"Ted?" It was Mitchell. "I'd like to see you for a minute or two before you leave. Is that possible?"

Ted hadn't known he was in the building, and it was just like Mitchell to catch him this way. He walked down the hall to his office. The door was open, and Mitchell was at his desk, on the phone. He waved Ted in.

"How about shutting the door?" he said with his hand over the mouthpiece of the receiver. Ted did so, and in a few minutes, he finished his call.

"I won't keep you long." Mitchell shuffled papers on his desk, looking intently at everything except Ted. "Sorry I've not been able to meet with you and Robert the last two mornings but this thing with Bates has taken a lot of time. I think they've been good meetings, very healthy and informative. Rudolph is very impressed with you, by the way." He looked Ted in the eye. "He thinks you have a very accurate grasp on things around here. In fact, he told me that of all the people he's spoken to, you were the only one who seemed to be objective in what you said. I appreciate that." He was looking again at the papers on his desk. "Ted, I'm going to be upfront with you. I know you aren't happy with what you're doing and probably not overly happy with me. I think it would be good for you to get away, you know, take a short leave of absence, go on vacation. Perhaps when you come back things will look differently. Bates thinks you need the rest too. He doesn't want to lose you and neither do I."

Ted couldn't believe his ears. As usual, Jenkins had figured out what he was thinking before he had the chance to say anything. It had happened countless times before and now again, after a two-day meeting with the chair of his commission, a meeting that could have been the end for him. Mitchell sat behind his desk very assured, confident the meetings with Bates were nothing more than an exercise, a cleansing after a challenging first phase of his career.

Ted didn't know what to say, but finally managed an answer. "I think that's pretty astute of Rudolph. I was going to ask for a leave myself, but don't want to go before the Logans are installed and the exhibition opens."

"I thought so," Mitchell replied, "typically commendable. Good old Ted, always in there 'till the last. Well, I think you should go whenever you wish. In fact, I've convinced Taylor that fall would be a better time for the exhibition to open anyway. There's time now for you to go and come back with a fresh outlook on things. When would you like to take time, end of the week? I can arrange it!"

His future was moving much too fast, and Ted tried to put on the brakes. "I think the end of the week would be too soon. It would take me at least ten days to get things tied up here."

The semester at Oberlin during which Ted was to lecture began in April and extended to the beginning of June. If he left at the end of the month, he would have time to get there after finishing his work at the museum. They agreed on that schedule.

"I think this will be good, Ted. I envy you having the chance to get away. I'll get you a letter tomorrow confirming this meeting. I'll run it by Bates and Sterling as well, but there will be no problems with them, it's just a formality."

Mitchell's positivity was killing Ted. He either had very good meetings with Bates and was assured of their outcome, or he had taken some of those pills he kept in his vest pocket. Ted excused himself and left. That night he called his friend at Oberlin and arranged his stay there. It would be wonderful to get away.

✱ ✱ ✱

The following morning there was another memo taped to everyone's office door.

> THERE WILL BE AN IMPORTANT STAFF MEETING ON FRIDAY, MARCH 9 IN THE MULTIMEDIA THEATER AT 9:30 AM. ALL STAFF WILL BE EXPECTED TO ATTEND. THERE WILL BE NO EXCUSES. REFRESHMENTS WILL BE SERVED.
>
> Mitchell Jenkins, Director

Ted read the memo a second time. It could only have to do with the Bates meetings. A decision must be coming, but he was supposed to meet with the full commission before anything was made public. It was already Wednesday. Ted called Bates. He didn't want to but decided under the circumstances he might as well be honest with him and admit he was confused as to what was going on.

"Certainly Ted, I completely understand. I've called a special meeting for tomorrow evening. It's to be held at Laura James' home and is just for commissioners; Mitchell will not be present."

"Does he know about it yet?"

"Why yes, I talked it over with him this morning, not an hour ago."

Ted thanked Bates and read the memo again. *A conclusion would be reached tomorrow!* Ellen wasn't in the building and would not be until after lunch. Ted wanted to tell her what he'd learned from Bates. Mitchell wasn't in the building either, but by eleven he had returned and shortly after was on the phone with Ted.

"Ted, I've decided you were right about Joe Mullens; he does deserve more than I wanted to do for him at first. I want to have a small party for him here and present him with an appropriate gift. I've spent the morning talking with his daughter who has agreed to help get him over here one day next week. I thought, well, since you are going away for a while yourself, we might combine the occasions. What do you think?"

He was high as a kite again, as he'd been the afternoon before. There was no telling what set of thought patterns he was operating under when he was like this, but Ted didn't want a going away party.

"Well, I'm glad you want to do something for Joe, but I think it would confuse the issue if you had a double party. Besides, I'd prefer that my leave be kept low-key. I'll tell the people who need to know, and the others can be told I'm doing research for a book on the Logan paintings. Do you think Joe will want to come back here for a party? You might want to consider an alternate site."

"Good point, Ted. He might not want to see us all standing around drinking to his health. I'll get back to his daughter."

He was off the phone, and Ted hoped he wouldn't have to deal with him again for the remainder of the day. He was sure the prospect of a closed commission meeting was scaring Mitchell to death. It would be the first time in its history that they met without him, and the issues they'd be discussing were hard for perhaps the first time.

Ted had much to do to finish business by the end of the month. He couldn't help but wonder what he would do when his leave was over, if he would return to Meriden or go elsewhere. He was also unable to decide about telling Mitchell where he was going and what he was doing. Certainly Mitchell wouldn't object to him working somewhere else for a while—it would be a credit to his resume and to the museum to have a curator who lectured at a prestigious university. Still, he wanted to be careful and not burn bridges heading out the door. In the middle of the afternoon Ellen called. Ted still wanted to tell her about his conversation with Bates and Mitchell's proposal for Joe.

"Ellen, you'll never guess what Mitchell's done now..."

"Listen Ted, I've got to talk with you in private. Something happened and you need to know." She sounded excited and nervous.

"Okay, you want to come here?"

"No, I want to go to that storage room of yours; can you meet me there in five?"

"I can if Martha's here. She keeps the key, you know."

"She's here, I saw her when I came in, typing something to beat the band. See you shortly."

She hung up and Ted told his assistant he would be out for a while and walked to Martha's office. As Ellen had said, she was making her typewriter smoke. Ted asked for the key, and she handed it over.

"I've got Mitchell's letter about your leave." She was smiling. "He wants you to read it over and sign it before you leave for the day."

"It sounds like some sort of contract,"

"It is!"

Ted told her he would get it when he came back from storage and left immediately. Ellen was waiting outside the door, which Ted unlocked, and they went in.

"Don't tell me my time has finally come and you're going to have your way with me right here among the museum's treasures!" Ted made a motion as if to remove his tie.

"You bastard," she smiled, "don't you wish! I had a long talk today with Morgan Coton."

This caught Ted by surprise. "About what?"

"The Logan collection, among other things."

Now Ted was getting nervous too as he remembered the conversation they had the night before.

"You didn't tell her my theory about the money."

She looked him in the eye. "I didn't have to; she already knew. Suspected it herself after Taylor told her how much he'd paid for the paintings and the manner in which he did it. She's mad as hell!"

"But how could she make that connection? She didn't see the money the courier brought, and Mitchell wouldn't have told Taylor about the extra commission unless he had to."

"It seems Mitchell has been asking questions about bank accounts in Switzerland. She overheard him one night talking to her father and Taylor offered to set one up for him. Mitchell said he had some extra cash from betting winnings he wanted to put there to avoid taxes. Taylor thought that was amusing and placed the call that night to his own banker in Zurich. Then Morgan said she wondered why her father was making so many purchases from the Bookbinder Gallery before the Logan paintings, and why her mother seemed to encourage it. She placed a call up there yesterday, told the secretary she was Laura James and asked to speak to Jack Grossman. Sure enough, Grossman came quickly on the line. She admitted who she was and asked if he was angry about the Logan purchase, then told him not to worry, she was sure her father would be back soon. Now get this, she said she assumed that when he was purchasing objects, Mitchell would receive his usual fee for bringing her father and him together, and Grossman assured her he would!"

The look of triumph on Ellen's face was the only thing that kept Ted from throwing up. It was true! Jenkins did receive money from the James purchases and the bag of cash he had seen that night was his.

"How long has she suspected?" Ted asked.

"Several months I suppose, since before they all went to Asia together."

"What's she going to do with the information?"

"She's going to tell her father as soon as he returns from New York on Friday. I told her about you and the money and the man with the gun. She went wild with rage and said she'd get Mitchell if it was the last thing she did."

"I see." Ted wanted to be happy but couldn't be for some reason, knowing that his suspicions were true. He just wanted out.

"I've taken a leave of absence, Ellen. It will begin at the end of this month."

"You can't go now! Taylor isn't going to let Mitchell get away with this; we'll need you more than ever."

Ted looked at her again.

"You and Morgan have missed the point of her conversation with Grossman. Laura knows about the money from Bookbinder's. She probably suspects some similar deal took place with McNeil. If she has condoned it so far, she won't stop now."

"But why would Laura allow that to happen? Mitchell is feathering his nest with their money."

Ted shook his head and walked Ellen back to her office. "Why does Martha Dyer defend him so fiercely? I don't know the answers to these questions. Laura is receiving something from Mitchell, we just don't know what. It's the same with Martha. I'm worried for Morgan, though. Mitchell thinks he's covered his trail with the Logan money even though I saw it. I'm not going to say anything unless I'm asked, because he can still hurt me professionally. But Morgan will go in with both fists. She has quite a temper."

Ted left Ellen and re-entered the office suite, meeting Martha Dyer heading toward him.

"Here's the letter from Mitchell. You're supposed to sign it at the bottom if it's agreeable. You can leave it with me if you'd like."

Ted scanned the letter as he stood there. It was typical Mitchell Jenkins, very formal, like an agreement for a corporate merger.

"Is Mitchell in his office? I'd like to speak to him for a moment."

"You just missed him; he's gone for the day."

"Has he gone home?"

She didn't want to answer the question.

"It's important that I speak to him."

The glare in her eyes made Ted wish he hadn't pushed the subject. "He's with Laura James, if you must know. But I wouldn't call him there."

Ted thanked her for bringing the letter and returned the storage room keys to her. Being polite was one way he could annoy her without causing a problem for himself. But that feeling of elation was overshadowed by knowing Mitchell was spending the evening with the Jameses the night before the commission was scheduled to meet.

CHAPTER THIRTY-EIGHT

Rudolph Bates was the last commissioner to arrive at the James home. Cocktails were being served by Louis Sterling from Taylor's large built-in bar, and Anne had a simple buffet dinner prepared in the dining room. As always, Laura was the perfect hostess, talking to each of her guests about their art collection newly rearranged by Mitchell Jenkins, and other topics of a more community interest. The discussion of Bates' series of meetings with museum staff wasn't to begin until after they'd eaten. Everyone asked about Morgan and married life. It was always a pleasant topic for Laura who had been surprised earlier in the afternoon when Morgan dropped by to get some things from her room. They had a short conversation, and now, as the dirty plates were being collected by Anne, she had completely forgotten about her daughter's presence.

"The purpose of our gathering tonight," Rudolph Bates began as Laura served Drambuie in small crystal glasses, "is to bring you all up to date on a rather serious turn of events at the museum between the senior staff and Mitchell. As you may recall, there have been personnel agitations there since Peter Rutledge left. Mitchell was concerned about tensions Rutledge and others were experiencing with another staff member.

Those tensions escalated, culminating in the series of meetings that Louis had with senior staff members who presented a statement of their frustrations with the same staff member and, dare I say, with Mitchell as well. Louis reported on this at our last regular meeting with Mitchell in attendance. I called this meeting without Mitchell present to discuss a subsequent series of meetings I had with these same senior staff members over the past week. The request for these sessions came from them and culminated in a two-day meeting Louis and I had with Mitchell. It's been a very informative week! I started with Ellen Maxwell, whom you all know, and ended with Mitchell. All comments were made in confidence and reflected each person's feelings about the museum's personnel problems and positive actions that could be taken to resolve them."

He paused as Laura re-entered the room and took her place at the table. He smiled at her, then continued his remarks. "The pervasive mood is that the museum has a definite short-term problem, as well as a long-term problem centered in the administrative branch. Mitchell, in our last meeting, detailed for us his new organizational chart designed to take more of the day-to-day pressure off of him and place it on two individuals who would meet with staff and troubleshoot areas of concern as they arose. Mitchell still feels strongly that this is a proper approach until he can hire an assistant director, a position that has never really been held by anyone.

"Martha Dyer has certain responsibilities in this area that are now more specific; at least that is what Louis told me after his meetings with Mitchell. The issue that precipitated the statement by Ted Martin, Ellen Maxwell, and Mary Griffin had to do with Martha's administrative role and Mitchell's inability to give it definition and scope. That was to have been remedied and was mildly under control in the opinions of each of these three. However, recently Martha seems to have maneuvered, in the opinion of some, the resignation of Joe Mullens, who was building supervisor for the past ten years. Joe left in reaction to an angry tirade Martha directed at him early one morning for no apparent reason. The feeling is Martha was in no position to act in this manner, and that if the new system Mitchell devised actually worked, this episode would not have happened. Robert Evans is the designated department chief with authority over building operations and didn't know Mullens had left until several days after the fact.

"What I didn't know was this wasn't an isolated incident on Martha's part. In fact, it seems she has been responsible, in some fashion, for the departure of at least seven other employees. Mitchell admits she has a personality problem but will not go as far as some of the others I've talked with in linking her directly to these resignations. According to Mitchell she's in counseling, but he feels there were other factors that contributed to Mullens' leaving other than Martha's outburst last week. I was unable to contact Mullens to talk with him directly, but I hope to soon. It's clear Mitchell thinks a great deal of Martha Dyer and doesn't want to be put in a position where he will be forced to let her go. On the other hand, three of his most important staff members feel she is clearly at fault here, and what is perhaps worse, see her performance with Mullens to be exactly like others in the past. I believe it's time we offer Mitchell some real, constructive guidance on this before he finds himself with an administrative assistant and no one else! However, I want to lay the rest of this out for you before we discuss specifics.

"Of all the people with whom I met this week, apart from Mitchell himself, the one who had the clearest overview of the current situation was Ted Martin. Ted arrived here when the new building was nothing more than a hole in the ground and participated with Mitchell in those early phases of growth, both physically and philosophically. He was privy to some of Mitchell's most important decisions and watched the effect those decisions had on other members of the staff, as well as people on the outside."

At the mention of Martin's name, Laura stiffened in her chair. Mitchell had warned her the night before that Bates had been impressed with some of the things his curator had said and that he was afraid Martin had fallen away from the goals he thought important.

"Martin made some very insightful comments about Mitchell and the museum that I would like to share with you. First, he believes Mitchell is a brilliant individual who is worthy of respect for past accomplishments. He said Mitchell told him once there are different types of directors, just as there are certain types of corporate executives, or physicians for that matter, which are necessary to a museum's growth and do specific tasks better than they do others. Mitchell's strength, according to Martin, is in creating and building, and once that's accomplished, the museum should be handed off to the second type of director who molds and shapes it into an entity of significance in a particular area."

As Bates talked, the commission members were joined by another person who kept to the very back of the room, yet within listening distance. She remained there, unnoticed.

"He feels the major concerns of the staff, outside of Martha Dyer, is there is never enough time to accomplish the internal things that need perfecting: the programs, collection goals, and projects for the school, which are essential to the growth of this museum and are listed quite clearly in its purpose statement Mitchell wrote years ago. Ted cites evidence of projects that Mitchell initiated in a continuation of his building need and never finished. It keeps staff constantly trying to keep up with Mitchell's drive without being able to properly complete the projects they've been forced to put in abeyance to take on something new. Ted paralleled for me the careers of Mitchell Jenkins and August Bishop, the former director of the Birmingham Museum and Mitchell's mentor. Ted believes Mitchell sees himself as another Bishop, with the same longevity."

"I don't see that aspiration as harmful," Laura James interjected. "August Bishop put his museum into the minds of everyone in this state for over twenty-five years. That was important to the state and the Southeast. Mitchell could do worse in selecting a role model."

"No one is arguing that point Laura, believe me," Bates said. "However, I would be the first to admit that when an executive of any organization is unable to change with the times or situation around him, the entire organization begins to suffer. Taylor would admit that too if he were here. He decided to move his operation to Alabama because it was the right thing to do for the corporation's growth and survival. It was a very bold move. Many people in his industry said it wouldn't prove successful, but it did. He was able to refine procedures and continue the excellence others had come to expect. But if he had come here and built, then found some other area to expand upon, and continued in this fashion without giving those working for him time to catch up, the move would not have succeeded. Ted Martin is saying the museum is being forced to continually grow and the staff can't keep up with the pace."

"Perhaps then those people should be replaced by people who can," Laura snapped.

"Perhaps so," Bates replied. "That's something we'll need to decide and counsel Mitchell on. But it also might mean Mitchell needs to look at his reasons for keeping things in a state of turbulent change and curb that tendency."

"But I don't understand," Laura interrupted again. "We can't fault Mitchell for his energy. He has built the best facility for the exhibition and collection of art in this state, perhaps in the Southeast. He has far surpassed his mentor and is only seeking to forge ahead. He's had support in this effort, and I would be less than candid if I didn't admit my family has been interested in this growth. But it was Mitchell who put it all together. The Logan collection, for instance, is a huge step toward enlarging the museum's prestige and will add tremendously to its annual attendance."

Bates had not wanted to talk about the Logan paintings because of the James tie.

"I suppose," Laura continued, "Ted Martin has something to say about that too!"

There was the slightest bit of anger in her voice in that last statement and Bates caught it. He liked Martin and didn't want to create an enemy for him out of Laura.

"I don't think Ted has any problem with the collection itself, Laura, but I do think he sees it as a major project that was pushed by Mitchell to ensure his own stability here a while longer. He feels Mitchell thinks his base begins to slip away unless there is something new coming down the pipe. And based on what the others told me, I think he's correct."

"You can't honestly expect me to accept the word of Ted Martin over what I can see with my own eyes, Rudolph! Mitchell is a very capable man. It would be foolish for us to deny what he has done for the art world and for Meriden. Ted Martin is a worker bee. He comes, does his job, and leaves at day's end. I'll admit, he's good at what he does, but his vision is limited to the here and now. If he were gone tomorrow, there would be a bump in the road, but nothing more; not like if Mitchell were gone."

"I agree, Laura. I used Ted's narrative of life at the museum because it was the clearest. The problem we need to discuss tonight is if Mitchell has lost the confidence of his senior staff, he will find it hard to operate."

Louis Sterling spoke up. He'd been very quiet all evening, fearing this kind of discussion would cause a rift among the commissioners. "Let's try to put things in perspective without getting too emotional. The staff asked for an opportunity to talk to Rudolph about some very specific problems—currently this thing with Martha Dyer and Joe Mullens. I think that while Martha may be very capable and helpful to Mitchell, she has some emotional stresses she is sometimes unable to keep under control. I think Mitchell should face up to that and replace her. In the short term, I think this would solve much of the unrest.

"None of us can question the fact that Mitchell has enjoyed a wonderful career here. Without his energy and drive, we would still be back in that drafty old building with little of significance going on. He shouldn't be replaced simply because he has difficulty seeing what I would consider smaller issues. He needs people around him who keep an eye on the future he seeks to create, but he should also give them the chance to attain closure on current work. This might cause him a bit of angst, not being able to move his agenda as quickly as he'd like, but in terms of what he still can offer, that is a minor consequence.

"Laura, none of us are going to deny the good you and Taylor have done for the community. You have given Mitchell a great deal of the resources he has needed to build what we all enjoy. The Logan collection is just the most recent example of this generosity and ability to recognize important opportunities. Few other people could have pulled that off as selflessly as Mitchell did. If that's an example of growing for the sake of growing, I think we can live with it. I feel the museum is really in a good position now and can be steadied by perhaps the removal of a few individuals who are causing friction. I believe that what is called for is dramatic action, and it should happen soon. Rudolph and I are attending a staff meeting first thing tomorrow to discuss the things we've heard. I think it would be good to already have that action taken by the time we go. Mitchell is aware of my view and that I would be telling you this. He's prepared to act accordingly if it's our wish."

"Thank you, Lou," Bates said. "We all know people come and go in any organization for a variety of reasons and that the change is generally healthy. I believe we, as the governing body of the museum, must look to its future and well-being. Particularly at this time when so much has occurred in relation to the importance of the James family in this growth. We must consider everything very carefully and make whatever changes are necessary for the good of the whole."

"Gentleman and ladies," Laura said, rising from her chair, "let me speak very clearly on the future well-being of the Meriden Art Museum. Our family money was used very wisely, I think, by Mitchell Jenkins to orchestrate the building of the facility. When it was completed, there were things installed within it that had significance and reflected the basic collection policy of the museum at that time. For eight or nine months, there was much enthusiasm in the community and the state about what was being accomplished. However, in time the newness of the building, as well as the artwork held inside, began to grow stale, despite Mitchell working hard to bring attention to the institution. Not for himself, mind you, but for the museum's future. We cannot afford the luxury of growth from within yet—we don't have the endowment, and the state funding has not grown appreciably. There simply must be things offered at the museum that can be easily appreciated by the public and deemed worthy of their tax dollars. The Logan collection is an example of that kind of attraction. For the first time in the museum's history there is something that will command attention from the outside, and Mitchell worked to get that for Meriden. We shouldn't condemn the man who worked that miracle, he deserves our accolades.

"The James family is tired of putting effort and money into things that get only mild community support and frankly, because Mitchell is a personal friend as well, we are tired of people taking shots at him for things he does in the name of the museum. So, I say to all of you, that if Mitchell Jenkins is forced to leave the museum for any reason, other than the most flagrant dereliction of his responsibilities, the James family will withdraw the collection of Axel Logan paintings and move it somewhere else. That is what we should deal with tonight so that tomorrow, if we have agreement, Rudolph and Louis can give Mitchell the vote of confidence he needs to carry on his duties, despite what might be said by his detractors. As Lou has said, it might be wise to take bold action in terms of some of the people there, but I think Mitchell's true feelings ought to be considered before Martha is released. The person in charge should have people around him he can trust!"

The silent figure who had joined the meeting, in secret, left her place at the back of the room unseen. There would be little said now by Rudolph Bates or any other member of the commission, as each knew the importance of the Logan paintings to their community and the museum's future. The evening would make a difference as to what her father would be told about Mitchell and her own role with the museum, now and after her parents were gone. Her revenge would manifest itself in her youth and the trust funds available to her when she turned thirty.

✻ ✻ ✻

Ted was not anxious to attend the staff meeting the following day; Mitchell was much too confident as he passed him in the hallway.

"Have you returned my letter yet, Ted? I'd like to discuss it with Rudy and Lou this morning before the meeting."

Ted had not but told him he would within the hour. "I'm going to be lecturing in Ohio," Ted said, "at Oberlin. It will give me some new experience and a small stipend to keep me going until I return." Returning was still something he thought about only as a last resort.

"Oberlin! Well, they have a good art faculty there I understand. You should be very excited. Is this confirmed?"

Ted told him it was. He was pleased he had decided to tell Mitchell. His reaction was better than Ted had anticipated, and he walked back to his office to re-read the letter.

Dear Ted,

In regard to your conversation of March 8, 1978, requesting a three-month leave of absence from your employment with the Museum, I am making the following recommendations to Louis Sterling, chair of our Personnel Committee, as well as Rudolph Bates, Chairman of the Commission:

That you be granted your request for the period March 30, 1978, through June 30 of that same year.
That the absence be without compensation.
That you communicate with me once each month of your leave to give a progress report and an indication of any plans you might have that would affect your expected return to employment on July 1, 1978.

That your rate of compensation upon return will not be affected by your absence.

If this letter and the terms of my recommendation accurately reflect the intent of our mutual agreement as discussed, please indicate this with your signature below. I will advise you of the outcome of my meeting with Rudolph Bates and Louis Sterling as soon as possible.

Mitchell continued the letter by saying he would miss Ted and looked forward to his return in July. Ted signed and returned it personally, refusing Martha's offer to take it to Mitchell herself. Mitchell had been much too confident for Ted to have any faith in something dramatic happening at the upcoming meeting. He had made his best move and hoped Ellen and Mary would do the same. Perhaps he would return with a new perspective on Mitchell and the way things at the museum seemed to work. But for now he was relieved; he was now off the hook, free for a while from the alarm he had come to feel being there.

As everyone gathered for the meeting, Ted purposely took a seat away from Ellen and Mary. He was passing problems on to them and no longer wanted to be reminded of the past, even though this meeting would be filled with those references. Martha Dyer was busy sorting paperwork for Bates and Sterling. Ted avoided her eyes as best he could, and in doing so saw Jenkins, Bates, and Sterling enter the theater together—Jenkins smiling broadly, Bates and Sterling rather subdued. The three of them sat at a long table at the front of the room. A moment later, Mitchell rose and walked to the podium to begin whatever was about to happen to the museum and everyone who worked there.

Mitchell began, "I want to thank you all for being here and changing whatever plans you might have had this morning. We'll attempt to have more of these sessions in the months to come. As I'm sure all of you are aware, some of us have been meeting with Mr. Bates about issues here. While I believe it is the director's role to work out these matters personally, I have come to view these exchanges as a chance for opinions to be aired in a fashion that might be difficult in private sessions with me. This is a healthy sign of our stability as we move rapidly into a new era of our growth and national importance. Without the complete confidence and support of the commission, this kind of atmosphere could not exist. It is to the lasting credit of Rudolph Bates that the commission acts as compassionately as it does to work with us. Rudy," he turned and looked over at the chairman, "I want to take this opportunity to thank you for your leadership and infinite patience." Mitchell applauded, followed by everyone in the room. "Before Mr. Bates makes his remarks, I have one or two short announcements to make."

The sudden suspicion Mitchell was going to say something publicly about Ted's leave caused him to hold his breath. It would be just like Mitchell to do this, even after Ted had asked him not to. He didn't want to be embarrassed by his remarks.

"Joe Mullens, who we all have loved over the years, left the museum ten days ago for personal reasons. At the time I was surprised by his action but determined to honor his request. However, after talking with Joe, I'm pleased to announce he'll be coming back to work on a part-time basis beginning the first of next month. I was sure you all would want to know of this very pleasant development. The second thing I wanted to mention," Mitchell shot a look in Ted's direction, "is Taylor James has decided a summer opening for the Logan Collection, which I would now like to refer to as the James Collection, would not fully take advantage of the massive press coverage it could be given if held in the fall. Consequently, he has decided to go along with the proposal I made to change the opening to October 4th, which will give us all a very welcomed breather. Your supervisors will discuss this change with you all in the next week. It's good news, believe me, and will allow us to prepare properly for this important event. Now Rudolph Bates will give a brief report on the meetings of last week as well as last evening's commission meeting."

Bates rose and took Mitchell's place behind the podium. He carried several pages of notes with him. "All bodies of industry," he began, "experience growing pains when faced with a new challenge or a series of them. This is a fundamental issue that should be expected by people involved in situations of dynamism. The meetings I have held with some of you brought these facts home to me once again. Outsiders to the workings of a place like this believe changes occur magically. Pictures appear on the walls overnight; programming happens on its own. They believe this, or they believe nothing new ever happens in a museum, and that the people who work in these places simply sit and grow the cobwebs they expect to find in the corners or on the objects themselves. Certainly, this is the way many of the members of our community think of us. However, now that the James Collection has come to be, minds are going to change, and visitors will see things as they really are.

"The growing pains I've alluded to can happen many times during the course of an organization's life. If large enough, they can affect things every time a new phase of an operation begins. The important thing is that they are recognized by the individuals who endeavor to make the organization work, as well as by those whose job it is to oversee its smooth operation. When this is done on both sides, things run smoothly, when it is not, there are issues. After discussing these facts with the other commissioners last night, I believe the current issues are the result of two sides not recognizing this yin and yang and suggesting surgery when only exercise is needed to make these growing pains subside. The growth of the last five years will level off, necessitating the re-thinking of ideas that were practical during our early years. But the leveling off will be productive and will reflect our current reality. It will be a time to take stock of what has been accomplished and to put that history in perspective. It will be a rewarding period, one filled with new experiences for us all. But it will be a distinct change from the past, and only those individuals who can adapt will be productive. As always, it'll be up to Mitchell to lead the way.

"We have been very fortunate to have a strong leader in Mitchell who didn't leave us to take other positions that were more attractive and certainly more lucrative. He has guided us through the issues of construction and fundraising almost single-handedly. Now he has brought this important collection of paintings to Meriden that will precipitate this leveling-off process while making the museum known throughout the world. I want to reiterate our continued vote of confidence in you, Mitchell."

✵ ✵ ✵

Ted didn't hear from Ellen until later that afternoon. The remainder of meeting was taken up with reports on the activities of individual departments. Rudolph Bates left shortly after his remarks, but Louis Sterling stayed until the end, leaving the theater with Jenkins.

When she called, her voice was hardly above a whisper. "I guess that's it?"

"Yep," Ted said.

"You're probably smart to get out now, even if it is just for three months. I wish I could go, but with the kids it would be difficult. Are you going to announce your leave?"

"No. I thought Mitchell was this morning though! I asked him not to." Ted paused. "I feel somehow as if my going were a sort of banishment, as if I were being punished for thinking and standing up for myself. I think Mitchell believes I'm the bad seed, and that life will be easier for him without me here. He's always tried to split the three of us up! We are to work together but not be friends."

"I think you're wrong about the troubles leaving when you do. Besides, you'll be back in the summer; it's not like you've been fired. Hell, you should be happy!"

They talked a bit longer before someone came into her office. Ted was happy it was Friday. He was going to try to forget about all of this over the weekend. He needed to stop thinking about it; it was making him crazy. He looked up and found Martha Dyer standing in the doorway looking down at him, her glasses perched on the end of her nose. She too had survived the morning meeting, though he was sure she wasn't happy about Joe Mullens coming back, even on a limited schedule. Perhaps that was a slap on her wrist!

"Mitchell wants to see you."

She turned and walked away, saying no more. Her tone and look destroyed the lightened mood Ted was trying to enjoy. He felt the tightness return to his chest. It was too soon after the meeting for reprisals, even if he were in full command again. Mitchell was sitting behind his desk looking pensive as Ted sat across from him.

"You had a very good day today," Ted began. "It must make you feel good to have the commission's full support."

He smiled thinly and nodded his head in agreement. "It does indeed Ted. It comes from knowing you've done the best you can; it's something we all should feel good about." He stared at Ted as if he were about to deliver some bad news, then looked down at his desk.

"Listen Ted, I'm sorry to say that neither Bates nor Sterling have approved your leave. I am personally shocked they've taken this attitude after my approval of it, but it's out of my hands now."

Ted felt his body hit the floor even though he was still in the chair, Mitchell's words ringing inside his head.

"I know you were looking forward to this time away. I'm sorry."

"I can't believe it!" Ted's throat was tightening. "Did they say why? Do they know I made plans that will be very awkward for me to change?"

"Yes, I told them of your lecturing at Oberlin. They felt they shouldn't give you the opportunity to leave and possibly find another job while we hold things for you here, as if you were on vacation. They said it just wasn't done and would set a bad precedent for others who might decide they want the same thing."

"They understand this is only a temporary assignment, right? How do they expect me to live while away? The leave is without pay from the museum—do they understand that? Do they think I'm wealthy?"

"No, not at all. They know what your annual salary is, but have denied the leave. I really am sorry!"

The tightness in Ted's throat gave way to anger and frustration. He was being cut out. They were forcing him from the museum instead of Martha Dyer or Mitchell. He had convinced them everything would be better without Ted.

"How do they justify all the bits of outside business you've been involved in then?" It slipped out; Ted could see him stiffen.

"I've always told the commission about each involvement I've had outside this office. My brief outside interests have not had anything to do with art or any aspect of the museum. If you wanted to go work at a clothing shop on the side, I am sure they wouldn't mind."

"I see." Ted felt the futility of arguing with him. With the meeting's outcome, it was clear Mitchell was in control, and Ted was no longer of any real use to him. Once the James Collection was installed, he would no longer need someone adept at organizing special attractions to interest the public and keep them coming in.

"What do you think you'll do? Stay or go?" Mitchell asked quietly, his own anger subsiding.

"I don't know. I need some time to consider. May I have the weekend?"

"Sure, but I'll need to know on Monday. Should you decide to resign, I could release you before the end of the month if that would help." He was anxious for Ted to be gone.

"I'll let you know first thing Monday morning."

CHAPTER THIRTY-NINE

Mitchell sat in his office a long while that night, thinking of the day's successes. He had been pleased by Lou Sterling's phone call the night before after returning from the commission meeting. Laura had played the exact card he hoped she would when it became obvious Bates had been affected by what he heard from Ellen and Ted. Sterling acted surprised by her using the collection as leverage to have her way in things. He still didn't understand the extent of her fondness for Jenkins. Everything had gone right; Martha was still on the payroll and Ted Martin was probably going to be off it and soon. Jenkins thought about the younger man who now had to decide between staying in Meriden or going away. Jenkins knew his will to stay was gone but wondered if he would have the courage to cut himself off from the relative security of the museum. He was prepared to make it very easy for Ted to go, and very difficult if he decided to stay.

What was next? Mary Griffin posed no real problem—a few harsh words in her direction and she would be back in the fold. She was bright and knew she was being manipulated, but with children to support, she wouldn't get in his way very often. Besides, he still hoped to get into her pants. Ellen Maxwell might prove to be more of a thorn in his side, but the real question was what to do about Rudolph Bates? He was a fair man who had been influenced by what he'd heard. Would Bates challenge him now? He tried to think through those potential obstacles.

"Here's to you, Laura!" He raised his scotch in salute. "May I always have you on my side." He swallowed the contents of the glass, placing it softly on the polished desk. He held a sharpened pencil in his hand while looking at the list before him. In a slow, deliberate motion he crossed through the name "Rudolph Bates."

✡ ✡ ✡

Taylor sat on the flowered couch in his daughter's living room. He had enjoyed dinner and even the pleasant anecdotes of his son-in-law. He appreciated the fact they were living within their means and could do so comfortably. Soon he knew she would have enough money to live any way she wanted. He had come to enjoy that privilege but felt money had certain responsibilities. He knew Morgan would define those for herself, just as he had done.

"Your mother would have enjoyed that dinner, Morgan. I'll be sure to tell her how elegant it was to make her not being able to be here even worse!"

She smiled and sat beside him on the couch, turning to face him. "Estephen still interested in working at that new school? I was speaking recently to several folks on its board." He fumbled with the pockets of his vest. "I could make my reply to them conditional if you'd like."

"No, I believe you should give opinions and money without strings attached. If you like the programs they're offering, that should be enough. Estephen would like a position there, but on his own merits. He thinks he needs to show you he can do something productive with himself, and I support him on that. Besides Daddy, you're giving enough money away these days." She smiled again as she said this, deciding she enjoyed toy-ing with her father in conversation.

"Have I given so much away this year? I think you're mistaken, my girl. Anyway, I have received tangible objects for my money this year, hedging for the future."

She knew he had no idea where she was leading him. "You really think the artwork you and Mother purchased these last couple of years will earn more money than other forms of investments? I suppose Mitchell con-vinced you of that."

She betrayed herself slightly with the mention of Mitchell's name. Taylor understood she couldn't forgive Jenkins for his interference in her marriage and probably felt threatened by the money he was spending on art. She knew most of the work would go to the museum in time, and that Jenkins had a hand in selecting them.

"This isn't really investing, my dear. I could do much better in other areas. But I don't necessarily want to make more money and the artwork is helping me do that. They're tax deductible if given to a museum. I get the deduction, the enjoyment of having had them at the house to view, and after they are gifted to the museum, the pleasure of replacing some of them. The museum gets new pieces for their collection, and the public gets something to see for the money they pay in taxes to support it. A complete circle is made, just as it is in any successful economic situation."

"And what happens when the museum no longer wants to accept what you have to give them?" she asked. "What happens if they suddenly decide to collect something else? A new director might have other ideas."

Taylor was enjoying the give and take with his daughter. It reminded him of the games they used to play when she was small.

"That will never happen. The museum will continue to collect the things it's interested in now. Mitchell assured me of that, and I don't think he's going anywhere. He's really very happy in Meriden."

"Especially now," she said almost sarcastically.

"I suppose any museum director would be happy to house an important collection of paintings by Axel Logan. Its merits are limitless, and it provides me a constant tax advantage. The museum is committed to that body of work now, no matter who the director may be."

"And Mitchell Jenkins?"

"What do you mean, Morgan? Mitchell does his job well. There are decisions he's made that I might not have, but he's capable enough. He also knows a good thing when he sees it."

Morgan smiled broadly at her father as he said that. "He certainly does Daddy."

Taylor was no longer smiling, tired of people seeing him as Mitchell's bitch. "You know Morgan," he sighed, "I've been dealing with people a lot longer than you and can take care of myself. Money isn't made by the timid. Ever since you heard that stuff from his ex-wife you've been angry with him. I'll admit that perhaps he shouldn't have done some of the things he did then, but it's over. He likes Estephen, he's told me so. Besides he can't afford to dislike any member of this family. I own Mitchell Jenkins."

"That's where you're wrong, Daddy. He's been getting rich off you and Mother these past couple years. Oh, it's been small amounts by your standard, but it has grown steadily. Your financials have a small hole in them. Nothing that will seriously affect your bottom line, but a hole just the same; and flowing from that hole is a straight line in one direction. Do you know who's at the end of that line? Mitchell Jenkins!"

Taylor looked puzzled. "What? I'm not following you. What do you think Mitchell's done?"

She was pleased he was listening, but not ready to tell him everything at once. "Why do you think Mitchell wanted to know about Swiss bank accounts?"

Taylor chuckled. "I didn't think you knew about that. What big ears you have! He said he had some money he wanted to hide from Uncle Sam. Betting winnings I think he said. I never asked him about it."

"What if I could prove it wasn't betting winnings?"

"Really Morgan, it's not our business where he gets money from. Certainly he's not getting rich on what he's making at the museum. What's your point?"

"Daddy, what if I told you every time you make a purchase at the Bookbinder Gallery, and likely at others, Mitchell Jenkins receives a check for steering you and mother through the door? He'd have a nice, steady income from that, don't you think?"

"I suppose he would, but I don't believe it. Where did you hear such nonsense? From Ellen Maxwell?"

"No Daddy. I called Mr. Grossman and asked. He was only too happy to confirm the information."

"Jack Grossman told you that? He's not stupid, Morgan, so even if it were true, a thing like that isn't discussed openly." He smiled broadly. "I've got you now. You thought you'd trick me with this. But the mistake you made was in saying you called Grossman yourself!"

"I didn't say I used my real name!" Now she was laughing with him.

"Who did you say you were?"

"Mother!" The laughter stopped. "You'll have to ask her about it when you see her next. Mr. Grossman acted as if she knew about this little deal. I'm sure Mitchell has grown to like his bonuses. I'll bet the one he received for the Logan paintings was enough to establish a retirement fund. He was paid in cash for that one. Ted Martin saw the money, though he didn't know what it was for at the time. Mitchell told him you were sending a final payment for the paintings, that the money he saw was yours."

"Who else knows about this?"

"I..." she checked herself, "I haven't told anyone else yet, but last night I secretly attended a special meeting of the commission. Mother made it very clear she didn't want anything bad to happen to Mitchell Jenkins. So I decided to tell you and let you handle things. I'm sure you're good at this, as you've said. There are a couple other things you should think about though. I've been silent about Mitchell and the way I feel about him for quite some time, per your wishes. But there will come a time when I'll be able to speak out or at least silently work against him, and when that time comes, Mr. Jenkins will see things begin to collapse around him. James family money has made him, and it will also tear him apart."

✲ ✲ ✲

March 12, 1978

Mr. Mitchell Jenkins
Director, Meriden Museum of Art
Meriden, Alabama

Dear Mitchell,

It is with sadness, that I submit my resignation as curator of the Meriden Museum, effective March 30 of this year. I hope this does not put the museum in a compromised position with respect to the important events of the near future; but feel under the circumstances, it would be better for all concerned if I terminated my employment at this time.

Sincerely,
Theodore Martin

It wasn't much of a letter. After five years, a paragraph would wrap everything up in a blanket of obscurity and become history for someone else. It was hard to believe. The weather this March had been turbulent, but soon it would be April. Even though the rain was falling steadily, the air was warm and beginning to smell of spring. Ted thought about other mornings he had arrived at the museum, of all the things that had kept him there and excited about the job. He didn't want his last days to be filled with remorse or sadness. What had happened between himself and Mitchell Jenkins was over. The anger and bitterness he once felt were now apathy and fatigue. He was completely drained. Still, it didn't seem possible he was next in a long line of friends and former museum employees to have a last day.

✵ ✵ ✵

The James Collection arrived, sequestered in the same secrecy as its acquisition. The paintings were delivered in a red van. Two attendants had made the trip in sixteen hours, stopping only for gas and food and armed like Tate McNeil's courier. Ted was to be at the museum to ensure their safe storage, and photographs of their arrival would be taken by George Whitmire and handed out to the press in packets orchestrated by Mitchell and Taylor. Taylor and Laura came to personally witness their arrival. There was something unusually tense about their manner with Mitchell.

In the following days, Taylor was in and out of Mitchell's office constantly. He encouraged staff to view the paintings, countermanding Mitchell's orders that the works not be seen, and arranged three different occasions where access was granted. It was an astonishing about-face from the Taylor James Mitchell had always described.

Taylor surprised Ted on one of these occasions when he took him aside to talk privately for a moment. "What's this I hear about you leaving?" His manner was very kind, as if the two were close friends and the snubbing of the past had never occurred. "Are you sure you want to resign at this time?"

"It's time for a change, Mr. James," Ted said. "We have all been here too long."

James mumbled something that was unintelligible, then nodded his head in agreement. He left Ted and walked back into the storage area.

Ted decided not to pack his personal belongings until late in the afternoon of his final day. He wanted it to be like any other Friday afternoon, conducting the business of his department without undue drama. In a week he would leave for Ohio and knew he would be asked many questions about the James Collection by both the Oberlin art faculty and curious outsiders who read about it in the newspapers. It wouldn't serve him well to talk badly about what had happened, but to discuss it as an important artistic event seemed absurd. Why would anyone in his position leave such an opportunity unless there were other issues not being aired? He was being used for the final time, not only by Mitchell Jenkins, but by anyone still working there who saw his departure as the answer for solving their collective distress.

He wanted no event to take place for his goodbyes—no luncheons, no drinks after work—though there were people who wanted to provide these artificial comforts. His leaving was not a happy occasion, as none of the others before his had been. He had prepared a short statement that had gone out to staff shortly after he gave Jenkins his resignation letter. He felt a need to say something to the people who had lived through the last years with him. After the meeting in which Rudolph Bates spoke for the commission, there had been a noticeable look of acceptance in the faces of people who were staying on. The challenge made to Mitchell by Ted, Ellen, and Mary was seen by the others as something long overdue. There was genuine support for it, but now that it was over, there could only be acceptance.

Mitchell kept a low profile where Ted was concerned after regretfully accepting his letter. His attention now turned to other matters related to his curator leaving, like the immediate issue of filling his position as group leader for the program side of operations. Though he had the commission's confidence, he wanted to go slowly in this and not rekindle dead flames. His first choice for the position was George Whitmire. Whitmire, Jenkins explained to Louis Sterling, was in an ideal position to oversee the activities of the curatorial department, the education department, and the school because he was handling publications for all three. He was already aware of deadlines and what programs were being initiated. He was also, according to Jenkins, a team player, someone he could trust with authority, someone who wasn't afraid to do the hard jobs. It didn't seem to matter to Jenkins that Whitmire had no previous experience working with a complex group of people and had only been working there four months. Sterling counseled against the move fearing Ellen and Mary would object.

The last person Jenkins wanted in that slot was Ellen, but she seemed to Sterling the obvious choice. His was a convincing argument for many reasons. Sterling had listened more to the remarks of Jenkins than he'd realized. After listing the apparent reasons for his choice of Ellen, Sterling listed a few that were much more attractive.

"You have often told me of her inability to supervise and get along with those in her charge. By giving her this position, which she clearly wants, you can give her the chance to show her inabilities. Once those are exposed, it'll be easier for you to pressure her out."

Jenkins agreed and the appointment was made.

Finding a successor for Ted posed no immediate problem. His position, as Jenkins had initially conceived it, had grown too large for easy supervision by the executive branch. He determined it would be better to rewrite that job description before filling the slot. He didn't want to repeat his earlier mistake. Martin's actual leaving caused Jenkins some concern. Word of his resignation had leaked to the press and was hard for them to understand, coming on the heels of the Logan announcement. Sensing trouble, the press was hot to know why the museum's curator was leaving at such an important time. Mitchell had already taken a few calls about it and knew Martin would also. It was on this subject that the two met during Martin's final week.

"Ted, I know you're busy getting your department in order, but I wanted you to know it concerns me that you might feel the commission wronged you in their decision to deny your Leave. They were only thinking of the good of the museum. I hope you will see it that way. They are concerned about your future and hope you will be able to stay at Oberlin or find something else that is as stimulating as being at a university. They wanted you to have this," he slid a folder across his desk, "as a token of their good wishes. They hope your leaving will not cause anyone any embarrassment and you'll be happy in your new life."

Ted stiffly picked up the folder, holding it without opening it. He could no longer look Jenkins in the eye and wanted the meeting to be over as quickly as possible.

"You'll likely be receiving a few phone calls from members of the press. They're already calling me about your leaving. Should they call you, you may respond however you wish, but I would hope you'll not say anything that would reflect badly on the museum or yourself. I would hope that neither I nor anyone else here would be forced into an ugly press interview. These things serve no real purpose and generate a lot of ill will, which would hurt us all sooner or later."

Martin said he understood and rose to leave. He held the folder under his arm until he was at his own desk. He opened it slowly, finding two checks enclosed, one for $2,700.00 with a note from Sterling explaining the commission wanted to compensate him with an extra month's pay, and the other for three weeks of accrued paid vacation.

By two thirty that afternoon, Ted began gathering his personal things, amounting to four small boxes taken to his car by museum custodians. As if on cue, his secretary left to do some filing and Martin sat alone at his empty desk waiting for five o'clock. The whistling he heard coming up the hall was a sign he wouldn't be alone for long. Mitchell came in acting as if it were just another visit. The tune, Ted recognized, was his collegiate fight song. He kept any expression from appearing on his face, and Mitchell, realizing the charade was over, sat sheepishly on the couch by his desk.

"I just came by to collect your keys and identification card."

It was a final humiliation for Martin, who had been entrusted with administering keys and identity badges for the entire staff since the move. He had, in fact, already turned the articles into himself, placing both the badge and keys into a locked cabinet to which only he and Jenkins knew the combination. He told Jenkins he had already relieved himself of those articles, but it didn't seem to matter.

"I'd like them anyway," Mitchell said. "I want to keep them in my office or with Martha."

Ted rose, retrieved the key and badge, and handed them over. Mitchell talked for a few more moments before standing to leave.

"You aren't leaving early, are you?"

Ted was disappointed the thought hadn't crossed his mind.

"We thought a brief party was in order at four thirty. I know you didn't want anything like this, but your friends asked for a chance to say goodbye. It won't take long. Oh, and one more thing." He stepped into the hall returning with a box wrapped in red paper. "We all wanted you to have something, so we got you this. Hope you like it."

In an hour, the first few members of the staff began wandering into Martin's office. It was an awkward scene, as no one knew quite what to say. There were many comments about the red box that sat unopened exactly were Jenkins had left it. Ted wouldn't have minded this informal gathering if he thought Jenkins and Dyer would not join in as the time got closer to five. They wouldn't leave their offices early for something that wasn't strictly business.

Their success with the commission had given them a new drive to do things strictly by the book. Martin noticed neither Ellen nor Mary were in attendance and wondered about their absence, but stopped as Martha and Mitchell entered the room. It was now official. Someone brought several bottles of chilled wine that were opened. Ted was given the first glass, and soon everyone was served and the light gaiety that had filled the room settled into quiet talking. George Whitmire came up to Ted and began talking about Oberlin and its fine art program. He had been on the campus for two days and could attest to its superior quality. He was getting itchy feet to move on himself, he said, but thought he would stay in Meriden a while longer.

Ellen finally appeared for a glass of wine and, as she said, "to see where all the noise was coming from!" She was being purposely funny, but her eyes were red from crying. She wouldn't look at Ted, and he didn't look at her. She didn't stay long. Others were leaving too; it would soon be over. Martha pulled a chair up to where Martin was sitting and spoke quietly to him without turning. The words were meant for him and no one else.

"I just wanted you to know that I'm sorry things worked out this way and that we aren't friends. The past few years have come between us as we've each chosen the way we felt we should grow."

Ted looked at her. She was still dressed severely, her hair cut short around her face. There were many things he couldn't forgive her for, but this was worst of all. She would not deny him his beliefs at this late hour by acting sad about his leaving. He wouldn't give her that comfort. She rose and left him for Mitchell's side. They had made their decisions and now each would have to live with them the best way they could.

Mitchell stood talking shop with George Whitmire and anyone else who cared to listen. They were discussing the James Collection and how it was to be handled to get the most benefit from its opening. Ted couldn't hear specifics of the conversation even though there were only a few people left in the room. He wondered if he could slip out himself, leaving Jenkins and the others to continue, but looking again at the red box, he knew he'd never make it. Ted decided to leave it behind as his personal bequest to whomever came after him. It seemed an appropriate gesture and he rose. Jenkins was watching and stopped Whitmire in mid-sentence.

"Come now, Ted! You haven't opened your gift. You can't go without letting the rest of us see it."

Ted sat back down and began removing the ribbon from the box. The people who remained gathered to watch, fascinated by the reality of this final gesture. The wrapping was thin and easily tore despite Ted's effort to make the unraveling take as long as possible. The outside of the cardboard box loudly proclaimed its contents in a modern, bold design that could be read from thirty feet: "10-Inch Black and White Portable

Television. Ivory case, molded handle. Model number HYT 578937654, made in Japan for J. C. Penny."

It was said afterward that Ted claimed it was just what he'd always wanted.

AFTERWORD

Neither Taylor or Laura James knew of the funds Jenkins was skimming from the art purchases they made from galleries in New York, nor from their Logan paintings purchase. They said they were greatly disappointed in him for demanding dealer commissions and were angered by the length of time it had gone on; they demanded he stop future extortion attempts. He did so for one year, then continued the practice until caught by Morgan Coton and Ellen Maxwell, who reported this activity to the American Association of Museum's Unethical Practices Committee. He was censured by that organization, which also recommended the museum's national accreditation be revoked. Shortly after, Mitchell Jenkins was fired by the commission.

The Jameses hired a part-time curatorial assistant to keep their still-growing collection's records and requests for loans to other museums and exhibitions. The Logan paintings were eventually given outright to the museum and was a popular public draw, limited only by the city's not being a larger metropolitan center with better public access. Morgan and Estephen Coton moved to Spain when Morgan's trust funds kicked in, returning to the US only for major family events, like Taylor's passing of a heart attack five years later. Laura survived him by an additional ten years, living alone with Anne, their cook and housekeeper.

Beau Britian continues to create art and is considered one of the greatest artists of his generation, with sales of his paintings at secondary market auctions reaching astronomical prices.

Ted Martin lectured for two years at Oberlin on contemporary American art before becoming director of a museum of American art in the Western Reserve of Ohio. He went on to direct three additional museums (as a "builder director") before retiring from a career spanning almost forty years.

Ellen Maxwell stayed at the museum through two additional directors before retiring.

Mary Griffin and David finally divorced. She remarried and had two additional children, staying on at the museum's school as its director.

ABOUT THE AUTHOR

Edwin Ritts' museum profession spanned 39 years, during which time he directed art museums in New Brighton, Pennsylvania, Asheville, North Carolina, and Dubuque, Iowa. He also directed the Historic Greenville Foundation in South Carolina, culminating in the construction of the Upcountry History Museum in South Carolina and the Thomasville Cultural Center in Georgia.

Edwin's interest in writing began at Wilmington College in Ohio, where he edited the weekly newspaper and wrote short stories published in the school's annual literary journal.

Edwin and his wife, Susan, have two grown children and four grandchildren. They currently live in Dubuque, Iowa with their four dogs and three cats.

Written four decades ago, then retyped into a computer over the course of a year, *Guardians of the Muse* is Edwin's first—but not last—novel.

www.ingramcontent.com/pod-product-compliance
Lightning Source LLC
Chambersburg PA
CBHW070149310726
48976CB00001B/41